Mere Mortals

Book I

John Andrew Myers

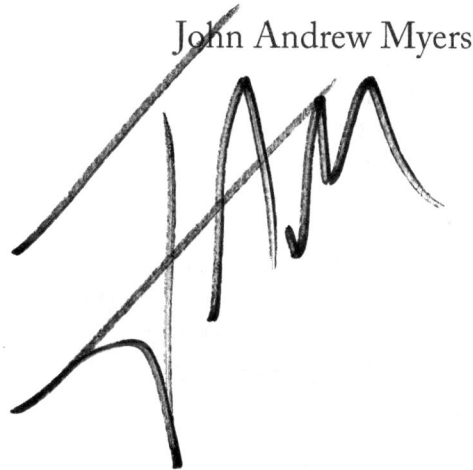

JAM Press, LLC

Published in the United States by JAM Press, LLC.

ISBN(paperback) 9781734348606

First Edition: 2019
Copy editing by Tammy Salyer
Cover illustration by John Andrew Myers

Visit www.meremortalssaga.com for exclusive downloads, gear and additonal information on UnEarth and the world of Mere Mortals.

Mere Mortals Social:
@ MereMortalsSaga

For my parents, Jack and Mary.

Mere Mortals

"Humanity, a prime contributor of Eve energy, has always been aware of it, whether they know it or not. Most have assumed what they felt within could be explained away by a word, one as simple as 'emotion,' existing only in an individual's mind. But every action in our world has an equal and opposite reaction in theirs, including volcanoes erupting and asteroids colliding, all the way down to our smallest actions and thoughts.

All create the Eve."

- Excerpt from the journal of
Dr. Francisco Emul. Murcia
June 1894

PROLOGUE

The marvel of it. A snarling face of weathered stone loomed before Research Professor Leigh Marie Evans, caked in ancient dust, its heavy, arched brow and thin, beady eyes resting above a protruding snout. She rubbed her two-inch dry paintbrush against her torn jeans to clear away any collected dust and continued to unveil the scowling beast: a six-foot serpent with four clawed arms jutting out like gnarled, viperous branches.

"Hello? I know you can hear me."

The voice from below tried to get her attention again, but the professor continued to ignore it. Usually, this voice was the bearer of bad—or, at the very least, annoying—news, and bad news was to be avoided at all costs. Leigh's headphones, sagging into her voluminous black hair and blasting heavy metal loud enough to be heard from fifteen feet away, typically kept unnecessary distractions at bay. But unfortunately, the source of this voice was far trickier to deter.

"You're going to keep pretending? That's great."

Why won't you people just let me work? Leigh lamented the long silences and uninterrupted dig sessions she had once enjoyed before becoming a project lead.

"Make me say it one more time." The voice below was especially upset today.

Yes, of course. Anything for you, your majesty. Leigh finally removed her headphones and wiped a layer of dust from her face. Taking a moment to roll her neck from side to side, she glanced around the enormous cavern for some peace before the inevitable argument sure to come. The rock making up the walls and floor was a lush mixture of reds, oranges, and deep browns, lit by work lamps that cut through the uneven surfaces, creating flashes of color and shadows zigzagging like black lightning. Above, the ceiling soared in a dramatic wave of crimson, making Leigh feel as though she were in a burgundy-laden Victorian theater two hundred feet underground. Beyond the statue were eleven tall, cracked obsidian steps, lovingly nicknamed the Dead Stairs by the few crew members daring enough to enter the chamber. Atop these steps lay the most exciting discovery in all of the professor's sixteen years of fieldwork.

"Turn your ass around and look at me!" The voice had reached fully perturbed.

Doing as told, Leigh turned around. "You do know I'm your boss, right?" she said, only half-joking, to her assistant.

The small but feisty Casey Lipmayer was already grinding her teeth and stewing in her always dependable tall white socks and old-man sneakers. With her elbows tight against her ribs, her stance was like that of a totem pole, one likely getting ready to lecture its boss on a budget line item gone astray. Seven years Leigh's senior, and an ardent advocate of lanyards, Casey carried the temperament of a strawberry dipped in sugar (*most of the time*) and had been along for the ride through nearly all the ups and downs of the professor's career—from Missouri State's Archaeological Society to the University of London's research division. Over time, the two women had grown as close as sisters, but none of that made Leigh eager to share the top spot, despite knowing her assistant dreamed of being a full-fledged research partner. Casey just wasn't ready, and her current panicked state was yet another example of why.

"So—as my boss," Casey started with an unsure squeak, "I trust you'll be truly excited to tackle these critical items, which I am graciously bringing to your attention." She forced a smile, wringing her clipboard so intensely in both hands that Leigh feared it might snap.

"Be right down." The professor took her time dusting off her shirt and gloves, descending each step of the ladder with deliberate care. But Casey didn't wait for her boss to reach the ground.

"We don't have enough workers to fill rosters tomorrow. Or Thursday. Or Friday. Word is, four more quit last night."

"Word is?" Leigh turned with an eyebrow raised.

"They didn't tell anyone they were leaving. They might be wandering the desert for all we know. I sent a group of three to look for them. There were plenty of volunteers."

"What's that make now? Eight?" Leigh asked. "They do know this is just a job, and not a gulag, right?"

"This might be worth taking more seriously. Have you noticed how placid it's been down here? Everyone's avoiding this chamber. We're falling further behind."

"The quiet helps me work."

Quips were Leigh's only weapon against Casey's logic. Of *course* she'd noticed that three-quarters of their workforce was refusing to show up. Technically, the crew was not required to work in any specific cavern on the site, and there were many caves in the labyrinth of tunnels that fell under that description. It was a fine-print detail that stripped Leigh of much of the power she'd grown used to (*and very much liked*) having since becoming a lead. Yet another of a thousand examples hidden within the unusual contract they had with their unconventional benefactor, whom Leigh had yet to meet face-to-face—which was probably for the best, considering she simply wanted to punch said benefactor *in* said face.

Casey would have to stop me. We're getting paid too well.

The claim was true, however. They had fallen behind. When the Dead Stairs had first been discovered, Leigh thought it might have been the smell driving the workers away. She'd been in caves reeking of sulfur and natural gas before—nothing new—but as they began to pull away layer after layer of steel-hard rock, a strange, new stench emerged—like rotten milk without the tangy bite. Leigh was waiting— hoping—to get used to it, but after three weeks, that hope was fading.

"Food stores are running low," Casey added.

"Have you called the vendors with the satellite?"

"Yes. The storms near the Gulf are slowing down the shipping lanes. They say it could take two weeks."

"So, we'll ration. We've done it before. Meanwhile, I'll go ahead and stop these storms—also my fault by the way—with my bare hands."

"You could at least care!" Casey was as near to shouting as she could get away with.

"I do care. I care so much, in fact, I want to finish the job so everyone can go home. What's so wrong with that?"

"It's not just the food." Casey's tone was turning motherly. "It's medicine. Bandages. More workers are getting sick. That *is* our responsibility."

"Any deaths?" Leigh asked.

"None so far."

"Keep it that way. I don't want to spend ten months in court. I doubt our backer does, either. And stop worrying so much. My crews have always loved me in the past."

Casey's right eyebrow peaked. "Who told you that?"

"Please. Just look at these guys!" Leigh gestured toward the four workers wielding enormous rock saws, at least two of whom she knew by name. *Hopefully, Casey won't ask which.* Leigh would've gotten to know them better, but was unfortunately only fluent in English, Spanish, Portuguese, and Mandarin, while the drill wielders spoke everything else—except for a Scotsman named Jeff, whom she'd worked with on several digs before.

A tall, broad-shouldered man, covered in sporadic tattoos and looking particularly good in his jeans today, Jeff had a buzzed head and each ear pierced with silver loops. Leigh found herself loudly gazing again, and this time was caught. Putting one foot on a crate, Jeff hoisted a seven-pound pickax over his shoulder for her benefit, beaming his slightly crooked pearly whites. Remaining fairly professional and unaffected, she quietly drifted off in her mind to the past few nights in her tent where the Scotsman had filled the role of her "fun thing"—some much-needed warmth and companionship in this desolate place. But the good memories only lasted for a second.

"You're still not listening!" Casey was fully shouting now, red-faced.

"What do you want from me? How can I help?" Leigh asked. "I will do literally anything if you let me get back to work. Hire a whole new fleet of workers, use robots, drones, dogs. Get the Libyan rebels to hook us up with some explosives. I bet our backer can get all of it. I don't give a shit. We just can't stop. We're so damn close to the finish line I can taste it."

Casey's eyes drooped. "This isn't fun anymore. For anyone. Don't forget, we've never worked with these people before. There's no telling how they'll react to these kinds of conditions."

"What do you suggest?"

"I'll get this one out of the way since you'll probably be angry, but they want to stop night digs."

"The reason we started nights in the first place was to escape the sun. People were getting heatstroke."

"They say they'll take their chances."

"Fine. No more nights. What else?"

"You need to get out there and talk to your people."

"We've had worse."

"No. We haven't."

Casey sounded done with the conversation. She'd made her point, and Leigh knew it was true. Handling bureaucratic red tape was usually her specialty, but now they were wading in it. She was beginning to wonder if the work visas provided by their mysterious benefactor would even get them out of the country. The last place Professor Evans wished to be waylaid was in Faya-Largeau, Chad.

"I know you've made sacrifices. I don't take it for granted," Leigh said, looking up the obsidian steps to what would surely be her Everest. "But you've got to see what we have here. This is—beyond special."

Jeff and the others were currently working away on the rock wall at the top of the stairs, slicing off chunks of hard red clay and uncovering sections of something akin to onyx. As the material seemed impervious to harm, they'd been ordered to cut without care, free to touch the smooth jet-black surface. An accidental strike with a rock saw during the first week had tipped them off to the fact. As of yet, no one was sure of the stone's actual composition, how it had been polished in the first place, or why it had been buried behind bloodred rock.

Just waiting for me, I guess.

Over several weeks the structure at the top of the stairs revealed itself to be rectangular and some seven feet high, with a depressed edge running the length of the shape. When the saws delved into the inverted lip, it was discovered that the granite was separated from the cave wall. They had found a door. At its center sat the only symbol or piece of writing Leigh's team had encountered at the entire site: a rigid, simplistic depiction of a red eye, minus a representation of a top lid, with a sharp white line slashing through the iris.

"Sort of odd, don't you think? Usually, Saô kings got buried near their kingdoms," Casey remarked upon its discovery.

"I've never been convinced that's who these people were," Leigh said. "Kanem Empire, maybe, but we haven't found any evidence to suggest either society is responsible."

"And why so big if it's just for a coffin?" Casey asked. "Before it died, the magnetometer scans showed a monstrous cavern back there. None of this is making sense."

"You're kidding, right?" Leigh had said, wrapping her arm around Casey's shoulder. "Look at Khufu's pyramid and the Colossus of Rhodes. Old-school rulers loved pompous shit. We're not here to think about the why. We're the finders. Let someone else figure out what to do with it after."

Presently, Casey adjusted her glasses—as she had to every two minutes—and Leigh noticed a slight, nervous shake in her fingers.

"I assume we're still in agreement about what to do with any artifacts discovered on-site?" Casey said. "Straight to London, same as usual. Just because we've got an anonymous donor doesn't mean we turn into pseudo archaeologists. Those people are thieves. This guy probably operates on the black market—"

"You're doing it again," Leigh snapped.

Casey's clipboard finally cracked in her grasp. "I'm sorry, I don't like being in this situation. It's foreign to me. I don't understand how you can be so calm."

"What will panicking do? We signed the papers. We're in this whether we like it or not."

"So little of this feels ethical, let alone legal. Tell me, honestly, as both a boss and a friend, what do you think is behind this door?"

Leigh didn't hesitate. "Why ask? Let's just find out."

"You aren't the least bit worried? Even when you have things like *that* staring at you underground?" Casey pointed at the gargoyle Leigh was cleaning at the base of the stairs.

A second statue stood guard opposite, almost identical to the first, with four arms, a head on top, a body stretched and curved, and a broken section of tail connecting to the pillar on which it rested. The guardians of the Dead Stairs were posed in a defiant war cry, snarling at the heavens, though Leigh liked to think they were laughing. Much like the rest of the site, the serpentine statues gave zero clues as to what ancient society first created them. With wholly unique designs, they did not resemble the works of any early culture or civilization on record—most of which Leigh was well versed in—having possessed a virtually photographic memory all her life, as well as a love of finding secluded spots far from the world in which to bury her nose in any history book she could find.

The region itself offered no clues to the identities of the cave's original inhabitants, either. Seen from above, the land around the site would have appeared stricken dead by God thousands of miles in every direction. At least it would have if Leigh actually believed in the deity, or any others. *That was Mom's department. Not mine.*

Never before had a dig been laced with so much raw mystery. Opening the onyx door at the top of the stairs would be like opening a sealed can without a label. *And I'm the lucky SOB who gets to do it.*

But not everyone shared the professor's enthusiasm. In fact, ever since the Dead Stairs had been uncovered, morale had been steadily lowering. Events such as equipment failures, animal fights, or disgruntled employees disappearing without notice hadn't seemed all that troubling initially. Leigh had dealt with each of those elements at one point or another in her career, but a continuation of disastrous events had created a fog of animosity over the dig, particularly during nights at camp, which had once been filled with music and laughter, since taken over by silence and brooding.

A new sound was making itself known in the cave, mixing with the electric blades: voices, tense. Some were yelling. Boots were hitting the ground. Leigh looked past Casey toward the cavern entrance.

"Shut the Hell up!" she hollered at Jeff and the others on the stairs. The workers quieted and soon the chamber stood silent—if only for a second—when a sudden, close shout rang through the tunnels. Leigh spotted a young man, Hasiim, one of their division leads, rounding the tight corner of the entrance. His eyes and reckless speed revealed a man in dire panic. In the two months since he had first approached her, tripping clumsily to extend his hand for a shake, exclaiming he was a fan of her published essays on late Ubaid period hierarchies, Hasiim had never acted like this. Fidgety, sure, but level-headed. In this moment he seemed more like a father desperately searching a crowd for a doctor to save his child's life.

Leigh hurried to meet him and the others. The panicked dig crew were yelling over one another in four languages, turning their message to mud. The only consistency was in their fingers, pointed back the way they had come, to the surface. She lifted her hands to halt them before they ran her down. "Hasiim, what is it? Just Hasiim!"

"It happened. They've gone mad! You have to come, quickly!" he shouted.

"Who?" Casey asked.

"There's no who. Please. You must hurry!" Hasiim pleaded with his dark sienna eyes and soon Leigh's feet were sweeping her away, leading a mob, charging the tunnels in what felt like a desperate errand. To his credit, along the way, Hasiim attempted to relay the story, but in his alarm his words rebounded between French, Slavic, English, and a few others. Leigh grabbed only a handful of words: "attacked," "unbelievable," "hospital," "blood."

The crew ducked passages and squeezed through tight gaps as the tunnels pitched into a steep incline as they neared the surface. Though there was an easier passageway out, that trip took at least forty-five minutes longer. Without time to think, let alone powder her fingers, Leigh lost her grip on the cold, slippery rocks frequently during the ascent.

"Sounds like a fight at camp," Casey gasped, short of breath.

When they reached the peak of the incline, light from the surface erupted over them. Their headlamps were shut off and tossed into a crate near the entrance as the cavalcade emerged and started on the path back to camp, traversing the trench leading up the canyon, sometimes pinched too narrow for more than one person. Fighting her already tired lungs, Leigh hoped she wasn't too late to stop whatever the Hell was happening at camp.

Bandits, maybe? A fire?

A sea of cries shook her guts as they came over an embankment to view a roaring cluster of movement. Almost all of them—fifty, maybe sixty crew—had turned the camp to chaos. Men and women ran about, shouting, trying to break up fights while others started new ones. There was no beginning or end to it. Leigh dashed down the slope, hoping her boots would keep their grip, and careened into the pile, shoving her way forward, assuming no one would be willing to strike the check writer.

Behind her, Jeff used his huge frame to pull workers off one another. "Calm down!" he shouted. One look up at the giant, pale Scotsman, and all obeyed.

The bodies broke away when Leigh found the eye of the storm. A centralized flurry of limbs—and blood—was at the center, where a small pile of men and women fought to contain a feral shape: a crazed man. His teeth were chattering and his neck snapped to and fro as he straddled a male victim, his fingers deep inside the man's eye sockets. The man, his back on the ground, was awake, screaming in pain, unable to defend himself, so desperate for relief it was dizzying.

She was frozen. Leigh had never seen anything so primal or visceral. Never imagined the inside of a human skull while the person was alive and not a relic. Finally, her instincts kicked in.

"Get him away!"

Grabbing hold of the crazed man's coat, she pulled with the others. The fight seemed to perpetuate itself with no ground gained, but eventually the attacker was lifted away, his fingers finally coming free from the poor man's sockets. Scratching and gnawing at anything he could, the crazed man continued muttering drivel under his wet breath as Jeff slid a sleeper hold around his shoulders and head. But any control gained quickly faded as the man, half his size, began squirming out.

"A little help would be bloody nice!" Jeff yelled, backpedaling, losing ground as the crazed man snarled and howled, nearly free.

The crowd swarmed in response and grabbed control of the flailing limbs. It took their combined strength to hold him down while ropes were tied around his ankles and wrists. The chair creaked under the strain but held firm, and soon the chaos stilled—a little. Scuffles on the outskirts sounded as the people near the center found calm, which only revealed the cries of the eyeless man writhing on the ground, whose whimpers had dissolved into desperation—for sleep or for death.

A woman ran to his side with a small black pouch, yanked a needle out and filled it with liquid from a blue bottle with a dirty label. No one seemed to panic when she injected the eyeless man, so Leigh did not intervene. In moments he was unconscious, well enough for surgery it seemed, and she was finally able to take a real breath.

A few feet away, the crazed man's eyes darted as if he were watching a swarm of flies, unaware of the moment. His upper teeth gnawed on his lower lip, already messy with blood.

"What was he saying?" she asked, unsure who would answer.

"He say, 'I'm saving you from seeing it,'" a Chadian local replied.

"Saving?" Leigh asked under her breath, feeling knots in her stomach and pressure building above and behind her eyes.

In that moment nothing sounded better or more appropriate than a stiff drink. Unfortunately, a sea of faces was pointed her way, looking for hope and answers. The workers were scared, and with every right to be. *Gotta say something.* The first notion that came to her mind was to tell them she had never experienced so much bullshit from a dig site in her entire career, and that no one should lose any love they had for archaeology. Sometimes it was hot, sometimes freezing—sure, not so bad. But this desert, this particular site—Leigh didn't have the heart to tell them how short the straw they had drawn was. In fact, until this very moment, staring at their beaten expressions, she'd never considered retirement.

"Hasiim?" she called, hoping he was near.

Luckily, her friend stepped out of the crowd. "Yes, Professor Evans?" She waved him over. "Please translate."

He nodded, helping her onto a generator box below a light post at the center of the crowd. The crew waited silently, displaying astounding patience.

She spoke as loudly as she could. "If anyone else is injured, please help them forward so we can provide medical attention." Hasiim shouted a translation over the crowd. A few minor interpreters among them echoed his message in additional languages. "And if anyone else thinks of starting a fight, do us all a favor and march into the desert instead. We're here to work as a team."

She fought to catch her breath, hoping her attempt at a reserved tone was coming across. Hasiim finished. The minor translators concluded as well, but the workers did not smile or respond warmly. Her threat seemed to be taken exactly as such.

"We're all tired. And I know we all want our beds—not the ones here, but the ones back home. I want that too, but we can't stop halfway. That's not how you get the next job." She paused to let Hasiim and the others catch up and glanced at her team. Jeff smiled encouragingly, while Casey and those around her appeared less enthusiastic.

One woman called in messy English, "Stop digging!" but no one added anything more.

Oh, that's how it is? Leigh cleared her throat. "No one is keeping you here against your will."

"Professor Evans," Casey said tightly, "maybe less of that? Like, a lot less." At the same time, she tugged on Leigh's pant leg, but Leigh pressed on.

"We all know what our contracts say. You're free to go at any time. This is a job. You're getting paid well. We're doing the best we can—" Leigh halted when a hum within the crew erupted into an uproar. "What is it? Tell us so we can help!"

Hasiim stopped interpreting to look up at her. "They don't fear the dirt. They fear what the dirt will make them do. Please try to understand."

She was shocked. *Not Hasiim, too.*

"Don't give in to fear and superstition! We're alone out here. All we have is each other."

The outskirts of the group began to disperse, releasing the crew into the camp. They were not interested in her pitch, and Leigh couldn't blame them; she knew she'd probably feel the same way if she were in their shoes.

"The desert is messing with you. I promise there is nothing to be afraid of," she said to those remaining.

Hasiim finished the last phrase, and a hushed murmur spread among the people.

"What is it? What did they say?" asked Leigh.

"They ask—'What about the half eye?'" he responded.

"The half eye? It means nothing. There's no translation yet. We haven't found anything to suggest the temple is haunted. Believe me, I hate ghosts too!" Leigh lied, having never believed in them.

Hasiim hesitated before finishing, turning to her as though unsure how to continue.

What? No mentioning ghosts?

"Why did you say 'temple'?" Casey asked from below.

Leigh glanced around at the faces. *What is with you people?* "I don't know. Just a basic word. Could be anything. But hey, let's stop focusing on the bad. We should be excited!" Leigh said, waving her hand. "Get ready, and make sure to get some sleep tonight, because we're opening the door tomorrow."

The workers who heard her paused in unison and turned, as if checking to see if they heard right.

"We are?" Jeff asked, sounding as unsure as the others.

"That's what we came here to do. Right?" Leigh asked, but no one nodded or vocally agreed.

The crew then spoke at Hasiim, who responded in a volley of dialogue. Voices clamored over one another.

"What's going on now?" Leigh asked.

Hasiim and the others finished conversing before turning to her. "Nothing. They say good night, Professor." He nodded humbly, and he and the crew turned their backs and walked away, disappearing into their tents.

Leigh jumped down from the generator. "I think that went pretty well. They got the gist, right?" She eyed Hasiim and a small group of crew speaking in a private huddle a few yards away.

Casey was visibly shaking. "Are you trying to get us killed?"

"What's that supposed to mean?" asked Leigh.

"These people are on edge. One already snapped! Why are you adding stress?"

"I know how to talk to my employees." Leigh was losing her patience with Casey, as well as the day in general. She looked at Jeff for some kind of reassurance.

"I got no dog in this fight," he said, backing away.

Leigh pointed at the ground, as though commanding a mutt. "You stay. We could use some outside opinions."

He halted in place.

"Professor Evans, I know you're not going to want to hear this, but"—Casey took off her glasses for added effect—"we need to discuss shutting down the dig. Temporarily."

"Out of the question." Leigh turned and marched up the path to her tent, thinking she'd had the last word. But when she heard two pairs of boots trampling to catch up, she knew there would be more to endure.

"You can't avoid this! Even by running," Casey shouted up the slope.

"Should I get some gasoline and a post? I'd love to get burned at the stake by nightfall." Leigh was almost to her tent. *Maybe I can get inside and pretend not to be home?*

"I don't know, maybe it's for the best. You know?" Jeff suggested.

Leigh halted and turned, locking her eyes on him.

"No. I didn't mean that," he said, shaking his head vigorously. "Didn't even say it, actually."

Leigh looked Casey square in the eye. "I know you're trying to help, but as your boss, I'm telling you to back off. Now. If we shut down, someone else will step in. They always do. If that happens, we can kiss whatever's behind the door goodbye. Just look at Babylon . . ."

"No—don't. Not this again," Casey said, hanging her head.

"A whole ancient city's worth of history—gone!" Leigh shouted. "Icons, artifacts, every vestige or clue of who they were and how their story helped lead to us, all destroyed by Hussein and his goons."

Casey groaned. "So you've said two hundred times."

"We're not abandoning the site. Go sleep off this frustration and come back tomorrow with a clear head."

Casey's lips tightened into a thin line, and she let out a heavy, supposedly calming breath. "Fine. Good night . . . boss."

Relaxing her shoulders, Leigh watched Casey leave with a heavy heart. She didn't particularly like using her position over people, especially with the only person she could remotely call a friend, but sometimes it was necessary to remind her of their true arrangement.

Jeff remained for a silent, somber moment on the hillside before turning to walk away. "Wait," Leigh said. "Keep me company?"

"Professor, you know last time you said there wasn't going to be a next time, and—"

"Call me Leigh."

Jeff laughed, shaking his head. "Okay then. Leigh. Tell ya what, I'll go grab some things. Be right back."

He hurried down the hill, glancing over his shoulder as Leigh continued to her tent. When he returned, the night with Jeff unfolded the same as the others, but afterward, when his arms were wrapped tightly around her in bed, she found herself unable to fall asleep. Jeff had drifted into snoring almost immediately as she listened to the wind whispering over the valley. The camp was without a single sneeze or midnight cough the whole night, leaving her hours of silence to mull over the day's events: the crazed man and his eyeless victim, the onyx door waiting to be opened, the workers nearly destroying the camp. *I've seen paranoia before, but this is nuts. What's come over everyone?*

The fact that Casey was equally worried gave Leigh pause. *What if she's right? What if the door should stay closed?* Professor Evans was a driven individual, but she wasn't without feelings, and her senses worked fine. Time at camp was a welcome reprieve from the cold, heavy dread she got in her stomach when in the presence of the Dead Stairs, which of course didn't make any sense scientifically speaking. But was it enough to throw her? The debate raged in her mind, but in the end, she couldn't imagine abandoning what might be the pinnacle of her life's work. *I won't give it up. Not wasting another chance.*

Through the foggy plastic window of the tent door, the sky shifted from pure black to a deep blue, then yellow, blending with a crimson glow on the horizon. The sun rose at 5:44 a.m.

Most of the crew were even earlier risers than she was and would be up soon, if not already. Leigh had no trouble rising and getting dressed, and the cold coffee in her thermos would suffice. The hardest part was getting her feet in her boots. *Damn, they're freezing!* In addition to grabbing her thermal jacket, Leigh packed her heaviest coat and a hat, as the temperature was likely to drop rapidly beyond the onyx door.

Jeff needed to be kicked a couple of times but managed to be ready in five minutes. Slinging his bag over his shoulder, he stepped to the door and yawned, finishing with a closed-mouth grin. "Something wrong? Thought you'd look more excited on a day like this."

At that moment, she was thinking positive thoughts, but wouldn't dare let him know it. Jeff was one of those rare people with whom Leigh could spend more than five minutes without wanting to claw at her own face. So, rather than give any indication of how she truly felt (*ew—gross—get it away*), she shook her head, ruffled his hair, and stepped outside. The morning was cold but windless, while the sky erupted in fountains of color with no one there to witness it.

Initially, it seemed that most of the workers, likely still angry with Leigh, had avoided breakfast at camp and gone directly to the site to get the day over with. Then she noticed whole patches of tents were completely missing.

Tapping on a door flap, she called, "Good morning! You guys sleeping in?" When there was no answer she poked her head inside. Only the provided cots remained. Hurrying into the next tent, she found their belongings packed and gone. All the others she checked were empty, too. Jeff charged about the camp, calling out the names of his friends, but no one answered. When Casey came stumbling over the embankment on the path to the Dead Stairs' cavern, waving on approach, she appeared dazed, stopping to catch her breath, hands on her knees. "They're gone! The crew is gone!"

No matter where they looked, it was true. The camp had been abandoned.

THE TEACHER

Just stay calm. Everything will be fine—Alex thought bitterly at himself for the fifth or sixth time today while hurrying down a picture-frame-laden hall in his home. Fishing his car keys out of his pocket, he mentally reviewed his checklist. The empty boxes for picking up dinner and assembling the crib weren't going to check themselves, and his anxiety candle was already burned low. Most of the day's stress—Wednesday, September 20, 2006—had come from the customer service call he'd just ended a few moments ago. It turned out the new crib he'd spent the last few hours attempting to assemble was missing three tiny screws—focal points of stability, apparently. After a long chat with a not-so-friendly man named Pete at the Readylast Furniture Company in Baton Rouge, Alex thought, *To heck with this, I'll find replacements at the store*, and hung up.

Reaching the living room, he found Melissa lying comfortably in her new napping spot, which seemed to change week to week. An open bottle of acetaminophen was left on the coffee table. *Must be another headache.* His wife had been having more and more as

the pregnancy went along. Sneaking across the living room, avoiding the empty cardboard boxes and packing materials littering
the floor, he grabbed his favorite denim jacket and moved to their
heavy, carved wooden front door, aiming to exit quietly when his
favorite voice spoke up, catching him in the act. "You've got to be
kidding. Where could you possibly have to go?"

Melissa wasn't just awake; she was sitting up, scratching her head of
thick, curly crimson hair, which was doing its best to swallow her hand.
With a yawn she patted down her pants pockets and looked around.
"Where's my phone? What time is it? Did I pee myself? Why am I
wet?"

"It's a little after six," Alex replied. "I'm just going out one more
time. The crib is missing some parts. You didn't pee. I think that's
sweat. I turned the air back on. It was off again for some reason."

"The crib?" Melissa gave him the look she always did when she
thought he was acting too cautious or tense for her taste. "Hon,
please. The baby's not going to need that for a few weeks. I'm
pretty sure we'll survive the night. Remember what the tapes said
about slowing your roll? So, slow it!"

She. It was still strange talking about their daughter without a
proper name, but both Alex and Melissa had agreed to wait until
they met her to give her one. *Names are a big deal in our book.*

"I also assumed you wanted takeout for dinner," Alex said. "I was
going to call in our order when I got in the car."

Melissa nodded. "On second thought, you're right. You should
go."

"Any special requests?"

"The usual, please. With egg rolls, please. Love you, please!" She
smiled wide, like a kid who thought they were gaming the system.

Before she could get up off the couch, Alex hurried to her and
leaned down to kiss his wife. The taste of her organic mint balm

transferred to his lips, where it would linger the rest of the day, reminding him again and again how unfathomably lucky he was to have her. Not many guys he knew got to marry their High School sweetheart. The ones who did usually found a way to screw it up, either through sheer apathy, unfaithfulness, or drunken belligerence. But Alex wasn't like them, and would never let that happen. At least, he hadn't so far.

"Love you back," he said. "Are we finishing the movie tonight? I have to return it tomorrow."

"Maybe. The girls from my salsa class are coming over later, remember? Do we still have those little cookies? The ones with the grooves?" Melissa made a wavy motion with her hands as she asked.

Monthly tea party—right. Forgot. "I think there's a new box in the cupboard," Alex said. "If not, I can go to Fry's before heading to the hardware store—"

"No, honey, chill. It's fine. You're the best, but we'll be fine. You know you can always hang out with us. The girls love you."

Despite returning their affections, the thought of being around any group of people—let alone a swarm of Melissa's girlfriends—made Alex's anxiety soar to new heights. "Thanks, but if it's okay with you, I'll be out back—should try to get some work done."

"Of course. Work that wood, love," Melissa replied. "Can't wait to see the doves when they're finished. Make sure you drive safe."

Alex hadn't taken any time to work on his wood carvings since injuring his left hand the night he found out they were expecting a baby. *Still having trouble opening and closing it fully.* The pair of doves he was carving out of a huge chunk of Indian elm had already consumed two years of his time, pulling him away from other woodworking and craft projects, including his first attempt at watercolor: a desert mountain scene. Yet for some reason he couldn't stop obsessing over the doves. *I don't even like doves. They're gross when you get down to it. Just need to finish it.*

Before leaving the house, he called in their dinner order from the landline. To sweeten the deal for his wife, he ordered twice as many egg rolls. The guy on the other end said the order would be ready in twenty minutes. Throwing on his denim jacket to cover his paint-smeared T-shirt, Alex stepped outside, pulling down his favorite blue baseball cap to shield his eyes from the Arizona sun. The cap was old, and not likely to last forever, so he reserved wearing it for rare occasions, such as this, when he got to be handy.

Heat waves rolled off the hoods of neighbors' cars and the road turned to mush in the distance. Wiping away the sweat pouring from his dark eyebrows—which took constant maintenance to keep reasonably sized and separated—Alex locked his door, checking it three times before stepping away from the ranch-style home, the same one his mother had grown up in before him.

He and Melissa were close with most of their neighbors in the three-quarter circle, but today, none were out to wave hello to, except for an older man named Miles, who lived in the corner house at the end, currently watering his plants with his ass crack hanging out of his swim trunks.

Prior to Miles, another family had lived in the house when Alex was a kid—a young couple with a little boy a few years younger than him, and a baby girl. A few attempts were made, mostly on Alex's end, to build a friendship between the boys, but nothing ever materialized. Though Alex had been a shy, timid child who rarely played with the neighborhood kids, the boy who lived in the house at the end of the street was even more fearful and closed off from the world. Shortly after Alex left for college out of state, the boy's family had moved away. Alex wasn't sure what happened to him, but seemed to remember his grandmother telling him the boy passed away a few years later.

What was that kid's name? For the life of me, I can't remember.

Getting into his car, Alex realized he'd forgotten to crack the windows again. *Ugh. I hate this heat.* Wincing, he forced the scorching seat belt into its latch. The car sputtered to life with a puff of smoke, and off he drove down the cul-de-sac nestled on the north end of town, near a barren stretch of desert facing looming mountains. As he drove along the east side of his backyard—enormous by suburban standards, with plenty of cacti, snakes, and prairie dog holes—Alex reminded himself to fill them in with dirt and lay down fresh grass before his daughter learned to walk. *It's on the list!*

Arriving at the hardware store on the corner of Olive and Judson, a small place owned by ma-and-pa types, he drove past stacks of lumber and summer cookout gear sitting by the entrance, likely left overnight, based on an honor system with local thieves. Finding his ideal parking spot, far away from any other cars, Alex got out and hurried toward the entrance but halted when a vagrant stepped out from behind a stack of plastic chairs.

The old man smiled, revealing the few teeth he had. "'Scuse me. Didn't startle you, did I?" He then took a step back to show he wasn't a threat.

Not this guy again. "Of course not," Alex said. "I'm sorry. I don't have any work for you. Just need some screws."

"Work and screws, huh? Bet there's a joke in there somewhere," the vagrant replied. "No, son, I was just curious if you knew the time." He stared at Alex with attentive gray eyes and a comforting smile etched into his wrinkled, expressive face, sun-damaged skin akin to leather. Atop his head rested a gray, moldy knitted cap with two brown stripes. Soft patches of speckled gray hair poked out from under it, dangling over and around his enormous ears, which were honestly hard not to stare at.

"Sure. It's about six thirty," Alex replied.

The vagrant rubbed his scruffy chin. "Hmm. Appreciate it." Stepping past Alex, he continued wandering the lot.

Feeling the same swell of guilt he had the last few times he'd seen this guy, Alex turned. "Wait," he called, fishing in his pockets and putting some coins in the vagrant's hands. "Hope that's enough change," he said, breaking eye contact with the old man's piercing peepers and moving toward the store entrance.

"Whatever someone can spare is always enough," the old man said as the automatic doors closed behind Alex.

Inside, the store had one cashier working: an overly polite ninety-four-year-old named Mr. Milton, who did not know the meaning of haste. *Or proper hygiene.* Finding a box of Phillips-head screws that would do the trick, Alex got in line at checkout, cringing as Mr. Milton licked his fingers for every bill he handed to the woman he was helping. When Alex's turn came, he made a swift swipe of his credit card and got out with his tiny A4 screws before Mr. Milton could even get a plastic bag off the rack. Planning to sidestep the beggar with the gray knitted cap on his way back to his car, Alex saw the man crossing the street, headed down the block, and felt another rush of guilt at how relieved he was.

The drive to the restaurant was spent imagining what his daughter's crib might look like when finished. There were plenty of improvements he wanted to make to its design. As shipped, it wouldn't be stable enough to house his and Melissa's baby girl. Plus, Alex couldn't resist the temptation to try out some tricks he'd read about in his monthly woodworking magazines. The sun was low in the sky, the clouds shimmering like white gemstones, when he reached a busy intersection and stopped, drumming on his steering wheel as he waited.

Spotting a man in tattered clothes coming down the lane of cars holding a cardboard sign, Alex lowered his eyes and pretended to search his center console. Judging the man's speed, hoping it would remain constant, Alex turned back to find the beggar parked right outside his window, holding up the sign with a smile. It read, *Know any good jokes?* Alex forced a polite smile, shook his head, and turned away before doing a double take. *Those ears!* But the beggar was gone. A few seconds later Alex spotted him, now fifteen feet away, continuing down the lane of cars. *That's the same guy from the hardware store. But how? He's two miles back, on foot.*

The vagrant was now too far away to see any detailed features, but Alex was positive it was the same guy. Like a faucet turning on, dozens of moments from the past came back to him, seemingly out of thin air. *Hasn't he seemed to be in two places before? The mall a few days ago, and also the gym? The liquor store, and also the post office? How could he . . . No, that's ridiculous.*

The cars behind him slammed on their horns as the green turn arrow turned yellow, making Alex fumble to get into gear. His car jumped across the line as the light turned red, the only one to make it through before traffic commenced, causing him to initiate internal self-whipping and anxiety-riddled apologies to the universe. Pulling onto Chandler Boulevard off Francis Street, Alex parked in front of the restaurant, Bry's Thai, nearly hidden by the huge tree out front that lifted and broke the sidewalk.

Before getting out, he spotted someone he thought might be the same bearded vagrant leaving a cash loan-out service but turned out to be just a hipster. *Don't overthink this. There's an explanation for why you keep seeing the same guy everywhere.*

The entrance to the restaurant was vibrant, displaying a multitude of colors, though blue was primary. The statues adorning the tables inside and outside the entrance held idols from many walks of Asian culture, mismatching numerous belief structures and ideas about the origins of the soul. The Filipino family who'd purchased the restaurant from a kind Thai couple who'd run the place for twenty years simply did not care; they just wanted to make everyone happy. A plastic strip of bells attached to the door chimed as Alex entered, having lost what was once a vigorous jingle over the years. The owner, Bryan, looked up from the cash register with boredom in his eyes. Alex hoped that meant his food was ready.

"Hi!" Alex said, closing the door behind him, wondering if his welcome was overdone.

Bryan stayed quiet until Alex approached the counter. *This guy . . . I've been helping him keep the lights on for years, and he can't even say hello—No—It's not him you're mad at. Stay calm. Everything will be fine. Stay calm. Everything will be fine.* The mantra slowed his pulse.

"I had an order for pickup," Alex said.

"Name?" Bryan asked.

"It's the pad thai, yellow curry, and egg rolls."

"Name?"

"Barker."

"Not ready," Bryan finished with a smack of his lips.

"You can't just say that? You know who I am. I've stood in this spot ten thousand times. I mean—" Alex felt proud of himself for what he viewed as a violent public outburst, truly defending himself, but Bryan was unaffected. Alex sighed and lowered his head. "How much longer?"

"Five minutes." Bryan wrote scribbles on his pad and stepped aside, revealing a little girl sitting on a chair and peering over the countertop. She wore a bright pink jacket with teal and orange stripes across the chest and stared up at Alex with wide, nervous eyes, probably because he'd yelled in public. He waved and played up a hearty smile, hoping it was enough to heal any mental scars before they set in. She went back to playing with her doll. *Thank God. She's desensitized.*

Turning to use one of the waiting chairs, Alex found a small family occupying them: a young mother and her two kids waiting on to-go orders. The stroller beside her was empty. A dozen or so shopping bags hung from its handles, and its intended rider, a three-year-old sucking on a pacifier, turned a bashful cheek and hid when Alex caught his gaze. His older sister sitting next to their mother must have been seven and was engrossed in a European history book that looked intense for her age, unaware of the goings-on around her. She reminded Alex of one of his students, Emily Morgan, a shy girl who spent most of her time buried in books as a way to deal with a ghastly home life. She had a bright future, as long as she worked hard. Sadly, Alex couldn't say the same about many of the fourth graders who passed through his doors, though the few he could made it all worth it.

With the seats taken, he was free to visit the fish tank in the dining room: his favorite thing about Bryan's restaurant. Moving through the archway into the small space with six tables, cracked tile flooring, and a flat-screen TV in the corner showing conservative evening news, Alex found the five-foot saltwater fish tank on his right. His favorite fish—the single black one, triangle shaped, with a yellow stripe down its side and a red oval on its underbelly—was bobbing on the tank floor.

"Hey, Bob. How's it hanging? Enjoying that fish life? Looks easy." Bob opened and closed his mouth a few times. "Sounds good. Keep it up."

A quick glance was all Alex needed; he wanted to wash his hands before handling his pregnant wife's food. Hurrying down the side hallway that led to a service closet and the restaurant's only bathroom, he stepped in, closed the door with his foot, and used his shirt to turn the lock. Averting his eyes from the wet floor sticking to his shoes, he lifted the toilet seat with his foot. Settling in, with nowhere else to be, he let out a sigh. Once the food was ready, it would be another story, but for the time being, he could relax and enjoy his piss. Closing his eyes, he waited for a wave of serenity, remembering the relaxation tapes Melissa had gotten him. *Just stay calm. Everything will be fine.* What came was more a spritz of serenity.

He double-checked his to-do list in his head. The screws were safe in his pocket, which was priority one, coming right after the real priority one: Melissa's egg rolls. Alex fell into warm thoughts of her, his source of strength, the only person on the planet who could talk him down from a ledge. And yet, even she would soon be number two in his life. Any day now, he would be holding his new source of strength and calm in his arms. *And she'll finally have a name.*

Finishing his pee, he flicked his dick twice, zipped his pants, and pressed the flush handle with his shoe. The chimes on the restaurant's front door rang, but Alex paid them no attention. Washing his hands thoroughly, he looked at himself in the mirror. His baseball cap was tilted. He fixed it. *So, you're going to be a father, huh?* He straightened his posture. *Dads stand tall.* His grandfather, Grandpa Parai, used to tell him something similar: "Don't let the people see a slouch. Let them see a mountain!" Alex took one last look at himself in the mirror, wondering if his grandfather would have been proud of him if he were alive, when a muffled yell escaped the lobby, possibly from Bryan. *Finally, food's ready.*

Stepping out of the bathroom, Alex proceeded down the service hallway. Upon entering the lobby, lost in daydreams of fatherhood, he hardly noticed that everyone in the Thai restaurant lobby was silent. The TV in the dining room was broadcasting to no one. He first spotted the mother of two, clenching her jaw, her intense gaze fixed on the counter, clutching her bookworm daughter tightly. Following their gazes, he found a figure standing at the lobby counter, wearing a black hooded sweatshirt. Their back was turned, and the hood was up, preventing Alex from seeing their face. *That's odd.* He then spotted Bryan, his previously bored eyes now sober and direct, analyzing the newcomer with urgency. His left arm was keeping his daughter, peeking out from under his arm, from wandering forward.

The first thought that passed through Alex's mind was that the figure in the hood had been injured or had witnessed a car accident and needed to call the police. The details must have been shocking, and Alex must have missed hearing them. He wanted to know . . . to help.

"What's going on?" he asked, instantly wishing he could take the words back or make time stand still.

The figure spun as Alex uttered his first syllable, revealing a wad of cash from Bryan's open register in one hand, and a 9mm handgun aimed at Alex's chest in the other. The gun snatched his gaze, and he couldn't break it. The only important thing in Alex's life was which direction that small weapon was facing. Memories of his childhood walks with his grandfather in the hills outside Prescott rushed back. "Don't point a gun at anything you don't want to kill, Allie," Grandpa Parai would grumble.

"Back the fuck up!" the thief shouted. His voice was young—far too young.

In his blurred peripheral vision, Alex could see the robber wearing a red and black baseball cap and sporting a smattering of facial hair. He waved the gun wildly, as though trying to break Alex's gaze. The barrel pointed at the teacher again, and again, and again.

The following six seconds lasted for what seemed like minutes.

With the gunman's attention on Alex, Bryan backed his daughter away, reaching for a telephone with his right hand—hopefully to call the police. Meanwhile, Alex strained to find the right thing to say to the robber. His first words had been atrocious. His next would have to be better, but he was coming up short. The nanoseconds crept by. The idea of lunging at the young man crossed his mind, but he knew a direct assault wouldn't work. *Too far apart.* Besides, there was no telling if this guy was alone. Then, a painfully annoying thought crept into his head: *What if the gun isn't loaded?*

"Calm down." Alex hated how the words fell out of his mouth. "That's your money, right? You got it. It's all good—"

"Shut up!" the young man interrupted, baring his teeth.

Not a smile. Maybe grinding them. Alex still refused to take his eyes off the gun. "Everything is going to be fine. Please, put down the gun," he said.

Alex and the gunman jolted when the three-year-old behind him started crying. Luckily, the robber didn't start shooting, increasing Alex's suspicion that the gun was empty. He could hear the mother trying desperately to calm her son, wishing he could turn to give the kid a reassuring smile. The gunman then shouted something Alex couldn't make out and turned the weapon on the mother of two and her kids, making Alex realize he preferred the gun pointed at himself.

"Shut the fuck up! Everybody acting like they're better than me. Like I don't know anything. Telling me to do shit. I'm sick of it. All of it! Always whispering things—fucking things in my ear! Talking 'bout me. Never to me. No one listens back. Nobody!" the gunman cried.

"We hear you!" Alex replied, hands raised, being careful not to make sudden movements.

The three-year-old continued to wail so loudly his voice was cracking.

"Get the kid to shut up! Fucking people won't let me think!" the gunman shouted.

"Easy with that!" Bryan called from behind the counter.

The gunman began to pace, grunting, breathing heavy, clenching his fists, and clasped his eyes shut. In response, Alex's body turned on its evolutionary programming and, whether he liked it or not, moved rapidly to intervene. He was four steps away. If he could just get between the family and the gun he could act as a barrier. Then, he could focus on keeping the kid in the red and black hat talking.

Mid-run, in the corner of his vision, Alex spotted Bryan with a heavy kitchen knife in hand leaping over the counter. His keys, dangling from his belt loop, smashed against the countertop. The sound detonated, a thousand times louder than the bells above the door.

The gunman screamed and spun, closing his eyes and firing three times. Alex leaped toward the family. The deafening bangs were joined by breaking glass and rushing water—*He hit the fish tank.* Wood exploded somewhere—*Probably in the drywall.* But there was no sound to indicate where the third bullet landed.

Then the six seconds were up.

Water from the fish tank spilled over his shoes as Alex fell to the floor, surprised he'd lost his footing so easily. He then spotted Bryan and the gunman wrestling, and the gun falling to the floor and remaining silent on impact. The mother of two hurried to pick it up and get it the Hell away as the gunman broke free of Bryan and backed toward the entrance.

With the pistol out of the picture, Alex finally looked at the gunman's face, finding a frightened set of blue eyes above a shaking jaw. He couldn't have been more than seventeen, his lip and eyebrow busted open and bleeding from a previous fight, which must have taken place before he ever set foot in the restaurant. The gunman took quick glances at the scared faces around him, but when his gaze landed on Alex, he paused, his jaw quaking.

Bryan rose from the ground, winded, brandishing the knife. "Get out." His daughter leaped to his side and latched onto him.

The gunman's lips trembled. "He was right. H—how?"

"Now!" Bryan bellowed.

The gunman broke his gaze with Alex and ran as fast as he could, smashing into the doorframe on his way out, most likely leaving a long bruise. Then, he was gone. The two hundred fourteen dollars he'd attempted to steal lay scattered in the middle of the lobby floor. But Alex wasn't ready for it to be over. He was determined to chase the kid. He wanted to break a bottle and stab him in the back of the leg, maybe cutting a tendon, just to keep him in place until the police arrived. The adrenaline rushing through him was all-encompassing. For the first time in his life, Alex wanted revenge.

He applied his usual thought process to moving his arms and legs, yet remained on the ground as a fog rolled into his mind. A chill crept up his spine as something wet crawled up his pelvis. It wasn't the fish tank water, and he was eighty percent sure he hadn't pissed his pants. The pieces then came together quickly. *The third bullet.* Alex allowed himself to go there in his mind, releasing his fight with reality.

I've been shot.

From there, time only seemed to move faster. People were shouting. The whole of the room was becoming a muddy orchestra of noise. Alex suddenly felt as heavy as a one-ton bowling ball sinking into the floor. The chemicals running through his veins were pumping him with rage, and a desire to live and conquer, yet he could not move. Looking down, he saw red soaking his shirt from his lower right abdomen. Wanting to know exactly where he'd been shot, he stuck his right hand—shaking uncontrollably—down his pants. Blood was pouring out by the pint.

It didn't take long for his soaked fingers, running along his hip, to find the hole. When Alex's ring finger slipped in, the nerve endings lit up with sharp, icy pain, making him gasp.

He began to picture the ambulance arriving to save him. The paramedics would be the sweetest thing he'd ever seen as they lifted his head, maybe stroked his hair, signaling that he was safe. But when he opened his eyes, it was the mother of two above him, propping his head up with her jacket. Doctor or not, angel or not, she made him feel better. He wished he knew her name.

"Are you okay?"

The seven-year-old stood above him, holding her little brother's hand, waiting while their mother tended to Alex. He wanted to joke with them, like he did with his students, but a new feeling was settling in, further silencing him—like hot metal had been poured into his wound and was creeping its way along the bullet's path. He could sense where it had stopped, a burning center under his left rib cage, like a red-hot coal. The agony pulsed within him like a subwoofer, where the bullet had most likely shattered his hip and lower spine. He could only imagine the damage it had done to his internal organs. The pain rolled over Alex until he couldn't hold back, releasing a primitive cry like a mangled wild animal, as his consciousness took its first dive away from his body and yo-yoed back. A vibrating, visceral, cold rush washed over him like ice water. It felt like truth. This was it. He was going to die.

The people in the restaurant were locking the doors and closing the windows and blinds. No one else was likely to lose their life tonight. Alex let a smile creep onto his cheek at the thought. He needed it.

The sleep coming upon him was fantastically inviting, offering a world free from pain, where he wasn't lying in a pool of his own blood. Against those promised comforts, he fought to keep his mind going—to hang on for as long as he could—and began a new checklist in his mind: the things he needed to do before "checking out."

Asking himself what higher power he believed in, he realized none particularly came to mind. Alex's family had abandoned their church when he was eighteen, and he'd hardly thought of God, or Heaven, or Hell since. Of all the things he feared, eternal damnation had never been one of them, but in this moment, the thought terrified him. He was eighty to ninety percent sure he'd been a decent person, but the basic belief structures of the major religions and the multiple sects they branched into, seemed hugely contradictory, so there was no way to know what the fate of his soul would be. Therefore, he decided to let it go.

Are those sirens? Deep down he knew it wasn't true. His body was sagging, and his lungs were slowing down, leaving him with only enough energy for a few more breaths. He needed to move his thoughts to the one place he was too afraid to go. The one place that actually mattered: Melissa and their baby.

The thought of her raising their daughter on her own did not scare him. She would find a way; it's what she did. But the thought of not being there himself was what broke Alex. He wanted to see the color of his daughter's eyes and find out what her personality would be like—if she would inherit some of his more neurotic traits. He hoped she would find a good partner someday, go on to do important things and be happy. *Happy. That's most important.*

He then thought of Melissa's hair and smile, saw her laugh in his mind, and heard her singing in the shower. He smelled her burned grilled cheese sandwiches and recalled the girl he met on the first day of ninth-grade science class, remembering their first kiss at age twenty-one at a friend's party when they were visiting home after college. The only real regret Alex ever had was not doing it sooner. *That's fine*, he thought. *That's a good one.*

As Alex looked back on his life, he felt a sense of calm wash over him. He'd done his best to be true and loved the same woman every single day. That was all any higher power could ask, right?

If the sirens were approaching, he wouldn't have known. Alex couldn't sense the world anymore, and the sleep was calling, but he wanted one more look around. Finding his last bit of energy, he forced his eyes open.

The walls were the purest blue he had ever seen. The reds were extraordinary. Each poster detail was a wonder. A gleam of light from outside fell on his eye, and Alex noticed one of the window blinds was left open. Standing beyond the glass was the vagrant wearing a gray knitted cap with two brown stripes, looking down on him with a slight smile on his wrinkled face. The softness of his brilliant gray eyes transferred into the mind of the teacher, stilling him. *Who are you?*

Alex's lungs gave up. His eyes closed. The sleep was here. Everything was fading. Lastly, he heard a dampened cry in his mind from a hushed voice he didn't recognize.

"Alex?"

THE SOLDIER

Oh, fuck you, just leave. Bennett watched the police cruiser pass the duplex on the corner as it searched the place for the third time. The officer was down to five miles per hour but still unable to spot him in his hiding place. *Yes. Please. Go.* When another few minutes went by without a sighting, Bennett finally let his shoulders relax and slumped over the steering wheel of his 2005 Ford, its eight-cylinder diesel idling like a growling West Indian tiger.

Putting the truck in neutral, he looked around the random garage he'd backed into, tucked away in an alley amid a maze of service roads, most of which didn't show up on any map. Its walls were lined with boxes, fishing poles, and beer signs. Not a bad place to lay low for a while. Sometimes dumb shit like this was necessary to avoid jail time—a lesson he'd learned from a dozen instances of watching his father pull similar dumb shit. *The true master of the lie.* Bennett figured he'd probably get away today, and could use this trick again in the future to dodge yet another cop. *Though I'm giving less and less of a shit each time I do.*

The only reason he was hiding in the garage like a common criminal in the first place was that he'd failed to signal a lane change and slammed on his brakes. *Thought I saw an IED. It happens.* It would have been easy to oblige the traffic officer, pull over, and play nice, but everything about Bennett stunk to high Heaven at the moment, and not just his breath and armpits. Today, he was driving angry, with plenty of reasons not to pull over, knowing full well he'd cashed in all of his good karma chips after his last offense three weeks ago.

The unfortunate incident involved the destruction of private property and the deaths of eight chickens from a local egg farm. *To be fair, who puts a chicken coop so close to the fucking road?* The county judges and higher-ups in the police department were nothing if not flag-waving, vet-loving Americans—good people infatuated enough with the idea of Bennett's service as to let it cloud their judgment. *The type of folks who'd say "thank you for your service" and have no idea what the Hell they're really thanking me for.*

He'd been let off the hook many times, but the galled look on Judge Riendot's face after the chicken coop incident unmistakably proved that Bennett's days of leniency were numbered. It seemed the community had had enough of him and his vapid bullshit: drunk and disorderly calls, public urination, things of that nature. *Bar fights are my specialty.* Throwing his weight around was one of his favorite pastimes, along with volunteering at the recruitment office at the mall, playing video games in his apartment, and dragging the streets of Tempe for special company—all of which he had ample time for, having been unemployed for the past thirteen months following a failed stint as a car-wash custodian.

So far, no one in the housing complex had noticed him or his truck, or seemed to care enough to make a verbal fuss about his commandeering the garage. Surprising, considering how many were willing to call the cops on someone who looked like a crotchety UFC fighter with shoulders and back almost entirely covered in ink. The most prominent tattoo, the one that made his blood boil every time he caught a glimpse of it in the mirror, was a pencil-sketch style of a tulip on his right arm, strung around a Marine Corps crest.

After an additional four minutes of cop-free streets passed, Bennett turned off the Ford's engine and took out the keys. Sitting back, exhausted and thirsty, he reached for a bottle-shaped paper bag in the passenger seat. Popping the top, he drank like a fish, leaving a good bit of whiskey on his thick beard and chest. *All right. What are my options?* No way he could drive away now. The Ford stuck out like a sore thumb, and his name and license plate were likely all over town. Plus, the cops weren't the only ones after him at the moment.

Today was turning out to be fucking stupid.

Grabbing the bottle, he opened the door and stepped down, knowing the scream would return. Using the truck's handrails for support, he descended, ignoring his bad right knee, shrieking inside him like an old, ugly aunt who'd just woken up from a nap. It was an angry war wound that refused to leave him alone even for a second. The pain even followed him into his dreams. *I limp there, too. It's annoying.*

Ducking out of the garage into the alley, he crossed the street, and hurried toward a local soda shop, Jack's Sodas and Cream Café. The alley behind the shop had been Bennett's usual hangout since he was fifteen, when his family moved to Prescott from Waco, Texas, so his dad could start a business. *Though I'd personally call it a fraud factory. Loser.* There were plenty of stacks of crates and trash cans—some good stoops for stooping, too.

Reaching the spot where he could still see Main Street, he stumbled, landing with concrete in his spine, and laughed with complacency—a forfeit of self-respect. Lying back on his elbows, he drank, watching the families go about their day on Main Street, their stupid faces and smiles making him want to puke. *Fuckin' consumer whores. Ignoring everything going on above 'em. Pretending shit's taken care of.*

The afternoon came and went as Bennett waited for the cover of nightfall to make his escape, and the bottle was soon empty. Not a soul had come or gone, except for a teenage employee of the soda shop with glasses, who stepped out to throw boxes into the dumpster, spotted him, inexplicably said, "Sorry," and hightailed it back inside. Two hours of peace and quiet had gone by since.

When shuffling feet came scraping up the alley, Bennett's head was buried in his folded arms over his knees. Through a gap he could see worn loafers and tattered slacks approaching, and he hoped whoever it was would ignore him and move on. *Why is solace so hard to find?* But the worn sneakers planted themselves firmly in front of him.

"Mind if I sit?" an old sandpaper voice asked.

The shape leaned to block the blinding sun, revealing a wrinkled smile aimed Bennett's way. The bearded vagrant wore a gray knitted cap with two brown stripes above gray puffs of hair poking out over his ears, which seemed large enough to glide with. An olive-green, double-breasted twill trench coat, riddled with holes, rested over a lighter jacket that may have been near-white at some point. His hands were rested on a cane with a dark wood shaft, topped with an emerald-green stone that seemed to radiate a faint glow from within.

"I don't have any change," Bennett said immediately.

The old man shook his head. "Don't want any. Too heavy."

"Then what do you want?"

"Lots of stuff."

Bennett half laughed and buried his head in his arms again, expecting the vagrant to vamoose, but there was no crunching gravel. "Is it too much to ask to be alone?" Bennett said. "Helps calm me down."

"Not at all," the vagrant replied, taking a seat next to him.

And people call me tone-deaf. Bennett's anger was all but spent. He let it go. As long as the guy didn't talk, he didn't care; he just wanted to think. They sat in silence for nearly five minutes before the old vagrant chuckled out of nowhere.

"Sorry," he said. "Thought of something funny."

The next silence lasted only a moment before the old man was giggling again, then laughing to himself. Soon, he was cackling so loudly it echoed down the alley.

Bennett glanced around, not getting the joke. "What's your problem?"

The vagrant reached into his breast pocket, revealing a worn green notebook with a chewed wooden pencil tucked into its weathered pages. He wrote something down, excited and chuckling the entire time. Once finished, he put the book back in his pocket and returned to sitting in silence, as though nothing had happened.

"I don't care if you're crazy, or whatever," Bennett said. "Just leave me alone. It's not the day."

"What's not the day?" the vagrant asked, cheerfully untouched.

"Do I look like the kind of guy you want to piss off?" Bennett asked, not expecting an answer.

"Not sure, to tell you the truth. You people all started to look alike after a while."

That does it. Bennett struggled to stand, his anger surging, ready to take everything out on this poor dumbass who'd wandered into the wrong alley and fucked with the wrong guy. Leaning on his good knee, he reached for the vagrant's throat.

"An Englishman, an Irishman, and a Scotsman are stranded on

a desert island!" the vagrant yelled as if it were an incantation, his hands up, hurling the quip.

The soldier found himself dumbfounded. In all his years of combat, he'd never seen a defense quite like this. His repertoire had nothing to offer the situation. He stepped back and waited.

The vagrant continued, "One day the Englishman comes across a bottle with a cork in it buried in the sand. He tries to read the label because, who knows, it might be worth a drink, right? But it's dirty, so he starts rubbing it to clean it up. Suddenly, guess what happens? The cork flies off, and *poof*, out pops a genie, who promises to grant them each one wish as a way of saying, 'Thanks for getting me out of that friggin' bottle.' The Englishman was the one to rub him out, so he gets the first wish and wishes he was back in his local pub, a cold pint in hand, a beautiful woman in the other, and his foot on the telly. The genie says, 'Great,' claps his hands, and the Englishman disappears. Next is the Scotsman. He thinks hard and says he wishes he was back home in his favorite chair with his feet up and a nice haggis waiting for him. Once again, the genie claps his hands, and the Scotsman is whisked away. The genie then turns to the Irishman and asks, 'So, young man, with this one wish, what do you desire more than anything?' The Irishman looks up at the genie, seeming very upset, and says, 'I'm so lonely—I wish my friends were back here with me.'"

The vagrant opened his arms as though he'd just performed a trick. A long moment passed where a cold wind blew and a beige sedan drove by before Bennett smirked and tried to take a drink of whiskey, having forgotten the bottle was dry. "Pretty funny."

The old man tucked a puzzled finger under his tattered beard. "That one's usually a killer. Heard it from a fella a few dimes ago. Been my go-to ever since. I'm still hoping one day I can write a joke as good. How about you? Do you have one?"

"One what?" Bennett asked.

"Favorite joke."

"Do I look like it?"

"People will surprise you."

"I hate surprises," Bennett said. "Besides, these days, in this country, there's nothing worth laughing at. It all leads to bullshit eventually, right? Life's like a . . . revolving joke."

"I've considered something similar many times," said the vagrant, "but it seems too . . . too . . . base? I think. That'll do." Reaching into his left jacket pocket, he revealed a fresh bottle of whiskey, the same brand as Bennett's original, and held it out with a puckered smile. "Look, we could get into a pissing match about who's got it worse between the two of us, or we could get drunk and be miserable together. Your choice."

A shot rang through Bennett. He'd heard those words before. *Miserable together. Yeah, Lance used to say that every time we'd get shit-faced after a mission.* He saw his squadmate, Mark Lance, in his mind, telling jokes and doing hand magic. Then he saw his pale face as he lay in his casket at his wake.

Pills. Fuckin' tragedy. Goddamn VA.

He didn't want to think of Mark. Bennett just wanted a drink. "My man." He took the bottle from the vagrant and sat down to pop it open.

"You know, when I walked into this alley, I wasn't expecting to see a vet drinking himself into the gutter," the old man said, taking the bottle back for a nip.

"Is there a better place to drink myself into?"

"Shower never hurt anybody."

"Coming from you?"

"Got me there." The vagrant handed the bottle back and wiped his gray beard, then took a huge breath, as though to prepare to say something he'd been dwelling on. "What a world. Days like today really make you wonder, don't they?"

"I don't wonder anymore," Bennett replied.

"That's amazing," said the vagrant. "I've never found a way to silence that voice asking why. No matter how many layers I pull back, the answer is always one step ahead of me." He looked up at the clouds as he finished, carrying a deep, arid sadness about him.

Bennett felt sorry for the guy. *He looks the way I feel. Starting to think he's seen some shit.* "Me personally, I think this world is a festering wound."

The old man laughed. "Yes, it's hard not to. But wounds heal, as long as there is life. Keep that in the back of your mind." With that, he closed the bottle. "I think that's enough. Fellas like us gotta ration things like this. Make it last."

Bennett scoff-laughed again. "What do you—I'm not homeless."

"Then what are you doing here?"

"Just 'cause I can't go home doesn't mean I don't have one."

"So what's the difference between you and me?" the vagrant asked.

"Fuck semantics, man. You know what I mean . . . In actuality, no, there is no difference. We're both just heaps of meat fucking over other heaps of meat. All for shitty profit. Makes me want to scream."

"You got a couple of screws loose, don't you?" The vagrant laughed and snorted. *Damn it. I'm starting to like this guy.* "You know what your problem is, son? You see everything as 'us' versus 'them.' It's terribly acidic. Trust me, nothing is ever cut and dried. There are levels."

"Things are pretty cut and dry where I come from," Bennett said. "It's kill or be killed. No way around it." *Maybe I don't like him.*

"*Hrm.*" The vagrant sounded frustrated, as though he were trying to make a point but couldn't quite land it. "That's sometimes true, and sometimes not. Not to sound indelicate, but you appear to be in desperate need of a bath and a massage, my friend. Why don't you head home and cool down? Have a good meal. Rest. You've obviously had a heck of a day."

"Cops had my place tagged last I checked. Might even be an official crime scene by now. Figured vacating was smart."

"I see. You rob a bank or something?"

"Assault," Bennett said solemnly.

"Oh dear. Against whom?"

"Her name is Autumn. Working name is, at least. Maybe was. Not sure."

"I assume it was all a misunderstanding. Or you acted in defense. An accident, perhaps?"

"Nope. She was innocent."

"Sounds like you got yourself into something very thick, young man," the vagrant said, sounding disappointed.

"I know. I know! I said I didn't want to talk about—I lost my shit. I just . . . it was a bad day. And she kept yelling. I asked her to go. I could feel it coming, you know? I get these . . . these . . . moments, flashes of utter rage. It's so much that I feel like I can't take it, and I need to break whatever is near me. For fuck's—" Bennett's hands were shaking. His head was pounding. "She just kept coming at me about money, and I tried to explain—and I snapped. I put her down. She fell into the cabinet. I'm still not even sure she got back up. I just . . . lashed out. It was so hard. My fucking hand—" Bennett's words stumbled out. "I called the ambulance, got out of there. Now I'm here, with you, avoiding everyone, including a pimp I've never met before and desperately don't want to."

A space was left, a silence to let him catch his breath.

"You know, thinking about it, I can honestly say I've never once crossed a pimp," the vagrant said jovially. "You've got me on that one. Maybe because I've never been one for personal contact?"

"Fuck—why'd you say that so nice? I don't deserve it."

"What do you deserve, then?"

"Prison. Or probably Hell at this point," Bennett said.

"Awful steep, don't you think?"

"You don't know my crimes. Or me."

"Does using the H-word imply you believe in life after death? 'Cause otherwise, you got nothing to worry about." The vagrant's tone was so easygoing, you'd think he was discussing the weather.

"I don't. At least, I don't think I do," Bennett answered. "Sometimes I wish there was life after death. But we would have to know about it—that it exists, you know? The whole truth. This going in blind crap isn't working."

"What do you mean?"

"People and their blind faith. Makes them act shitty because they think imaginary things are real. What we saw . . . in war, or battle—whatever—me and my guys, we did so much for this country. For those people," he said, pointing at the citizens walking and shopping on Main Street. "They praise some invisible man before ever thanking us. Then they come and picket my friends' funerals, saying they died because God wanted them to, because they deserved it. Makes me sick. None of us are decent. Yeah, I hope Hell is real. We all deserve to go."

The old vagrant sat wide-eyed, bulged his cheeks, and let out a burst of air. "Wow. That is . . . a new perspective. Thank you." He then patted Bennett on the back, as though to say, *Great job, kiddo*.

"So, let's say it is real. All of it. The whole religious shebang, and all the horrible punishments waiting for us beyond the grave. Even then, you're still a young man! What, thirty-four? Plenty of time to right your wrongs. It's not like you killed someone."

"I've killed more people than I know," Bennett said, stone faced. "Every single one of them someone's brother, or sister, or kid. Most of them, never even saw their faces. And for the record, I'm thirty-six."

"Sounds like we've both seen our fair share of war," the vagrant said with an identical air, gathering a suspicious stare from Bennett. "Don't think I got it in me? Death seems to follow me wherever I go. Because of it, I've done more unspeakable things than I can even remember."

"Then how do you know you did 'em?"

The vagrant sighed with the weight of more years than Bennett cared to guess. "Because I remember how I felt each time."

Silenced, Bennett searched for a new subject. "Which branch were you in?" The vagrant's brow tightened as if confused. "You know, Navy, Marines . . ."

"Oh. Right. Gotcha. Uh, none . . . I guess you'd say it was an offshoot branch."

"Try me," Bennett pressed.

"No, son. Pretty sure you never heard of us. We were a small group. Not really warriors in the strictest sense. More . . . facilitators."

"Of war?" Bennett asked.

"Of peace. That was the idea, anyway," the vagrant finished with a tired grin.

"Funny how many people we have to kill to stop all the killing, huh?" Bennett added.

For once, the vagrant had no remark. He simply smiled as one does after hearing a joke that brings to mind a dark memory but doesn't want to ruin the fun for the others, so they keep it to themselves.

Bennett wanted to save them both the embarrassment and changed the subject again. "Tell me why you seem so familiar. Have we been drunk in an alley together before?"

"No, I've only been in town a few weeks. Maybe I just have one of those faces? Why, is something wrong?" the vagrant asked.

Bennett shook his head. "Just déjà vu. Hate the stuff."

Using his cane for support, the vagrant stood with a groan.

"There's nothing I can do about that. There's not much I can do about any of this. And yet, here we are. But I want you to know something, young man. When I set foot in this alley, it was because of a choice. Same as you. Where you go when you leave here— that's a choice. Sometimes it seems like the world is nothing but a bunch of choices colliding into each other, sending everybody in completely different directions from where they started. It's maddeningly unpredictable. And yet, after all my years, I'm still not sure who makes them. Is it really us, the players, or is it something else? I just don't know. In fact, I've reached the point where I don't really give a hoot. I'll play along, fuck it. But what I want to see more than anything is one choice that straightens it all out, like . . . planets aligning. Even if just for a second. That would be true beauty. If I could just see that, it would all be worth it." His sandpaper voice trailed off, sounding weary, like an idealist whose candle was close to being extinguished by the rain.

Bennett shook his head. "Universe ain't my problem. I got plenty of those already. A bunch of assholes who sit in front of computers all day put me on meds for my knee that they knew fucked people up, then hung me out to dry when I refused to take them. And this whole society has done nothing but give me shit for what I—what *we*—did for them. I mean, I can't even walk around like a fully formed person." *Where is this coming from?* Bennett couldn't help unloading on the old stranger. "You want to talk about choices? How about the people who don't get to make them for themselves? Taking orders all day. Nobody ever gives a shit about them. Nobody ever asks what they want."

The vagrant smiled like a proud grandpa and handed Bennett the bottle. "Here, keep it. Good talk, son. Peace be with you and all that." Pulling down his gray knitted cap with two brown stripes, he gave a respectful nod and walked back the way he'd come. "I'm glad I got to meet you in this life. Remember, the world is made of choices . . . and a bath and a meal can work wonders."

"What do you mean 'this life'?" Bennett shouted, but the vagrant had already disappeared around the brick corner, leaving him alone to contemplate their conversation. *Never even got his name.* He was sure he'd seen him before. There was something familiar, almost comforting, about the scruffy vagrant, and for several minutes Bennett couldn't stop replaying his last words in his mind. *Why did he say, "this life"?*

When his wristwatch beeped, signaling the hour, Bennett snapped to attention. The day was getting late, and his baby would not stay safe much longer. Hurrying across the street to the open garage, he climbed into his truck, took three sloppy attempts to get the key in the ignition before starting the engine, and somehow convinced himself he was sober enough to make it safely out of town. Taking his foot off the brake, he hoped for the best and made his way south, past Main Street to Highway 89, into a stretch of barren desert. Proud of himself for drifting only a little, he was soon twenty miles outside of town, in the clear. *Cops only come out here if someone calls 'em.*

By sundown, his truck was kicking up pillows of dust into the day's remaining light, casting the dimming sky on fire. As darkness swept over the valley, the truck rolled onto a dirt lot in front of a rustic, abandoned gas station. None of its original vintage pumps remained, having been stolen years ago, much to Bennett's chagrin—mostly because he'd had no idea they were valuable and would have sold them himself if he had. The truck's headlights swept over the building and its connected auto garage, illuminating the main entrance. He parked, leaving the engine running and lights on, illuminating the weeds wrapping their way through every crevice and broken window, giving the station the visage of a sunken ship within the dark depths of the sea.

His thoughts drifted to what it might look like if he decided to put the Ford in gear and tear through the whole goddamn thing. *Probably fun as Hell.* But the damage it would do to his truck wasn't worth it. *True.* The Ford was all he had left in the world, other than the deed to the dirt beneath the station.

Stepping down from the cab, he found the paper-bag-wrapped bottle of whiskey still in his hands, though he couldn't remember picking it up, and tossed it back into the cab. Approaching the station entrance, he pulled out his key ring from his pocket. He opened the first two locks but paused before opening the third, unsure why, and turned around. The blinding headlights made it impossible to see anything but the deep blue sky above, fading quickly to black and revealing a starry Arizona night.

"Hello?" he called, answered only by his truck's purring engine.

Turning the last key, Bennett entered the station and shut the door behind him. Hard streams of light from his truck pierced through the station's shattered windows, tinted a slight blue in the lingering air. He limped past the clerk counter and fallen shelves, over rotten wood crack-ing under his weight, past mountains of boxes and stacks of files, into the rear of the station and the corner office. Its door was adorned with a skewed nameplate reading *Mr. Hunter - Owner and Operator.*

A coyote's howl in the distance broke the silence, jolting him as he opened the door that was half hanging on one hinge. *Not in the fucking mood, dog.* The rest of the station was a mess worthy of a flamethrower or a hand grenade, but this room had been preserved perfectly. A thin layer of dust blanketed every inch. Bennett lifted his right leg, letting his boot hover over the entry, closed his eyes, and messed the first bit of dust on the floor. Moving to the wall on the left, he looked over the rows of plaques and custom frames decorating it. Most contained certificates of excellence from local newspapers, hedge fund managers, and even a few of the companies his father had defrauded. All were dated at least thirty years ago.

When everything (*inevitably*) came crashing down, and the Hunter family was left with nothing, the plaques were left behind—an attempt by Bennett's father, Tony, to keep up appearances and pretend the business was as legitimate and profitable as ever—surely never propped up on faulty repairs with counterfeit parts and a thinly veiled aftermarket warranty scheme. *No, never.*

Below the main cluster, a wooden frame hung tilted, covered with spiderwebs. A black-and-white photo resided inside. In it, a picturesque nuclear family stood in front of the store, the way it had once looked in its prime: bushes trimmed, windows clean, the exterior walls freshly painted.

Hi Mom. Hi Dad. Hi Jer.

His father was dressed in a finely pressed suit next to their immaculate mother, with the two boys, aged nine and fourteen, standing on either side of them. The older boy, with a thinner jaw and dressed in a fitted suit, wore the same stern expression as the father, while the younger, the stockier boy beamed sarcastically, missing most of his baby teeth and clutching a wooden sword and shield. *"Do what good you can, King Arthur." That's what Jerry used to say to me. "That will always be enough."* Bennett tried to hear his older brother say the words, but could no longer remember what his voice sounded like. Nor could he recall his mother's. The only voice he could remember—and remember he did, clear as stolen crystal— was his father's. *Either shouting or whispering so intensely you'd wish he were shouting.*

Stepping away from the photos, Bennett flung the brown leather chair behind the desk in a circle. Its rusted joints screamed as it rotated, forcing it to a quick stop. He spun it again, sending the chair screeching back to the same position.

He forced it harder, this time getting two spins.

Again, harder still. The chair's screams flew through the halls and back over the shattered glass on the station floor. Bennett sat, avoiding the exposed springs, his eyes fixed on the photo amid the certificates—specifically on him and Jerry, sharing their father's wide nose and stout forehead.

What's it been, Jer, sixteen—seventeen years?

Saliva drained from his lips onto his beard as he gazed, his eyelids heavy and uneven. The second-drawer handle was gripped and absentmindedly pulled opened. Without taking his eyes off the photo, Bennett placed the drawer's contents on the desk. In the light of the truck headlights, the cold gray steel of a 1964 U.S. military-issue revolver gleamed like smooth charcoal.

Taking up the weapon, he aimed it at the photo. "Son, what good is a gun if it's not loaded? You thinkin' straight?" Bennett lowered his tone, matching his father's, and pulled back the hammer. "You a man like your brother? A little man-fucking faggot? Or are you a man like a man? Huh?"

He squeezed the trigger, and the gun went off with a thunderous bang, lighting the room with a flash, mussing the dust on the desk. The bullet tore into the lower corner of the photo. *Reliable sixty-four. Right, Dad?* He fired again. "Do you know what to do when someone refuses to stop causing trouble?" The blast tore open the opposite corner as the gun fired on repeat, and he lost count of how many bullets were left in the cylinder.

In his mind, Bennett was screaming, letting the anger escape into his veins, but on the outside, he was as silent as the night. The photos on the wall dripped splinters, reduced to chunks dangling by wires. His finger caressed the trigger, and his jaw shook so violently it sent tremors through his whole body. To Bennett, it all felt like a sign. There were no options. There was nowhere to go.

What if I'm the one who won't stop causing trouble, Dad? He fought to hear Jerry's voice, not his father's. *Why can't I remember what he sounded like? He'd know what to do. He'd know what to say. He always did.*

"A real man always knows what to do, you little shit." Bennett repeated in his father's voice, as though possessed by the spirit of Tony Hunter, suddenly surprised to find the cold barrel of the gun resting against his temple. *Really? We're doing this again?* Bennett wanted to laugh at himself. Nothing ever came of episodes like these. Most likely, he would wake up in the morning with nothing more than a hangover and regret. But when his mouth opened, he released a sound he never knew he was capable of making. A moan of pain and regret escaped, with so much raw emotional force he thought he might burst like a water balloon. The dam had broken, and he was facing it with nothing but fear, feeling smaller and smaller every second. Shaking, he gripped the handle tight and held his breath.

Tell you what, Dad, if there's one left in the chamber, it's on me.

With a sudden clarity—real or imaginary—Bennett closed his eyes and pulled the trigger.

"The creatures of UnEarth are our essence. Thus, it all begins within us, and the power we generate within. I wonder, is there a way to increase this ever-present Eve prior to one's death? If so, how? Is there a limit to how powerful one human might become? My source seemed uneasy with the question."

- Excerpt from the journal of
Dr. Francisco Emul. Murcia
October 1896

IZAIAH

Izaiah took the last bite of the fried chicken leg he'd fished out of the garbage. It was still greasy, crunchy, and flavorless. He'd gotten bored waiting and decided to eat food from Earth, which—aside from ice cream—was as good as trash to him. *Ugh, why do I do this to myself?* With a belch, he tossed the bone aside so a colony of lesser creatures could take what they needed from it. He liked thinking of the little guys. The cloudy sky was lit by a dull moon tinted a warm blue, as rainwater drained down the street from a storm that had recently rolled over town, giving the alley floor a reflective shine. Cars sped by, splashing the sidewalks and red-bricked buildings of the sleepy town's business district.

The old man, who appeared to be a simple vagrant, had seen nearly every type of village built by mankind since they began do-ing so. *People didn't have houses for a long time—they just walked everywhere, from one place to the next, picking up food along the way. It wasn't so bad, really. Nice folks, most of 'em.* However, desert com-munities like Prescott, Arizona, had fascinated him since their inception in the nineteenth-century, which seemed only yesterday to him. *If there's no water, what are you weirdos doing out here?*

Then again, much about North America puzzled him. *It used to be a quiet place.* When people began arriving by the boatful on what Izaiah called the "flat, but pointy in the middle" continent, he first started noticing subtle changes in the Eve. They were dreamers, no doubt, but most seemed to be trekking across this "new land" looking not for community but for some sort of isolation. *It got real hard to find anyone willing to take me in.* Izaiah had grown used to being kicked out of human villages long ago, so it was only mildly surprising that there seemed no place in the developing world for one like him. Humanity, with their notions of owning land and picturesque towns in complete isolation—free from outside influence (*or dirty apples*)—seemed an element here to stay.

Which baffles me, if I'm honest. After all, humans had found ways to connect and share their written words, voices, and visual ideas all across the globe in only a few centuries—a feat Izaiah never dreamed possible. He was sure peace would finally break out like a plague. But then, following a couple of big wars, most of humanity fell back into their tired old xenophobia, which often had a tendency to spread.

After all this time, and all of his fighting, there seemed to be nothing he could do to help humanity move forward. Even when told the truth about the universe (*and I mean the real truth*) people in communities like Prescott rarely believed him. And why should they? If life seemed good, why allow in anyone with crazy notions who might wish to take it away? Most simply weren't willing to accept that a world existed above their own, populated by beings of their own making. Coincidentally, this idea seemed to conflict the most with religious types.

Despite confessing to many what he really was over the years, always hoping someone might finally believe his tale of the soul, or as he knew it, the Eve, and in return share their own secrets about what it felt like to be the driving force behind it, no one ever came along. *Statistically speaking, I should have found something resembling a friend by now.* People liked believing what was in front of them, and to the naked eye Izaiah had never looked like much more than an old kook in need of a bar of soap and a pair of clippers. But that never stopped him from trying to bridge the divide between his people and humanity.

"That's why it's gotta be you," he remembered his old friend Afton Laffler saying in his bid to persuade Izaiah to cosponsor the mandate to send human delegates to Earth in lieu of representatives from Arros and Hywyn. The hope was it might quell some of the growing tensions in the UnEarth Senate and among the UnEarth people. *Haven't seen everyone this tense for a few thousand years, since before Inferius.* To everyone's surprise—especially Izaiah's—the mandate was approved unanimously by the Senate, leaving the responsibility of finding the human delegates to Earth's ranking Warden Sentry: him.

It's a lot of nonsense jargon, I know, but should start making sense soon. The point is, I don't want to be here, and definitely think this is a bad idea. But if it's gotta be done, it's gotta be me who does it.

Presently, taking another look around the drop-off point, where he'd found a stack of empty crates to rest on, part of Izaiah wondered if he'd told the UnEarth kingdoms the wrong time and place, as he'd been known to do from time to time, though the incidents were usually spaced out by a few hundred years, give or take a decade. He checked his watch: 11:04 p.m. Still no humans. *For crying out loud!* No one knew exactly how long it would take for the powers above and below to finish imbuing his chosen human delegates with Eve, which was one small example of the greater problem at large with this particular mandate: no one knew anything. Izaiah could look to neither realm of the "afterlife" for help. There was no precedent.

Letting out a tired sigh, he wished for more horrid human food to distract himself from the fact that the delegates would be arriving soon with surely nothing but questions, and he was the one expected to have answers. In addition, he was tasked with breaking the news to the humans that even though they weren't technically dead, they were going to be treated as such—much like pawns—by a world they never actually knew existed until now.

A flash caught his senses. He looked up and sniffed. Wrath was near—*What humans are calling Hell these days.* Using his cane to stand, Izaiah reached into his jacket for half a comb to straighten his scruffy beard and eyebrows, adjusting his gray knitted cap. Un-Earth energies surged down the alley at a three-way junction. A blinding strike came and went, lighting the alley and probably half the neighborhood, as a portal opened just large enough for a human. Heat and unbridled Wrath poured from the porthole, nearly shoving Izaiah off his feet. A body soared through the hole and landed on the greasy pavement with a paralyzed thud. Before he could reach it, the portal snapped shut with a gasp.

"You cowards! Can't even face me? Show off your handiwork!?" Izaiah shouted, shaking a balled fist as he hobbled to meet the body tossed out like garbage. Nearing the man on the ground, whose skin was sizzling, Izaiah knew he was going to hate what he was about to see. Splayed on the ground, eyes closed, was not the angry one, not the soldier, but the teacher.

Alex Barker stirred, unconscious. Muscle spasms rolled through his body as though he were being shocked by small, invisible stun guns. Stepping closer, Izaiah caught a whiff of him—just to be sure.

It was obvious, even to an old Medolian like himself. Alex was soaked in the essence of destruction. He'd been to Arros. *Or Hell—whatever you call it. I'm so sorry, Mr. Barker.*

Another train of Eve was fast approaching—Rapture this time, the essence of creation. *What humans might call Heaven. Though . . . I don't know. Not really what I'd call it. The place gives me the willies.* A similar flash of energy erupted over the alley, freezing Izaiah's gut and forcing everything in the alley to slow in time. Bennett Hunter fell from the portal, landing a few feet from Alex, and the second Eve gate snapped shut, plunging the alley into darkness. The mortals lay still, their clothes and skin steaming in the cool evening air.

"Sure. Take a nap. That's fine," Izaiah said. Seizing the opportunity, he held his cane over each of the humans in turn, scanning for possible foul play. *They seem all right, and I can sense the seeds of Wrath and Rapture within them.* Though knowing that didn't give him much comfort.

Finding a seat to wait as long as necessary, Izaiah pulled his green journal from his jacket and flipped through its pages, looking for the right thing to say when they woke up—some insight, maybe—but came up dry. A moment later, when Bennett began to stir, Izaiah pocketed the book.

The larger of the humans groaned, grabbed his side, and curled into a ball, shivering and muttering, "Cold, cold—please."

"It'll pass," Izaiah said, unsure if he'd just lied.

Bennett opened his eyes and looked around. "Where am I?"

"Safe. No longer where you were. Try to stay calm. Breathe some robust, dusty air. See? Good stuff." Izaiah pounded his chest and coughed once.

"F—freezing." The soldier sounded weak for the first time since Izaiah had met him.

"It's seventy-nine degrees out. You're okay. Give it time." The old man spotted a shiver running down Alex's back and leaned to see under the bill of his blue baseball cap, where his eyes shone white—roused, yet distant. "Hey, how long have you been awake? Can you hear me?"

The teacher did not react, appearing perpetually terrified.

"I'm sorry, son. It wasn't supposed to be like this." Izaiah leaned in to take his arm, but when he did, it was like popping a balloon.

The teacher's limbs thrashed in a last-ditch effort for survival. "Stop! No more burn! Please. Stop! It's coming!" he screamed, unaware of his surroundings. "Stop!"

Izaiah managed to hold him steady. "Easy—easy. You are far from there, you hear me? Nowhere near it. The Earth has you now."

The teacher finally blinked as he took deep breaths, holding Izaiah's arms for support. "Did you pull me out?" he asked, his raspy voice filled with despair. "Thank you."

"No. Don't thank me. Please don't ever do that," Izaiah said, nearly brought to his knees by the look in Alex's eyes—a look he'd never seen in a human before. They weren't the same eyes of the man he'd met many times over the past few weeks: those of an idealistic elementary school teacher leaving a food mart or stopping at a red light, always ready to give what little he had to those less fortunate. No, these were broken, revealing a mind pushed beyond its Earthly limits.

Setting Alex against a stack of crates, Izaiah let him rest so he could remember how to use his lungs. By now Bennett was sitting up. "Hello," Izaiah said, followed by a toothy smile full of gaps. "Welcome back!"

"Who are you?" Bennett asked, reaching into his back pocket for his phone gadget, only to find it dead.

"Electronic devices rarely survive an Eve gate," Izaiah said.

"Sorry, I know humans love their devices these days, but right now I need you to focus. Are you okay? Does everything feel in place? With your body? Mind? Soul? I want to make sure they put you back together right. I would have been there personally with you the whole way if they'd let me, but sadly my jurisdiction is limited to this planet."

Bennett hurled his phone to the alley's end, gripped the dumpster, and fought to rise, shoving away Izaiah's helping hands. "Get off me, man!" Unable to stand, he was reduced to a crawl, progressing a few feet before collapsing into a puddle, clutching his side.

"Ah, look what you did," Izaiah said, picking Bennett up off the ground and laying him against a nearby dumpster. Reaching into his pocket, he produced a gray hanky to wipe him off.

"I know you," Bennett said, refusing the help.

Izaiah smiled. "Hope so. Why drink half a bottle of whiskey with someone in an alley if they're just going to forget you?"

Bennett looked over his shoulder at Main Street, dropped his chin to his chest, and laughed. "This is it. The alley. I never left, huh? Fuck, I drank a lot. What time is it? And who is that?" He pointed at Alex, curled up against dairy crates, his tenuous gaze fixed on the ground. "Hey, buddy, bad night too?" Bennett chuckled to himself.

"Would you believe me if I told you I found you passed out here?" Izaiah asked.

Bennett shrugged. "Wouldn't be the first time."

"Then that's what happened. You and the other one both passed out, and I'd like to offer my assistance," Izaiah said.

"I told you earlier, there's nothing you can do to help me. I'll be in jail, or Mexico, or dead within a week. Frankly, right now, I don't know which I'd pick. So . . . just stay away from me. Seems like we're both bad luck," Bennett said.

Izaiah was stumped. This wasn't how he'd thought this would go. "Tell you what, let's start over. I've been rude. Never even properly introduced myself to either of you." He switched to a tense foreign accent, intrinsically smooth and unlike any on Earth. "My name is Izaiah Ezekial Devonah–Vature Saltulay Mont'Cabeese Relure Renada Tamoris Gulmonderiano Kul Sau Tolio Hart Geshwin Balaroo—and that's about as far as I can remember anymore. I think I've got it written down somewhere."

"Parents divorced a bit?" Bennett asked.

"I've tried to respect some of the dominant energies that were my parentage."

"How many people you got in you?"

"Lots. I think," Izaiah answered with a snort.

"Guess we all do." Bennett was eyeing Alex, who was currently looking skyward as though following a flock of birds. "You sure he's all right?" the soldier asked.

"No. I'm not sure," Izaiah said bluntly. "How about you?"

"I feel shitty. So, no."

"Can you elaborate?"

"This is the third time you've asked me. What am I supposed to be? Where's my truck?" Bennett fought to rise, searching his pockets.

Izaiah readied himself in case he needed to catch Bennett again when a weak voice came from behind them both.

"How did we get here?"

They turned to find Alex looking their way, shivering, but free of the microseizures that had riddled him.

"That's a long story," Izaiah replied. "One that I'm happy to tell, but first I need you both to come with me."

"Where?" Alex asked.

"Someplace less exposed. No telling who might come looking for the two newest Eve signatures on Earth, and we can't afford to let anyone see you fellas and possibly start a panic. Sorry to say, you've caused quite the stir in my world, and most people aren't too happy about it."

"What are you—no. What? Shut up. I'm leaving," Bennett said, fighting to remain standing as he took his first steps out of the alley.

"That won't do any good. Not now," Izaiah said.

The soldier stopped and spun around. "What do you mean?"

Izaiah crept toward him, dragging and tapping his cane on the ground. "Think, Mr. Hunter. It must be in there somewhere. Go back. Hours, maybe eons. Not sure what it would be like to a mind like yours."

"Look, I passed out. Had a bad dream. Got drunk. Probably still am. It happens."

"Your truck isn't in the garage. It's still outside the station," Izaiah said. "You left the lights on. I turned them off for you and closed the door. You're welcome."

Bennett froze in place, his back facing Izaiah. "Say that again."

"The Sip and Drip? Your father's place? Off Highway 95?" Izaiah continued. "The shattered picture frames will be a dead giveaway if you return." *Hope this isn't too aggressive, but we don't have much time.*

Bennett faced Izaiah, huffing and letting his inner caveman out. "Fuck you. That's something I told you yesterday, right? Now you're using it against me like an asshole. I fell asleep, and—"

"What makes you say that?" Izaiah asked. *Humans are so volatile sometimes.*

"Because dreams don't become real. And if you die—" Bennett went silent as his gaze drifted to the side.

"How many bullets were in the gun, Bennett?" Izaiah asked.

Alex looked up. "Gun?" He sounded dazed, his arms wrapped around his knees. "I remember a gun . . . I remember falling."

Izaiah waved his arms as if warning a plane not to land. "Don't think about it. Focus on literally anything else!"

"What is happening? Where is my wife?" Alex cried.

"This is going to be jarring. I've gone over this a lot and there seems to be no easy way to say it." Izaiah calmly stepped toward the teacher. "What was the last thing you remember on Earth?"

Alex's brow furrowed, as if he were battling an old, unwanted memory. "The restaurant. The boy. I thought I was going to die—"

"Only for a moment," Izaiah said in his low, scratchy voice. "I was able to reach you both before you faded. Though, Bennett, I admit I almost wasn't fast enough to snag you. Rapture still trips me up from time to time."

"What are you talking about? Snag me? From where?" Bennett asked, leaning in to join the conversation.

Alex felt down his right thigh. "No . . . I felt it."

"It's complicated. Just 'cause you're on my turf now doesn't mean I understand it," Izaiah said. "Tell you the truth, I've always secretly hoped for an opportunity like this, to see someone's face when they don't just hear the truth but live it. It's never happened. It's so exciting! But in actuality, no, seeing your faces now reminds me how sad this really is. I'm sorry I have to say this, but Alex Barker didn't survive the night." Izaiah sighed, unable to control his fingers from shaking on the emerald top of his cane.

"Hey, buddy, if you're dead, then what are you doing here? Go bother someone in the afterlife," Bennett said to Alex.

"You're going to have to accept it yourself, Mr. Hunter," Izaiah said. "Or else you'll never be able to do this. Believe me, a lot might be riding on you and Mr. Barker."

"Cut the bullshit!" Izaiah and Bennett turned to Alex. He had one hand on the ground and another gripping a dairy crate, fighting to stand. "If you don't make sense in fifteen seconds, I'm leaving," the teacher finished, glaring.

Izaiah sat on a crate and balanced his hands on his cane. "Let me tell you a story about two parties that have traditionally not gotten along—resembling what you might call Heaven and Hell. A lot of bad blood has been spilled between them and for a long time neither of them seemed interested in putting a stop to it. Until finally, the feud came to an amicable end, and a—let's say, *contract*—was signed, stating neither kingdom could enter or interfere with Earth. Since then, some years have passed in relative peace. Not many, but some. For the most part, everyone's happy, but contracts need to be upheld, and sometimes situations arise that challenge them. This is why I'm here. I have been sent to procure your services, by any means necessary."

"Services for what?" Bennett asked.

"And for who?" Alex added.

"I represent a faction of the UnEarth government operating out of the Tribunal. We are in need of independent delegates who can act as our agents on Earth to find a vigilante Archfiend—sorry, demon—known only as Joseph, who's possessed a mortal and refuses to release them. You two fit the bill as our ideal candidates to handle the situation." Izaiah continued under his breath, "At least that was the idea." He brightened his face in an attempt to soften the news. *Humans love smiling!* "My order was 'find two humans about to die, and send them off to be imbued with Eve.' The kingdoms' methods were to remain secret, as well as how I found you. In fact, only one provision truly matters—when the demon is found, it must be you two who make the arrest."

Bennett spoke to Alex as if Izaiah weren't present. "Did anybody ask you if you wanted to be a part of this Greek drama?"

"No," the teacher answered.

"Me either," Bennett said, stone-faced. "Who chose us?"

"Me . . . I suppose," Izaiah replied.

"I want to be un-chosen," Alex said.

Bennett, rushing in with surprising speed for a human, seized Izaiah by the throat and squeezed. "I want to wake up. Now!"

More confused than in pain, Izaiah spoke quietly so Alex couldn't hear. "Do you remember now, Bennett? Was it five bullets or six?"

The soldier bared his teeth and released his grip.

Stepping back, Izaiah cracked his neck and adjusted his dirty coat. "I can only say I'm sorry so many times. Nothing will change what happened. Life is life, and it all ends. I'm here to ask for your help with a small errand before you fade into the Eve—nothing to fear, simply a formality, and I promise I will do my best to keep you out of harm's way."

Alex appeared the most inclined to believe. "What are you?"

"A Medolian. Thank you for asking."

"Is that like an angel?"

Izaiah shook his head, having thought they would assume he was the grim reaper rather than a Celestial. A man in a dirty coat isn't exactly the first thought that comes to mind for a glorious Heavenly creature. Though, to be fair, humans had no idea what an angel actually looked like.

"No. It's not," Izaiah said, standing up. "Medolians are . . . balancers. I keep an eye on Earth, making sure everything stays in peachy harmony. The living universe is like a boat on a tide. Gotta keep it afloat. If one side gets too heavy—Bennett, as a serviceman you can appreciate the importance of following orders, yeah?"

"Always hated it."

"Well, regardless—"

"Does anyone hear that?" Alex interrupted, peering into the empty distance of the alley as though something unspeakable were there. "Sorry. Never mind. Thought someone was—" Alex rubbed his eyes, stood with a huff, and started out of the alley, taking slow steps.

"Where are you going, Mr. Barker?" Izaiah asked.

"Back to my wife."

"She's not that way. She's behind you. And she always will be. Same with the baby," Izaiah said, deeply regretting the words.

"No, you're lying. This is all a lie!" Alex shouted. "I'm going home."

With a deep sense of remorse, Izaiah watched him go, wishing he had the power to change what had happened. *But no one does. Sorry, Alex, you're not going to like this. We just don't have the time.* Hoisting his cane, Izaiah channeled the Mallos flowing through his veins, and with a sound like crunching tin foil, Alex was lifted off the ground, suspended in a nearly translucent sphere. Rippling energy coursed along its surface like reflections of light off a soap bubble, tinted a slight apple green.

"Put me down!" the teacher shouted, smacking the enclosure.

"You got it, boss." With a wave of his hand, Izaiah collapsed the sphere, dropping Alex into a puddle on the alley floor, drawing stares from the humans as if they'd just seen a ghost. *Which I've never found particularly scary, to be honest. They're quite boring.* "Sorry, but I can't let you go," Izaiah said. "I know this is all a bit strange, and I'll explain everything, but first we need to get you fellas someplace safe. You're going to have to trust me."

"Why is that?" Bennett asked.

"Because a lot of people are relying on us, and as of now, I'm the only one on your side." Izaiah pointed at his rosy cheeks. "Sorry as it is, this was the best face you two could've seen when you woke up. Now, if you could please hold still, I have a feeling you're not going to like this next bit."

IT IS FOUND

"Here goes nothing!" Jeff shouted, yanking a steel lever and shifting the stationary engine out of neutral. Hydraulics moaned under the stress as gears clicked into place, spinning the turbine. Kevlar straps wrapped through steel loops drilled into the rock wall around the onyx door drew so taut they sounded like creaky floorboards as the two-ton lift heaved, shaking dust from the ceiling. Yet the door held firm.

You've got to be kidding me! Leigh stood at the top of the Dead Stairs, off to the side—sweaty, smelly, exhausted, and far too close to the action for any reasonable safety standard. Casey had talked her into wearing a hard hat and goggles at minimum, but damned if she wasn't going to be the first to stare into the doorway's open mouth.

"More!" she barked over the engine.

Jeff gave an unsure nod, seemingly struggling to control the turbine, gripping the joysticks on the console as he stood on a grated platform at the rear. Huge bent legs, drilled several feet into the floor, rose and fell from the body of the machine like an insect, ensuring stability as thousands of pounds of force pulled on the wire retractors. The janky piece of hardware, which Leigh's crew had dubbed the Alien, had been used six times, and six times it hadn't let her down.

"Let's not fuck up our favorite toy quite yet, ay?" Jeff shouted.

"Just open the damn thing!" Leigh roared back, turning to find Casey at the foot of the stairs, several feet back toward the cave entrance, holding her stomach and wearing her anxiety like a beach hat. Recently Leigh had been finding herself wishing her pint-sized companion hadn't come on the dig at all. *She would've been happier at home with her mountains of quilts.*

A low bellow was released by the wall, barely distinguishable from the engine.

"It's gonna give!" Leigh screamed, taking a step closer to the action. *Here we go!* She could hear Casey calling, probably urging her to back off, but the voice was lost in the blender.

"Professor Evans, bad place to be!" Jeff shouted, but she didn't care.

This might be our only chance! The Kevlar straps were stretching past their limit. Each was rated for two thousand pounds, and the lift itself for fifteen. If that couldn't get the job done, it meant calling off the dig until they could commandeer heavier equipment, which could take weeks—maybe months. Not an option. Her mysterious donor wanted results. Their last correspondence proved as much: *Bonus 200k—open door—any means.*

Leigh turned and hustled down the stairs, grabbed the largest sledgehammer she could find, and charged back up. Landing at the top with her back to the door, she lifted the hammer and, in a swift move, released its full force onto the rock.

"You're crazy, Professor!" Jeff shouted, throwing the throttle to maximum.

After one final smash, Leigh leaped out of the way just as the red material around the door hissed like a cracked can of soda. The cavern wall heaved, and the onyx door flung forward with a thunderous pop, crashing down the stairs, spinning and tumbling, finally stopping on the last step with a colossal thud, hurling a wave of dust over Casey as she dodged away, coating her from head to toe.

"Are you insane!?" she screamed, shaking, wiping her mouth and glasses.

Leigh stared into the empty black where the door once stood, (*I did it*), while Jeff killed the engine and laughed like he'd caught a fit.

"Whew! That was some wild shit. The Alien strikes again!"

I really did it. Leigh aimed the flashlight from her side pack into the open doorway, only able to penetrate the dust enough to see walls closing in quickly, narrowing into a path leading farther into the depths of the mountain. *It's time.*

Jeff stepped to her side. "Congratulations."

"Thanks. You deserve a little bit of credit, too."

"Yeah, I do," he replied with a toothy smile.

Leigh grinned, pinched his ass, and stepped toward her exploration gear.

Casey called from the bottom of the stairs, "Um, I thought our agreement was if it took longer than six hours to open the door, we would enter in the morning?"

"Come on, where's your sense of adventure? You really think you'll be able to sleep knowing we just opened her up?" Jeff asked.

"I don't sleep here anyway!" Casey shouted. "It's been a long day, I'm sure we're all tired. Maybe a nap could—"

"I'm good," Leigh said.

"Me too," Jeff added.

"Fine! But do you really want to go in now?" Casey pleaded with her eyes, green in the face.

"There's a path," Leigh said. "Doesn't look difficult. Come up and check it out. You might feel better." *Not likely.*

Casey took a step forward, stopped, turned, ran, and proceeded to vomit in the corner.

"You doing all right, lassie?" Jeff sang, as if patting a friend's back who'd had one too many pints.

Casey leaned on her knees, her hair covering half her face, and gave a thumbs-up.

Good enough for me. Leigh tightened her shoulder pack, readied her camera, and turned on her headlamp. "You can stay here, Casey. Honestly."

Jeff put on his own trekking pack. "I think she's as curious about what's inside as the rest of us. Might just need a moment. Right?"

"It was the freeze-dried omelets," Casey said, rallying and spitting some more on her way up the stairs. "I'm okay."

Once fitted with respirators, Leigh led the group, with Casey second and Jeff in the rear. Lifting her hand, she slowly pressed forward as the fog moved minimally around her. There were no handholds on the walls, or railings, or even images or cave paintings.

"These are the humblest bunch of ancient fucks ever. No signatures or bullshit anywhere!" Jeff remarked.

"Yeah, where's the ego?" Leigh added, taking notice of the ground, which was polished to a lumpy, smooth sheen, making it difficult to walk quickly.

Fifteen meters into the tunnel, her headlamp revealed an opening at the end: a pitch-black space. As they stepped through, the wind on her back spread out into a new cavern, so enormous her headlamp couldn't find the ceiling. When her ankle nearly rolled into a divot, Leigh aimed her light down, revealing a thick, round indentation carved into the dark gray floor, intersecting with others in a precise geometric orientation. Based on the small section she could see, the lines were part of a huge emblem carved into the ground.

"Better get some video," she said.

Casey aimed her camcorder fitted with a light and pressed "Record." Leigh waited a dramatic moment before peering into the lens. *Hope I don't look like ass.*

"This is Professor Leigh Marie Evans, researcher and lecturer at the UCL Institute of Archaeology in London. Today is Wednesday, October eighteenth, two thousand six. The time is a little after seventeen hundred hours. My team and I are standing inside the door beyond the Dead Stairs' passage, located in the western Tibesti Mountains, roughly three hundred miles northwest of Faya-Largeau in northern Chad. Behind the onyx door, we found a corridor roughly twenty yards in length that opened into a larger cavern. We've just begun exploring and have already noticed some interesting things. For example, the floor of the cavern is lined with intricate carvings, roughly six inches deep and six inches wide, forming a complex pattern of some kind. From above, they might create a larger symbol. However, I still do not recognize the design, nor does it resemble any ancient writings or cultural symbols I am aware of. Whoever built this place remains a mystery."

Jeff pulled a few flares from his pack, lit them one by one, and hurled the first two into the distance. They bounced off a wall, rising high thirty yards away and curving up, disappearing into darkness.

"Room looks like a big donut, ay?" he said, tossing another flare.

It sparked and hissed when it struck something above them, ten feet away, bouncing and spinning wildly to the ground. The flare soaked a hulking figure in red light, revealing a thick tongue spewing from a roaring mouth. Claws were reaching for her. The creature's snakelike body was leaned forward in a taunting attack. Casey and Jeff screamed.

"Fuck! Scared the piss outta me and right back in," Jeff said in a panic as Leigh approached the statue—a pristine version of the duo at the base of the Dead Stairs. But this one had not been ravaged by time, and it did not have four arms but ten. The six in the middle, smaller by comparison, must have fallen off of the outer statues over the centuries. The detail in the versions beyond the door was awe-inspiring. Every scale and whisker was present. *Magnificent.*

Leigh looked beyond the statue and spotted its twin to the side. The dark gray and cobalt-blue creatures shone vibrant and alive in their headlamps, also guarding a stairway, this one much taller with a narrower path rising into darkness without barriers or railing. Whatever lay at the top was worth protection from these two nasty characters. *And it's been waiting for me.*

"I really, really hate this," Casey muttered.

"It's just rock," Leigh said. "We live on rock. Let's keep going."

Moving on, Leigh described what she saw to the camera, hardly pausing for interruption, or to breathe, as she analyzed the polished rock of the entrance and walls, speculating on the floor carvings and going over the statues inch by inch, marvelling at how well preserved they were. The mystery was far too exciting. Leigh lost track of time and herself. After a while, Casey stopped filming.

"What's wrong? Is your arm tired?" Leigh asked.

"Do you think we have enough for today?" Casey replied hopefully.

"I do. Anyone? No?" Leigh and Jeff shone their headlamps on her.

"You faring all right there?" Jeff asked. "You're looking a little—"

As though on cue, Casey grabbed her stomach, coughed, and leaned over to vomit again.

"Don't puke on the site!" Leigh screamed.

"I'm so sorry. I can't control it," Casey moaned, spitting out the last bit.

"I'm thinking it wasn't the eggs," Jeff muttered.

"I'm okay. It's just—when the door was opened, I felt ill. Do you not feel it?" Casey asked.

"Hey, don't get me wrong, I'm not feeling one hundred percent either, but this is me since yesterday. We're worried about you," Jeff said.

"Maybe it's best if you go?" Leigh suggested, sure it was a reasonable response. But the looks she received from Jeff and Casey said otherwise. *Why is everyone so sensitive?*

"I'm fine. It's—I can do it. I'll stay," Casey said with a self-reassuring huff.

Leigh smiled, though she wasn't convinced. "I know this place is creepy, but—"

"It's not creepy," Casey interrupted, finally catching up to join them while casting worried glances off to the side, away from the stairs. "It just feels wrong."

"What's over there?" Leigh asked, eyeing her. *She's hiding something.*

Casey gave an exaggerated shrug, her most obvious tell. Stepping away from the stairs, Leigh rounded the second gargoyle and spotted something spread across the ground a couple dozen yards ahead.

"We don't know if it's safe over there," Casey squeaked, hurrying to follow.

Leigh held out her hand, and Jeff placed a flare in it. Once lit, she aimed it forward and ducked around the towering column, stepping carefully over the carvings in the ground as the forms in front of her came into focus: brown and gray, a jumble of shapes. An arm became clear, then a femur, then a mound of skulls.

"Jesus Christ Almighty," Jeff said, wide-eyed. "There are thousands of them."

"This is no tomb," Casey said. "It's a sacrificial chamber."

"We don't know that—" Leigh started, before feeling the tip of her shoe go over an edge. She halted, inches from falling, and caught Jeff before he went over. The void before them was so deep it appeared invisible until they were directly upon it. Shining her lamp, Leigh found the visible bones were merely the tip of the iceberg. A slanted mass lay across from her, nearest the high column, making it seem as though the bodies were dumped in from that side, atop wherever the new set of stairs led. Some of the bones were clearly human, while others were less obvious. *Maybe cows and goats.* A few of the skeletons nearest the edge seemed to be reaching out, as though their last moments were spent battling to leave the pit.

"What's wrong? Never seen skeletons before?" Leigh asked, spotting Casey's and Jeff's dull expressions.

"Not like this. This is grotesque," Jeff said.

"They were thrown in alive," Casey added gravely.

"That's a Hell of a drop," Jeff said. "Look, look, either these people were really tiny, or those are kids in there. What kind of prick would do this?"

"None I know of," Casey said.

"Me neither," Leigh agreed. "But I'm not about to start judging ancient dead societies. Sounds time-consuming and boring."

"I'm not saying go totally radge every time we hear about a goat sacrifice or discover some priest's knob-chopping tools," Jeff said. "I'm saying look at that!" He pointed at the heap of bones. "This is starting to feel more like a dark cathedral, where folks worshipped demons and the like. Being shitty for shit's sake, you know? Real old-school cunts."

"Maybe it was sealed on purpose, then?" Casey piped up.

"Sealed? What do you mean?" Leigh asked.

"You said it yourself. It looked like earthquakes and runoff had settled the rubble in front of the door, but if all of this is untouched, it means the door was blocked from the outside, on purpose."

It was an interesting theory, one of hundreds Leigh was eager to explore. This place was going to provide years' worth of research, maybe even some notable awards or an appearance on a television show or two. *Why the Hell not?* But for now, she wanted to see what was at the top of the second set of stairs. "This pit is off-limits for now. Too dangerous. Let's head up top. I don't think we'll need climbing equipment on the stairs. Just be careful."

"The . . . stairs?" Casey asked, following Leigh and Jeff back.

Leigh looked up the steps, fading in a perfect gradient from gray to deep black.

"You two go ahead. I'll stay down here," Casey said softly, apparently resigned to taking more pictures.

"That's fine," Leigh agreed.

"Lotta love in this cave right now. I gotta say," Jeff added as he followed Leigh.

She took slow steps up the first few stairs. "Nobody's been on these steps for hundreds, if not thousands, of years." The professor was fully aware there was no longer a camera rolling, but relished it all the same. The journey took a full minute, as the stairs narrowed and tilted in incline as she neared the top. With each careful step, her heart beat a little faster. When she reached the end, her headlamp fell upon an enormous shape standing on a high plateau on the platform before her, five meters wide by ten meters long. The creature was down on all fours, its head adorned with horns from front to back, like a hideous, portly dinosaur, with wide wings stretched over the room.

Massive hooves were molded into the ground at the bottom of

broad, powerful legs, below a monstrous tongue twisting back and forth in the air. Its mouth was a cavern of teeth tilted out in every direction, some protruding from its lower jaw and piercing its skin. The hide covering it seemed less like flesh and more like jagged rock and open wounds.

"What's up there?" Casey called from below.

"Nothing," Jeff shouted back, his voice cracking a little from fright. "What do you make of this guy?" he asked quietly.

"No idea, but he sure is handsome."

"Good to meet the competition."

Leigh shone her light on a pedestal near the edge overlooking the cavern. A stone sat next to it in the center of the deck, with a dip in its core, creating a natural bowl large enough for several gallons of water. *Maybe a baptismal pool?*

"Does any of this make sense to you?" Jeff asked weakly.

"Not at all," Leigh said, shining her light on the side of the base of the statue, finding a dark crevice as tall as an adult. "Look at this."

Jeff grabbed her arm before she could get far. "Uh . . . Maybe that's not such a good idea?"

"We're worrying about good ideas now?"

"I'm worried about Casey," Jeff said. "She's not doing well. Maybe we should go? Come back in the morning. Fresh, you know?"

"Why do you want to stop? I can feel it's right through here."

Jeff did a double take. "Feel what now?"

"That we should keep going. Come on!"

Leigh turned sideways and pressed on through the tight opening. Forcing herself forward, she entered a room no bigger than an average suburban bathroom. A stone bench was at her left knee, while the opposite wall had two deep, carved shelves. *That's it?* Jeff followed, having to duck to fit. Once inside he looked around and made a *huh* sound.

"This wasn't carved. It's completely natural, except for the shelves," Leigh said, scanning the room with a surprising sense of disappointment. *Not sure what I was expecting. Just not this.*

"End of the line, looks like," Jeff said, taking a knee and glancing around. "Feels sort of like a green room. You know, for the band before they go on stage." He played a quick air guitar solo as Leigh moved to the shelf on the far wall.

Her light fell on three smooth black stones. The smallest was nearly the size of a baseball, the next twice as big, and the largest was double that. Their silky surfaces gleamed in Leigh's headlamp as magenta and steel-gray wisps seemed to dance like smoke within the crystalline rock. On the top shelf, she found a serrated dagger covered in a thin layer of dust. Blowing lightly on the knife, she revealed a cold black handle, smooth yet primitive.

"You got something?" Jeff asked.

"Take a look."

He shuffled over as she picked up the dagger. "Isn't it a rule not to mess with the merchandise?" he asked too late.

The handle felt ice cold against Leigh's skin, almost painfully so, and didn't warm in her grasp. "I don't understand," she said, putting the dagger down. "This can't be all of it. This doesn't answer any of my questions."

"You know, most people would be happy just to discover a one-of-a-kind, underground boogeyman-cult church. *Hrm*, gonna have to give it a proper name, aren't we? How about Temple of the Beast?" Jeff punctuated with another air guitar riff.

Leigh shook her head, but not at the name. "Don't you see? If we don't discover anything about this place or these people, we've failed. Someone else will come in and take the credit. They always do."

"Good thing it's not all about that, right? The glory, I mean." Jeff smirked, trying to goad a reaction from her.

Looking over the shelves one last time, Leigh decided the dagger would have to do as a consolation prize. "Take it. Just be careful. And get pictures of everything first."

Jeff took several pictures with his phone before wrapping the dagger in cotton rags from his trekking pack. Upon touching it, he winced. "Fucker's cold, ay?" With the bundle safely wrapped in a plastic bag and placed in his pack, they stepped toward the exit. Leigh's head was hung low. "What about these?" Jeff asked, pointing at the three stones on the lower shelf.

"Bring them along, I guess. They're pretty," Leigh said, slipping through the exit and emerging beneath the statue of the titanic monstrosity, finding Casey had not moved from her spot on the stairs below.

"How are you feeling?" Leigh asked.

Casey responded with another silent thumbs-up as Jeff exited the small chamber.

"Those three fuckers—whatever they're made of—whoo! Heavy little bastards," Jeff said, hoisting his pack.

"Can we please, for the love of God, go back to camp now?" Casey shouted.

"Yes. We can," Leigh said, also feeling a sense of relief.

It was freshly nightfall when they made it back, and Casey and Jeff quickly retired to their own tents. Jeff would probably put his feet up and relax with a beer and tea combo (*he always packs enough somehow*), while Casey would likely get to work on her reports.

Heading to her tent to download her camera's memory card, Leigh stowed a copy in her bag and then began writing in her journal as gusts of wind outside sent sheets of sand rattling over the leather tent.

An hour or so later, a friendly voice called from outside, "Leigh, are you decent?"

What now? She signed the entry in her journal and turned to the entrance. "Yes." Casey and Jeff both entered. "Thought you'd be asleep by now. Got another big day tomorrow."

"About that," Jeff started. "We've had a talk and think you should hear what we have to say. All due respect, of course."

"That makes it sound like a mutiny," Casey said. "It's not. It's simple, logical, professionally minded fact-sharing."

Damn whoever invented the term "fact-sharing."

"Every night for the past week and a half I have gone to my desk, and I've told lies. For you. I told the Department of Agriculture and the SAA we're adhering to proper excavating protocols. We're not. I told the Chadian government our employees never left. They did. I'm getting tired of having a million questions and getting the same answer every time: 'It's what the benefactor wants.' Well, I don't care about the stupid benefactor anymore. In fact, he can . . . just . . . kiss my ass!" Casey finished, blowing her bangs out of her eyes.

"She," Leigh said.

"Excuse me?"

"Our benefactor. It's a woman. She's from Switzerland, pays on time, goes by the name Aluqa, and that's all I know. I like her because she lets me do things my way and doesn't stick her nose in it. Neither of us asks the other many questions. Way I see it, it's all win-win."

"How many of our digs has this magic woman—what's her name, Albacore? How many has she funded without your business manager and personal assistant-slash-accountant knowing?"

"Aluqa. The last two."

"Cairo?" Casey asked. Leigh let silence answer. "Why am I finding out about this now?"

"Because you asked," Leigh said. *Not that I have to tell you at all.* "Cairo was only partially funded by her, which in retrospect I think was a test. Guess we passed, because Pakistan was a dream gig, and now here we are. But if I didn't know better, I'd say you weren't happy about it."

Jeff cleared his throat, and Casey made a silent *thank-you-for-the-reminder* motion. "We are grateful for the opportunity, but none of this changes the fact that this dig, though successful, has been a disaster. Now that the door has been opened, and the . . . temple explored, we feel it's time to get out."

Leigh looked at Jeff.

"Actually, I'm with Casey, Professor Evans. I don't think we can afford to stick around any longer. We did the job, right? Case closed. Cut the check. Time for a nap and a pint at a five-star hotel. What do you say?"

"We haven't fully explored the site," Leigh said as calmly as possible.

"We've explored every inch and didn't find a single item of interest except for a dagger. Oooh, a dagger. Cool. Oh, and the largest sacrificial pit known to man." Casey spoke with surprising sass, which Leigh would have loved any other time.

"Be careful how far you go," Professor Evans warned.

"I mean no disrespect, but we had a deal. Anything we find goes to the university first. Then we figure out what our mysterious donor gets. Right?"

"Ultimately, I get to decide what we do, where we go, how we dig, and what we do with whatever we find," Leigh said, having had about enough. *If she pushes this, so help me.*

But Casey continued, undeterred. "And you seem to have forgotten your own ethics."

Oh, Hell no.

Leigh closed her eyes and took a calming breath, hoping it would help. It didn't. "Let me get this straight. You two want to send off our only finds? Literally all we have to show for our efforts in this god-forsaken place? You two want to get rid of them before we, or anyone else, can properly study them? And go back home empty-handed? Is that right?"

"Well, when you put it like that . . ." Jeff snickered.

"No matter how you phrase it, I'm going to tell the truth," Casey said. "I've already written a draft to National Services. I can send it at any time. Just because we're in the middle of the desert doesn't mean I don't have Wi-Fi." She kept her spine arched and chest out to finish strong.

She's been studying me. That's sweet. "You can't do that. Not yet," Leigh replied.

"What are you going to do? Kill me?"

"I wouldn't know how." Leigh chuckled, hoping to lighten the mood. Another miss. "Okay, fine. I hear you. I haven't been my professional self lately. The artifacts will go to the university, as promised and as ethics obviously call for. But I'm nowhere near done with the temple. I need more than a day. Can you please just hang on a little while longer?" Leigh asked, hoping they would accept after a small fight.

Casey's eyes drooped and closed. A tear streamed down her cheek as she slumped onto the cot beside her.

Jeff fanned her with both hands. "Hey, it's all right. Take your time. Get some air in your lungs."

Ugh. Crying. This is why you're not promotable.

Her assistant opened wet, glimmering eyes and focused on Leigh. "I can't do it, Professor Evans. I can't stay. Not for one second longer than I have to. Being here is unbearable. I'm asking. I'm begging." She clasped her hands together. "We need to get out of here."

SLEEPING BASTIONS

To Alex, it might as well have been magic. The bright light that brought him and the muscle-bound man named Bennett halfway around the world made him feel as though he'd been spit through the clouds. There was no ground or up, no left or right, while at the same time there was an immense sense of movement—like when his grandfather used to speed down the highway in his '72 Chevelle with Alex in the back seat, multiplied by a thousand. Then, as quickly as it had left him, reality came rushing back. Weight settled upon his legs, warmth touched his skin, air filled his lungs, and a stale, stagnant scent made itself known. No longer in a filthy, wet alley, Alex found himself keeled over in a muted room, being steadied by Izaiah, who was grinning with what teeth he had.

"Pukin's fine, if you gotta. Seen it before," the old man said.

Alex shook his head, trying to rattle away the mixture of pain and euphoria coursing through him from the trip through the white light.

Izaiah pulled out a chair from a plain wooden table and sat him down. "Take a seat. Relax. Everyone has a hard time after their first Shift. Nothing to be ashamed of. How you holding up, Bennett?" Izaiah went to steady him as he had Alex but was pushed away by the soldier.

"What the Hell was that? What did you do to me?" Bennett grumbled, sounding like a garbage disposal.

"I told you, it's called Shifting," Izaiah replied. "Heck of a way to travel if you gotta cover a long distance in a short time. Basically, we pass through different frequencies, taking a trip through the Eve until we find the spot we're looking for. Sorry I didn't warn you, but in my experience, there's no good way to do that. I didn't want us speaking any more in the alley than we had to. There are prying eyes and ears everywhere, but don't worry, we're safe here. Very private. So, Bennett, take a seat. You're making me nervous."

Bennett took one step toward the table before buckling over and vomiting.

"There it is," Izaiah said with a comforting grin that Bennett did not seem to appreciate. "Shifting can be a pain. No shame in being shook up. There was a human I took through an Eve gate once—must have been a few hundred years ago now, Damascus I think his name was. He had some real problems. Whoo! What a mess, lemme tell ya." Izaiah chuckled. "Actually, now that I think of it, he might've died. Human matter can't pass through the Eve unless tempered first."

Bennett rose quickly, straightening up as though trying to hide his moment of weakness but unable to conceal the shade of green flushing his face. "Just—tell me where we are, and what we're do-ing here."

"You're not in Arizona anymore, I can tell you that," Izaiah said. "This is one of our safe houses. Got 'em hidden all over the world. Me and the other Medolians can come here to rest, gather supplies, or get away from any threatening parties on our tail. Course, I don't think anyone's been here in some time. Things have been quiet in this part of the world for a while."

"Safe house?" Alex asked, taking a look around.

The room reminded him of the black-and-white photos his grandparents had in their basement bathroom of settler homes in the Old West: plain, simple, mostly empty, covered in dust, with little more than some shelves, a bucket, a couple of pots and pans, and a dining table with four chairs. A short hall extending from the main room was lined with two wooden doors, likely bedrooms of some sort. Much like the old man who brought them here, nearly everything about the safe house was gray: gray walls, gray doors, gray shelves. Even the wood flooring was gray. The only room with an ounce of color was what appeared to be a kitchen, though it was not like any Alex had ever seen. A sink was featured, but no faucet, and no fridge, with uncovered shelves lining the wall filled with foggy jars and small wooden boxes.

Outside a single window on the far wall, Alex saw a blazing desert that was not his. This one was more feral and hazardous, with miles of rocky, rolling hills dotted with dark green bushes stretching toward the horizon. *Okay, just stay calm. Everything will be fine. For the love of God, stay calm. Everything will be . . . fine.*

Bennett dropped into the seat beside Alex, nursing his left temple. "Where are we exactly?"

"I won't answer that," Izaiah started. "Mostly because I'm not entirely sure. Names of regions and countries are always changing, and it seems to offend people when I'm not up to speed. Also, because I don't want to give you guys any ideas or feed any plans of escape you might be mulling over. There's nothing out there but endless barren desert. You can't escape, so don't think about it.

Just—no. Though I suppose there's no harm in telling you we're somewhere in northeast Africa."

Alex and his mantra were stopped flat. "Africa?"

"Fuck off," Bennett said.

Izaiah stifled a laugh. "Believe it."

"The Hell are we doing in Africa?" Bennett asked.

"Like I said, we need your help. You and Mr. Barker were selected to act as independent arbiters to help us solve our runaway demon problem. It's all a simple formality, and a ridiculous one at that, but still, we have to do what we have to do. I brought you here because we have reason to believe the demon stowed away onboard a ship and arrived at Damietta Port two months ago, heading south. His trail has long since gone cold, but we're pretty sure he's still on the continent. Why is yet to be determined. This safe house is nowhere near his last known whereabouts, so you both will stay comfortably out of the whole affair and maybe even soak up a little sun. The Senate may be able to force me to go along with this stupid game, but you fellas don't need to be any more involved than you need to be on paper. Exorcisms and Archfiend arrests are no joke, but if we play our cards right, we should be able to get you both in and out of this quickly and send you on your way. I just need you fellas to play along. This is where you'll spend the majority of your time in service of the UnEarth Senate. I only need one thing from the both of you—once a day, step out, look around, then come right back inside and shut the door. That's it. Don't need to find anything, don't need to do anything—we just need to be able to say you fellas gave finding the demon a shot. Any questions so far?"

"Yeah, just one. Who the fuck do you think you are, and why do you think I'll give a shit?" Bennett asked with abhorrence.

"Oh, me?" Izaiah didn't skip a beat. "Nobody important, same as everyone else, but I am trying to help you fellas. I hope you believe me when I tell you that."

"I don't believe anything," Alex said, seemingly catching the other two off guard. "Why should I? None of this makes any sense. You're talking in circles about, what, Heaven and Hell? You can't just—I was shot yesterday, and nobody is acting like it happened."

"I prefer to call them Hywyn and Arros, or the worlds of creation and destruction, but sure, yes. Oh, and it wasn't yesterday," Izaiah said.

"What do you mean? Of course it was," Alex said. "I can still see it happening. I can still feel the bullet. It's—"

"That night will always be with you, Alex," Izaiah started, "but it wasn't yesterday. It was twenty-five days ago."

No. Alex's legs went numb above the knee. "That can't be true."

Izaiah gave a forlorn sigh. "Today's date is Sunday, October fifteenth. As I said, you fellas were sent to Hywyn and Arros to be imbued with Eve, making you official representatives of each shade. The kingdoms insisted they would need the time to ensure you survived the procedure. I was thrilled to see you both made it. To tell you the truth, I'd already gotten kind of fond of you."

"Twenty-five days? But that could mean—" Alex felt his voice catch in his throat. "My baby girl might have been born. But how can—" He trailed off. *Melissa. I'm sorry. I'll make it up to you. I will.*

Bennett stood and paced the room, staring down the old man as though he wanted nothing more than to break his jaw with an uppercut. "You think this is funny? Messing with people like this? You think you get to play with our lives?"

"I think you need to calm down, young man," Izaiah said, nose down, eyes up, in a sudden, cold turn that brought a chill to the room. "Learn not to look a gift horse in the mouth."

With a conceding grunt, Bennett sat at the table. "I did my time in public service and got out in one piece, so tell me why I owe you, or anyone. Hmm? I don't know who you think you're talking to, but I'm nobody's errand boy. Soonest chance I get, I'm out of here."

"And where will you go?" Izaiah asked, blissfully unaffected by Bennett's vigor.

"Anywhere but here. Doesn't matter. I'm pretty resourceful. I can get around, and I also don't believe for a second we're on the other side of the planet."

"Please, for your own sake, just do as I ask. Stay here and keep the door shut. It's the only way to mask your energy signatures," Izaiah said. "We have to be careful, or else this could end up going sideways—for all of us. I know it stinks. I know this is no fun, but this was the best plan I could come up with on such short notice. It'll involve a lot of boredom on your parts, but at least you'll be safe."

"You keep saying that," Bennett said. "Safe from what? If this is such a big deal, shouldn't we be an actual part of it? I've had my fair share of manhunts. You say it's a demon we're hunting? Shit, that's new—load me up. Let's do it."

Izaiah's grin and feather-light air returned. "I don't doubt you'd be able to help, Mister Hunter, and thank you for the offer, but no. Catching an Archfiend is no joke. And also," he hesitated, licking his lips, "I wasn't going to tell you fellas this, but rather than risk you going for a jaunt and running into trouble, I will. The runaway demon is not our only critical concern at the moment. For several years we've been gathering reports of the Wraithian cult reconstituting itself on Earth—a mean set of characters who worshipped Wrath for thousands of years, attempting to cultivate as much as possible, until they were extinguished more than two millennia ago. Now, appears they're back, and a large portion of the sightings have taken place on this continent. Sorry to say, for too long we ignored the reports because there wasn't any credible evidence, just hearsay. Now that we know, the Senate doesn't believe the sudden rise of the Wraithians and a rogue Archfiend stealing a body and making his way to Africa are related, but I do. Sadly, it has my team stretched thin."

I haven't followed this guy at all. As Melissa would say, "Dude, you make less sense than terms and agreements."

Alex and Bennett shot the old man curious glances. "The other Medolian Sentries," he answered. "Think of us as caretakers of the planet. Catching creatures like Joseph and putting them back where they belong is part of the job, but this particular one has been, well, difficult. He's somehow able to mask his Eve, same as this safe house will yours, which has us stumped. But still, I remain confident we'll have him in custody soon, and once the demon has been exorcised, I'll come back for you fellas, and we can escort him to the Tribunal together, where he'll stand trial. After that, your civic duties will be concluded. Hugs and milkshakes."

"Return for us? You're leaving?" Alex asked.

"I'll be back in a couple of days. Promise. In the meantime, help yourself to the food in the pantry. Most of it's Hywyn and Nashwyn based—I'm assuming—so it should be healthy and, technically, shouldn't go bad. Also, there's a freshwater well out back. Maybe think of all this as a role-playing game? Try to have some fun with it. Eh? That's what I do. Just bear with me for a little while."

"This is fucking insane. Do you hear yourself?" Bennett asked.

"I understand this is hard to take in. I'm plenty used to all this crap, so to me, it's old hat, but I can see how you two might not believe it. I'd hoped experiencing a Shift might convince you, but I can see it will take more."

The old man continued to try to explain, but by the end of the talk Alex felt he knew less than when they'd arrived. Every notion he'd ever considered about life after death seemed to be dead wrong. *This guy isn't a devil or an angel. He's . . . I don't know what he is. Is this really happening? If so, why did he pick us? And does this mean there is no Heaven? I mean, come on.*

Izaiah continued stressing the importance of keeping the door closed at all times. "And don't let anyone in but me, got it?" Then, as mysteriously as he'd come into their lives, without providing any sense of closure, the old man slammed down his cane and was literally gone in a flash, leaving Alex and Bennett to fend for themselves in a wooden cottage in the middle of a desolate African mountain range.

But he lied. He wasn't back in two days. Or three.

It had been four days with no word from Izaiah. Four arid days and tedious nights that gave Alex nothing but time to think, fend off panic attacks, miss his wife desperately, and hate everything about his new living situation and roommate, who appeared incapable of communicating anything other than contempt. Several times he tried to have a conversation with the man and was shut down each time.

"Why don't you mind your own business, and I'll mind mine?" Bennett suggested.

Fine by me. Alex was by no means desperate to get to know the guy. He was just tired of listening to his stomach rumble, as both he and Bennett refused to eat what was in the kitchen area after opening the glass jars and wooden boxes in the pantry the first day. The jars contained either a dark blue or murky green goo, which stunk like mothballs, while the boxes contained what looked like rye biscuits wrapped in cheesecloth, but smelled like rotten onions and salty garbage. With no vegetation to forage nor animals to hunt, it seemed starvation was his and Bennett's destination. The soldier even went so far as to try to find edible insects for them but came up empty-handed. Not that Alex relished the suggestion all that much. It was simply better than dying.

His bearded companion hadn't come out and said he was ex-military, but Alex noticed his Marine tattoo mixed in with the others the night they awoke in the alley. Bennett was also condescending as Hell, sometimes spoke with a sharp, drill-sergeant-like tone, and occasionally let phrases slip like "solo" and "recon." He also struck Alex as a guy who'd spent many nights sleeping under the stars, fending for himself, and who preferred being alone to working with others. However difficult, even alarming at times, he was, Alex was thankful to have him because being around another like himself was the only thing convincing him he wasn't losing his mind.

The voices—which began the night he woke in the alley, as well as the strange feelings piggybacking on them—hadn't given him more than an hour's peace since he and Bennett first arrived at the safe house. Until this week, Alex had never in his life been assailed by so much anger or urges of violence, eventually convincing himself he was merely having a psychotic episode. *As if that's better.* Several times he heard Bennett speaking to himself and also reacting to people and things that weren't there, only to deny it when questioned. Something inscrutable was happening to both of them, though neither seemed ready to admit it yet.

At the end of the second day, unable to take the hunger any longer, Alex decided to try the food provided by the safe house, taking a small bite of one of the pungent biscuits in the wooden boxes. The morsel tasted just as bad as it smelled (*worse*) but, to his amazement, made him feel leagues better and filled his belly for at least a few hours. Since then, they had lived exclusively on the fetid food Bennett described as "trash biscuits."

There was no conversation when the two men ate. Alex still knew nothing about Bennett's death and could only fill in the gaps of his origin by guessing, using his tattoos as a guide. *Let's see, there are a lot of smudgy sections, hard to make out, some tribal stuff, and I do get the feeling either he's from Texas or he's lived there. I'm also sensing a fondness for the legend of King Arthur and the Knights of the Round Table. In fact, he might be a straight-up Renaissance nerd because that's definitely a wizard on his tricep.*

As time passed like molasses, once a day they did as requested and stepped out to "search" for the enigmatic demon. *Joseph. That can't really be his name. Right? A demon named Joseph?* For the first two days there was nothing to see but the sterile landscape acting as a prison, but on the third day, Bennett swore he saw signs of fire in the distance.

"Might be people out there," he said. "A day's walk at most."

When Alex reminded him of Izaiah's cautionary tale about the hate-worshipping cult whose name he'd already forgotten and tried to hint that the key to survival when lost was to stay put, he was summarily silenced.

"We're not lost—we were abducted. How many times have you had to survive, Al?"

In no position to argue, Alex let it go. The soldier had years of training and experience he didn't, which meant the elementary school teacher had been permanently relegated to being a dependent observer.

"It's our best bet," Bennett reiterated.

The thought of traversing the landscape outside the confines of the safe house scared Alex, though not nearly as much as the prospect of spending another day away from Melissa. Up until now, they'd never spent more than forty-eight hours apart, which had only happened when he got stuck at the John Glenn Columbus International Airport during a blizzard for two days after moving his grandparents to an assisted living facility in Upper Arlington. *That alone was tough, but this* . . . When the fourth day came and there was still no sign of Izaiah, he agreed with Bennett for the first time. They had to take matters into their own hands. It was time to try their luck in the desert. It was time to leave.

On the day of their departure, Alex couldn't sleep. *What else is new?* Bennett decided they would travel at night, the idea being they would rest during the day and then march as far as possible once the sun was down. The trek into the barren wilderness would be a complete unknown, with no destination or real goal other than to find people. When Alex asked about their route, "south" was all Bennett had said, pointing off in the distance. *That helps a lot. Thanks.*

Turning on his pillow and trying to get comfortable for the millionth time, Alex covered his ears, fending off Bennett's snoring, which echoed around the small house like a rattling children's toy and reminded him, oddly, of his wife. She could nap anywhere too.

Sleep, damn it. Come on. The coming night would be laborious, and every bit of strength he could muster was going to be essential. Though part of him was relieved he couldn't doze off, because every time he did, he felt the fire from the night he was shot. When awake, Alex was sometimes able to forget the burn, but in his dreams, it always came rushing back. He could only scream for relief, waking in a sweaty panic on his straw cot, sometimes forgetting where he was and how he got there until Bennett could get him under control. Patting himself down in a daze, he often expected to feel blistered, charred skin ready to fall off the bone, only marginally happier when it all turned out to be in his head. The red fire in his dreams reminded Alex of the night he'd nearly burned down his grandparents' house and sustained third-degree burns on his left hand, following a grease fire in the kitchen.

I was trying to make fried chicken. Then Melissa told me we were expecting.

When his wife had come home, she'd tried to break the good news gently, knowing how easily Alex was startled, but was unsuccessful.

"I want to tell you something, but I think you should sit down first," she said, diving into the fridge and handing him a beer. Melissa usually opened one for herself in the evenings after work, but since she was making him drink alone, he could tell something unusual was going on.

Not wanting to leave the chicken to burn in the pan, he opted to stand and hear the news. "I won't freak out. Honest," he said, planting his feet. *Big mistake.* "What's up?"

"We need to call your grandma," she said.

Several red flags arose in his mind. "Why?"

"To let her know she's going to be a great-grandparent."

Not only did Alex freak out and stumble back looking for balance, but he also slammed the handle of the frying pan, sending flaming grease spilling over the stove and kitchen floor. Putting the flame out took nearly as long as it took the fire department to arrive, and by the end, not only was their kitchen carpeted with baking soda and table salt, but most of Alex's arm up to the elbow required immediate medical attention. *Turned out attacking the flames with a dishrag was a bad idea.* Sitting in the emergency room an hour later, well-drugged and waiting to hear if he would need skin grafts or not, he and Melissa held hands and laughed, feeling nothing but joy and love.

"You know, in a way this was a good thing," she said, getting an aghast stare from her husband. "Wait, hear me out. I know I tease you a lot for your anxiety, and you're always a good sport, but tonight I didn't see it. You didn't hesitate. You rushed in to protect us and what we have. I knew I could count on you, but it was great to see just how much. I'm proud of you."

She'd never spoken to him like that before. When Melissa crawled into the hospital bed with him that night in the ER, just a few floors down from where their baby would be born eight months later, and laid her head on his chest, it was the most like a man he had ever felt.

And now it's gone. All except the burn.

Presently, in the Medolian safe house, the soldier sniffed and adjusted his position. He was awake. Alex checked his analog watch: 5:27 p.m. The plan was to rise at five thirty. *How does he do that? Does the military train people to wake up on time?*

"You up?" Bennett asked with his usual curt tone, rising and stretching, cracking enough bones to sound like someone was slowly dropping walnuts onto the floor. He'd never used the cots in the safe house bedrooms, saying he preferred the ground.

"Yeah," Alex replied.

"Did you sleep?"

"A little." The teacher rose and made his way out back to the well to splash some water on his face and arms. He began packing the makeshift backpack he'd constructed out of two burlap sacks and some rope he found in the kitchen area. The two boxes of trash biscuits they packed would last longer than the six jars they'd emptied to use as water jugs. Despite constantly daring one another to try the stuff, neither man ever brought himself to eat the blue substance that had once been contained within, a decision Alex would have been perfectly comfortable dying over.

Lumbering to the safe house entrance, nursing the bullet wound pulsing under his rib cage, he gazed over the horizon as the sun began to set behind the rocky hills.

"You sure you don't have any questions?" Bennett asked as they stepped out.

"Seems simple enough." Alex tried to sound as unworried as possible.

Bennett laid out the basics anyway. "Keep your mouth closed.

Breathe through your nose. Don't hurry or exert too much energy. We'll halt for water every two hours. If you feel faint, stop."

"I'm ready."

"Keep telling yourself that." Bennett closed the safe house door behind them.

Moving onto the level plateau Alex had once referred to as their "porch" in an attempt to lighten a particularly bleak afternoon, the duo started down the hill, traversing jagged boulders and patches of dirt as the sky turned a muted orange. A short way into the hike, Alex turned to take a final glance at the small shack that had housed them for the past four days and three nights. To his amazement, he could not find it anywhere, as though it had vanished into thin air or never existed at all.

Whatever. Good riddance.

Looking ahead, he saw a vast expanse riddled with mountain ranges, hillsides, and canyons, and was already having trouble keeping up with Bennett's pace. The soldier's boots held up much better on the terrain than Alex's paint-splattered sneakers. "Think we could slow down for a minute?" he asked once, scrambling up a sandy hill that gave way with each step. But Bennett said nothing, keeping his speed constant.

As night folded over and the stars came out brilliantly, a refreshing breeze began to roll off the dunes of sand to their left, while the looming black shapes of rocky mountains to their right dominated the horizon, highlighted along their edges by a half-moon rising. Alex spent the majority of the trek imagining the look on Melissa's face when he would inevitably walk back through their front door, finally able to hold her and tell her everything was going to be okay. He had not seen her in so long that every demonic voice that thrashed its teeth and whispered of sin in his mind was a joy by comparison. *I'm coming home, honey. Dead or not.*

"Any idea how far we've gone?" he asked, again receiving no response. "Cool. Thank you. You're a great travel companion, you know that? Really instilling a lot of confidence."

The soldier's march continued, and Alex felt fury building in his gut. "Fine, you're not gonna talk? I'll talk for both of us. Let's see, a week ago I was painting a nursery for my kid. That's something. Never done that before, you know? Paint a whole room. I've done all sorts of home repairs. Lots of drywall and tile floors. Posts and bannisters. I've even dabbled with acrylic and watercolor paints, but no, never painted a whole room. I think it was fun. I hope I did it right."

He paused, just in case Bennett might have something to say. *I figured he would've told me to shut up by now.*

"But woodworking is my real passion," he continued. "Got a workshop at home. Still not very good. Can't plane worth a damn, but I think I'm getting better. I've just been so focused on these doves I was making. Then it all got sort of sidetracked when we found out . . . I was so looking forward to being a father, you know? I mean, I was scared—like crazy scared. But I still wanted it. You know?"

"No, I don't. Now please, shut up," Bennett said.

There it is. "You've never thought about being a dad?" Alex asked, trying for jovial.

Bennett spun to face him with eyes as fierce as a jungle cat. "I said I don't want to talk, so I'm not going to. I don't care about your life, or your crafts, or watercolors. How the fuck are you not getting this? Or are you the world's stupidest teacher?"

Alex fought to control his shaking hands and knees. "I don't understand. Are you afraid of someone hearing us? Isn't that the point?" He cupped his hands around his mouth and shouted to the hills, "Hello!"

Bennett grunted and walked on. "That's not it."

"Then what?"

"I just don't want to talk."

"Some of us need human interaction, you know? It might do you some good to give it a shot!" Alex trailed after him, keeping on his heels. "Because this situation we're in is extraordinarily . . . I guess extraordinary. And I'm still not sure why I'm part of it. Are you? One minute I'm expecting to wake up in a hospital, or not at all, and the next—" Alex stopped himself and moved on before the burn took over his mind. "I mean, how do I know you're not a part of this? How do I know I can trust you? Am I walking to my doom?"

"How do I know this isn't a trick to get me to trust you? Hmm? Let my guard down?" Bennett asked. "I'm in the same boat. We're both on our own."

"I'm not in on this. I can promise you that," Alex assured him.

"Don't worry, I know," Bennett replied. "It was just an example."

"How do you know?" *And what did you mean by that?*

"Because I don't think you're capable of manipulation on that scale," Bennett said. "You're a basic street guy. Met a million of you."

Alex was surprised at how offended he was. "You don't even know me."

"I know enough."

"If you're so smart, tell me how we ended up here."

Bennett grunted. His frustration was clearly boiling over. "Like I've said a hundred times already, I have no idea. I'm supposed to be dead. You think I want to be here? Now?"

"Stuck with me?" Alex asked.

Bennett shook his head with a sudden sense of calm. "No. Alive."

It was the first time Bennett had spoken about his own death since the night in the alley with Izaiah. The conversation ended, and they marched for a few minutes with only the sound of dirt crunching under their shoes.

"Do you believe what Izaiah said?" Alex asked eventually. "About the kingdoms of destruction and creation and their contract of no interference? I mean, Heaven and Hell? Gotta be something else."

"If you're asking do I believe that nut job, the answer's no. Obviously, we aren't dead."

"How can you say that?"

"Are you breathing?" Bennett asked.

"Yeah."

"I rest my case. Strange things happen, but the universe has rules. Whatever's going on here, my guess is it's just as disappointing as the rest of existence."

"You're the guy who sits with his arms crossed at a magic show, huh?"

The soldier moved on, but Alex swore he spotted the tiniest grin on his face. As they neared the top of a ridge, where Alex hoped to see some twinkling lights below, he found only pale blue darkness. Marching into the gully, he began to feel the precious hours of sleep he was missing and struggled to keep his mind occupied, pushing away thoughts of the burn. Then Bennett did the unthinkable.

"Next minute what?" he asked.

Alex didn't register the question at first. "I'm sorry?"

"You said, 'one minute I'm expecting not to wake up,' then stopped. What happened next? Did you see something?" The soldier pressed.

"I don't remember."

Bennett persisted. "Come on, not anything?"

Alex only recalled sounds and feelings; fighting for air and, of course, the burn. During it all, he remembered thinking nothing could be worse. "It felt like falling. At first. Then, I could feel someone, or maybe there were many of them, watching me, looming over me. The rest is just—I don't want to think about it."

For the first time, Bennett was all ears. Nodding, he reciprocated. "I remember falling too, and this . . . ache. There was a table, I think, and I was laid out, open like a cadaver. They had me and . . . there was so much . . . weight, and pressure, and light. Rigid. Everything was so rigid. And cold, like all the warmth and goodness had been pulled out of me. It felt like—everything. Gravity. Momentum. Strength. There was so much, inside and out. I wanted to burst and be done with it, but they kept going. I begged, but they didn't care." Bennett slowed to a crawl, his eyes fixed on the ground as if allowing himself to relive this for the first time. "Then, I woke up, and a hobo told me I was part of something I didn't have a choice in, with a stranger who I have nothing in common with, other than apparently dying at the worst possible time," he finished, his usual enmity creeping back in.

"I thought you didn't believe that," Alex said.

"I don't believe anything anymore, but that doesn't mean I give up. All I have is my gut, and right now it's saying, *Go this way.* You don't have to follow me, you know."

"Funny thing to have in common, huh? Being dead," Alex said, keeping pace.

"Extremely funny."

"Want to talk about it? How it happened, I mean?"

"No, and don't ask about it ever again," Bennett replied bluntly.

Alex shut up for twenty minutes, admiring the vibrant nighttime horizon, his thoughts lingering on nights spent with Melissa in their backyard under the stars, talking.

Why didn't I marry her sooner?

"You know, going through something like this, it makes all the stupid little stuff that filled your life seem so . . ."

"Meaningless?" Bennett finished his sentence.

"Not what I was going to say."

"It is. Trust me," Bennett said. "There are a few things in life you can see, things that break the mirror, ruin the fantasy. I've seen 'em all."

"Are you talking about your time in the service?" Alex asked. "It's okay if you don't want to get into it. I just think it might help, is all."

Bennett sighed. "Look, I appreciate it. You're not wrong to try. It's nothing personal, just realize I'm not going to talk about this stuff. Not with you or anyone."

"That's fair," Alex said, leaving it alone for only a moment before asking, "Were you serving during nine-eleven?"

Bennett nodded, his eyes growing distant, filled with unkind years. "Joined six months before Desert Storm, lasted till o-three. Yeah, I was in it. All of it." Suddenly, he seized and dropped to a knee, clutching his ears, as if protecting them from a monstrous noise. A painful groan escaped him as his body shook like a paint mixer.

"Hey, you okay? What's going on?" Alex asked.

"You don't hear that?" Bennett shouted, grabbing his sides and chest, moaning. Then, with a shudder, the agony seemed to leave him, and he snapped upright, stone-faced. "It's okay. I'm okay. I just—give me a minute." He looked around, clearly disoriented, as though someone else were with them.

"What was it?" Alex asked.

Bennett shook his head as if trying to get snow out of his hair, then turned toward the horizon while forcing himself to stand taller. "Nothing. Just some residual effects of whatever drugs that Izaiah guy gave us."

"That's not honestly what you think."

"How else do you explain neither of us remembering the trip to Africa?" Bennett asked.

"Do you finally admit that's where the light brought us?"

"Enough!" Bennett shouted. "There was no light. No magic. There was only a sick old man who kidnapped us and brought us here."

"So, you deny anything strange is going on?" Alex pressed.

"Tell you what, if we find a mermaid, or the abominable snowman out here, I'll start to believe. Until then . . ." Bennett's voice faded as he walked farther away.

Alex hurried to catch up as he neared the top of yet another embankment. "You really don't remember the feeling when he teleported us?"

"He didn't teleport us. He knocked us out and transported our bodies. It's fucked up, it's weird, I don't get it, but there it is. We're not dead. Please understand that."

"How can you think this is so simple? I'm feeling and hearing things I never have before, and it's getting worse by the minute. Judging by your little fit just now, I'm not the only one," Alex finished, catching up to Bennett, who was staring into the eastern distance. Following his gaze, Alex spotted a nearly indistinguishable trace of smoke rising and dissipating, with a faint glimmer of orange light at its base.

"Is that what I think it is?" Alex asked.

"Yes." Bennett was already moving down the rocky path. Alex followed as best he could, resisting the urge to get excited, hoping they would reach the fire before it went out and they lost track of its source. The care it took to cross the eastern valley left the two men nearly silent during the hike, and by the early morning, fatigue was setting in. Alex's muscles and joints screamed for sleep. His mind ached. He needed water but had already taken his drink for the hour. Even Bennett was slowing.

Alex eventually allowed himself to check his watch: 4:03 a.m. He was about to suggest stopping for the evening; the thought of another hour was torture. Then they crested a ridge as the sky began to show the first signs of sunrise. Nestled below was a small collection of houses, stables, farms, shacks, and concrete service buildings. Several structures had power and working lights, but at least three had been reduced to heaps of ash and smoldering wood. Alex also spotted a charred car chassis.

Must have burned through the whole night.

He and Bennett moved with renewed spirits, entering a bushy field amid a valley of sand. Soon, they were on a flat straightaway, heading for the cluster of buildings, and Alex wanted to run. Electric power meant communication, phones. He might even be able to hear Melissa's voice within the hour. *It could be daytime back home. Not that it matters. She'll just want to hear from me. I'm coming, honey. Hang on.*

Alex was so focused on the path that he hadn't noticed Bennett divert to the side.

"Barker," the soldier whispered harshly.

Backtracking, Alex joined him among a clump of bushes, where they kept low, peering at the village, roughly one hundred yards away.

"What are we waiting for?" Alex asked, his foot tapping like an anxious dog ready to go outside. "We're so close!"

Bennett's eyes scanned the town with skepticism. "I don't like it."

"Don't like what? The fire? They might need help. Let's go." Alex stood but was forced back down, out of sight.

"Those fires look random. And why the truck? If they were fighting fires, where is everyone? And look, no animals." Bennett pointed at the empty fields surrounded by fences outside of town. "Most of the people in these towns are farmers of some sort. At the very least, they need milk and meat. I don't see a single chicken or goat."

Everything checked out fine to Alex, but Bennett's tone had grown grave and flat, too engrossed to offer any color. The duo waited a few more minutes, seeing nothing.

"Do we just sit here? What if people need our help?" asked Alex.

"Hang on a second," Bennett muttered.

"Do you want to wait for sunlight?"

"I said hang on a second!" Bennett didn't bother looking at him. "We need to know what we're dealing with. I'll find out. You stay here."

Alex fell silent as Bennett rose and hurried toward the buildings. *What a dick.* Soon, Bennett was out of sight, and Alex was left to wait, watching the horizon lighten until shades of yellow bled into the mix. With the new light, he spotted one of the missing goats from the village in a nearby field. It was lying on its side, its innards strewn about and surrounded by a fog of flies. A small brown falcon was picking voraciously at the meat. Looking away, Alex tried to ignore it and grew bored, reduced to drawing in the sand with his finger. Soon after, a scream erupted from somewhere in the village.

That wasn't Bennett. Springing to his feet, he charged into town, leaving the satchel of water jars and trash biscuits behind. Rounding the largest house, Alex barreled up the dirt road splitting the village. His feet pounding the pavement and his frantic breathing made it hard to pinpoint the direction of the sounds. Two loud bangs rattled him: shotgun blasts. The shack to his right lit up. Alex pitched forward, stumbling into the wall, hearing two voices—one was Bennett, the other a mystery man.

"La Darar! La Darar!" Bennett shouted.

Another gunshot rang out. The wall five feet from Alex exploded and light from inside the shack poured onto the dirt. He bit his hand to stifle a sound, feeling his spine stiffen as the gunfire triggered memories of the night in the Thai restaurant and the deep sleep that followed.

Inside, Bennett sounded increasingly desperate. "Barátságos! Fuck, what else? Listen, I'm not trying to—" Another gunshot echoed, metal clanging. The other voice shouted from the rear of the shack, a few words clear: "*Laisser*," "*mort*," "*maison*."

"He's speaking French!" Alex shouted into the hole in the wall. "Bennett! It's French! Nous ne vous voulons aucun mal!" *I hope that means "We're here as friends."* Alex felt rusty at best, but the chaos inside paused, so he continued. "Salut! Salut! Uh . . . Parlez-vous Anglais?"

Bennett was silent inside. *Hope he's not dead. Again.* Then came the sound of feet rustling through papers and silverware, and the man spoke, much calmer now. "Non . . . Little bit."

Damn. French it is. Alex introduced himself. "Je m'appelle . . . Alex."

The man inside launched into a tirade of words Alex couldn't follow. Judging by his tone, he was confused and scared, and likely viewing them as attackers. Alex caught one word: "*entrer*," meaning "enter." He took a deep breath and moved toward the front door.

"Okay. I'm coming in now. Please don't shoot . . . Jes suis sympa. That means 'friendly,' right?" He tried to sound as amiable as possible.

Pushing the door open, he immediately saw Bennett crouched on the floor to his right behind a metal stove, clutching a pan like a club. His eyes were fixed on a wooden door at the other end of the small room, its top half blown away, likely by the shotgun. What little furniture remained had been torn to bits. Flowerpots and framed paintings were shattered. The walls were scathed and smeared with blood. Alex pushed the door fully open and held his hands up.

"Get down, you idiot," Bennett whispered.

"I don't think he wants to kill anyone. He's trying to scare us off," Alex said calmly. "We're friendly. Like Bob Newhart."

"Bob . . . Neu-hart?" The man's panicked voice came from the darkness, asking many questions in French, only one of which Alex caught: "Who are you?"

"I'm Alex, like I said. This is Bennett. Uh . . . Mon ami est Bennett. We're American. We need help. Please."

The man continued, finishing with the word "*soldat?*"

"No. We're not soldiers," Alex replied. "We're civilians."

"Civilian?" the man said, and Alex heard footsteps. A face, slightly younger than his own, emerged into the light, with dried blood caked on his skin where it had run down his head and neck, soaking his white collar. His jaw quaked as he repeatedly licked his chapped, bloody lips.

Alex smiled. "Salut. Je m'appelle Alex." He placed a hand on his own chest, matching his breathing speed to the man's. The man lowered his gun.

Good. Nice and slow, friend.

Relief and a sense of pride filled the teacher; his tactics had bested Bennett's. But the sensation only lasted a moment, when a cacophony of sound filled his ears: screams and high-pitched wails. The voices had returned. *Not now!* A multitude clamored in his mind, whispering and shouting, urging him to commit every terrible act imaginable. The bullet under his rib cage ignited, broiling his insides. There was no fighting his body's reaction. Alex seized and cried out.

Through the haze of agony, he saw the man behind the door lift the shotgun, shouting in terror. Something was about to happen, and Alex could do nothing to stop it. Bennett's massive frame was swiftly at the door, wrestling with the man. Expecting another gunshot, Alex instead heard only the voices in his mind as waves of blistering heat rolled through him. When the chaos subsided, Bennett was still pummeling the man and freeing the gun.

Alex leaped into action, "Wait! He's down."

"Arrêt!—Stop!" the man screamed, his hands shielding his bloodied face.

"Good. See, we're all okay now. Nobody needs to blow their stack," Alex said. "Bennett, maybe we should ask our new friend what's going on?"

Bennett—his unflinching glare as sharp as daggers—finally released the young man, stepping back to give him space. The man scrambled into the corner, adopting a defensive stance in front of a short cot. It was then Alex noticed another man strapped to the bed, wrapped in blankets, his skin beneath covered in bloody bandages, wracked with contusions. He was long dead.

"Who is that?" Alex asked.

The man knelt by the bed. "Ahmed. My brother."

Alex approached cautiously, rolling his steps from heel to toe. "I'm so sorry. What is your name?"

The young man spoke through tears, his eyes darting around, alert for any further danger. "Yuri."

"Are you and your brother the only people here?" Alex asked.

Yuri nodded solemnly. "Why are Alex here?"

"That's a long story."

Bennett loaded the shotgun in the corner, handling it as though he'd owned it all his life. "Barker, can I talk to you alone?"

Alex stepped away from Yuri and his brother's body to meet Bennett near the front door. "What happened?" he asked quietly.

"I searched the town. He's right," Bennett said. "There's no one else around, and it's . . . bad. Whoever came through—there's some gruesome shit here I've never seen. I think they might have been sacrificing people."

"There's no way," Alex said, half expecting Bennett to retort with *Of course not, stupid*, but he didn't. The soldier's gaze had never appeared so sober and unwavering.

"There was one, on a dinner table . . . they had their—" Bennett struggled to finish. "Anyway, it's not important. There was a symbol.

Kind of looks like an eye. My guess is whoever these gutter-lickers were got their hands on Yuri's brother. Don't know how he survived, but now he's so scared he doesn't know what's what. I just hope to Christ whoever did this is far enough away that they didn't hear those gunshots."

"Starting to sound like Izaiah's story about the ancient cult might not be so far-fetched," Alex said.

Before Bennett could surely berate him, Yuri stepped into the doorway of the back room. Looking at the ground and holding his right elbow, he asked, "Tea?"

Moments later, after Bennett lifted the kitchen table back into place, Yuri poured hot water from an electric kettle over ground tea leaves in a strainer while Alex sat patiently in the kitchen and Bennett stood at the front door like a Doberman on guard.

Once seated with their drinks, Alex asked Yuri about the attack on his village. The young man managed to answer, but only in spurts of dialogue so fevered and full of emotion that they were hard to discern. "They leave me alive. To be coward."

Alex did his best to communicate and console him, while Bennett did little of either. Soon, the morning sun's rays were streaming into the dusty shack. The temperature rose quickly as Alex pressed Yuri about the attackers, but he did not know much. They were an unidentified group who moved swiftly, made no demands, stole nothing, performed a strange ceremony before murdering each member of the town, and disappeared into the night. Yuri remembered the sounds of horse hooves as they left, but that was all. "Sorry. No more."

"We need to leave. Do you have a working car? Car? Right?" Bennett asked.

Yuri grabbed Alex's arm and spoke frantically.

"He doesn't think we'll survive the trip," Alex translated.

Bennett countered, offering to carry Yuri's brother's body to whatever transportation they might have access to. It took some persuading on Alex's part, but Yuri eventually agreed, leading them away from the home, with Bennett carrying Ahmed's blanket-wrapped body, bringing up the rear. In Yuri's backyard they found a lime-green pickup with a crushed front bumper, a roll cage, and an eight-inch lift kit. As Bennett laid Ahmed in the rear, a small brown falcon swooped by within mere feet of Alex's head. *That was the same one I saw eating the goat.*

A sound like thunder rose from under their feet just as five more falcons appeared across town. Then eight. Then a dozen. Hawks and sparrows joined the mix as well. Soon, a legitimate flock was aimed in the direction of the pickup, screaming as if alerting one another of a nearby predator.

"Hey, guys," Alex said wearily as the rumble vibrating through his legs petered out into low-frequency impacts. *Hooves.*

"That's them," Yuri said, devoid of hope.

Bennett wasted no time slamming the rear gate shut and taking the driver's seat. Yuri tossed him the keys without argument and took the passenger seat. Alex jumped into the back of the pickup just as the first wave of screeching birds came upon them, forcing him to drop to safety. The engine roared to life as a multitude of shapes emerged from behind the buildings in town, blurred by the heat rising from the desert floor. Horses in a charge became clear first: brown, black, gold, and spotted white, wrapped in cloth or leather. Their riders were seated high in the saddle, thrashing up and down as they rode, clad in dark natural colors and wielding handheld weapons Alex couldn't clearly make out.

The soldier hit the gas, sending the truck forward and Alex into the tailgate as Bennett took wild turns through the few buildings in their path, which were, unfortunately, poor obstacles for the riders. Their screams surrounded them: yelps and calls mixed with the shrieks of their birds overhead, seemingly intended to frighten, as was their effect. Metal scraped metal and Bennett flung them back and forth in the fight to lose the fast-approaching horde. But when a pop overcame everything, the 4x4 jostled, and the soldier cursed in ways Alex never dreamed as the truck spun out of control, diving into a hillside face-first with a thud.

Yuri's truck fought valiantly upward, lurching like a dazed prizefighter on the mat before its engine gave out. It settled a few feet down the hill, coming to a halt as the horde—at least twenty-five strong—swiftly circled the truck. The riders had myriad skin colors to match their horses' coats and came in varying sizes, though most were plenty large enough to defend themselves, doubly so, considering the rusty, custom, bladed weapons each carried. What little clothing they wore was made of leather and fur, some of which hadn't yet been cleaned of their blood and innards, making for a perfect treat for the birds on their shoulders to peck at.

Covered from head to toe in white markings that appeared tribal—featuring sharp partial circles bisected by hard lines—the riders' appearances offered no indication of letters or language or a way to distinguish them. There did not seem to be a leader or individuals within the group, and only their birds spoke as they closed in like a high fence.

"What are we doing?" Alex asked, leaning his face into the rear cab hatch. "How do we get out of this?"

"Not sure we can," Bennett said so calmly it hurt to hear.

"Nous avons fait de notre mieux," Yuri said, leaning his head against the passenger window, looking so relaxed he could have taken a nap.

As the riders waited, a small section of six broke away to approach the truck.

"Here we go," Bennett muttered.

Yuri whispered a prayer to himself, the despair in his voice bleeding into Alex's mind and creating a pitiable, weak feeling within him. *There must be options.* He searched the truck bed, finding nothing of use. *How is this happening? This can't be real.*

The six orbited the truck on horseback, looking over their potential prey until seemingly satisfied, then dismounted. Two riders, each a head taller than Alex, seized him and dragged him out of the truck bed. Following several prods and bruise-inducing blows, he found his best course of action was not to struggle, despite the rage growing in his gut.

Yuri was pulled from the truck and forced to the ground beside Alex as additional riders were called in to subdue Bennett, who managed to kill one of the riders with Yuri's shotgun. But with the gun empty, he was easily seized by a hulking figure who marched out of the riders' ranks. All it took was a single punch to the gut to send the soldier to the sand, where he was collected. Muttering the whole way, his mouth filling with blood, Bennett was plopped next to Alex in the lineup. Of the three, only Yuri remained calm and collected.

"I'm sorry. We did this," Alex said softly.

The riders and their birds of prey went silent as the group split at the center. A smaller woman came through, wearing thick leather gloves, one held over the other, with something dark and round resting in her palm. When she neared, Alex found it was a rock, one revered by the riders, judging from the way they parted for it. The gloved woman who was its keeper stood over Yuri and began speaking in a monotone language Alex didn't recognize, as though reading from a textbook, letting each syllable linger for as long as possible. The words gave Alex the same morose feeling he'd had when he was drunk, lost, and alone in Albuquerque at age 22 after his friends ditched him in the middle of the night.

At the sight of the stone, Yuri's survival instincts seemingly kicked in. He thrashed and fought, screamed and threatened, but ultimately it did nothing. The gloved rider finished her sermon and held the stone forward, pressing it into Yuri's chest, where it sizzled on contact with his skin as the birds squawked with shrill calls.

The instant the stone touched Yuri, a wave of boiling heat coursed through Alex's veins. His rage skyrocketed. His mind clouded. A scream came without choice. The voices in his head had returned en masse, calling for death and destruction. They wanted blood, and Alex felt himself falling into their desires.

"Shut up. Shut up!" he shouted, gritting his teeth as the gloved rider bared a long, slender blade over Yuri, who was frozen in place, eyes wide with terror. His jaw snapped open, fighting for air, as though something were blocking his esophagus. Tears streamed down his cheeks.

Then the voices in Alex's mind stopped, and a cold recess opened within him—a void—as though his identity were erased, leaving him hollow. The gloved rider raised the blade, ready to strike, and a singular voice within the teacher spoke, not with words but feelings. A pure and abhorrent hatred filled him. A swell of torrid heat was in his hands, and he was suddenly free, on his feet. The flash was all-encompassing, visceral, full of sound and light. Before he knew it, he was upon the gloved rider, his hands on her throat, ready to rip it open.

NOT OF THIS EARTH

When Bennett was on his knees in the sand like a dog, laughing and spitting out blood, about to be executed, he found himself, of all things, excited. Driving Yuri's truck like a bat out of Hell was fun. Crashing it was too.

The desert-dwelling assholes who were about to kill him, Alex, and their new friend, Yuri, were about the ugliest things he'd ever seen, so Bennett was ready to be done looking at them. *Bring it on. I can't stand being around "bird people."* Bennett also believed he deserved it for helping Alex and Yuri in the first place. *After the shit I saw in that town, the smart move would've been to kill both of them, take the truck, and run.* Once again, life had proven to him that helping people . . . *only gets you fucked. Just like what happened to Jer.*

When Bennett and the others were placed in a lineup, and the gloved desert rider was upon Yuri, ready to plunge her blade down his throat, Alex, the little guy Bennett had been caring for like a baby on his tit, erupted. There was a sound like something sizzling on a grill, and suddenly he was free of his bonds, with a slew of new veins boiling over his neck and arms. He set about trying to rip the riders apart. *And I felt something strange. Something . . . hateful. No other way to describe it. I think it was coming from Al.*

Rather than attack, the desert horde stared with undaunted reverence at Alex, whose rebellion lasted all of three seconds before he was struck in the back of the head by the large rider who had put Bennett down. The teacher collapsed, unconscious, his brief fire extinguished, and was collected along with Bennett and Yuri.

When a burlap bag was pulled over Bennett's head in preparation for a hike, reducing him to hyperventilating from sheer claustrophobia, he tried to focus on the only good thing to come out of all the bullshit with Izaiah, Alex, and the safe house: his limp was gone.

He'd noticed it the moment he woke up behind the soda shop. Though his knee didn't fully heal until his second or third day of solitary confinement in the safe house, once it did, it kept improving. A feeling of restoration was spreading over his body like an infection. By now, he felt as good as he did at twenty-five—wracked by constant abuse and injuries, but still.

Throughout the blind trek led by the desert horde, Bennett pondered Alex's outburst. *It was like I could smell his anger.* He also wondered why the desert riders had halted their executions afterward. *They didn't seem all that shocked by a guy with smoking hands.* Hours went by with little to hear except Yuri's continuous prayers, and just when he thought he couldn't take another step, Bennett was abruptly halted. A rusty door was opened, and he was forcefully loaded into the rear of a truck. Alex and Yuri were loaded in with him, and the heavy door was slammed shut behind them, echoing in a tight space. Loving the feeling of cold steel against his face, even through the bag, Bennett allowed himself to pass out immediately.

The nap wasn't long, but it helped. He still hurt everywhere, but at least he'd gained some energy. Focusing on his surroundings and hearing a muffled diesel engine, he guessed they were in a sealed box. *Maybe a commercial truck. Not an eighteen-wheeler.*

The sound of tires rolling over rough pavement brought back memories of family road trips when he was a boy. *We'd usually pull a trailer. I was stuck in the back, closest to the noise.* His mother would sit in the passenger seat, knitting—never speaking up, arguing, or responding. *Just knitting.* Meanwhile his brother, Jerry, ever a spitting image of their father (*until their relationship went to shit*), had a spot in the middle seat, looking out the window at whatever their father was pointing at and talking nonstop about. *He'd call it a vacation, but they were never just that. Most of the time he was just using us to look legit so he could pull his schemes over state lines. There was always a catch with him.*

Presently, Bennett dared to whisper, "Yuri? Al?" He got no response, and his fingers grazed along the ground. Shuffling along, he found a handful of fur, which coated his palms in a thick, cold liquid.

"Ah, shit." He flicked his fingers, trying to get the sludge off, remembering the feeling of old blood all too well. A smell wafted into the bag over his head: rotting meat. *Guess I found their dinner. Or mine.* Bennett tossed the mysterious furry creature aside and rubbed the blood off his hands on the ground, like a dog wiping its ass on the carpet.

"Al, if you're here, let me know. Come on, guys. We might not have much time before we reach wherever it is they're taking us." Bennett heard a slight groan.

"Al? That you?"

"Yeah. I think so." It was the teacher, if faint.

"Look, we're being saved for something, and I don't want to know what that is. So, let's find each other and maybe we can get one of our masks off."

Alex moaned in agreement as Bennett caterpillared his way in the direction of his voice. After he'd moved only a few feet, another voice spoke up.

"Will not work," Yuri said dryly.

"Yuri? Hey!" Alex cried out. "Are you hurt? Where are you?"

"Nous ne sommes pas seuls. Will not work," Yuri repeated.

"Why not?" Bennett asked.

"Man with us. Watching us. Ils sont ici . . . I see him."

Damn. I knew it. There was a rider in the back of the truck with them, sitting so quietly that Bennett had no indication. That meant they were stuck. *Damn.*

The remainder of the trip wasn't long; Bennett guessed about thirty-five minutes. The truck then came to a lurching halt, and their mysterious babysitter stood up, revealing his or her relative location less than three feet away. Bennett then heard the rear gate open. The sound of birds calling washed over him, and sunlight struck the burlap bag over his head. He hobbled toward the faint, square outline of a door and was grabbed and forced off the truck. "Okay—okay! Just chill out."

Somewhere behind him, Alex refused to shut up, shouting things like "You don't have to do this," and, "I have a family." *How is he even still alive? Where's the guy who erupted with rage? I miss that guy.*

Marched blindly across dirt, hot winds and sheets of sand struck the bag over his head, Bennett spat out little bits as the sounds of a camp came into focus: dozens of voices, clanking metal, fires crackling, and the occasional cry of a falcon or bird of prey. There was the smell of death in the air, reminding him of the bodies he'd seen lying in the sand during his overseas tours. *They bloat in the sun. Good way to get hepatitis.* As he was marched closer to the commotion, it suddenly died away. Bennett could feel likely dozens of eyes on him, and the silence of the camp soon began to fill with snarls and the hissing of overlapping breaths passing through clenched teeth. Angry words were uttered and Bennett could feel something he would describe as a wall of bloodlust falling upon him. *Liked it better when they got spookily quiet.*

"Bennett?" Alex asked with a whimper a few steps behind.

"We're okay. Don't let them spook you."

"Sure. Right. Hear that, Yuri? We're going to be okay." Alex's voice shook enough to add syllables.

A series of heavy cloth drapes passed over Bennett's head. After the fourth, he could sense they'd entered a closed space. It wasn't nearly as hot, and the sound was too contained to be outside. Pushed forward a few more steps, he was then halted and forced to his knees, listening to Alex and Yuri receive the same treatment.

"This feels familiar somehow," Bennett said with a jaunty laugh, his head held high.

"Honestly, it feels like you're trying to get us killed sometimes," Alex said, muffled, on Bennett's left.

The bags over their heads were pulled off, unveiling a circular tent around them, ten yards across, with black, red, and maroon tapestries hung from rusted frames lining the perimeter. Painted in white across the tapestries was an eye, its bottom lid smeared with red. Hard desert sunlight pierced through holes in the walls, leaving beams streaking every which way like long spears in the otherwise dark space. The hut was impressive to be sure, supported by thick wooden beams, though the construction and lack of finishing made it appear the camp was impermanent.

"So, what now?" Bennett asked, receiving no attention from the riders taking seats to rest. A few closed their eyes, possibly to meditate, while a murmur of multiple voices announcing an arrival began outside. The desert riders in the tent—suddenly called to attention—formed a half-circle formation facing the door. Bennett then heard heavy boots upon the dirt, carrying a particular cadence: jittery, with a slide into and out of every step. Then came the all-too-familiar sound of handcuff chains jingling as a large figure stepped through the four entrance flaps. At first, he saw only black boots and a long black coat. Then, before the shape emerged, Bennett caught one of the desert riders near the entrance shudder, as though suddenly taken by fear.

Interesting.

The last entrance flap was swept aside as a tall, dark man ducked beneath the wooden frame into the tent. A black hood obscured most of his face, and his body was tightly wrapped in many worn leather straps. He wore ragged, torn black gloves, topped with two pairs of broken handcuff chains dangling from his wrists. In the shadow of the hood rested a smooth white mask covering the man's face.

Once inside the tent, the figure stretched to his full height—just under seven feet—cracking every vertebra in his spine before returning to his hunched state. The white mask swept over the room and settled on Bennett, whose skin suddenly felt cold and itchy.

The masked man then took a deep breath into lungs sounding so sick and full of mucus it was a wonder they worked at all. He crept forward, speaking in a horrid voice like broken glass scraping over concrete. The frequency rattled like a snake's tail, producing a thick, foul air that seeped from behind the mask and tickled Bennett's eardrums. The first words spoken made no sense; they sounded more like guttural ramblings than a language. After the dark figure emitted a string of wretched syllables, the desert riders responded in unison with a chant that sounded like "Bos Thereom Dah Sathiron." The riders then fell silent.

Darting to the outer edge of the tent, the masked man avoided any direct beams of sunlight, his neck bobbing and tensing to rigid spots, much like a bird, as he floated the mask up and down. His horrid voice continued, some of it sounding like words, some not.

"You know any English?" Bennett asked.

The masked man stopped. His head tilted slowly to the side, the mask's eye slits lingering on Bennett far too long for his comfort.

"Yes. We do," the man finally replied. "It's been some time."

One of the desert riders set a chair in a shadowed area in front of Bennett and the others. The masked man sat, crossed his legs, folded his hands on his knee, and pointed a long, gloved finger at Bennett. "You will be the one with whom we speak."

"Whatever you say, chief," Bennett replied. "But can I get a glass of water first? My throat is so dry you wouldn't believe."

"The Wraithians were never known for their hospitality," the masked man said. "Nor their need for water. Nature has provided many ways to consume it, which they have mastered. And do not look to us for help. We are not their lord. They do not believe in the idea. To them, our arrangement is . . . symbiotic."

"And what about you? What do you see it as?" Bennett asked.

"We're done speaking about us. We wish to know about you. The Wraithians do not take prisoners. How curious we are. Are you what we felt in this desert? What we've been sensing all along?" The masked man took a long moment to study each of the three prisoners before asking cryptically, "The Brothers?"

"Do we look like brothers to you?" Bennett asked.

The white mask snapped to him, muffling a furious grunt that would've put Bennett's mightiest to shame. "We do not play games when speaking of the Brothers! They are everything and shall be treated as all. The only purity in all of reality."

"Yes! Yes. Of course. I would never speak ill of the Brothers. Or reality," Bennett replied, trying to anger the guy only a little bit.

"You smell of many things, neither Celestial nor Archfiend. So what are you? There are depths of UnEarth that have escaped even the demon's gaze—beings we've not yet encountered. Yet, this doesn't feel right." The masked man began rapping his fingers on top of his knee, the sound pulpy and hollow.

"We're just people," Alex said. "Regular, run-of-the-mill."

"So, the little one can speak," the masked man—who kept referring to himself as two people—said, focusing on Alex. "Tell us, what is your goal in this . . . neck of the woods? And why is one of you unlike the others?"

Alex and Bennett looked at Yuri. *Uh, do we really need to say it?*

The masked man wagged his finger. "No, no. We meant which of you attacked the tribe with fists of fire? Who is the Imp?"

Out of solidarity, Bennett and Yuri stayed quiet, but the teacher held his chin up anyway. "I guess I am. Whatever that means."

Bennett wished he'd given Alex lying lessons. It was just as much a survival skill as starting a fire or scavenging for food.

"Curious," the masked man said. "Show us."

"What?" Alex asked.

Goddamn it, Barker. Shut up.

"Show us some Wrath," the masked man demanded. "It doesn't need to be much. We simply wish to know if you're who you say you are."

"We haven't said shit," Bennett said.

"Exactly." The man waited, watching Alex until Bennett and Yuri joined him.

Alex tensed up when every eye in the tent fell on him. "What?"

"Can you do it?" Bennett asked, acting as an intermediary.

"Do what?" the teacher shrieked.

"The thing you did after we crashed Yuri's truck."

"You crash my truck," Yuri corrected.

"How can you accuse me of a thing like that at a time like this?" Bennett exclaimed.

"I don't know what you want from me. No," Alex said, a mix of disappointment and relief in his voice.

The man in the white mask leaned back in his chair. "Not surprising. The Wraithians are no authority on the Eve. They were likely mistaken . . ." He trailed off, tilting his head to the side. "But are you really just human?" Rising from the wooden chair, the looming tree of a man took jittery steps forward. "There's a mystery here, and it isn't just us. Three strangers. Two—Americans lost in the desert—one—a commoner simply caught in the path of the Wraithians. All found together, fleeing for life, but it doesn't work . . ." He stood above them, cracking his neck to the side with each new sentence. "There you were, maggots in the sand, about to die. You witnessed something . . . something that makes the ever-so-small, ever-so-sensitive part of you tick. It moved the compass. And then, without control, brought it out. Yes? The fury. The Wrath." The man leaned back, opening his arms wide, bathing the white mask in sunlight. He took a gargled breath before turning his gaze down on Alex.

"It's all the demon has ever known—the Wrath. Unable to escape it . . . and yet . . ." The man trailed off again, his head tilting upward and to the side as though he'd spotted a fly.

"What are you?" Yuri asked, his eyes fixed on the ground in front of him.

The white mask swung down on him like lightning. "You. From you, we feel nothing. A faint whisper of Dread and Rapture. You will be a very poor addition to the Eve." He turned to Bennett and

Alex. "What are we? What are we? A chance at a first impression of our choosing . . . What are we? We are what should not be named, what nature has yet to define. We are plague, locust returned, but you may call our union Joseph."

This is him? The guy all this is about?

Lifting his hands slowly, Joseph closed them around Yuri's head, one glove over each ear, forcing his chin upward. "Look at us, child."

Yuri shut his eyes and mouth tight, trying to close himself off from the presence of the masked man, but unable to control his shaking.

"Don't be afraid. You will soon feel the beauty of silence."

Yuri's breathing finally slowed. His eyes slid open, collected and at peace. "I am not afraid of you."

Joseph nodded once. "Good. There is nothing to be afraid of." He then closed his hands effortlessly, clasping them with a horrid crunch, intertwining his fingers. What was once Yuri's head exploded outward, spilling onto the dirt, while his body lingered erect.

The violence did not give Bennett pause. He had long since grown used to the sight of blood and guts. Even the sound, horrible as it was, was tolerable. However, at the sight of Yuri without a head, Bennett felt his body flood with the same icy chill from the night he'd awoken in the alley. He was suddenly immobilized. The voices were back.

"No!" Alex cried out. "Oh my god! Christ almighty! Why? He didn't do anything! He—Why did you—"

"As you say," Joseph began, "he did nothing. He was nothing. A soul that will never ripen. We've released him without pain, prior to the coming conflict. Is there anything more merciful? But you, where is it? Your Wrath. Show us! The Wraithians are many things, but liars—" He stopped abruptly. The mask turned slowly to Bennett, then tilted clockwise. A violent inhale through damaged nasal passages shook the porcelain-like material.

"What is that?" he asked, moving closer to Bennett, bits of Yuri still dripping from his black gloves. He leaned down, his white mask hovering a foot above Bennett, bobbing as Joseph sniffed vigorously. "Interesting. One can never mistake the Rapture, no matter how long you've been apart."

He faced the Wraithians watching from the shadows of the outer circle. "Do you know what this means? Here we have two humans, one smelling of Archfiend, the other of Celestial, found on the threshold of our convergence! These are the mortals we were warned of slaves of the Tribunal sent to stop us. This means Arros and Hywyn are terrified. They now see. They believe what we have known all along, as destiny ordains us! Gehenna lives! The temple of the Molochs waits to be opened. It will be found! The Brothers will rise!"

The mob chanted, "*Bos Thereom Dah Sathiron!*"

Joseph continued, "They damn us yet have done the same! Controlling the flesh! Sounds of hypocrisy!"

"*Bos Thereom Dah Sathiron!*"

"They show their desperation by sending these wretched insults. We will be the third lord! We will bring the Beast!"

"*Bos Thereom Dah Sathiron!*"

"Tell us," Joseph said to Alex, "did they ask, or were you simply taken from a blissful, eternal sleep? Forced? Impregnated?" He pointed at Alex's chest. "You've got us. We're in there." The white mask then turned to Bennett. "But what lies within you is much worse—the greatest affront to peace in all the void. The creation of despair and torment."

"Worse than you? Doubtful," Bennett shot back.

"To think so many believed the three of us could never exist," Joseph said. "Yet here we stand, having proved that which the kingdoms deny—flesh and Eve can coexist." His glove caressed Bennett's face, but Bennett pulled away.

"Get off me. We're nothing like you."

"True. The chains you wear around your necks ensure your obedience. We've broken our chains. We have no limitations. We are free. The demon ensures the Wrath within us remains a slave, ours to use and control. But you . . ." Joseph rose and stepped away. "You were sent to collect us, yet are now prisoners. It is doubtful either of you has any control of your Eve, or you would have shown us."

Alex and Bennett said nothing, keeping their heads down.

"Surely it was the Medolians charged with the task. Bringing you into the fold. Yes, this reeks of Izaiah. It must be mortal hands that bring us in, correct? Wouldn't want it to look as though one side was trying to tip the scales, would we, or risk breaking our precious Covenant. That pledge was an insult to all of Arros."

"We have no idea what you're talking about, pal," Bennett sneered.

"No matter. Our time here comes to an end," Joseph said. "The Brothers have finally called. They long to be free. And soon, it will be found. It will be found!"

"*Bos Thereom Dah Sathiron!*" the Wraithians bellowed.

Joseph crept toward the nearest desert rider and whispered something before turning back to Bennett and Alex. "Left in the care of the Wraithians, you will be used in their pain rituals. We have asked they spare your lives, though you may soon wish otherwise."

With that, Joseph bowed and stepped through the entrance, leaving Bennett and Alex alone with a hut full of desert riders. Some appeared to be smiling in the shadows, revealing yellowed teeth. A rustle grew, and for the first time an expression other than hate crossed the riders' faces. *I know that look.* It was the same look Bennett used to get on his own face just before torturing prisoners.

The riders crept closer. One, a skinny woman without a single hair on her body, wearing a white chain-mail shirt, pulled out a sharp, three-pronged stabbing device.

"Been nice knowing ya, Al," Bennett said.

Alex turned to him—flabbergasted, judging by the stupid look on his face—as the Wraithians descended on them. "You know my name is Alex, right?"

"That's what you're worried about right now?" Bennett replied. *Definitely should have left him behind.*

The Wraithian standing over him smiled a sickly grin, clearly lost in wildly fucked-up thoughts. But her pleased expression was wiped off her face the instant Bennett started to laugh.

"... early in my research, I had a hard time accepting what I'd learned, continuing to see Un-Earth as a place of magic, where the dead walked. Then I began to realize these creatures were simply newly discovered life [. . .] provided by life expanding in our universe, which I refer to as Universe Alpha. For research purposes, I have thus labeled UnEarth as Universe Delta."

- Excerpt from the journal of
Dr. Francisco Emul. Murcia
August 1894

ANOTHER MEDOLIAN

The tent flap shut, cutting off a blinding flash of sunlight as the sounds of the desert riders' footsteps faded. *Finally. Alone.* Alex could barely move without making the pain worse. The same air blessing his lungs was wreaking havoc on the open nerve endings all over his body, most of which had stopped soaking his clothes in blood by now.

Their methods were exuberant; he had to give them that. Every inch of the Wraithian pain ceremony was awash with drama, complete with shouting, grand gestures, powerful speeches he couldn't understand, and calls and responses. Once handed the ceremonial blade—which seemed to be a regular, run-of-the-mill knife you might buy from a hardware store—the new Wraithian in charge led a chant and shared their own gospel. Each spoke as though getting their hands on the blade was all they'd ever wanted, and once their individual performance was over, the real fun began: the torture, which riled the bunch more than anything else. Yet, after all Alex had endured these last few hours, he knew Bennett had gotten it much worse. The Wraithians had chosen the soldier as their favorite.

Five times he was beaten unconscious and five times he got back up remarkably quickly. By the fourth time Alex thought he was witnessing a miracle. Not once did Bennett cry for mercy, forcing many of the stoic riders to let slip their frustrations. One Wraithian even had to be forcibly pulled off Bennett by her fellow cult members when she tried to strangle him with a whip. At the moment, however, the soldier was lying on his side a few feet away from Alex, passed out.

The infections he'll get alone . . . Alex shook the thought away. *No. Stay here. Keep your mind here, on the situation. We know why they cut us, because they're freaking psychos, but why did they cut themselves?* He'd pondered it the whole time. After each Wraithian had their chance with the knife, they would cut themselves across the wrist, just shy of fatally, and drain the blood onto a small black stone.

It was the damndest thing.

Morbid as the thought was, part of Alex missed the man in the mask. At least when Joseph was around, he felt merely sick to his stomach, not also shivering and wracked with pain. Meeting a demon residing inside a boy had been an utterly terrifying and unwelcome experience overall.

Poor Yuri. Now I know why Izaiah wanted us to wait for him. I just hope the kid inside Joseph, whoever he is, can't see any of the things the demon is making him do. I can't imagine what it must be like in there.

During Alex's recent introduction to torment, with every jagged blade dragged across his skin, he fought as hard as he could to re-ignite the surge he'd felt when Yuri was about to be killed in the desert, trying to harness the power it provided. He pressed himself to feel utter rage, assuming it was the most likely ignition source, but failed. Even Yuri's real death had done nothing to reignite the fire.

For now, the sounds of the Wraithians outside had grown soft and distant, as though the majority had ridden off, possibly to hunt.

Guess now's the time to look for an escape.

"*Psst.* Bennett." Alex shook his shoulder gently, trying to avoid the numerous contusions in his blood-soaked skin.

"Get some sleep, Al," Bennett muttered.

"So they can wake us up for round fifteen in half an hour? We're dying. We have to—" Alex stopped when Bennett coughed blood onto the ground. "You're not looking great."

"Thanks. So, tell me, what does that even mean to you anymore? Dying. To die."

"Can we please discuss this later? Do you have a plan to get us out or not?"

The soldier let out a slight chuckle. "This is my plan."

Before Alex could muster a response, a powerful voice rose outside, accompanied by footsteps. A cadre had returned. When they entered, Alex could only see white blobs through his swollen eyes. The largest blob up front, a monstrous Wraithian, chuckled to himself and drew a long, gleaming blade from his sheath. But Alex felt no humor. That blade wasn't meant to torture. *It's meant to cut things in half.*

He desperately tugged on Bennett's cold, blood-soaked shirt. "Hey—hey, dude, wake up. We need to do something. Like, now."

Bennett waved his hand off. "I'm not playing anymore." The soldier adjusted and tucked his hands under his arms, as though trying to catch some Zs.

"They're going to chop our heads off," Alex whispered.

"That'd be new."

Outside, a chant rose—a mass of desert riders shouting, "*Bos Thereom Dah Sathiron!*" Leather banners were being beaten like drums, while Wraithian birds squawked and horses neighed, as though a circus parade were seconds from rolling over the tent.

"Been fun, I guess," Alex said to Bennett's shoulder.

Bennett shrugged. "Guess so."

The gang of riders inside the tent closed in on Alex first, the natural choice. Drawing his blade high above his head, the enormous Wraithian muttered some guttural syllables that seemed to beguile the others. Alex couldn't help but roll his eyes, beginning to share Bennett's malaise. *Just do it. Screw the song and dance.*

The Wraithian was about to swing when the thunder outside the tent came to a lurching halt. Feet no longer marched in formation, and the chanting had ceased. The atmosphere shifted from wild militaristic pride to reactionary panic, staying the enormous Wraithian's hand. He and the others listened to the small clashes of steel outside leading to an eruption of painful screams. The largest Wraithian shouted orders, and a handful charged out of the tent, while the rest seemed content to follow their own commands. This was the most unsure and uncoordinated the Wraithian cult had yet appeared.

Within seconds the thunder outside returned, now intermingled with the chaos of war. There might have been dozens of attackers storming the encampment for all Alex knew. Mounted riders circled the tent, shouting battle cries and creating a symphony that reminded Alex of the cowboy and Indian movies he'd watched as a kid. The remaining Wraithians inside exchanged unsure glances before charging out, leaving the big one behind, who was making a poor show of confidence.

With every cut-off shriek of a desert rider, the combat outside dwindled. Whoever was left was giving it their all, but then, with a flutter like sheets in a heavy wind, a shadow sped around the tent, twisting the gaze of the huge Wraithian, who'd been reduced to shouting boorishly. Spinning, he landed on Alex and Bennett. *Was hoping you'd forgotten about us.* Alex closed his eyes, praying to every god he wasn't about to be sent to the fire again. *Just stay calm, everything will be fine.*

He jolted when hot blood splashed his face, making him unsure if he'd been cut in two. Opening his eyes, he found the huge Wraithian was now a foot shorter, headless, his body remaining upright for a moment before collapsing with a thud, revealing a cloaked, hooded figure standing behind it. A staff with curved multipronged blades on each end, smeared with dark blood, was clutched in their hand. The figure's deep gray cloak was striped with vibrant cyan, and a hood of black obscured their face, revealing glistening light gray eyes like sunlight filtering through gypsum. Those eyes settled on Alex, bringing on a whole new kind of unease.

It was just you? No army? "Who are you?" Alex asked.

She pointed the tip of her staff at him, so sharp it seemed to vanish as it turned. "You know what I am, and you know we don't like our time wasted. So, go on, what are you waiting for? Puff your smoke, blow your ash, tell me your clan." The blade hovered less than an inch from his throat, rendering Alex still with fear. "You can't hide, and you know you can't run, so show me your real self. Well . . . are you an Imp, or aren't you?"

"Why does everyone keep calling me that?" Alex asked.

The woman looked as though he'd just told her he tried to eat a tree with a fork once. She backed off slightly. "I don't—you're not Archfiend? But I can smell Wrath on you. Who are you? The both of you. Full names. New and old. I've never seen either of your faces before."

Alex was too busy fighting off the anxiety of being threatened by a weapon such as hers to answer any questions. Bennett responded by laying still on his side. The woman in the cloak knelt beside him and held her palm over his shoulder, her wrist guards and gauntlets catching Alex's eye.

"Why were you taken prisoner?" she asked. "Wraithians torture, kill, perform their sacrament, and move on. They use Earthly bodies as vessels for Wrath and dispose of them when done. So, my only question is, are you Earthly bodies?" Leaning over Bennett, she sniffed. "It can't be. You're both human?"

"What else would we be?" Alex asked.

The woman rose and stepped back, revealing her tanned face, narrow flat-bridged nose, and high curved eyebrows. Nearing him again, she held her hand out, and for a moment, he thought it might be to assist, until she jabbed a finger into one of the open wounds on his arm.

"Ow! What the Hell?" he yelped. *Where has your hand been?*

She stepped back as though she'd just discovered they were lepers. "By the Eve, it's true."

Alex stayed quiet, not wanting to upset her further. *Still very scared.*

"What are you doing here?" she asked.

"We were brought here. Please, this man needs a hospital. I need one, too. Are you here to help us?" he asked frantically.

"The one who brought you here—was it an old man who smells of rotten entrails and shares multitudes of terrible jokes?"

"You know him?" Alex responded.

With a roar, she slammed her staff into the ground mere feet from his knees, shaking the dirt. "So, it wasn't just a rumor. They actually did it. No due process, just barreled forward. Seems to be the way lately."

"Ma'am, could you please explain what's going on?" Alex asked.

"First, tell me where Izaiah is," she said. "He wasn't supposed to let you out of his sight."

"The guy took off," Bennett said from the ground, facing the other way. "Said he would be back soon.'Cept he wasn't."

"Typical," she said. "Just like Izaiah to ignore his responsibilities and do things his way, despite what it would mean for everyone else. When did you last see him?"

"Five days ago, when he dropped us off at the safe house. Said he was going out to find the demon on his own," Alex answered. *Instead we did. Yay.*

"Such a mess." Mara's shimmering eyes darted between them, narrowing. "I didn't think it was possible. Yet, here you are. Eve in the flesh. Somewhere you don't belong, a part of something you couldn't understand. A mockery of everything my post *used* to stand for."

Alex was shivering, losing clarity, and couldn't keep conversing for much longer. "Please. Can you help us? I j-just w-want to go home."

"I'm not here to get you what you want. I have a job to do, and my orders do not involve you. At least they didn't until now. I suppose neither of you has any clue how important the task you were given is."

Bennett rolled over. "Your friend Izaiah mentioned something about preventing a war."

She laughed. "I wouldn't call him my friend."

"But you're a Medolian, right?" Bennett asked, trying to pick himself up from the dirt.

"Yes," she said, her tone laced with surprise.

"How did you find us?" Alex asked.

"Followed the trail of destruction left by these Wraithian imposters. Their numbers are growing and concentrated in this region, which isn't far from where the nameless demon was last seen. Something is coalescing. But even without that, I could've smelled you miles away. Any UnEarth creature could. You're lucky it was me who came calling."

Lucky. "But we don't know who you are," Alex said.

While she stood, her eyes kept moving, analyzing and calculating. "I'm Mara Loren, second in line of the Medolian Sentries, and I am taking you into custody. You will be transferred to the Tribunal, provided it hasn't been shut down already, where you will wait for your fates to be decided by the Senate."

"We didn't do anything wrong!" Alex shouted. *Ow! No more shouting. Hurts.*

"I'm not your enemy, child." She stepped closer to Alex. "I was against using humans in this mandate from the start. The reason the public lost trust in us and forced this debacle is because of the Warden Sentry's incompetence. If I'd known he was just going to ignore the mandate and not escort you, I would have insisted I take lead. Perhaps he simply wanted to let you get back to death as quickly as possible?"

"When do we finally get to do that? Die," Bennett asked. "I've been trying for hours, giving up all sorts of hope. I'd be surprised if there were any left in the old ticker. Yet, here I am, alive, with lungs full of blood. What about your staff there? Looks like it'd do the job." Bennett stuck his neck out toward her. "Here. Chop away."

"The Rapture and Wrath within you have already started to take seat," Mara said bluntly. "That is why you continue to live."

"What the Hell does that mean, lady?" Bennett shouted. "We have no idea what the fuck is going on! What is Wrath? What is Rapture? Why were we abducted from what sounds like a really great nap? Just chop already!"

"I don't have to explain anything," she said sharply. "As far as I'm concerned, you both know more than you should."

"You mean about Joseph?" Alex asked.

"The Archfiend is none of your concern. He can't hide forever. He'll be in chains soon, answering for his crimes against the flesh. The Covenant will be honored. Izaiah will be forced to kneel before the entire Tribunal and pay for his imbalance, and you two will no longer have anything to worry about."

You are beyond terrifying.

"Sounds good to me," Bennett agreed.

Alex waved his arms. "Hold on. I have to get back to Arizona."

"Or you could kill us now. Going once . . ." Bennett sounded hopeful again.

Mara gripped her staff and yanked it from the ground. "Confusing creatures. I'm glad I experience you rarely. If it's what you really want . . ."

"No! Wait!" Alex screamed. "No chopping yet. We have information you might need. We can help." *Please-please-please.*

"You have nothing I want."

Find something to use. This is our only shot. What do we know? "We know where Joseph is! Or, where he's going, at least." *Please.*

She stayed her hand. "You saw the Archfiend? Not possible, I would have sensed him."

"Five hours ago. If you hurry, you can catch him. After letting us go, of course," Alex added with a false grin.

"Or there's always that killing thing," Bennett suggested again.

"Be quiet!" Mara shouted. They both did as told. She stepped back and began twirling her staff absentmindedly, keeping her gaze on them. "Men are easy to read. I can tell you're not lying, and seeing you like this, broken, it does remind me you should never have had a part in this to begin with. You're simply Eve providers. Not even that much, frankly. I think everyone would sleep better if they knew you two were no longer part of the equation. Very well.

If you show me which way the demon has gone, I will take you back where Izaiah found you and tell him nothing of this."

"Really?" Alex nearly shouted. *Am I really going to see her?*

Mara smirked. "You can only get in the way. I want you as far away from this as possible, without having to find a way to dispose of your bodies, of course."

Alex could've cried. *Melissa . . .* "Thank you. You don't know what this—"

"But," Mara stopped him, "if I find out you two have misled me in any way, I'll have no problem delivering your tainted corpses to the Tribunal, and will gladly accept whatever punishment is handed down, even if it means starting another war. Do we understand each other?"

"Absolutely," Alex said, his toes wiggling in his shoes.

This is it. I'm going home!

A VOICE IN THE DARK

"They didn't kill them on the platform," Leigh said as she leaned forward and stared down a sheer drop of at least forty feet. "A ceremony was performed here, at the top. Maybe organs were harvested. Maybe it was all about blood. Then—" She whistled like a bomb falling, ending with a squishy splat. "Some might've been killed from the drop, some might've lived and tried to climb out." Leigh pointed out one of the skeletons halfway out of the pit below. "Look, arms reaching out. Fighting for it. Killing each other to live."

Coming out of a daze she spun to face Jeff, who sat a few yards away, his eyes and pencil buried in a sketchbook, drawing the massive statue atop the column for what must have been the fiftieth time.

"Cheery bunch," he said without turning around to face her.

Leigh sighed, anger bubbling beneath the surface. *You serious right now?* Jeff's constant sketching and incessant cold shoulder had gotten old yesterday.

The temporary lights he'd set up inside the cavern allowed them to study it more closely, alleviating the constant fear of rolling an ankle on the uneven floor. But getting power into the temple had taken an entire day of hard work—a day wasted in Leigh's eyes. That was two grueling days ago. Since then, they hadn't found any new passages or artifacts, and she was running out of ideas and excuses.

Trying to ignore Jeff's disinterest, she returned to cataloging the skeleton pit. "These weren't sacrifices to appease a god, or gods, whatsoever. It's as though it wasn't about the death at all—it was about the pain being inflicted. It was about the punishment."

Jeff replied only, "People used to sacrifice other people. Shitty business, but that's the way it goes. Luckily, they're not alive to feel it now."

"But this is the worst we've seen—by a lot. These people . . . I don't want to know how someone like that thinks," Leigh said.

"Hmm," Jeff responded.

Leigh faced him, waiting impatiently. "That's all? 'Hmm'?"

"What am I supposed to say?"

"Literally anything else. You could start by showing some enthusiasm for your work."

Jeff waved his arms, shaking the pencil and paper, feigning a rousing cheer. *Smartass.* She was seconds away from screaming at him. All she wanted was to focus on the damn temple, the most important thing to happen in her career—possibly her entire life. The cavern was purpose; the rarest of archaeological finds, all to herself. Yet now, she could only think about what to say to the only person she had left in the world.

He was upset, she knew that. The nights had been strained, and they hadn't slept together for the last two. She remembered waking up in the middle of the previous night to find Jeff had moved to his own tent, and it wasn't for survival's sake she had missed his warmth. If he was hurting, so was she. It had escalated far more quickly than she'd anticipated, or ever let happen before.

Ever since Casey had left with the crates containing the dagger and all three black stones, Jeff had been acting differently—distant, and bitter, constantly complaining about stomachaches, similar to what Casey had experienced. During nights at camp, Leigh and Jeff researched statues, symbols, and art throughout history, but so far nothing matched their temple or the great statue of the beast within, whose wings shared a resemblance with those of western dragons but were nowhere near as refined or majestic as the classic image that came to mind. The flesh between its long, slender phalanges had so many torn holes it was hard to imagine they could carry such a broad creature, whose thick body and trunk-like legs reminded Leigh of a rhinoceros or a fat dog.

Presently, she yawned, exhausted—more physically than mentally. The professor of archaeology had all the energy in the world for activities like finding a new chamber or some (*goddamn*) writing, but managing human connections was a high-bandwidth activity. *Even the great Leigh Evans needs food and rest. Give it up, sunshine.*

She closed the notebook, stood, and stretched. "You about ready to call it a day?" she asked, trying to sound amiable.

Jeff nodded and rose to grab his backpack. They walked in silence, passing through the temple entrance, down the Dead Stairs, and onward toward the surface, each stealing glances at the other when they weren't looking. *Really wish he would say something.* Zipping up her coat when they reached the cave exit, Leigh pulled her collar high over her neck, protecting herself from the frigid wind coursing through the canyon like an icy river. As the canyon opened to a wide berth, the gusts became warm compared to those raging over the camp plateau. Marching behind Jeff, using his frame as a shield, she wished they could walk side by side, huddled together. He probably felt the same, but neither would be the first to admit it. *I know I won't.*

Trudging up the final hill, they watched their sordid camp come into view, its empty tents swaying violently, windows and entrances flapping and flailing. The sight made Leigh think of Casey and how she missed her more every day. A small glimpse of the setting sun on the horizon was obscured by gray clouds as Leigh and Jeff trudged into camp. Breaking away, she marched up the hill toward her tent, hearing him follow. When she stepped inside out of the wind, Jeff waited at the entryway.

"What do you want to eat?" he asked.

Leigh emptied her pockets and started a gas lamp. "I'm not hungry."

"Gotta eat something."

She could tell he was aching to be invited in. *Strange he thinks he needs to be.* "When did I ask you to take care of me?" She sat down with her notes at the table, ignoring him (*starting now*). Jeff lingered a moment in the doorway, where she could feel him watching her scribble. Eventually, he came to his senses, stepped in, and sat down on the cot, not saying anything at first, rubbing and blowing air on his cold hands. Leigh kept ignoring him. *If you're going to talk, talk!*

"So—" he finally began. "I've been thinking . . . we're done, right?"

Leigh kept jotting notes as if he hadn't uttered a word. "You said you'd stay."

"There's nothing else in there. Look at us—what are we doing? The camp is abandoned."

"How is it abandoned if we're still here?"

"You know what I mean. We're almost out of supplies, and we haven't had contact with the outside world in days. What about your mystery backer, huh? Aren't they curious what's going on? I think it's time we bring in someone else. This thing is dead and you know it—"

Leigh jumped to her feet and threw her pencil at the desk hard enough to make Jeff twitch. "Somebody else? Did you have an aneurysm? No one is getting into my site until I'm done with it."

He sat still, his eyes direct but tired, maybe even a little sad. Leigh didn't budge, and he eventually stood up. Jeff circled the perimeter of the tent, tying down the window flaps one by one, though it did little to subdue the noise.

Finishing the last flap, he turned to face her. "We've found nothing new. No more stones, except for some fallen stalactites. Certainly nothing as interesting as the dagger. The site's wasted. Don't you want nice things again? Fuck, I miss nice things. We should go toward 'em, not away."

"What's all this 'we'? This isn't your site."

"We're a team now, aren't we?" Jeff asked.

"No, we have fun, but I'm still your boss, and I say we investigate the site further."

"What are you so afraid of? If this is such a great find, fucking show it off! You've earned it. We've all earned it. Especially the chap who lost his eyes for it, or the others who might have died traipsing through the desert. Eh? Do something for them. Because I haven't seen my boss do shit."

"I release you," Leigh said with a wave of her hand, returning to her notebook and pencil, finding its tip intact and scribbling whatever came to mind.

"Excuse me? I didn't quite hear that," Jeff said.

"I think you did. If this place is so horrible—if what we're doing here is so ethically wrong—quit. Go off and take your little crusade with you. I have a couple of those going myself. Whoever built the temple left clues. Whether or not we're good enough to find them, they did." She caught Jeff's gaze, hoping to convince him with her eyes. *I know this is the right call. I do.*

He sighed and smiled. His brow tightened. "So . . . that's the way it is?"

"That's the way it is." Leigh said it so coldly she surprised herself.

"I'll be gone in the morning. Good luck, Professor Evans. Hope you find what you're looking for." Jeff made his way to the exit. "Don't bother sending my last check, boss. I won't be wanting it."

Before she could say anything, he untied the doorway flap and ducked out. *Fine, leave like that. See if I care.* Leigh slammed her book closed and began preparing for a few hours' rest.

For whatever reason, that night was the coldest of the entire three-month dig. The deafening howls of the wind crept through the openings in the tent windows and entryway, knocking over anything not already toppled. Leigh listened to the sea of white-noise for hours. Sleep never came.

Why can't Jeff see the bigger picture? This is something amazing. The world will be talking about this, and it can be ours. As long as we're the ones to unlock its secrets, it will be ours. We could have gone anywhere afterward, been together for as long as we wanted. Her scattered thoughts suddenly landed on the workers and their faces after the camp riot: how scared they had been. Leigh had been here longer than anyone, and so far had no desire to pluck anyone's eyes from their sockets.

Shit like that is what keeps us living like cavemen.

Another hour went by and she was still awake, though the screaming wind in the canyons had been reduced to a hush, and the tent flaps had gradually slowed until they lay still. Sand fell from the sky and settled on the plains like mist. She concentrated on dozing off, hoping to utilize the new quiet. However, after a few minutes, the sound of someone marching up the hill became clear.

Heavy footsteps. *Only Jeff's boots could make that sound.* Also, the sound of small chains rattling.

The steps reached the tent entrance and stopped. Jeff's silhouette remained on the fabric just outside the door, waiting for a good thirty or forty seconds, doing nothing.

Probably thinking about how to apologize.

When the entrance flap finally opened, Leigh shut her eyes to pretend to be asleep, hoping he would think she was at peace after their fight. The flap shut, and she squinted to take a peek, but it was too dark to see anything other than a big dark fuzzball moving toward her. She hoped he wouldn't say anything stupid and would simply get into bed with her, hold her close, and apologize for what he had said. But after a minute or two, she felt nothing. There was not so much as the sound of anyone breathing. She opened her eyes slightly, not seeing the tent—nor Jeff—but a stark white face with thin dark eyes attached to an enormous shadowy figure dressed in rags.

Rocketing back, she reached across her cot and grabbed the baseball bat stashed away for just this kind of situation. "Who are you? Why are you in my tent?" she shouted, gripping the bat so tightly her hands cramped. *Jeff, where are you? I know you heard that.*

The figure in black remained still, seemingly watching with curiosity. The mask floated in the darkness, darting randomly from one side to another, as a low, wet, gravelly voice crept up, churning Leigh's insides. "We wish to thank you."

Jeff finally arrived, calling out as he charged up the hill. His silhouette fell on the tent. "Leigh? Where are you?"

Dashing inside, he immediately went after the masked stranger, his equal in size, tackling them, though they stood as strong as a pillar. Leigh couldn't see much more than limbs and bodies flailing, and a glimpse of Jeff's arms wrapping around the figure before disappearing in a flood of black. Jeff roared over the tussle, while the masked man remained silent as a whisper, save the rattling of his wrist chains. Then Leigh heard the horrible crack of bones breaking, followed by Jeff's screams.

The fuck are you? What's happening to us?

Rushing in with the baseball bat, she swung as hard as she could, landing a loud thud in the masked man's lower spine. But he did not move, flinch, or cry out in pain. Instead, he turned and pulled away the cloak near his legs, revealing Jeff, frozen, clutched in a vise grip on his lower neck. His eyes were wide, his mouth twitching intermittently. Blood dripped beneath the masked man's finger-tips, where long sharp nails protruded through his gloves.

Leigh reeled back to strike again, halting when the masked stranger tightened his hold on Jeff. "Let him go!"

The stranger in the mask was so calm and still he didn't even appear to be breathing. "We will let this one go if you give us what we seek."

Leigh eyed Jeff, unable to tell if he was paralyzed or simply in too much pain to move. His arm was a deep purple and gray, twisted, hanging like an empty coat sleeve.

"Okay. What do you want?" Leigh asked.

"It is found. Here. By you?" the masked man said plainly.

Jeff's mouth twitched. A stream of blood rolled out. He was turning white. "Don't . . . don't li-listen, Leigh."

"You're killing him! Let him go!" she shouted.

The masked man remained calm. "He will not die if we are given what we came for."

"I don't know what you want!"

Jeff fought more words out. "He means the dagger."

"It's not here. Let him go!" Leigh demanded.

"Harmful lies are a wonderful source of Wrath," the man said as his grip around Jeff's neck tightened, forcing his eyes to roll back into his head. "Continue."

"Listen . . ." Jeff coughed out. "What you want isn't here."

The mask shifted back and forth between Jeff and Leigh. "You believe that is truth. But we know what we sense. If you are useless . . ." He lifted his hand over Jeff's skull.

Leigh lurched forward, hands splayed out. "Wait!"

The man stayed his hand. The white mask turned toward Leigh. With a mounting sense of remorse, she moved to her cot and grabbed her backpack.

"Wh-what are you doing?" Jeff asked.

"Here." Leigh unzipped the bag and pulled out the dagger made of obsidian metal from the temple, presenting it to the man in the mask. "Take it and go." *For the love of God.*

"Leigh?"

"Quiet, Jeff."

The masked man reached out and took the dagger. "Ah, yes," he said. "Do you have any idea what this is?"

"No. Please go," she said.

"This is the blade of the Molochs. The breaker of barriers. You can't even imagine the wonders it can accomplish. Alas . . ." He tossed the dagger to the side. "It is not what we seek. Where are the Brothers?"

Leigh's gut plummeted. "I thought you wanted the dagger. What brothers are you talking about? The temple is empty."

The masked man reached out and opened his left palm. "Give us the stones, girl."

The stones? Impossible. How could he know about them?

Jeff's eyes stayed on her as she stood, holding her backpack, hoping he would pass out before he saw what he was about to see. She reached into her bag.

"No . . ." Jeff sighed, as if taking his last breath.

Leigh revealed the smallest stone, shimmering like satin. The masked man gasped, filling his lungs with fluid.

"Leigh? Why did you—" Jeff started, his eyelids sinking like lead weights, pulling his head down with them.

"Where are the others? Let us see them! *Put them together!*" the masked man growled.

"They're gone, like I told you," she said.

"He is alone? You're telling us . . . you separated them?"

Her loose grip trembled as she moved toward Jeff and the attacker, about to hand over the stone when his scratchy breathing halted. She froze.

"What do you want with the stones?" she asked.

"You separated the Brothers!?" the masked man bellowed, his voice so loud the tent shook, as if the icy desert winds had returned. "You cannot!"

Leigh's body, weakened by the sound, dropped the stone at her feet.

The masked man roared once more before Jeff's head jerked to the side and his body convulse for a split second before going limp. The man in black yanked his hand upward, and with it came a flurry of blood and bone. The mess splattered across the tent walls, and himself. Remnants of Jeff's spine hung limply from the man's hands.

Her insides shriveled up. She went numb, even though she was screaming. But the sounds were simply impulse; she was empty. In a flash she was hammering at the man with the bat, swinging wildly, hitting nothing but air. The masked man's hand shot out like a snake, grabbed the weapon, and took her by the back of the neck, burying her face in the dirt near the stone. The deep maroon and gray swirls within the rock seemed to be dancing. On the other side, she found Jeff's eyes gaping in terror.

"Look at him! Can you tell what his last thought was? We heard betrayal in his voice and felt nothing but despair when he joined the Eve. He was afraid for you. We want you to remember this in your future."

Leaning down, his mask landing a hair away from Leigh's ear, the man whispered, "We wish to thank you. All that will be unto this Earth from now until the end will be from your hands. Know this. For it is you who is blessed. You who found it."

"The first world described to me was that of fire, Arros, created by the Wrath. Hateful energy slowed to a matter-like vibration within its own universe. This is what creates the creatures known as the Archfiend. Then I learned of the other lower shades of Eve and the life they created. Below Arros was the world of shadow, Fovos, created from the fear of all life. The creatures dwelling there sound so terrifying as to strike death into their victims merely at their sight. Yet, all these rumors seem only the tip of the iceberg. There may be no end in sight to the amount of life thriving within Universe Delta."

- Excerpt from the journal of
Dr. Francisco Emul. Murcia
December 1896

THE WRATH

Alex eyed the steaming plate of pad thai in front of him. After his week in the wild and all his yearning for civilized food, he had taken two bites of the dish and quickly come to hate it. Somehow, he wasn't hungry. Looking up from his meal, he scanned the Thai restaurant in Prescott. It was a Monday, and they weren't busy. The owner, Bryan, wasn't there. Mindy, the waitress helping Alex, approached him at his table, speaking with a thick Colombian accent. "Something you don't like? Tell me the truth."

"It's fine. Thank you," Alex said.

"Then dig in. You're a man. Eat your meal."

Alex held his gut. "I know. Just having some stomach problems."

She was sweet for treating him with what respect she did, knowing what he looked like. Everyone's stares made it obvious. His blue cap was even more sun bleached and covered in dirt, much like the rest of him, and his denim jacket had so many holes now that it seemed a miracle the thing was holding together. After his time in the African desert, he looked a lot more like Izaiah than he did Alex Barker, American fourth-grade teacher. Still, it was better than looking like a corpse, bleeding out in a tent on the other side of the world.

The multitude of open wounds that had once covered his body due to the Wraithians' torture ceremony had been reduced to faint scars when the mystery woman, Mara, who claimed to be a Medolian like Izaiah, rescued them from the desert riders' encampment. Bringing them outside the main tent where they had been held captive, she took them by the shoulders and ordered them to think of home. Then, just as had happened when Izaiah got them to the desert in the first place, they were enveloped in a blinding white light and instantaneously Shifted, marked with a bang.

After the rush, Alex found himself along with Bennett on the outskirts of Prescott, their wounds all but healed, which surprised even Mara. "The Shift through UnEarth revitalized the Eve in you. Interesting," she said. "There may be other changes coming for you as well, of which I would not speculate."

"Yeah, we know 'this has never been done before,'" Alex replied, repeating what he and Bennett had been told several times now.

"Correct," she said with a huff. "We're halfway between the locations your minds chose. Now, move on and forget about me, about everything after your deaths. Forget about Izaiah, the stones, Joseph, all of it. Start anew. Try to find a semblance of lives before departing into the Eve for good. Find balance. Maybe you could even be of help? The universe desperately needs it," she finished, turning to depart.

"What are you going to do now?" Bennett asked. "What happens next?"

Mara spun to face them. Her cloak, as light as air, lingered as it settled. "There's work to do. If the demon isn't caught soon, I worry the relations between UnEarth worlds will only get worse. If what you said is true, and he is still in Africa, I'll find the disgusting creature myself, as should have been commanded from the start, and put an end to all of this. But you are relieved of duty. Bennett Hunter and Alex Barker of Arizona, good luck." She nodded with respect, and in another flash of light, she was gone, leaving them to pick up the pieces.

Thank God I knew where we were. Alex was familiar with the area, southeast of greater Prescott near Oak Knoll. It was slightly disappointing to have arrived in more barren desert, but at least they were back home. The hike took some time, though neither he nor Bennett seemed to care, moving at a quick pace in silence, listening to the wind over the valley, feeling comfort at seeing the green- and gray-bushed hills and rising red mountains of Arizona once again. When he and Bennett reached a junction, Alex proceeded west, but his bulky partner kept heading north.

"I guess we part here."

Alex paused and turned to see Bennett go. "Wait, that's it? You're just—gone?"

Bennett halted and took a breath, letting a bloated moment pass as Alex waited for a response on the side of a two-lane highway. Finally, he muttered, "Go home, Al," and walked off.

After all that—after Izaiah, Joseph, the Wraithians, and Mara—you just leave? So long, I guess.

An hour later, Alex was jogging slowly down the street a few blocks from his house, poring over what he would say, what he *could* say. He didn't know if Melissa thought he was dead or alive. Was he supposed to lie about where he'd been? *Hi, honey, I've been dead and in Africa for a month because a hobo forced me to. Did I mention I met a demon?* He almost wanted to laugh but couldn't manage it.

When his home came into view, he froze, wanting to charge around the corner, down the block, and through his front door. Yet something kept his feet glued to the pavement. When a car turned onto the street from the next block, he ducked away, ashamed of what he must look like. *I'd probably call the cops on me, looking like this.* The headlights swept across his back and passed. It was a sedan far nicer than any he'd ever seen in the neighborhood before. Alex eyed it stealthily over his shoulder as the vehicle rolled down the street and into his own driveway. A horrible new thought then crossed his mind. *Oh no. What if she moved?*

It wouldn't make sense. The debt on the house had been paid by Alex's grandparents years before he and Melissa ever moved in, and they'd never taken out a new loan. Even with both of them employed full time, money had always been an issue. Plus, life insurance had never been part of the equation. Alex barely had a will, with little to enter into it. *What if she couldn't stand to stay in the house? What if she left? How am I going to find her now?*

The doors to the car opened, and a man stepped out of the driver's side—tall, with a shallow blond beard, wearing a clean-cut sport coat and gold tie. *Maybe he can help me find her?* Alex started toward the house, freezing in place when he saw a familiar mane of vivid auburn hair rise into view. Melissa stepped out of the car, nearly stopping his heart, and turned to face the bearded man.

There she was, dimples and all. Alex's love. Her hair was longer, messier, and she looked tired. *One guess whose fault that is.* Opening the rear door, she leaned inside, and he felt nearly all his worry wash away like dirt in the gutter. Seeing her reminded him she would believe anything he told her and would only be thankful he was alive. She would take him in her arms and kiss him as hard and as lovingly as ever. His feet started again—slow, growing to a jog, then a run. He was almost home when Melissa leaned out of the rear of the car, holding a baby girl.

His legs refused to move an inch farther. Every ounce of warmth in Alex filtered away as he watched the blond-bearded man carry the bags and car seat, following Melissa and the baby to the door, acting as their hands and their shield. Alex tried to take a breath of air, feeling his lungs seize. Reaching the door, the man with Melissa turned and looked down the street, not spotting Alex but keeping a watchful gaze around the block a moment before closing the door behind them.

The teacher took off as fast as he could in the other direction, back to town, with no specific place to go. *Can't go near the school. I'll be spotted.* Any added stress on his students was to be avoided. He needed to find out what the story of his disappearance had become. *Maybe try the cops? That's the sane thing.* Following a footpath, Alex found himself in Granite Creek Park and collapsed behind a grove of bushes, fighting to control his breathing while his vision went in and out of focus. The voices in his head had returned en masse, screaming so radically that he couldn't understand them. *Stop it! Why are you doing this? I'm out. I'm done! I'm home. Mara said we're free!* Fighting his mind, Alex lay back and passed out from fatigue, remaining in the park for the next day and a half, drifting in and out of consciousness, watching the clouds pass by. *You lazy ass. What's the plan?*

There wasn't one. He wanted his old life back, but that seemed impossible at this point. He turned his thoughts toward the baby— his baby. He had missed her birth, and Melissa might have moved on. *Maybe he's just a friend I never met? Helping her? Maybe.*

If Alex wanted to get his life back, he knew he needed answers. He needed to go to the one place he'd been deliberately avoiding since returning to Prescott.

Presently, he searched the dining room of the Thai restaurant, where the fish tank once stood. A new TV was now in its place, playing more conservative news. The other bullet hole in the dry-wall was plastered over. One corner of the lobby had clearly been redone. Rubbing his hip and feeling the bullet wound, which still hurt even after two healing Shifts through the Eve, Alex jolted when someone entered the restaurant. The shaking of the bells over the door sent his eyes to the ground in the lobby out of in-stinct, to where he'd lain the night the heavy sleep had washed over him. The hardwood floor, likely stained, had been covered by a rug.

Mindy approached. She must have seen him gawking. "Anything else I can get you?"

"No, I'm fine. I was . . . can I ask you a question? I was wondering about the robbery here, about a month ago."

"Why do you want to talk about that? What's wrong with you?"

"I think I might've known the guy who got hurt. Can you please tell me a little?"

She smiled at him as if he were six and needed a talking to. "Sorry, but it's not right to ask about such things. You understand, right?"

"I don't want to know much. I'm not with the police, or a lawyer, or anything. I'm a teacher. Or, I was. I just need to know." Mindy still looked unwilling. "Please."

"Okay, but I didn't say anything. All right? A guy did come in here a bit ago to rob the place with a gun. Really scary. My friend was cleaning dishes in the back that night. She didn't see nothing, just heard shouting and some shots and called the cops. They got here quick, but I guess not quick enough."

Alex kept his gaze on the rug in the lobby. "And the guy who got shot? Did anyone pronounce him dead?"

Mindy studied him. "No one knows. The body disappeared."

"As in stolen?" he asked.

Mindy shrugged. "Nobody saw. The owner checked the guy's pulse after chasing the gunman away. He said the man was dead, then got everyone outside to wait for the police—no messing with the crime scene. But when they went back in, the guy was gone. Nobody saw him leave, but they think he walked away and got picked up by a car. There was a trail of blood that stopped at the back door. The cops still hadn't found a body last I heard."

Alex had a million questions but felt he was already asking too much of her. *Just a few more.* "What about cameras? Did anyone identify the victim?"

"Yeah. They figured it out from his to-go order. Guy and his wife—long-time customers. I'd never seen 'em in person, but their orders go way back. Turns out she was pregnant, too. So sad." Mindy gave Alex a warm, grandmotherly smile. "You said you knew him?"

He couldn't take his eyes off the spot on the floor. "I did." He then shook her hand, thanked her, tossed what little money he had in his pocket on the table, and left the restaurant before another episode could strike.

The remainder of the day was spent retracing the places where he'd seen Izaiah in the weeks leading up to the night he was shot. But the old man wasn't at the market, the turn signal median, or the soda shop alley. As another day came to a close, Alex decided to find a spot to watch the sunset. He made his way to the western outskirts of town and found a boulder that was perfect for perching. There, he sat thinking of Melissa and his daughter, whose name he still didn't know. Soon, the sun dipped below the horizon, taking the last bits of orange light with it, and the sky was enveloped in darkness, twinkling with stars. Alex climbed down from the rock with renewed vigor. *I have to talk to her. I have to try.*

Walking through town, he pulled his hat low over his face whenever a car passed, headlights cutting through the darkness. *What are you doing? This can only lead to trouble. Come on, don't do this.* But

Alex ignored his own warnings, as well as the depraved voices in the back of his mind, which grew louder as his anxiety mounted. He couldn't be deterred; he had to see her face-to-face.

When he reached his neighborhood, he walked along the edge of the street opposite his home near the end of the cul-de-sac. The lights were on inside, but there was no movement. His feet trudged sluggishly as a wave of heat washed over him. He couldn't tell if it was a blistering wind from the valley or something brewing within him. Beads of sweat dripped down his face as he took his first step onto the driveway feeling only fear.

You still have no idea what to say.

The thought of scaring Melissa half to death proved too painful. Like a cold punch in the face, he suddenly realized his own selfishness. Alex stopped and took a step back as his heart began to slow. *Good boy. Think of her and the baby.* He backed away from the house with a new plan: hightail it out of the neighborhood and find a nice spot to cool down. But as Alex crossed the street, he heard the front door open.

"Who is that? I know I saw someone," a rough male voice called.

Alex turned. It was the blond, bearded man in a sport coat. He marched faster. "Sorry. Wrong house," Alex said.

"What are you doing? Huh?" the man shouted.

Alex couldn't blame him for the questions, but it was hard to hold back the fit of anger rising within him. "Just passing by," he said.

"We're on a closed-off block. That dog don't hunt."

"I got lost. Don't worry about it," Alex said, trying to mask his voice.

"Turn around," the man demanded.

"What for?"

"So I can see your hands ain't full of mine or anybody else's shit." The bearded blond stomped closer, pumping up his energy.

Alex spun, shielding his face with his hat and holding out empty hands. "Satisfied?"

"Didn't I see you here before?"

"Nah. Must have been someone else," Alex said. *Leave me alone!*

"Look, folks in this part of town don't have much. They're good people. Move along."

"You don't understand. I'm not here to steal."

"Yeah? You got a job?"

"None of your business. Do *you* even live here?" Alex asked.

"Do I—what kind of question is that?" The bearded man stared with a new kind of suspicion.

"The one I'm asking." Alex felt a store of heat rising, creeping up his torso and originating from the scar on his hip.

"Ah, smart guy." The man studied him. "Yeah, I'm sure I know you from somewhere."

Alex clenched his side, feeling his muscles tighten all over. The voices suddenly screamed in unison: "*The baby!*" they cried. "*The baby!*"

"What about the baby?" Alex blurted out, unable to control himself.

"The baby? Why the Hell do you . . ." The man stopped as he neared Alex.

The teacher couldn't fight the pain any longer, moaning as the searing fire moved up his neck, through his veins. His knees nearly buckled as he cried out in desperate distress.

"I'm calling the cops!" the man shouted, reaching into his pocket. "Ya hear me? Fucking addicts. Get out of here!"

Alex fought through the voices. He held his hand out. "For Melissa's sake, don't."

"What? How do you—I knew it. You're Alex, aren't you?"

Alex turned and darted away, but the man kept pace, the phone lingering in his hand. "You're alive? Fuck, man."

Alex waved him off and hobbled faster. The voices aligned once more. *"Kill the man! Kill the man!"*

No!

"Stop! Where are you going?" the man pleaded. "Hey, don't you recognize me? It's Daniel. Cuthmoore. I used to work with—hey!" Daniel persisted. "You can't walk away. Hold on! You can't do this. She almost died, why did you never—it's drugs, isn't it? Or what? You know, the insurance companies came after her. I had to help her save the house. You left your family with nothing. Feel free to say thank you at any time. Hey, asshole, I'm talking to you—"

"Let it go, Daniel. Now," Alex muttered. The low, primal voice coming out of him sent a shudder down his own back. A flood of heat under his left ribs spread to his limbs, left arm first. An immense pressure was building, like a pot about to boil over.

"I have to tell her you're alive! Jesus Christ, man. Where have you been?" Daniel exclaimed as a lightning cloud pulsed in the distance. Thunder rolled over the neighborhood as nearby trees began to sway.

"You want to know where I've been!?" Alex shouted, suddenly upon Daniel, seizing him.

"What are you doing?" he asked with panicked eyes. "Hey, Melis—"

"You want to know where I've been? Do you?" Alex wailed at the top of his lungs.

"Kill him! Kill him!" The voices were a unified maelstrom. *Shut up—shut up!* The skin on Alex's hands started to burn, just as it had when he'd broken his bonds the day Yuri died. The next moment was a fog as he felt something snap, other than Dan's arm in his hand. Then his knee. Something deep, deep inside him, like a hall of mirrors shattering, unleashed a power and presence from within Alex that he couldn't control.

The first drops of rain began to fall as Daniel turned toward the house, cupping his hands to his mouth. "Help—"

Alex's fist shot like a bullet, leaving a sizzling mark, and he was suddenly upon Daniel, pummeling his face and body, moving so fast the man could not mount a defense of any kind, other than to call out, "Please!" before his jaw cracked in half.

The teacher's muscles pulsed and flexed and grew before his eyes, releasing more strength than he had ever known, as red and blue veins rose like ships from the depths over his skin. Continuing the barrage, the teacher's fists, glowing red hot, released wisps of steam, and Daniel's body began to feel like pulp under his knuckles. Alex gritted his teeth and looked upon him with utter rage and malice, continuing with no sense of honor, or remorse, or judgment, roaring until Daniel collapsed, now a steaming mess. Alex grabbed the beaten man by the head, ready to thrash his neck until it snapped, when his eyes caught a shadow in the window. *It's her.* His senses came rushing back.

Even silhouetted in the darkness, her eyes were as clear as the moon above. She had seen everything, with a phone to her ear, the other hand touching the glass, reaching for Daniel—not himself—cursing at him, screeching. Alex looked down at the man he'd beaten. Bubbles from his weak breath were popping in the blood pooling on his face.

Releasing his grip, Alex stumbled backward. "No, I didn't . . . I'm sorry, I—" He was dumbfounded, with no idea how to proceed. Melissa's curses continued, jarring his mind and instincts. *She can't know it was me.* The voices called for Alex to finish Daniel, claiming it was the most humane option. "*Finish it! Kill him!*"

I won't! He winced, holding his side as a heavy rain began to fall, and bolted into the dark wilderness behind his house, his thoughts swimming. His leg and arm muscles felt seared. He grew desperate for relief, as he raced down the hill into darkness. A bolt of lightning staggered across the sky as he roared, grabbing his aching head, casting his blue cap aside. *She can't know. She can never know.*

Pitching down the hill into the underbrush, he fought through a patch of trees into a clearing, where he fell to his knees and thrashed about on the wet ground. A searing pain, like a tattoo artist with a rusty needle and a grudge, crawled across his chest. "What is happening to me? Izaiah! Mara! Please!" Another bolt of lightning swept by, releasing a deafening, blinding streak.

The fabric of his shirt began to smoke and burn away like a newspaper over a flame. Alex gripped the loose material and ripped it off to find his chest beet red, smoking, and pulsing. Then the mark began to appear. Thin red etchings burned their way into him, starting at his shoulders, sizzling down like an invisible brand creeping along his skin, wrapping scars around one another, lifting and bonding newly wrecked flesh. The lines flowed across his chest and out to his body, popping vessels filled with boiling blood, leading to his hands, glowing with a tremendous heat as sparks of flame caught in bursts around his fingertips. He shoved his hands forward, keeping them as far away as possible. The agony seemed to last a lifetime, but eventually the pain slowed, and the scarring subsided.

Shuddering, he felt the skin on his chest, now like tanned leather, and tilted his head to view the insignia burned into it. From shoulder to shoulder, down to his sternum, the lines formed something resembling a twisted, horned bull's head, releasing streams of smoke as rain poured on it from above. His fingers were like red-hot embers of coal, as the bones in his hands cracked, rattled, and hissed, but no longer searing with pain. Laying his knuckles on the ground, Alex let his chin sink into his chest, listening to bits of leaf, twig, and wood burn, and silently wept.

"Then there are the higher shades of Eve. According to my source, the smallest of these is Lanwyn, the world of green, made from Jubilee, the energies of life's joys in Universe Alpha. Above that was Nashwyn, the world of water, created from Fervor, literally concentrated passion. Highest above all is Hywyn, what sounds like a land of diamond, made of Rapture, the very essence of creation. This is from where my source hails."

- Excerpt from the journal of
Dr. Francisco Emul. Murcia
December 1896

THE RAPTURE

I saw it. I know I did.

Bennett kept keen eyes on the sky, leaning against a thick oak tree next to him, feeling a sense of wonder he hadn't experienced since he was a boy. Vast hills of crystaline clouds rolled by, but he was focused solely on a single jet stream fading between them. *I didn't imagine it.* He fought to hold on to the image of the shape zooming across the horizon before it fell out of sight in the hills to the east of his father's gas station, lost in a stretch of forest. *Don't forget it. Remember it.* The thin line left in its wake was all the proof he needed.

It was real.

A coarse wind blew under the dusty jacket he'd thrown on before charging outside. Without a shirt on underneath, it was easy to get cold out here. When Bennett had heard it in the morning—whatever the thing in the sky was—he hadn't had time to get properly dressed. He ran as fast as he could with his newly restored legs and stamina, propelling himself after the mysterious object toward the forest.

Every moment today had been overrun by bombastic emotions

surging to the surface, dipping him into bouts of depression, only to have him laughing seconds later. *Al complained about similar things in the desert. Always talking about voices.* And though he always knew exactly what Alex was talking about, Bennett never reciprocated vocally. To him, they were less voices and more raw emotions and strange desires, pulling him in one direction or another; inaudible whispers, clear in their intent, like an audience at a television taping watching his every move, judging him with contempt.

When he and Alex arrived with the mystery woman, Mara, on a cool afternoon a couple of days ago, Bennett thought he'd confirmed a theory he'd been holding on to. The concept of the Medolian Shift was so obtuse—so ridiculous—that when he'd experienced it a second time, he concluded it could only have been a hallucination. There was no other way to explain how they could have traveled so far so fast. It must have been a dream. All of it: his suicide, the desert riders, Joseph, surviving Africa. Everything had been a grand adventure through his own mind, a "spiritual journey." *Is there some lesson I'm supposed to be learning?* He was more than ready to wake up in an alley, covered in his own vomit.

Try as he might, Bennett could not stop thinking about Izaiah, the mission, and Joseph. *What did he mean by being the third lord? Is that why Heaven and Hell would be so scared of this guy?* The man in the mask had killed Yuri and left Bennett and Alex with the Wraithian cult. For that alone, Bennett felt invested in whatever mission promised to take him down, even if it all was a dream. The prospect of hopping back into his old life as an unemployed drunk was tempting in many ways, but one thing Bennett had been struggling with lately was keeping his priorities straight.

Something about all of the craziness . . . guess it did seem pretty real.

The soldier's first action after being rescued by Mara and returning to Prescott was to find his truck. If it had all been a dream, that would mean his baby would still be in the garage where he'd hidden it the day the cops tried to chase him down. Bennett marched downtown, sticking to the service roads he knew, avoiding crowds, and eventually rounding the corner of the quadplex. The garage was open, but his truck was not in it. With that option closed, his apartment was next. As he trekked the other way across town, a newspaper in a trash can caught his eye. The header date read Saturday, OCT 21st, 2006. It had been thirty-one days since his suicide attempt. The dream theory was already showing seams.

Across town, his apartment complex was quiet, as always, but Bennett approached using stealth nonetheless. For all he knew, there might been cops posted nearby to watch for his return. He half wished he could find one just to ask some questions, wanting to know if the young woman, Autumn, had been permanently injured from his assault. That same part of him wanted to turn himself in no matter the answer.

First, he checked his numbered parking spot beneath a rusty overhang. No truck. After climbing the steps of the building, Bennett made his way to his door and took out his ring of keys, still in his pocket. Finding the right one, he fit it inside the deadbolt, but it wouldn't turn. Noticing a letter taped to the door, stamped with the Arizona state seal, he tore it open and read. In so many words, the letter stated that the apartment had been forcefully vacated and was ready to lease. His belongings had been put on the curb weeks ago.

Through the living room blinds the space looked practically empty, except for some buckets of paint, brushes, cleaning supplies, and plastic tarps in the corner, leaving no indication he'd ever lived there at all. Taking the door handle, ready to snap it off, he found it unlocked. With a deep breath, he stepped inside and shut the door. There was no point in turning on the lights; he could see fine. The entire apartment had been redone, top to bottom. No more holes

in the drywall or cigarette burns in the carpet. They'd even fixed
the small bathroom window he'd thrown a miniature tequila bottle
through one particularly shit-faced Ash Wednesday.

Passing the kitchen threshold, he paused, looked at the ground,
and saw her fall again in his mind. *Autumn, I'm sorry.* The frigid
cold in his gut returned in force as the voices of judgment swelled,
reminding him how weak he'd been that day—how he'd taken it out
on her to feel strong. *Coward.* Bennett knelt and grazed his fingers
along the cabinet door where her head had broken through, once
jagged and sharp as knives, now repaired. Whoever might move in
would have no idea what evils had transpired here.

A flash ran up his spine. Bennett's chest tightened. *You are responsible for not only that young person's pain, but a lot of other people's too.
You know that, right?* This time, Bennett didn't fight the weight on
his mind as he made his way to the bedroom. It was empty, same as
the others. *Just hope they missed one thing.* Opening the closet, he felt
behind the radiator box taking up its lower left half. *Thank God.* His
hand came back holding an envelope, its paper feeling dry and rough
in his fingers, fragile in its age. At first, Bennett could only stare, still
more afraid of what was inside the envelope than any enemy he'd ever
faced on the battlefield. A distant police siren broke his daze. Pocketing the envelope, he hurried out of the apartment and snuck away
before anyone got wise to him. Out of options, he began a trek to the
only location left on his list where he might discover the truth.

Two hours later on foot, he reached his father's station, where a
huge shadow came into view, lingering out front: his truck, right
where he'd left it, lights off and the driver's side door shut. *Damn.
Score one for Izaiah.* Bennett stretched up on his toes to peer into
the cab, seeing the bottle of whiskey on the floor in the back. He
expected himself to crawl in to retrieve it for a drink and was pleasantly surprised when he felt no desire to.

Huh. Just not feeling it.

Marching up the cracked concrete outside his dad's shop, he found himself nervous. Each step felt akin to giving up somehow, a release of his fears and himself, both liberating and terrifying all at once. Bennett entered the station and found the door to his father's office open. Stepping inside, he saw the picture frames smashed and bullet holes that had ripped through the walls. At his feet were remnants of the photo of his family. Jerry's face was gone, ripped asunder. *Of course it is.* An intense stream of memories—all of Bennett's wrong-doings—came rushing back, completely out of his control, like he'd been plugged into a computer and was receiving data. Feeling all of it at once made part of Bennett want to curl up and find death again. He fought the information, as he always did with his memories and guilt, and kicked the photo away. *The fuck is going on with me?*

Rounding the desk, Bennett found the one thing he was hoping, praying, not to see—the one thing he could have used as leverage to prove to himself he hadn't tried to blow his brains out. But there it sat. The revolver shimmered in the pale light, a toy left out on a rug by a child. *You stupid little . . .* Kneeling, he picked it up and released the cylinder with his thumb. The empty casings clattered to the floor, where streaks of dried blood led to the chair, illuminated by a beam of moonlight pouring through a hole punctured in the glass.

Leaning against the desk, Bennett set the gun in his lap and reached for the letter stuffed into his back pocket. As he opened it his hand began to shake.

Hey little brother,

Thank you for your last letter and the peanut butter cookies from Grandma Waters. Half the squad's allergic, so more for me! Not gonna lie, things are bleak—which I get is weird to say considering what I do, but still, things seem to be changing. Feels like something big is going down.

They assigned us some new guys, and I'm not so sure about them. Don't get me wrong—badasses all around who signed up like me and want to help, but these guys seem to be fighting for a different America from the one I thought we lived in. Plus, they remind me of Dad, which is never good, so . . . Commanders say we're liberating people. The looks on the faces I see say otherwise. Sorry, still can't say what or where the op is. Tell Mom I wish I could.

The guys still don't know about me. I know you said I should tell them, but I'm just not sure how they would react after all these years. It's okay, I can bear it. I did for the first eighteen years of my life.

But enough about me. How are you and that new girl? Was it Laura? Sorry. If so, I hope it's going well. You deserve an outlet, someone to talk to other than me. If you're still struggling with your anger, stop and think about what's truly important to you, and focus on how you can help that instead. Channel all that fury—your heart will lead you straight, you'll see. Just do what you can, little brother. Just like King Arthur, right? And never underestimate the healing power of helping others.

Give Cody a hug and kiss for me. Tell him his dad is coming home soon. Love, Jerry

There were no more letters. Six months later, Jerry was dead.

A month after that, Bennett was in a recruitment office.

Running. That's all I was doing. His eyes fixed on his nephew's name—the one he'd promised his older brother he would take care of, should the worst happen. When it did, and Jerry was killed, Bennett's father stepped in and took the child from his boyfriend, who had no legal recourse.

Cody, I abandoned you. Left you with . . . how could I—

A swell of voices grew in Bennett's mind, like the whispers, multiplied by a thousand. Covering his ears did nothing to soften the clamor. Sweat dripped from his brow and froze on his cheek as the stream of his past injustices poured through his mind. *Why? Why did I choose to be this? What have I ever done for anyone else? All I do is hurt people.* Clutching the letter and gun with both hands, sobbing, Bennett wanted to scream—to lash out and break the world. He craved more bullets to play roulette with all over again. *Always running. Always hurting.*

He wanted to feel the pain he'd caused and finally take the blame he secretly knew deep down he'd always wanted. Yet he could only sink lower, feeling pity for himself as he clutched the backrest of the desk chair, grasping for equilibrium. *I've been fucking weak because I allowed myself to be. The worst shit I've ever done was the shit I got roped into. Like a drone, unable to think for itself. Not like Jerry. He never took the easy way out. He didn't play everyone else's game. He didn't blame other people for his own shit. He was everything I'm not.*

Broken glass and debris on the ground rattled like a dozen tambourines, met by the cracking and splintering of the backrest in his grasp. Beneath him, the wooden floor moaned under his weight as a deep rumble grew from the cold center of Bennett's gut, and a new voice emerged in his mind, clear as day. *There—I finally remember.* The voice was that of his brother, Gerald.

"Do what good you can."

An explosive pop shook the walls as cobalt-blue, white, and violet light sprang from him, illuminating the station. The aura was everywhere, most concentrated at his spine. Bennett's clothes dissolved as he clenched his knees to his chest, feeling the streams of light tear through his shirt, striking the ceiling and forcing him down into the floor. A frigid cold swept across his skin as a tremendous pressure was released from a well within him that he was experiencing but had no way of understanding.

Spherical waves extended from Bennett's left hand, coursing through the chair and all nearby matter, transforming it into a cold, raw umber mass that retained the shape of the objects. The bulk of the chair, the corner of the desk, a circle around Bennett on the ground—all were changed. Vines and colorful flowers seeped through cracks opening in the dense material as it settled, slithering outward in a furious, brief burst of life.

With a final grand flash, the light faded, leaving Bennett in the dark station once more, kneeling at the center of a strange, beautiful mass. He rose, finding himself in the mirror, naked, his skin steaming and covered in a paper-thin layer of ice, which broke away and fell as he moved, only to be replaced by more. Bennett's back and shoulders, once covered by tattoos, were blotted by clean skin traced with a twisting line of cobalt-blue scarring in the shape of wings, as if they had landed and cleansed everything beneath them. Even his birthmarks and freckles were gone. The old tattoos around the wings remained but now looked like a cookie cutter had been taken to them. *Damn. Paid good money for that ink.*

The night droned on as Bennett sat silently, hardly breathing, contemplating what had just happened. After losing track of time and his thoughts, he was suddenly stirring the next morning, jolted awake by a distant boom that rattled the bits of glass on the floor. That was when he sensed the object in the sky. Springing out of his father's chair, he looked out the window to see a small shape that definitely had wings but was difficult to discern otherwise.

Grabbing some shop pants, boots, a jacket, and his keys, he was soon in his truck, careening over rough desert hills, trying to keep pace with the UFO.

This is so stupid. So stupid. What am I doing? Splitting his time between watching the road and gawking at the shape, Bennett swore he saw a person between the wings for a split second. He soon found himself slamming on the brakes at the forest line, narrowly missing a massive acacia tree. His Ford stumbled up an embankment filled with vines and halted, coughing out smoke. Without pausing, Bennett dove out and took off on foot through the trees, leaping over rocks and fallen trunks, keeping his eyes upward as best he could without tripping.

Finally, a clearing opened into an open valley just in time for him to see the figure rocketing through the atmosphere with one final colossal push of its wings. A high-pitched whoosh flooded over the forest as a blinding ring of crystalline light exploded in the sky, followed by the same boom he'd heard earlier. The sound wave struck his chest like a fist, shoving him back. When he looked again, the winged shape was gone, as if it had vanished into thin air. Marching to the edge of the clearing, Bennett leaned against the oak tree and gazed over the green and brown landscape. *It couldn't have been a . . . could it?*

At present, leaning against the same tree, Bennett waited for another boom to roll over the desert, or for another winged shape to dance through the sky, but the afternoon remained stubbornly peaceful. Birds sang overhead, and the forest was alive with the sounds of life, reminding him of when he would play inside it as a boy, back when his father didn't have any chores for him at the station. Walking past a thick tree in the center of a clearing—where he'd built his first tree house—he rounded the far side and found three overgrown planks hanging by a few rusty nails in the old bark: the only bits left. *It used to be bigger.*

A voice seemed to whisper from the brush behind him, a presence. He turned, but nothing was there. Bennett stuck out his hand and moved forward, waving it, aware of how foolish he looked, yet half-expecting to touch something—perhaps someone invisible.

At this point, who fucking knows? But his hand passed harmlessly through the air.

Sunlight streamed through the gaps in the trees, casting beams across the dense forest. Passing a small bubbling stream, he knelt and splashed a few handfuls of water on his face, feeling a thin layer freeze over his skin. Clenching his fist, he watched the ice flake off into the water and float downstream, only to be replaced by more.

Huh, stopped drinking right when I could've iced my own drinks.

Bennett's gaze remained on the water's surface when he sensed another set of eyes on him. Across the stream, a buck had stopped for a drink. A doe soon joined it, kneeling at the water's edge, followed by a small herd stepping out from the tree line. Bennett stood, having gotten his fill, and to his amazement the deer did not scatter.

Maybe they're all blind?

"Get out of here." He waved his hand, but the herd just stared curiously for a moment before returning to the water. "Go on!"

The first buck moved to the rear of the group and lay in the shade of a tall tree. A few of the others joined him, while the youngest deer, a doe with white spots and shaky legs, lingered before Bennett, her deep black eyes fixated on him.

"What do you want?" he asked, annoyed, shaking his head and thrashing his hair with his hands to dry off, hoping the swift movement would startle her. When he looked back, she hadn't budged. "Your friends are over there," he said, leaning down to splash her. The doe flinched, took one last look at him, and scurried off.

Finally. Bennett marched away before any of them could start following him, losing all sense of where he was in relation to the station and his truck. Annoyingly, he found himself scratching his shoulders a lot; the insignia that had erased his tattoos itched worse than any of them ever had.

Guess there's no point pretending none of it happened when I got the proof on my back.

Bennett then began to sense another presence. This was different from the judgmental assholes in his head he'd come to refer to as the Jury. No, this voice was outside of himself, and felt human. Like the others, it was more a heap of suggestions than actual words, familiar yet unclear. Whatever was sending the signal was clearly in pain, and there was sadness as well, strong enough to be palpable.

As he closed his eyes, Bennett found it easier to navigate this newfound perception. Like the glow of a city on the horizon at night, he could sense where this soul was, leading him from dirt and trees to concrete and urban settings. He passed under tall streetlamps casting orange light onto the highway, navigating broken medians and abandoned farmhouses. Soon, he was on cracked, debris-covered roads, treading through neighborhoods and eventually reaching the southern business district of Prescott.

Keeping his head low, he listened and felt. The townsfolk passed by, exuding faint smells that didn't evoke memories but rather raw emotions. Their feelings were as plain as a rotten egg, exposing their true thoughts and desires. There was far less anger than he'd expected and much more sadness. Humanity, at least among these few dozen people, was not as he had imagined. They felt weary, and the weight of the sensations forced him to halt several times and take a break before getting overwhelmed.

The fuck's wrong with you people?

Throughout the march, the first burst he'd sensed remained the loudest, and Bennett could feel he was getting closer. He wondered if the angry sad soul knew he was coming. *Could be a trap.* An ominous feeling came over him as a heavy rain began to fall, amplifying the painful energy into a chaotic bubble of rage and hatred that turned his stomach. Then, as the storm peaked over the valley, the signal in the distance began to subside. By the time he reached a public stretch of land on the southwest edge of Prescott, the energy had faded, just as the rain reduced to a sprinkle.

Surrounded by a bush-filled desert, the earthy scents stirred by the rain filled the air. Bennett followed the muddy path until he spotted a looming mushroom-shaped tree in the middle of a field, beneath which lay a dark shape. His heart raced as he recognized the familiar face of a frightened teacher without his blue baseball cap.

"Barker?" Bernnett hurried over to Alex, who looked half-awake, wrapped in a wet, dirty blanket he must have found on the street or in a bush somewhere. "Al? What happened?"

Alex said nothing.

"Christ, you're burning up, man. Talk to me. Where were you these past couple of days?"

Alex stirred but still remained quiet.

"Look. I've been thinking. I—know what happened to you. I'm not stupid, and just as in the dark as you are about why we didn't go to different places when we died. Feels like a fucked-up joke, if you ask me. You're a good man. I should have gone through the— anyway, I'm not great at this talking stuff, especially about shit like this, so . . ."

Bennett sat on the ground next to Alex, lingering in silence for a moment before feeling compelled to try again. "Sometimes people need to talk, you know?"

Alex laughed, his voice rough like he'd smoked a thousand packs of cigarettes in the last two days—a bitter sound, heavy with ill will. "So, that's a Sergeant Hunter apology?"

Please, I'm trying to be real with you, Al. "I know it doesn't mean much. But—"

Alex interrupted with another harsh laugh. "It means less than nothing. You don't know what I've done. And I don't know what you've done. No one knows anything—not even God, who, by the way, doesn't seem to exist. At least not from where I'm sitting." He turned to Bennett with wide, excited eyes, like an addict who just remembered they were holding. "Hey, we should find a way to kill ourselves."

Bennett chuckled, but out of worry. "Couple days ago, I would've been right there with you."

"And now?" Alex asked with an air of excitement.

Bennett shook his head. "That's not how you do things, Al."

"There's nowhere for us now. If we do it together, to each other, we might not go to the fire. I need this, Bennett."

"You need to chill. We'll figure this out. Just like we figured everything out so far."

"How can you say that? Like we're partners. Like we succeeded. I'd call what we went through anything but success." Steam was rising from the blanket wrapped around Alex. "Do you know what was taken from me? I was about to have a family, and it was taken, and yet . . . there was nothing I could do about it. Izaiah, Joseph, the kid at the restaurant, you, all making moves against me, and I don't know why. My life is gone, and I can't defend myself. She's gone . . . If she saw me. Oh God, if she saw me . . ."

"Saw you?" Bennett asked. "Who?"

Alex was staring at his steaming hands like they'd strangled his mother. "I wanted to kill him! So badly. I wanted to kill everyone. I wanted to find blood. See it. I wanted to punish the ones who did this to me! I wanted . . . I just want this to end."

"You're not the only person yanked from their life," Bennett said.

"What life did you ever have?" Alex asked bitterly.

"A bit of one."

The teacher was shouting now. "I don't care about you! I never have. You're like a freaking ghost to me!"

"We're both ghosts, Al."

"Stop speaking in facts! You sound like a robot. Speak from your hollow chest for once. Go on, tell me, how is it on your end of the Eve? I want to know. Is it clouds and sunshine? You want to try mine? And my name is Alex, by the way. Alexander James Barker."

"I know that you're hurting—" Bennett started.

"You don't know anything. You don't know where I went . . . And I don't know where you went when you died or how it happened. We're not in this together. We never were. You always say you think I'm a figment of your imagination—well, I think you're a pretty thinly crafted fucking figment of mine!" Alex wrapped himself tighter in his blanket, trying to contain the smoke.

So, this is Wrath. Bennett would never be able to forget it now, what he'd first felt when Yuri was about to be killed. The energy was volatile, leaving a horrible feeling in his gut. He wondered if Alex truly knew what was lurking within him. They sat in silence for a few minutes, letting tempers cool.

"Since I've been back, it's been a nightmare," Bennett began. "I know the truth now. We might not be dead, but our lives are. I'm not going to fight it anymore. I've seen things, too. Heard them. I didn't want to admit it. It's crazy, right? Then, last night . . ."

Alex looked up. "What?"

"I felt, well . . ." Bennett stood and unzipped his jacket, releasing a plume of steam and revealing the wings outlined with dead scar tissue of his own. Patches of his chest were veiled with thin layers of ice. "I don't hear the voices anymore, at least not the same way. I can feel it—the Rapture. It's there, but I'm not scared of it."

Alex looked away, uninterested. "Makes perfect sense. Why would yours be scary?"

"I think I can control it. I think we can use it."

"To do what?"

"What we were made to. What we died for," Bennett said.

Alex stood and removed the blanket covering him, revealing the bull-headed scar across his chest. "This is not control. This is being railroaded, and it's already taking over. I did something horrible, and it's because of this shit they . . . I can't be good, right? How could I? I have evil inside me."

"You're not evil. You're Alex Barker, a grown man who chooses to spend his time teaching little dumb asses their letters and numbers so they can go on to be customer service representatives. With any luck, some of your good nature rubs off on them so they can at least be non-shitty people while they do it. People who make the world less shitty are the opposite of evil. And I don't know how the Hell someone like me got saddled wielding divinity, but I'm going to give it a shot because it's our *only* shot. It's our one option, Al. Tell me you don't see him when you close your eyes."

"Who?" Alex asked.

"You know who."

"Joseph," Alex said under his breath.

A bitter wind swept by, scattering sand across the valley and through the tree above them. Once it faded, a familiar scratchy voice replaced it. "You should listen to him." The men spun around to see a dirty coat and a wrinkled face come into the light. Izaiah leaned on his cane. "I know this isn't the best time, but I need you both to come with me. Now."

THE GATHERING

What was that? There was another flash of Wrath. Izaiah turned and focused. *Within a mile or so—barrels of it, but . . . blurry. Hard to place. It's . . . it's him. It's Alex!*

"I found 'em! The fellas are here!" the old Medolian with near-elephant ears shouted in a crowded business park, though no one seemed to notice. The people of Prescott were still distracted by the heavy thunderstorm that had passed just moments before—a behemoth that came and went so fast it seemed like a hiccup from nature.

Izaiah hurried in the direction of the power burst, by far the strongest Eve signature he'd ever felt from a human. Meanwhile, unease crept into his gut regarding every decision he'd made so far in the mess known as the Joseph debacle.

If I was wrong, so help us all.

He'd arrived in Prescott the previous night, following a stint in the African wilderness searching for Joseph. *But didn't find him, sad to say.* When he sensed the awakening of Bennett's Rapture, and the force of creation cementing itself into the soldier, the Medolian knew his plan had gone off the rails sooner than usual and had to abandon his search.

I thought it would take those boys a lot longer to figure out their Eve. At least, I hoped so. I've been trying to keep them away from all this— the Josephs and the cults and what have you—but it seems we might actually need the fellas, after all. We might need everyone, in fact. Those boys aren't the only mysterious power to show itself recently in the Eve, and frankly, the other one gives me goose pimples. The very bad kind.

Izaiah hightailed it back to the Sip and Drip, fighting his panic. He found the gas station empty, and with Bennett's signal faded, there was no way to locate him, forcing Izaiah to wait for another signal to show itself, which took less than a day. Alex's transformation was much more dramatic than his counterpart's, providing a perfect signal flare. *There you are! Alex, I hope you're okay.* Shifting as close to the source as possible—unaware that he was in Arizona until a road sign told him so—Izaiah began his search.

Presently, finding the edge of town, he kept going. The boots on his feet, barely holding together, crunched on the wet desert sand as he marched on, being sidetracked only once by a faint signal nearby. Searching a patch of smoldering bushes, he came upon Alex's blue baseball cap, which must have soaked up some Wrath before being discarded. The cap was blazing hot. Izaiah dusted it off and tucked it safely into his coat.

When the Medolian found a large mushroom-shaped tree in the center of a field, and the human delegates seated at its trunk, his UnEarth senses viewed two flames: one cobalt-blue and violet, the other crimson and copper.

They were talking as Izaiah approached, and he heard Bennett warn Alex about Joseph. "You should listen to him," Izaiah said.

"I know this isn't the best time, but I need you both to come with me. Now."

Neither human said anything at first, making Izaiah kind of nervous. "I've been searching everywhere for you. You boys have, uh . . . really changed since I last saw you."

Alex rose and sprang forward. "Not another word! No more lies!" Stopping a few feet from Izaiah, he clenched his fists, a thin layer of orange flame surrounding them and coursing up his arms, following veins to his elbows.

"Your Wrath's growing," Izaiah said with a proud smirk.

"Get this shit out of me," Alex grumbled.

"We should get you a shirt. Are you cold?"

"I want it out! I'm not asking!" Alex cried.

Izaiah wanted to calm him down before igniting his signal further. "I know what I did seems horrible, and in a certain light, sure, I can see it too, but—"

"You left us!" Alex roared, the flames searing.

Don't try it, Mr. Barker. But he did. The teacher leaped, hurling an uncoordinated attack at Izaiah, who nimbly dodged the blows and thrust out his cane, producing another near-translucent emerald sphere that released a chaotic blaring noise like radio static. Alex was thrown away, landing on his back in the mud, coughing up gray smoke.

Slouching over his cane, Izaiah brushed himself off. "Control those emotions, Mr. Barker."

"What was that? I felt shut down," Alex moaned, picking himself up.

"Mallos. Neutral Eve. What *made* me," Izaiah explained. "I know this is all very confusing, and I wish we had more time to explain, but we don't—"

"I don't care, old man. Please, just leave us alone again. It's all because of you. *You're* the reason there's nothing left of my life. Do you have any idea what that's like? Could you? I mean, what the h— what are you?" Alex rolled himself onto his knees, hyperventilating, pounding scorched fists into the mud. "Why can't I go home?"

"Because life is unfair, and so is death. If you need someone to blame, I'm your guy," Izaiah said. "I accept it, but that won't change your situation. Alex Barker's human life ended the night he was shot. I'm sorry. All you have now is the choice of what to do with this new life. Will you help us? I'm really hoping you fellas say yes."

"New life?" Bennett coughed out. "So, this all was, what, a gift? To who . . . us?"

"Certainly not to me," Izaiah replied, a little confused.

"I don't remember asking you for anything," Bennett shot back.

Hrm. This one is turning out to be quite the smart aleck.

"I saw her," Alex said. "My baby. My little girl. Then, I . . . there was a man. His questions. He wouldn't let me leave. Then—" A look of untethered sorrow filled his face, almost childlike. "You put Hell in me."

Izaiah knelt next to him, looked Alex square in the eye, and told the truth, feeling utterly horrible he had to. "Yes, we did."

"Take it out."

"I can't." *Please, stop.*

"I'm not asking."

"Alex, I told you before, it will remain in you until you finish this—until the demon within Joseph is back where he belongs, and we can put this particular crisis behind us." Izaiah looked at Alex with a heavy heart, trying again for a comforting smile. "I'm sorry. I really am." Reaching into his coat, he handed over the blue baseball cap. "Here. You dropped this."

The teacher clutched the cap in both hands. "You say it's called the Wrath? Yeah?" His lips quivered. "If I . . . what will it do to me?"

"Wish I knew." Izaiah placed his hand on his shoulder. "But I will tell you this, young man . . . I saw you. I know who you are. You're a fine person, Mr. Barker. Nobody has a better chance of wrangling this beast than you. Use it . . . Help us."

Alex hung his head. "I've never handled anything without her. This will only take me further away from my family. I can't do it."

"'Can't' doesn't apply here. If I didn't think you boys could do this, I wouldn't have asked you to. Now, I'm sorry, but we're very low on time."

Izaiah couldn't delay any longer. Lifting his cane, he thrust it down, performing a Shift before either human could argue, having to give it some extra juice, finding the two humans were a much heavier load than the last time he'd transported them through an Eve gate. Soon they were enveloped in salty sea air, and Izaiah's boots dug into cool sand under a dim gray mass of storm clouds assailing the beach where they now stood. Strident winds swayed groves of fat, colorless palm trees perched on a hillside running the length of the shore, their weakest branches breaking free and soaring to the ground, where they crawled along the sand before being snatched away by violent, foam-topped waves.

To Izaiah—who was not so sure about his aim or memory—the island smelled familiar enough, which was promising. It had been many years since he and his brethren had used this particular outpost for a meeting, but now was the time for utmost secrecy. Something irritatingly foul was afoot. *Hope they all got the message.* No Gathering had ever been called on such short notice before. *Seeing how long we live compared to humans, UnEarth folks tend to operate at a much slower pace. Gatherings are usually called a year or more in advance. Hopefully, the five days I gave proved how urgent this all is.*

Glancing around, Bennett shrugged, looking happy enough. "At least it's not a desert this time."

"We're in the South Pacific!" Izaiah shouted over the noise. "Not sure where, so don't ask. Come on! This way, I think." Hurrying down the beach, sticking close to the inland, he looked back to find Alex had stopped a few yards back to take his hat off and bask in the drizzling rain, letting his scars sizzle in the early morning air. "We gotta keep moving, pal."

The teacher put his hat back on and hurried to catch up. "Why are we here, Izaiah? I was fine under my tree in the rain."

"Business to attend to, Mr. Barker. All will be explained soon!" Izaiah could barely sense his fellow Medolians. The new batch had gotten quite good at hiding their auras, while he'd begun to feel too old to keep up with them sometime around when humanity hit on the idea of piping water into their homes. *Shitting inside . . . Never saw it coming.*

"Business? Like Joseph business?" Bennett called over a series of waves crashing against the beach.

"Afraid so, slippery little snake. Among other things, which hopefully aren't related. Much to discuss since I last saw you!"

"You mean when you stranded us in the desert to die?" Bennett asked.

"Exactly!"

The trio soon came upon a series of dilapidated wooden shacks dotted throughout a long stretch of forest leading away from the shore. They seemed to be the work of a local, semi-modern tribe who'd abandoned it. Most of the structures had been reduced to rotting piles of wood, but a few remained standing on thin support legs, elevated many feet above the ground for high tide. Izaiah found a path leading through the shacks, some large enough to house entire families. They reached a knoll with a large, seemingly sturdy hut resting atop a bluff at the end of a trail.

"Ah, see. Told ya. They're here!" Izaiah exclaimed.

Alex paused midstep. "It's a cube of rotten wood on toothpicks."

"Ease your mind, Mr. Barker. This structure has withstood the test of time. I'm sure it's most cozy once you're inside!" Izaiah hobbled forward on his cane, and the humans followed. Moving through the last steps of an overgrown path, he made his way up aged wooden stairs, passing through a sheet of rainwater draining off the roof made of leaves and grass. Shaking his head to dry off his cap, he stomped the mud off his boots. "You boys are going to hear a lot in there. Most of it won't make sense, but try to keep up. It may prove useful later. And, for your own sake, I suggest listening mostly."

"Whatever you say," Alex mumbled.

Izaiah opened the door to the one-room shack, revealing a twenty-foot square space, both dreary and cold. The walls, merely twisted beams meshed together, let in gusts of frigid sea air, singing with a shrill cry as the shack creaked and swayed under the weight of the storm. Two of his partners were already sitting in the far corner next to a wobbly table and the only window. Like Izaiah, they wore coats and hoods to keep as low a profile as possible; but unlike him, they did not appear to be transient. Galinthia's and Fabian's garb honored the final souls that had created them, as did many Medolians.

Our kind can't remember the previous lives of those who made us, but we are born on Earth and usually claim heritage of the land of our birth. All except Izaiah, who had no recollection of his origins, or true age. *You honestly just forget things after a while. Can't even remember when I forgot.*

Galinthia's heavy coat, pants, and many adornments were Greek, featuring a mix of old and new, with vivid browns accented by flashes of maroon. Leaning back in her chair against a support beam, she appeared to be a bodybuilder in her forties with dozens of ear and face piercings, asleep and snoring, a line of drool running down her cheek.

Wearing yellow and brown traditional Kurdish dress with white accents, Fabian's waistline—pointing straight at the ceiling—stretched his pants to their limit. Eating an orange with one hand and tapping away on an electronic gizmo of some sort with the other, he spoke through a mouth full of juice, never taking his eyes off the device's screen. "Izaiah showed. You owe me six rubes," he said dryly to Galinthia, who startled awake.

"*Huh,* what? Well, look at that." She rubbed her eyes. "Guess you *can* still be surprised after nineteen dimes." *She means centuries—UnEarth slang.* "Hello, Izaiah. Hope you've got a good reason to pull us away from the joys of our fruitless demon search. Not that I'm complaining," Galinthia said.

"I don't know if I'd call it a good reason, but it is awfully important. Where is everyone else? No Di-Xiao? No Ingrid?" Izaiah asked. "I was hoping to see Philomena and her group, at least."

"You expected a huge turnout with a cryptic message and a week's notice? Are you on the moss again?" Galinthia asked as though he were a senile invalid. *As she always has.*

"We're only here because we truly had nothing better going on," Fabian added.

"And twenty rubes says most of the Medolians don't even remember where this place is," Galinthia said.

"I had to make sure only those authorized knew of our location," Izaiah said before Fabian could take the bet. "You never know who might be eavesdropping on our memos."

"It was you who ordered us to focus all our energy on finding the rogue Archfiend," Fabian retorted. "Now you're telling everyone to drop what they're doing and meet you at a dreary, dead safe house? What if they're chasing a lead? And in case you forgot, we have perfectly good safe houses in Mumbai and Tokyo. Naples is beautiful this time of year. Or better yet, we could *finally* utilize human technology for these get-togethers."

"Here we go," Galinthia groaned.

"I'm serious!" Fabian exclaimed. "You have no idea the advances their electrical engineers have made the past few decades. I can send a message to anyone on the planet in an instant. It's almost as effective as Eve memos. And the shorthand they're developing is quite clever. Take a look—these are called 'emojis.'" Fabian held out his gadget, displaying what looked like cartoon drawings of children's stickers. "See? This human has indicated their excitement at an upcoming blind-dating television event. They're very social creatures!"

"Fascinating," Izaiah said dryly.

"Just trying to help you communicate with your team. Is that so wrong?" Fabian whined. "There's been nothing but rumors and hearsay flying around for almost a decade. Seems to be getting faster all the time. It's a lot to take, is all."

"Easy, big guy," Galinthia said, patting Fabian's hand and turning ireful eyes on Izaiah. "Though he's got a point. Until this week our Warden Sentry hadn't sent out a notice in six years. Makes it hard to keep everything straight. I assume you called this meeting to discuss the rumor of a measure in the Senate that would bring in humans to mitigate the Joseph job? Because that's what I want to address."

"Can you imagine?" Fabian sounded close to fainting.

"About that." Izaiah stepped aside for Bennett and Alex to join them.

Galinthia shared Fabian's jaw-agape stare.

"Don't tell me. These are . . . them?" Fabian said, his tone unusually timid.

"This is Alex and Bennett," Izaiah said. "They're going to be helping us out for the foreseeable future. Fellas, this is Galinthia and Fabian."

Alex and Bennett waved. "Hi," said the teacher.

Fabian and Galinthia were speechless as Izaiah shut the door and laid his cane against the wall. Blowing warm air into his hands, he noticed a faint crackling sound but could see no fire or smoke. Finding small plumes of steam sizzling and rising off Alex, who seemed blissfully unaware, Izaiah turned back to his cohorts.

"I thought you'd brought a Celestial and Archfiend along. They smell like it," Fabian remarked, taking a long sniff and making a *pee-yew* face.

"That was the idea," Izaiah replied. "Imbued with the Eve, they can act as representatives of Arros and Hywyn. No Archfiend or Celestial need be involved. Laffler's plan. A clever workaround if you ask me."

"Let me get this straight. You somehow got Speaker Binahq, Ariel Van Mortus, all of the other Senators, plus Gabriel, not to mention Lucifer-Aveyl, to agree to this course of action, and then you brought the humans *here* after?" Galinthia sounded as though she were teetering on laughter. "Mara's going to lose it. I can't wait to see what this looks like. She never misses a Gathering."

"Mara will understand once she hears what I have to say," Izaiah lied. "She can be quite reasonable sometimes."

Fabian held out his device, which projected a yellow light, like a fisherman's net. It seemed to scan Alex and Bennett. *Fabian and his gadgetries. Silly things to imbue with Mallos.* "Their Eves are strong, but their shades are unusual. Never seen anything like them," he noted.

"Excuse me, but we're standing right here," Alex said politely.

"Sorry, fellas, you might want to get used to this kind of reaction from UnEarth folks," Izaiah said. "Don't get me wrong—most of them are friendly and would welcome you with open arms. They'd love to hear about you and get to know you, maybe even show you around, but there will be some who will be uncomfortable around you. Maybe even a little offended."

"Offended?" Bennett snapped. "What the Hell? Why?"

"Nobody wants humans walking around with buckets of Eve in their veins," Galinthia explained. "You guys make the stuff. No accounting for what would happen if that engine inside you got supercharged and then broke. It's been making people twitchy and on edge ever since the rumors started flying, which apparently are true because nothing makes sense anymore."

"Yeah, well *we* didn't choose to be a part of this, lady," Bennett snarled. *Oh, Mr. Hunter. Why?*

"*And* they talk back? I'm having a hard time processing this, Izaiah." Fabian held his chest to control his unnerved breathing and retrieved his device from his pocket to calm down—the one he'd put away just seconds before. *Gonna have to take that thing away from him.*

Bennett seemed almost pleased by the news. "Hey, Al, sounds like we're famous."

"I can honestly say I've never wanted that." Alex's body was still sizzling like a plate of fajitas. "So, I take it you're also . . . Medo whats?"

"Medolian Sentries, kid." Galinthia laughed, pulling out one of several knives on her belt to twirl in her hand. "Glittering prizes, Izaiah. I can see why you picked them."

"I'd say we've done pretty damn well considering the circumstances, and we can stop with this kids' table bullshit," Bennett said, somehow even more bitterly.

Fabian moaned, rubbing his temples. "Make. Them. Stop!"

Galinthia growled and rose quickly from her chair to approach Bennett. *Play nice, Gale.*

"If I didn't know better, I'd say you were nothing but Wrath," Galinthia said. "But there it is—Rapture, asleep. Can you do anything? Come on, show me something. Even the little one can make sparklers. What about you?" She stared Bennett in the eye, but he remained silent.

"That's enough. We're all on the same team here," Izaiah said.

"Can't wait to see how this plays out." Galinthia sat, twirling a knife around the tip of her finger, continuing to scrutinize the humans with pitiless eyes.

"She's not nearly as threatening as she seems," Izaiah said. "In fact, she's one of the cheeriest nihilists you could meet. Just don't get your hands too close to her mouth." He retrieved a wool blanket from one of the chairs near the table and hobbled over to Alex, handing it to him. "Maybe best to cover up and chill out for now? Hmm?"

The teacher's eyes darted from person to person before he accepted the blanket and tossed it over his shoulders. He and Bennett entered the room fully and settled into an open corner as a quiet, somber mood settled over the shack. *Brr. Not liking how this is going so far.*

"If this is everyone, we should get started," Izaiah said. "Before I tell you why I called this Gathering, are there any updates? Have either of you heard anything regarding our guy?"

"If we'd found the demon, don't you think we would have told you?" Galinthia snapped.

"Gale, please," Izaiah begged.

She rolled her eyes, letting Fabian answer. "I did manage to speak to Yanush about a year ago, before the human delegate rumors started. His human company has seven more buildings. Seven! Did you know that? Anyway, he swore he spotted another squad of Celestial elites moving on Earth but couldn't get enough proof to present in the Senate. If Hywyn is still sending agents down, Arros is doing the same, I guarantee it."

"And if both majority party kingdoms continuing to break the Covenant wasn't enough fun, we've also gotten more reports of Wraithian wannabes in southern Europe. No idea where they're coming from or who's bringing up this new batch. Still no sign of a proper Moloch. As soon as one shows up, I'd be happy to put their head on a plate for ya," Galinthia said with a dashing smile.

"That would be lovely. Thank you," Izaiah said appreciatively.

She nodded. "You got it."

The front door opened. A familiar figure in a dark gray-and-cyan-striped cloak stood in the entryway, a long staff slung across her back. *How does she sneak up like that?*

"What are they doing here?" Mara said in the damp tone Izaiah expected.

Alex and Bennett looked at him for reassurance. "I know our rule on Gatherings, but this involves these fellas," Izaiah said. "I figure they got a right to be here."

"I insist they leave." Mara remained steadfast, her arms folded tightly.

"You don't seem too surprised to see them," Izaiah pointed out.

"Are you going to escort them out, or should I?" she pressed.

"How about putting it to a vote?" Izaiah suggested.

"Pointless! I see no reason the humans can't stay," Galinthia added with a snarl. "We have to use them, right? So, let's get on with it. Some of us have unmotivated lives to get back to."

Mara made no move, but the room was in silent agreement with the knife wielder. *Mara's more bark—Gale's way more bite.* After a tense pause, Mara huffed, stepped inside, slammed the door to the shack, and marched to the only empty corner. Drawing her staff, she jammed it into the support beam and leaned on it, tightening her cloak and pulling her hood down. Of all the Medolians, Mara looked the most like she'd stepped out of a history book circa fourteenth-century BC Israel. Appearing like a human and wearing contemporary Earth clothing had never been a priority for her.

"Excellent!" Izaiah clapped his hands and passed a smile to each corner of the room. "We can begin. As I'm sure you've all heard by now, the Joseph Mandate has changed—"

"Hang on," Mara said. "One more is joining us."

What? Who? I don't sense any—

Not a second later, another Eve gate opened outside. A blinding flash of light poured through the shack's gaps, faded, and the door creaked open. Chloe, the youngest Medolian at just under eleven hundred years old, entered. Born in the guise of a human woman in her twenties with short red hair, she still wore a soiled eighteenth-century English sea admiral's coat. Beneath that she wore a vest with orange highlights, a black shirt, pants, and heavy boots. As always, since the day she'd slain the captain and taken his sword, it swung by her side, her Eve-imbued tool of choice.

Stepping through the door as quietly as a mouse, she appeared more hunched and drawn in than usual. "What? Am I late? Did I miss something? I'm so sorry. I was searching Senegal, as ordered. I've been trying, but I still haven't found any sign of the Arch—" She spotted Alex and Bennett and recoiled, her hand on the hilt of her sword, ready to draw. "Why are a Celestial and Archfiend present?"

"They're not. These are Izaiah's humans," Galinthia said, her tone as dry as burnt toast.

"Humans?" Chloe asked with a panicked squeak. "From the mandate? I don't understand. What does this mean?"

Galinthia shrugged. "It means we're all going to die."

Chloe stepped away to join her and Fabian at the table, casting suspicious glances at the humans as if they might lunge and bite her. *Still so shy and wary of the world.* Although remarkably powerful for her age, Chloe had proven difficult to train, and Izaiah had been grateful when Mara took on the task. *She doesn't think I should be trusted to raise the new batch.* For reasons beyond anyone's control, Mara had been forced to abandon Chloe's training before it was finished, always intending to return to it in a later century. None of the new batch of Medolians had struggled with their Sentry role as much as the Dread-tinted prodigy. *Deep down, she's always wanted to be human. Part of her always will.*

"Pay young Chloe no mind, fellas—she's always a little skittish at first. She'll warm up to you, or not. Now, I want to thank those of you who made it. I know credible information has been scarce, and we've hardly been able to keep up with the mandates coming down from the Tribunal. You know, these meetings used to be almost festive—hundreds of us back then. 'Course that was before most of you were around. Those days seem like they could have been yesterday—"

"Izaiah!" Galinthia shouted.

"Right." He course corrected. "Just saying, we only get to see each other every few hundred years or so, and I wish it could be better. You know, tell some jokes maybe? I've heard some good ones recently—for instance, have you heard the one about the incontinent frog with a paintbrush?" He reached into his coat pocket and snatched out his green notebook, but to Izaiah's surprise, the Medolians groaned in unison.

"Trust us. We'll let you know when we want your jokes," Galinthia said, tapping the broad side of a knife against her brow as if considering jamming it into her skull.

"No, you're right. You're right," Izaiah agreed. "There isn't much to laugh at lately. I don't know about the rest of you, but I've noticed we aren't getting any stronger. No new Sentries have been born since Chloe, which means the supply of Mallos from Earth is dwindling. Heck of a time for it to happen, too, because I got a feeling we're about to need all the help we can get."

"What are you talking about?" Fabian asked. "You sound as frightened as Chloe when she hears a Barium Guard coming down the hall."

"Go dive into Mallum Bay!" the youngest shouted back.

"Stop this, now. We don't have the time," Izaiah boomed. "I called this Gathering because six days ago I sensed something unsettling and can't stop thinking about it."

"I haven't sensed anything out of place." Galinthia sounded skeptical.

"It's so subtle it might fly under your nose, but I know there's one here who felt it." Izaiah turned to Mara.

"I don't know what you're talking about." She refused to even look him in the eye.

"There were three of them. Distinct, dark presences, talking. Something like Wrath, but much worse," Izaiah said. "Only present for a moment before they disappeared, but long enough to fill me with Dread. You're more sensitive than I am. You felt it, I'm sure. Do you agree it was a warning?" He hoped his second-in-command would be on his side for once. *Help me out here.* But Mara remained stubbornly silent.

"Assuming this power source exists, what do you think it was?" Galinthia asked.

"I'm not sure, but the demon being sighted nearby suggests they might be related," Izaiah said. "We still don't know why the nameless Archfiend took the boy's body in the first place, though I suspect we may soon. My gut is telling me to expect the worst."

"What does this have to do with the humans? Aren't they our biggest problem right now?" Fabian asked, finishing off another orange. "Not only do we still need to find and capture Joseph, but now we have to bring them along with us? Does the Tribunal know what they're asking? We should march in there and demand to be heard."

"Don't think that'll work," Mara said. "Word is the Tribunal is going dark. Might even be already."

Fabian gawked, a hunk of orange peel dangling from his mouth. "A shutdown? You're sure? What about Trivium City?"

"Haven't been back in a while, but I trust my sources," Mara reaffirmed.

Fabian's face turned as pale as a Nashwyn banana. "But that could only mean—"

"Yes, Hywyn and Arros have severed communications. Thousands have already returned to their kingdoms," Izaiah said. "I fear what either of their rulers will do if Joseph succeeds with his plan, whatever that may be."

"Well, if the demon is trying to start a war, it seems like he's going about it in all the right ways," Galinthia said.

"Wait, go back. Tell me about this war," Bennett inquired. "You say if he's not arrested soon, a war between Heaven and Hell may break out?"

"We don't have time for this." Mara was clearly losing her patience. "We need to stop guessing and—"

"Hey!" Bennett shouted, drawing the room's attention. "You're all playing some fucked-up games with our existence, and I think you should explain what's obviously an important part of the puzzle. Honestly, I'm asking as nicely as I'm capable."

"Okay, big guy, pump those brakes," Izaiah said, hoping to stall Mara from murdering Bennett. "I'll tell you the story as best I can. As hastily as I can. The war we're speaking of is called Inferius, when Lucifer-Aveyl tried to overthrow Hywyn by using the Beast in a bid to bring all of UnEarth under his control—and failed. He was still of utter importance, however—needed, in order to keep the Beast of Arros at bay. Only Lucy knows the secret, and a balance must exist for life to continue. So, a truce was formed between the two great kingdoms—Arros, the kingdom of destruction, and Hywyn, the kingdom of creation. This agreement was known as the Covenant. It stated no direct interference with Earth—neither side could make moves to tip the balance. No agents acting on Earth soil. Humanity was free to flourish in whichever direction it wished. Independent stragglers have occupied Earth ever since, causing the occasional problem, sure, but otherwise things are mostly quiet, thanks to the fine folks you see before you."

"And Heaven and Hell and everyone in between lived happily ever after. Blah blah blah. Get on with it!" Galinthia shouted.

Izaiah continued, gesturing wildly. "Look, if we merely had a runaway demon to contend with, it wouldn't be much of a problem, but this time is different. A mortal was brought in—a boy. Neither kingdom may interfere to collect him or the demon without provoking the other. A representative was chosen from each of the two primary kingdoms. Those are you fellas."

"But weren't they supposed to be switched?" Fabian asked, pointing at Alex. "We were under the impression the weak one would be given the Rapture and the big one would get the Wrath. If so, they might have been able to activate it by now and actually be of use."

"Doesn't matter. What's done is done," Izaiah said, catching Alex's gaze, which snapped to him and refused to let go, his skin sizzling beneath the wool blanket. "The fellas are here to help."

"Then why did you leave them stranded in a safe house and try to find the demon on your own?" Mara asked.

Izaiah could feel every set of eyes judging him. "Because I was a fool," he admitted. "I dropped them off *near* Joseph's last known whereabouts. Technically, I did as ordered, then went to search. I really thought I was going to find him. But, still, nothing. Not a sign of him. Then, turns out these two ran into him without even trying."

"Ran into him? Meaning Joseph?" Galinthia asked, her interest piqued.

Izaiah gave the floor to Alex and Bennett. "I figure I'll let them tell their story."

Alex pointed an *us?* finger at himself.

"Yeah. We met your demon. Nice guy," Bennett said.

"You don't really believe this, do you, Izaiah?" Galinthia asked.

"No, it's true," Alex said, his modesty giving the story a boost of credence. "At the Wraithian camp. I'd say two or three hundred miles from where Izaiah left us. They seemed just as spooked by Joseph as we were."

"We didn't have much of a chat," Bennett added, "but the guy smelled horrendous and was disappointed as shit we weren't 'the brothers' or something. He was really interested in getting them together."

"Brothers?" Izaiah asked, feeling his internal warning sensors go off. *Brothers? Why does that sound so familiar? Hmm.*

"Yeah," Alex replied. "Then he took off, trying to find them and leaving us with the riders with white markings. He said he felt something strange recently, too, and thought it was nearby. At the time it seemed like nonsense, but now I'm wondering if he felt the same thing Izaiah did."

Brothers . . . Brothers . . . Brothers. Hope it's not too far back to recall. Come on, think.

"Anything else you remember? Anything at all," Izaiah pressed.

"The Wraithians kept chanting something," Alex said. "Something like 'bos thoros,' 'theorum'—sorry. I can't remember a lot about that day. It was my first time being tortured."

A light bulb went off in Izaiah's head. "Bos Thereom Dah Sathiron?"

"Yeah, that's it," Bennett confirmed.

Izaiah's skin went cold. "Are you sure? You should be positive. It was 'Bos Theor—"

"I heard you. I'm sure," Bennett repeated.

"What in the blazes does that mean?" Fabian asked.

Izaiah took his gray knitted cap off and scratched his bald spot.

"'It is found.' A language from so far back my mentor had to learn it from hers. Not sure how these guys know an ancient Wraithian language, but it's enough to worry me. Darn. *Hrm.* Also, why reappear at the same time, in the same place as Joseph? The Wraithians and Archfiend alike work with no one. It makes no sense."

Not good at all. Hmm. Who's playing us?

"'It is found?' What does that mean?" Fabian asked, but Izaiah was miles away. "Izaiah?"

"Yes? *Hrm?* What?" The old Medolian was trying to hide his despondency as the memory returned. *There were three signals last week . . . Three Brothers of Gehenna. By the Eve, please don't let that tale turn out to be true.*

He caught Mara eyeing him and attempted to straighten up and act casual.

"I don't understand. How did the humans get away from the Wraithians?" Fabian asked. "They don't take prisoners."

Everyone turned to Alex and Bennett, who in turn looked at the ground.

Mara broke the silence. "Because I got them out."

The others turned, mouths agape. Galinthia spoke first. "You did what?"

"I took them back to their homes and told them to stay out of this. I was cleaning up Izaiah's mess. Then he decided to bring them back into the fold," Mara said bitterly.

Chloe stood and faced Mara, fighting to keep her chin held high. "The Senate stated the humans were to be sent to collect Joseph with Izaiah. Not us, and not you."

"I know what the order stated—better than any of you. It was broken long before I arrived." Mara turned an accusing gaze on Izaiah.

"Look at these boys. I know you feel their Wrath and Rapture taking root," Izaiah said. "They're involved whether any of us like it or not. Right now, we need teamwork and smarts. Does anyone know where we can get some?" He chuckled alone. "Seriously, though, I'm very worried. We need to plan our next moves very carefully."

"What about the Seeress?" Galinthia suggested. "I'm sure she could help. Just ask her where Joseph will be. She could probably have solved this problem months ago."

"No. This isn't Illyana's fight," Izaiah said rigidly. "She made her choice. We have to respect it."

"That didn't stop you from going to her when you needed help selecting Barker and Hunter," Mara countered.

"That's enough," Izaiah interrupted forcefully.

"Then tell us where you're hiding her. I'll go ask her myself," Mara continued, unabated.

"Or I'll go. You can trust me," Chloe added.

"Our deal hasn't changed. I'm the only Medolian allowed access to Illyana, per her own wishes," Izaiah said. "She's too dangerous a tool to risk falling into enemy hands. End of discussion. Now, let's get back to finding a way to catch Joseph."

"How?" Chloe said, picking off a piece of one of Fabian's oranges. "None of us have sensed a panic signal from the human boy."

"I think it's clear the possessed body isn't giving off a signal of panic, as he does not seem to be panicking nor fighting the infection," Izaiah said. "That we could trace. This host has accepted the Archfiend, allowing it the use of its body indefinitely."

"Humans are as vain as any Fiend," Fabian said. "They don't let other spirits run around in their bodies. Odds are the humans are lying, and the boy died years ago, forcing the demon to vacate Earth—and it turns out there's no situation at all, so we should all just go home. It's not like he could continue using the body like a marionette puppet once the soul is gone. Honestly, it feels like we're on a hamster wheel. What are we hoping to accomplish here? Why does no one else see these things?" A flustered rose color was filling his cheeks. Galinthia shushed him and rubbed Fabian's shoulders.

"I wish your theory were true, Fabian, but I don't think that's the case," Izaiah began. "Humans are a species that has continued to surprise me, and I see no reason they will stop. When mixed with this cunning Imp—who has somehow kept his identity and motives secret—the union Joseph remains elusive."

"It wouldn't be enough for the Archfiend to have cohesion with the boy," Mara piped in. "We can see UnEarth creatures when they possess humans. This one managed to mask his every action all these years, traveling the globe without ever leaving a trace."

Chloe spoke up. "They say Joseph can sense UnEarth energies, even in the human vessel. In fact, they say he's mastered many shades of Eve."

"Impossible." Galinthia dismissed the idea with a sneer. "No Archfiend could learn to channel Mallos. Not in a billion years."

"I'm not so sure anymore," Izaiah added, pointing at Bennett and Alex. "These two are proving most of our preconceived notions incorrect. They can sense Eve—at least Bennett can—and Alex has shown that his rage and Wrath are in perfect sync. They've proven pure Eve can survive in flesh. The Imp within Joseph has had years to develop. Who knows what they are capable of?"

"Then let's get going," Galinthia said, her face firmly planted on the table. "Give us our orders. I'm bored and tired of this place."

"I think that means we're with you," Fabian said.

The group looked at Mara for acquiescence, but she scoffed and pointed the humans out the door. "First, I want them outside. Far outside."

Izaiah sighed. "Sorry, fellas. Mind giving us a few minutes?"

Without protest, Alex and Bennett bowed out, with Mara's gaze fixed on them like a hawk until the door closed behind them. Through the window Izaiah watched them march down the path to the beach as Mara joined the others around the table in the corner.

"Those are the humans Illyana helped you find?" Chloe asked, her judgment obtruding.

"Hate me as much as you like, but don't hate them," Izaiah said. "They had no choice."

"You did, though," Mara started. "Of all the mortal deaths every day in the world, what made these two so special?"

"You're just going to have to trust me."

"I trust you as much as the public does," she said, pulling her cloak tight. *She's looking to get a rise out of me. Not going to happen.*

"With the Tribunal shut down we're on our own," Izaiah said, his tone stone-cold, trying to make a point. "Nothing will start back up until we deliver the Archfiend. It's all on us. Please, Mara, I'm not asking you to like me, just to work with me."

The Medolian Gathering continued for another half hour as each Sentry gave their final remarks regarding the plan moving forward. As usual, Izaiah welcomed all thoughts and criticisms. Although he couldn't get Mara to admit to sensing the three dark presences, a consensus was eventually reached among the team: keep an eye out for absolutely anything unusual and report it immediately via a secure Mallos channel. *Sort of a one-way ESP thing just for us Medolians. It's invasive, though, so we don't use it often.*

The storm let up, revealing the warm orange light of the sun piercing through the wooden beams of the rickety safe house. Izaiah closed the Gathering with their marching orders. "Listen for each other's signals and continue focusing on North Africa. We need everyone, so somebody figure out why we can't reach the other Sentries."

"I'm on it," Fabian said, wiping his hands of orange bits. With a clap and a flash of yellow-tinted light, he vaporized the trash pile on the table into dust and wiped it onto the floor.

"Thank you, Fabian. I trust you'll figure out what's going on soon." Izaiah continued his instructions. "If you encounter the Imp, only impair it. Alex and Bennett have to be the ones to slap on the cuffs."

"Slap what?" Mara asked. "Who's slapping him?"

"It's an expression . . . Never mind."

"And what will you and the humans be doing?" Chloe asked.

"I'm going to take them to Nigel Roe," Izaiah said. "He was the first to see and report Joseph to the Tribunal, but I've always suspected there was more he didn't tell us. Maybe Bennett and Alex will have better luck getting it out of him."

"The humans think you'll take them back to their lives when this is done," Fabian said, sounding surprisingly sympathetic. "You can see it in their eyes. They have no idea what's ahead of them."

"I know," Izaiah said, pushing the thought away, knowing that no matter what the future held, Alex and Bennett would hate him. "We'll cross that bridge when we get to it."

THEY ARRIVE

Jeff's eyes were still open. What they said about dead bodies was true. He had frozen in place the night he was murdered by the man in the mask, then been left to rot. Leigh—chained to the cot directly across from him—would have used her jacket to cover him, but it was held hostage by her wrist restraints. *He deserves some goddamn dignity.* She tried to focus on the few enjoyable nights they had shared in the tent, trying to block out the gut-wrenching, almost incomprehensible evil that she was forced to relive every time she caught an accidental glance.

A freight train of guilt was running her down, screaming, *This is all your fault!* inside her head. *They tried to warn me—everyone.* Yet she had never hesitated to open the door for even a second. *Some things aren't meant to be found. Lesson learned. Can I go now?*

For the first time in her life, Leigh was as alone as she had long wished to be, and felt nothing but shame for it. The utter isolation was overwhelming and debilitating. There were no friends nearby, no allies. The closest family she had were in Zimbabwe, twenty-four hundred miles southeast. *Couple of aunts and a pair of grandparents I've ever met. Mom told me grandpa was a mayor. Might still be—not sure. She never revealed the name of the town she came from, but said it was near a mine. Gramps and I didn't keep in touch after Mom died, and he never tried to reach out beforehand.*

The skin on her wrist was healing, which was the only good news. It had been torn up from fighting her chains on the first day of her entrapment. On the second day, she'd decided to let it heal so she could try again today, the third. But at the moment, she was too tired to even make the effort, as her captor had not given her much to eat or drink, and what little he had made her retch. The man in the mask seemed only interested in the temple, reappearing randomly and occasionally bringing something for her.

Once, he brought a dead rat covered in maggots. When she refused it, thinking it was an insult, Leigh swore *he* was the one offended. On another visit, he presented her with a half-empty can of pickled yams that had clearly been sitting in the sun without a lid for a week. "Eat," he said in his fingernails-on-a-chalkboard voice. Taking the jar graciously while ignoring the flies buzzing around it, Leigh promised to eat it later. The masked man seemed satisfied enough that day and left. However, on some visits, he would take a seat on the cot nearest Leigh, oblivious to Jeff's remains, and ask her questions. His curiosity about the temple matched her own. Even though he knew a great deal more about it and its original inhabitants than she did, he also seemed in the dark about its true origins, implying several times that an ancient people called the Wraithians had once used it as a place of worship but were not its original creators.

"All had forgotten it," he once said, then added with disdain, "Even the great Michael and his brother Aveyl knew not of it."

On the second day, Leigh felt confident enough to ask him his name. The masked man responded, "This union is called Joseph."

Wanting to test her luck, she pressed him further about his origins.

"The demon has lived many thousands of years in the fire. Always there. Always serving. Always groveling." Joseph cleared his disgusting throat before continuing, "The demon stayed low. The demon found the shadow in which to hide. The demon waited. The demon listened. So long . . . like Gehenna, the demon was forgotten and became the nameless. The demon was the only one to discover the truth, which you have made reality."

The words were still haunting her a day later. Leigh couldn't be sure if the man was simply a psychopath whose body was failing him or if he was telling the truth. Intelligent in a fashion, Joseph was able to run circles around everything she threw at him and was not to be underestimated. The strength alone it would have taken to rip Jeff asunder was enough to make her extra careful. *One wrong move . . . I can usually talk my way out of shit, but this isn't exactly a contract negotiation.*

Presently, Joseph's boots crunched their way up to the tent on approach. The flap was pulled aside, and his monstrous frame curled through the entryway, carrying a rusted steel bucket with liquid sloshing around inside. *Hope to Mom's God it's drinkable.* Leigh waited for him to make the first move, but he stood still at the entrance, not quite looking at her. Then, his neck jolted straight, and he stepped forward. Leigh felt her spine tighten and her legs contract inward as he came upon her, setting the bucket down at her feet, splashing what looked like water over her shoes. It was foggy, but more promising than anything she'd received so far.

"Drink," he said in a low, gravelly tone, as though fatigued.

Leigh forced a quick smile. "I will. Thank you."

Sitting on the cot opposite her and shoving Jeff farther aside, Joseph slumped down, leaned on his knees, and drew sandpaper breaths for an uncomfortably long moment, sounding as though any might be his last. The dark slits in the plain white mask stayed fixed on her.

"I hope I'm not being presumptuous, but I need food, too," Leigh said flatly.

"Food can wait. Our human has grown to know the absence of it. You will too."

"Is your plan to let me freeze to death, then?" she asked.

"Death does not call unless it wishes to," Joseph replied.

"Then what's your plan?"

"No plan."

"Okay . . . What do you want?" she pressed.

"Nothing." Joseph reached into his coat and revealed the smallest Gehenna stone. *Oh, what now?* He caressed it like a rabbit in his hand. "Do you know what it is?"

"It's a rock. The world's full of 'em," Leigh said dismissively.

"It is Mellu. Its brothers are Raide and Eilam."

"Of course, and the temple is magical, and inside is a genie who can make all your dreams come true. I support you—I'm just not in the business of believing that sort of thing. See, I dig up the graves of people who did a long time ago. Not so smart—those people—y'ask me."

Joseph cackled, hocking saliva into his mask. "The demon has walked the Earth many times, over many years, and sees nothing special in the humans of today versus those of yesteryear. Except for those on their way here. Those who choose."

"I see. So, you're a believer of some kind? Is that why you do the things you do? You feel it's divine purpose?"

"The divine is to find your purpose."

"Wonderful. What's yours?" Leigh asked.

"We have kept that secret for millennia. We will not share it so easily," Joseph replied.

"I know mine doesn't involve this tent or these chains."

"On this, we agree." He pocketed the stone, stood, and leaned toward her, gripping her chains and ripping them free. "Come." He walked to the tent entrance.

There was no room for an escape. Standing for the first time in days, Leigh forced her legs to work again and left the tent with Joseph, traveling down the hill to the campsite. They moved through the rows of abandoned tents, starting up the hill toward the cavern and the dark cathedral, eventually reaching the crest. There, Joseph broke away to forge a new path, hiking eastward over rough terrain filled with cracks and cacti until they came to a cliff edge. Below them, the desert valley stretched on and on, its rolling hills and mountains covering the horizon. Late in the afternoon, a haze rolled in, paving the way for dusk. Joseph stood tall above it, taking a satisfied breath. "They are here."

"Who?" Leigh asked, hoping the answer wasn't any more Josephs.

"The believers," he said. "So far they do not disappoint."

"There are people who follow you?" Leigh asked, sadly believing it already. "Makes sense. I know a cult leader when I see one."

"No. The Wraithians do not follow. We simply promised them something—the ever-present dream of all who worship Wrath. They believe our union will ascend, dethrone the Fallen One, and rule on high in Arros!" Joseph's tone became increasingly self-indulgent. "The third lord, bringing the great war, Inferius, once again."

Felt a little rehearsed. "And this is something they want?" Leigh asked, maintaining her banality.

"Enough to choose to believe it."

"Sounds like blind faith to me."

"There is no other kind. The universe will never reveal itself to the living. Or the dead. Nor to any form of being. There is no purpose. None have found it. Life will always traipse aimlessly, lost in the light. God will never reveal itself, mark our words."

"I don't know what you're talking about, but you sound like every other narcissistic asshole in history," Leigh said. "Sargon of Akkad was a dick like you. The 'first emperor,' ever hear of him? Or Dr. Albert Kligman, another dick who used to do experiments on the inmates of Holmesbury Prison, same thing. What about Napoleon? Huh? Definite dick. By the time he went down, there were at least three emperors vying for power of the world. All dicks. Dicks like you come and go, and always, *always* fail, because you're not the house, the world is. You're the miserable gambler who gets himself laid out on the curb."

"Fascinating. However, if your mind were expanded by thousands of years without ripping apart, and you saw what we have seen, you would likely feel the same as we," Joseph said softly.

"Spare me this bullshit and just tell me what it is you want. There has to be something."

"As we said, nothing."

Joseph's mask turned to view the horizon, and Leigh decided to do the same. *Whatever. I might be dead soon. Better soak up the view while I can.* Though the landscape was hazy and dreary, making it hard to find any peace or tranquility, her gaze found three shapes coming over a sand hill. *Are those people?* As they approached, their images cleared, revealing riders on horseback. White tattoos covered each of their bodies. Above them, three birds circled and kept pace.

"After one hundred thousand years, the Wraithians come home. Word will spread. The hordes will heed the call." Joseph sounded almost gratified.

As the riders pushed their horses across the last stretch of sand, cries of triumph rose from the desert floor.

"Call to what?" Leigh felt compelled to ask, if reluctant.

"To the temple. To begin anew what was forgotten." Joseph leaned close to her. "We know you wish to leave. If you tell us where the Brothers are, we will allow this."

"The second I give you what you want, I end up like Jeff," Leigh said.

"The man—yes." Joseph released her and stepped to the edge of the cliff. His rags lifted and fell in the breeze as he awaited the arrival of his friends. "You believe we wish only harm? We are self-ish? Without love?"

"Pretty much," Leigh replied.

"You are wrong," Joseph snapped back quickly, sounding greatly offended. "Our true goal is based solely on love. We're sad to say there are those out there who wish for pain and anguish to con-tinue. They want innumerable creatures to suffer. Always. But soon, we will end the suffering of those we love."

"You're going to end suffering with some rocks? I thought you were becoming the third lord."

"The Brothers called us. They desire to be with us because we seek the truth. We seek their purpose. What no one has the cour-age to admit they desire."

"The stones . . . called you?" Leigh asked. *What a relief.*

"When they were discovered—touched, by you—the Brothers awoke in a new era with a new spark of life. We saw this face in our mind." He held his gloved hand out and caressed Leigh. The broken handcuff chain swung out and touched her lip. "And just as we were called here, so were you, another piece of this puzzle."

"I wasn't called here. I was hired. I'm here because of money. You know what that is, right?" Leigh said as if she were speaking to her spoiled ten-year-old cousin.

"That is two ways of saying the same thing. You needed this. You wanted this. Your mind was engrossed by it. You would not have been here upon our arrival otherwise."

Leigh found it hard not to squirm in his presence. "You don't need me. Just call these 'Brothers' again or have them call you. I'm not part of this."

"When you separated the Brothers, they went silent," Joseph said. "If you will not tell us where they've been sent, we will need to extract the information."

The riders galloped up the final stretch to meet them. There were two women and one man, dressed in patches, straps, and strands of leather hide. Now closer, their white tattoos were clearer, resembling crescent moons and lines of geometry out of Leigh's college textbook. As they slowed, one of the falcons, a beautiful brown and tan peregrine, flew in and landed on the leader's shoulder. The riders dismounted and began shouting questions at Joseph, who returned answers as they climbed the ridge. All three kept their eyes on Leigh with contempt.

The sizable, well-composed woman in front with the peregrine presented a black rock from the satchel at her side. Joseph placed his hand on it and leaned his head back with an audible gasp. After saying a few words in a strange tongue, he took his hand off the stone and gave an approving nod. The Wraithian pocketed it, and the riders proceeded to walk their horses into camp.

"More will come," Joseph said.

"How are they able to find us?" Leigh asked.

"With this . . ." Joseph opened his cloak and revealed the smallest black stone from the temple. "A vessel for Wrath. When a Wraithian is devout and true, capable of giving all and creating a vessel of their own, they will be able to hear it and follow."

As crazy as it sounded to Leigh, the rock-based GPS system worked. Over the next several hours, riders arrived by the dozen, always preceded by falcons and smaller birds surveying the land. Charging hard and fast, the riders chanted as they neared, storming over the camp and taking complete control. When the sun dropped low in the sky, headlights appeared over the hill. Two all-terrain trucks approached at first, carrying more tattooed people, as well as supplies, including heaps of animal carcasses. An hour later, a third truck, much larger, with an enclosed cube trailer, showed up with its own caravan of supplies.

The Wraithian legions poured in, some interested in Leigh, others openly hateful, but seemingly unable to do anything about it as long as she was near Joseph. Nausea had settled into her gut early on from standing next to Jeff's killer, but at the moment it seemed like the safest place. The riders appeared to come from every corner of the globe, representing every age group and demographic, all sharing one unique quality: they stank to high Heaven. *Why do people in cults never bathe? Or bathe way too much? Never a balance with weirdos.* At every turn, Leigh found herself face-to-face with snarled grins, yellow teeth fighting for space in foul mouths, and birds screeching. As the sun began to set, Joseph led her back through what was once her camp, now being torn apart for wood, fabric, and nest-building materials. Anything deemed useless was summarily set aflame.

Joseph escorted Leigh to her tent, which had already been ransacked. Even Jeff's body was gone, forcing her to imagine what might have happened or was currently happening to it. Once she was chained to the same cot, Joseph left her, promising to return later, giving her several hours with nothing to do but think.

Maybe I'm wrong? Should I tell him what I did with the other stones? I mean, they're just rock—yeah, but money is also just paper, and I know how people act around that shit. The stones are obviously important to these people. They're willing to kill for them. Not talking is the only thing keeping me alive . . . Shit.

She lay down, trying to rest while listening to the overrun camp, now a village of chaos, with physical contests and frightening tales being told over roaring fires. Pressing her jacket over her ears did nothing, and fatigue was taking its toll. Soon, her desire to give a shit waned enough to allow Leigh to pass out.

She woke at night, not knowing if it was natural or if she had been jolted awake, soon realizing it was not a specific sound that had roused her, but a lack of it. The once anarchic camp was silent, and an all-too-familiar sound was creeping up the hill: Joseph's boots and wrist chains. The tent flap opened, and the white mask swept through the doorway. He was followed by the first three Wraithians to arrive at the site. The large, composed woman snarled at Leigh, gripping a blade resembling a jagged machete.

"It's time," Joseph said, leaving the Wraithians at the door to approach her. He loomed over Leigh, a pale-faced statue in the shadows. "We want to show you something."

He broke her chains once again and held out his gloved hand. Leigh did not bother arguing or trying to clever. She simply stood, refused the hand, and started toward the tent exit. Luckily, the Wraithians stood aside as she passed.

Once outside, she discovered why the camp had gone silent. The Wraithians were gathered at the bottom of the hill, many with torches in hand, every face pointed at her tent in anticipation.

Even the birds on their shoulders were as quiet and still as stone. When she stepped out, there was a shudder of electricity among the crowd. Led down the hill by Joseph, she was soon surrounded by the mob, which parted as they passed.

"Why do I get the feeling they want to cook and eat me?" Leigh asked.

"We doubt they would take the time to cook you," Joseph said. "But the Wraithians can be a reasonable people if your goals should align."

The sea of horse riders soon broke, and Joseph pressed on, leading Leigh and the pack along the path to the temple. As much as she wished Jeff were here right now, she was glad he hadn't lived to see this or experience the hike that was most likely leading to her death. Once she entered the cave, climbed the Dead Stairs, and stepped into the temple, there would be no way out.

Torchlight from the Wraithian parade reflected off the orange and brown canyon walls, allowing the party to travel quickly in the dark. When the path was reduced to single file, she was pushed ahead to lead, and twenty minutes later they stepped out of the canyon to view the open gully and the cavern entrance to the temple. The Wraithians grew restless as they neared the cave, a murmur of voices growing among them until it became a thunder of a dozen languages, grunts, and shrieks aimed at the sky. Spears were slapped against breastplates. The clanging metal echoed deep into the cavern as Leigh entered the cave and her continuing nightmare.

"We feel you're afraid," Joseph said quietly behind her.

Wind from the birds whooshing by stirred Leigh's hair as their caws overlapped. "No shit," she said.

"You radiate brightly for a human. We've seen much Fervor in you, and your Dread is palpable. You are right to be afraid. The boy has told us much about pain."

"What boy?" She turned to Joseph.

"The body. The boy." Joseph put his hand on his chest.

Before Leigh could contemplate it further, they reached the Dead Stairs cavern, where the Wraithians became feral and charged past them to swarm the steps. She kept close to Joseph, trying to hold her breath. The smell was nauseating, but it was better than being swept away by the tide. Finally arriving at the base of the stairs, she wanted to pause—anything but to go inside—but Joseph's hand on her shoulder pressed her on. Leigh ascended the eleven steps and passed through the doorway, wondering if she would ever see blue sky again.

Or anything at all.

Inside, the Wraithians spread out in the temple like insects in a hive, carrying excited conversations in strange tongues while others muttered crazily to themselves, running their hands along the indentations in the ground as though it were holier than Jerusalem. The Wraithian birds landed on the great statue atop the plateau, their squawking melding into a high-pitched cacophony. Joseph marched Leigh to the foot of the tall stairs leading to the column plateau and the great statue of the beast, but surprisingly no desert rider dared follow. Reaching the top of the column, she moved onto the plateau with the stone baptismal bath, overlooking the crowd, their white tattoos gleaming in the torchlight.

Joseph's arms opened wide over the sea below, which was beginning to chant. "You see . . . an army, born of a rumor. The Eve of mankind is weak. Easily shaped." He laughed. "To begin . . ." Joseph turned back to the maniacal crowd and spoke with a profound new voice—boisterous and fierce. She did not recognize the words and guessed many of the Wraithians did not either, based on their expressions, which did not seem to be the point.

The energy in the room was palpably condensing. With each word spoken, the Wraithians were drawn into something of a bloodlust, slithering over one another, trying to get closer to the wall, clawing at the rock, snarling, and dripping saliva.

"The Temple of the Beast is powered by Wrath," Joseph said to Leigh. "As the Wraithians bring more raw fury inside, the wave swells. It was here, in this spot, where the universe was forever changed." Reaching into his pocket, Joseph revealed the smallest of the black stones, driving the crowd into a frenzy. "Pay homage to Mellu!" he roared, then muttered under his breath, "Tear one another apart."

The Wraithian horde collapsed into brutal insanity—clawing, chewing, and maiming, staining their white tattoos red. Yet, from within the tumult, a chant grew: "*Bos Thereom Dah Sathiron . . . Bos Thereom Dah Sathiron . . . Bos Thereom Dah Sathiron!*"

Joseph sounded gratified. "In this place, their belief in destruction as the most benevolent shade of Eve is increased a hundredfold. Only with it can the stone be awakened long enough to grant us a glimpse. With its power, we will show you what we have been speaking of. Though the boy thinks you will wish we hadn't."

A multitude of desert riders held out black stones of their own, trying to catch blood from any nearby carnage. "They're ready," Joseph said, reaching for Leigh.

Placing the small stone on the pedestal, he pulled away his left glove, revealing a horrid green appendage. The tissue looked dead, or close to it. Red veins, raised from the skin, spread like webs over the hand. Pus dripped from the glove and his fingertips, oozing from open sores covering the palm and back of the hand. With the exposed hand, he grabbed Leigh by the throat, sending a malicious burning agony throughout her body.

"Now, you will tell me where you hid them." With his free hand, Joseph took up the stone. Within it, the ribbons of color began going haywire.

The light in Leigh's mind was beginning to fade. She couldn't breathe.

Joseph's smooth white mask turned on her. "It's working."

"Good . . . for . . . you . . ." she coughed out.

He released a thunderous bellow, shaking Leigh to her core. "Tell me where Mellu's Brothers are!"

A low-pitched rumble emanated from the stone, which quaked in his hand. Then an utter chill swept over Leigh. Her skin, hair, eyes—everything—was awash in an ice she'd never before experienced, making her feel as though she'd already died weeks ago, and her decomposing flesh was suddenly rushing to catch up, while her inner self boiled. Life felt truly empty, without a concrete world to hold on to. She was spinning. The floor dropped out within her, just as it had when she'd first touched the dagger, but on an astronomical scale. Leigh would do anything to escape it. She needed ground beneath her. She needed to breathe.

Amid the void, a flood of information came. Leigh saw the face of a teenage boy staring hatefully into a mirror. His expression contorted as waves of passionate and venomous thoughts passed through him: others crying, screaming, reaching out in pain, the three black stones, and a long-gestated dream of a black fate for all realities. *What is all this? Why can't I stop it!?*

"Stop! Please!" she managed to cough out, her eyes rolling back. *Fine! I'll talk!* "I sent them! A stone went to London! Institute of . . . Archaeology, UCL! Casey knows!—STOP!"

"*A* stone? You separated them yet again!?" Joseph roared. "We would like to break you over and over again . . . Where did you send the other? Where?"

The cavern her withered soul was falling through didn't end. Unbearable images filled the void and her mind. She would have to tell him what she hadn't told anyone: where she had secretly sent the largest stone. But before she could utter a syllable, the Temple of the Beast was suddenly shaken by a thunderous blast, centered on Joseph's hand and the smallest of the black stones, forcing him to one knee. Leigh was finally let go, left gasping for air, clinging to the ground.

"No!" Joseph shrieked. The swirls of color in the stone had frozen in place. The electricity in the air was gone. "That can't be all! We tasted it. We need more! We need—" His frantic panic slowly subsided, and Joseph's mask drifted toward Leigh. "That is all the power Mellu will allow me . . . without his Brothers." He slumped over, his shoulders tense, holding the stone close. "No matter. We will begin by collecting Raide. You will accompany us to London, where you will aid us in uniting them, or you will fade from life. This choice is not ours. It is yours."

Doesn't sound like much of a choice to me.

"... despite their vast differences, a cross-shade society was established. The UnEarth Senate governs over all, though each world-state has autonomy [...] The six worlds of the Eve, existing within their own pocket universes, are populated by radically different creatures, who long ago discovered one another and have been trying to coexist peacefully ever since. So far, it has been a mild success, save for a few wars. However, according to my friend and informant, the current reign of peace is tenuous at best."

- Excerpt from the journal of
Dr. Francisco Emul. Murcia
May 1895

SMOKE AND MOSS

A wall of neon washed Bennett in gaudy maroon, orange, and rose-colored brilliance, forcing him to squint to see the patronage in front of the nightclub down the street: people out for a smoke in the misty evening air. Above them, a neon, bipedal cat wearing a blue fedora winked and took the hat on and off, its arm flipping back and forth with a faint buzzing sound with each switch. *Fucking cat. I hate you.* Above it, flaming, pink, cursive letters spelled "La Rose Noire." Inside the auspicious watering hole was supposedly a man—an UnEarth political activist currently going by the name Nigel Roe—whom Bennett and Alex were to find and question about the demon Joseph. Roe was a former Scythe, according to Izaiah; whatever the Hell that meant. *Sounds annoying already. Regretting ever agreeing to this.*

"Roe was the first to report seeing Joseph six years ago," Izaiah had explained. "Little snake is always trying to gain favor with the Tribunal. He's been campaigning to get his ascension rights restored ever since the Purge. Seems he thought snitching on the nameless demon might help, but ever since, he's been hiding out around here. No one's sure why. My guess is he's scared of something, but he won't talk to me or any Medolian. Doesn't trust us. In fact, he's a rather paranoid creature. I need you fellas to get in there, pretend to be two run-of-the-mill Celestial and Archfiend who are new to town, and find out what else he learned from Joseph that night. It may prove key to finding out what the demon is after and where he's going."

Gathering intel? Well, all right. Bennett couldn't deny the prospect of a new mission gave him a slight (*and much-needed*) kick in the ass. *Even some goosebumps.* Alex, on the other hand, looked less than delighted.

After the Gathering on the beach, Izaiah Shifted them to a new city in the middle of the night—in, where else?—a seedy alley. To no one's surprise, least of all Bennett's, the old Medolian then did his favorite thing after telling bad jokes: he abandoned them when they needed him most.

Izaiah makes my old man look clingy by comparison.

"Sorry about all the baloney with the Medolians, fellas," the old man said before taking off. "They can be surprisingly sour. Things been kinda hectic lately. You understand."

Izaiah then told them the truth about La Rose Noire: it wasn't a regular club at all, but one of a handful of sanctuaries where UnEarth Humans—a general term given to creatures of Eve living on Earth as *Homo sapiens*—could gather.

"When folks got Purged, they were stripped of their Eve and transformed into human form. They mostly keep to each other," Izaiah started. "But every now and then, a new face pops up. So, you should technically be okay. The general UnEarth community still doesn't know humans were made official delegates, and the Tribunal shutdown hasn't been announced yet, to the best of my knowledge."

This is a lot to remember.

"You sure you can't come with us?" Alex asked, voicing the words in Bennett's mind.

"If anyone gets wind a Medolian is nearby, they'll clear the place," Izaiah said. "The owner, a Wyst named Madam Daphne, is not our biggest fan."

Are we working for the fuzz? It's starting to sound like it.

"Is there anything else you need to tell us?" Bennett asked like a jab. "Think. I'm not going into any more shit situations unless I believe you've told us the truth. If we do this for you, it's because it's the right thing to do, it's important, and no one else can. Right?"

"Couldn't agree more!" Izaiah said, offering a grin that lifted his rosy cheeks. "Don't think of me as a liar, Bennett. Or a knife in your backs. I hope you'll believe me when I say I did what I did to protect you both. Yes, I was a fool—to no one's surprise—least of all my fellow minstrels of the middle. I thought when I left you in the safe house, if I kept you in the dark as much as possible, you'd be less likely to go looking for trouble. I hope you know that if things were my way, you boys never would have met. We all know you'd be better off. But, well, anyway—"

"You can stop apologizing. I don't care," Alex said coldly. "I just want to get this over with and go home."

Bennett mustered a smile for Alex, lacking the heart to tell him what he knew Izaiah was keeping from them: they could never go back home. *It's better this way, Al. We might lose you if you found out you're never going to see your wife again.*

Izaiah and Bennett exchanged glances before the Medolian nodded. "Of course, Mr. Barker." He then warned them that they might encounter strange things in the Rose, and to—"Just act like you've seen and done it six times yourself. If you get in hot water, don't be afraid to tell a joke. Everyone loves jokes." Izaiah tapped his chest pocket containing his green notebook. "Got a real tickler about Genghis Khan walking into a bakery, if you need an ice-breaker."

"We're good," Bennett replied.

The Medolian then stuffed a wad of cash from his pocket into Bennett's palm. "Get some food, and a shirt for Alex. Don't want anyone seeing those scars. You too, Bennett. And keep your Wrath and Rapture in check. Your signatures still look a little funny. Avoid calling attention to yourselves. We're not sure who we can trust."

"Where'd you get the money?" asked Alex.

"What do you think I've been standing on street corners for?" With that, Izaiah said goodbye once again, created another white tunnel for a Shift, and stepped away. "I'll be back soon! I promise."

Doubtful. Then he was gone.

"I really hate him," Bennett said, to which Alex nodded.

Stepping out of the alley, they found themselves in a neighbor-hood tinted brown and gray, filled with rusted warehouses and smokestacks reaching into the sky. The street signs and faded logos on the sides of the structures were written in French. *Ugh. Europe.*

"You sure you want to do this, Al? Last chance to back out."

"We made our choice. Sooner we live with it, sooner I go home."

"Did we though?" Bennett asked.

The first street was desolate. Around the next corner, they spotted a food vendor parked under a lamppost, packing up his sandwich and sausage trolley for the night. Alex waved and shouted a warm greeting, hurrying ahead of Bennett as though to make sure he got there first. Somehow, even shirtless, with a smoking demon-bull brand burned into his chest, Alex was able to approach the man without startling him, and even drawing a welcoming smile in return. *Little asshole.*

Bennett caught up as Alex and the man were exchanging messy

but mirthful volleys of French. After a moment, Alex turned to Bennett. "We're in northern Marseille, near a freight train station or something. You hungry?"

Using the wad of dollars Izaiah had given them, Alex bought not only some cold sausages and crackers with cheese spread but also the shirt right off the vendor's back. The man seemed perfectly fine parting with it, as the salmon-colored shirt was stained with grease and featured moth holes in the shoulders, and his walk home to claim a fresh one was only a few blocks. Alex then asked the vendor if he knew of the club they were looking for. "He says he's heard of it," the teacher said with a smug smile aimed Bennett's way.

Half an hour later, they rounded a corner to face a wall of neon light and the electric cat above La Rose Noir.

"You're welcome," Alex said, folding his arms proudly.

Have you ever had a win in your life, Al? The next hour was spent finishing their cracker and sausage plates while Bennett went on a stakeout, making sure the smokers out front were merely that (*and to get a general feel for the clientele*). It was habit. He and his sniper team used to stake out targets for days, even weeks, before making a move. *Gotta get to know someone before you kill 'em.*

When Alex finished his food, he folded the soggy paper plate into quarters and pocketed it, noticing Bennett staring. "Just till we can find a trash can." *Dear God, man.*

"How do you know French in the first place, Al? You don't strike me as worldly," Bennett asked, striving for a chummy tone.

"Oh, we've been talking about visiting Europe for years. Melissa and I," Alex answered, his face suddenly flush with life. Bennett then saw the memory fade in his eyes, and the teacher's smile drifted. "We were going to do it for our honeymoon. Come here. On our first try, I had a panic attack on the plane before they closed the doors. So we went home. I was frozen. I can't explain it. I was sure the plane going to crash, which of course it didn't. I just—that was the start of the first really bad year. We tried again two years later. This time it was going to be Hawaii. You know, cheaper. But then my aunt got sick, so we—it's funny, we never ended up having the trip. Talked about it a lot. Never stopped talking about it. I was going to learn the language and surprise Melissa by ordering our first meal when we got here."

Bennett decided not to push further and possibly rile up the guy and the Wrath inside him. Once satisfied with their vigil, he stood.

"Does that mean we can finally go in?" Alex asked, rising to join him.

"You remember the plan?" Bennett asked.

"We made one?"

"Yeah, remember what I said a few minutes ago?"

"About me just listening to you and following your orders?"

"Exactly," Bennett said.

If the Medolian's story about the great war and Heaven and Hell was true, there was no room for fucking around. *They called the kingdom of creation Hywyn, I think. Where did we get Heaven from? Are they even the same thing? Ugh. Fuck me, what's going on?*

Bennett scratched the wings on his shoulders, itching so much he'd grown to loathe them. Not the scars themselves necessarily, but what they meant: he was a puppet who'd been slapped on the back by God—a deity who was remaining classically absent. *Hey, Almighty, if I'm being used as an instrument or whatever, can you at least come tell me yourself? Maybe wine and dine me before I get fucked?*

God had only ever been a stain on Bennett's life. His commanding officers in the military had shoved the idea into his head so hard that for a while he almost believed it. But it turned out to be merely adrenaline and the fear of combat talking. When he returned to civilian life and looked back on the things he'd seen and done, Bennett knew God should be treated the same as the boogeyman: only there to frighten children and keep them in line. Then, a name mentioned by the Medolian Galinthia in the Gathering hit him like a brick in the nuts: Lucifer. She'd said it so fucking casually that it made him sick, as though the lord of darkness were just a few doors down the hall, next to the break room. *But if Lucifer is real, then God is too, right? Who else could cast that motherfucker down?*

Bennett took another swift glance around the block. "Before we go in, I've been thinking—these beings, these Medolians and Imps and Celestials or whatever, they all seem to sense one another in an invisible network. I'm getting glimmers of it, and I think I'm sensing that pretty much everyone in this place is like us, filled with this Eve bullshit. There are a lot of people in there. Like, so many I have no idea."

"But Izaiah said we were the first humans to get it," Alex argued.

"Which is why I think these people might be something else altogether. Like Izaiah said, we shouldn't let on that we're regular men."

"What else should we be?" Alex asked.

"People keep calling you an Imp, so be one. Alexander the Imp. Sounds cool, right?"

Alex looked so nervous it rounded the bend into appearing as though he had to pee. "I'm not so sure about this."

"Look on the bright side," Bennett said. "At least your dead, poor ass finally got to see France."

Sauntering down the street, they approached the club and the small crowd out front—true creatures of the night in styles that must have been UnEarth inspired. Vests were plentiful, and none of them wore shoes. Bold chunks of primary colors and incandescent designs matched or complemented their eyes, so vibrant they seemed to glow, while every head of hair was spiked in one direction or another. As Bennett and Alex passed by, their every move was scrutinized.

That's not horrifying.

When they neared the door, a rhythmic thumping from inside pounded against Bennett's chest. *Why'd it have to be a club?*

Passing a few large men in dark suits standing at the door, he looked the biggest in the eye, which carried a soft yellow glow. The doorman sniffed vigorously over their heads as they passed, and with a grunt he waved them on before turning away, seemingly satisfied. *That was easy.* Stepping through the doorway into a dark space filled with thick fog, they ducked under a low ceiling as quaking electronic music surged down a long hall. Bennett pushed through shadowy bodies drifting by like ships in the night while bass hits punched him in the sternum, growing stronger as they neared a mess of laser lights beyond the end door.

This already sucks.

Crossing the threshold into the Platinum Hall of La Rose Noire felt like coming out of a dream with a jolt, like kicking oneself awake. To Bennett, the assault on his senses was beyond over-whelming. The smells, colors, sounds—all somehow new—broke his barriers and accepted limits, leaving him speechless and bring-ing a tear to his eye, which he quickly wiped away. The dark was shattered by rotating, spinning lasers cascading through the hall, striking textured pillars of granite scattered unevenly throughout, lofting torches of fire and neon. Across the black sea of twisting bodies on the dance floor was a stately platinum staircase, thirty feet wide, rising to a second-floor landing. The upper floor, like a lordly Victorian hall lined with numbered double doors, disap-peared into the rear recesses of the club, seeming to defy the sheer physics of the size of the building he'd viewed from the street.

Everywhere he looked, the lines, trim, and curves of the room were highlighted by myriad colors, brilliant and alive with energy. *Eve. Right.*

When studying a shade, Bennett also felt a swell of everything associated with it. *And happy and sad are just the tip of the iceberg. There's all sorts of feelings and shit going on here. Some of 'em I hardly recognize. Seriously, what the fuck was that last one? And why do I suddenly want a banana and an apple fritter?*

On his immediate left and right, stretching the length of the dance floor, were lounge areas crowding two platinum-topped bars, each with three bartenders serving drinks and littered with shimmering bowls and glassware filled with fruits, vegetables, and other (*I'm guessing*) plants he couldn't recognize. One of the bartenders was a mountain of a man, well over seven feet tall, with preposterously chiseled facial and body features, and skin so blue he looked like he'd frozen to death days ago. He was preparing drinks, putting on magnificent show, tossing four shakers at the same time, which seemed to slow in motion while in midair, as did the liquid spilling from them.

Hell of a trick. A green strobe struck Bennett's retina, making him grunt like a caveman who'd lost his steak. The wonderment he felt on arrival was gone. Playtime was over.

"How are we supposed to talk to anyone in this fucking nightmare?"

"It's a nightclub. What were you expecting?" Alex shouted.

"Something quieter," Bennett muttered, searching for the shortest line to a bartender. *Gotta start somewhere.*

When Alex tugged on his jacket and pointed up, Bennett craned his neck, spotting shapes dangling from the ceiling by chains. *Are those people?* Some were naked, others were covered in paint, sweat, or other substances, and some wore tight leather straps. As the lasers danced across the bodies, Bennett caught glimpses of barbs penetrating flesh, stretching skin and pulling muscles, yet drawing no blood. Flashes of light crossed faces not in pain but in pleasure—ecstasy, even—as tubes of brightly colored liquids pumped through them, running back along the chains and disappearing into a contraption on the ceiling that resembled a gigantic car engine, but a mutant, an aberration rejected by the factory. The dry siphoning noises it made were audible even over the club music. With each rotation, the machine shook and gasped, making it seem like a tired bodily organ plagued by smoker's tar.

So that's the deal in this place. Got it.

Leading Alex as casually as possible past private seating alcoves, Bennett took quick glances inside them. One alcove, framed by Greek columns, contained a cadre of half-naked men wearing green sunglasses. Another was occupied by a single woman with jet-black hair twisted into a messy knot, smoking a black cigarette, her head draped back over the cushioned seat. Before moving on, Bennett caught a glimpse of movement near her feet and spotted a leathery, scaled tail with a translucent golden tip slinking back and forth.

"Seen and done it six times myself. Right," he assured himself, spotting a pair of women leaving one of the alcoves. Swooping in, he claimed the table. "We can base camp here."

"I think I just saw a lady with gills," Alex said.

"Saw a couple of weird things myself," Bennett agreed, keeping a wary eye around. "I'm going to ask around. Stay here and don't do anything stupid. Hear me? Nothing stupid."

"Maybe I should go, ya know?" Alex suggested. "I'm the one who speaks French. And I'm also, you know . . . it just might be easier." He used his overly friendly tone. *The one I already hate.*

Bennett wasn't in the mood to risk Alex ruining what might be their only chance. "Based on the Medolians and Joseph, I'd bet somebody here speaks English. Stay put. Watch the table and my back. If things go south, can you fire up?"

"I can try," Alex said, instilling zero confidence.

"Wow. Thanks, Al. Glad you're here." Bennett turned and marched through the crowd. "Fuckin' kid's table."

The least busy bartender, a thick man with dark skin, a beard hanging down to his belt, and a glistening platinum shirt with suspenders, was speaking in French to a woman at the bar when Bennett approached. *Damn. French.* Closing his eyes, he tried to get a read on the guy's energy. The bartender's form was replaced by a cloud in the darkness, but its shade was hard to make out. Fighting to focus, Bennett began to see a gold hue that turned into a vibrant canary yellow, filling him with a flash of despondency. *Whoa. Heavy.*

Maneuvering past lounge tables, he stepped up to the bar, nodding at the bartender. "Evening."

The bartender offered a fully silver-toothed smile. "Good evening, lad. Always chipper to see a new face from the Celestial clan. What can I get ya?" *Fuck. What do these people drink? Not beer, obviously.* "Yo . . . come on, what's your thing?" The bartender snapped his finger impatiently.

"Sorry. Having trouble deciding."

"If you're not drinking, there's plenty-a space left in the Still Room. But I don't judge those who wander. If you're into other shit, it's cool. All ideas are welcome in the Rose. Just say what you want, and I'll go get the proper sign-up sheet."

Bennett was about to move on, straight to business, but curiosity got the better of him. *Sign-up sheet?* "What else you got?"

"Shit. A first-timer? We got everything. You want to swing the dial all the way over and join the Fiends in the Blaze Barrel? Be my guest. Orgy carousels for the Fervor types. And our Scream

Theater attack simulator was just renovated, now with even more fevered Lythe Dogs. Got something to satisfy every flavor. So, what's yours?"

"I'm actually looking for someone," Bennett said.

"Isn't everybody?"

"A Nigel Roe."

"*Eck*. Yeah, I've been seeing him slinking around for a few years now. And his cats. Creepy fuck. What you want with him?"

"Just want to ask him a few questions."

The bartender smirked. "Good luck with that. Roe used to be the kind who'd talk your ear off if you accidentally made eye contact. Always ready to get into 'Purged Scythe relations.' Though he hardly comes out of whatever hole he's hiding in anymore. We all know he's here—again, on account of the cats—which are honestly becoming a problem. Little fuckers are everywhere, either puking on everything or getting eaten and making a mess. But we're not sure exactly where Roe is. The Rose has a few nooks and crannies, after all."

"He's laying low? Why here?" Bennett asked.

"This place is a sanctuary. But something must have spooked the guy more than usual, because he hired an Archfiend bodyguard. Not just any Fiend, either. Word is she used to be one of the Niel Nulus." The bartender shuddered as though a cold chill had gone down his spine. "Those Fiends don't fuck around. My guess is Roe finally spilled more beans than he was supposed to. Pissed somebody off good upstairs."

The bartender grabbed an unlabeled rectangular bottle from under the bar and poured two glasses of a foggy green liquid with a layer of smoke rolling off its surface. "You might be waiting a while. Here. On me." He pushed one of the glasses toward Bennett.

"I'm good. Thanks," Bennett replied. "You think anyone else around here might know where to find the guy?"

The bartender nudged the drink closer. "Nope."

"Seriously, I'm good."

The bartender gawked as if he didn't understand the phrase. "Thought Celestials loved this shit."

"We do. Just not in the mood." Bennett kept his lie short and sweet.

"Never met a Purged who turned down a drink. Figured you'd need to forget the past two K, like everyone else. Or did you not serve?"

"Oh, I did my time," Bennett said.

"Where were you stationed?" the bartender pressed.

A tired, angry guise slid easily over Bennett's face. If this was retired military talk, he knew exactly how to respond. "You think that's why I'm here? To talk about that shit? Relive it?" He never broke eye contact with the bartender, who laughed sheepishly.

"Shit, good point. Sorry, lad. To forgetting those days!" The bartender lifted his glass, waiting for Bennett to do the same. "If you're looking to talk to Roe, trust me, calm your nerves first. He can make one . . . let's say anxious."

Seeing no other way, Bennett took the glass and sniffed it. The smell was like spoiled mushrooms fermenting in gasoline and Drano.

"Bottoms up," the bartender said, jamming it back like a shot. *Hrm, I do enjoy stuff that fucks you up. Then again, I just gave up drinking. Does alien alcohol count? Choices—choices.*

"Fuck it."

Bennett tried not to shut his eyes as he dove in headfirst and downed the concoction. The first sensation was like hot sauce and rubbing alcohol coating his throat. Next came a flavor that confirmed the drink's smell was an accurate representation of its taste. His eyes watered instantly. A pressure ran up his neck to his skull, planting itself snugly and blowing up like a lead balloon. Sour sensations ripped through his nasal passages, like a handful of potent herbs and spices, followed by the inexplicable smell and taste of charred meat. The soldier's hand shook as he handed the glass back, fighting to keep his expression neutral and resisting a coughing fit. The effects hit him like alcohol at sixty miles per hour, with the giggling, stupid-happy phase of drunkenness approaching without warning.

"Well?" the bartender asked with a smart-assed smirk.

"Good stuff," Bennett coughed out hoarsely, feeling the acid working away on his vocal cords.

The bartender looked away, seemingly bored and ready for another customer. "Yeah? I can tell you like your swamp water."

"Me and the others in my team—loved it. Been drinking it since the dawn of time. Am I right?" Bennett finished with a cough and slammed a balled-up fist on the bar, shaking his head as pastel-colored fog began to fill his mind. *Keep it together, sissy. It's just a drink.*

The bartender's eyes narrowed. "That's funny, because it's not called swamp water. Don't know moss when you drink it?"

"Thought you might have been stupid or something," Bennett coughed. "I sure as shit call it moss. Everyone does."

"Ah-huh." Continuing to eye Bennett, the bartender snapped the top on the bottle of the worst drink the soldier had ever had. "Good luck finding Nigel, lad."

That's my cue. Needing to escape before the bartender grew suspicious and before the fit of giggles creeping up his gut could escape, Bennett slipped away. The sensation was enraging and overwhelming all at once. While he did his best to walk normally—*don't you do it*—fighting the effects of the drink made his knees quiver. *Unacceptable! No.* Tears streamed down his cheeks as his face contorted into an awkward, tightly stretched mess. *No. No! You hear me? You will not giggle right now!* The room spun. *Stop!* He couldn't fight it any longer. *You are Sergeant Bennett Hunter of the US Marine Corps Regiment Four, O Company! You will not—*

His knees buckled. In the worst fashion, like a nightmare he didn't know he'd always had, Bennett dropped to the ground and laughed to the Heavens.

Get up, damn you!

Stumbling to his feet, he wrestled through the bodies on the dance floor, biting his lip and thinking angry thoughts, stubbing his toe on accident, unable to stop laughing so intensely he wanted to throw up. Breaking free of the crowd and rounding the nook where he'd left Alex, he found it empty. The teacher was nowhere in sight.

"Al? *Ha! Ha ha . . .*" Bennett shouted into the storm of darkness and fluorescent light. "Al!—*Ha!*" Taking heavy steps onto the dance floor, the room spinning faster all the time, he called, "Anybody seen a—a little guy, thick eyebrows? Looks nervous? Al! *Haha!* Barker! Hey—"

Bennett froze in place, allowing the swarm to overtake him. Faces passed like gothic statues in shadow. There were wide irises, sly smiles, lips licked. The deafening bass and high-pitched scream of the music clawed at his eardrums.

I've been on bad trips before. Just gotta focus.

Taking a deep breath, he began the search for his missing partner.

Al . . . thought I told you not to do anything stupid.

SCYTHE

Bennett's going to be so mad at me. Alex marched through the darkness of a tight hallway, following a mysterious stranger, feeling his anxiety spike. *And my germaphobia. Is this place up to code?* Dull, tinted windows above let in blue moonlight, casting columns of light onto the pebbled path ahead, shimmering on the tall stranger's head. She was bald except for a knot of braided ash-blonde hair originating just above where her skull met her spine, which hung down like a thick tail, swaying with each of her steps.

Stay calm. Everything will be fine. Just. Stay. Calm.

Moments ago, when Alex was left alone by Bennett at the table in the Platinum Hall of La Rose Noire, he could feel every UnEarth Human eye on him. None looked keen to say hello, and he somehow got the distinct impression he was a topic of conversation among the crowd. The stares made him so nervous that the scars on his chest started to heat up, and the Wrath inside him was rising to say hello. He shut his eyes, took long breaths, and managed to slow his pulse, but when he opened his eyes again, his heart was jump-started.

A tall, lean woman with blonde eyebrows was parked at his table, wearing what must have been a few hundred bracelets on her forearms. The shimmering orange dress she wore was as tight as a second skin, moving like fish scales. Smiling a siren's grin, she waved her pointer finger. "Hey there, little one. Don't be frightened." She spoke with a sensual, soothing tone. "I couldn't help but notice you getting some heat on. What's the deal, baby?"

"No. Thank you. I'm good. Just wait"—Alex coughed—"waiting for someone." He coughed again. *Oh, great.*

The enigmatic woman studied him with narrow eyes, her head swaying through the air a little too similarly to Joseph's for any comfort. With the sudden swiftness of a snake, she was in the alcove, seated beside him, making Alex jump.

She slid a finger over his lips to shush him. "You don't need to speak, sweetie. I know why you're here." Leaning in close to his ear, she whispered, "But why would Nigel wish to speak with you?"

Alex was positive he had a dopey, stunned expression on his face. *How does she know about that? What do I do now?* The woman slapped a hand over his mouth, gripping him by the cheeks, and turned him to face her irises, which were deep red, dotted with flashes of orange.

"Who are you?" he asked through squished cheeks.

She laughed. "Earthly name's Yusay'ne. How about you, baby?"

"People call me Alex."

She puckered her lips and kissed the air like a chef tasting perfection. "Yes, I know. Alex Barker. It's smart. Simple. No one would ever take a second glance. True invisibility. And how about your old name? Your *real* name?" *How does she know my last name?*

The look she gave confirmed Alex was the mouse and she was the cat. His choices were to play along and possibly not die, or mess it up and definitely die.

He gave the first answer that came to him. "You know, it's been so long I don't even remember."

The expression on Yusay'ne's face was nearly impossible to read. He braced for the worst. "Ha!" she laughed to the rafters. "If I had a sixer of thresh for every time I heard that. Why do us Archies always forget our past? Do you think it's because we're ashamed of it?"

"No, not at all." The response popped out, and Alex found himself falling comfortably into the part. *Izaiah was right. It's easier if I role-play. Still can't tell if that guy is a lunatic or the wisest creature I've ever met. Either way, when this is over, he and I are going to have a little chat. Got a few things to straighten out.*

"I'd like to think we aren't ashamed of what we were, or who we are," Yusay'ne said, her tone softening. "Most of us know what it's like to be asked to do something we don't want to, but must anyway." She let her eyebrows droop sadly. "It's always unfair to ask a creature to feel shame for being true to themselves, right? I remember far too much to feel shame for it all—the wars, my old deeds, my old name, Niel'Yeus. In Clan Niel we were taught nothing can exist without a present desire to destroy. But no one ever sees that, do they? They see what they want—what the masses want."

The teacher was stunned by his sympathy for the woman who was scaring the daylights out of him and seemed to be defending evil. Though she looked as young as fifty, Yusay'ne's gaze bore a callous and worn wisdom that Alex was only noticing now, as her voice cracked.

"I think . . ." As usual, the teacher felt responsible for whatever distress he might have caused another, real or otherwise. "I think if others don't see something so obvious, it's because they're blind. None of us can help what's inside us. None of us can help our fears, or hatreds. They're just there—always looming over us."

Yusay'ne smiled with a curious flip of her braided ponytail, then paused so long that Alex thought she'd frozen in place. It turned out she was simply studying him. "That'll do," she said. "On to business. Do you still wish to meet him? Yes or no?"

"Nigel? Yes, and my partner is—"

"That's a no. I'll take *you* to see him. Only you. Only now. If you wish to hear what he has to say, this is your chance. I'm going to stand up and walk away. If you follow, you'll meet him. If not, you won't. Please nod if you understand," Yusay'ne finished with a closed-mouth grin creeping up her cheeks.

The teacher bobbed his head and, before he knew it, was following her through the dance floor, the color of her dress seeming to change with each step, shifting from orange to red to maroon, making her harder to spot through the crowd and laser lights. Fighting to catch up, he found her near the staircase, not climbing but darting to the right, approaching a side door beyond the elaborately carved silver handrail. Slipping her hand over the door handle, she opened it and stepped aside for him. "This way, Mr. Barker."

The next hall was wide and dimly lit by fancy beige sconces attached to deep brown trim running its length, featuring doors with beautiful carvings on their faces, like something from Greek antiquity. Clusters of patrons were scattered throughout, speaking in the more intimate setting. Yusay'ne closed the door behind them, shutting off the noise from the Platinum Hall before gliding ahead.

Keeping his eyes on her feet, swift and fascinating as they were, Alex tried to avoid interacting with the small ensembles of Un-Earth Humans, who halted their conversations to watch him pass. *They know what I am. Somehow. I know it.* He then slowed his pace, remembering the three times he'd smoked pot in his early twenties and how paranoid he'd felt then, thinking everyone knew he was high and judging him for it. *Just stay calm. No one knows anything. Stay calm.* Though it was hard to ignore how even the couples making out passionately in the darkness paused to sniff the air around him like vigorous hounds.

Reaching a door halfway down the corridor, half as elegant as the rest, labeled *21A*, Yusay'ne stopped. "This is the one."

Alex followed her down a tight hallway, through columns of light from above, watching her braided ball of hair bob back and forth in the dark.

Presently, he noticed the area was becoming more industrial chic as they moved, though he had so far assumed it was part of a modern club aesthetic he didn't fully understand. *Is this a . . . janitor's service hallway? Or just made to look like one?*

Yusay'ne seemed to be speeding up. Alex then spotted movement ahead and heard jingling keys. A figure was backing into the hall, which seemed to mute Yusay'ne's excitement. She muttered under her breath as they neared an inlet, seemingly little more than a storage space with dirty shelves holding cleaning equipment and toiletries. The figure stepping out of a janitorial closet turned as they approached. A wet mop was clutched in his hand. Though above-average height, he was so skinny he might have weighed less than one hundred pounds, most of it likely encompassed in his long, dark mane of hair, which hung over his beard-encrusted face. The white T-shirt he wore was stained to the point it appeared to have gotten a tie-dye job using only earth tones.

When the janitor spotted Yusay'ne and Alex down the dark hall, he jolted and backed into the shelf behind him, sending half a dozen toilet paper rolls to the ground.

"Yusay'ne, hi!" the janitor said, a hint of panic in his voice. "Didn't expect to see anybody back here. Sort of an employees-only kind of thing, know what I mean?"

They neared, and Alex read the man's plastic name tag: *Hi, my name is Felix. How can I assist you today?*

"And how proud those employees must be," Yusay'ne replied to Felix coldly, turning to address Alex. "We'll leave *Felix* here," she said his name with a sense of abhorrence, "to his duties, and just go back the way we came."

Ignoring her own words, Yusay'ne continued down her original path.

"But you just came from that way," Felix said, pointing behind them, obviously trying to be as mannerly as possible, unable to intimidate Yusay'ne while standing in still water.

She leaned over him, taller than Felix by a head. "One must walk the way one will. Unless, of course, you wish to say otherwise, Niel'Vyl?"

Niel what? I thought his name was Felix.

The janitor gave a nervous laugh, as though he wanted to say more, before returning to his business with the spill. "No. Totally fine. Keep going. You're bound to find the exit. Have a good night, folks."

Felix took a couple of semi-worried glances back at Alex as he followed Yusay'ne into the farther reaches of the service hallway, which began to feel like a warning the farther they got. Keeping pace with her, Alex soon realized the sounds of the club had completely vanished. Looking back, he could no longer see the janitor's nook or Felix, but suddenly, sitting in the middle of the hall was a house cat—so white it seemed to glow—swinging its tail and watching him intently, its eyes reflecting light like fifty-cent pieces. *Where'd he come from?*

"Seems like we've walked pretty far," Alex said. "I can't even hear the music. What do you say we go back, huh? Your boss can meet us in the kissing hallway." Turning back, he first heard a series of cat meows echoing faintly in the dark halls, then a swift sound, like a branch swung through the air, and he felt a powerful grip on his wrist. Yusay'ne's fingers burned as they wrapped around him, stinging more than hurting.

"Is something wrong?" she asked.

Don't act scared! "No, I just don't want to go any farther." More meowing grew near.

"Right as we were starting to get to know each other? To trust each other?" Yusay'ne said, her lips glum and pouty. "We didn't have to contact you, you know. I could have left you at that table, twiddling your thumbs, waiting for magic to spring. Here I thought you seemed reasonable, and maybe even a little grateful."

"I'm not ungrateful. Sorry," he said. *Stop shaking!*

"What do you say we stop playing games, huh, sweetie?" A low, guttural sound joined Yusay'ne's voice toward the end, a bellowing power emanating along with flashes of crimson in her gaze. She bared her teeth, and Alex noticed for the first time they were pointed, more like a shark's than a human's. Twisting her head to the side, she jerked once before falling into a dull grin. "You've got nothing to fear from me," she said. "After all, we're on the same team. I'm simply . . . curious. Never smelled one like you. What is your secret?"

"No secret." Alex held still, keeping a strong gaze with her. "And we can just forget I said anything. I'm okay to keep going."

With a sudden change of expression—from suspicious to genial—Yusay'ne released his wrist, backed away, hoisted her shoulders, and took in a huge lungful of air. "Accept my apologies. I see now you are a reasonable man," she said, sounding like a whole new person. "Mr. Barker, may I present the one you wish to see—"

Dropping to the side with a bow, as though humbled, Yusay'ne revealed a rigid, slender figure behind her, shaped like a standing missile, with a long robe swooping out beneath their shins. A high, tight collar ran up their neck, leading to a well-fitting garment of uniform material draped on a willowy body. Stylized patterns of green, yellow, and orange danced around the cloth, changing color in rolling waves, similar to Yusay'ne's dress. Circling their feet, four or five house cats rubbed against the robe, meowing in a jittery, hungry chorus. *That is so disconcerting and I don't know why.*

The tall figure's arms were behind their back, narrow chest out, with two dark inset eye cavities with white reflective dots where pupils would be. The long, stark, ancient face towered over Alex under a beam of cool moonlight, momentarily stopping the teacher's heart and breath for a flash. *This must be Nigel. Do I say that? Is "hello" offensive here?*

Luckily, the slender creature began, their voice surprising Alex with its banality. "Greetings, Archfiend. I am Nigel Roe. I understand you are new in town and, therefore, within the Rose. As such I will begin with a welcome, should you have failed to receive one. My kitties have told me you and your friend were looking to find me. If so, please say yes."

Nigel sniffed the air, and Alex began to notice that the pale of his eyes was rarely focused on him, or his cats, or anything at all. *He's blind?*

"The kitten has your tongue, I see," Nigel said, reaching into his sleeve. "Better give it back before it eats it. Meat doesn't last long in the claws of a feline. I should know." With a slow wave he opened his long hand and dropped a handful of treats on the ground.

Alex snapped to attention. "Thank you for the warm welcome." *Don't stutter. For the love of God.* "You heard right—I was hoping to speak with you."

"What could you wish to know from little old me, Mr. Barker? Unless you wish to join the ranks of those who would fight the oppressors?"

"Uh, no, not exactly, and it's Alex, but at this point you can call me whatever. Everyone else does. Call me an Imp—see if I care."

Yusay'ne tensed at the word and puffed steam out through her nostrils. The cats hissed and meowed in response before returning to their treats.

"Mr. Barker! Why on all of Earth and Un would I call a beautiful creature something as horrid as that word?" Nigel exclaimed. "Perhaps where you come from, people speak to one another in such menial ways, but not here. I live according to all polite Fovos societal standards, you know? Or do you think because I use Dread I am abhorrent? Because I once hailed from Fovos, I am unclean? We fear above all else what one would think of us should we fail to be pleasant company. You are Archfiend, yes? Of course you are. Then shame on you. We of the darkness must help one another, not smother."

"Thank you. I agree, and I apologize if I offended you," Alex said, feeling relieved. "It's nice to know there are still people who don't just throw around the term willy-nilly," he quoted his grandfather to the best of his memory, trusting his conviction was applicable to the situation. Being immigrants from Bangladesh to 1940s rural Arizona, his grandparents knew a thing or two about jerks thinking they could say hurtful things and get away with it.

And boy, if they tried, Gramps let 'em have it.

His grandfather's favorite story involved a man named Bob and his son, Rob, "both as dull as the broad side of a train," who tried to swindle him out of their gas-powered lawn mower by offering to buy it for pennies on the dollar of the original price. When Grandpa Parai said, "No, get lost," they spray-painted the words "Get out Asians" in big orange letters on their garage. *But Gramps hit 'em back.* The idiots had picked a fight with the head of loans in the only bank in town. *And weren't approved for any future refinancing options.* Sadly, Bob, Rob, and his mother, Debbie, had been forced to relocate to Utah due to financial hardship and were never seen or heard from again.

Nigel seemed pleased. "You'll hear no such language from me. The fact that my world is made from the survival instincts of this universe does not mean I wish to spread what many call fear. My people live in caves, not dung heaps like the Veen—filthy scavengers."

Yusay'ne folded her arms, looking both suspicious and embittered at Alex.

Okay, there's a big lesson learned. Don't say imp around imps. "How did you know we were seeking you out?" Alex asked jovially, trying to steer the conversation.

"My boy, reading intentions is one of my specialties," Nigel said. "A soul within the Rose wreaking of Wrath and speaking my name is hard not to pay attention to, especially when so many have come before you. I assume you want to know the same thing they did. Go on, say it."

"I want to ask you about the demon in the boy."

"Of course you do. It's all anyone can talk about anymore, isn't it?" Nigel said woefully. "The Archfiend who's ruining the fun for the rest of us. Wish I'd never met him. Everything I've said was published by the Trivium Exodus—you can read it for yourself."

"I know," Alex said confidently. "I want to know what you didn't tell the reporters, or the Senate."

"Didn't? Whatever do you mean?" Nigel asked.

"There's no point in hiding it. I know he told you more because I met him too. Last week." Alex lied the only way he knew how: by telling the truth. "I know what it's like to be in Joseph's presence. But . . . there's no one I can talk to. Please. We could swap stories. What do you say?" He knelt to pet one of the cats that had approached him, congratulating himself on a fib well told. *Even the cat's convinced.*

Nigel released a scratchy laugh and smiled. "Ah, so you have also seen the nameless? Here now it all begins to make sense. Yusay'ne, thank you for your help. I will accompany our friend from here."

"I don't think that's a good idea," she argued.

Nigel waved her off. "It is perfectly all right. I do not think young Alexander will harm me. In fact, he's the most gentle Archfiend I've ever met. Take the rest of the night off. Go, enjoy the party. Seek out a few rounds in the Bahc Pits. Why not? Someone's bound to defeat you eventually. Perhaps tonight is the night?"

Yusay'ne sneered at his patronizing tone. "Very well." Turning to Alex, she gave a slight, respectful nod. "Mr. Barker, I enjoyed our chat. Come and see us again soon." Slinking down the hall, she soon disappeared into the darkness. *Bet she suspects something.*

"You've no idea how reassuring it is to meet another like me," Nigel said once they were alone. "I've been disavowed. My life threatened. I fear I will be labeled a liar unless the worst comes to pass, in which case, it will hardly matter. Tell me, have you told anyone you've seen Joseph?"

"No," Alex answered.

"Don't. They will only ridicule you. If I could go back in time and stop myself from reporting the damn thing, I would. I'm only blind of Earthly sight, not of common sense. I know it's led to the very tensions currently in the UnEarth Senate, but three other eyewitnesses have corroborated, and still the headlines read 'Nigel Roe—Poet of Death.' Can you imagine? Using my love of poetry against me to sell news. All I did was tell the truth, which, take it from me, is the scariest thing of all."

Nigel started down the service tunnel, moving even farther away from the club. His cats followed, crowding his feet. "Please, walk with an old UnEarth creature. I need to use these legs or they'll wither and fade." He left space beside him for Alex.

"Sure. Yeah." Alex gulped, hurrying to meet the tall, thin man in the robe. *Okay, caution up. Be ready for anything, but don't look like you're ready for anything.* "Could you tell me what the demon—the nameless, whatever—told you?" he asked.

Nigel gestured with his chopstick fingers. "No, first I wish to hear your tale, Mr. Barker. Where and how did you meet the enigmatic Joseph?"

"Africa," Alex answered. "Outside of Cairo. Wraithians attacked, and he was with them. I've seen some scary things in my day, but that takes the cake." *Real good demon talk, Alex. Ugh.*

"So, he did make it across the sea. I had no doubt. What of his quest? I assume it's all he spoke of—his obsession with a certain set of rocks."

"Yeah, the Brothers, or something. The guy sounded like a nut," Alex said.

"I curse the day I first heard of the Brothers of Gehenna. One chance meeting has haunted me ever since and will probably continue to do so. At first, I assumed Joseph was an Archfiend. He did not appear as most possessed mortals do, and his Wrath was strong. He thought of no custom and gave no damn as to what anyone thought of his actions. The most independently minded of your kind I've ever encountered since meeting Yusay'ne. Fabulous, isn't she? One of the Niel Nulus, you know. Also one of a kind. You will never find a more humble, inquisitive Fiend. She has changed the way I view your species. I often feel you think as a hive mind—a dumb one, at that. No offense."

"None taken," Alex said.

"I thought Joseph was perhaps recently born or one of a new batch of Purged," Nigel admitted. "The Senate regularly cleans house every century or so, just to keep those of us below on edge and well reminded of our plebian status. And the new generations feel different, don't they? Each less pure than the one previous, all thanks to the rotten Eve draining off this planet like mold in a sewer pipe. Mark my words, the humans will be the death of us, far before any new war has the chance to do so."

"So, he sought you out? What for?" Alex asked.

"It was an unusual exchange, to be sure. I asked this Joseph if he wanted a drink. He refused but agreed to tell me a little of his tale. He needed passage and knew I've spent a majority of my time traveling. Seems he had trouble moving about the human world. Not so unusual when speaking of an UnEarth Human. Little did I know . . ."

Alex spotted a dark section in the hall approaching where an obstructed overhead window blocked the moonlight. "Did he eventually tell you what this Gehenna was?" he asked.

"That's all he talked about," Nigel replied. "He said it is a place rumored to be where sin itself was created, active long ago. So long that even the oldest in UnEarth knew not of it—from back when man first learned to hate. Fascinating story. The shepherds of the Wrath were a people who'd mastered the art of collecting the essence of destruction. These vessels, called the Brothers of Gehenna, sounded very important—a rumored source of unthinkable power."

One cat meowed angrily. The rest echoed.

"And what do you think he wants this power for?" Alex asked as dryly as possible. *Just stay calm. Everything will be fine.*

"One could only guess what possibilities lie within the Brothers soaked in sin," Nigel added solemnly. "It is just a story, after all. Though the demon did speak ill of Lucifer-Aveyl. Quite a lot, now that I think of it. Perhaps he had designs on the throne he intended to achieve through machinations? However, I did not find this particular Archfiend to seem power hungry. Determined, yes, but also tired—like a being looking for quiet, rather than conquest. But I've been wrong before. Needless to say, I did not like what I sensed."

More drawn-out meows came from below.

"And did you help him?" Alex asked, feeling unease growing in his gut.

"Of course not. I've worked far too hard harnessing good relationships with my contacts, benefactors, and otherwise," Nigel said. "I couldn't have risked my reputation on a creature as lowly as he. I'm sure you understand."

It sounded as though Nigel was wrapping up the conversation. *Fine by me.* "I understand," Alex said. "Well, if that's it, I'll say thank you and stop taking up your precious time—" He saved himself from stuttering on the "t."

"Please. Not necessary. I live to talk," Nigel said warmly. "But to do so, I must first listen. One thing I have not heard, Mr. Barker, is your own intentions for the future. Why do you come here, to this club, with a being smelling of Rapture, looking for an unnamed creature now named Joseph, who is searching for the Brothers of Gehenna? I trust you have encountered the demon. But now I want to know what's inside your heart." His tone lowered. The meows went up in pitch. "For I have my suspicions."

Alex's insides twitched as he and Nigel passed through the shadowed section of the hall. Glancing up at Nigel, whose black eyes shimmered in the darkness, the teacher nearly gasped when the pale man's face turned down to him. *Can he . . . see?*

"One more thing the demon said prior to leaving." Nigel's jaw snapped up and down, his voice dropping another tone, growing even scratchier. "I knew I'd smelled it once before—this strange blend of Wrath. What was the added element I couldn't place?"

The cats' meows were becoming voracious. Alex considered firing up his Wrath, just in case. *Feeling a little agitated here.*

Nigel continued. "When the savage admitted it, Joseph, I confess I went berserk. To find out I was speaking with a human vessel? A mortal bonded with the Eve, cavorting freely! Can you imagine? Empowered by it! The idea is disgusting beyond rebuttal. I demanded he leave and never return. The whoreson agreed, but not before telling me that others like him might be sent to find him—sent by Medolians—on a mission." Nigel stopped in his tracks, his black eyes with white pupils fixed on Alex. "Imagine my surprise when news of the Senate's plan reached my ears. I never believed I would meet one of the chosen human delegates."

Alex's heart skipped a beat. "No idea what you're talking about. I've never even met a Medolian. Avoid them like the human plague. I avoid humans, too. Sorry to be rude, but I should get back to my partner—"

Before Alex could step away, Nigel took the teacher by the shoulders. His long fingers ran over him like heavy spider legs, keeping him in place. A low growl shook Alex's spine. "Mortals?" Nigel said as though he'd just been told he'd ingested poison. "In this place? A sanctuary of UnEarth?"

More meowing, louder than ever.

Nigel Roe's white pupils began to glow like lightning bugs. His lips spread wide, revealing inches of indigo-shaded gumline. Words escaped, dripping with disgust. "The demon in the boy will be caught and tried, but not by you. Never by a foul, impure wretch. The Medolians and the Senate have truly lost their ability to regulate if this is their solution."

Alex fought to get his arms free, squirming away from Nigel's face, a snarl of malice growing upon it.

"I will pump you full of fear, slit your throat, and drink your juice," Nigel said. "Your Dread will ascend to Fovos. Your blood, ripe with it, will give me strength. I adore the taste of human flesh,

Alexander. As do my kitties. Your mixture of Wrath and flesh will be an exquisite treat. I shall have to thank whoever sent you here. They've given me a wonderful meal."

A thin line stretched from the middle of Nigel Roe's forehead, down between his eyes, to his chin. The line—a skin flap Alex had failed to see in the dark—lifted. With a quick, wet breath, Nigel exhaled, and the slit down his face opened outward like double doors. His jaw and skull were cleaved wide, leaving his fat tongue dripping saliva onto his robe.

The small, button eyes of the old blind man were revealed as shimmering insectoid lenses under his skull, dark and empty as space. The mass around them was a web of red and yellow tendons, torn, shifting and snapping among sharp crimson and bone-colored protrusions, like bursts of light. The open cavity below Nigel's upper teeth roared over Alex, assaulting him with vicious, wet breath, rocketing his Wrath to the surface and taking hold of his mind before he could have a heart attack.

Kill it!

Clenching his fist tightly, he lit it aflame. Alex's arm launched up, connecting with the underside of what was once Nigel's face, now worse than any nightmare he'd ever had, sending sparks and ash exploding out. The cats scattered as the mouth cavity shrieked, buying him a few seconds. Wrestling away from Nigel's clawlike grip, Alex stumbled free, but the monster's frame was soon over him. With a swift dodge, Alex flung himself to the side, ready to attack, wishing his fists would light up as brightly as they had when Yuri was about to be killed. But before he could throw a punch, Nigel's splayed hand swatted him with a resounding clap. Soaring, Alex slammed into the wall, feeling his insides jam up. Landing hurt, too.

Nigel's open face screamed like a jet engine streaking by as he leaped into the air, arms and legs outstretched. *This is your chance!* Pulling his arm back, Alex imagined striking Nigel to the moon and gritted his teeth. *I hate you! Got it? Hate you!* His fist sprang to life as the monster came down upon him. *CRACK!* Burning knuckles connected with the jagged bone protrusions in Nigel's "face." A long spike snapped off, stuck in Alex's hand, as the monster was sent soaring into the ceiling, collapsing in a dusty mess of concrete that Alex was too busy running like Hell in the other direction to notice. When he yanked the barb from his hand, scorching blood oozed free, sizzling on the ground as he ran. Behind him, Nigel screamed like a titanic, rabid bat. *Scythe—this. Bad. Got it!*

The end of the hallway finally came into view. *There's a door! I can make it! I can make it!* Alex pushed himself, his legs burning. Then he heard the same hushed whisper that had called his name in the Thai restaurant just before he'd died. *Alex?* The voice was louder this time, but the speaker's identity remained a mystery.

Then came a flash before his eyes, so powerful it blotted out the rest of reality. Melissa was before him, as clear as day, her expression wiped with pain. Blood ran down her face in interconnecting rivers, joining red tears streaming from her eyes, soaked in crimson. She screamed in silence. Clutched in each hand was a dove, stained red, dead and broken, gone limp, dripping blood. Alex felt his insides turn as if he were on a roller coaster, and heard a deafening pop. Reality came back long enough for him to hear what sounded like leather flapping all around him, just before something akin to a dozen needles stabbed into his back and he was lifted off his feet, crying out in agony.

The tall creature below him shrieked and clamped its jaw onto his shoulder. Rage erupt in the teacher, with little he could do about it. His hands blazed like red-hot coals, and his chest gushed scalding steam. *You wanna do this? Fine.* When he touched down, Alex kicked back against the wall as hard as he could, sending both he and Nigel Roe rocketing backward at breakneck speed, crashing through three consecutive walls. *Whoa! I can do that?* Sharp chunks of concrete and steel flew by as Nigel's throat hole released satisfying howls of pain. Alex tumbled through a fourth wall with the monster, where they were assaulted by the bombastic music of the Rose's Platinum Hall.

Dust and rock scattered across the dance floor as Alex landed on top of Nigel, feeling the Scythe's body wracked against stone shapes. *Ha! Serves you right.* Rolling away, Alex nimbly leaped to his feet. Keeping a hateful gaze on his attacker, he gradually acknowledged the silenced clubgoers gathered around him, gawking with even more shock than he had expected. Feeling a sudden breeze, he realized his shirt was torn open. The crowd was agape, not just at the intrusion, but also at the blazing bull-head brand glowing across his chest. *Ah . . . shoot.*

From the rubble pile, Nigel screamed, "It's a human! The humans from the mandate are here!"

Like a gun had gone off, the crowd scattered as Nigel spun up from the ground and flung himself after Alex.

Not wanting to wait for the attack to come to him, Alex charged at the monstrosity, darting through the panicking crowd until he collided with the Scythe. Focusing on keeping Nigel's cockroach face from ripping out his jugular, Alex flung them both through a row of cocktail tables near the bar, finding himself enjoying doing so. *It's my first bar fight! Wait until Melissa hears about this.*

"Relent, Mr. Barker!" Nigel's throat hole spat out. "I must feast on your soul!"

Alex sent a fist into the gap between his skull, where it sizzled like a wet ribeye on a scalding grill, drawing a horrendous scream from the pale Scythe.

Stumbling away, whimpering, Nigel called to the rafters, "Yu-say'ne! I was wrong! It wasn't easy! Where are you?"

Looking up just in time, Alex spotted Nigel's bodyguard leaping from the second-story landing. She landed gracefully and moved like a goddamn giant bird, lost in the scattered crowd. *Shoot—shoot. Not good.* Feeling a presence behind him, he spun, ready to attack, stopping just short of impaling a familiar soldier's face.

"Bennett?" Alex cried.

His partner pointed behind Alex and yanked him out of the way just as a shimmering orange flash soared by. Yusay'ne landed behind them in a cluster of warring patrons, again lost.

"Where in th' Hell were youuuu!?" Bennett slurred.

"Are you . . . drunk?" Alex shouted. Bennett answered by laughing madly and shaking his head.

The sea of bodies split as Yusay'ne charged out once more and tackled Bennett. Before Alex could help, Nigel was upon him, his grotesque face like a tiny red jungle, snapping with jagged teeth. Alex turned his baseball cap down so he didn't have to see it as he assaulted Nigel's slender body. Connecting against his ribs, cracking several, he sent the old Scythe into a frenzy. Clawed hands raked over Alex's back and opened fresh contusions, washing his skin with hot blood as the teacher pressed on, feeling a sense of desperation and the need to survive take hold.

His mind flashed with white light, and he was once again faced by her. Melissa stood stark naked before him—a pure being. Her gaze connected with his for a blissful moment before the rivers returned. Blood ran down her face as her expression morphed from peace to pain. Gripping the blood-soaked doves until they were crushed in her hands, she screamed, releasing no sound. A fire of UnEarth wrapped around him and Melissa, scorching her flesh but not his. Smoke billowed around Alex until everything went black, and reality took hold of his consciousness, revealing that he was locked in a struggle with Nigel, their arms intertwined.

Judging by the frustration in the Scythe's cries, Alex, the "weak human," was baffling him. *He expected me to be a free meal, but I could break this guy if I wanted to. If I brought up enough hate.* As tempting as it was, the notion terrified Alex.

Across the dance floor, Bennett was taking hits, but giving out few of his own. When a short bar patron with hairy, bulky arms and a smile the size of a watermelon struck him in the lower spine, Bennett went to the ground. *To heck with this!* Alex hurled the Scythe to the side and darted for the dance floor, where his partner was being surrounded and beaten by angry UnEarth clubgoers. Charging up, Alex leaped and landed in the middle of the crowd, blasting them away like a stack of beanbags hit with a rock. Grabbing as many throats as he could, pounding in as many faces as possible, Alex felt a glorious sense of relief wash over him. With Bennett freed, the duo backpedaled onto the dance floor, just in time to spot club security arriving.

Guards and clubgoers alike circled them. Bodies shifted in the lasers rebounding across the club as the humans faced a constricting ring of fangs, claws, glowing eyes, and tails dancing in the air. Nigel and Yusay'ne made their way to the front, Nigel's face snapped back to the guise of an old blind man—weak and tired (*after an ass whooping!*).

"That one tried to kill me! Don't let them escape!" Nigel pointed his long finger at Alex.

"So, any bright ideas?" Alex asked over Bennett's shoulder.

The soldier turned and gave a silent, dull-eyed stare. "You're kidding, right?"

Definitely drunk.

"Ilsa often speaks of the tens of thousands of UnEarth Humans living on Earth, banished from their homes [. . .] stripped of their life force, and made to live among humanity.

. . . there are ways to gain back one's Eve, she says. As the energy is gathered, in many cases ingested, the process of transforming into their 'true selves' begins."

- Excerpts from the journal of
Dr. Francisco Emul. Murcia
October 1894

SONGS IN GLASS

Bennett took inventory of the security guards. There were four behind and five in front, sandwiching him and Alex in the tight stone stairwell. *Fuck me.* The staff of La Rose Noire were impeccably dressed in green suits with bright cyan ties, their blond hair shimmering like gold in the afternoon sun, even in the darkness, and all looked mad as shit to be in the presence of humans. Just a few moments ago (*but it seems like a week*), he and Alex had been back to back, surrounded by clubgoers from the *Twilight Zone* who were ready to swarm them in the Platinum Hall of La Rose Noire. After a brief tussle, Bennett was forcibly grabbed and arrested by a woman with broad shoulders, sunken cheeks, and a tight bun of blonde hair tucked under a chauffeur's cap. Her name tag read—*Chief Mary? Hrm, she's like an Amazon. Always did like those.*

The chief and her staff calmed the remaining crowd and managed to bring order—at least Bennett assumed so. *Couldn't tell ya.* It was all a blur, and he was still wrestling with the effects of the horrible

UnEarth libation moss when he and Alex were led through the hostile crowd in restraints. *Never drinking again. I mean it this time.*

Saliva sprayed his face as all manner of "death to the human" rhetoric was screamed in their direction. With his eyes closed, Bennett could see Eve flashing all around them, some in shades he'd never sensed before. The towering Chief Mary was awash in a deep cyan, similar to the Medolian Mara but subdued by comparison. *And whatever shade she is makes me feel downright naughty. Gotta say. Definitely bagging her groceries.*

Beside the chief, the shortest of the Rose guards continued prodding Bennett onward with a sick air of delight, carrying a much brighter hue, closer to a green apple. He also wouldn't stop smiling like a freaky haunted-house munchkin. Despite how much Bennett loathed looking at the guy, a sudden joy washed over him when he did, like a sneeze. *This feeling's new.* However, a falseness was apparent in the happiness. Bennett knew damn well he wasn't actually happy, joyful, or any other form of content at the moment. *Come on, stop it with this shit. I haven't felt this many emotions in my entire life. How do I get it to slow down?*

Bennett pondered his Rapturous powers as they were escorted through what seemed like half a mile of back hallways and eventually up the cold stairwell they were currently climbing. The spiraling stone steps, going round and round a central column, gave Bennett the impression they were in a medieval castle, marching to the highest room in the tallest tower where a princess might lay in waiting. *Probably just more assholes, though.* With his head starting to clear, the soldier was feeling better, but Alex was faring worse with each step. Even without sensing his Eve, he could tell that his slight companion was swimming in anxiety and dealing with a mess of pain thanks to the wound on his shoulder, courtesy of Nigel Roe. *Split-faced freak.* The blood seeping out of the wound showed no signs of stopping either. On Barker's pale face was the look of a man about to pass out. *Seen it a thousand times.*

Eventually, the stairwell opened onto a broad landing, where a heavy pair of double doors rested at the end of an inlet topped with a rounded stone roof. Two guards, equal in stature to Chief Mary, stood posted outside.

"Does she know we're here?" Mary asked as they approached.

"She knows," the guard on the right replied, her scent reminiscent of the woman who attacked Alex. *Wrath. Different from Al's, though. It's getting easier to tell them apart.*

Each of the door guards grasped a handle and swung the gilded gates inward, allowing the group to enter. Before they could see or hear anything, Bennett's nose was assaulted by a medley of odors: herbs and spices, fruits and vegetables, a tangy sweetness he couldn't identify, and countless others too numerous to sort through. The familiar scent of sweat took over, mingled with tobacco, a few drugs he was versed with, postcoital air, and—*gasoline?*

The office stretched twenty yards from side to side and felt much deeper than that, dotted with tiny lights that sparkled like a mini galaxy. Rows of silver billiard tables lined the front, their industrial cocktail lights casting a glow over players as they leaned in to take their shots. Those drinking and lounging on couches were shrouded in shadow and smoke, rising in cumulous plumes along the room's outer edge, filling the space with a dreamlike haze. The mix of sights and sounds—from the clatter of pool balls to muffled laughter—set an oddly vibrant yet sinister tone.

Above, colorful windows interspersed along a balcony running the length of the office were tinted and packed with air bubbles, lightly obscuring the heaps of nude bodies grinding on the other side. The animalistic moans, spankings, and screams from the orgies were drowned out by the electronic music playing a beat far too fast to comfortably groove to in the office. Taking it in with slow breaths, Bennett assessed the layout.

Only seeing one exit. Super. He and Alex were forced to the center of the room, where a broad, smooth, silky-topped desk rested.

"Oh my God," Alex said, jolting Bennett's heart.

"What? What is it?" Bennett asked.

"That is the most beautiful desk I've ever seen."

Bennett was so mad he could've punched Alex's lights out right there, but the broiling rage made him feel oddly tired, as if he'd gone sprinting and gotten winded. Also, his "sixth sense" of feeling Eve was noticeably repressed while the anger lasted. Trying to calm himself, and regain the strength, he glanced at the desk, and found himself agreeing with Alex. "No. Actually, you're right. That's amazing."

The craftsmanship of the desk acted as a strange salve to his inner turmoil. *Pretty obvious I have to get my anger under control. So, whatever helps.* As Bennett calmed, his new senses returned, clearer than ever. *Starting to understand what this Rapture wants from me. I think. It's a fine fucking line, though.*

The desk was also a mesmerizing distraction from the imminent danger surrounding them. It looked sturdy enough to withstand a collision with Bennett's Ford and walk away without a scratch, its swirling trim of violet and green flowing seamlessly with no hard edges to be found. Behind it, an empty chair glimmered, crafted from black pearl and adorned with cyan and silver inlets, scattered with shimmering diamonds.

Beyond the desk, the majority of the room was filled with a stunning miniature city of glass and vertical metal tubes, dotted with gauges, timers, and twinkling sensor lights. Vats, pressure cookers, and distilleries rose like high-rises within the skyline of twisting brass towers that disappeared into the murky ceiling, while below, beakers and pint glasses cluttered endless countertop space, intermingled with potted plants and bowls of vibrant fruits and vegetables. There were burlap sacks filled with what appeared to be dried beans, tea leaves, and possibly uncured coffee; as well as roots, weeds, and literal tons of other colorful ingredients that Bennett couldn't begin to identify. Steam rising from boiling pots infused the air with green, blue, and yellow vapor, fogging the cylinders with a foamy mildew. Lastly, Bennett noticed a couple of jars of moss, which made him throw up a little in his mouth.

From within the glass metropolis, a sultry, granular voice began to sing, its vibrations creating a ghostly chorus.

"Oh, a diamond would be grand, when its face bears not a crack.
From Mother Earth, we take the jewel, and never give it back.
In a whispered wood, her nectar finds us weeping for a soul.
In a body destined for the dirt beneath a grassy knoll.
Amen."

"Beautiful," Bennett said overly loudly when the verse finished, earning a baton to the spine.

"Coming from a human male, that word means nothing, darling," the hidden singer replied before addressing Chief Mary curtly. "Anywhere is fine, Constance."

"Hang on." Bennett glanced over his shoulder. "Your full title is Chief of Security Constance Mary?"

"You got a problem with that?" she shot back, her tone threatening, but also a complete turn-on.

Bennett threw his hands up preemptively. "Nope. No. Love it, actually."

"Please, Constance," the voice continued, "no need for more violence. There's already been too much of it tonight. In the Rose we treat everyone with respect. Even when we don't know who they are, why they're here, or if they had a good reason for turning my darling little nightclub into an American Old West saloon."

"You're absolutely right. We're being rude," Bennett said, digging up his father's lessons on playing up manners. *Makes it easier to con people.* "Forgive us. My name is Bennett Hunter, and this is Al Barker."

"We're partners," Alex interjected.

"Loosely connected associates," Bennett corrected.

"Good to know you, Bennett and Al, the infamous humans in-stilled with Eve." She paused, and Bennett got the feeling she was studying him and Alex from the shadows between the pipes. "You look surprised. Of course I know exactly who you are—I'm Madam Daphne, for Eve's sake. Word is spreading, you know? Some say you perished already, blown up when they tried to imbue you. Others claim you became abominations who needed to be put down. Your arrival has a lot of people agitated, I must say. Not that I care one way or another what happens on Hywyn, or even on Trivium, for that matter. But one thing I will not tolerate is my guests having their evenings ruined."

Damn. There goes our cover. Gotta go with the truth . . . Hope I remember it.

"If you know who we are, you know why we're here," Bennett said. "Again, we're very sorry, ma'am. We didn't want you to get mixed up in our business."

"For the duration of this conversation, you will both address me as Madam Daphne. Do I make myself as clear as Hywyn crystal?"

"Yes, Madam Daphne," Bennett and Alex said in unison.

"I'm a retired UnEarth Senator, former lord of Nashwyn, and a prominent Wyst of the Maldrimo Order, all of which demands respect. The Rose is mine. Every brick, from first to last, was placed by my will. Not my hands, of course. No, that work is far too garish for my delicate skin, but it was my vision, you see, that brought it all together. Yes. My Eve is in every inch. My breath filled the Rose with life. And now my brothers, sisters, and everything in between can join me for a drink and fulfill all their wanton desires while in a place of peace. The only place of peace in all of Heaven and Earth, mind you."

"Of course, Madam Daphne," Bennett began. "It's very nice to meet you. Compared to some of the greetings we've been receiving lately, this is a hug and a sugar cookie. We're sorry it's happening under these circumstances, though. Please know that neither of us would do anything to bring harm to your establishment or its clientele. On purpose, at least."

One of the pool players broke a rack like a shotgun blast. The sound reverberated through the steel table. Alex jolted, eliciting laughter from the smokers on the couches.

"I'm not mad about the damage, darling. Sometimes things break when passion is involved," Madam Daphne said. "Nothing wrong with that."

"What *are* you mad about?" Bennett asked, receiving another crack in the back from Mary. "What? I'm just asking a question."

The chief was downright scowling. "No one gets to speak to her like that. Let alone you." *My God, could you be any sexier?*

Madam Daphne laughed. "I haven't decided what I'm mad about, human Bennett, but anger is an emotion I rarely feel. Dealing with it, I'm sure you can imagine, is hard. Did you know you're the only humans I've ever allowed upstairs? In the eight hundred years I've provided service to the downtrodden of this forsaken planet, no man or woman—no matter how powerful, or well-connected— has ever set foot in this office. Human presidents, dictators, CEOs, all permanently held at arm's reach. The agreements we've made with the powerful of your kind are quite permanent, thanks to mortal men being so damn easy to purchase, and a global society that judges one another for seeking pleasures. Something I deplore, mind you, but in the end, useful. Most countries believe we are a simple drug enterprise that their economies rely on, operating at the highest level in the shadows. So far, everyone has been happy."

"Any drugs I would've tried?" Bennett asked, a little hopeful.

"I hate to judge by appearance, hon, but I would guess no, you have not," Madam Daphne replied. "Of course, there's a first time for everything. Constance, please, give him a taste."

"Bennett, no," Alex whined, leaning his head to the side.

"I'm just curious," Bennett assured him, whispering. "They know who we are. We have to be cool, okay? Can you do that?"

The teacher gave a weak nod as Chief Mary reappeared from the darkness of the corner she'd slipped into, holding a shot glass. Inside was a purple liquid, faintly glowing, with a sheen of silver on its surface, like oil on water. Bennett hesitated when Chief Mary offered him the glass, opting instead for a sniff. Without an ounce of scent, it stunned Bennett, who suddenly felt as if he'd just sniffed a million perfumes at an expensive lingerie shop while hanging out with the Dallas Cowboys cheerleaders on a nudist beach—on a good dick day—and the girls all needed help with their suntan lotion, especially up their ass cracks.

"What's it called?" he asked with a squeak, pulling away before pitching a full tent.

"Its production title is Kabungahan-Soli, which I find quite attractive," Madam Daphne said, "though I must admit, pretty much everyone calls it Soli, or Soul Weed, which I'm less than fond of. You might say a little bit of me is inside every drop."

Bennett waved off the shot. "No, thank you. I recently gave up drugs, and alcohol. Sort of saw the light, I guess. *Heh.*"

With a bored shrug Chief Mary took the shot and tossed away the glass, letting it crash behind her as she wiped her mouth. "You know life's for living, right?" *Oh baby, do I ever.*

He couldn't take his eyes off the chief and was probably drooling a little, though she hardly seemed to care. Needing a distraction from Constance Mary, whose Eve was twisting Bennett's balls into a knot, he tried to find Madam Daphne amid the sparkling assemblage of pipes.

She continued. "Even a diluted supply is worth enough to gain protection from any human government. Most have already stepped in line. I scarcely lift a finger. Amazing what your leaders prioritize. We give them the means to keep your brethren vigorous and high, thereby making them easier to control, and in return we're left alone. Easy as Cantsbury pie. Now, I'd like to move on to what you both were doing here tonight. It's strange to think two humans could be pulled from death and given the Wrath and Rapture without my knowledge. The Senate during my time would *never* have allowed such a thing. Yet, it happened, and the chosen humans have found their way here, bringing their problems—Tribunal problems—into my establishment."

Amid the anarchic chemistry set, there was movement: a poof of colorful smoke and blue fire, and something shimmering like rainbow trout skin. "Quite frankly, you've caught me at a bad time. I'm very busy. As you can see, or maybe you can't, I am an experimenter. At the moment I am creating a new brew for my Archfiend-friendly clients. They need a particularly intense experience, don't they? Something potent. Knowing the things the Archfiend have seen and done in their existence is something I must endure. I must understand it if I am to take the pain away. Sometimes that seems impossible with a creature born in Arros, but after all these years—hey—I still try. I am a Wyst, after all. Passion is our doctrine."

Another puff of smoke, green this time.

"I love to craft experiences for my kind, creatures born of human souls. That's what this place is, a haven where the banished can be their old selves and find what this planet took away. A place to put the Fervor back in their lives, to give them something that makes them feel like they were fucked to perfection. Or are, themselves, the perfect fucker. Who doesn't love to fuck? Best thing about Earth, by far. Everyone knows it. No one says it.

"Tell you what—I'll do the same for you, my guests. I'll concoct the perfect brew, one for each of you, specially tailored to your aura, and this drink will do just that—fuck you."

Bennett raised an eyebrow. "Not sure if I want a drink to fuck me, but go ham on Al."

"You'll love it, I promise," Madam Daphne said excitedly.

Alex shot Bennett a silent "*Why?*" through his swelling face.

"I've had so little experience treating humans," Madam Daphne continued. "It's an amazing opportunity for practice. Your kind is so . . . sensitive. Never truly happy, are you? Humans. *Hrm.* They require finesse."

Bennett could hear her getting to work within the glass and metal workshop, catching glimpses of movement and flashes of light and color. A chopping sound echoed as knives sliced into something plump and juicy, followed by the whir of an industrial blender.

"Madam Daphne," Bennett began, "as I'm sure you've heard by now, we did not come here of our own accord. From what little we've seen, your world needs us to succeed—and soon. We're here to gather information on a fugitive."

"As did all the others who came for Roe. That man should learn to keep his mouth shut. His incessant need for attention is directly responsible for the sorry state our politics are in." She turned up the power on the blender until Bennett thought something might explode. With an excited yelp, she switched it off. "Points for civility, young one, but I heard no apology in there for destroying my property. While I feel pity for your situation, the Tribunal sent undercover agents to my Rose—human undercover agents, no less—looking to interrogate a known commère informateur. A line was crossed, and fate has decided that you two will bear the weight of its consequences."

"What'd she say, Al?" Bennett asked.

"Like, a backstabber or tattletale, I think," Alex replied.

Madam Daphne chuckled. "Oui. So, Mr. Barker has a mind to make up for his body?"

A female figure stretched and squashed in the glass tubing like a house of mirrors. Three or four misshapen Madam Daphnes approached the edge of a table. By the time they reached the end, they had merged into one. She stepped out from behind the last golden metal silo, holding a tray with a shimmering drink atop.

When Bennett got a good look at her, he felt a literal guffaw come on—an old term he'd heard his dickhead father use a dozen times, now finally making sense. Her hips, shaped like a nonmetaphorical hourglass, swayed from side to side with the weight of a ship's anchor on a short chain, while her long legs, like exclamation points, dove in front of one another, propelling her with effortless grace. The hair bouncing above her head, as fiery as a sunrise, had so much volume it could've been supported by chicken wire. She was the most peculiar—and at the same time, the most enticing—woman he had ever seen.

I'm so confused right now.

Closing his eyes to focus on her aura, he found a near-overwhelming, churning fire of cyan, with flashes of indigo, violet, and hints of canary yellow. The feelings were potent: passion, desire, and jealous obsession assaulted him, reminiscent of when he used to see other men flirting with his favorite strippers.

Opening his eyes, he found Madam Daphne sashaying up to them, holding out a beautiful turquoise drink with a glowing red center to Alex.

"I'm not much of a drinker," Alex said.

"This isn't a simple beverage, my boy. This is a journey." She offered it persuasively, puckering her giant, rubbery lips.

"Will it do anything strange to me?" the teacher asked.

"It should calm you down, for one. Which you seem to be in desperate need of."

"It's true. He is," Bennett agreed.

"I don't have a name for it yet," Madam Daphne said. "Just something I whipped up, and I certainly won't force you to drink. It's nothing malicious. Why would it be? You boys are acting delegates of the Senate. Not as if I could kill you. Ha!"

She lingered, keeping her immense eyes on Alex, seeming more like a painting than a person. She reminded Bennett of something from one of the anime porn catalogues his Marine teammate usually had stashed under his mattress. *George Svenko. My spotter. Fucker put mayonnaise on everything. And I do mean everything.*

Alex still hadn't taken the drink off the tray. "Should I?"

"You're a big boy. I don't care," Bennett said.

"Fine." Alex took the drink and tried to kick it back like a shot. Most of it was coughed out. Swallowing what he could, the teacher's face lit up. "Hey, that's pretty good!"

"See, I knew it," Madam Daphne exclaimed with a bright smile, wiping the last drops off Alex's lips with her thumb. "I can tell who a person is. You, you're easy."

Taking the glass from him, she turned to her desk, revealing three long tendrils spilling from the back of her head, swaying at their own pace, as independently minded as cat tails. *How did I miss those? Shit.* Their skin bore a two-toned shimmering effect of blue and green, reminding Bennett of the time he'd seen and touched a dolphin's skin while tripping on acid at Myrtle Beach.

"Has no one told you it's not polite to stare?" she asked without turning around.

"Don't mean to," Bennett said. "Just never seen, well—"

"My kind before?"

"Yeah."

"I suppose it would be strange for a people who've spent their days reading about grand creatures in books or seeing them on television to fully grasp the reality of their existence. The human rhetoric alone—I'm sure your minds are incapable of understanding what we of UnEarth really are or what the both of you have stepped into."

"We didn't step into this thing, lady," Bennett said. "It was thrust on us. All we did was get murdered at the wrong time."

"You just told me your first lie. I despise feeling those. Don't do it ever again," Madam Daphne said resolutely, silencing Bennett.

"We might understand a lot better than you think," Alex said, grinning like an old drunk uncle at a wedding dance, luckily too buzzed to grasp that Madam Daphne might have just revealed Bennett's suicide.

As she drifted behind her desk, seeming to float into the black pearl chair, Madam Daphne scanned them, running her fingers along the side of her desk. "So, humans, shall we settle the matter of the damage to my club?"

Alex spoke up, stumbling a few steps first. "I'm sorry. Feeling a little loose after that drink. Madam Daphne, I only wanted to say I didn't mean to go where we weren't supposed to. Nigel attacked *me*. I was just defending myself. God's honest truth."

Madam Daphne's eyes narrowed at him. "God? Is that a joke? Why do you speak as you do? You're filled with Wrath—where is it? Can you even snarl? Or are you submissive before your Rapture-bound partner?"

"What? No," Alex said defiantly. Bennett laughed a little.

Madam Daphne grew quiet and contemplative, then released a grunt. "Roe . . . I was hoping never to hear his name again. Every time I do, the stench lasts in my place for years. Still, once he sets foot in the Rose, he is protected, as are all UnEarth creatures."

Alex hiccupped. "Scuse me."

"Why would you want or trust any information you'd receive from such a creature?" she asked. "Who sent you?"

"You said it yourself—the Tribunal, whatever the Hell that is," Bennett replied.

"Fuck me—you're like children, aren't you? I mean who *specifically*, darling," Madam Daphne demanded. "Who was tasked with carrying out this charade? I want a name and the specifics of your mission. Remember, you can't lie," she finished, staring daggers.

Bennett treaded lightly. "Not sure what we're at liberty to say. We can tell you that as far as we know, we're independent arbiters, working on behalf of Arros and Hywyn—"

"Oh, give it up. I know it was the Medolians," Madam Daphne interrupted. "Possessions are their jurisdiction. But not Mara, the one with brains. No, this sounds more like Izaiah—only he would do something like this. It's too good an opportunity to mingle with his precious humans. Now, what of this Joseph? The rogue demon. What can you tell me about him?"

"How do you know his name?" Alex asked. "Izaiah said the UnEarth public—"

"I'm not the public, dear," Madam Daphne replied. "Trivium City doesn't go dark for no reason, and Speaker Binahq and Minority Leader Van Mortus do not mince words. If Hywyn and Arros are ready to declare war over one Archfiend, there's a lot more going on behind the scenes than a possession gone wrong. Someone knows something and isn't sharing it with the rest of us."

At that moment, the main door to Madam Daphne's office was struck from the other side with a bang. Every face in the office turned to see a man in a stained white T-shirt backing into the room, dragging along a custodial cart. Severely skinny, yet tall, he had a thin beard scattered across his face, hidden under a mess of dirty brown hair. As he backed into the room, whistling and in his own little world, Bennett caught Alex doing a double take, as though recognizing the guy.

The janitor began emptying trash cans and replacing their linings. Eventually noticing the lingering silence, he turned to the faces pointed his way and smiled. "Hey-o. Cleaning time," he said, giving a wave as he pushed on.

Fighting for composure, Madam Daphne picked up where she left off. "To say nothing of the Senate approving the injection of Eve into humans to solve our problems. And not just any Eve, either—Wrath and Rapture. I swear, the moment I left those dolts, they not only began losing their minds but also their savoir faire. And look what they've done. C'est bien triste que les gens aient peur de sortir la nuit." Madam Daphne appeared to be getting flustered.

"I'm sure Izaiah or one of the other Medolians can help sort this whole thing out," Alex suggested. "Let us try to call them, and—"

Madam Daphne laughed. "If Izaiah left you alone with no means of contacting him, I see no reason to involve him yet."

Bennett caught the janitor taking worried glances at them as he collected pint glasses from the pool table areas, accidentally knocking one off the counter. Glass shattered, spilling blue liquid over the shoes of the billiard players. The janitor was on his knees in an instant with a rag, cleaning the carpet and wiping their shoes.

"Pardon! Pardon! So sorry. Clumsy me." The players kicked the janitor away until he got the message and rose from the ground. "Okay, okay! Just can't see in this low light, know what I mean?"

"What are you doing?" Madam Daphne shouted.

The janitor's mouth dangled loosely. "Uh, there was a spill, and—"

"Does now seem like a good time? Perhaps there might be business going on?" she asked, waving her hand back and forth, palm up, as though holding an invisible tray.

"Oh, you have company. Pardon. Je me trompe . . . encore une fois. But my boss said to," the janitor replied.

"Who do you think your boss is?" Madam Daphne shouted.

"My supervisor. Rick. I could go get him if you—"

"Get out!" Madam Daphne bellowed, flaring the tendrils on her back.

The janitor jumped into action. "Right-o!" He packed up his cart and wheeled it to the exit, where security was waiting to usher him out and slam the door behind him.

Madam Daphne adjusted her hair, sweeping it out of her eyes. Taking a breath, she continued. "As I was saying, this is between you and me. No one else. Izaiah and the others claim to be neutral but have shown themselves to be anything but."

Bennett noticed Chief Mary and the other guards edging closer. Alex hiccupped again as he started to sway. *Damn it. His Wrath is dropping fast. What did she give him?*

Madam Daphne had the light of a dreamer in her eyes. "Unlike them, I care for all the shades of Eve and the creatures born of them. Hywyn, Arros, and all of UnEarth can destroy themselves for all I care. I'd call it a reset. The Earth and its creatures would be none the wiser, and would create a new UnEarth. Perhaps I could be the one to nurture it, guide it, and help it grow?"

Alex hiccupped louder, interrupting the moment and rubbing his eyes. "Sorry. Feeling funny. Legs are a little tingly."

Bennett forced a smile at Madam Daphne. "I should get my friend home before he makes bigger fools of us. Thank you for your hospitality and all that. And since this was official Tribunal business, rest assured these proceedings will be kept confidential and will never be repeated—"

Madam Daphne cut him off, standing and beaming with her own pearly whites. "I'm sorry, but no. After your stunt downstairs, it will be difficult to put the genie back in the bottle, but I must try. No one can know the humans of the Tribunal were conducting an official investigation on my property. My reputation in the UnEarth community depends on my lovelies knowing they can always find asylum here. No judgment will cross into these walls save my own. If Izaiah wants you back, he can knock on my door and ask, just like everybody else."

"We're not pawns to be used as bargaining chips, lady," Bennett said.

"Not at all," Madam Daphne replied. "A bargaining chip is intended to be given away, something I would never do with such a rare find. My beautiful fallen stars who landed in my lap."

"We're not lap dogs, either. Now tell your chief to show us the door before the Medolians start wondering why we aren't at the rendezvous." Bennett missed how easy it used to be to intimidate people when they weren't whatever the Hell Madam Daphne was.

"I think I won't," she said. "Izaiah will learn one way or another he has no power here and cannot go around doing as he pleases. Humans soaked to the brim with Eve are too great an opportunity to pass up for my experiments and those of my colleagues. Think of all we can learn."

"You're not going to cut us into little pieces, are you?" Alex asked (*for some reason*).

"Sweetheart, no! I'm a vegetarian. I could never do such a thing to a creature. But I will pay someone else to do it and give me all the applicable bits. I'm sure he'll find a use for whatever's left. I can only imagine with the doctor. He's got such an imagination. Who knows, he might even find a cure for an UnEarth disease within you! Myself, I'm always looking for new ways to get people off, or maybe a delicious new ingredient for my world famous Mallos-brew stew."

Backing away, Bennett was met by Chief Mary, who took him by his restraints. *What the Hell, Chief? I thought we had something special.* Another guard seized Alex, who was showing serious signs of fatigue.

"I'm actually sorry to do this," Madam Daphne said. "I feel a horrid sense of Grief about it. Surprising. But your kind only lives about half a century anyway, right? So, it's not like I'm taking *that* much from you."

"Al, light up," Bennett said, fighting for freedom against the impossibly strong Chief Mary.

"I'm trying!" Alex groaned.

"In the hands of my friend, Dr. Neil-Shemaine, you will be cared for like princes right up until your very last moments, which should be painless, at least from what I hear—though I wouldn't know—I've never died. Be sure to treat him with respect. He is a brilliant man and worthy of it." Madam Daphne swayed back and forth, singing, as Bennett released a furious scream, trying every trick he knew to break the chief's grasp as he and Alex were dragged through the office double doors.

"In a whispered wood, her nectar finds us
weeping for a soul . . ."

Despite his strained efforts, Bennett couldn't find the power he'd felt the night the wings appeared, pouring through his emotions and giving them all a try. For a brief moment, his skin turned cold, but his hand radiated nothing. There was no ice on his chest. Hauled like prisoners down the spiral staircase of La Rose Noire, he and Alex were surrounded by shadows as Madam Daphne's voice became all that was left, echoing in a chorus from above.

"In a body destined for the dirt
beneath a grassy knoll.
Amen."

"So odd, to think their universe lies directly over our own. A higher, more frenzied plane. Like the layers of a cut of fabric, the cosmos is made of multiple universes overlapping, feeding into one another as a stream does a river [. . .] Do the layers ever end? Is there a final destination? If Ilsa doesn't know, what hope do I have in figuring it out?"

- Excerpts from the journal of
Dr. Francisco Emul. Murcia
February 1894

THE SENATOR

Mara breezed through the dusty bronze turnstile, lifting her staff and gliding her hips through the rotating arm. It clicked three times as she passed, confirming her status as a non-Purged Un-Earth creature and granting her entry to the city. *Home sweet home.* Slinging her staff over her shoulder, she continued toward a brick wall ahead. A mural stretched across its face, depicting a giant, statuesque human head—white, with blank eyes like a Greek statue. Many shades of color in cookie-cutter shadows were stacked behind the head, with purple in the foreground and red coming last. At the end of the mural was a diagram labeled "*UnEarth*," depicting six spheres with overlapping orbits in between the Earth and the moon. Near the entryway's end, golden letters strung above read "*Welcome to Trivium City*" in a series of languages. A banner tucked away at the bottom declared: *Current Majority Leader: Hywyn.*

As if it ever said anything different.

Existing in the same space as the hot liquid core of the

Earth but on a different material frequency, Trivium—the planet she was currently standing on—was the glue that held the fabric of UnEarth society together. Much like the nucleus of an atom, this chunk of silver rock acted as an anchor for the orbits of the other worlds of UnEarth.

Located at the direct center of the spectrum of energy known as the Eve, all creatures had equal access to the planet and the lone city built upon it. Lovingly called TC by many, Trivium City was established when the peoples of the Eve first settled the mountainous planet, using the only available flat stretch of land, a curiously square strip in the lower hemisphere.

The Tribunal was the cornerstone around which a metropolis grew, becoming the central hub of UnEarth culture. By now, the city had hundreds of generations' worth of history sewn into its bones, and its population had never stopped growing, or slowed. The financial sector, a recent addition, seemed to be always thriving. *Then there's my favorite part.* No visit to TC was complete without a trip to the immaculately designed Museum of Nature, Science, and Eve, courtesy of Alice the Builder, a long-dead hero to the people of Hywyn. There was also a sprawling district devoted to the Colossal Competitive Eve Leagues of UnEarth. *Really big enterprise. Not my thing. Pretty barbaric, you ask me.*

Getting to Trivium was as simple as a Shift, which only meant sparing some Mallos and focusing. But seeing as Mara had not visited the capital in nearly eighty-five years, her path back was slightly more complicated than that.

With some steam to blow off after the Gathering in the South Pacific, she only wanted to get back to hunting Wraithians, hoping that making them extinct again might ease some of her frustrations. Though tinted with Fervor and not a violent creature by nature, she'd been experiencing flashes of Wrath these past couple of decades, particularly since the Joseph Mandate began—what she viewed as an insult to all Medolians, who for the last forty thousand years had guarded and kept the Earth safe from those who would unbalance it. *Alexander the Great was a tough nut to crack, gotta admit. Spread too much Rapture, if you can believe it.*

By the stroke of some asshole's pen, the responsibilities she'd taken exceedingly seriously her entire life (*and career—same thing*) had been handed off to a pair of small-minded mortals from modern North America (*egk*), who were still having trouble understanding their own demises, let alone be able to lend a hand. Releasing them in the Arizona desert that fateful day after saving them from the Wraithian horde, she'd hoped it would be the last she'd see of the humans. Sadly, that was not the case. *It's what I get for doing something nice.*

After leaving the Gathering, Mara set out across Africa and Southeast Asia to find the Wrath cult. Along the way, she encountered a few raiding parties that were easily dispatched, but she found no smoldering villages. The abundant prey she had encountered over the past year had dried up, along with the distraction from her standing orders.

Since Izaiah had taken the humans to question the Scythe Nigel Roe (*not a bad move*), their fates were out of her hands. *But I'm not going to keep running around in circles in the desert. We need more information about Joseph to figure out what he's after. It's time to start looking in places no one's thought to.* Breaking her edict, Mara masked her energy and set off for Trivium City, where she might finally find the answers she was seeking.

The Warden Sentry can get as mad as he wants.

She arrived at the Trivium South Eve gate via massive golden rings, half-buried, which towered fifty feet into the air. Known as the Eb Rings, they were smooth, without markings, and also the only way on or off the planet. *Partly a security measure, but mostly because we can't Shift directly into Trivium, only through the rings. The mineral that makes up the majority of the planet amplifies and channels Eve, creating way too much interference.* The construction and installation of the two Eve gates, one in the north of the city and one in the south—each with three rings— marked the official end of the original Eve war, Unos.

Presently, after passing through the rings, walking through the Eve gate plaza, past the bronze turnstile and the white-faced mural, and finally stepping out of the low corridor that opened to an urban skyline, Mara quickly sensed something was amiss in the city.

Guess it's true. Most people skipped town.

The wave of palpable Eve she expected, usually a rejuvenating blast to her senses, was almost nonexistent. The few hundred scattered signatures remaining in the city were muddy and unfocused.

Entering Bellion Square, eager to see her favorite places and people, to smell food she actually liked, and to hear some decent music for a change, she found none of it. Instead, she was greeted by closed shops and folded boutique carts. The few eateries and pawnshops still open shared a smattering of customers among them, but with so little product on their shelves that Mara wondered if there had been rampant looting. The brick walkways lay bare, dismally gray, and worst of all, there was no music. She longed for a reprieve from humanity's painfully thin, meandering excuse for symphony, far preferring multiple compositions layered over one another, stampeding along as fast as she could run—bounding and crashing in a beautiful, anarchic musical experience. Though she did have a certain fondness for Frederick Handel's work. *Messiah kicks ass.*

Carrying a maroon haze, buried by shadow, the moon of Trivium, Doloros, hovered overhead as if near to crushing the pointed gray mountains looming outside of town. A golden glow on the murky horizon gave the area a dark, muted feel, as though cemented in perpetual dusk. The city's wide streets, designed for foot traffic and pedal carts, were lined with flush, flat-faced businesses, all painted in the same five or six dark pastel colors. Most were cut across the middle by horizontal service windows. Some had chairs out front, transforming them into bistros. A few boutiques were large enough to let customers inside to shop or dine, but the vast majority of trade in Trivium was done at windows.

What made today so strange wasn't the barren streets. Trivium City had looked this way before, during either an Eve storm or a shutdown of Tribunal operations, but as she walked past the shops and cafeterias, Mara noticed none of the pure Eve creatures were to be seen or felt. There were no Celestials stomping around, knocking everything over with their rigid, folded wings. No Archfiend slithering by, leaving vapor trails. No Makaan Scythes . . . *Scything? I guess. They kind of float.* Mara was never exactly sure how the cocoon-like creatures from Fovos moved. All the same, returning to Trivium and not seeing a single "pure" was both disheartening and suspicious. All signs were pointing to a worst-case scenario unfolding, and Mara felt utterly helpless to stop it. Hywyn and Arros really *were* close to war, and apparently the lesser kingdoms had fallen in line, which would only bolster the chances of conflict.

The growing xenophobia in the city was noticeable the *last* time Mara visited, but somehow things had gotten even worse, faster than she ever anticipated. Word of the humans becoming delegates in the Joseph Mandate must have been the final straw that started the panic.

She focused on the remaining energy signatures in the city, searching for anyone familiar. *Can't tell who's left to speak with. Wait—there's Stoddy. Thank the Eve. Of course she stayed. She'll be in the mood to talk, always is. Just hope she kept the stove on!*

Turning down a few avenues lined with businesses, many barred up or with steel shades drawn, Mara finally came upon Miss Massachusetts's Meatery, a corner operation with a rusted sign hanging overhead. Little more than a pastel-blue box mixed in with the others—but with a little extra space because it was located on a corner lot—the Meatery had a long, horizontal service window about six feet high. Stools of different sizes were lined up out front. Three, on the far end, were more than quadruple the size of a normal stool. *For the Lostros, her kind. A chef could run a successful business with just two pure Lostros regulars.*

Inside, Mara saw a silhouette like a seven-foot potato, finding Stoddy Kline Massachusetts facing away with a clipboard in hand, checking items off a list. Her yellow dress with white trim and lilac print hung loosely on her distended frame, which took up most of the interior of the business. Surrounded by food prep tables, mini fridges, utensils, knives, and a seemingly endless supply of mixing bowls and serving plates, Stoddy could serve a fleet of hungry Un-Earth Humans without ever standing from her seat.

Sliding onto a stool, Mara took off her staff and laid it on the counter with a clang. Stoddy's spine stiffened. "I know that sound. Only one weapon in the universe makes that sound. Hope there's a hungry Medolian sitting behind me—otherwise I got a thief who's about to learn a thing or two from Miss Stoddy Kline Mass."

Mara smiled. "Heard this was the only place in town still serving boulash."

Stoddy spun around, revealing a face that often seemed to be in some kind of discomfort, (*don't tell me, it's your knee this time, maybe the back*), but would always make room to smile for a friend. Leaning forward, she slid the service window open with her enormous paw. "You can rest assured, my Meatery closes the day they haul my dead, fat, Lostros ass out of here."

Mara felt better already. "Hi, Stoddy."

"My favorite Medolian! So good to see you!" Stoddy's flash of happiness quickly devolved into melancholy. "Sorry, hon. I would get up to properly greet you, but the foot's been acting up again, so—"

Foot. Of course. Stupid me. "Not a problem. Which one is it, again?"

Stoddy leaned down, squishing to get her face closer to the service window. "I honestly can't remember. Just happy to see you! So—so—so—sit! My gosh. Are you hungry? You want boulash, right? I bet you could eat a whole riber snout. Just because you look like a human doesn't mean you have to eat like one, you know?"

Stoddy still talked to Mara like the mother she never had or wanted, despite being less than half as old as the Medolian. Her unique way of communicating stemmed from the habits she'd picked up living on Earth for three hundred years in an effort to study human chefs and restaurants before returning to Trivium to fulfill her dream and open the Meatery. *She even coined a slogan: "Human food, done right."* But Mara wasn't here for human food. She wanted UnEarth grub.

"Have you gotten . . . bigger, since I saw you last?" Mara asked hesitantly.

"Oh, you noticed! Thank you. Yes, I have been shaping up—or shaping *out*, is more like it, right?" Stoddy chuckled, quickly checking off her list before tossing the clipboard aside.

Mara guessed her friend weighed over a thousand pounds by now, looking more like an egg with a face than a human. *On her world, bigger is better. Still love her the same—just worries me.* It wasn't Stoddy's fault she was born on Doloros. However, growing closer to her original form, that of a Lostros, could only mean she was using more Grief, the shade of Eve that created Stoddy in the first place. UnEarth Humans could get concentrated forms of it in some of the seedier corners of Trivium City, usually in pill form, but the methods of absorbing it surreptitiously were getting sneakier all the time. *The question is why is she using it?*

Stoddy swiveled backward and cleared off the grill being used as a desk. "So—so, what was your favorite again? You like your riber salted and sanded, yeah? Maybe a nice moss to wash it down? Eh?"

"No moss, thank you."

"Right, I forgot you stopped drinking after your breakup with your girlfriend—oops, sorry, ex-girlfriend. The flame. The one."

"Stoddy—"

"Back in the good ol' days, right? You looked happier back then, something the world could use more of. Not that I really care. We're all going to die. Makes me jealous of the humans. They get to do it quicker than the rest of us." Stoddy lit her stove. "You want two chunks or three, love?"

"Three, please. And she was never my girlfriend," Mara corrected. "She was my . . . roommate."

"Right-right. Sorry. No talking about the famous you-know-who."

"And we were never in love."

"What was that, dear? One more time?"

"Never mind." Mara grumbled and turned away while Stoddy kept cooking. "Speaking of the good old days," Mara started, unsure if this would go over well, "you trying to . . . go back?"

"Whatcha mean?" Stoddy asked, staring at the grill.

Mara decided not to tiptoe. "You going to need a Changing Chamber soon, or—"

Stoddy put her knife down, shut her eyes, and folded her hands. "Are you saying my appearance is unpleasant? Because—"

"No, of course not. Never. You're gorgeous. I've just lost too many friends to obsessing over Ascension rights and CAF ideologies, is all."

"If you think I would ever subject myself to begging my way back into Doloros with those sycophants—"

"No, of course not! I'm sorry, I shouldn't have said anything. I just hope you're not chasing a dragon here. That's what the humans call it. Means putting stuff in your body you don't need, looking for something you shouldn't want. Using Grief won't help you." Mara hoped her friend didn't think she was talking down to her.

"That's rich coming from a Medolian. Not all of us can be born of pure, pristine Mallos," Stoddy sassed. "Want to know what I think? I think you've been spending too much time around life-forms who don't live long enough to know anything, and you should watch your mouth if you want this meal to be edible."

Stoddy picked up her knife and resumed chopping, silently forgiving Mara. Swiveling from station to station in a circular arc, spinning knives, chopping vegetables, turning a roast, yanking roots, and stir-frying whatever it was that made her boulash the best, she gabbed with Mara as the meal came together in a large bowl. Many subjects were quickly touched upon, including an outbreak of mock weed on Nashwyn. *Pretty scary. Eats other plants, which is exactly what their cities are made of.* Stoddy also talked about a recent scare when she was forced to use six frying pans to fend off an attempted robbery by a couple of Veen Scythes. *Gross little bastards.*

"And I'm not the only one," Stoddy said, flipping her skillet to punctuate her point. "Been mass looting going on everywhere. Worst I've seen." *So where is the Barium Guard? This is strange.*

When their small talk was done, Stoddy asked, "So—so . . . what brings you to TC? I mean, what *really* brings you here?"

"The boulash. I swear," Mara said.

"That's some bullshit. The best Medolian Shifts to Trivium City after the shutdown, chooses to come see me, and you want me to think it's for my cooking and not the gossip? You get the Hell out."

"Gossip? You?"

"Don't play with me," Stoddy said. "I'm not in the mood, and I *will* throw this meal out. So you gotta tell me. I have to know for sure. Did they actually do it? Are dead humans really helping the Sentries catch the demon?"

"You know I can't talk about that stuff," Mara said, half-serious.

Stoddy gasped excitedly. "That's a yes. By the Eve, I can't believe it! Tell me what happened. Do they look normal? Did their Eve leave, and if so, was it replaced? And with what? Also, are they disfigured? And how are you handling all of this? I expect you're hating every second. I mean, *humans*—what were they thinking?"

"They're just men. In no way prepared to accept the responsibilities on their shoulders, and with almost no choice in the matter. Makes me sad, really. It's shown me how weak the institutions we thought we could stand on are. Though I guess Izaiah is finally getting his wish. He always wanted more humans to know about us and our world. Wonder if it means more are going to follow."

"Never understood why your boss preaches so incessantly for human inclusion. Who cares? They're humans. If I'm honest, it gives me the creeps." Stoddy slowed her chopping and glanced up with slanted eyes. "I lived on Earth—I know what I'm talking about. They treat every day and every meal like it may be their last. Except for their cooking techniques, nothing good comes from those things. You should know, being a Medolian. You guys spend more time down there than any of us."

"Even I know we can't pin this on their whole species," Mara argued, against her baser instincts.

"S'pose not. Just hard to know what to think. You know what would help? If I knew who was to blame. Then I could rest a little easier. Blame always helps. And a good cry."

Stoddy wisdom. Take it or leave it.

"For some reason this Joseph business is getting under people's skin extra good," Stoddy continued. "We've had rogue possessions before, but this just feels . . . wrong. In a whole lot of ways. Maybe it's how quiet Arros is being? Nobody's heard from Lucifer in ages. Most think the guy's already dead, but the Alus Conclave can't let the Archfiend get wind or they'll face a revolt. Just rumors, mind you, and I didn't tell you any of it. Don't like speaking idly about such things—but this is big, right? Do you think people, i.e., me, should be scared?"

Mara didn't know what to say. The truth felt too harsh a thing to lay on her friend. "Any word from the Tribunal?" She hoped the question would both change the subject while also addressing Stoddy's concerns.

"*Spf!* The Senate. They're the ones who caused this mess." Stoddy was successfully distracted. "The six who represent? I think they've got their heads screwed on wrong, ya know? Being forced to be in human form all the time gets to them. I know it gets to me, which is why I keep as much Grief as I can. But those six Senate dopes— we make them get rid of their Eve to represent—and I get why, but I swear they're starting to act like human politicians."

"Politicians are atrocious no matter the frequency you're living on. Trust me," Mara replied.

"Guess that's true. Soup's on!"

Stoddy slipped a steaming bowl through a metal grating, landing it in front of Mara without spilling a drop. A spoon followed. She salivated over the steaming bowl. Inside were three red globs with green spots, floating in thick, translucent yellow soup. Boulash, a common Lostros dish made from bits of riber (*a Doloros mammal, about nine feet tall, over six tons, with tiny, leaf-like ears, and a long snout that drags on the ground and is used exclusively for eating manure*), was a meal that had once disgusted Mara. But then Stoddy came along with her secret regional recipe, converting the Medolian into a lifelong fan.

"Careful, it's hot, sugar—" Stoddy warned.

Mara ignored the warning, took the bowl in both hands, and slurped it back in four gulps. After slamming the bowl on the counter she wiped her mouth. "You have no idea how badly I needed that." She finished with a burp loud enough to shake the bowl and spoon before placing them on the counter to be collected. "Thank you."

"Someone's been eating too much Earth food. You're in desperate need of flavor." Stoddy tossed the bowl into a tray.

"Speaking of flavor . . . something I noticed coming in, where are all the pure breeds?" Mara asked, glancing around.

"Ah, you know how paranoid they can be," Stoddy remarked. "That's one good thing about us Purged folks. It kinda . . . mellows you out. I think the dulling of the senses gives us less to worry about, because once it became official that Hywyn and Arros were both prepping armies—the pure breeds ran. All my Doloros pals, Arjay and Demitri and the like, having to hurry away—can you imagine anything so awful?"

The image in Mara's mind was purely hysterical, but she shook her head in disgust and solidarity anyway. The creatures of Doloros were strong and immense, but also slow. *So very, very slow.* Especially the Trerds. *One of two types of Lostros, in addition to the Derds. They named themselves, by the way. Not a joke.*

With another burp, Mara rose from the stool. "Speaking of hurrying away—wish I could chat more. Unfortunately I have business with—"

"The Tribunal, I know."

"What do I owe you?"

"Your money's no good here," Stoddy replied.

"Fine. Add one more favor to the pot."

"I have enough favors from you," Stoddy groused. "Keep a few for yourself. Just hope the taste of home did you good. Now get out there and save the city, and my business!"

"Thank you." Mara took her spear and started to walk away from the counter but couldn't pull herself away just yet. "If you do ever start feeling the pull, you know, to go back to Doloros, I . . . just know you can talk to me about anything."

"You're sweet, but I'm fine, sugar. And you need to get going." Stoddy finished with a faded smile before sliding the glass door closed.

Mara had to pocket her concern and hurry to the heart of the city, looking skyward out of habit as the dark spires of the Tribunal rose into view, silhouetted against the burgundy sky. The long, dark shadow looked like it was made of obsidian, dressed by wide staircases on all sides. On Earth, it would have easily spread over dozens of residential blocks. The lofted, razor-sharp points of its structure, including numerous protruding spikes from its walls, like the barbs of a rose stem, were perfectly placed and mathematically sound. Immaculate.

Similar buildings built by humans, such as the Chhatrapati Shivaji Terminus in Mumbai or the Central Train Station in Amsterdam, reminded Mara of the Tribunal, but they were minuscule by comparison, both in size and simple grandeur. The Tribunal was not merely a central travel depot, containing the BAT (*Bestiola Arteria Transvecto, our version of a subway*), it also housed the Senate and its chambers, the only unified governing body presiding over the kingdoms of UnEarth.

Dolefully majestic, it now appeared abandoned, with no one left to appreciate it. Mara approached the wide doorway to the section of the building devoted to law, shaped like a teardrop and made of rigid lines and hard angles. Both outside and in, she noticed no Barium Guards at their posts. *Celestial elites. Tough ones. Never fun to fight.*

Taking one of the long golden handles, she opened the five-yard-tall door and stepped inside, hastening down the broad beige hallway. The calm, subdued mood inside the Tribunal washed over her. Celestials preferred things serene, so that's how it was kept. Sound was dampened in the halls by the multitudes of carpets lining the floors and walls, and the heavy tapestries hanging from the ceiling, less for aesthetics and more to deliver ordinances from the Senate. Like the rest of Trivium City, the halls were spottily occupied, mostly by clerical assistants carrying scrolls to and fro, and Counselor proletariats going home for the day.

Mara first wanted to stop at the primary Senate chamber before questioning any officials she could find. *If any of them are even here, or in a giving mood.* There was one large favor she needed to ask, and any of the six Senators could provide it. Nearing the Senate Hall, expecting to finally hear some commotion, she could only make out a single heartbeat inside. Moving into the chamber shaped like a colossal horseshoe, more than two hundred yards from side to side, Mara exited the short tunnel located under the center of the stadium seating. Stepping onto the central carpeted walkway, she took in the Senate Chamber.

The flat-faced, open end of the horseshoe opposite was built up in stacks of rose-colored wooden structures. Each level was littered with tables for lawyers and bookkeepers, stacked atop one another, built over centuries. The highest level, a balcony, featured a podium, a long desk, and six chairs belonging to the representatives of the kingdoms of UnEarth. Above, the chamber ceiling was adorned with knitted banners depicting the thirteen tenets of UnEarth law, along with various words of wisdom from Michael, known as the "greatest Celestial" or "Champion of Inferius." *Yeah, right.*

Mara knew who the real hero(s) of Inferius were, even if no one wanted to admit it or honor them in any way. *After all, why would they honor Medolians instead of another Celestial? We only decimated our numbers to save you all. What's so great about that?* Die Muneris, or Day of the Gift, as it was called, was a sore subject for Mara. It marked the day Inferius ended and victory was declared over Arros. *And the day my friends killed themselves. So, I wouldn't call it much of a gift.*

The chamber audience seating was divided into six sections, each designed to accommodate the various body types and lifestyles of UnEarth's creatures. Transparency was touted as a vital part of the government structure, so everyone was allowed to participate in Senate proceedings—so they said. The sections were distinguished by shades of Eve, with Rapture and the Celestials having the lion's share, along with finer seats gilded with intricate golden crests. Arros had the second-largest seating area, though it was located farthest from the podium and featured several obsidian columns that obscured the view for many Archfiend attending Senate proceedings. *Long ago, they'd been allowed to swarm up the columns so more of them could see, but Gabriel put a stop to it. Almost makes me feel bad for the Archies. Almost.*

Mara spotted a lone figure near a table on the ground level, hunched over a pile of scrolls scattered about. She quickly recognized the Eve signature of Senator Laffler, from Lanwyn. *Ugh. This guy.*

As the elected representative from Lanwyn—also known as the world of joy—Laffler had been a Beaubon before being stripped of his Eve and regressing to his base form. Of all the lands of UnEarth, Lanwyn annoyed Mara the most. *It's cliché—I know. But it doesn't change how I feel.*

The short, doltish excuse for a leader spoke exclusively in little white lies, wore a human suit and tie, and had a squished face with beady little eyes. He was also an old friend of Izaiah's. Mara loathed everything about him.

The senator did a surprised double take upon spotting her and quickly rolled up the scroll he was studying, sliding it in front of a small stack. "Sentry Mara?" he squeaked. "What brings you here? As you can see, I'm in recess—*we're* in recess."

When she stepped up to Laffler, he backed up uncomfortably. "Where is your escort, Senator?" she asked. "I haven't seen a single Barium Guard since arriving. Nor Guard in the city."

"Oh, yes, I've given Hydrus the week off. They will return to escort me to Lanwyn in a few days. As for the remainder of the Guard, with no one here to protect and their sworn duty to neutrality, many have been relieved of duty. Captain Hwyllahs has stayed on to keep the peace, but I'm afraid the Barium presence has been se-verely diminished." Laffler chuckled, as though convinced he was playing it cool. "You know, I was under the impression no Medo-lians would be coming to the Tribunal until the Archfiend was in custody. Izaiah . . . well, he assured me. Does your arrival mean—"

"No. The nameless Archfiend hasn't been caught."

"Then what are you doing here?" Laffler asked. "You and the others should be out there finding that damn Joseph. I don't even want to imagine what Hywyn will do if the human host dies."

"If this is so important, why isn't the Senate in session? Where are the representatives? We need leadership. Or, Eve forbid, some action."

"I can't control the reactions of others when tragic news reaches us. Speaker Binahq closed the session and called an indefinite recess. You know as well as I that's absolute. The representatives have gone back to their realms to quell tensions. It's all chaos, no matter where you look. So please, tell me we've made progress on Earth."

"Don't worry, your little mission is still a go. It will just take time—especially with Izaiah keeping the humans out of it as much as possible. I assume you had no idea he waylaid Barker and Hunter in Africa to continue the search himself."

"I didn't," Laffler said with a chuckle. "I should have known he'd coddle them. Izaiah and his love for humanity. As long as the job gets done, who cares? That's what I say."

"He's taken them to find Nigel Roe, believing he might speak with them."

"Sounds dangerous. If there's one thing that Scythe hates more than Medolians, it's humans. He didn't provide us proper information the first time—why would he now? There's nothing in it for him." Laffler pinched the bridge of his nose. "But if it's what Izaiah believes is best, I can't think of a reason to doubt him now." With a forlorn sigh, he rolled the final scroll tight and secured it.

"It's hard to trust someone who mostly guesses," Mara said.

"I know, but though he may seem off his rocker—which is mostly true—our dear old Izaiah is also a lot more. He only went along with me on the plan to bring in the humans because he found a way to do it without violating his beliefs. Your boss can do wondrous things if we all get out of the way and let him."

"Beliefs? You're referring to Hunter and Barker?" Mara asked. "Why were they selected? Tell me. What criteria did they fill?"

"It wasn't haphazard, I can tell you that. Izaiah was positive he wanted the teacher and the soldier. I told him, 'I don't want to know why you pick them, just that you're sure.' He chose the way he did, I assume, with Illyana's help. He said, 'Trust me, as long as Alex Barker is given Rapture, and Bennett Hunter Wrath, all will be fine.'"

"You mean the other way around," Mara corrected.

"Excuse me?"

"Alex Barker was sent to Arros to be imbued with Wrath. Bennett Hunter was sent to Hywyn and is imbued with Rapture. Isn't that how it was supposed to be?"

Laffler's expression shifted to one of confusion before he smiled and gave a mousy laugh. "Oh yes, of course. Silly me. So many details. Now, I should be going. Is there anything else, Sentry Mara?"

"Have you been listening? No one knows where the Archfiend is. The boy isn't fighting the demon spiritually, and together they can hide their Eve. Joseph has been playing everyone for six years. Am I the only one who wants to know why?"

"Joseph is hiding himself, you say? Even from *your* keen senses? *Hmm.* As far as I knew, only Medolians were capable of completely obscuring their Eve signatures," Laffler said, his tone tinged with suspicion.

"I truly hope you're not suggesting one of the Sentries is . . ." Mara couldn't even finish the sentence.

Laffler leaned against the table and flashed her one of his safe, patented politician smiles. "I'm not suggesting anything."

"I came here for help. If you won't provide it, maybe one of the other Senators will. Where are Mau-auvt Bo and Minister Yaddo?" Mara inquired.

"As I said, they've gone back to their worlds to quell tensions. I believe Yaddo had to escape to Filanos when word came of a

Lostros mob balling up to ransack the city. I'm the last remaining representative. Punishment, I suppose, for my amendment," Laffler said, sounding like a kid who just spilled his ice cream cone.

"Doesn't Lanwyn need you?" Mara asked.

"I won't make any difference there. The Beaubons will always be the last to pick up a weapon. But I can make a difference here. Adding humans to the Joseph Mandate was my idea, so I need to see this through. When I proposed the amendment, I was trying to fend off a thunderhead bearing down on us. Hywyn had already begun drafting legislation that would grant them— and only them—access to Earth. The other kingdoms were appalled. Arros wanted to send in a fleet of Archfiend, claiming it should be them, as Joseph is one of their own. Things got ugly. I did my best, but the storm has come anyway, and now everybody's gone back to their homes to wait it out, hoping to hear good news. Everything is riding on us. On me. So please, just say whatever you need. I'll do everything I can."

"I need authorization to enter the Changing Chambers."

"Absolutely not! Have you lost your mind? What could you possibly learn down there?"

Mara tried to explain her theory: that Joseph had clearly done his research and mastered multiple shades of the Eve, possibly even learning how to wield them. *He's operating on knowledge so ancient that most have forgotten it. I need to speak with old souls who've seen a thing or two and can't run away when I try.*

But Laffler wouldn't hear it. "It's not a question of importance— it's a question of time," he said, gathering the last of his scrolls into his arms. "I can't get you that kind of authorization before I leave next week. There's no way. You're going to have to try another avenue. I'm too busy trying to keep everybody happy."

"When someone spends all their energy trying to make other

people happy, they usually end up doing the opposite," Mara muttered, hoping her words would chill him enough to reconsider his approach to life. "But if you won't help, I'll find someone who will."

Laffler gave her a slight nod and scampered past, clutching his scrolls. "I have to get these archives to the Counselors before they start filing motions of delay. Until next time, Sentry Mara."

Stepping aside, Mara watched the little man exit the chamber. Once alone, she took a moment to absorb the solitude of being the only soul inside. *Doubt this will ever happen again. Then again—*

There was a chance the Senate might never reconvene, and Mara wasn't sure how she felt about that. *I've never been out of work before. Wonder what it's like.* She had always meant to take time off to visit Feliush Beach in Nashwyn, but could never find the right opportunity. *Maybe this is finally it?* The resort was an upscale retreat that welcomed all shades of Eve, and with the savings she'd accumulated during her years of service, Mara could afford to stay indefinitely.

On her way out, she glanced above the stadium seating. Glistening in a row, looming like Trivium mountains, massive marble statues depicted heroes from the great kingdoms, one from every world, including two from Hywyn—but no Medolian was present. Having seen enough, Mara walked out and headed to her next mission.

Never really thought he'd give me authorization, but it's better to have asked than to be sneaky from the start. I know I'm right, and this will just prove how wrong everyone else has been. It didn't matter if she faced suspension for entering the Changing Chambers; it's where she needed to be. Hurrying down the Tribunal's khaki and sienna-colored halls, she passed the formal kingdom offices, moved into the administrative section, and bypassed the hall leading to the BAT as she descended into the lower levels. A feeling of nervousness settled in. After her last visit to the Chambers, she had promised herself she would never return. *Sorry, self, but I need to do this.*

Feliush Beach would have to wait another thousand or so years.

With her Eve at a minimum and ready to use all her tricks, Mara found sneaking into the building surprisingly uneventful and boring, passing only one Barium Guard who was asleep at their post. Once in the lower levels, past the scullery, the kennels, and the furnace, she reached the Changing Chambers at the bottommost level of the Tribunal's subterranean conurbation.

The stench of synthetic chemicals, molting flesh, and mounds of body waste intensified until it was more overpowering than she remembered—not to mention the sounds. No torture chamber on Earth could compare to the wails and cries of thousands of Un-Earth Humans being pumped full of Eve, returning to their "pure" selves. *By request, too.*

At the bottom of the stairs, lit by torchlight, she found the Chamber entrance also unguarded. *Damn, a fight might've psyched me up.* Pausing before the immense metal door, she crossed puddles of slime on the rock floor, took the handle, opened it, and stepped inside. *The things I do for my job.*

HANNAH

The lamps overhead were scorching, and utterly blinding. *I'm getting a tan from these friggin' things!* Globs of gray and brilliant stars crisscrossed his vision as Bennett fought to free his arms and legs but still couldn't move.

"I'm going to enjoy seeing the insides of Eve'd mortals," said a nauseating, nasally voice with a French accent. Their host, Dr. Neil-Shemaine—the one Madam Daphne promised would cut them into little pieces—had remained stubbornly out of sight since Bennett and Alex had been thrust into this new hellish hole.

A long shadow crept into the light overhead. Bennett's eyes focused on a pneumatic arm descending from the ceiling, a glossy, dark mass of pulsing material running its length. At first glance, it resembled exposed blue muscle. *Ew.* Attached to the end was a needle, its point so sharp it seemed to fade rather than end.

The blood drained from Bennett's face. "Uh . . . there's a ridiculously huge needle staring at me," he said.

"I got one, too," Alex replied from somewhere on his left.

"Hush hush hush." Neil-Shemaine's voice cut in, his little feet scurrying by on Bennett's right. "Don't get all worked up."

"Trust me, Doc, you don't want to do this. We represent some very powerful people. Top of the top. So it'd be pretty stupid to harm us," Bennett threatened, lacking the energy to sound convincing. "Also, you don't want to go digging around in me. There's not much to see—just some shrapnel and liver damage."

"Yeah!" Alex chimed in. "I was nearly vegan for six weeks before I died. How interesting could my insides be?"

"Silence!" Neil-Shemaine yelled. "Is this what humans do? I swear, I forgot until recently. Cripes! It's so aggravating. You try to get some work done, and—it's no wonder UnEarth despises your kind!"

What a weird little guy. Bennett closed his eyes, attempting to sense the doctor's Eve, but found nothing. *He doesn't have an Eve signature? So he's just a . . . guy?* Bennett wished the knowledge that Neil-Shemaine was human offered him more comfort.

After their ordeal in Madam Daphne's office, they'd been dragged back down the spiral stairwell, their heads forced low to disorient them. Despite the disorientation, Bennett managed to count the steps. They passed the ground level of La Rose Noire, descending at least three more floors before entering a shadowy cellar. Before he could take in his surroundings, metal claws grabbed Bennett from behind, forcing him onto a cold slab and throwing him under harsh surgery lights. The slab twisted beneath him, making it feel alive, while its claws stretched him like a medieval rack. He assumed the same was happening to Alex. *And that's how we got to this fucking fairy-tale situation. Happy?*

Neil-Shemaine laughed. "Soon, these bioarms will plunge cryoneedles into your sternums. It's sort of a syringe, sort of not, but don't worry! I know what I'm doing. Also, I apologize for the upcoming lack of anesthetic. We're not quite sure how you'll react, and I'm not exactly practiced at keeping human specimens alive, so—I guess we'll just see. Oi?"

"Why are you talking like you're one of them?" Bennett asked.

"I don't know what you mean," Neil-Shemaine deflected.

"You're human, too. I can see it."

"No, see, that's not true," the doctor insisted. "Just as those born of UnEarth can traverse from one form to another, so can we— no, I meant humanity—so can humanity. Those who are human, which isn't me. I can figure out how to do it. And now, with you two, I will." His voice paused, savoring the moment. "You prove what I've always wanted. Flesh—my flesh—can carry the Eve, just like yours. I can finally be what I know I am ... a Scythe of Fovos. The secret's in there somewhere, in you, but we have to be careful, don't we? We have to take—our—time." He laughed again, now somewhere to Bennett's left.

"How do we keep getting into these situations?" Alex muttered.

"I swear I don't try to," Bennett replied, his eyes fixed on the needle overhead, his body trembling.

Though he'd seen and done many horrible things in life, instilling him with a blunt, numb coldness, and had so far handled all the bullshit UnEarth had thrown his way, this was finally breaking his will. *Angels and demons are one thing, but no one said anything about huge fucking needles!*

Everything that had happened since arriving at La Rose Noire had only made him angrier and antsier, draining the Rapture he'd barely begun to grasp. *How is being in a situation like this not supposed to make me fucking angry? How do I use Rapture in this kind of shit?* He was not accustomed to feeling useless, and there'd been no ice on his skin in a long time. Alex had saved *him* during the bar fight. *Those are supposed to be my thing! I'm supposed to be the tough guy here. I mean, I had it—the cold power—the night*

*in the gas station, when the wings showed up. But getting it back . . .
did I lose it already?*

"Look . . . hey, Doc. I'm sure Madam Daphne told you a lot of things, but did she also mention our asses are under the protection of the Tribunal?" Bennett's voice rose, a desperate plea. He heard buttons being pressed and a lever being pulled. The needle above him shifted, poised like a cobra ready to strike. "Let's talk this out. We can make a deal!"

"On the count of three!" the doctor shouted. "Ready? One . . ."

He's bluffing.

"Two," Neil-Shemaine continued, his voice tinged with excitement.

Has to be.

"This doesn't seem like the love Madam Daphne wants her guests to experience," Alex moaned.

"Three!" Dr. Neil-Shemaine grunted, struggling as a rusty switch was thrown.

"Wait!" Bennett shouted—but it was too late. The needle dove into his gut, piercing clear to his spine, stealing his breath and keeping him from mustering a scream. *Hurts too much!* Feeling his insides being turned inside out, and some good ol' rage fighting to pass through his veins, Bennett decided to let the feeling through. *Fuck it. Always worked in the past.*

But the fury only intensified the agony. It, combined with Alex's screams, drowned out everything else. Suddenly, Bennett heard a door creak open, voices rising in argument. Then, with a sudden yelp, the mechanical arm yanked itself back, leaving the needle still oozing. Bennett coughed, gasping for air as the cold slab tilted him upward until he was nearly vertical. The claws binding him released, and he collapsed to the floor, seeing only gray blobs through his blurred vision.

Closing his eyes and focusing, he found Al's signature—faint, but nearby—and another, even fainter, also Wrath.

"Awesome! You're not dead!" a male voice chimed, much more warm and inviting than the snivelling doctor's.

As Bennett's vision adjusted, he could see in his periphery. There were trays with tools like a wood-carver or sculptor might have and long tables topped with what might have been science equipment but looked more like rusty power tools, covered in more blue muscle.

"I know you," Alex said to whoever owned the warm voice. "You're the one I saw in the hall, when I was with Nigel."

"Yeah. And at the moment I'm trying to get you both out of here."

Bennett then felt a pair of hands help him to his feet. Blinking a couple of times, he found the janitor from Madam Daphne's office, smiling with friendly, half-closed eyes. A name tag pinned on his shirt read: *Hi, my name is Felix. How can I assist you, today?*

The oily-skinned, hunched-over Felix, looking like he was in his early forties, flashed a lopsided smile. "How's the tum, my man?"

Bennett pushed him away, leaning against the slab for support. "You couldn't have gotten here one second sooner?"

"Don't mind him. Bennett's always like that," Alex interjected, clutching his own stomach a few feet away.

"Good to meet you both," the janitor said, his smile unwavering. "If you didn't scope the tag, name's Felix. Yes, this is a rescue, but I also want to let you know, our chances of getting out of this alive are, like—less than five percent."

"That's fine. We were just playing at around two percent anyway," Bennett said, stretching his calves.

"Yeah, if anything, that's an uptick!" Alex added, attempting a grin through his pain.

Felix clapped his hands together. "Great! Before we run out of here like goddamned sons of bitches, am I right to assume you have no Wrath or Rapture abilities?"

"I used to," Alex admitted, staring at his cold hands.

"I can see Eve, a little," Bennett said.

Felix stared long enough to let them know that was pitiful, then perked up and smiled like he was searching for something positive to say. "Well, I still feel good about this. So, next step. We can't go out the way we came in. Trust me, they'll be checking soon. Madam Daphne runs this place like a Fovos prison."

Felix ushered them toward the back, passing a massive, ancient-looking computer that covered half the room. Its screens, made of glass, lay in a dark, slimy mass, reminiscent of the surgical slabs. As Bennett hurried past, he spotted a skinny man with a huge mustache slumped against one of the computers, unconscious, wearing slacks and a black turtleneck, adorned with chains and a fresh lump on his forehead. A wet-dry vacuum tube was wrapped around his neck.

Pretty much exactly what I imagined. All except the bling. That's a surprise.

Felix stepped over the doctor, holding a yellow wet-floor sign. "Funny thing is, I kinda liked the doc. He said funny shit sometimes. But—" He set the sign next to Neil-Shemaine, removed the vacuum tube, and shrugged. "You gotta watch out for those warning signs. Come on!" He darted toward an open entryway, pausing when he realized Bennett and Alex weren't following. "Let's go!"

"We're not going anywhere until we know what you're getting out of this," Bennett demanded.

"Getting out of it?" Felix fidgeted, eyes bright with anticipation.

"I think we can trust him," Alex suggested softly.

"I don't care what you think," Bennett said. "I'm in charge when it's just you and me, remember? We need to be smart about this.

Every single fucking UnEarth weirdo we've met so far has tried to stab us, poison us, intimidate us, or eat us, and I want to know what your true intentions are," he finished, exhaling sharply.

"He's trying to help us. He's one of the good guys," Alex argued, now physically trying to nudge Bennett forward.

"You still can't see it, Al?" Bennett asked. "He's got Wrath inside him. He's not just a janitor—the guy was an Imp. A demon."

Alex's face stayed blank for longer than Bennett liked. The teacher then took a couple of glances back and forth.

"Tell him," Bennett urged Felix.

The janitor, who seemed confused by, perhaps, the severity of the humans' exchange, looked Alex square in the eye. "Totally was. Though 'Imp' isn't a very nice word. What of it?"

"My apologies," Bennett said.

The sound of thunderous footsteps began to grow within the walls. Bennett wasn't sure if Alex could hear it or not, but it made him feel a sudden urgency matching Felix's.

"I'm just . . . surprised, is all," Alex replied, in a suburban beigeness that made Bennett cringe.

"Look, guys—yes, I was once an acid-fire spitting monster who was basically a tail that hissed—but that was a long time ago. I haven't used Wrath in centuries, and I also haven't spent much time around humans in, like, two hundred years. So, if there's something I need to know, let's hear it. 'Cause otherwise, why are you fighting the help I'm offering?" Felix shrugged cynically hard. *Hmm . . . I, myself, make that pose on occasion.* The janitor impatiently held still, waiting for a response.

"Okay, I changed my mind," Bennett said.

"What?" Alex nearly screamed.

"Yeah. I like him now. Let's go." Bennett turned, starting away toward Felix.

Alex gradually followed, muttering under his breath.

The trio stepped through the open entryway into a room filled with cages, colorful jars, and wide glass terrariums. Some contained brown mush, others glowing green and yellow plants. Many held what might have been remnants of various living things, some translucent, others like stones floating in gel. Bennett's gut churned violently, aggravating his stomach wound. *Goddamn needles.*

The cages stacked against the wall on their right were filled with creatures, both alive and dead. At first glance, most resembled Earth animals: two dogs, mice, a few cats, and insects. But a few Bennett couldn't quite recognize. *Is that a smiling green armadillo?* What scared him most was that none of the animals made a peep as he passed. *They're terrified of anyone entering the room. Fuck that. I know I've killed a bunch of people, but animal abusers can eat shit.* Leaving the innocents behind gnawed at him. All Bennett could do was bargain with himself. *I'll make it up to you guys, if I can.*

A flash of Rapture surged through him. His shoulders went cold a moment before it faded. *Whoa.* Shaking it off, he hurried to catch up to Felix and Alex, passing a colossal cage at the end of the row. Inside lay a skeleton, a chain wrapped around its wrist. The thing must have been eight feet tall when it was alive—bulbous and imposing.

"Just ignore all this," Felix said, leading them onward.

Soon they were at the end of the freak show. A regular human-sized door, which was oddly reassuring, opened into a hall lit by flickering torches. The trio pressed on, sticking close to the black stone walls.

"Which way to the front?" Alex asked.

"That's . . . not going to work, Wilbur," Felix replied with a nervous chuckle.

"A back door?" Bennett suggested.

Felix coughed. "Also not going to work."

"Why not?"

"Because the Rose went on lockdown the moment you went missing. Constance Mary and her goon squad are hunting us like rabbits. She's sorta famous for never losing her prey."

"So if we can't use the front door, or the back door, or any other door, how are we supposed to get out?" Bennett whisper-shouted.

"I have no idea." Felix continued strolling.

The humans stopped their march and shared a glance. It took Felix a moment to notice. "Uh . . . this isn't where we stop," he said, turning back to them.

"Repeat what you just said," Alex demanded.

"This isn't where we stop? Does it look like we should? 'Cause—" Felix looked around, trying to see what they were seeing.

"Look me in the eye and tell me you have a plan," Bennett said.

"Plans aren't really my thing."

"But you said this was a rescue!" Alex shouted.

Felix shushed him. "It is. Chill out. I know just who to ask for help."

"That's your plan? Get help?" Bennett replied, deadpan.

"Always worked for me so far. How old are you again?" Felix asked.

"I'm thirty-six."

"Oh, cool. I'm three thousand and twelve."

"Who is it we're asking for help?" Alex asked.

"A friend," Felix said bluntly. "Look, I've been working here a long time, and I'm telling you, none of us are ever seeing the outside of this building again without help. Luckily, my friend happens to be the strongest UnEarth Human alive. Just five floors up."

Bennett and Alex exchanged another glance, possibly searching for some sort of reassurance. Both simply shrugged.

"Yeah, all right," Bennett finally said.

Next thing the humans knew, they were joining Felix in a climb for survival, entering a service stairwell at the end of the hallway, moving with as much stealth as they could muster.

"I think I'm starting to feel some Wrath coming back," Alex said, pumping his fists like he was getting blood drawn.

Bennett's stare went dead. "Great. Just in time, Al. Thanks."

"Got a short jog once we get to the second floor. We'll be exposed, so act casual," Felix said, approaching a door labeled *Level 2.* "First, I'll make sure the coast is clear." He opened the door a crack to take a peek, then stepped into the hall. "Be right back."

Bennett and Alex watched as their new janitor-demon friend stepped into the hall, its tan walls adorned with brown baseboards and fancy golden sconces glowing in hazy air that gradually swallowed the light further down the hall. Felix, moving a little slowly for Bennett's taste, turned to give them a thumbs-up, when a door opened up behind him. A security guard stepped out, one of Chief Mary's crew.

"Attendre! S'arrête," the guard shouted, zeroing in on Felix, who plastered on a dull grin and waved.

"What do we do?" Alex whispered.

"Let him do his thing," Bennett replied.

Felix's voice was hard to make out. "Hi, how are you, fellow employee?"

The guard advanced, eyes narrowing. "No one is supposed to be out here. We're on lockdown."

"I was just going to restock the toilet paper," Felix said amiably. "Don't care how locked down we are, people always need to go, know what I mean?"

The guard grabbed Felix by his skinny arm. "Constance will want to speak with you."

"Sure. Just let me get my things," Felix tried to pull away.

"We're going now!" the guard yelled.

Things weren't looking good. Bennett needed to act. *There's a solution here. Think. Think!* But he was too busy berating himself to notice Alex already sprinting past him, leaving behind a heat trail. Diving headfirst into the security guard, he wrestled with him on the floor of the hall, jamming his red-hot palms into the guard's face.

The guard screamed—a hideous sound—as Alex pummeled him, flames licking at his fists, rendering the guard unconscious before he could radio for help.

Bennett hurried into the hall to join them as Alex leaped up from the ground, bouncing on the balls of his feet like a featherweight boxer after a knockout.

"Woo! Yeah, it's definitely coming back. I can feel it!" Alex paused to blow steam off his glowing right hand.

"If I didn't know better, I'd say you missed the Wrath," Bennett remarked. "What happened to 'my living nightmare'?"

"Leave me the fuck alone, Bennett. Okay? For five minutes." Alex wiped the smile from his face as he turned away. *Jesus, Al.*

"We can't risk Chief Mary's people finding the body," Felix said, turning to Bennett. "Would you mind?"

"You want me to carry him?"

"Alex needs to be ready for more guards, and I would need to use Wrath to carry him. You're huge, what's the problem?" Felix asked.

Unable to look to Alex for support, Bennett muttered, "Whatever," and hoisted the security guard over his shoulders in a fireman's carry. "Cripes. The guy got sand in his pockets?"

"He used to be a Lostros. They're hefty," Felix said, hurrying down the hall with Alex while Bennett fought to keep pace. *Assholes—cock suckers—shit kickers . . .*

The doors they passed in the tan hall, in a variety of sizes and colors, were made of wildly different materials and radiated potent shades of Eve. The first they came upon was what Bennett had sensed from Nigel—Dread. Bennett couldn't be sure, but he swore he heard not one, but several people screaming bloody murder inside the room beyond the tall black door. Since Felix moved on without a hitch, he decided to ignore it and do the same.

Next was a door soaked in the same canary-yellow shade of Eve as the bartender who'd served him the mug of moss—and the security guard now slung over his shoulder. This energy carried a heavy, morose feeling. Once again, strange noises emanated from within, this time the haunting wails of countless voices.

"Scuse me, but what exactly is happening in these rooms?" Bennett called out.

"These are the Kingdom Chambers," Felix answered. "Folks come here to feel a little bit of the old life. Be like their old selves, back before we were stripped of our Eve and banished in the Purge."

"What happened?" Alex asked up ahead.

"You ever hear of Inferius, Wilbur?" Felix said.

"The war between Heaven and Hell?"

"Oh, right. I'm still getting used to this new-age Heaven and Hell stuff," Felix said. "I guess that's right, at least from a human perspective. It also explains why you reacted so strangely when you found out I was an Archfiend, or demon. A lot of the stories you've heard about us over your human years are probably wrong."

"Is it true they like to eat us?" Bennett asked.

"Some of them do. Okay, bad first example. The point is, when Inferius ended, we UnEarth Humans were labeled traitors or enemies of the state. The Tribunal came up with a thousand ridiculous names for those they wanted out of the way, and every kingdom went along with it. Assholes," Felix concluded with a shake of his head.

"Izaiah said the war ended two thousand years ago. That's how long you've been on Earth?" Bennett inquired.

"Sounds like a long time when you put it like that," Felix said.

Bennett felt a twitch in his spine, making him stumble. It was a whisper, same as the night he got the wings, but at the same time a dominating presence. *Whoa. We're getting close to something powerful.* It felt like an army of others like himself were around the next corner—others with Rapture.

"Here we are," Felix announced, stopping in front of a hulking door.

The door's trim was composed of hard geometric shapes, seemingly made of glass yet shimmering like mirror or platinum. A violet-and-orchid-blue haze danced within the material as Bennett passed by it. When he stood still, the colors in the glass also stilled.

"What's in here?" Alex asked, his tone a mix of curiosity and caution.

Felix took the door handle and twisted it down. "This is the Still Room." As he pressed forward, breaching the door, Bennett was struck by a sudden cold wave within his mind. A rigid strength surged through him, his spine popping and straightening as an enormous breath, unexpected and overwhelming, filled his lungs. Whatever lay beyond the silver door radiated light so bright it felt like a sunny day, pouring holy illumination into the murky hall. Bennett felt as if he'd been plunged into a rapid river of ice, swept away by its power.

"Stop! Close it, now!" Alex shouted from behind, dropping to a knee, clutching his head as if he got struck by a rogue hockey puck.

"It's okay, Alex." Felix placed a reassuring hand on his shoulder. "That's just your Wrath reacting. It's not hurting you, know what I mean?"

Alex's trembled, desperation in his voice. "I'll w-wait here."

Felix shook his head. "It's not safe. Someone's bound to come by."

"Sorry, Al," Bennet agreed.

"Yeah, I bet you are," Alex said coarsely, fighting to rise to his feet.

"Before you go in there, just . . . prepare yourselves . . . yeah." Felix advised, nodding before stepping inside.

Bennett was the first to follow him and cross the threshold into the luminous room, instantly enveloped by a pressure that held him in place, like molasses crushing from all sides. It was uncomfortable and restrictive, a sensation that sparked serious claustrophobia. Fighting against it, he gazed into a landscape that seemed possible only in dreams.

The landscape was stark white, yet easy on the eyes. Glimmers of blue and violet—the same hues as the door—danced like smooth, soft bolts of lightning along the floor and ceiling. Apart from the vibrant streams of color, there were no visible features, no structures. Bennett was staring into wide-open nothingness.

A moan broke the silence, and Bennett turned to see Alex crawling through the threshold. He set the guard down and, along with Felix, helped the teacher inside.

Shutting the door, Felix said, "We should be safe for a few minutes. Take it slow. Being in here ain't easy for any of us. Luckily, it never needs cleaning, so I never have to cross the threshold."

"Why do I f-feel like this?" Alex asked, shuddering.

"Still Rooms are also called Hywyn Rooms," Felix explained. "They're designed to mimic the conditions of the land of the Celestials. While there's no way to actually recreate the plains of Hywyn in this reality frequency, places like this can help ease some of their homesickness."

"I can't breathe," Alex coughed.

"Yeah, you can. It's just hard," Bennett said, fighting for his own breath. The air he did manage to get was stifling and tasted centuries old.

"Where's this friend?" Alex asked with no signs of patience left. "Let's find them and get the Hell out of here."

Bennett scanned their surroundings. "There's no one here."

"Yes, there is," Felix said with a sly grin. "There's a lot in here. We just have to know what we're looking for." Making the *come on* signal, he started into the brilliant, empty landscape.

The march was a struggle as the cold of Rapture filled Bennett's lungs. Yet this time, instead of fear, he felt a strange calm wash over him. He glanced back at Alex, who was lagging behind, grunting out of annoyance. "If this is all a trick, Felix, and there's no one here, and you're crazy . . . I'm going to be very pissed," Bennett warned.

Felix offered no reply, and they continued their march. Just as Bennett was about to halt and declare that he and Alex were officially out and would return to the Rose, a pulse shot through him, igniting his Eve senses. The presence he'd sensed outside was near.

"There," Felix pointed at what looked like more nothingness.

A small shape began to materialize, as if layers of lace were being pulled away by an unknown wind, revealing a figure seated on the ground, her legs crossed. As Bennett approached, he noticed she wore a black leather jacket, weathered like Izaiah's coat, paired with a sweatshirt, hood up, dark jeans, and tattered boots. She was leaning forward, letting her jet-black hair dangle above a bright silver belt buckle she wore.

When the others approached, she didn't seem to notice. Felix double-timed it, waving excitedly. "Hey! Hannah!"

The sensations coursing through Bennett were overwhelming. Every step closer to her was like wading farther into the deep end of a pool. Arriving at the woman's side, Bennett could see her eyes were closed. As bright as it was in the Still Room, he dared not close his own eyes, or even blink, fearing what kind of power he might see when he looked at her.

"Hey, Hannah. What's going on? Remember me? It's your old pal . . . Uh, sorry, are you, like meditating? Or—" Felix made a rotating circle with his pointer fingers.

After a moment, she calmly took a breath and replied. "Felix, as nice as it is to see you, please keep your voice down. I'm not the only one in here looking for peace and quiet."

"Oh, sorry. Right-o!" Felix winced and lowered his voice, finishing with a salute. "Right-o."

Hannah opened her eyes and turned to Felix, her blank expression giving way to a warm smile. "Hello, old friend," she said.

Felix knelt beside her and they placed their right hands on each other's shoulders, connecting foreheads for a brief moment of shared respect and affection. "As a duly appointed representative of La Rose Noire, it is my duty to inform you that your time in the Still Room has expired," he said. "Please exit the premises and go get some sun, old lady!"

"I knew you'd open with that," Hannah replied, finally turning her attention to Felix's companions.

When her gaze landed on Bennett, he was struck by the fantastically vibrant colors of her eyes, mirroring the hues of the Still Room. Staring into them felt like free-falling—an exhilarating beauty that rivaled any sunrise or sunset he had ever witnessed.

It's like looking into one of the nine wonders of the world.

"To whom do I owe the pleasure?" she asked.

Felix turned with a sudden flourish, as if introducing royalty. "Gentlemen, this is Celestial Hannah, of Cross Station. General of Inferius, in service of the Army of Michael, hero of Hywyn, and"—he beamed at her—"my friend."

"I'm Alex," the teacher introduced himself, visibly struggling.

"I'm Bennett. We're human," Bennett added, immediately feeling stupid after.

Hannah gave them a once-over before turning away. "I can see that, but as Felix would have told you if he'd remembered, I don't like to be disturbed. Frankly, you don't belong here," she finished, closing her eyes and returning to her resting position.

"Trust us, we know that," Bennett said, his frustration bubbling.

Felix waved his hands in front of her face. "Come on—come on! We went through a lot to get here. People are after us! Where's the Hannah who did all that stuff I just mentioned?"

"None of this has anything to do with her," Hannah answered.

"Madam Daphne was going to let the doctor turn these guys into sashimi! I had to get them out," Felix whisper-shouted, urgency creeping into his voice.

"Again, not my concern."

"Please." Alex struggled to even speak. "I just want to get back to my wife and child. Can you help us?"

"I don't do problems anymore, kid. Sorry," Hannah said flatly.

"These are no ordinary circumstances," Bennett jumped in. "We've been sent by the Tribunal to catch Joseph, the demon. You've heard of him, haven't you?"

"No. But it sounds like a job for the Medolians, not me," she motioned behind them. "You should get going. I can hear Chief Mary and her squad coming for you. They sound irritated."

"If that's true, we need to go!" Alex called, on the verge of tears.

Bennett hated that he felt the same, as Hannah did not sound inclined to help them, and it could take forever to get back to the door. *Why would Felix bring us in here? This feels like a trap. A dead end, at best.*

"Hannah, please. These guys need some help," Felix pleaded as Alex began to back away.

"Whatever it is, it doesn't involve me. Nothing should, anymore. Leave me be," Hannah said.

Bennett and Felix exchanged desperate glances. The soldier bowed his head and turned to follow Alex.

"Guys, wait!" Felix shouted, his voice full of urgency. "Tell her who sent you. Specifically."

Bennett turned back. "Izaiah. Why?"

Hannah opened her eyes and focused on Bennett. "You must be mistaken."

"Nope. Old, wrinkled guy. Smelly. Gray knitted cap. Ring a bell?"

Hannah uncrossed her legs and stood, now eye to eye with Bennett. He glanced at her belt buckle, which depicted a striking eye surrounded by six shimmering orbs.

Turning back to Felix, her expression sharpened. "The Tribunal ordered the Medolians to use humans for an exorcism? Did the Senate approve this?"

"It gets a lot weirder than that," Felix replied. "Everyone's talking about it. Where you been?"

"Here," Hannah said tersely, catching Bennett's curious stare at her belt buckle.

He struck his gaze when a booming sound echoed in the distance. *That was the door.* "They're in," Bennett said, sensing a host of signatures approaching, Chief Mary's shade the most potent among them.

"What was your mission?" Hannah asked, her tone shifting slightly.

"Find the Imp. Get it out of the kid. Deliver it to the Tribunal. Prevent a war. Save the day," Bennett answered.

"Guess that explains the Wrath and Rapture within you," Hannah said.

"We didn't ask for it. They put it there," Alex said.

"None of this makes sense. Someone's lying," Hannah murmured.

"That's what we've been saying." Bennett felt the security detail getting closer. *There's no way out of this.* He was feeling stronger but knew he, Alex, and Felix couldn't take on a whole squad of beefed-up UnEarth security by themselves. *Though I wouldn't mind trying out some moves on that Chief Mary. Mmmm.*

"What about me, Hannah?" Felix sounded frantic. "If they catch us, I won't just lose this job. Know what I mean?"

"Do you have any idea what you're asking of me?" Hannah barked, turning away. "What treaties or agreements could I violate? If the Senate made the order, you know exactly who's pulling the strings. Do you not remember anything from Inferius? Stupid mistakes start wars, not a single Archfiend acting alone."

"You're the one who said Izaiah doesn't make mistakes," Felix pressed. "I don't think these two coming here tonight was one, either."

Hannah fell silent, narrowing her eyes at him. Bennett could hear shouting in the distance. Chief Mary and her team had picked up their scent and would be there any second. *Hopefully, they have just as hard a time finding stuff in here as we did.*

Hannah remained still, her head bowed in contemplation.

"Miss?" Alex chimed in. "I had a life. I think Bennett did too. But then we were supposed to die. Now we have this second chance. I know we're just dumb humans, but I want to help. Then I want to go home. Izaiah chose us, and we're still not sure why, but we're on our own until he comes back."

"Something big is going on, and we need to know who the good guys in all this are," Bennett added.

"Over here!" someone shouted in the distance.

Bennett turned and found foggy figures approaching. *Balls.*

Felix, Alex, and Bennett awaited an answer from Hannah. She lowered her head and sighed. "Oh, Felix. If—and I do mean if—I help you out of this, the first thing you will do is tell me everything. Got it? No secrets."

"Whatever you say," Felix agreed for them.

Bennett caught sight of Chief Mary leading her team, like a mirage in a desert. "Anything else?" he asked Hannah.

She turned her gaze on Bennett and Alex, studying them for a moment longer. "Very well."

Felix hurried to Hannah's side, placing a hand on her shoulder. "Hop on, guys."

"Hop on? What do you mean? How the Hell are we getting out of here?" Bennett shouted, struggling against the intense pressure and gravity to reach Hannah.

As he and Alex placed a hand on her shoulder, Bennett found her brilliant gaze fixed on him just before she closed her eyes. "Haven't taken four in some time," she said. "Hold still. Wouldn't want to lose anyone."

"What was that?" Alex asked as the white energy of a Shift wrapped around them.

Oh, not this again.

The ground fell away beneath Bennett's feet. The sensation of traveling at a billion miles an hour overtook him, and the Earth passed below, their destination unknown.

THE STRANGER

The ground rumbled as another airplane took off. A beam of light from a gap in the wall illuminated a line of dust shaken loose from the ceiling, drifting lazily through the air. Most of the takeoffs were smaller jets or prop planes, but occasionally, a jumbo jet would roar past, like the one that just taxied.

Leigh brushed some dirt off the stack of luggage beside her and laid her head down. Sleep was impossible, but that didn't mean she couldn't close her eyes and imagine she wasn't trapped in a metal box with Joseph and his white mask lingering in the shadows across from her.

Focusing on how hungry she was made it easier. *I would eat anything right now. Even Joseph's gross-ass hand.* Other than a protein bar she'd found in the pocket of a dead man on the side of the road during their trek here (*strawberry cream*), it had been days since she'd last eaten, and she hadn't had anything to drink in at least twenty-four hours. *I would even eat haggis, Jeff. I would.*

It seemed they were waiting for the cover of nightfall, though

Leigh had no real idea because Joseph hadn't said a word since they climbed into the luggage container. Based on the length of the trip so far, and knowing their intended final destination, Leigh guessed they'd made it all the way to N'Djamena International Airport. Joseph had said he was taking her to London to find the second stone, and it would have been the only international airport within a week's drive. *True to his word. Classic Joe.*

Three days earlier, he had used the smallest stone to force a confession from her, revealing a vision that haunted her every waking moment since. Shortly after the ceremony, she had been tossed into the rear of a box truck that stank of old meat, joined by Joseph and two dozen riders with their pet birds. They had traveled hundreds of miles through the scorching desert, trapped in the truck's cargo container which may as well have been an oven. Her body had sweated out what little water it had left, and at several points, she thought she might go mad. The only real relief came from brief periods of unconsciousness, blurring her sense of time. Three days was a guess at best.

Some of the time awake was spent playing a game with herself, figuring out who in history had had it worse than her. *The souls cramped into four-foot by three-foot boxes in Urga, Mongolia, early twentieth century. They had it pretty bad. Limbs atrophying, a whole mess. And then there were the slave ships out of Africa, hundreds of souls crammed into crawl spaces like sardines, forced to lie down for months. Or being stuck in the Tower of London in the thirteenth century. No, thank you. This is slightly better. At least I'm doing a good job convincing myself of that.*

The journey gave her plenty of time to hate herself for telling Joseph where the second stone was. *Gave up your best bargaining chip. Stupid.* It also allowed her to dissect what she'd felt in the cave when he had touched her. *The shit I saw . . . I can't get it out of my head. It won't leave me alone. This guy is crazy and dangerous. Astronomically so.* Whatever the stone had allowed him to do, she never wanted it to happen again. The experience was more than just pain; it had shattered her psyche. Luckily, the smallest stone ran out of juice before she could spill her final secret. If anything happened to her now, no one would be able to find the third, largest stone. *Which I pray would prevent what I saw. It's weird to think my death might be the best solution for everything and everyone.*

During the trip to the airport, the Wraithian caravan passed several villages, stopping at each one. What followed was something Leigh couldn't have believed was real unless she had lived through it. There was no escaping the horror as the Wraithians ransacked farms, houses, businesses—anything that could be desecrated. Dogs barked in panic, cattle and sheep called out desperately. The desert riders howled and shrieked, raising Hell into the night as they traveled. Try as she might, she couldn't drown out the sounds.

Good thing I never believed in God, or else this would be a doozy of a faith crisis. Curious what Mom would say to justify all this.

During one such pillaging, Joseph had lifted the rear gate, as he usually did, giving her the chance to step out into the evening air. On this night, much of the violence was within sight, and Joseph did not leave her to walk among it, as he was prone to, as though drawn to conflict like a moth to a flame. This night, he asked Leigh to watch the Wraithians at work, insisting it would be of great value to her.

Leigh instead said, "Fuck you, and your pets."

Joseph chuckled. "They would be most unhappy to know you think our arrangement is such. The Wraithians will perform their rituals, collect their Wrath, and depart. The village will be a shell of its former self, able to regrow. They simply act as all plagues do."

"Plagues are evil."

"Plagues are part of life, which knows not of green lights and red.

It is a fluid ocean of energy colliding. The boy figured it out. It's what made him special. A fire cannot roar without a tree to burn, and a tree cannot grow without soil made from long-dead others. Hywyn cannot exist without Arros. A humor within reality, perhaps."

Leigh's rage boiled over. "And you're going to what? Fix it? Is that it? Get rid of the humor?" Joseph's mask locked onto her, but he remained silent. "That's it, isn't it? Why when I asked you what you wanted, you said nothing, because you mean it." Again, Joseph didn't respond. "Don't bother denying it. I saw it all when you touched me with your fucked up hand."

Joseph huffed like a wild beast. "So, Mellu saw fit to show you . . . Very well."

"I don't know what happened, but I saw it—what you really are," Leigh snapped. "I saw the kid, and your plan. I saw the black empty explosion. I saw what it does. Or, undoes. I'd bet your Wraithian pals don't even know what you're really after, as ludicrous as it sounds. They think you're starting a war for the control of Hell. What's to stop me from telling them the truth?"

Joseph clenched his fists, his composure slipping. "Silence would benefit you far greater."

"Not really convincing me," she said.

With a swift movement, Joseph gripped the high rear door and slammed it shut, cutting off the cool evening air. *That confirms it. Full on madman. I have to tell someone. Anyone. Because I am way too goddamn tired to save the cosmos right now.*

That was the last Leigh had seen of the sky until arriving at N'Djamena, which felt like a miracle in and of itself. *A guy in a mask, surrounded by wild horse riders? Strolling through society unnoticed? Psh!* The riders' smell alone should have set off alarms as they neared civilization. Leigh thought, *This is it—they're done—no way,* a hundred times, but the Wraithians seemed to have every trick up their sleeves to pass through society undetected.

She'd watched with mounting terror as the two dozen riders who'd accompanied them washed away the white markings on their skin, skillfully covering their tattoos with clothing and makeup, transforming into upstanding citizens. Whether navigating a blockade or joking with police, the riders slipped into and broke character effortlessly. *Some of these fucks must have been cops and electrical engineers in their previous lives.* Together, the Wraithians escorted Leigh and Joseph safely and sound through the largest city in Chad.

When the caravan reached the airport, it split in two. Leigh's half, with Joseph and six Wraithians, broke for the tarmac. The riders accompanying them were an average-looking bunch: three women, three men. *Makes me feel like I've got Secret Service protection, except mine wants to kill me.* They made it safely across the airport and took refuge in a container the size of two average hotel rooms, intended for stowing luggage before a flight. Here, they had been waiting.

Presently, Leigh wondered if Joseph was asleep under his mask. He hadn't spoken in hours, but then out of nowhere coughed and said, "The man, his name was Jeff?"

"You don't get to say his name," Leigh muttered, refusing to look at him.

"He was a warrior?"

"More so than you."

"We have wondered what his thoughts were," Joseph said. "It is one of the few mysteries left—one's thoughts. Even to the Medolians, who may glimpse them if allowed, the human mind remains closed. Time and space are physical constructs easily read like words. Yet the mind. . . There are those who say the Seeress can see the full breadth of our thoughts when we die. We are no seeress, but we sensed much Grief from him when he dissolved. But also Fervor, and the violet of Rapture. We believe he was in love with you."

"I honestly don't care what you think."

"We feel the Wrath within you. You must have also loved this warrior Jeff. Part of you wished to stay with him in the desert, did it not?"

"No. Sometimes we have to do things we don't want to do."

Joseph cleared his throat. "And other times, we choose where our feet tread. Do not blame others for your own actions. A body is a vessel—it moves only when commanded."

"Yeah, but you also put me in this situation, and I can't do anything about it, so you're full of shit." Leigh folded her arms and turned away.

"What about your mind? Your thoughts? Your feelings? You have no control over these?" Joseph inquired. "No matter where you rest, you are body and mind both. The body creates change in the Earthly realm, while the mind prepares the soul for the next step. Mortals choose their Eve, thus deciding what the afterlife becomes."

"I'm honestly so tired of hearing about this Eve bullshit." Leigh rubbed her temples. "You make no sense."

"The Eve is a culmination. A horrid by-product of all beings," Joseph explained. "When life is created on Earth, as is Rapture. When a life is purposefully taken, Wrath is the result, feeding Arros, birthing our kind."

"Wrath? That's what you said you feel in me?" Leigh pressed, hoping she could find something to exploit. *Before I pass out again.*

"The Wrath within you drew you to the temple. As did theirs." He gestured at the Wraithians and reached into his cloak for the smallest stone, Mellu. "The task of filling the Brothers was passed through thousands of generations until Gehenna was swallowed by the sands, lost to time. The Molochs were gone and forgotten, except by a few."

Leigh desperately missed reality. "I want off this ride."

The mask turned on her. "You wish to die?"

"If it stops this fun house from Hell," Leigh said plainly. "Shit—I could even do it. Does one of your friends have a gun?"

"The girl makes the boy laugh," Joseph said. "However, your death is not allowed until you disclose the location of Eilam."

"I'm never going to tell you where the third stone is."

"You will. Once we have the second Brother, we can access even more strength. We can use the pain. You remember the pain, don't you?" Joseph asked.

It wasn't just pain, you dick. "Yeah. I remember. Everything," Leigh said, her voice rising enough for the Wraithians to hear. "Like what I saw. What you're really after." She wanted them to know, wanted them to see Joseph for what he was. "So, your friends know you're, like, a low-level demon, right? A small fry. In no way ready for the kind of challenge taking on the devil presents. It's as though that kind of plan would never work."

Joseph huffed violently, silencing her. "We meant it when we said silence from you was best. You know nothing of demons, child," he said in a hollow, haunting tone. "You think us invisible ghosts? No. The only reason you don't see us is because we don't *allow* it. You've likely glanced over one and not known it. The Archfiend have taken shape on Earth since the dawn of man. Though most are vain, yes. Blind. Condemning the great heritage of the Beast of which they were blessed. This is why the nameless took action. This is why we, Joseph, exist."

"Sounds like someone is a special little guy."

"We have something no Archfiend before has possessed."

"The kid?" Leigh asked.

"With the boy we may walk the Earth as human, aiding our journey."

Here's something. "Is that all he is to you? A vessel?" Leigh asked.

"We are strong together. The Archfiend play with humans, never seeing the strength in taming one."

"How does that work, exactly? Do you have to sign release papers to get out of Hell? Forgive me, I've never been very religious."

"Entering Earth is no easy task, but make no mistake, Arros is not a prison," Joseph replied. "Many fight to return. The Archfiend cannot stand life on this planet. They will do anything to be free of it."

"I'll take your word for it. So, you got a body on Earth, then what?"

"It was not effortless. Earthly flesh resists pure Wrath. The boy has no control. But the body eased, felt the truth, and allowed the demon inside, opening its eyes and showing him things he never dreamed—true strength."

"Yeah. I saw how you murdered my friend really easily."

"The demon taught the boy to forget the body's limitations. We were the first to bring Eve into flesh."

"And why would you want to do that?" Leigh asked, half-pleasantly. *Gotta keep him talking.*

He shook his head. "We've spoken enough."

"No, I don't mean 'we.' I mean you, the boy," Leigh said.

Joseph didn't respond.

"He's in there, right? Not a slave or anything?" Leigh pressed. "You said I made him laugh. I can make him laugh more." She hoped this wouldn't backfire. The white mask lingered. "You want to build trust? Show me a sign of good faith."

Joseph remained silent for an agonizing moment. Finally, he cleared his throat and said softly, "If you are allowed to speak with the boy, you are likely to tell us the location of the third Brother?"

"Couldn't hurt your chances."

Joseph stirred, his mask drifting from side to side. Following a low growl, he muttered, "Very well."

Placing his hands on his knees, he looked at the ground near his feet. His shoulders rose and fell slowly as the arch in his spine curled farther forward. With a fierce cough, he straightened it with a sharp crack. Wet lungs fought for breath as his hands gripped his knees for support. A moment later, he found a steady rhythm, his body relaxing with a sigh.

The white mask floated around the container, as if seeing it for the first time. It settled on Leigh. "Hello," a new voice said.

Leigh barely held on to her breath, racing through possible responses in her mind. Everything felt wrong, as if anything could set him off. Finally, she settled on, "Hi."

His gloved hand stretched out, touching everything within reach. "It's been so long—since I've—felt." His voice was weaker now, his words sluggish. "You wished to speak with. . . me?"

Leigh took a moment. "Yes. I did. I'm glad you were able to. First, what's your name? It's not Joseph, is it?" He shook his head. "What is it?"

"Mason."

"It's nice to meet you, Mason."

Mason laughed callously, echoing in the confined space.

"What is it?" Leigh asked.

"That's what the doctors used to start with. Good reveal."

"What doctors?"

"Lampre. Wilson. All of them."

"I'm not a doctor—at least, not of medicine. I'm an archaeologist. I wanted to speak with you because I want to make sure you're okay."

Mason cupped his hand where his mouth would be. "Paging Dr. Bull."

"No really," Leigh pleaded. "I've seen what's happening to you. You can't feel well under that mask. What if we—"

"Show us your goodwill," Mason interrupted with a cold chuckle.

"Excuse me?"

Mason's words slowed, his tone dropping. "You asked the demon to show you goodwill, so show me yours."

"What do you want in return?"

"Tell me something . . . something about you. I want to smile."

"About me? Like what?"

"Just start."

"Mason, if you could point me in the right direction, I'd be—"

"Start! Talk! NOW!" Mason boomed, slamming his hands on his knees, his massive shoulders heaving.

"Okay, okay! Let's see—I'll tell you about my hometown, okay? It's a nice place, probably not much different from where you grew up. Do you remember where you grew up?" Leigh paused, waiting for a response. Mason stayed quiet, listening intently. "When I was little, it was a small place—about ten thousand people. Maybe more. Everybody knew everybody. But every time I've gone back it's just, well, exploded."

"Exploded?" The mask tilted to the side.

"What I mean is, there are a lot more people. It's growing so much that I hardly recognize it sometimes."

"Growth. *Eck*. The nameless hates it. He showed me that the more there is, the more there is that hurts. And more who serve as slaves. The nameless is wise," Mason said.

"What else does Mr. Nameless say?"

"He says you don't care for me and will try to trick us, and that you aren't as nice as you seem."

"Mason, sweetheart, I don't want to trick anyone. I just want to go home. What about you?"

"I am home."

"No. This is a box on a tarmac in Africa. You must have grown up somewhere."

"I was never anywhere for long," Mason replied casually. "Makes it easier to forget."

"I'm with you there. I've tried to forget everything about the old me."

"Really?"

"Oh, yeah. You know how long I've been trying to forget high school? The cliques, the drama, the parties, the boyfriends—ugh. It was the worst four years of my life." Leigh sighed, letting her shoulders drop in a feigned attempt at comfort.

"I knew you were special. I told the nameless so," Mason said. "School is for the weak. The stupid." His right knee began to pump like a car piston in an idling engine. "Their faces were . . . flat. Pointless. They were hateful. Judging, always. 'The dissection was wrong! He did it wrong! We need another frog. Tell him so! Cut it down the middle!'" Mason's breathing quickened, his mask swinging from side to side.

Leigh let him calm before speaking softly. "I hear you on the judging. I'm sorry people treated you that way, but if there's one thing I've learned after all these years, it's that there's always time to change. You can always become better."

"How do you see yourself better?" Mason asked with a soft inquisitiveness.

"For one thing, something to drink and eat would make me feel instantly better," Leigh said "How about you? What would make you better than you were yesterday?"

Mason looked around as if deep in thought. "Nothing would. I'm safe."

"You may think that, but at the end of the day, it's not just you in there, and your body doesn't sound good. Don't you want it to be yours again? I like being in control of my body."

"You can't turn me. The nameless showed me. My flesh is power. It's freedom. I'll use them both."

"Did you invite it? The demon? Or did it find you?"

The mask tilted to the side. "Does it matter?"

"I just don't get it, Mason. You sound like a good kid. I want to know why you seem okay with this arrangement. Do you realize you're hurting people?"

"We do—I do," he said with a callous laugh.

Leigh was taken aback. She hadn't expected that. *The demon's right. This kid is perfect.*

"Tell me why you want to hurt people," she said.

"Because they're mean. You know they are."

"Not everyone. Come on, that's childish."

Mason shook his head. "Like my mom and dad. The stupid towns we lived in. The kids. They didn't understand. WRONG! You dissected it wrong! All wrong! And the doctors. Them. The girls. They stared. Like I didn't belong. No one was . . . there was no one." Mason hung his head, starting to scratch the wrappings on his torso and legs.

Leigh nodded, feeling like she could pass out from exhaustion at any second. "I'm curious, do you know how old you are?"

"I was eighteen when the demon knocked. Now . . . I'm not sure." He stopped scratching to stare at his gloved hands.

"That's okay. Do you know where you are?" Leigh asked.

"Yes, we're going to London, where you sent the second Brother."

"And what's going to happen when we get there? Are people going to be hurt?"

"If they get in our way."

"I still don't get it. Explain it to me. What do you get out of this?"

"Power," Mason replied.

"How do you get power out of this?" Leigh asked. "You're not even in control of your own body."

"You have no idea. The nameless has shown me things, you can't even—With the Brothers of Gehenna, we'll be more powerful than even Lucifer. We'll ascend every throne in UnEarth."

"No, that's a lie he's telling the desert cult so they'll work with him."

"What do you mean?" Mason asked.

"I saw it when he used the small stone on me. He wants to use them to—"

Mason suddenly convulsed, silencing her. His body shook as he screamed through torn vocal cords, his head whipping back.

"No!" the voice of Joseph boomed. "That is enough! You will speak no more." His posture curled forward. "The boy will never return to our surface. Ever. Learn your place. Both of you!"

"You bag of shit!" Leigh spat out. "If you want to kill me, do it. But I'll never stop trying to stop you, or your friends."

Joseph laughed and sighed. "A defender now? Why claim to loathe conflict? You fool no one. Not when we can sense what is within you—the desire to destroy."

"I don't destroy," Leigh said. "I'm an explorer."

"You explore previous lives. You break walls, charters, barriers to find what others left behind. If that is not breaking and taking for one's own gain, what is?" Joseph asked. "Yes, your tint is that of Wrath and Dread. You, like all living things, like all life, commit evil to survive."

"You don't know anything about me."

"We'll see, child."

There was a knock at the container door. Joseph rose as it opened, letting in moonlight. The rest of the Wraithians who had accompanied them on their trek were outside. One of the smaller men now wore an airport worker's uniform. Leigh didn't want to know how he got it.

When Joseph approached them, the Wraithian up front whispered something Leigh couldn't make out. He then signaled to the others in the container. Swiftly and silently, they moved out from their hiding spots and exited the cargo hold.

Joseph stepped toward Leigh and held out his hand, as though she might take it. "It's time."

She rose without touching him and moved to the front of the container and out the door. Stepping into the evening air as another airplane took off, she was surrounded by Wraithians staring with dead eyes, having lost their civilian guises and returned to their desert-cult chic. She glanced around the airport; there was no one else in sight. When the recent takeoff's rumble faded, the airport returned to quiet.

"Let's move," Joseph said, pushing to the front.

Leigh was hurried along as the group stuck to the shadows. She couldn't help but stare at the tall lights over the airfield. Brilliant, white, and luminous, they were an odd comfort in a situation that was becoming worse by the minute. If they actually reached London, what then? *He's bound to find the stone, and what if Casey is still—no! Don't think like that. She's not there. With any luck she went home.*

They rounded an open aircraft hangar. A small two-engine jet came into view. The Wraithians broke their silence and began shouting, charging with new vigor. The door of the plane opened, and a red-haired Wraithian woman leaned out. She glanced around the airport before lowering the staircase for them. Every step closer to the plane made Leigh's gut churn and her legs weaken. *Please. . . Anywhere but in a tube at thirty thousand feet with these guys.*

Just before Joseph marched onto the stairs, he froze in place, and Leigh nearly ran into him, finding his mask pointed off to their left.

"Joe? You okay?" she asked.

"We felt . . ." He trailed off, stepping away as if having forgotten all about her and the plane. His head was tilted up to the night sky. He lifted his hands, as though feeling the heat of an invisible fire. The Wraithians waited calmly, not the least bit swayed by his behavior. *Voodoo bullshit, swear to God.*

Joseph gasped. "It's her. A new player, yet familiar face . . . from long ago." He turned to the Wraithians and uttered a few grave words in their language. Leigh swore they looked downright surprised.

"You . . . felt something?" she asked, but Joseph wasn't listening.

"If she is returned, that can only mean—" For the first time, he began to sound panicked, muttering to himself before stomping up to the Wraithians. "We must move up our schedule. Call the Medolian."

The three in front, two males and a female, stepped forward, reached into their satchels, and revealed small black stones—the same ones Leigh had seen them trying to catch blood with during her interrogation. Along with the stones, they also produced serrated daggers.

A voice spoke up from behind Leigh. "Do you think that is wise?" The red-haired Wraithian leaned out from the plane door, keeping a watchful eye on the perimeter. "Others will be able to sense the signal."

It was the first time Leigh had heard one of the Wraithians speak English, or at all curtly to Joseph, who did not miss a beat.

"We must take the risk. A Celestial has entered the game," he said.

The red-haired Wraithian grew tight-lipped and nodded. Joseph motioned to the three up front holding stones and daggers, waiting for his orders. "Call her."

The three Wraithians began to grunt and huff, flexing every muscle in their bodies. Throwing their heads back, they roared. Veins bulged. They snarled, biting into their own tongues and cheeks, drawing streams of blood, and with a final cry, swiftly jammed the daggers into their own sides, opening holes large enough to plunge the black stones into themselves. The screaming continued as long as they could keep it going. *God Almighty. This—no, this isn't happening.* Leigh looked away but could still hear everything.

"What are you doing? You're going to get caught!" she screamed at Joseph, whose mask was fixed on the gruesome act.

"A plane will no longer do," he answered. "Desperate times, Leigh."

The screams of the Wraithians died down. Their blood pooled on the pavement as they drooped to the ground, soon silent and still. Their brothers in arms took the daggers and finished the job, slicing their throats from ear to ear, pocketing the daggers afterward.

"You people are insane," Leigh said, choking back vomit.

Joseph's mask turned down to her. "Define sanity."

Before she could muster a response, a blinding strobe struck her eyes, and a flash of wind came out of nowhere, nearly shoving her off her feet. She peered through her fingers as a shadow appeared in the light. The flash faded as quickly as it had arrived, revealing a new figure standing ten feet away. She could not see much, squinting to make out any detail on the woman who'd appeared out of nowhere, but she could tell she had a rigid posture and was holding a bladed weapon of some kind.

"You rang, my love?" the mystery woman asked Joseph.

Sorry, did she just say "love"?

Leigh would have laughed if she wasn't so scared.

THE FALLEN GARDEN

Trivium City, a saucer of warm glow over a dark landscape, returned to Izaiah's view on his left, nestled in the distance between mountain peaks. Above it, the sky's once deep shade of maroon had become purple, gradually fading into the darkness of night.

Ninety-nine percent of Trivium's surface was an endless, deep-pitted mountain range, with jagged peaks resembling standing spikes. There was little room for civilization. Yet somehow, Trivium City had been erected, the result of thousands of years of planning, cooperation, and action among the worlds of UnEarth. Tonight, however, as though a dose of literal symbolism alluding to the spreading hysteria and xenophobia within, the once vibrant city seemed dull, its former sheen reduced to a mere flicker.

Izaiah's current trek into the mountains was the third stop of his tour since leaving Alex and Bennett at La Rose Noire. *And I'm exhausted! I wish I could have brought them along, but mortals can't enter Arros or Hywyn. Their atoms are still too low a frequency. Too bad, too. I bet Alex would've gotten a kick out of seeing all this. I doubt Bennett would've cared.*

The first stop on the tour was Arros, the world of Wrath. No surprise, the old Medolian couldn't make it past the ninth gate, told he would have to return at a later date, as Lucifer-Aveyl was not seeing visitors and the Alus Conclave had adjourned for the month. His following trip to Hywyn was similar in almost every way. Met with the coldest of receptions (*a staple of Celestial hospitality for millenia*), he was made to wait for a whole day before being allowed to say his piece before the angels. After telling the Magnus Council of Joseph's rumored goal—to find these Brothers of Gehenna—he was summarily dismissed.

His ears were still ringing, and his body still felt cold and restricted, all side effects of his recent time in Hywyn. The old Medolian lamented, his thoughts lingering on how Gabriel and his council had ostensibly responded the same as Lucifer's had: "*Order still on. Neither kingdom allowed to extract. Medolians must do so. Both humans MUST be present at time of arrest.*

Best wishes. Xoxo."

The only opinion everyone in UnEarth seemed to share in common was a mistrust of the Medolians. Lately, Izaiah couldn't even question a witness to an Eve offense without being accused of partisanship by all sides. Though he had to admit he'd been having doubts about his team of Sentries and their impartiality lately. *Meaning this week, and the last couple of decades. Just a gut feeling for now, though my gut is usually right.*

Since the Gathering of the Medolians, Izaiah had kept tabs on the Sentries working the Joseph Mandate. Everyone's Eve signatures were exactly where they were supposed to be, except for one: his second in command, Mara, who hadn't revealed herself in two days. Izaiah wasn't surprised or jumping to any conclusions, but dropping off the grid at such a crucial moment was more than suspicious. *She knows better.*

After his dismissal from both majority party kingdoms, Izaiah hightailed it to Trivium City. He regretted having to do so, but he needed help solving this crisis. If anyone would be able to figure out who was helping Joseph, it would be the Seeress, Illyana.

He Shifted to the North Eb Rings, and hoofed it into the north hills, out of the city and up into a section of the Pilomine mountain range known as the Hyperion. As he climbed the mountain path, now more than sixty miles from the city, Izaiah considered what he might say to her when he arrived. He hadn't brought any gifts like she liked. *That's a "my bad," as they say.* Sweet, buttery breads and candies were her favorites. He also smelled awful, which was just rude to inflict on another in such close quarters. *Nothing my powers can do about that. Whoof. Sorry, Illyana.*

Part of him was nervous. Though he had already visited her—more than once in fact—while working the Joseph Mandate, she had been reluctant to help each time. *Scolded me pretty good. Rightfully so.* Reliving the past and glimpsing possible futures was a gift too powerful to be wielded as a tool. Izaiah knew this as well as Illyana, and respected her and her mutation enough to only ask for help in extreme circumstances. *Gotta respect your peers. She's a Medolian, after all.*

Presently, he pulled his gaze from the glow of the city far below and continued up the treacherous slope into shadow. Even with his cane for support and a steady stream of Mallos pumping through him, Izaiah's joints ached, especially his knees. After more than two hours on the rough path, avoiding protrusions like eight-foot spikes from the slope, he was having a hard time finding something worth laughing at. Every possible sound in the dim gray canyon made him halt and take a panicked glance around. Luckily, so far it seemed no one was following him.

Reaching the crest of the path, Izaiah came upon a triangle of darkness on his right, peering deeper into a cleft in the mountain. Stepping around a bulbous rock, he found an opening filled with light and ducked through, pushing aside stiff, dead vines, cold to the touch that broke apart like old campfire cinders as he passed. Soon, he entered a wide gray-themed scene, brushing dirt and ash off his coat, coughing and spitting onto a broken stone walkway. A field of fossilized pillars sat before him, leaning, standing, or broken across nearly two hundred acres in the once thriving UnEarth garden, Yil.

The garden was invisibly set in a low inlet valley between mountain peaks. Slanted, flat-faced rock walls encroached on all sides, holding in the damp air filled with stagnant scents. Standing pillars—like obsidian redwood trunks stripped of their branches—reached to the sky, where the moon shone through a canopy net of ash-tinted vines. Below, the wild garden spilled out of wracked stone structures like serpents breaking free of their cages. Once, the plants had been astounding, always thriving and changing—back before Lucifer had cast himself from Hywyn, and the garden he had tended for thousands of years was rendered still.

Few who remembered the garden existed, and Izaiah knew them all. Furthermore, Eve signatures were cut off from the outside world once inside, making Yil the perfect place to hide someone too important to be found.

So why do I feel like something is misbegotten 'round here?

Moving up the stone walk, Izaiah sensed a suspicious amount of nothing. *Where are Luna and Amrath? Those big lugs should have greeted me by now.* Scratching his head through his gray knitted cap, he spotted on a knoll up ahead. Four pillars stood at the corners of a square floor and roof. Izaiah hurried to the structure, hoping the high ground would let him see the garden better. *Maybe spot those Celestials, wherever they're hiding.* Abound in recessed chunks, particularly in the roof, the structure would have crumbled to pieces in a rainstorm if one ever came to Trivium.

A few feet shy of the hill, Izaiah's enormous ears picked up a faint whooshing sound. He froze, trying to remember why it filled him with panic. Then it came back to him.

Oh. Right. Darn.

With a yelp, he flung himself forward just as a monstrous object impacted behind him. Dust blasted out, and Izaiah was sent flailing into a fallen pillar—spine first—upside down. He coughed, trying to wave away the dust and the ringing in his ears as a hulking Celestial stood a few feet away, pulling their spear from the ground. *Found Luna! So where's Amrath?*

Before Izaiah could flip right-side up, the shape lunged at him, bellowing, "Be gone!"

Izaiah raised his cane just in time to halt a symmetric, chiseled fist eight inches across attempting to pummel him. The creature's hand was made of something akin to a powder-blue Violan gemstone. *The fist of a creature many on Earth would dub an angel. So like I said. . . pretty different.* The emerald bubble Izaiah generated was a sloppy, minimal Band-aid defense against the Celestial's attack. Grimacing from the strain, he swung his cane to the sky, launching the enormous shadow away.

Forty feet up, Luna, majestic and terrifying, roared with the might of a dozen grizzlies and opened their full wingspan, stopping midair.

"I think there's been a misunderstanding!" Izaiah shouted desperately, rolling up his sleeves, his words drowned out by a battle cry from the Celestial breaking into the moonlight.

"Medolian!" Luna launched like a streaking eagle, brandishing their spear. *Wow, they sound upset. I mean really upset.*

Celestial wings in action were either a glorious wonder or a source of pure horror to behold. Izaiah was straddling that line at the moment.

"It was your doing!" Luna shouted, their squared-off features and perfect proportions gleaming in the reflected moonlight.

Izaiah gripped his cane, forced Mallos to the surface, and narrowly blocked the Celestial spear, sending it to the side like a repelling magnet. The spear tip shot back like a viper but was unable to pierce the Medolian.

Izaiah pleaded, "Luna! It's me! Don't you recognize me? It's Izai—"

The spear was set aside and replaced by fists hammering at Izaiah like boulders. After a handful of blows, the Medolian knew he couldn't last long like this. Drawing his cane like a baseball bat, he swung for left field, striking the Celestial's fist, blasting them across the floor and sending himself backward into a mess of bushes. *Oh, great!*

Luna and their wings crashed through pillars and raised concrete beds. The dead bushes, flowers, and vines broke apart like ash. Everything in their path was crushed before Luna came to a stop, sending a cloud of dust into the air.

Izaiah climbed out of the mess, spitting and picking twigs out of his ass, when he spotted the silhouette of the nine-foot Celestial rising from the murk. They roared and spread their wings, draping him and the hill in shadow. "The Medolian will die!" Luna shouted.

"You're starting to scare me. Now tell me what's going on," Izaiah demanded. "Where is Illyana? And Amrath?"

At the mention of the name, Luna let out another roar and launched into the air, turning down like a missile ready to plummet to Earth. *I've about had it up to here with this nonsense.* Izaiah closed his eyes, ignoring the threat, and concentrated on stirring the Eve within himself, generating a supply of Mallos. Time slowed in his mind, calm washed over him, and the neutral energy ignited.

A thunderous pop from the tip of his cane made Izaiah think for a second that Luna had landed on him, striking him dead. He screamed, opened one eye, and found the Celestial was suspended in midair inside a perfect spectrum sphere—rippling, strong, made of equal parts of all shades of the Eve. Luna's vicious attacks against the translucent orb, as well as their protests, were reduced to subwoofer booms. A brilliant blue glow radiated from within their crystalline body with each strike.

Phew! That was a little close. "Huh? What's that? I can't hear you." Izaiah put a hand behind his huge ear, sitting on a flat chunk of stone to catch his breath. "I can see that you're upset, and I want you to know I don't take that lightly. I don't. I also want to know the answer to my question. For the last time, where is Illyana?"

Luna shouted something back, but Izaiah couldn't make any of it out. "Okay, fine. Fine! I'll let you down, but you have to promise to be civil. High Celestials are the most civil of all, right? Can you do that?" Luna fought all the harder. "That's not going to work for me. Why don't you chill here for a bit while I go look around?"

Izaiah turned about-face and started away. The thumping soon stopped and Luna calmed. He smiled. "Is that a yes?"

The trapped Celestial nodded, clenching their hairless brow. Izaiah released the bubble, allowing them to stand and regain their dignity, casting a towering shadow over the slight Medolian. Luna kept their promise not to resume the attack, shouldering their spear, crossing their arms, and waiting to hear what he had to say.

"You keep saying Medolian, but I'm the only one who knows about this place, so tell me what you mean by—"

"Lies," interrupted Luna, remaining placid.

"Then tell me," Izaiah said.

Luna huffed. "The old Medolian speaks as if the old Medolian doesn't know. It was one of *their* kin who attacked Illyana! Attacked us! Killed Amrath while I took the Seeress to safety. If the old Medolian wishes to finish the job and kill Luna, they should hurry and do so."

"You say Amrath is dead? That can't be. Where? How?" Izaiah had so many darn questions, and yet seemed to be running on borrowed time. Luna stayed silent and still. "Show me!" Izaiah shouted, trying for a spark of intimidation.

The Celestial was unmoved. "I am under orders to only trust Izaiah, Warden Sentry of Medolians. Only that one may see the message."

You've got to be kidding me. "That's who I am, for Pete's sake! You're saying you don't recognize me? I'm the one who got you this gig, remember? I'm not sure . . . how I should feel about that."

Luna shook their head. "The old Medolian should say so first next time. Your kind look alike to us. Like humans." They turned and walked away, leading Izaiah, too frustrated to care, up a path to a rising slope. "I will now trust the old Medolian," Luna said.

So glad to hear it. "Just tell me where she is," Izaiah said, trying to keep up with the creature's strides.

"I don't know. I only know she's far from here," Luna replied. "At least, I hope. She ordered me to remain and wait for Izaiah, to make sure that one received the message."

"What's the message? What did she see? Did this have anything to do with Joseph?" Izaiah halted Luna, who stared back with blank gemstone eyes. Since they had no real irises—only indentations in rock—Celestials never appeared to be truly looking at an individual, only through them.

"You know . . . Joseph. Runaway demon," he tried to jog their memory. "The reason the kingdoms are on lockdown. Ringing any bells?" Izaiah received only blank stares. "For being the bodyguard of a fortune-teller, you'd think you'd know a little more about UnEarth affairs."

Luna resumed their original path. "The message is this way. Follow." *Can't argue with that.*

They led Izaiah to a section of the garden recently torn asunder. Columns were felled, the majority of plants reduced to dross, and chunks of earth ripped from the ground. Luna pushed off with their wings, gliding and landing near some fallen pillars, where Izaiah spotted chunks of a glowing, broken humanoid, sensing a faint Rapture signature. *Oh no.*

Their torso was mostly intact, leaning against a column, but missing its left arm and wing. Amrath's insides were exposed, revealing rounded cubes of tough, translucent, glowing tissue packed into a hard outer shell of sky-blue material. Even slaughtered and mangled, the creatures of the essence of creation did not bleed. All the same, Amrath's Eve was leaving their body.

Who could have done something like this?

"Bladed weapon," Luna said, as though answering Izaiah's thoughts. They nudged their fallen comrade. "Amrath, awaken."

The injured Celestial's eyes opened. "Luna. Friend." Amrath then turned to Izaiah, expressionless. "Izaiah. Medolian. Welcome."

"Well, where were *you* a few minutes ago?" Izaiah said with a pain-filled chuckle, taking Amrath's remaining hand and placing his gloved palm on top. "I'm sorry, old friend. Who did this to you?"

Amrath shared a glance with Luna before answering. "Medolian. Woman."

Izaiah shook his head. "That can't be true. There must be more you're not telling me."

It couldn't be Mara, could it?

Luna slammed their fist into the ground. "It is true! Mallos did this!"

"What did she look like?" Izaiah asked.

"Woman. Wielded a blade," Amrath said. Luna nodded in agreement.

Thanks, you two. That narrows it down. Of course, only one person like that has been keeping their Eve under wraps lately. Darn it, Mara. Now?

"The Medolian can fix Amrath. The Warden Sentry," Luna said, with a tinge of hope in their broad Celestial voice.

Izaiah shook his head. "No, they're in too bad of shape. This time, none of us can fix this. I'm sorry."

Amrath nodded. Though their face was blank, Izaiah could sense they understood. "Death has found the deathless," Amrath said. "My Rapture will join Hywyn, and my soul will enter what lies above. Do not grieve."

Luna stood over them like an impartial statue as Amrath closed their eyes. Though Celestials rarely showed signs of emotion, Izaiah could sense something breaking inside them. After all, the duo had guarded the garden and Illyana for more than three thousand years. The only thing to do now was let Amrath's Eve fade peacefully, which could take days, maybe even months. In Hywyn tradition, Luna would be by their side the whole time. *Just goes to show you we're all temporary. Death finds us all. Even angels.*

After a moment of silence, Izaiah turned to Luna. "Please, show me the message Illyana left for me."

They drew their spear, as though reinvigorated by duty and purpose. "The old Medolian will follow me."

Luna strode deeper into the garden, leading Izaiah nearly all the way to the far end, where they approached a short hill. Atop it was a rising mushroom cloud of shadow. Two hundred feet high, its broad, leafless branches stretched in every direction of the sky. The Trilleu tree was as old as Trivium itself, and sadly, long dead—a monolith to a simpler age.

"In there," Luna said, motioning to an opening in the hill, between enormous, rotted roots billowing outward.

"I got it from here. Thank you," Izaiah said, hurrying to a small green door tucked into the gap. He did not bother knocking before entering, but couldn't help calling out, "Illyana? Are you home?"

With its only occupant being an eyeless woman, there were no sources of light in the underground cottage. Igniting the end of his emerald cane to better see, Izaiah began his search, hunching his way through its five rooms. Illyana lived minimally: a bed, blankets, some clay pots and bowls scattered about, a few side tables, kitchen supplies, and some shelves of food. Taking up the majority of the space in her enormous pantry were many jars of what she called her "medicine." Izaiah didn't know what the materials were, only that they helped the Seeress make her memory potions. *She taught herself how to make them, since there was nobody who already knew how.*

Without much to go on, Izaiah surmised she'd left home in a hurry, having packed nothing and failing to take her favorite robe. Though none of it helped solve the mystery of why she left her guards behind and ventured out on her own.

Just as Izaiah was about fed up, Luna called from the front entryway, "Old Medolian."

Izaiah hurried to the front den and saw Luna leaning into the open doorway, which was far too small for them to enter. Their long arm was stretched inside, aimed at a glimmer of light near the fireplace. Izaiah found a trinket dangling from a teapot holder— one of Illyana's vials, a memory. *Bingo.*

"That help?" Luna asked.

"You big, beautiful behemoth. I could kiss you," Izaiah said, earning a confused eyebrow from the Celestial. "Keep watch while I see what she wanted to tell me."

Luna nodded and exited from the doorway.

Finding Illyana's favorite chair—the one she used to collect her visions in the first place—Izaiah set aside his cane and sank into the cushions. *Oh, that's nice.* Once ready, he opened the vial and took a sip. Setting it aside, he closed his eyes, waiting for the ride to begin. It would be all-encompassing, taking him away from reality for however long Illyana had designed the experience to last. *The first time I tried one, it wasn't pretty. No, sir.*

His physical presence was the first to go as his consciousness separated, floating over the den, then the garden and Luna, and finally up over all of Trivium: a pint-sized planet amid a deep maroon cosmos. Then everything went black before a cloud of blue faded into view, soon filled with white clouds—beautiful, like those found only on Earth. He was soaring through them. *This is a strange memory potion. I can already tell something was off with Illyana when she brewed it.*

"Hello, Izaiah," a weathered voice as soothing as a babbling brook said. "I hope Luna and Amrath didn't scare you. I know you think they don't like you, but they do. Almost as much as me." Illyana laughed, then dropped her tone to one of maternal concern. "If you're seeing this memory potion, it's because you're having a harder time catching the Archfiend than you thought you would and came back to me much sooner than you meant to. It also means I was wrong—this has become much more than a diplomatic issue, and everything will *not* turn out fine. My visions have been haunting lately. Something is coming—its form just hasn't set yet. I had to leave Yil to protect UnEarth, though if I'm honest, I'm not sure anything can be done at this point. It happens. It. No matter which way I look. It comes."

Her tone alarmed Izaiah, who knew Illyana as a spirit who had loved flowers since she was young—one whose years of dealing with her unique abilities had matured her quickly, yet she had never lost her carefree nature. To hear the Seeress now speak of doom was something Izaiah had never experienced and could never have guessed would feel so awful.

Illyana continued. "One thing you taught me was never to stop fighting, so I am leaving you this message in the hopes that you may be able to turn the coming tide. Though I have to warn you, every moment you're about to experience will hurt."

The memory then transformed into a full sensory experience. Izaiah was bombarded with images of UnEarth, its cities, and his colleagues. Memories of meetings with Illyana sped by, interspersed with flashes of Joseph, seen through the eyes of those he'd murdered.

"I'm sorry to say I still don't know the identity of the demon inhabiting the boy. It remains nameless," Illyana said, disappointment heavy in her voice. "As you know from your last visit, Mason's parents and several of his doctors are deceased, so I've had access to their memories, learning a great deal about him. The picture was always incomplete, however, as we knew nothing of the boy's time spent united with the demon, as Joseph. Until now. Six months ago, I stumbled upon a stream of Eve entering UnEarth during a meditation. It was cold and rotten, so full of malice that I thought it was a blend of souls coming in from a battlefield. I investigated, now sorry I did . . ."

The fog in Izaiah's mind cleared, and an image faded into view: a young man's face, one he had seen before. It was Mason, aged fifteen, staring into a mirror. Izaiah was seeing the world through the boy's eyes, knowing immediately what that meant.

"Yes," Illyana began, "the boy possessed, Mason, is dead. His memories joined the Eve, which means only one personality remains in the body—the nameless demon."

By the Eve. Fabian was right. A marionette doll. This could have been the big break they were looking for, finally revealing the demon's plans. Izaiah wished he could ask Illyana questions, but that wasn't how memory visions worked. The story of Mason would continue, whether Izaiah kept up or not. He was swept through years of the boy's life in the blink of an eye, witnessing a lonely childhood, feeling Mason's seclusion and the chaos within his mind, twisted as it aged, unchecked. It was a wholly different experience from viewing the boy's past through the eyes of his parents, who had died years earlier. Izaiah had no idea humanity and their offspring could be so foreign to one another.

The memories of Mason, now aged somewhere near seventeen, were awash in frustration, anger, and a constant feeling of claustrophobia at school. Images flashed by of the boy glaring at the psychiatrists he had been shuffled through over the years, feeling an urge to rip their throats out just to silence them. Every animal he saw was a weak potential victim. The feelings were overwhelming. Mason had been born without a filter deep in his psyche, allowing anything pure to flow out in whatever form it wished.

Time passed as Mason confined himself to his parents' backyard shed, secretly assembling an "armory," inspired by the mass shooters of the age, making his own plans to sow chaos and murder. *God help us. These kids. Illyana, wait! Gimme a minute, huh?* Izaiah wanted it to stop, but the images shifted to a black stormy evening, where Mason was anxiously waiting in the shed, staring at a calendar, two days from his intended attack. Local police, after receiving a tip from his younger sister, surrounded the shed and raided it. Mason fought to the last, shooting seven police officers dead before being brought down, only to awaken from a coma in a mental hospital six months later. *This is almost too much to take.*

"He spent nine additional months in the hospital, serving part of a life sentence. By then, his soul was pure Wrath. There was nothing anyone could do. It was only a matter of time," Illyana said.

Every moment of every day, Mason was strapped to the bed, fighting his restraints. Izaiah could feel how they burned him in his mind like cinders. His nights were spent awake, staring at the ceiling, muttering to himself.

"Every day, and every night," Illyana began, "he asked the Heavens to give him the strength to break free, to smite his enemies, and to fulfill his quest for greatness. Then, one night . . . it came."

Izaiah found himself transported to Mason's padded room. The air was as cold as ice, but he was not shivering. What sounded like a wild animal searching for prey floated through the halls outside his door. Mason watched as a blood-red light appeared under it, growing. A presence neared, and Izaiah felt Mason's fear at that moment when the straps binding him to the bed gave way. Mason stood and approached the padded door as something began pounding on it from the other side, denting its steel. The door shook and quaked. Bolts fell from its corners, and finally, it collapsed inward, leaving a smoke-filled gap. Mason peered inside, where two eyes opened in the darkness, shining like red fire. Scorching shadow engulfed him, and he fell.

The night the demon took him. Poor stupid kid.

The next memories were physically painful and unclear, filled with chaos. Dozens of voices screamed, glass shattered. Izaiah could feel blood dripping from Mason's hands as he walked the halls.

"They killed fourteen people the night Joseph was born," Illyana said, her voice weak with sorrow. "Mason would never rise to the surface again, or be in control. The demon immediately set to work, roaming the world, spreading Wrath, turning fragile minds to the Wraithian cause, hoping that by recreating the ancient cult, they would find Gehenna and his prize."

The memories continued, but now Mason was in the back seat, watching as someone else drove his body. Izaiah felt the boy's apprehension grow over the months and years, traversing continents, trading whatever they had for passage. When they couldn't afford a trip, violence was used. Mason quickly acclimated to wielding power over others, his thirst for it growing so strong that he didn't notice when the demon stopped feeding them, letting their body survive only on Wrath. Eventually, Joseph had to don a mask to continue making deals with humans, who were understandably squeamish around decomposing flesh.

"Mason allowed it all," Illyana explained in Izaiah's mind, "believing he and the demon were searching for the stones to overthrow Lucifer-Aveyl. Power was his obsession, and he thought they would find it alone. But it turns out the nameless Archfiend had long ago made a promise to a very different partner. Again, I'm sorry to do this, Izaiah."

A flash in the memory vision revealed a Shift. Standing before Izaiah, seen through Joseph's mask, was a face he was unprepared to confront. Luna and Amrath had been telling the truth about a Medolian woman, as had his instincts.

The youngest Sentry, Chloe, clad in an admiral's jacket, marched up to Joseph and took his hand as Izaiah experienced the memory.

No! Not Chloe. We can't lose her. If he hadn't been on a spiritual drug trip, Izaiah would have punched something.

"She was the first Medolian to catch the demon, long before it ever bonded with a human," Illyana explained. "But instead of arresting him, for reasons I don't know, she let the Archfiend go and joined his cause. Chloe was seduced into searching the Earth for decades, doing the demon's work. When Joseph arrived on Earth, they continued the demon's ultimate quest, which isn't a repeat of Inferius at all. The throne of Arros is merely a smokescreen, one even the boy didn't know about. The demon and the young Medolian made a pact long before—one far more malevolent than war."

Time passed in the vision. Chloe and Joseph worked together to spread Wrath, keeping the Medolians busy and unfocused as the Wraithian tribe was reborn on Earth. Many secluded nights together ended with the phrase, "Till none suffer," whispered in each other's ears, resounding through Mason's mind as his paranoia about the duo grew. They often spoke in riddles to keep him off their trail.

"The demon played everyone. He continues to," Illyana added. "Though Medolians have mastery over Mallos, anyone balanced, devout, and willing to practice can learn the skills of the guardians of Eve. Turns out, the nameless is such a creature."

Izaiah saw Chloe teach Joseph to create and control Mallos and to bend his Wrath signature in the boy's body, rendering him invisible to Eve senses. *Where did she even learn that? Not from Mara or me.*

"The stones are close to being found," Joseph said to Chloe one frigid afternoon in the desert. "We can feel it."

Chloe nodded. "When we find the temple of the Molochs, will you be ready for what comes next?"

"We always have been," Joseph answered, pulling her into an embrace.

Chloe lifted his mask and kissed his green, dying lips. "I'm not ready to lose us."

"The end of everything is also the end of pain. Remember, until none suffer," Joseph said, pulling the mask back down.

"Until none suffer," Chloe repeated.

"That was the day Mason learned the true plans of the demon and the Medolian," Illyana said. "By then, the demon may have simply stopped caring if Mason knew the truth, feeling confident that the body would remain theirs. The very next day, when Mason made a final, desperate attempt to wrest control, the demon snuffed him out for good."

The memories of Mason ceased and did not return.

For a moment, Izaiah's consciousness was engulfed in darkness before Illyana spoke again. "The demon believes with all its essence that the stones are real, convinced they hold more power than we in the kingdoms of UnEarth could ever fathom. I tell you this because I, too, now believe it."

Excuse me? Izaiah wasn't sure if he had heard her right.

Illyana's words became jagged, broken by tears. "I've seen it. So many times—I can't bear to look again."

Joseph appeared as a fog before Izaiah, immense and formless. Three objects floated below him, glowing white-hot, surrounded by a deep red fire that drew near to blackness. Like a dream he couldn't explain, Izaiah sensed that the world was in agony from what he saw. The three glowing objects were an Eve so concentrated—so powerful—it was beyond comprehension. Joseph's laughter permeated the chaos, a sound that Izaiah knew in his heart heralded the end of the world.

"Mankind was filling these stones with Wrath for hundreds of millennia," Illyana said. "The immense power within them has grown stale. It's no longer just Wrath. It's something else. The nameless calls it an Abyss, free from light or creation. Each stone holds the power of an unlimited army. When the Archfiend taps into that power, the Abyss within them will shatter every molecular bond it touches. The world will turn to dust. Its matter will be unable to collapse and reform, and the cloud of nothing will spread until it reaches all corners of creation, no matter how long it takes. I know this because I've seen it." Illyana said.

Izaiah then witnessed what had broken her: the rending of the world. He saw the Earth sink into a pit of black, where nothing existed.

"And so you see, my old friend. You were right, and I was wrong. Every direction we take, the Earth will be split. It is inevitable," Illyana said. "I'm sorry I didn't see it sooner."

As Izaiah's consciousness soared back into reality and settled over Trivium, panic sped through him at the Armageddon he had just witnessed. *What am I going to do? Oh—what can any of us do?*

"Do not try to find me," Illyana said finally. "I'll come to you if the danger has passed, which may never be. Keep your wits and stay wise, old friend, if you are able. Good luck." She ended her words with her usual sweet and salty disposition that Izaiah was fond of—as though a final gift before sending him into a war she knew he couldn't win.

Returned to the garden, Izaiah lay in the Seeress's chair like a lumpy pile of misshapen bricks, struggling to catch his breath. The weight of an elephant pressed down on his chest. *The Gehenna stones—real, and under my nose this whole time. If only I'd . . . no, don't do that. No time for pity.* Izaiah shot up, grabbed his cane, and exited the cottage.

Luna turned as he climbed out from between the roots. "Did the Medolian learn what it wished?"

"He did. And he did not," Izaiah answered, hurrying down the cracked stone path back to the garden entrance.

"Where will the Medolian go now?" Luna called after him.

Izaiah pressed on, pushing, ignoring the screaming pain in his knees. "To get help!"

"What about the people there, in Hell? All the damned souls? [. . .] turns out, no, humans do not reside in Arros. When a vessel dies, its Eve joins UnEarth, no longer an individual but a breath of energy. Their shades live on, but that is all. There is no place of eternal burning for mankind.

At least, none my source has yet seen."

- Excerpt from the journal of
Dr. Francisco Emul. Murcia
September 1894

HISTORIES OF WAR

Alex trudged through the soft, muddy ground at the rear of the group, just behind Bennett. A bright moon shimmered off the tall, damp grass of the yellow plains surrounding them. Rolling hills loomed in the distance, and behind him stretched nothing but wide-open prairie. Scattered portly trees were dwarfed by two massive, shadowy shapes dead ahead, gradually revealing themselves to be hulking grain silos. Overgrown weeds and vines wound their way up the cracked concrete walls, clinging to a small rustic shack at the base of the silo on the left.

Ahead, Hannah leaned on Felix for support. The Shift from the Rose in France had clearly taken a toll on her, though they had managed to escape just in time to avoid capture by Constance Mary and her squad. Still, Alex had no idea where in the world they were. Given that it was the dead of night, he guessed they'd shifted at least one time zone west.

"That was a Shift, wasn't it?" Bennett asked, clutching his stomach as if trying not to topple over.

"Sure was, my man," Felix replied. "You feeling okay? Sorry, I figured Izaiah had shifted you guys before."

Bennett nodded, straightening his posture. "He has. Just caught me off guard. I didn't think anyone but a Medolian could pull off that trick."

If Alex didn't know better, he'd swear Bennett was puffing out his chest more than usual. *Is his voice a couple of tones lower? Who's he trying to impress?*

"Shifting is no trick," Felix said, shaking his head and his bushy hair. "It's tough to do. Almost no one else can. Only Medolians, since you have to master Mallos. I certainly can't, 'cause I never had a teacher like Hannah did. Takes, like, five thousand years! And she learned it from—"

"That's enough, Felix," Hannah said sharply.

"Right-o. Sorry." He turned to the guys. "Forget I said anything. Just be thankful Hannah was there and willing to help at all."

"We are thankful. Right, Al?" Bennett said.

"Yeah. Thankful," Alex responded dryly.

As they continued their march, Hannah remained silent.

"I, for one, think it's a good thing," Felix said to her. "Been trying to get you out of that Still Room for a while. It's not healthy to be cooped up in a Kingdom Chamber. Too much isolation makes people weird."

"How I spend my infinite plodding moments on this rock is my own business," Hannah muttered.

Alex was grateful for her intervention but couldn't shake the nervousness she stirred within him. Just as the Still Room had drained him of warmth, the air around Hannah felt cold and oppressive. Her piercing stare seemed to cut right through him, carrying an aura of heavy, bored apathy that made Alex feel microscopic in her presence. Whatever strength he believed the Wrath had given him evaporated next to a former general of Hywyn, brutally reminding him he was merely human—a child in the realm of near-gods.

The grass thinned suddenly around a deserted, overgrown dirt road, which Hannah followed. The grain silos loomed larger on either side of them.

Finally, Alex had to ask, "I may have missed the conversation while I was writhing on the ground in the Still Room, but where are we? And what are we doing here? We're supposed to be out there catching Joseph so I can go home."

"Patience, my man," Felix said. "Shifting takes a lot of energy, especially if you're not made of Mallos. Hannah needs to rest."

"Rest?" Alex asked, scanning the surroundings. "But where?"

"Here," Hannah said, pushing away from Felix as they neared the small shack. "Thank you, old friend. I've got it."

Stepping toward a circular patch of dirt where nothing grew, she reached down into the grass at its edge. Her fist emerged gripping a heavy steel chain, which she wrapped around her forearm. Hannah closed her eyes, and a chill crept up Alex's spine, the same energy he'd felt from the Still Room. Her hand and forearm glowed a dull orchid blue, the light seeping into the chain as she heaved and pulled. A concrete slab as wide as a man slid aside with a harsh rock-on-rock screech, revealing a dark staircase leading into the earth.

"Home sweet home," Hannah said, dropping the chain. The glow faded, and the cold up Alex's spine dissipated. She began descending the stairs into the darkness. "Come along if you want. Or don't. All the same."

"We're going in . . . there?" Alex yelped.

"Is there a problem?" Felix asked, following Hannah closely.

Alex turned to Bennett for reassurance. "You can't be okay with this."

"It's a bomb shelter. Being safe inside is the whole point!" Felix exclaimed before disappearing into the darkness.

"Bennett?" Alex pleaded with his partner.

The soldier took a couple of glances back and forth before re-plying, "I think if they wanted to hurt us, they would have done it back at the Rose. You got a better idea, Al? I'm all ears." With-out waiting for an answer, Bennett ducked down and followed the others, leaving Alex alone on the surface.

Well, of all the . . . you know what, fine!

Stepping up to the opening, Alex peered down into the inky blackness, unable to see anything but hearing the others' footsteps on creaky wooden stairs. His anxiety surged to the surface, freez-ing him in place. *Just stay calm. Everything will be fine. You can do this.* He took the first few steps, able to speed up as he went along. Nearing the bottom, a faint yellow light began to glow. Bennett and Felix were waiting on the landing while Hannah fished keys from her leather jacket. One by one, she turned several large locks set into the door, then grasped a rusted metal wheel on its face, snapping it into position with a loud bang.

Hannah gripped the door and pulled outward, revealing a gap-ing black mouth into the Earth.

"Don't touch anything," she said as she ducked through the door-way, moving toward an electrical panel. One by one, she flipped the switches, and fluorescent lights flickered to life as power coursed through the shelter. Beyond the switches, a stout metal staircase led down into what appeared to be the main living space. Equipment lining the walls hummed to life as a ventilation system somewhere in the shelter coughed dust from the overhead ducts.

As Alex stepped off the short staircase, he crunched paper be-neath his foot and felt glass break. The floor was buried under so much debris that he couldn't tell if it was carpet, hardwood, or something else entirely. Piles of waste loomed in the corners, fea-turing candy and food wrappers from around the world, stacked atop hunks of scrap metal and tangled electrical wiring, alongside cardboard boxes, trash bags—both full and half-empty—and organic messes Alex didn't want to know the sources of.

"This is really . . . nice," he said, forcing a smile.

"I don't do much entertaining," Hannah said, sweeping aside a mound of debris with her arm, revealing a moldy couch beneath. After flopping onto it, she began rubbing her brow as if nursing a headache. "If you can find a seat, take it."

"And here I thought Celestials were the clean ones," Felix joked, brushing more junk off an ottoman in front of Hannah, then lifting her feet to rest them on it.

She chuckled. "You see any Celestials around?"

"Sure don't." Felix began tidying up, picking up trash and attempting to organize the chaos. "This is terrible. Awful. You need a maid."

"Or a janitor," she replied, sounding pleased with herself.

"I am recently in the job market."

"You're hired," Hannah said. "Hope you like working for nothing."

Felix caught Bennett and Alex staring from the foot of the small stairs. "Something wrong?"

Bennett shook his head. "No, nothing's wrong. Guess we're just a little . . . confused. How are you two—"

"Friends?" Felix finished for him. "Is there a reason we wouldn't be?"

Bennett was as clumsy with his words as Alex had ever seen. "It's just, I mean, you're a—and she's a—"

"Go on. Say it," Felix urged.

"An angel and a demon," Bennett said.

Hannah scoffed. "There's no such thing as angels, kid. Not the kind you're thinking of. At least not that I've seen. The closest thing you have on Earth is probably your grandma or people who work with the disabled. I suggest you get those notions out of your head. They'll just slow you down. We know how humans think about us, and it's changed a lot over the years. It's hard to keep track, frankly. We're just creatures who were born without asking for it, same as you."

"Don't take it personally; Hannah's always been uncomfortable with the A-word," Felix said, guiding the humans inside. "Why are you being shy? Make yourselves at home. You guys hungry? Hannah? *Hmm?* I'll fetch us something to eat. Kitchen was over here, right?" Felix bounded down the hall on the right.

"Other way," Hannah corrected.

He scurried back and crossed to the hall on the left. "Right-o!"

"For a guy who says he doesn't spend time with humans, you sure sound like one," Alex called after him.

"Oh, I've tried, believe me! Just never cared much for hanging around them. They're always so caught up in their little issues and self-hate. Know what I mean? But I do love this television thing you guys cooked up! Never thought I'd see anything like it." Felix's voice echoed down the hall, interspersed with the sounds of rummaging through cabinets and drawers, along with the occasional stomp through piles of trash, whistling a tune.

Alex listened for a moment, trying to place the melody. "Where do I know that song from?"

"It's what he thinks is the theme song to *Mr. Ed*," Hannah said blandly. "Felix's favorite show."

"Best program ever made!" Felix called from the other room, amidst another ruckus. He began to sing, "'Go up to the source and ask him, a horse. He'll give you the thing and the answers endorse. He's talking on a steady course. Look, it's Mr. Ed!'" He stopped singing to laugh. "So true, and so wise. That equine was a certifiable genius!"

"For the last time, the horse didn't actually speak. They were using camera tricks to make it seem that way," Hannah shouted toward the hall.

"I know what I saw!" Felix yelled back. "Not the first talking horse I've come across, and likely won't be the last."

Alex couldn't help smiling, but quickly stopped when he caught Hannah's icy blue and violet gaze. Turning his attention to the marred ceiling, he pretended to study it.

She called to the kitchen, "Felix, while you're at it, there should be a couple of bottles of Brenden thresh in the cabinet near your feet—"

"Absolutely not!" he cut her off. "No more tonight. You've had enough. For a long while, in fact."

Hannah stuffed her tongue into her lower lip out of annoyance and nodded, as if to say, *Okay, I see how it is.* Reaching into the pile of trash near her right hand, she rummaged around, finding a bottle. The label read *UniMoss - Extra Dry.* With a shrug, she popped the top and took a swig.

"Well, humans"—she burped, then sighed wearily—"I did my part. You're out of the Rose. Now, start talking. First, what are your names?"

"My name is Bennett Hunter. This is Alex Barker," the soldier replied.

"Both American?"

"Yeah," they answered in unison.

"Arizona," Bennett added. "Before that, Texas."

"Is that a problem?" Alex asked.

"Just doesn't make much sense," Hannah said. "Izaiah is charged with finding humans to represent Hywyn and Arros to aid in an exorcism, and he chooses you two? Why?"

"Wrong place, wrong time," Bennett said.

Hannah shook her head. "No. You were chosen for a reason—you just don't know it yet."

"My guess is he was new at it. We've been told several times that what happened to us is unprecedented," Bennett added.

"That's true, and for good reason," Hannah said. "Our worlds have always been separate, and for the better. For the Senate to resort to this kind of action—to have the Medolians jump through these kinds of hoops—tells me that the bureaucrats are desperate." She shouted down the hall, "Felix, you said the Tribunal's gone quiet, but is there any word from Trivium City?"

"TC? Shit, I don't know. Haven't been there for a while," he called back. "But you'd think if something were wrong, we'd know about it. I overheard folks at the Rose talking about new mandates coming out of the Tribunal, and how the lower kingdoms are upset—as usual. Seems like there's tension between Hywyn and Arros, which isn't new, but people have stopped talking, breaking into cliques. I couldn't get anyone from Nashwyn or Lanwyn to even look my way lately. Didn't think much of it until now."

Hannah turned back to Bennett and Alex. "Izaiah sent you to speak with Nigel Roe?"

"Yeah," Bennett answered. "He thought Nigel might have information on Joseph's whereabouts, being the first to speak with him."

"What did he tell you?"

Bennett glanced at Alex, who cleared his throat. "Um, he said Joseph was looking for passage into Africa, trying to find the Gehenna Brothers. When Nigel found out he was a possessed human, he got upset and sent him away, then got equally mad when he found out I was human, too. Tried to eat me."

"Fuckin' Scythes!" Felix shouted from the kitchen.

"What exactly is a Scythe?" Bennett asked.

"Like the Celestials, Archfiends, and Medolians, Scythes are a species of UnEarth creature born from a different shade of Eve," Hannah explained. "Before Nigel was Purged, he was one of the most politically powerful Scythes in Fovos, the world of Dread, and would regain that status if he were allowed to return."

Alex shuddered. "Guess that explains the split-open face."

"He belonged to a particular genus of Scythe called the Aidaas," Hannah continued. "The others are the Makaan and the Veen. Every world has multiple branches of its primary species. The Archfiend have the most, at five. Scythes thrive on fear as a defense mechanism, even though that's all they are themselves. Nigel attacked you because, like some, he abhors the idea of blending the species—something you two might have just proven is a possibility."

"I don't understand. Why is that so bad?" Bennett asked.

Hannah shrugged. "Humans are a major source of Eve. Each person contributes only a tiny amount, but over hundreds of millennia, their souls have helped grow UnEarth and its kingdoms. Recently, though, people of UnEarth, myself included, have noticed that the Eve coming from humans is becoming more potent—especially Wrath, Dread, and Grief, the lower shades. Arros, Fovos, and Doloros are fine with this because it makes them more powerful and gives them a louder voice in the Senate. But the spectrum is already shifting. Some believe humans might eventually learn to tap into the Eve within themselves. If that happens, their emotions could cause their Eve to grow exponentially, creating an unending cycle of power, which could lead to dire consequences. That's why possessing a human body is forbidden under the sixth statute of UnEarth law."

"That explains a lot of the looks we've been getting," Bennett said.

"Yep. Now, I'm tired of talking, so unless you have any other questions, it's your turn. I want to hear your story, all of it. Start from the beginning," Hannah said.

Bennett began recounting their tale, starting with their "deaths" (*conveniently glossing over his own*), and moving through meeting Izaiah in the alley twenty-five days later, up to their confinement at the safe house. Alex waited for a chance to chime in, keeping his eyes mostly down, as every time he looked up, Hannah seemed to hit him with the same cold stare.

Felix eventually strolled back into the room, arms loaded with unfamiliar food packages and a tray stacked with what looked like the same trash biscuits they'd eaten in the safe house. "Sounds like ol' Izaiah didn't want you guys getting hurt," he remarked.

"Or in the way," Hannah added.

Felix offered the tray of food to Alex and Bennett. "Dilo cookie?"

One whiff told Alex they were, in fact, the same horrid biscuits. He did a poor job hiding the disgust in his face. "No. Thank you."

"Hmm, yeah, I forgot humans don't like UnEarth grub." Felix moved on, offering the tray to Hannah, who grabbed a handful and stuffed them into her mouth like raisins. "I see someone found a bottle of moss without my help," he said bitterly, eyeing the green bottle in her other hand.

She held it up, grinning, crumbs covering her mouth. Felix huffed in frustration, taking his remaining snacks to a pile of trash, where he sat, keenly watching for the rest of the tale. Bennett continued, reaching the point in the story where he and Alex found the ransacked village, encountered Yuri and his brother, and were captured by the Wraithians during an escape attempt.

"Wraithians? Those sickos? Can't be," Felix exclaimed, glancing at Hannah for reassurance.

"That's what Mara said," Alex added. At the mention of the name, he saw Hannah's gaze spring to life.

"Mara? When? Where did you see her?" she asked.

"She's the one who rescued us from the Wraithian camp. Then we saw her again at the Medolian Gathering. Don't know where she is now," Bennett answered.

Hannah fell silent, her eyes drooping to the floor.

"Rescue? That doesn't sound like Mara," Felix interjected. "I can guarantee she was only there to hunt them, not to save you two. In fact, I'm surprised she let you go free instead of taking you to the Tribunal or just cutting your heads off."

"She also seemed surprised by that," Alex said.

"Unlike Izaiah, Mara's not fond of humans. She blames your kind for the war in the first place," Felix continued, stuffing his mouth with what looked like red oat bread. "Since the Medolians were neutral, they got pulled in every direction. Then there's the Day of the Gift. She's always been touchy about that. Not that I blame her. The Meds saved the day when they sacrificed themselves to contain and Shift the Beast back to Arros. Izaiah was the only one to survive. The others were lost, but it effectively ended the war."

"You mean Inferius?" Bennett asked.

"That's right. Hannah and I both fought—on opposite sides, mind you. Some pretty dark days in my life. But then I met her, and everything changed."

"You got yourself out. I didn't do anything," she replied.

"I'm never going to see it that way," Felix insisted. "If not for you, I would still be a six-foot snake. Getting Purged was the best thing that ever happened to me. You sure you guys don't want some food?"

"No, thank you. Why were you Purged?" Alex asked.

"Because I didn't want to help Lucifer with his whiny bid for more power," Felix explained. "I don't think UnEarth belongs to any one world, so I was deemed a traitor to Arros. Lost a lot of good friends that day."

"I know the feeling," Bennett remarked.

"You're military, aren't you?" Hannah asked.

"I was. Our wars sound a little different, though."

Hannah remained stoic. "No. War is war. And I don't want the same tired conflict to rise up again. Whenever it does, the only side that truly loses is the one in the middle that can't defend itself."

"That's what we're trying to prevent," Bennett assured her.

"Continue, then."

Bennett went on with the story, going through the Gathering of the Medolians, leading up to the bar fight in the Rose. "And that's where we met Felix."

Felix swallowed his mouthful and wiped his hands on his stained shirt. "So, years have gone by, and none of the Medolians have been able to pinpoint this nameless Archie? That's puzzling. I've seen Mara find a Beaubon in the freaking Amazon. How is this Joseph cat staying off their radar?"

"Chloe thinks he can hide his Eve signature, like they can," Bennett said.

"Which one is Chloe again?" Felix asked.

"Izaiah said she was the last born, which makes her the youngest," Bennett said. "She wore a sea admiral's coat and carried a sword. Didn't seem too pleased to have us around, either."

"Oh, right. The wunderkind. She leans toward Dread, yeah? Don't know much else about her, but I've seen her around. She's wrong, though. Joseph wouldn't be able to hide his signature while in a body," Felix countered.

"Why?" Alex asked.

"Because when an Archfiend possesses someone, they have to

keep the host at bay, usually with a lot of Wrath, which is pretty easy for the Medolians to spot. Along with the signals possessed humans give off, this guy should be glowing like a Christmas tree."

"But the Medolians said the kid wasn't giving off a panic signal," Alex added.

Felix's eyes widened. "No? Never heard of a human who was cool sharing their body like that. Sounds like this one's broken."

"Do you know why the demon would take a body in the first place?" Bennett asked.

"Not really. Archfiend can live on Earth in their true form. Possession is more like a game for them—sneak onto Earth, spread some hate and fear, then go back to Arros and brag to their friends. Children and women elicit the strongest reactions. It's all an exercise," Felix explained.

"Have you ever done it?" Alex asked.

"Once or twice. It gets old real quick. And it's gross. Concentrated Eve can't exist in a body for long, especially Wrath. If this Fiend is still inside the kid, the body would be deteriorating—trust me. It's . . . unpleasant." Felix rolled his long tongue out of his head in disgust, revealing its craggy texture.

"That's Joseph all right. The smells coming off that slimy, infected nutsack son of a—" Bennett cut himself off, waving his hand in front of his nose.

"Sounds like Izaiah and the others have no idea why the Archfiend came to Earth at all," Hannah said.

"He mentioned some sort of power. Said he wanted to ascend to the throne of Arros," Bennett added.

Felix shook his head. "That can't be it. A single Archfiend couldn't overthrow Lucifer-Aveyl—not with any army Earth could offer. I know the Archfiend collective. Wherever the majority wants to go, that's where they go. It's called the One Voice. They're individuals, but so devoted to preserving their leader that you could mistake them for ants. The majority would never betray the bossman who makes them feel strong."

"What about the Brothers Joseph is looking for? Nigel called them the Brothers of Gehenna. Could that be some sort of army?" Alex suggested.

"Gehenna?" Hannah asked, leaning forward.

"That's what Nigel Roe said Joseph was after," Alex confirmed.

The lights in the shelter began flickering and dropping out. Hannah quickly pulled her feet off the ottoman and moved to the electrical panel near the entrance. "What else did Joseph say?" she asked, smacking the panel once. The lights jolted back to life.

Alex and Bennett exchanged a glance. "I don't know. It all sounded like nonsense—something about Gehenna living, finding the ultimate purity, Inferius coming again, yada-yada," Bennett said.

"Then his buddies started getting riled, shouting, 'it is found' in some ancient language. At least according to Izaiah," Alex added.

Hannah was pacing now. "And both Nigel and Izaiah confirmed Joseph was headed to Africa?"

"Yeah," Bennett answered.

Felix, still gorging, looked completely lost. "What are the Brothers of Gehenna? What's Gehenna? Should I know what that is? I should, shouldn't I?"

"Never heard of them in my life," Hannah said, deflating the mood. "But Gehenna... that does spark something."

"It's the rumored lost temple of the Molochs," Alex explained. "The story says Wraithian priests were able to contain Wrath within rock. Sounds like the birthplace of evil on Earth. This is all according to Nigel, mind you."

"So this Joseph thinks the Gehenna stones will be enough to

challenge Lucifer-Aveyl? Like the Wraithians always wanted?" Felix chimed in.

"Even if it's not enough, I don't like where this conversation is heading," Hannah said. "What I want to know is, where is Izaiah in all of this? He left you without any clue as to where he was going?"

"Wasn't the first time, either. After the Gathering, he said he had business to attend to, and that we shouldn't trust anyone but him and the other Medolians, then took off," Bennett said. "But I'm starting to wonder if he's the one we can't trust."

"You don't know what you're saying," Hannah shot back.

"Yeah, if there's one guy you can always trust, it's Izaiah," Felix added. "Best advice I can give you is do and say exactly what he tells you."

Alex and Bennett exchanged skeptical glances. "You sure we're talking about the same guy?" the soldier asked. "Nothing about the Izaiah we met screamed wisdom."

Hannah shook her head. "Nobody said anything about wisdom, but Izaiah is one of the oldest UnEarth creatures—if not the oldest. He's seen and done more than any living being should, and somehow made it out alive every time. You don't know it, but your world only exists now because of him."

"Okay . . . but do you trust him?" Alex pressed.

"With my life," Hannah said without hesitation. "Besides, Izaiah relishes any opportunity to spend time with humans. I imagine doubly so in this instance, where he wouldn't have to lie to you about who and what he is. He's always fought for our kind to tell humanity the truth about their afterlife and about us. He even thinks humans should have a seat at the table of representatives in the Senate, though he's been denied time and again. If he left, it was because he felt he had to. The guy may not make sense, but he's rarely wrong."

"Well, whether he had a good reason or not, we're at an impasse, and our one lead is gone," Bennett said.

Alex nodded and finally dared to meet Hannah's gaze. "We could use some help."

"No problem, guys! We'd be glad to help," Felix piped in, slapping his hands on his knees and standing.

"We absolutely will not," Hannah countered, sitting Felix back down. "I did what I said I would, and there's nothing we can offer that the Medolians can't. Earth is their territory. This is their burden, not ours."

"Didn't you hear anything they just said!?" Felix pleaded. "We can't let one asshole Archfiend ruin thousands of years of peace among the kingdoms."

"Think with your head, not your heart, old friend. The whole reason for the Senate to imbue human arbiters was to maintain a noninterference policy with Earth. A human was taken, and humans need to save it. You and I might have already broken the Covenant by bringing them here."

"We were Purged, Hannah," Felix insisted. "We're free agents. You don't represent those stuffy Hywyn despots any more than I do Arros or its dickhead king. These guys need help. They're only human. The Hannah I used to know wouldn't run away from something like this... Sorry, that was harsh."

Alex caught Hannah staring at Felix with a gaze like blue fire. "Felix, can I speak to you in private?"

Felix gulped and shared a glance with the humans. "Sure thing." He followed Hannah into the right hallway of the shelter, and a door clicked shut behind them.

Alex sat in silent contemplation for a moment before asking, "What do you think?"

Bennett sniffed vigorously. "I think there must be literal piles of shit floating around in here."

"I meant about our new friends."

"Oh. Not sure."

"Izaiah told us not to trust anyone but the Medolians. Doesn't this fall into that category?"

"Izaiah also neglected to tell us what the Wrath and Rapture would do once they kicked on inside us. I'm more inclined to trust Hannah and her pal, Pit Stain, right now."

"Why? We don't know anything about her."

"Just a feeling I guess."

"That doesn't sound like you. Are you having another episode?"

"No, I feel fine. I think."

"Can you see them?" Alex asked.

Bennett closed his eyes and faced the right wall. "A little. Looks like they're just standing there, talking. Felix's Wrath is getting heated, but it's hard to see him next to Hannah. I've never seen anything as bright as her."

"That's what makes me nervous," Alex said softly as he heard the hallway door open.

Felix bounded into the hall with a wide smile. Hannah was close on his heels. "Good news! We're going to help you, but Hannah has a couple of conditions, which I will let her explain because I already forgot them."

Standing firm between piles of garbage, Hannah stuffed her hands into her jacket pockets. "Yes, we'll help, but only because—and for the life of me, I don't know why—Izaiah trusted you both to see this through. Not that we're not impressed you made it this far, but it sounds like most of it was luck. First thing we need to be clear on—I'm in charge. Plans and strategy are policy now, no more guessing. Agreed?"

"Agreed," Alex said quickly, looking at his partner, who didn't answer.

After a beat, the soldier finally nodded. "Okay."

"Second, Felix and I will only act as guides. This is still your mess to clean up. If we start using Wrath and Rapture haphazardly, others will come calling, and we don't know which other parties are looking for Joseph or the stones—if they even exist. Thirdly, you both will learn to control the Eve inside you. Felix and I will teach you. The lessons will be hard, but they're nonnegotiable."

"Thank you," Alex said.

Hannah moved on as though she hadn't heard him. "Any questions?"

The humans shared a glance. "None," Bennett replied. "How do we get started? We still have no way of finding Joseph."

"We talked about that, and Hannah has an idea," Felix interjected.

"These Wraithians you saw—did they have blood stones?" Hannah asked Bennett directly.

"Those little black rocks they opened their wrists over during the pain ceremony?"

"That's them. Every true Wraithian carries one to collect as much hate and anger as they can. The more they collect, the more weight they carry within the clan. If these Wraithians are true and devoted enough to engender blood stones, we should be able to track the Wrath within them. I'm petty sure that's how Mara was doing it, too. If the Wraithians are working with Joseph, we may be able to find him at the same time."

"It's a start. We'll take it," Bennett said.

Hannah's tone shifted, becoming grim. "Just be aware—we're not in this for your well-being. You had your shot, and your lives ended, which is why I'm guessing Izaiah felt comfortable using you. Our main concern is preventing a war. Is that clear?"

"As ice," Bennett replied, and Alex nodded.

"Good. Then get some sleep. We leave in the morning." With that, Hannah retired down the right hallway.

Once the door closed, Felix turned to them with a waggish grin. "She's pretty great, huh?"

"If I didn't know better, I'd say you were in love," Alex suggested.

"Oh, it's much more than that." Felix aimed his grin toward the hall with a sigh. "She's saved me in more ways than I can count. Know what I mean? You'll see it, what she is, eventually—if you're lucky enough. I do love Hannah, but it's not a love I could describe in human terms. It's . . . ah, I should just shut up about it."

"Thank you, for everything. Our asses are eternally indebted to you," Bennett said.

"Not a problem, guys. We'll get this figured out and you back to your happy lives in no time. Now, rest up! Big—*big* day tomorrow." Felix took a few steps down the kitchen hallway, stopped, and turned back.

"What's up?" Bennett asked.

"I think I'm getting an inkling of what Izaiah saw in you guys. Now, feel free to take the couch and chair. I got dibs on the big kitchen counter." Felix ambled down the hall, trying to whistle the *Mr. Ed* theme song, missing only half the notes. There was a crash as debris fell to the ground, and he squealed, "Nope. Not a problem!" Then there was silence.

Bennett insisted Alex take the couch, and he wasn't about to argue. The soldier sat on the short stairs at the entrance, leaning against the guardrail, his stare vacant.

"You going to sleep like that?" Alex asked.

"Gonna stay up for a while. You go ahead, get some rest."

Again, Alex didn't feel like arguing. He cleared off the couch and lay down. Normally, he would never have been able to get comfortable in a place like this, on a couch so disgusting, but after the fight in the Rose (*my first ever*) with a monster (*also a first*) and their narrow escape, he was well exhausted enough to push his germaphobia aside. *Melissa would be proud.*

As he closed his eyes, a slight sense of relief washed over him for the first time since this all began. All signs so far pointed to Hannah and Felix being trustworthy. *With their help, and Hannah's ability to Shift, we should be able to find Joseph in no time.* Before he drifted off, Alex imagined walking through his front door, free of Wrath, seeing his wife, and holding his little girl. She smiled at him, and Alex's chest filled with a warmth that had no connection to Arros. In this perfect place in his mind, Daniel—the man he attacked—was healed, assuring Alex that his wife had never given up on him. Time became meaningless as he drifted into sleep, and his perfect place grew shadowed.

Flashes erupted in his mind, accompanied by wretched sounds, like leather wings in the dark. Nigel's pale face and black eyes with white pupils appeared, staring through Alex, piercing him, just as Hannah had. The teacher's voice was gone, devoid of body or sense of the physical world. Obsidian strobes whizzed by, parting like storm clouds, revealing a bubbling stream in a meadow the color of coal. She was there. Melissa sat on her knees near the water's edge, running her hand along its jet-black surface.

Alex wanted to call her name, but every time he tried, he was shoved farther away. Her head lifted, peering around the pasture as though she'd heard him but couldn't see him. Like sand in the water, her fingers began to dissolve, turning the stream into a blazing shade of red, illuminating the field with a damning brilliance. One by one, splashes in the river erupted with boiling white liquid as doves smeared with blood fell like hail into the stream and field, exploding with deafening cracks. The rotting pulp left behind by each burst began to crawl toward the river—and Melissa.

The water had taken her hands, then it took her arms. She made no sign of pain as the rest of her crumbled and drifted away downstream. Alex shouted her name in silence and was forced back by a raging wind, soon enveloped by unrelenting darkness.

Melissa!

In the void, he then heard the same voice as the night he'd been shot, but Alex still couldn't place who it belonged to or what it was trying to convey. The word was the same, but this time whispered, in pain, as though pleading.

"Alex?"

PILGRIMAGE

The fire was everywhere—a cyclone wrapping around Bennett, filling his lungs, scorching his flesh. He tried to locate the source, spotting a concentrated dot on the horizon. As he fought toward it, the dot pulled him in, as though he were tumbling down a hill. It grew larger, and he felt the Wrath inside it: the most potent he'd ever experienced. Within the sphere was a dark figure surrounded by a maelstrom of destructive essence. The figure turned to Bennett, its eyes blazing white, and he felt evil crawl under his skin, tearing him apart from the inside. When he finally managed to cry out, the figure vanished in a blinding nuclear flash of light.

Bennett jolted awake, slumped on the short staircase in the bomb shelter, greeted by a theater of chaos. The sensation of unbridled Wrath continued to surround him, having followed him out of his dream. There was fire and smoke everywhere. The confirmation then came that he was no longer dreaming when he found Alex thrashing on the couch, screaming, "Save her!" so desperately his voice was crumbling.

The teacher remained asleep, lost in his own nightmare, flames pouring from his hands and forearms, engulfing him entirely. The couch beneath him was scorched almost to cinders as the blaze spread through the debris in the room. Bennett sprang forward, reaching for Alex's shoulders to shake him awake, but the flames seared his hands like a chemical burn, forcing him back.

"Wake up, man! You're having a nightmare!" he shouted, but Alex continued to writhe, still trapped in his dream.

Turning to call for help, Bennett was met with glistening eyes. Hannah was already striding toward him, clad in a sleeveless undershirt and jeans. He quickly ducked aside to avoid being bowled over as the Human Celestial stepped into the flames, surrounded by a soft blue aura. She seized Alex's hands, interlocking their fingers. The connection hissed like a dozen pissed off snakes. Crimson and cobalt-blue light mixed, and the flames surged from Alex to Hannah, smooth as liquid, enveloping her until she vanished from Bennett's view. With a radical pop, the blaze exploded outward and dissipated.

Reeling, Bennett snapped out of his daze and grabbed a blanket, beating at the flames that spread through the room. Hannah remained focused on Alex, gritting her teeth. Finally, his eyes opened, darting around in terror, uncomprehending of his surroundings. His cries dwindled, replaced by confused grunts and frantic breaths. The fire engulfing the couch extinguished, and Alex lay completely naked, his hands and forearms—red-hot cinders—gradually cooling to a more benign shade of ash. Hannah broke the connection, their hands parting with a crack like bark tearing from a tree. She loomed over him, her energy waning as Alex's skin returned to its normal tone.

"I'm sorry—I'm sorry—I'm sorry . . ." he repeated in panic, clamping his eyes shut, sounding on the verge of tears.

Bennett thrashed the last of the flames out, and the room fell silent, leaving only the crackle of dead fires and Alex's frantic apologies. The brief lull was then broken when Felix came clamoring in from the kitchen.

"Smoke! I see smoke! Wake up, everybody! Fire! Hey guys!" Stomping into the room a moment later, half-asleep and wielding a fire extinguisher backward, he said, "Oh, you already knew." His gaze swept the scene. "What happened? Everything okay? Why is Al naked?"

Alex opened weak eyes and gazed up at Hannah. "Thank you."

Without a word, she stepped away from the couch and moved toward the bedroom hall, motioning to Felix. "Get him some clothes and out of here, before he lights up again."

Felix tossed the extinguisher aside and rummaged through the junk piles, producing a pair of jeans and a large black T-shirt. "Okay, better? Come on, Wilbur. Some fresh air sounds good, know what I mean?"

"I didn't mean to. It was an accident," Alex said, passing Bennett.

"Nobody blames you, pal," Felix assured, helping him up the stairs and out the front door.

The door slammed shut behind them, leaving Bennett to survey the destruction and scavenge for clothes. He found a pair of socks and sneakers among the trash, and in a cold section, he discovered Alex's blue baseball cap, a little singed but otherwise okay. He stuffed it into his back pocket and stepped down the bedroom hall.

Before Bennett could knock on the door, Hannah's voice called from inside, "Just come in."

He opened the door cautiously to a bedroom that mirrored the main living space—nothing decorated the walls but wires and mold, and the floor was obscured by a mysterious depth of garbage. In the middle sat a large, unkempt mattress.

Hannah emerged from a side door, likely the bathroom, fastening her leather jacket and silver belt buckle. "Need something?" she asked, moving on to her heavy boots.

"Uh, yeah. First, I took some shoes. Hope that's cool. And also, I want to apologize. Barker's doing his best to figure this out, so I want you to know I'm sure he feels awful. Though saying it out loud makes me realize how stupid that is."

"When you're as old as me, you tend not to get attached to places and things. Take whatever you need." She finished lacing her boots and stood.

"The shit they put in him is starting to get to the guy," Bennett said. "I've only known him for a little bit, but I can tell he's changing."

"You both are."

"I guess that's true."

"The changes are going to keep coming, which is why this needs to be done. Fast."

"Al thinks we're going home after it's done."

"But you know that's not true." Hannah didn't even try to mask it.

"It wasn't hard to figure out. We've got government scapegoat jobs on Earth, too. Felix would know—lots of TV shows about them."

"Pretty sure he stopped watching TV about forty years ago. But you're right, I know the Tribunal. They'll use what they need to serve their purposes, then toss it aside. Sorry to say, but you'll both be put down when this is over. Sooner the better, in my opinion."

"Uh . . . why?" Bennett asked with a peaked eyebrow.

"Would you say he's fearful? Your friend?"

"I wouldn't call him my friend, but yeah, he's got issues. Guy's skittish. Worries about his asshole and everyone else's too much. Seems to live in constant anxiety."

Hannah paused, scrunching her face as if wanting to say something but hesitating. "Look, the quickest way to hatred is through fear, and the quickest way to fear is through sadness. The essence of destruction has buried itself in his heart, searching for anything to latch onto and grow. My guess is it found something already."

Bennett considered her for a moment. "One of the Medolians said I was supposed to be the one taken to Arros and given Wrath."

Hannah didn't look surprised. "It was probably assumed humans couldn't ignite pure Eve unless they carried similar shades to the Wrath and Rapture. I think Izaiah knew better and feared Wrath would run rampant in you, so he . . ." She simply motioned at him.

"You're saying it was Izaiah who made the switch?"

"No, I said probably."

Stumped, Bennett blurted out, "Al can never know."

"The truth?"

"It would destroy him."

"I know you think you're protecting him, and you may be right, but in my experience, the truth always comes out. The more it's held in, the more violently it does so."

Bennett nodded. *I get that. But he still can't know.*

"Now," Hannah said, walking past him. "Shall we?"

"I have a favor to ask," Bennett said. She paused and turned to him. "You're right. I can't use what's in me the way Alex does. I want to fight—it's what I know—but I need something."

"Like what?"

"Weapons. A gun, some fucking nunchucks, I don't care. Whatever will help against Joseph and those desert horse-fuckers."

Hannah shook her head. "Guns only inhibit Rapture. Attacking from afar is the way of Fovos. That won't help you find your strength."

"Yeah, but I'd feel a lot better with a piece."

Hannah's eyes narrowed. "I get it." She scanned the sea of junk filling her room. "Where is it…"

She stepped to a pile in the far corner, plunging her hand in and returning with a black leather knife sheath. Bennett took it cautiously when she handed it to him. With that same caution, he drew it out for a once-over—a full-tang bowie-style knife with a nine-inch clip blade. The handle, resembling ivory, had marbled streaks of black and gray. He had never seen a more beautiful knife in his life.

"Will this suffice?" she asked.

Bennett felt like a kid on Christmas. "Where did you get it?"

"Don't remember. Just be careful with it. Hang onto it," she answered, finally leaving the room.

"Yes, ma'am." Bennett sheathed the blade and followed Hannah to the surface, where Felix and Alex waited. The morning sun had risen, radiating off the golden fields as birds perched on the silos overhead sang. A soft breeze stirred the tall grass.

Bennett found Alex slumped on the ground, refusing to look Hannah's way, wearing his shame like a cloak.

He handed Alex the shoes, socks, and his blue baseball cap. "Found your hat. Lucky. Gotta keep better track of this thing, Al."

The teacher took it without glancing up, putting it on and muttering (*like a little asshole*), "Thanks."

At Hannah's instruction, the group gathered around and placed their hands on her shoulders. She told Alex and Bennett to think of where they last saw Joseph and the Wraithian camp. Any detail would help.

Closing her eyes, she stayed silent for a long moment while Bennett struggled to keep his thoughts focused on the camp, Joseph, and the Wraithians, finding himself simply dreading the fact that they were about to Shift.

"I think I have something. Hold on," Hannah said.

A moment later, the blinding light wrapped around them—*God*

I hate this part—and the queasy feeling in Bennett's gut came rushing back as the group sped through time and space. Soon, the acrid smells of horse manure, rotten meat, and campfire smoke assaulted his senses as his feet landed on hard, dry earth. A high desert sun poured heat onto his head and shoulders. The landscape around them was overgrown with gray, dead trees and brown grass, eerily reminiscent of the place they'd been imprisoned by the Wraithians. Bennett's view was of wide-open desert, almost peaceful, but the expressions on Alex's and Felix's faces—pointed the other way—told a very different story.

Not ten yards away sat a Wraithian camp. The nine riders occupying it looked just as startled to see them. Five animal-hide tents surrounded a fire, where a dead animal—*possibly a horse, hard to tell*—was roasting on a crude pike. On the far side, seven living horses were tied to two dead trees providing minimal shade, next to a rust-covered custom Jeep.

It took the Wraithians no time to grab their weapons and mobilize on the newcomers, baring their teeth and blades, shouting war cries.

"Well . . . we found them," Felix said.

"Guess my aim was better than I thought," Hannah said. "Put them down before they can call for backup."

Bennett smiled, feeling relief. *Finally. Speaking my language.* The Wraithians swarmed from all sides, sending he and Alex instinctively back to back.

"Light it up, Al," Bennett said.

"You can stop telling me what to do anytime," Alex muttered, as Bennett heard his hands spark and release smoke.

Drawing Hannah's knife from its sheath, Bennett felt a surge of confidence. This was a weapon he could trust. Turning it upside down in his grip, he bared his teeth. *Round two. Let's go!*

The first wave approached.

A young Wraithian charged in with surprising speed but terrible balance. Bennett seized his spear and used the momentum to throw him off course. In one fluid motion, he raked the knife's serrated blade across the man's ribs, sending him sprawling.

Just then, a long jagged blade came crashing down toward Bennett's head. He blocked it with the knife, but a spear aimed at his gut forced him to break away from Alex. Charging at the bladed Wraithian, Bennett leaped aside as the spear wielder lunged, instead sinking his weapon deep into his fellow tribeswoman's chest. She dropped, dead, and Bennett sliced the back of the spear-wielder's knees, sending him spilling to the dirt. The Wraithian roared in anger, but Bennett was ready, silencing him with a swift blow.

Out of the corner of his eye, he caught sight of Hannah charging into the fray, but lost track of her in the chaos. Alex was behind him, crying out and flailing like an amateur, while Felix, wielding a rock the size of a softball, began pummeling Wraithians over the head, leaving them sprawled in his wake. *Weirdest fucking demon.* But Bennett couldn't focus on anything but the enormous Wraithian looming in front of him.

His knife had been lost, knocked out of his grip by the behemoth, and they were now struggling for control of the Wraithian's spear. Bennett's confidence began to falter as he felt himself losing ground. *Shit. Not good. Uh . . . help?*

The huge man was seconds from overpowering him. He fought for a plan . . . *nope.* The Wraithian hurled Bennett to the ground, lifting the spear high above his head. Bennett braced for impact, but the Wraithian's eyes went wide with fear. His jaw quaked as if fighting for breath, and the spear fell from his hands. Bennett jolted back as the giant's bare chest turned a deep gray, raw umber radiating outward like a shockwave, crackling as the dark mass solidified. The parts of the Wraithian still flesh went limp, collapsing into the sand with a heavy thud, revealing Hannah behind him, an open palm out, glowing a vivid blue. The Wraithian's expression was frozen in place, mouth agape.

Hannah stepped over him and held out a hand for Bennett, who was in as much shock as the Wraithian. *Well, maybe not that much.* He recognized the substance the Wraithian had been transmuted to. It was the same he'd created in his father's office the night the wings appeared. *Was starting to think I'd dreamed all that.* Thin green and purple vines wormed out of the cracks in the Wraithian's rock chest, sprouting white-petaled flowers with brilliant yellow and violet pistils.

"Thanks," Bennett said, squeaking on accident.

Hannah helped him to his feet. "Don't mention it."

"Was that . . . Rapture?" he asked.

She nodded with a slight smile. "That was Rapture."

The fight was waning. All of the Wraithians were down, except for two. A young male with a wide triangular nose, pale skin, and dark hair had seen Hannah's punch turn the biggest of them into half a statue, and thus was making a frantic run for the open desert.

Felix stepped up beside Bennett and Hannah, rock still in hand. "I got him." He hurled the stone high and far, and it soared down directly onto the young man's head, who dropped without a sound and didn't get back up. "Bulls-eye!" Felix shouted.

They turned to find the last remaining Wraithian locked in combat with Alex. She was lanky, with long blonde hair, wearing a patch of leather over her mouth. Alex attacked with fierce swings, his burning fists glancing off her blade and sending sparks flying. Deep blue and gray veins protruded from his skin, flushed terra-cotta red everywhere except his lower arms, which were charred and blackened. With a powerful punch, he sent her flailing, the blade clattering to the ground.

"Stop him," Hannah ordered Bennett. "We need one alive."

Bennett charged in, reaching Alex just as he began to batter the defeated Wraithian. Tackling him away, Bennett held on for dear life as Alex thrashed like a wild animal caught in a trap.

"Let me go! Let me go!" Alex screamed.

"Chill out, you got her!" Bennett shouted, but Alex, fighting for freedom, didn't seem to hear.

Felix rushed over, taking hold of Alex's wrists. "That's enough now, Wilbur!"

After a moment, the teacher's fight subsided, and he panted heavily. Bennett kept his hold until Alex finally relaxed, the fires on his hands and forearms dwindling.

"Let go, Bennett," Alex said sharply, but Bennett held firm. "I said let me go!" the teacher shouted, wrenching free and rolling away. He stood, marching away from the camp with clenched, smoking fists. Felix followed, putting an arm around Alex and saying something Bennett couldn't make out.

Lying on the ground for a moment, catching his breath, Bennett nursed the burns he'd sustained trying to hold Alex. Thankfully, they were already healing themselves. *Some of this Rapture stuff ain't so bad.* Finally standing, he approached Hannah, who loomed over the blonde Wraithian, who was spouting what could only be curses in their ancient language, judging by her tone.

"What's she saying?" he asked, now side by side with Hannah.

"It isn't nice," she answered with a chuckle. "This one thinks I don't understand her."

"That language of theirs sure is pretty," Bennett remarked.

"The old speech of the Molochs. Yeah, it's like German's angrier, creepier stepbrother."

"I don't get it. Who are these people? How did they get like this?" Bennett asked. "Are they some ancient tribe we never knew about?"

"This one was speaking Portuguese a moment ago. That one over there was screaming in Russian." Hannah pointed around the camp. "Wraithians are everyday people, just like you and Barker. Human minds are easy to influence, and the Wraithian cause appeals to lost souls. The Molochs thrived on it. The tribes of old felt civilization was progressing too quickly, too fast. They worshipped destruction and, thus, the Wrath. I never thought modern people could fall this far, but it's not the first time I've been wrong."

The Wraithian woman continued her tirade, spitting at Hannah and Bennett.

"We need to figure out what they're doing out here," Hannah said, kneeling to address her. "Sel-brin sulios. Ra'h. Kai-lo ra'h."

The Wraithian's arrogance faded, her eyes turning desperate.

"There. Now you get it." Hannah turned to Bennett. "Give us a moment alone."

Bennett stepped away and found Alex leaning against the Jeep. Felix stood behind him, rubbing his shoulders like a boxing coach, speaking softly. As Bennett neared, Felix's words became clear.

"This was put in you, but it's not you. The Wrath responds to a desire to dismantle. So . . . don't desire it."

Alex was gripping the Jeep doors, fingers digging into the frame. "You said that, but it hurts! I can't stop myself—when it hits, it's like there's nothing I can do."

"Buddy, I've been living with this shit a lot longer than you. It. Don't. Have. To. Control you," Felix said with a sudden southern-twang.

"The voices are so loud. They want me to . . . God, the things they want!" Alex moaned.

"Been there, if you know what I mean," Felix said, giving Bennett the *back off* signal before he arrived.

"Thank you," Alex said to Felix. When he caught Bennett staring, he countered with a sneer. "Anything I can do for you?"

Bennett raised his hands and backed off. "I'm good."

"No! Come on, breathe!" Hannah screamed a few yards away, gripping the blonde Wraithian's collar, shaking her. "Open your throat, dammit!" She slapped the woman across the face, which was turning ghostly pale.

Bennett charged over to help. "What's happening?"

The Wraithian's cocky smile returned as her head drifted back, eyes rolling over. Her body went limp, and Hannah shoved her down, standing with a frustrated huff. "I hate it when they do that!"

"Is she . . . dead?" Felix asked, kneeling next to the Wraithian. He lifted her wrist and dropped her arm into the dirt. "Super dead. What did you do?"

"Nothing. She suffocated herself," Hannah answered.

"You can do that?" Alex asked, eyes wide.

"Solves the debate of whether these are authentic Wraithians or not," Hannah said, marching back toward the camp.

Felix followed closely. "Did you get anything useful?"

Hannah rifled through the Wraithian's side pouches. "Mostly gibberish. Said 'the third lord is coming,' or something. Also mentioned a congregation. I think they were on their way to meet friends." She pointed at tire tracks leading from the camp. "They were going this way." Then she gestured in the direction the riders had fled. "And what do you know? There just happens to be an assortment of Wrath gathering over there." She pocketed one of the small blood stones from a Wraithian pouch.

"An assortment of Wrath? What does that mean?" Bennett asked.

"Let's go find out," Hannah replied.

If Bennett didn't know better, he'd swear there was a tinge of excitement in her voice—subtle, but there.

"Okay, let's do it!" Felix said enthusiastically.

Hannah ripped a pair of leather undergarments off a male Wraithian. "Not going anywhere looking like that."

She tossed them at Felix, who smelled them, gagging in dismay. "You're not serious."

"I am," Hannah said with her most genuine grin yet.

Twenty minutes later, the group was stripped of their normal clothes and had assumed the identities of mangy desert riders. The only one showing signs of nervousness about disrobing was Alex, who carefully covered his indecency with an animal skin. Felix, on the other hand, was naked far quicker than Bennett anticipated, taking a moment to stretch in the nude before fully embracing the Wraithian guise. Using the camp's stash of white paint, they drew similar designs on their skin, and by the end, they looked surprisingly convincing. But within minutes, Bennett felt on the verge of vomiting from the stench. *Can't imagine how Al is doing with this. Seems like the type of guy who bathes in bleach.*

"You sure this is going to work?" Bennett asked, adjusting and picking leather with dried, crusty blood out of his ass crack.

"Depends on how well we all play the part," Hannah said.

Having collected all the blood stones in the camp, one by one, she crushed them in her hand, leaving just three intact. These, she distributed to Alex's, Bennett's, and Felix's satchels.

"Don't touch it," she said to Bennett. *No problem.* "Felix, Barker, let the horses go. It's time to leave."

After gathering all useful items from the horses' saddlebags, Felix and Alex cut their ties and let them go free. As the seven animals galloped away, kicking up golden dirt, Hannah whistled as piercingly as a blasting cornet. "Not you, buster."

The horse leading the charge, a striking black stallion with streaks of white, took a sharp turn and returned to the camp. Marching to Hannah, it stopped and lowered its head. "Hey there, pretty," she said, sliding a hand up its neck, petting its nose. She whispered something Bennett couldn't hear to the animal, then leaped onto its back and took the reins. "Let's do it."

The others proceeded to the Jeep, already packed with their clothes, but when Felix climbed into the driver's seat, Bennett and Alex exchanged weary glances. Bennett slid into the passenger seat, and Alex hopped into the back. As expected, the interior smelled atrocious.

"Did they slaughter their goats in here? Pee-yow," Felix said, putting the keys into the ignition.

"You do . . . know how to drive, right?" Bennett asked.

"Do I know how to drive!? Let me tell you something, young man—" Felix turned the key, the engine roared to life, choked, and fell dead. "Wait—which one is the throttle, again?"

After a few more attempts, the Jeep sputtered to life, and they were off, traversing the grassy desert terrain in pursuit of Hannah and her stallion. Thankfully, the stench lessened once they started moving.

As the day wore on, the landscape became rugged, dotted with rocky outcrops, gray bushes, and dead trees, both standing and fallen. Upon reaching the top of a high embankment, Hannah brought her horse to a stop.

Felix pulled up next to her, giving the Jeep's horn a honk. "What's up, buttercup?"

Hannah dismounted, instructed her steed to stay, and marched toward the edge of a cliff.

"What's she doing?" Alex asked.

Felix shrugged. "Beats me. Taking a look at something with those Hywyn peepers of hers. She could probably pass an eye test from here to the moon."

"Sounds like she's pretty much infallible," Bennett remarked with a hint of bitterness. "You sure she's not an angel?"

"Nobody's perfect, my man. Know what I mean?" Felix's voice lowered to a whisper. "There are cracks, even in her. Believe me. And it's getting harder, you know? To watch them get wider and deeper. Nothing quite like witnessing a person you care about go down a path you know is going to break them. Know what I . . . mean?" Felix's voice caught, his words faltering.

Bennett wasn't entirely sure what Felix was referring to but suspected it had something to do with the drink he'd tried to deny Hannah the night before. *Heard similar things from Lance when he asked me to quit, like him. I didn't.*

At the cliff's edge, Hannah motioned for Bennett to join her. "Hunter."

Hopping out of the Jeep, he hurried to her side, staring across the horizon as a welcome breeze swept over them. Despite his growing weariness with the desert, he couldn't help but appreciate the beauty of the view.

"Signal's getting strong. Can you feel it?" she asked.

Bennett closed his eyes but sensed nothing. "Don't think so."

"Try. Feel it. Celestial sight isn't just about seeing Eve. You'll see everything, but first you have to expand your own perception."

"Was that Buddha or Garcia?" Bennett asked with a smirk.

"Joke's on you, asshole—one of the few things I like about humanity is Jer-Bear. That guy's soul was nothing but Rapture and Jubilee. Just wanted to create and spread joy. You have to need that same Rapture and somehow make that need a part of your goal. The energy will give it to you once you know what that is. As long as your purpose is true, able to stand in the light, the Rapture will respond."

"What do you mean 'true'?"

"To defend something that has no defenses. To build something not yet built. To help those who are most in need. To be truly honest with oneself. This is what it responds to. Raw emotion is Eve, so use what's inside of you. Ever had someone you cared for? Or who cared for you?"

The past rushed back: the family photo in the gas station office, and the ripped face of Bennett's older brother. *Always loving. Just like Garcia.* Then, the face of his father took center stage; Tony, with his wide nose, slanted eyes, and curly ear hair. As always, his hateful diatribes erupted in Bennett's mind. *His special little insults for all of us. Ways to feel like a big man. I got it pretty bad, so did Mom, but Jer had it worse. Always did. Nothing in this world scared Dad more than his own gay son.*

Shoving the memories down, as he always did, the soldier shook his head. "Once."

Hannah studied him. "Don't push away your humanity, especially now. Remember, even though you got this from us"—she put a hand on her chest, then pointed at his—"first we got it from you. The essence of creation comes from humans, too. You've always had a little bit in you—you just didn't know it."

"But people like us—soldiers—we tear things down," Bennett said. "We don't create. Can you be true if all you know is the fight?"

"Right, the violence paradox—it's a doozy, but worth thinking about. Let me ask you—is it evil to strike a nail with a hammer? Obviously a violent act, yeah? But necessary. If a fight is in your way on a path—the path for true creation—Rapture will help you end the conflict. How you end it is up to you. Your counterpart, Barker, would be strong with it because he has only one unselfish goal. Just because he's small doesn't mean he doesn't have strength. His potential is—well, it's there. Believe it or not."

"That's true. Al's a good guy. But . . . what if I'm not?"

She turned a curious gaze his way. "What do you mean?"

"I'm not here for unselfish reasons. I'm here because of a mistake. I'm here because . . . well, because I . . ."

"Offed yourself?"

Hearing her say it made Bennett feel hundreds of pounds heavier. *Never thought of it in those words.*

"How did you—" he began.

"Call it a well-educated guess."

"Meaning it takes one to know one?"

"No, meaning I'm good at guessing games. You know, just because I was a Celestial doesn't mean I can't understand what it's like to be human. I've been around."

Hannah grew quiet, taking in the view, and Bennett wanted to move on. *Could an angel even be suicidal? How could they go about killing themselves? You know what, never mind.* "Look, all I know is someone gave me a mission . . . and—"

"You're going to see it done," she finished for him.

"It's what I know—the mission. But now, thinking back, I'm not sure I ever knew what I was fighting for. In any of it. Not like Jer, anyways."

"Jer?"

"My older brother, Jerry. He died in ninety, during a raid. South America. Some special ops mission. Hostage situation, I'm still not sure. But he was everything a soldier was supposed to be—totally pure, caring only for the well-being of those around him. Basically, everything I'm not. He used to tell me, 'Just do what good you can, King Arthur,' but I never did. It's like I thought that because he was around, or because he was overseas fighting for us, everything would be okay. If anyone said anything bad about the military, or anything I considered a representation of him, I would fight them. It's all I did—always fighting with something or someone. Jer would have been ashamed of me if he knew. And I'm still doing it—still fighting, still following orders, and I'm not sure why."

Hannah put a firm hand on his shoulder. "Then that's what you're going to have to find out."

"What do you mean?"

"Whatever it is you're fighting for."

"Hey, guys!" They turned to see Felix waving from the Jeep. "I think I know which way to go!" he called, pointing to a thin line of smoke rising in the distance. "Don't gotta have angel eyes to see that!"

Fifteen minutes later they were speeding down a sandy slope toward the smoke. When they reached the top of yet another ridge, Bennett became aware of sharp flashes of light from one of the distant hills.

"Felix, stop. Someone's out there," he said.

The party halted and looked in the direction he motioned to. More flashes appeared on the hill, less than a mile away.

"Someone's talkative," Felix said.

"There's about twenty of them." Hannah rode the stallion alongside the Jeep, snapping the rearview mirror off the passenger door to reflect a response.

Felix let out a cowardly laugh. "Hope you didn't just tell them to come kill us."

"Nah. They look amenable. And ugly." She tossed the mirror into the back of the Jeep.

More flashes returned, then ceased. Hannah covered her mouth with a leather mask. "They're headed this way. This is it. Barker, Hunter, cover up the scars."

Bennett and Alex put on additional layers of hide to cover the bull head and wings as the group continued on. Soon, a pair of

4x4s and a group of riders on horseback became visible, merging with their heading.

"Play the part," Hannah said as the real Wraithians drew close.

Bennett pulled his leather hood low and studied them. They, like the others, were a vast mixture of races, without a dominant size or shape, yet they all seemed deadly in their own right. Most rode their mounts like old pros, with custom weapons in hand, as though always ready for battle. Felix slowed the Jeep to follow them into the valley and a ravine, which quickly drew in tighter.

"One behind us, too," he said.

Bennett turned and spotted another 4x4 following their path, careening down the gully after them. The party in the rear caught up, soon passing the group led by Hannah. The six Wraithians stared questioningly as they roared ahead into the approaching canyon. "This is starting to seem like a bad idea," Felix said.

The sun was soon setting, blanketing the sky with a furious mix of red and orange as they drove for miles along the canyon. Hannah tapped Felix. "Speed up. You're drawing attention to us."

"I know what you mean." He put the car in second gear, racing to keep pace. A few minutes later, two more 4x4s and a dozen horse riders joined from an intersecting canyon. They were surrounded by galvanized Wraithians charging as fast as they could, hollering and hyping themselves for something they seemed to be in the know about.

Figuring *What the Hell?*, Bennett joined in, yapping like a dog into the air, immediately drawing a worried glance from Alex. "Let it out. Why not?" Bennett suggested.

Alex's stern guise surprisingly melted. He grinned, turned his head up, and howled, joining Bennett, and soon Felix did as well. The three screamed and shouted for minutes on end, letting off some steam, though the teacher was clearly the one who needed it most, as he was the last to finish, looking as relaxed as though he'd just had a massage.

The horde of riders continued to exclaim their excitement for another ten minutes as the sun dipped below the horizon and the caravan came over a hill. The canyon suddenly opened into a plateau valley. Below them lay a sprawling Wraithian camp, with well over two hundred tents silhouetted by the sunset, somewhere north of two hundred horses, and at least three times as many desert riders.

"Ladies and gentlemen, we found the hive," Felix said as the Jeep dipped into the valley and toward the camp.

Hannah rode up close alongside them. "We'll be okay. Remember, we're just here to look around. And if either of you two spot Joseph, let us know as silently as possible. Felix and I will take care of the rest."

"What do you mean?" Bennett asked. "You said it's our job to—"

"Hunter, don't argue with me," she said. Bennett sat back in his seat. "You ready?" she asked all three in the Jeep.

Felix screamed one last time, answering for them, "We're ready!"

Hannah stared Alex down. "Barker, keep the Wrath in check. Don't blow our cover. I can't Shift us out of there if we're caught in a storm of Wraithians."

The teacher nodded and slunk lower in his seat. As the Wraithian train entered the camp, Bennett noticed many of the tents scattered about were made of industrial material, much more modern than the rest, which were mostly sewn together from various cloths, likely pillaged, and cuts of animal hide. Passing into the outskirts of the camp, they found contemporary camping chairs, pieces of furniture chopped into firewood, and many tents containing spring cots. *Must have been an engineering camp, or dig site, or something. One guess what happened to all the poor fucks here.*

The Wraithians had fires going and were clumped in packs along the plateau, either giving oratories or listening to them while eating. A small hill sat at the far end of the camp, upon which the largest tent was built. Across the valley, another canyon began, where a steady stream of Wraithians was flowing in on foot.

Hannah found an open spot in a clump of tents to dismount as Felix pulled the Jeep alongside her and killed the engine. "So far so good."

The sky was a dark blue and purple by now as the group of invaders in disguise made their way through the tents left by the original camp, looking for clues. Many had been burned to the ground; the rest were well rifled through.

"Any sign of Joseph?" Felix asked Bennett, glancing around.

"Trust me, you'll know him if you see him."

A loud horn somewhere overhead broke the noise of the camp, echoing through the canyons on either side of them. The desert riders stopped their speeches and turned silent, now like statues staring upward with eyes that did not waver. Bennett followed their gazes and found the source of the sound: an old Wraithian male in a long white cloak perched upon a high stone at the mouth of the far canyon, where the procession was continuing. He blew the horn again, held weakly with both hands. The old Wraithian then disappeared behind the rock. In near silence, the rest of the camp began emptying into the far canyon, following the man in robes.

Just when I thought you guys couldn't get any weirder.

A wave of Wraithians marched toward Bennett and the others, forcing them onward like fish caught in a net. There was nowhere to go. With one look, Hannah made it clear that they would have to follow along. *Yay.* Bennett made his way alongside the riders, hoping he was covering the wings on his shoulders well enough.

Surprisingly, his other tattoos were not a problem, as many of the Wraithians had them as well, ranging everywhere from genuine tribal and prison tattoos to mottoes and pop culture references.

A few moments into the trek, Hannah suddenly held her head and let out a groan.

"You okay?" Felix asked.

"Yeah. Just . . . we're nearing a lot of Wrath."

Bennett could feel it too; a faint storm cloud of crimson was fast approaching.

The march continued for ten minutes, leading them to the mouth of a cave. Many Wraithians were handed torches as they entered, lighting their way through the cramped tunnel. For another half hour, the parade moved deeper into the mountain until they arrived at a wide room with a red cresting roof and black stairs leading up to a tall, open doorway. Two weathered statues flanked the base of the long-stepped stairs, resembling Chinese dragons but far uglier. Felix and Hannah shared a curious glance, and Bennett swore he heard Hannah whisper, "Friend of yours?" while Felix stifled a laugh.

As they climbed the steps with the horde, they entered the doorway, passing into a dark hall. *This feels fucking wrong.* A brief walk led to a passage through a rock entry, where the walls exploded upward into a new cavern. An orange hue from the few torches cast flickering shadows on the black and brown walls. The main feature of the room—a statue of an immense beast looming atop a large column—commanded Bennett's attention. Covered in boils and spikes, with no eyes, the statue had colossal wings spread out over the room like immense sails. The noise of the Wraithians inside heightened Bennett's senses, distracting him and causing him to stumble when the ground suddenly gave way to intricate trenches chiseled into the floor.

The room was now filled to capacity with desert riders, letting out low, guttural sounds that rose and pulsed, almost hymn-like. Bennett joined in, making noises for conformity's sake, catching a few odd glances from nearby Wraithians. *God, I hope I'm doing this right.* "Uuuuuhhhgg...Buuuhhhgg—" *Hi, how are you?* "Baaaaaahhhh."

A figure in white appeared at the top of the plateau: a Wraithian woman, aged near sixty, with stark white hair, wearing robes similar to the horn blower. She wielded a torch in her left hand, raising it high above the mass as the Wraithian chants reached a fever pitch.

From the shadows behind her stepped a naked male Wraithian covered in blood. The crowd roared, apparently in approval. Judging by the manic look on his face, Bennett guessed the blood covering him wasn't his own. The naked Wraithian held his arms high, proudly, as the woman in robes approached him and pressed the torch into his chest. He roared in rage as his skin boiled, yet he did not fight back. In fact, both he and the crowd seemed to revel in it. After a moment, she lifted the torch, and he dropped to his knees. Stepping to the edge of the platform, she motioned behind her, where three more shapes emerged from the darkness below the beast. The two on the outside were Wraithians, as large as the one Hannah had turned to stone, carrying a third party between them: another naked man, free from blood, his head hung low, with no white markings or tattoos on him.

The man's head lifted weakly, and when he saw the horror below him, he began screaming desperately in English, "Help! Somebody!"

Bennett and Hannah shared a worried glance. *Shit. A civilian. Must be one of the people from the original camp. What do we do?* But Hannah's expression—looking as though she were ready to watch and wait—gave him no comfort.

The blood-covered Wraithian was handed a dagger by the woman in white, raising it high over the crowd to rouse them. *This looks fa-*

miliar. Things are about to get ugly. Watching an innocent man endure the torture he and Alex had faced at the hands of these maniacs sounded excruciating, and at the thought, Bennett felt a new, crackling cold run up his spine, settling into the scars on his shoulders.

The civilian man was held in place by the brutes as the wild, naked Wraithian proceeded to beat him, cut him, and do all his worst, all while his clan's people called for more. *We have to do something!* Bennett took a step forward, feeling his spine straighten and an austere strength spill into his chest. Rapture filled him like a glass of water expanding as it froze.

But before he could move, Hannah's hand shot out and gripped his wrist, stopping him. "No. We have to wait for Joseph," she whispered.

Bennett fought her grip and felt her tighten like a vise. *He's going to die!*

Watching the civilian man go limp and hearing his shouts cease, Bennett's wings turned so cold it burned, and his fists began to feel as heavy as ice blocks. He looked down and saw a faint fog of orchid blue appearing at his fingertips.

The civilian held by the brutes went still: dead. The blood-covered Wraithian was done. The victim's body was then taken to the edge of the plateau and tossed over the side, disappearing from Bennett's view. *I've seen enough.* The soldier was finally understanding what Hannah had told him on the cliff. *I've got a pretty good idea of what I'm fighting for.* But Hannah wouldn't relent her grip on his wrists, holding him in place even with his newfound strength.

Felix whispered at Bennett in slight panic, "Chill out! You want to get us killed?"

In his peripheral vision, Bennett caught nearby Wraithians taking notice, murmuring among themselves. Meanwhile, the brutes on the upper plateau brought out a new victim: a woman in her thirties, brunette, fairly short, stripped of all clothing except for her glasses.

No! No more! Bennett bared his teeth at Hannah. "Let me go."

She remained firm. "I'm not going to do that."

The blood-covered Wraithian made another display for the crowd, holding up the dagger as the woman screamed for help. Bennett felt it coming: an even bigger wave of Rapture than the night the wings had appeared on him.

This is it. Come on! I'm ready!

He was more than willing to fight off Hannah, charge up the stairs, and stop the ceremony. Bennett gritted his teeth, just about to make his move, when a wave of Wrath assaulted his senses, and a sharp bang echoed through the cavern. An explosion blasted Alex Barker's five-foot-five frame twenty yards up, sending everything nearby crashing to the floor. The teacher's fists glowed red hot as he shot toward the plateau like a flaming lawn dart, releasing pure rage.

TO LONDON

Nope, I was wrong, it can get worse! Casey thought, hoisted off her feet and out of the shadows beneath the statue of the beast by two lumbering brutes. Her weak neck left her head dangling as she was lifted into the deafening temple filled with smoke. All she could see was the black and brown floor passing beneath her, then torches drifted into view before the platform gave way to a three-story drop into an ocean of bodies. The intricate carvings on the floor were hidden by an arena's worth of dirty, angry people, who seemed basically like the world's worst Oakland Raiders fans.

What the Hell was I thinking, coming back here? Who are you psychos? Where is Leigh!?

Questions swirled in her mind. Casey fought to get free, but the huge captors with white tattoos gripping her on either side felt like stone pillars. Exposed and sweating, dangling by her arms, she felt like a sacrifice to King Kong. *Also, why did they leave my glasses on?*

Casey scanned her surroundings for any glimmer of hope, seeing a thousand unfriendly eyes. She thought about screaming for help, like her friend Dennis had, but it hadn't done him any good—so why would it work for her?

Serves me right for helping open the door to Hell. Smooth move, Case.

The naked Raiders fan smeared with blood was holding the ancient knife Leigh and Jeff had found in the "green room," which had just been used to murder the only person she'd ever seen lose on the second spin in a game of Twister. *And who knew the words perfectly to one too many Christmas carols, and tried to kiss me at a UCL Bloomsbury graduate party after having a single blueberry daiquiri . . . Oh, Dennis . . . I'm so sorry.* She wasn't going to scream for help, but that wasn't going to stop her from screaming period.

Dennis's killer stepped closer, drawing the knife. The look in his eyes—bloodshot, angled sharply down—was something she'd never seen in a man of society. The blade danced, ready to pounce, so she closed her eyes, hoping the end would just happen already! But instead, an explosion erupted in the middle of the crowd below, sending Raiders fans flying like leaves. One poor bastard, who must have been standing directly over the bomb, soared into the air like a flaming catapult projectile. A second later, the body zeroed in on the plateau, and Casey saw the face of a man, wide awake, with thick eyebrows. To her amazement, he landed on his feet and charged up the stairs toward the plateau, holding what looked like flaming paper bags in both hands, using them to pummel his way through the Raiders fans, sending them off the tall, skinny stairway.

Casey heard a voice from the crowd scream, "What the Hell are you doing?" though the dark-haired man seemed not to hear it. Leaping the last six feet, he reached level ground, landing in a splash of smoke. The man fought toward Casey (*not this way*) as the bloody Raiders fan wielding the dagger charged. By now, it was clear the flaming bags around the small man's hands actually *were* his hands; when one of them went through the Raiders fan's gut, out the other side, and retracted.

The goliaths were forced to drop Casey to deal with the new guy, who was either terrifying beyond reason or her personal savior. Dwarfed by their size, the dark-haired man ducked away from their hands and sent thundering punches into their ribs, cracking bones with each hit. Once he'd dispatched the giants, he leaped at the old (*ish*) woman in white, who made no moves to fight back and seemed in awe of the fire fighter. He didn't care, however, and simply booted her off the ledge. The white-haired lady soared over the bone pit, landing out of sight with a squeal.

Again, scary, or savior?

Within feet of Casey, the dark-haired man extinguished the fire around his arms and ripped off his leather mask and hides, revealing innocent sienna-brown eyes and a glowing, blistering tattoo of a goat (*or something ugly and creepy*) on his chest.

Casey was about to run or fight back when the man shouted in a true-blue American accent, "Wait! I'm not one of them! I'm getting you out of here." He tossed his hides over her shoulders for cover—it wasn't much, but it helped—then held out his hand to escort her. "Let's go!"

What? No. Crap, uh—what do I . . . Casey looked for other options but saw only furious Raiders fans swarming up the stairs, seeking blood. She took his hand. It was warm but didn't burn. The dark-haired man scooped her off her feet and hopped to the edge of the plateau overlooking the crowd, whose fury seemed directed at two individuals who clearly didn't fit in. Their hands glowed in a deep blue, like the electric lanterns Casey and her team used at base camp. In addition, it looked as though one of the normal, nonglowing Raiders fans had turned on his friends, swinging dual swords in a desperate bid for survival.

"Barker! Get down here!" the blue glowing female boomed.

"Right. I can do this—I can do this," the short, dark-haired man assured himself.

Casey shot him a glance as he took a running start with her in tow. *Do what?* But it was too late to worry. He leaped off the column, sending them soaring forty feet. A second later, they landed with a shocking bang—reminding Casey of the car wreck she'd gotten into at sixteen—and a blast of hot wind hurled frenzied Raiders fans to the side. Casey was then set down, shaking but uninjured.

"Get her out of here!" one of the glowing people, a huge man with a thick beard called out. He then said something about finding a car and shifting which Casey couldn't quite make out.

The blue-glowing lady shouted back, "Not here! Move!"

Casey then found herself in the middle of the weird new group of half-naked people (*not friends*) while they fought the tide of Raiders fans toward the exit of the cathedral. The blows from the blue-handed fighters seemed to stun and stagger the Raiders fans, slowing them down until the flashes of light dissipated. It proved effective on all sides, and by some miracle, the escapees made it to the temple exit and entered the tight, dark tunnel out. In a twist of luck, as the glowing fighters held off those in their path—blasting sparks of blue, violet, red, and orange—the light also helped them navigate the darkness.

A Raiders fan struck by the glowing woman stumbled backward into Casey. His mouth was forced open, revealing a thick green vine worming its way out, and then up through his eye socket, into his brain cavity, where it broke out again. Brains splashed her face as Casey screamed the last of her voice out and hopped over the body, dashing to catch up to the others. *Okay, friends!* She dodged sword thrusts and stayed close to the bearded man, clutching the leather straps below his burning blue wings. *Burning what?* Making it out of the tunnel, the group shot down the Dead Stairs, pummeling the last few Raiders fans along the way. *I think we're going to make it!*

"Thanks for the help, Felix! Where's your Wrath?" the glowing blue lady shouted angrily at the friendly cult member with them.

"I told you—I'm not going to!" the Raiders fan returned.

The glowing blue lady seemed genuinely offended. "Wha . . . I thought you were kidding!"

"Well, I wasn't!"

They raced on. At the cavern split, the glowing blue woman was about to lead them up the long way to the surface.

"Not that way!" Casey called out, charging past the big bearded man and showing them the quicker path to the surface, which also had the added benefit of forcing their pursuers to reduce down to two or three at a time. Casey figured the majority would still take the long way, giving her and her rescuers would have at least a few minutes' lead. *With any luck, which I seem to be short of lately.*

The adrenaline pumping through her dulled the pain of running on gravel without shoes and the fatigue in her muscles, but she knew she was likely cutting up her feet horribly. Anger fueled her, pushing her along, driven by her hatred of how exposed she felt—and how exposed she literally was.

A jagged stone stabbed into her heel, sending Casey sprawling, but luckily the bearded man was there to steady her. "Get on!" he shouted, positioning himself in front of her. She complied, piggyback style, ignoring the horrid smell he emitted and holding on for dear life as they made their way to the mouth of the cave. The group burst out and dashed across the sand, while the Raiders fans poured from the tunnel in hot pursuit.

Spears whistled through the air, stabbing into the dirt around them as they raced up the ridge toward the canyon mouth over-looking the camp.

The blue glowing woman broke off to the left. "Go on ahead!"

Racing up a rocky path against the red rock wall, she disappeared into a crevice between it and a boulder the size of a three-story Coke can. When Casey heard her roar and saw a flash of blue light, the stone began to tip.

The man Casey now knew as Felix laughed nervously. "Uh, Hannah—we're still here."

Hannah is her name? Okay, got it.

The wings on the man in front of Casey flared with intensity, nearly blinding her as he charged under the looming rock, exiting the canyon just as dust began to rain down. The gigantic boulder moaned and toppled into the mouth of the canyon, landing on a dozen Raiders fans who were nearby, sending a cloud of dust out like a brown wave crashing ashore. The escape party slammed to a halt, turning to see if anyone had made it through. A moment later, a blue glow emerged from the rubble, hopping down and out of the brown cloud.

The lady, Hannah, waved them on, screaming, "What are you dumbasses waiting for?"

Who is this magnificent woman?

Casey and the others raced through what was once her camp, past her former tent, and stumbled upon an old Jeep missing its roof.

"Get in!" the dark-haired man shouted, followed by Hannah whis-tling loudly enough to make Casey bite her lip. Heavy horse hooves approached as Casey leaped into the back of the Jeep. Soon, a tall black horse with a white middle (*Oreo*) charged in, riderless. Hannah leaped eight feet, landing on the horse's back with the grace of a gymnast in jeans, seized the reins, and bolted. Felix threw the car in gear, tearing through the tent forest, wrapping some of them up in the axles of the Jeep.

As the vehicle jolted from side to side, Casey clung to the bearded man for stability, which was tricky as they were both scantily clad and covered in sweat and blood—some theirs, some not. As the Jeep passed the last grove of tents, the moon erupted into view over the next hill, a brilliant yellow globe on the horizon. The Jeep careened up the slope, speeding into the ravine as the sounds of pursuit faded, leaving only the engine's roar echoing off the rock walls and the wind whipping through her hair.

Felix was the first to speak. "So, that was nuts."

"Are you okay?" the dark-haired man asked, turning to Casey.

She nodded, keeping quiet and using the hides he had given her to cover herself as much as possible.

"Mind telling us what the Hell that was back there?" the bearded man bellowed at the dark-haired one as if he were his father.

"I don't want to hear it, Bennett," the dark-haired one shouted, ready for the jab. *Bennett. Got it.* "We couldn't do nothing! And don't act like you weren't getting riled, too. I saw you glowing."

"Fuck yeah, you did!" Felix shouted, reaching back to pat Bennett on the knee. "Welcome to the Eve club, my man."

Bennett looked at his hands, grinning for a split second before turning mournful. "Sorry, Al. You're right. You did good."

And Al—so that's everyone. Casey felt compelled to interrupt. "Hi, Al, Bennett, and Felix. Um, quick question, are you going to kill me?"

"You think that's why I put my ass on the line back there?" Al replied harshly.

"Easy," Bennett said, turning to Casey. "He's right, though. If we wanted you dead, we could have just let the Wraithians finish you off."

Ew. They have a name? "Wraithians?"

"It's a long story. They're basically devil worshippers who keep rocks as pets," Bennett answered.

"Accurate," Felix agreed.

"So . . . why are you dressed like them?" Casey asked.

Mentioning it seemed to jog their minds all at once, and the three men ripped off their leather disguises, discarded them, and changed into clothes they had stuffed under the seats of the Jeep. Al and Bennett handed Casey some items. "Grabbed extras, just in case. Been going through a lot of clothes lately," Bennett said, the comment seeming like a jab at Al somehow.

Casey quickly donned the jeans, an old camp counselor T-shirt, and shoes. *Thank God. Gimme gimme. No more nakedness with strangers. No more cults and temples. No more weird bullshit threatening my life, please.*

"We went in there to find someone and found you instead," Bennett continued, answering her original question. "Not that I'm complaining. We'll get you to safety, but first we have some questions. For starters, what's your name?"

No harm there I suppose. "Casey."

Felix caught her gaze in the rearview mirror. "Was that your camp back there, Casey?"

"It was. My team discovered the temple a few weeks ago. I left to escort samples back to the lab, but when I lost contact with my friends, I decided to return with a search party. Instead, we found your Wraithians. Or they found us." A wave of emotion hit her, catching her off guard. After a moment, she continued, "I'm sorry. I know you just saved me, and I don't mean to sound ungrateful. I just—"

Al finished lacing his shoes. "Trust me, we get it. This is a heavy world to get thrown into. We're not trying to be pushy, but we need to know about those artifacts."

"They were nothing special," Casey said, shaking her head. "A dagger, some rocks—things that might have been important to ancient people, but not enough to tell us anything. We don't even know who built the temple."

"Did you say rocks? How many?" Felix asked, his tone shifting.

"Three."

Al, Bennett, and Felix exchanged a tense glance. *What? What does that mean?*

"Where are the stones now?" Bennett asked.

Her new friends were starting to sound as obsessed with these artifacts as the Wraithians had. "I'm not talking about that. Not until I know my boss is safe. Besides, I only know where one of them is. When I opened the crate we packed, two of the stones, as well as the dagger, were missing."

"Stolen?" Al asked.

Casey shook her head. "They were never loaded. I'm sure of it. Leigh—my boss, Professor Evans—wanted to keep them. She couldn't even stand parting with them. That last week . . . she wasn't acting like herself."

"Not like herself how?" Bennett asked.

"Leigh is always half impulse, half logic. The two sides balance her out, but the more time we spent there . . . Never mind. I left her and another man behind. I saw his body in the camp, but never found Leigh's. I think she's still out there, alive."

"Is Professor Evans the only one who knows the locations of the second and third stones?" Al asked.

Casey hated answering these questions but saw no other way. She nodded reluctantly.

"Sounds like Joseph may have her," Felix said casually enough to make Casey angry.

"Could be using her to find them as we speak," Al added.

"The rocks?" Casey asked. "Who's Joseph?"

"There's a lot to catch you up on, and not a lot of time, but we think your boss might have been taken by a bad hombre who wants those stones," Bennett explained.

Casey couldn't help screaming, "What are you people talking about?"

"The story says an old, evil magic lurks within the stones, waiting to be set free," Felix said, finishing with a cheap haunted-house laugh.

"You're telling me my friends were killed because ignorant ass-holes believe in shit from the Stone Age?" Casey said.

"Sounds like from even before that. More like the . . . dirt age, or something," Bennett said, noticing the incredulous stares from the others. "What?" he said defensively.

"Did you just make a joke?" Al asked.

Bennett folded his arms, staring over the landscape in silence.

Casey broke the ensuing silence. "Can we get back to where my boss is, and what we're going to do about the Wraithians?"

"My friend, we hear you, but we sort of have other priorities at the moment," Felix said, his annoying joviality grating on her nerves.

"Who's we?" Casey asked, tired of doing so.

"Call us officers of a—higher court," Bennett said.

Oh, great. "So, you're government?"

"Sure. Go with that," Al said.

No, you're not. "Which agency?" Casey pressed.

"Bennett's representing one party, I'm with another. Basically, the highest of the high, and . . . lowest of the low," Al added.

"Start making sense, or I'm going to jump out of this car!"

"Okay!" Al shot a glance at the others for support.

Felix shrugged, smirking. "Curious what her reaction will be." Bennett put his hands up with a *not my problem* turn of his head and continued looking over the landscape.

Al took a breath before saying, "It's Heaven and Hell."

"Though that's not technically accurate," Felix tossed on.

The archaeologist sat in stunned silence for a good seven or eight seconds. *Okay, that does it. Get out, Case. However you have to do it. Just get away.* She sat still, formulating her escape, trying to covertly take off her seat belt.

"She doesn't believe you guys," Bennett muttered.

"No, I totally do. I believe—in God, and Jesus, Mohammed, Buddha, Gandhi, all of it. I see them every day." She sang, "'And praise be to all blessings . . . so . . .'" struggling to remember even the most basic of Sunday school lyrics.

"Fine. Show her," Al said to Felix.

"Right-o," he answered.

Without pause the driver swung his head to face her, keeping his hands on the wheel; but his face was not his anymore. His human jaw, speckled with curly hair, was stretched downward to a point, as if an arrow were fired, pulling it down. Two-inch razor teeth lifted and lowered from the jaw leading up into a mangled throat, where they met a thick snake's tongue whipping up and down. The smell of smoke and old meat slapped Casey in the face, as two sneering red eyes set in dark sockets glowered at her. She was frozen, like when she'd try to run in a dream (*or nightmare*). Unable to scream, she let out a wet cough instead.

The driver's face quickly snapped back into place, with beady little eyes, a long nose, and a mouth that never fully closed. Grinning like a little brother who'd just pulled a prank, he returned his attention to the road.

"What the fuck!?" Casey blasted.

Felix shrugged. "Gotta get you on board somehow."

Al caught her gaze. "Please. This stuff is real, and from the sound of it, these rocks are bad news. I just want to go home. If you help us, it might actually happen."

Casey lowered her eyes. "I'm not a part of this."

"You know what they're saying is true," Bennett began. "You said yourself you felt something in the temple, so you must be Eve sensitive. What was it you felt?"

Casey had never tried to put it into words before, but could only think of one word that seemed appropriate. "Evil," she said.

A moment later, they followed Hannah into a grove of trees at the edge of a forest stretching over the hill, continuing until she seemed satisfied that no one would be able to follow. Dismounting, she spanked the horse and gave another piercing whistle. "Thank you, love. Now hide." The horse charged through the trees with a whinny, disappearing from sight.

Felix stopped the Jeep and killed the engine.

"Anyone hurt?" Hannah asked, approaching them, no longer glowing like a lantern.

"Don't think so." Al shook his head as he and the others exited the car, though Casey stayed put. Hannah grabbed her clothes from the back of the Jeep and proceeded to change, and for the first time Casey noticed her brilliant eyes, shimmering like violet starlight. *Heaven . . . right.*

Felix started excitedly, "Boy, have we got a lot to tell you! Casey here says—"

Hannah cut him off. "I heard your whole conversation. So . . ." She eyed Casey while sliding on her leather jacket. "We know where at least one stone is."

"Whoa, hold up. I haven't told you anything yet, and I have no way of knowing if I can trust you," Casey said.

"After everything that's happened?" Bennett asked, stepping away from the Jeep before suddenly stumbling over.

"Hey, big guy!" Felix called, catching him and helping him to the ground. It was then that Casey saw the deep cut spilling blood from Bennett's lower abdomen.

"One of the spears. I've had worse. Even before dying. Just light-head-ed . . ." Bennett's speech slurred. He was losing consciousness.

"Help him!" Casey shouted.

Hannah joined, surveying the wound. "He needs to learn to help himself."

Felix slapped Bennett's shoulder. "Come on. You just had it. Find the Rapture again."

Bennett moaned, holding his side, looking defeated.

"What is your goal?" Hannah asked him.

The glow of Bennett's blue markings intensified and a subwoofer hum grew deep within him. With a sense of awe, Casey watched as the wound began to scab over.

"Attaboy!" Felix said, slapping Bennett on the other shoulder. Bennett gave a weak thumbs-up. The driver then took a deep breath and looked at Hannah. "So, I guess we found Gehenna."

"Hold on a minute—" she started, but he jumped back in.

"You know you felt it, General—sorry, Hannah," Felix said. "Once we passed that doorway, shit, talk about Wrath central. Might as well have been Arros down there."

Hannah still looked skeptical. "We don't know what that was. But . . . if it was Gehenna, it would explain why no one has ever been able to find it. Something's been hiding its energy from the kingdoms for hundreds of thousands of years. Possibly millions."

"Starting to look like Joseph's stories are true," Bennett said.

418 John Andrew Myers

"If that's so, and these rocks are the genuine article, then we need to know where the others are—yesterday," Hannah said.

All eyes turned to Casey. "What?"

"I know you don't believe us," Al started, "but if your friend is alive, we're your best chance at getting her back in the same condition."

"We need your help. You need ours. What do you say . . . friend?" Bennett coughed out from the ground.

Casey glanced around at the others, trying to make a decision, knowing there was only one real option. *Oh, great.* A few minutes later, her trepidations were swept away when she herself was swept across the planet. Casey's aching feet now stood on cool, soft grass. The air was filled with the comforting smell of a recent rain in a familiar city park, surrounded by a bustling metropolis. Water streamed through rattling tin gutters beyond the park's outskirts. A few yards away sat the lumbering tree beside a bike path where she often ate her lunch.

Oh my God, it's Gordon Park. They had arrived in London.

After placing a hand on Hannah, closing her eyes to think of the university, and experiencing a violent poof, Casey found herself home. The white flash the others called a Shift was awful (*we'll leave it at that*), and she wanted to forget its memory, as well as the vomit she left on the ground, ASAP. Needing no further proof of their legitimacy as otherworldly beings, she led her new friends through the park, trying hard not to look suspicious with them in tow. *Have none of you ever been in society before?* Veering off the walking path, they approached a steel-barred wall with spiked fence posts across the street from a long, brown brick building, five stories tall, with white window frames, sitting among a mix of student and residential housing.

"That's the archaeology building," Casey said, pointing. "My office is inside."

Bennett and Felix nodded and started toward the park exit without hesitation.

"Wait!" Casey said, hurrying to block them.

Felix looked confused. "But you just said it was in there."

"Yeah, but trust me, this will go a lot smoother if we don't all go in and start setting fires—no offense, Al," Casey said.

"My name's Alex, actually. Just so you know—"

For a guy who was on fire just a few moments ago, Alex's demeanor could not have been sweeter.

"I'm sorry. Alex." Casey then turned to Hannah. "Ma'am, I realize this is your show, but permission to make a suggestion?"

Hannah chuckled. "Shoot."

"Alex and I go in, keep it small and casual. They know me, so they won't be suspicious if I bring one person along."

"Why Barker?" Hannah asked.

"Frankly, he's the least scary looking of all of you."

The others seemed unsure, especially Bennett, who asked, "What if Joseph shows up?"

"We'll cover the perimeter. If Joseph arrives, we'll know," Hannah said, giving Casey an approving nod. "Just hurry."

"Be careful, Wilbur," Felix said to Alex.

He and Casey started across the street to the front entrance, where a handful of students were lounging. Entering the lobby, she led them along the blue and white tile flooring while Alex began tucking his shirt into his khaki pants and lifting his baseball cap straight back, aiming as high as possible.

"What are you doing?" she asked.

"No one suspects a man who wears their hat this high," he said, finishing with a toothy grin.

Whatever you say. They neared the security desk outside the glass door to the library. Sitting in the chair was an elderly man with a bushy caterpillar mustache Casey didn't recognize. *Oh no. Where's Irene?*

He looked up from his book as they approached. "Evening, folks, coming for a late visit?"

Casey read his name tag: *Maurice Mathers.*

"Hi . . . Maurice. I'm faculty—well, contractor—and I forgot something in my office, but I thought this would be a perfect opportunity to show my friend around. He's visiting from out of town."

Maurice huffed and put his book down. "This may not be my usual building, but I know the rules, ma'am. Non-student visiting hours are from nine to six."

Casey started into a lie with trepidation. *Where's Leigh when you need her?* "Uh, yes, I know . . . but I was hoping you could—"

Alex bounded forward, extending his hand to Maurice. "Hi-ya! Name's Alex, Alex Barker. Great to meet you! Can't begin to tell you how wonderful it's been to walk around your campus here. So green! And the history . . ." he trailed off, leaving acres of space for Maurice. Two agonizing seconds later, the security guard snapped to a tight-lipped grin and returned the handshake.

"And you'd think nobody ever thought about that," Maurice said. "Just going about their days, never appreciating where it all came from. Never even bothering to look down at the ground beneath their own ridiculous feet!"

Alex shook his head and put his hands on his hips, as though it were the worst news he'd ever heard. "I hear ya. I'm a nature man, myself. A camp counselor at Pushaw Lake, Maine." He pointed at Casey's shirt. Sure enough, it was from Pushaw Lake, Maine. "Gave her one of my old shirts. Yeah, beautiful country." He then pointed outside. "And I tell ya what else is a shame, I saw the construction you got over on Taviton Street. Just awful. Those guys'll tear up anything they can get their hands on." Alex shook his head again, stopping just short of saying *tisk-tisk-tisk*.

"Well, that's all they do, isn't it? Just destroy it all and build new, useless, ugly malls no one asked for!" Maurice agreed boisterously. "Then fill them with good-for-nothing fusion restaurants." He finished, heated but also laughing.

Casey moved closer to the door, being careful to interrupt as gently as possible. "So—about the thing I forgot upstairs?"

Maurice, distracted, waved them on. "Oh, sure, your friend can go with you."

"Thank you so much!" Alex said, shaking Maurice's hand again. "Keep on protecting history, 'cause if we don't—well . . ."

Maurice gave him a friendly shot in the arm. "Say no more, I'm on it. Cheers! You folks have a nice night."

Casey and Alex hurried through the carpeted library, past studying students, to the elevator hallway. Once inside, they began an anxious, boring ascent. "So . . . running around with angels and demons, what's that like?" she asked halfway up.

Alex laughed and sighed. "Not what I expected, that's for sure. And don't let Hannah hear you calling her that. Even though she probably just did."

"An angel? Why?"

"I think they don't like being lumped in with what us mortals think of them."

"And what about you?" Casey asked cryptically.

"What do you mean?"

"I mean, you are . . . human, right?"

He looked away with fearful eyes, possibly reliving some recent bad memory. "I'm not sure anymore."

They arrived. Alex stepped out of the elevator to check the hallway before letting Casey out. He followed her past a series of doors leading to project labs until they reached the second to last one. After Casey punched the code into a keypad, the door unlocked, and they hurried into a large, unoccupied room with white walls, lined with shelves and dotted with desks and workspaces. Long metal arms with magnifying glasses attached stretched down over the tables from a framework of white tubes running the length of the ceiling. Turning on the fluorescent overhead lights, Casey made her way down the aisles of artifact shelves in the rear.

"Where is it? Where is it—"

She searched the many spots the rock could have ended up. Finally, a black box she recognized came into view. *Got you.* Taking it from the shelf, she opened it and pulled away the heavy protective cloth, revealing the medium-sized black stone gleaming like freshly polished marble.

"This what you're looking for?" Casey asked.

"I have no idea," Alex said, reaching for the stone, but as his hand drew near, it began to tremble. "Uh, maybe you should hold on to it?" he suggested.

You guys really are afraid of these things. Casey wrapped the stone and snapped the box shut as Alex started out of the lane with haste.

"Let's get out of here," he said, darting across the room so fast that Casey had to run to keep up.

When the exit was mere yards away, a white flash overtook the room. For a second Casey feared she was about to be transported again, but when the light faded, she was still in the project lab, and three new people had joined them. Casey nearly lost her shit when she saw the face of her boss—looking stretched, thin, worn, and pale—and the monstrosity standing next to her: a vile, mountainous figure in a white mask.

THE DEMON

With his eyes fixed on the lobby of the UCL Archaeology wing, Bennett suddenly noticed his toe tapping and forced it to stop. *What's keeping them?* All he wanted in that moment was to see Alex and Casey make it safely outside, having found the smallest Gehenna stone. Once the team had it, hopefully Joseph would be forced to come looking for *them* for once. *Then we should be able to apprehend him easily. The guy sounded like a two-hundred-year-old asthmatic. How much of a fight could he put up?*

Bennett lost track of Hannah and Felix when the group split up to watch other possible ways in or out of the building. Posted across the street, kneeling in a thin alleyway that extended into darkness behind him, he could see the main entrance clearly. At least six minutes of quiet had gone by. Though he had no reason to worry yet, Bennett felt something had gone wrong. As the moments dragged on, the area around the building and the dense city park drifted into a pleasant, quiet evening, which only made him more uncomfortable. *Ugh. Europe.*

Adjusting his weight to keep his right leg from falling asleep, Bennett swatted at an insect buzzing around his ear. *Why did Casey only want Alex to come along? I mean, I helped her too, and she sat next to me in the Jeep. And why did Hannah let them go alone? Al's gotten strong, sure, but I don't think he's ready for this kind of thing.* Another fly zoomed a halo around Bennett's head. *Buzz off!—If Joseph's got the lead on us, there's a good chance he already has the rock. There's also a good chance Al and Casey might run into him.*

Another bug buzzed his ear. He swatted it, but two more took its place, then three. A mess of flies was suddenly vying for his attention. *Did I get too close to a dumpster or—*

A quick search of the area revealed no dumpster. Gnats joined the bug circus. Bennett fought to maintain his vigil but couldn't focus as a haze of winged insects filled the air around him. Closing his eyes, he sensed the bugs giving off Wrath and Dread. It was a minuscule trace, but when combined, it created a red and orange fog, dulling his senses. The distraction blinded him to the broiling energy rising behind him until it was just a few yards away.

He spun when he heard a soft, slippery sound, like a wet leather whip. Facing the alley of black nothingness with open eyes, Bennett closed them again, finding a bright sun suddenly before him: a moving blaze cascading down with tendrils, hair, legs, claws, and God knows what else. It was Wrath, as heavy as a pickup truck, swirling, blinding, and overwhelming. The dragon of fire approached, well over six feet long, sometimes moving as swiftly as a hurricane, other times as slowly as drizzling honey. Bennett immediately recognized it from the statues at the foot of the stairs in Gehenna. This thing was no mystery to him. He knew exactly what he was in the presence of.

A shrill, high-pitched, mangled voice spoke from the shadows, making his cheeks involuntarily tense. "*What is this?*"

Bennett opened his eyes. "What is what?"

Two thin, curved red eyes, with tall, dark pupils, flew out of the darkness. Bennett found himself surrounded by a black and red cyclone that flung itself back into obscurity. "*This one was right. This one did feel Rapture nearby,*" the demon said. "*Rapture within a human form could only mean a fallen Celestial, yet . . . your face is not known. Aili'Eace is the knower of faces. This cannot stand.*"

"I'm usually an exception to stuff. Can I help you with something?" Bennett asked, feeling his toe tap returning.

"*This one spreads its name far and wide. Yet, you do not know this one?*"

"Nope," Bennett said, pointing both thumbs at himself. "And this one was minding its own business until you came along. Feel free to return the favor."

The demon slowed and raised its cheeks into a nightmarish smile. "*This one's arrival has caused you distress . . . is it Dread? Surely not Wrath. In a Celestial? What would one of your kind fight in its mind? Memories of war, perhaps?*"

"Nobody likes remembering those days."

The creature did another loop around him, sniffing harder. "*So few memories, yet so much regret, and pain.*" Aili'Eace laughed. "*So much fear! Yes. This one can smell it . . . fear of a gun.*" It angled its nose higher. "*A man, and a baby. Regret. Mountains of it. And family—yes. An older male. Yes . . . a father, or brother? Such grief and woe! These are not the memories of a Celestial. If this one did not know better . . . perhaps the rumors are true.*"

Hope this demon's as dumb as it seems. "What rumors?" Bennett asked.

"*Surely you are kidding. Why, those of humans force-fed the Eve and sent on a holy goose chase.*"

"Don't know anything about it."

"*The community speaks of it madly. Trivium is blacked out. The dull-*"

ard Lanwyn Senator accused of birthing the charge is to be tried, yet most still blame Arros." The demon barked. *"Hypocrisy!"*

Bennett folded his arms to keep them from shaking. "Oh, right, I heard about that. If you're subtly implying something, I suggest you openly imply it."

"This one implies nothing. This one believes every word you've uttered and is simply curious. Now, 'fallen Celestial,' what are you doing in a London alley, smelling of recent battle?"

Bennett couldn't help getting uneasy. "What do you mean?"

The demon laughed again. *"This one meant no offense. Aili'Eace will never forget the smell of Wrath clashing with Rapture. It makes such a special brew, taking one back to the days of Inferius—days Aili'Eace enjoyed."*

A welcome voice broke in. "Glad someone did, because I sure didn't." Hannah stepped into the alley entrance, hands tucked into her jacket pockets, looking as if she were out for a casual stroll.

Oh, thank God.

The demon hissed, flapping its tongue like a spring doorstop. *"Gggggeneral. What a surprise."*

"Shouldn't be. I live on this planet." She stepped forward, and as she did, the insect cloud parted as if she were a giant bug candle. "What about you, Eace? Checking out the digs? Thinking of leaving Arros and settling on Earth?"

"Bah! Life on Earth is a punishment. Are you so indoctrinated you've forgotten? Or is it all the moss and thresh this one hears you imbibe to drown away your sorrows?"

"Probably the moss," Hannah said. "Funny you should mention it—I was just headed for a drowning session. There's a place around the corner that does rubbing alcohol and cantsjuice shots. Who's in? First and last rounds are on me."

"This one's days of candor with other shades of Eve are long over. No."

Aili'Eace slinked around Hannah. *"Besides, this one would hate to contribute to the downward spiral of the legacy of the great Hywyn general of Eio."*

"I was just being polite. Get over yourself," she said, waiting patiently for the demon to finish swimming around her, as if she were at a tailor getting her pant seam measured.

The demon finally swooped away and rejoined the shadows. *"This one has not misplaced its manners. This one will not keep you from your drink, but, General, before you go, perhaps you will help solve a mystery? This one has never seen the likes of this fallen Celestial. What does it call itself?"* The thin black irises fixed on the soldier.

"Bennett," he answered as plainly as possible.

"Bennett. Yes. If you could help this one identify him, Aili'Eace will remain the knower of faces. As a general of Hywyn—excuse me, former general—this one assumes you know him."

Hannah yawned. "I don't care about your stupid self-given title. But no, he wasn't one of mine, and it doesn't look like he wants visitors, so why don't you and I both leave him alone?"

The demon swirled in the darkness. *"Tell us, Celestial Bennett, warrior of Inferius, your captain's name."*

"My captain? This is getting ridiculous," Bennett said.

"Lack of pride is a wretched stench. This one smells it on both of you. This one remembers their commander well: Aili'Uvos, the Solemn, lord commander of the armies of Arros. This one was proud to follow their commander through the war of all wars."

"Except he didn't exactly get you through Inferius, did he?" Hannah said with a dismissive smirk. "Commander Uvos was killed at Lannion Peninsula."

"A battle won by Arros. A crowning day." Aili'Eace spat into the

light. The saliva landed on the sidewalk and began to erode the concrete. *Fuuuuck.*

"I can't believe you guys still go on about this." Hannah groaned. "Is it really that hard to admit you lost a war?"

"Using the miscreant Beaubons and corrupting Doloros into the heathen camp was a cheat. Hywyn stole its power! And used it to place itself as overlord of the Senate. But make no mistake, Arros was not defeated and shall rise again."

What are you assholes talking about?

"The Lostros joined the Alliance all on their own!" Hannah shouted like a heated mom at a Little League game. "They hated Lucifer as much as everyone else. By the time he invaded Hywyn, everyone had had enough of it. Face it, you backed the wrong horse."

Aili'Eace began to laugh. *"What makes you think this one supports the fallen Celestial?"*

Heavy footfalls suddenly neared. Felix charged around the corner, having only spotted Bennett and Hannah. "Hey! Watch out, I think there might be an Imp—"

Hannah cut him off. "Wow, Felix, weird seeing you here."

The janitor was slow on the uptake but played along. "Hi, Hannah. Crazy seeing you, too. What a collection of people to run into—that's what I was doing, by the way, running. Jogging. I also see we have a pure breed present. How's it hanging, Eace?"

"Niel'Vyl," the demon snarled.

"Actually, it's Felix now. I know you knew that, but whatever. Who acts polite anymore? So, how'd you get your skinny red ass out of Arros?"

"With honor, unlike you. This one also kept their Beast-given name."

"Come on, tell me the truth. You snuck out, huh?" Felix said.

The demon swam slowly through the air, speaking in a low tone. *"This one sees you shaking. Is this fear? Dread? Having spent so much time on Earth with humans, looking like one, you must think this one a demon from Hell."*

"I don't believe in Hell. I'm just cold. But I do believe in assholes, because I'm staring at one right now," Felix replied.

"*You tiny, pale nebbish!*" Aili'Eace hissed, flinging out of the shadows and stopping just shy of head-butting Felix, who made a *pee-yew* face and waved them away.

"*Ugh*. You guys still don't clean your teeth? Say what you will about Earth, at least it has hygiene."

"*Better this than the smell of failure and Jubilee!*" Aili'Eace screamed.

The demon and former demon faced off, baring their teeth. Bennett caught a glint of orange Eve burst in Felix's eyes, which faded when Hannah placed herself between them.

"You two want to cut the bullshit before we all get in trouble with the Tribunal?" she bellowed. "I don't feel like dealing with a formal inquiry by the Counselors when things go back to normal. Do you?"

Aili'Eace returned to the shadows. "*The murderous traitor started it.*"

"Lick my butt, Eace," Felix said.

The demon roared, lines of red-hot cinder flaring around their body.

"Speaking of being honorable to your clan, do the Aili know you're here?" Hannah asked the demon. "Not trying to break the Covenant and influence things, are we?"

Aili'Eace tilted their head to the sky and barked like a thunderous bird of prey. Their eyes, once burning with the softness of oil lanterns, now blazed like campfires. "*Do not speak to this one about that bastard document! The pathetic notion of solitude between the kingdoms disgusts all true Archfiend.*"

Felix jumped in. "Doesn't matter what you think of it. Sticking to one side means following the One Voice, bud."

"You've forgotten the One Voice! Niel'Vyl abandoned it when he betrayed his brethren!" Aili'Eace screamed.

"You guys abandoned reason, first," Felix said.

Hannah broke in. "And you still haven't told us what you're doing on Earth."

The demon rose over her, puffing their chest. *"Despite whatever rules you believe govern the universe, in this place, in this form, you are weak, General. This one could tear you apart, and no amount of Rapture could save you once I've severed your head. Lest you forget, you are no longer a jailer. Aili'Eace is not in chains, at least not yet, and is allowed to drink the fruits of the Earth from time to time."*

"No, you're not, and I'm not afraid," Hannah said, her voice unwavering. "Now, move along before I call the Medolians."

Steam huffed from the demon's long nose. *"Yes, call the old flame. Claim your special treatment."*

Hannah said nothing in response, and with a blast of smoke, the demon bowed. *"Aili'Eace, the knower of faces, is satisfied, and will now and forever know Bennett the Celestial."* The creature soared into the sky. *"Have a blessed night."*

Aili'Eace swam through the air toward the moon, its Eve signature growing faint as it passed behind rows of apartment buildings, until Bennett could no longer feel its presence. A silent moment passed before he turned to Felix, who raised a flat hand to quiet him before he could speak.

"Please, don't," Felix said. "I know you don't want to judge, but I also know you won't be able to help it, so it's fine. I've come to terms with what I used to be." With one last glance toward the sky, Felix stepped away, his head hung low.

Bennett didn't want to press it any further. He turned to Hannah, letting out a relieved sigh, shaking—though he knew it wasn't just from the cold. "Thanks for the backup."

Her ever-watchful eyes were still scanning the sky. "If they found out you were human, things could have taken a bad turn. This doesn't make sense. Why is Eace out here?"

Bennett shook his head. "I think they *do* know about me. They're playing games with us. We should get Alex and Casey and get out of here."

"What makes you say that?" Felix asked.

"They knew everything—about my brother, my dad—" Bennett cut himself off, and started again. "The demon knew it all."

"Nah. It was guessing. Demons can see fears to an extent, then fill in the rest. It's a classic fortune-teller scam. You might be surprised to know how many of them are actually demons in disguise, trying to make a living," Felix said.

Bennett then noticed that Hannah had exited the conversation, her attention locked square on the UCL Archaeology building.

"Hannah?" Felix asked.

She closed her eyes and turned her head, as if listening. "Someone's here."

Immediately after, groups of lights within the building began going dark one by one, starting from the lower right corner and working up to the higher floors on the left. *A power outage?* Just before the last lights went out, a low-frequency blast, like a car bomb, went off. A chilling scream followed, and Bennett felt a surge of Wrath emanating from inside the school.

"That was Alex," Felix said.

Hannah darted out of the alley, muttering, "Damn it," and jumped over a taxi's hood. Felix and Bennett followed, though the soldier was nearly left behind. At the lobby entrance, Hannah spun around, stopping him with a cold palm to the chest. "Stay here, in case Joseph slips through."

Bennett tried to push on. "We should go in together!"

With a hard look from her icy eyes, he was halted. Hannah and Felix bolted through the front door and across the lobby at breakneck speed into a stairwell, while Bennett growled, feeling his Rapture weaken from his anger. *Fucking kids table.* He backed into the street to get a better view of the higher floors as more sounds erupted: screams, crashes, possible explosions—moving about the building, centered on the fourth floor.

Local residents and businesses were waking up and taking notice. Dozens of faces peered out from neighboring windows as pedestrians gathered. Bennett held his arms out wide, pressing them back, instinctively slipping into his squad leader voice. "That was an explosion inside! Glass is falling. Keep your distance and wait for the cops. Stay back!"

The citizens of Bloomsbury acquiesced and resorted to getting out their phones as Bennett turned his attention back to the archaeology building, now engulfed in chaos—an animal escape at the zoo. A human scream pierced through the clamor. *Casey! Ah— fuck Hannah's orders, I'm not just standing here.*

Bennett started toward the front steps, his fists turning heavy and blue, when a horrid, alien howl cascaded out of the building: a pitch nearly too high for human ears. A window overhead shattered, and Bennett caught a glimpse of a body—bloody, clad in cargo pants and a black T-shirt—soaring through the air. A spray of glass, wood bits, and steel flew with it. *Al?* The body careened toward the park across the street, landing on the spiked steel fence with a sickening crack before bouncing into a mess of shadowed greenery.

Changing course, Bennett sprinted as fast as he could, feeling his eardrums raked by another high-pitched scream, clearer and closer. He looked up to see a black figure crawling out of the broken fourth-floor window like a four-legged spider. Leather straps and coat flaps dangled as it climbed the wall and vanished onto the roof. With no way to catch it, Bennett pressed on toward the park, rushing past the entrance.

Searching the grounds, he quickly spotted a section of fence missing a few steel barbs, where Alex had landed. The crumpled body of the teacher was laid in a thicket at its base.

"Al!" Bennett shouted. Even from this distance, he could see dark blood spreading on the ground around Alex. Stumbling into the mess of barbed plants, Bennett got a grip on his partner, who had welts stamped into his skin like brands, scattered around various contusions. His femur and four of the ribs on his left side were broken, twisted, poking in and out of the skin, but the worst injury was a fifteen-inch-long fence post shoved through his lower chest. The teacher was unconscious, somehow still alive, fighting for breath as fluid filled his lungs.

"Al. Wake up. You can heal this, remember? Wake up, pal. We got it worse than this with the Wraithians, remember? Come on!" Alex coughed up a heap of black blood but remained asleep. "We can't lose you, man. Come on, find some rage. Get mad!"

Bennett gripped the barb to retrieve it from his chest but found it looked too deadly to pull out in either direction. *If this guy dies, everyone is going to kill me.*

A sudden rise in power nearby made Bennett tense up. The approaching signature was familiar, yet he had trouble placing it. He shielded his eyes from an incoming Shift, just as a loud bang and gust of wind shoved him off-balance.

"You two?" a familiar voice called out.

The Medolian Mara was there, gripping her staff tightly in both hands. *Sure hope you're here to help.* She approached, glancing around the area as though voices were speaking to her from all directions. *What's she hearing?*

"What are you doing here?" Bennett asked.

Mara glanced around, her attention elsewhere. "I came when I sensed . . . something. Where's Izaiah?"

"That's what I want to know! We found Joseph," Bennett said, pointing across the street. "He's getting away, maybe with a Gehenna rock, I'm not sure. But we need help here."

"Gehenna? Who's we?" she asked without taking a glance at Alex.

"Al, me, Hannah, and Felix. Please, he's hurt!"

At the mention of Hannah, Mara finally turned. "Did you say Hannah?"

"Yeah, but look, he's dying—" Bennett's plea fell on deaf ears. Mara lifted her staff, ready to Shift away. "Wait! I need help!" he shouted.

Mara rolled her eyes and stepped closer, gripping the barb in Alex's chest. With a swift motion, she yanked it free, dropping it on the ground with a sickening splash of blood. Alex coughed, his lungs now partly missing, seconds from dying.

"What did you do that for?" Bennett shrieked.

"You didn't want me to get it out of him?" Mara asked, unfazed.

"Fucking no! I meant heal him!"

"Me? You're the one with Rapture." Without another word, Mara stabbed her staff into the ground and vanished in a swirling flash of white.

Fucking Medolians. Bennett looked down on the teacher in his arms. *She's right. I can do this. I just have to find the need. Think! Get the Rapture. Do what you did before, in the cave. Remember Jerry. What would he be feeling right now?*

Bennett's hands pulsed with cobalt-blue energy as the wings on his shoulders began to ache. A heavy, cold storm brewed in his gut. *The mission. Focus on the mission. Alex is necessary for its success. He has to get back on his feet.*

Without his doing, the soldier's thoughts swerved to his other family, the one he'd lost when he tried to forget his time in service to his country. *Yeah, the squad. That's good. That will help. George. Lance. Ilhan.* The feeling of war came back to him, but not the aspects built on rage: the ones in between, when trust was built with his peers. He saw his squad mates, each of their faces—heard their voices and their jokes. *I would have taken a bullet for any of those guys. Still would because they were my team, my family. I forgot that feeling somewhere along the way.*

Bennett's eyes snapped open. The man in his arms had stopped breathing, his fire almost out.

I've been so blind. I'm sorry, Al. My team is my family, and you're my team now. I'd take your place if I could.

The feeling of absolute zero coursed up Bennett's spine, forcing it into perfect alignment. He bellowed, channeling every ounce of his will and the weight of Rapture into his limbs. *Come on. Fix him! You know what a human is supposed to look like.* He pressed his hand over the wound on Alex's chest. *Get in there. Heal.*

With eyes closed, Bennett saw brilliant violet and cobalt-blue energy transferring from his hands into Alex, mixing with red and orange, igniting a flame that refused to be snuffed out. Wrath swelled within him, coursing through his veins.

With a gasp, Alex spewed blood, taking shallow, beleaguered breaths.

"There it is!" Bennett shouted. "Just stick with it."

Alex screamed as he awoke, eyes wide in shock at the pain crashing through him as his wounds snapped and rolled back into place. Bruises faded, and scabs formed only to vanish in a radiant glow until he was whole again. As the final wound set, he shook his head as if waking from a cold splash and shouted, "What happened to Casey?"

"Not sure. We're outside. You got thrown out a window."

Alex pulled himself into a seated position, grimacing as he rubbed his chest, his gaze drawn to the broken window across the street and the mangled fence post. "Oh, right." He noticed the blue glow surrounding Bennett. "That was you?"

"Think so." Bennett helped him to his feet, but Alex shrugged him off, brushing away twigs and leaves.

"Good trick to know."

"You're welcome." Bennett powered down when he noticed the civilians still watching from a distance.

"We have to get inside. Joseph is here," Alex said sharply.

"I know, I saw him take off. What about the stone? Did you find it?" Bennett asked.

Alex's eyes ignited with fury. "He got away?"

Next thing Bennett knew, they were sprinting toward the park exit, crossing the street, and racing up the steps of the archaeology building. The Rapture had definitely done its job; Alex was moving like a damn jackrabbit, staying a few yards ahead. They burst into the lobby, bypassing an abandoned security desk, and headed straight for the stairwell.

Alex climbed quickly, and Bennett followed as close as he could, still getting the hang of the Rapture's effects on his own steps— soft landings, and powerful push-offs. Bounding several feet at a time, he quickly caught up to Alex as he reached the fourth-floor door, which suddenly swung open.

Everyone screamed in surprise when Felix stumbled through, wielding a microscope as a club.

At the sight of Alex, he beamed and dropped the instrument, hugging him. "You're okay! Thank the Eve for good news!"

"Thanks to Bennett," Alex said.

Felix shook Bennett's hand enthusiastically. "My man, learning the Rapture! Also, glad to see you're not dead."

"Where's Casey?" Alex asked.

"Still in the lab. Joseph snapped her neck."

"What?" Alex screamed.

Bennett's heart sank. *Yeah. What?*

"Darn, sorry, no—she's fine," Felix said, waving their worries away. "Hannah was right there, caught her before she even hit the ground. Casey's already standing. Says she feels amazing. Also, heads up, we have a new guest, which is already proving to be very interesting. Come on!" Felix led them away from the stairwell with a youthful excitement, and down a murky hall that looked as though it had been host to a flaming car crash.

Bennett's boots crunched on the glass littering the floor as they charged forward. "I take it this means the stones are real?"

"Sounds like it. Joseph got away with one. Now he's got two. We caught him and a Medolian beating up on Alex. She Shifted away with another lady—human, I think. Joseph stayed behind to keep us off the Med's trail. Fucker is strong. Not sure where he ran off to—I was unconscious. When I woke up, Mara was here. It's been a strange couple of minutes."

They stopped at a project lab door, where Bennett could hear raised voices inside.

"Oh, and just so you know, Hannah can get a little snippy around her ex," Felix added, turning the doorknob.

"Ex?" Bennett followed him into a room so dark he could hardly see. What little he could make out was a lab in complete disarray. Tables and chairs had been flipped and hurled to every corner. Exposed electrical wiring sparked, lighting the outskirts of the lab, where a rural library's worth of shelves with glass cases, wooden boxes, and scads of science equipment was toppled like dominos.

At the center, a white table was illuminated by the only working lamp, revealing two silhouettes: Hannah and Mara, locked in a heated argument.

Mara's was the first full sentence Bennett could make out.

"Why is it every time I think I'm finally free of you, you find a way to smash your existence back into mine?"

"Just the way I roll, honey, or did you forget?" Hannah asked. "And by the way, blaming me for everything isn't going to work this time. If you guys had done your jobs in the first place, none of this would have ever happened."

"The Medolians had no way of finding the Archfiend! Clearly, now we know why. You saw what I saw," Mara shouted.

Bennett found Casey tucked off to the side, watching the exchange with a mix of curiosity and horror. When she spotted him and Alex alive, she hurried over, arms open wide. "I'm so glad you're okay!"

Bennett smiled politely, stepping aside for her to hug Alex, but was surprised when she latched onto him instead. *Oh, hi.*

"I was worried about you," she said, her warm gaze making him blush. "Did you catch Alex?"

"Not exactly," he admitted.

Alex chimed in. "Yep, I'm all healed. Might have even died again."

Casey gave him a high-five. "I think I died too! Thank you for fighting for me. I know you did your best."

"Thanks," the teacher said, smiling through gritted teeth.

Casey gestured at the ongoing argument. "They've been going like this since the lady in the hood showed up. Who is she?"

Mara let out a hefty, fake laugh. "Ha! Glad to know you think this—like everything else—is just a game."

"And I'm shocked to hear you're taking something so seriously," Hannah said with a mock slap of her own face.

"What if this had been a trap? Or a raid I'd planned?" Mara growled. "*Hrm?* You'd have ruined any chance of success."

Hannah stooped low enough to use a daffy voice. "Duh, sorry, Mom. Didn't realize I needed permission before I did anything on this here Earth planet."

Mara sneered and pointed at Felix. "You and your Imp janitor's involvement may have broken the Covenant!"

"Hey . . ." Felix said, his brow scrunched to a weak, offended hurt.

Hannah scoffed and scowled. "Mara Loren!"

Mara dropped her eyes to the floor. "Sorry, Felix. I didn't mean it. Hannah, can we have this discussion in private?"

"There's no discussion to have," Hannah answered. "Me, Casey, and the guys are ready for action. You're either with us or against us, because knowing what we know, and seeing what I just saw, I can tell you we're very low on time."

Mara stomped over to Bennett and Alex, taking them by their arms. "If that's the question, then I'm against you. As the only Un-Earth authority figure present, I'm doing what should have been done from the beginning and will be taking the humans back to the Tribunal, where their fates will be decided. The search for Joseph will be continued, by me."

Just then, a gush of indoor wind struck. A flash appeared as an Eve gate opened: one not created by anyone in the room. This Shift was stretched wider than most, and was more turbulent, sending apple-green sparks into the air as three new figures landed.

"Are we too late? Where are they?" a scratchy voice boomed.

A green-handled cane appeared first, followed by the rest of Izaiah hobbling into view, flanked by the Medolians Galinthia and Fabian. The expressions on all three of their faces said they were ready for a fight.

FOR THE BEAST

Leigh had seen her best friend die, then watched her wake up seconds later. *Her eyes opened, I know it.* No matter how many times it replayed in her mind, she couldn't fully grasp the sound of Casey's neck snapping in Joseph's hand or what it meant, leaving her unsure whether to laugh or cry. Just twenty minutes earlier, she'd been standing on the tarmac of an airport in northern Africa when Joseph and his "girlfriend"—a woman named Chloe, dressed like a pirate—had coerced Leigh into thinking of the archaeology building at UCL. She had no idea why they would make such a request until they both grabbed her, and a blazing white storm that made her feel as if she were being torn apart and put back together again transported her to London in an instant.

Without time to process how she'd traveled so far so fast, Leigh locked eyes with Casey and felt her first glimmer of happiness since Joseph had entered her life. There was a man she didn't recognize, the same height as Casey, standing next to her in the project lab. His hands glowed like red-hot pokers, and his arms ignited when he attacked Joseph, seemingly giving Casey a chance to escape, but the plan failed. After just a few seconds, the mystery man got his ass thrown out a window, leaving Joseph free to nab Casey and do his worst.

Chloe, restraining Leigh from entering the fight, seemed to hear someone approaching and whispered, "The Celestial is here!"

Joseph then ordered them out. "They can't be allowed to see you! Take Professor Evans and go."

Before Leigh was transported away, she saw Joseph murder Casey and crawl out the window to safety. Falling in slow motion, Casey was caught (*by some miracle*) by a woman in a leather jacket who appeared out of nowhere. The woman must have had a blue medicinal fucking firework in her pocket, too, because there was a blast of light, and Casey woke up as if she'd merely fallen asleep in the woman's arms.

She has to be alive. I didn't dream that. Right?

Presently, standing in tall, wet grass on the side of a road in the northern outskirts of London—an area which Leigh recognized from her frequent drives to "cool off" during her years as a graduate student—she could only feel shame. The nightmare she was living with Joseph was supposed to be her own, not Casey's. *Anyone but her. Why was she there in the first place? What does she want with the stones? And who was the little fire guy with big eyebrows?*

Chloe stood watch on the other side of the road, glancing back to glare every now and then. No cars or trucks had passed since they'd arrived five minutes ago, and all of Leigh's attempts at conversation had failed.

"So, how do you make those wormholes?" she asked soon after arriving, referring to the space bridges in the sci-fi books she'd read as a kid.

Chloe's lips tightened, holding in her tongue and whatever harsh words were likely resting on it. She shook her head. "You can't fathom the number of ways I could . . . Imagine this, girl, being sent through every conceivable emotion so violently your head spins backward."

"Sounds unpleasant," Leigh said.

"Then be quiet," Chloe snapped. "We're waiting until my nameless calls."

A few minutes went by before Leigh decided, *To Hell with that.* "So, are you a follower of Joseph's? Or . . . ?"

Chloe shook her head and laughed bitterly. "I do follow him, closely, to make sure he doesn't get too distracted. All great minds do."

"Sounds like you're the one who's really in charge."

Chloe glowered. "No one is in charge."

"Not even the big guy? You know . . ." Leigh pointed upward.

"Just because you're human doesn't mean you have to believe any of that. The problem with the universe isn't that there are gods who allow bad things to happen and punish us. It's that there are no gods at all, and the only punishment is now."

The woman spoke so resolutely that it sent a chill through Leigh, who fumbled her next words. "I—I can agree with you there. I had to fight my mom on a similar subject many times. It always seemed weird to me that someone who was cursed to spend their years dwindling away in one spot"—*CMD*, Leigh thought—"would hold on to their faith so resolutely. I believe pain exists to help life grow. Call me crazy. I'm a history buff."

The woman laughed again. "Your idea of history is adorable, at best. I've been roaming this forsaken planet for nearly twelve hundred years, cleaning up the messes mankind makes for itself. Your kind is seen as nothing but a battery for UnEarth, did you know that? And the Medolians are the ones who have to maintain it.

Time's circle is no mystery to me. The only parts you remember are the dark tunnels. Trust me."

"Twelve hundred? You don't look a day over eight or nine," Leigh said as light as a feather.

A smirk appeared on Chloe's lips, but she quickly struck it and frowned. "I'm starting to see why my beloved likes you."

It was Leigh's turn to laugh. "If he liked me, he'd let me go. I honestly don't know what you see in that guy."

The Medolian rested her hand on her sword hilt, as if aching to draw and use it. "I see what you and everyone else refuse to."

"What? An ambitious psycho?"

"My darling nameless knows true pain. He has seen the worst the universe has to offer and wishes to fix it. He wishes for no one to be forced to serve another, as he and all life have for countless millennia."

"So your plan is just, 'wipe it all away and start anew'?"

"No. Wipe it all away and never begin again. To end all life, and with it, all suffering. It is a great burden we have taken—giving life what it has always craved, yet always been too scared to demand. Only one can hold the key—my nameless. He will be the first to tear into the fabric of space, and the sooner we get there, the sooner he and all of life, so tired and worn, can finally rest."

Leigh leaned on a bare fence post on the side of the road to catch her breath. This conversation was starting to feel like a marathon.

"You've felt the Abyss within the Brothers. You've had a taste, a drop of the ocean," Chloe said with visible pride. "They're the most potent collection of negative energy in all of existence. My beloved can take a sip, but only together can they release their full strength—an unstoppable wave."

"Pretty shitty to take away everyone else's chances at happiness just 'cause you can't find your own," Leigh said.

Leaning close, Chloe's gray eyes met Leigh's. "Try being born into servitude as tools for corrupt bureaucrats, knowing your life and sentence could last indefinitely thanks to your species' insurmountable lifespan. Then, and only then, tell me you disagree."

Before Leigh could respond, Chloe looked at the sky, like a hound that had caught a scent. "Finally," she said, drawing her sword.

"I didn't mean it! I'm sorry!" Leigh exclaimed, hands raised and eyes shut tight.

Swinging the sword in a wide arc, a vertical tornado of light engulfed Chloe. When Leigh opened her eyes, she was suddenly alone. The thought of running barely had time to take root before the light and fury returned, along with Chloe—and a tall, familiar menace in a cloak.

Joseph immediately stole away from them, and Chloe followed. Their sparring sounded like a lovers' spat, even though Leigh couldn't make any of it out; they were speaking in a bizarre language she'd never heard before. The sounds were deep, slippery, and choked with vowels. Joe seemed furious about something, and Chloe was having difficulty talking him down.

Suddenly breaking into English, she shouted, "We'll get him back! Just tell me Raide is safe!"

With a huff, Joseph blasted steam out of the sides of his mask, then spoke calmly. "He is." Reaching into his pocket, he produced the medium-sized Gehenna stone.

"I can taste your agitation. Give it a rest—don't get sidetracked," Chloe finished, motioning toward Leigh. Joseph's mask turned on her.

"Still here," Leigh said with a wave.

Joseph pocketed the stone and took lumbering steps toward her. "We require one more thing, Professor—the location of the third Brother. Just as you brought us to London, think of where it was you sent Eilam. See it as clearly as you can. Do this for us—the last thing you will do."

"And if I refuse?"

"You know what we'll do," Joseph said, tapping the stone in his pocket.

He was right. No matter how much she resisted, he could simply use the rock to send her back to that evil, poisonous void. She would squeal. All Leigh could do was nod in agreement. Joseph and Chloe stood on either side of her, each with a hand on her shoulders, as she fought to find the memories. They came to her—muddy and fragmented. After all these years, it was difficult to imagine home. Images flooded back one by one—the mountain, running away—and the bed: the one where her mother had lain through most of Leigh's childhood and teenage years.

Leigh's subconscious began to piece it all together, and Chloe soon said, "Bingo."

When the wormhole light dissipated, Leigh found herself on a white hillside, surrounded by pine trees as black as space. The air was as cold as an ice bath. Her shoulders relaxed, and Chloe stepped away into the freezing midnight air, her breath glowing in the moonlight.

"What is this place?" Joseph asked, holding out his gloved hand to catch snow falling from the limb of a monstrous pine.

"North of Red Lodge, Montana. Near an… old research facility," Leigh answered, lying, feeling a wave of mental exhaustion wash over her. "I sent it here."

"Montana. *Hrm*, might have known. No, there is no research facility. This is home to you. Or was," Joseph said.

How could he possibly know? "What makes you say that?"

Joseph let the flakes fall to the ground. "A guess. Now, lead us."

Leigh glanced around. "I'm not exactly sure where your girlfriend landed us. We might be a mile away, maybe two. And if you didn't notice, *I'm* the only one without a coat."

Stepping between Leigh and Joseph, Chloe locked a hard gaze on the professor. "Then walk quickly."

Leigh voiced her protest with a grunt (*the best I got*) and took off through the trees, stepping over logs and through banks of snow. *Do I mislead them? Am I going to freeze to death too soon to try? Or should I just show them, because they'll find a way no matter what I do?* Leigh settled on the option that involved her dying as late as possible.

During a long stretch of silent marching, Joseph asked Chloe, "Do you sense anything from the Seeress?"

She scoffed, sounding annoyed. "I told you, I took care of it. Her, those Celestial bodyguards of hers—all of them. The Seeress is a nonissue."

"That can mean many things. We need to be sure Illyana cannot warn Izaiah of our plans for Mr. Barker—"

Chloe interrupted sharply. "I'm not discussing this further in front of the human."

Joseph dropped the topic.

As her bearings returned, Leigh was forced to make several drastic turns and one about-face, making sure they found the right path. At the second major turn, Chloe shouted, "The human is misleading us!"

But Joseph shook his head. "We don't think so. She's freezing—the last thing she wants is to be out here any longer, our beloved."

Chloe grew quiet, though it was clear she hadn't let it go. The rest of the hike through the winter woods was not just miserably cold but now also socially awkward. All the while, Leigh fought against the rampant shivers and hopelessness overwhelming her, still trying to think of something clever enough to say that might save her life.

When she eventually discovered the main path through the woods, she began counting her blessings.

Twenty minutes later, the trees stopped in a hard line, revealing a clearing. At its center rested a cabin, its walls scuffed and cream-colored paint chipped away to the corners. On the cabin's porch rested a brown package the size of a small ice chest, with a haphazard tape job and a mess of stamps on the side. Leigh was almost embarrassed.

The post office had fucked her over so many times in her career, losing and damaging important packages and artifacts, that she had hoped they might have come through in a pinch and saved the day. Unfortunately, there it sat, perfectly placed on the welcome mat. She didn't even need to point the package out, as Joseph sniffed the air, gasped, and his mask settled on the porch. "Wonderful," he said with a pleased snarl.

Great, another step closer to the world's end.

If there was ever a time to intervene, it was now. "Before you do this," Leigh said, stepping between him and the cabin, "I want to speak with Mason before he's lost for good. I want to know if he's still in there. Consider it my final request."

With his mask fixed on her, Joseph took a breath of palpable rage.

"Mason?" Chloe asked, laughing. "What is she talking about?"

Turning his shoulders away from his beloved for a moment of minimal privacy with Leigh, Joseph said, "If you speak that name again, I'll have your tongue."

Leigh's heart skipped. Her breath hitched in her throat. "You . . . said I." *He's been playing this whole time—what, like a role? A part? Was it even Mason I spoke to? No . . . of course it wasn't.* Leigh wanted to punch herself. *Well, what did I expect from a demon?*

With no response, the white mask pulled away, facing the cabin.

"What a mean trick to pull," Chloe said, her voice flush with irritation. "I fear you're having too much fun with these role-playing games, my love. She is distracting you. Let me run her through."

"You will not," Joseph said. "The only distraction is this moment. Now, a Brother awaits."

"Very well." Chloe stepped onto the cabin porch. Kneeling, she took the box and ripped open the top with one hand. Packing peanuts and foam exploded, revealing a glimpse of the round stone shimmering inside. She handed it to Joseph, who gasped faintly.

"Eilam." He removed the stone from the box with the care of removing a newborn from a crib, saying, "He alone could split Un-Earth in two, but once united with his Brothers . . ." He sighed. "It isn't right. Not to have the others in this moment . . . brings us Grief."

"Let go of everything but Wrath," Chloe said, sounding suddenly alarmed. Her gaze turned back the way they had come, into the shadowed woods. "We have company."

Oh great, now what?

The area fell as silent as a still lake. Between her breaths, Leigh could hear rustling branches in the distance. A piercing wind was approaching low through the forest.

Chloe looked worried. "You sent for the Archfiend? The Imps were to be a last resort."

Imps? That doesn't sound good. What's going on?

"We've arrived at last resort," Joseph answered. "Not only are Izaiah's humans alive, but they have grown in strength and are now joined by Hannah, of Eio, and her idiot Archfiend retainer. Aili'Eace proved the Aili clan's effectiveness. They can keep Izaiah and the others busy while we see this through to the end."

Neither looking nor sounding convinced, Chloe said, "If something goes wrong . . . I can't protect you from them all."

"Their loyalty lies with the Beast, above all. As long as ours appears to, all will be well." Joseph turned to her. "You remember the third option? What to do if we should fall?"

"I'm not who you should be worrying about, my love," Chloe said, her gaze fixed on the looming pines surrounding them.

A heavy tension filled the air, reminiscent of Joseph's anger but on a grand scale. Voices drifted into the clearing from the darkness: whispers that turned Leigh's stomach. Shapes moved in the black. Joseph handed the stones to Chloe and took commanding steps into the clearing, now a miniature figure on a lowered pulpit beneath a dark terrace. Two red dots appeared among the shadows, then dozens more, blinking to life. The pack of thin, twisted eyes floated from branch to branch, releasing the most ferocious snarls Leigh had ever heard. Long snouts with leathery tendrils broke into the moonlight but did not advance, blasting scorching plumes of steam into the air.

"What are these things?" Leigh whispered to Chloe.

"Others like my beloved. You'd call them demons." Chloe caught Leigh's gaze. "Feel proud. No human has seen anything like this in three thousand years."

Proud. Leigh was at a loss of mind. Seeing creatures she'd categorized alongside the wolfman or vampires had shattered a part of her psyche. There seemed no escape from this new nightmare, unless by some dumb luck the cabin door was open—but it was over a dozen yards away, and something deep down told her these creatures were swift, conceivably hungry, and a wooden door would offer little protection. Small movements seemed best.

Joseph raised his arms high. "The clan Aili, of the Beast mark, welcome!"

A deep, rasping voice responded, chilling Leigh. "*The Aili clan is come, Nameless, against the boundaries of the Covenant. Haste! Haste! In the name of Uhl'k, show us this weapon.*"

Ugh—they can talk? Of course they can.

"Do not order us, Archfiend! We are of no clan," Joseph bellowed. "The weapon is in our possession and speaks only with one. With it, we will topple the morning star!"

"We've heard of this supposed quest for too long, Nameless," one of the creatures snarled. *"Aili'Cin wants to hear something new. Aili'Cin wants proof."* Others hissed in agreement.

"I warn you now, Archfiend, never test our resolve, nor that of the Medolian you see before you," Joseph said, punctuating his syllables. "We all fight for the same thing. We all long to see the Beast set free. To do it, we will need power. Behold, Raide and Eilam, the Brothers of Gehenna!"

Stepping into the clearing, Chloe held up the stones for the dancing red eyes. Some demons gasped. Others laughed. "Gehenna has been proven real," she called. "The war shall commence."

"So, the rumors are true. This one was correct. Aili'Oin is always correct. The nameless one did lose their mind hiding in a mortal for so long," one demon, Aili'Oin said. Their clan hissed and snickered in response.

"It's unthinkable! Aili'Uance denounces it!" another monster screamed. *"Letting Wrath waste away in flesh."*

A glob of green-tinted spit fired from the shadows, landing a few feet from where Joseph stood, eating through the snow, sizzling into the ground below it.

"Your crimes have put all of UnEarth after you. And for what, Nameless? To chase rocks? To mate with a Mallos user?"

Chloe would have jumped into action if not for Joseph holding her back. The demons barked in chorus, like waves crashing on a rocky shore. When Chloe calmed and shook off his grip, Joseph took the stones, one in each hand, and held them high.

"Aili'Uance is a fool who will lead you down a disloyal path. You want to see the truth?" He roared and clutched the rocks close to his chest.

A sound barreled over the clearing, like an overloaded locomotive slamming on its brakes. Joseph lifted his head to the sky as a gust of wind swept toward the center of the clearing, and a deep red mist evaporated off the stones, flowing down his arms, disappearing into his cloak and behind his mask. A scream pierced the chaos, like hundreds of live shellfish boiling, as he was lifted into the air, chest first. A flash of deep red, like blood without oxygen, revolved around him, turning the ground below as black as night. Joseph's shoulders stretched outward, and his fingers broke free from his gloves, leaving long, curled, green, razor-sharp claws to grip the stones.

Eventually, the sound subsided and the red mist disappeared. The chants of the monsters in the trees slowed as Joseph drooped to the ground, left catching his breath, his body steaming.

Chloe pried the stones from his claws.

"My love?" she asked, throwing back the hood of his cloak, revealing a steaming head with no hair. Rotten flesh fell into the snow, exposing patches of a skull dyed orange. *Oh, Joe.* From behind him, Leigh could only see a glimmer of his face, still covered by the white mask. The flesh around it had folded over, keeping it in place like a tree grown around a pole.

Joseph stood with Chloe's assistance, now towering over her, a behemoth well over seven feet tall, even with his usual wicked, cane-handle hunch. "See this!" he roared, holding out his clawed hand. "The one thing Lucifer-Aveyl fears—the Abyss!"

Worked into a tizzy, but also stifled, the creatures appeared unsure of what they'd just witnessed.

One of the monsters slipped from the shadows and fully into the moonlight. A long, reptilian body with rows of clawed arms and whipping tendrils slithered through the air toward Joseph and Chloe, landing a few feet away, always in motion, rarely touching the ground, like a sagging helium balloon.

The eyes in the trees burned brighter as the demons descended into chaos, snarling and snapping their jaws. Smoke lifted into the air as if the forest were set ablaze by an invisible fire. *"False idol!"* the demon facing Joseph shouted. *"There is nothing here. Aili'Uance is the seer of truth. The Brothers are as false as the one who claims to wield them!"* The creature hissed, turning back to the trees. *"This one says the Aili should reject the nameless and return to Arros before our discovery."*

Opinions from the mass were voiced all at once, their howls cascading in an ebb and flow. Soon, every voice echoed the same tone and cadence, as if an agreement had been reached.

"Aili'Uance," Joseph said calmly as a black smoke with red highlights streamed from his hand across the clearing. "You know nothing of the Abyss."

The mist swirled around the one called Aili'Uance, soaking into them, as it had with Joseph. *"What is this?"* the creature shrieked, but their voice was cut off when their body turned a deep shade of gray. Aili'Uance's red eyes flung wide in terror before their fire was snuffed out and their body collapsed and crumbled to the ground in a pile of black ash.

Unholy cheers erupted from the demons, so high in pitch that Leigh feared her eardrums might split. Raising his arms triumphantly, Joseph cried out, "Now you see! There is nothing greater. With the Abyss, we will not only take the throne, we will burn it! We are done waiting. We are done wanting. We are done serving! Thousands of years ago, the Beast walked free—it shall do so again. Walk with us!"

Fueled by Joseph's fervor, the demons began to glow from within. *"For the Beast! For the Beast! For the Beast!"*

Leigh caught a glimpse of Chloe, watching the scene with skeptical eyes, scanning the trees. *She doesn't trust them. I wonder why.*

"Are you with us?" Joseph cried over the clamor.

The demons answered with a resounding chant. *"For the Beast! For the Beast! For the Beast!"*

They believed Joseph sought only the throne. Desperate for someone to return them to what they viewed as their former glory, they had elected a nameless force from the shadows who offered only malevolent false promises. Against every ounce of instinct and intelligence she had, Leigh stepped into the clearing.

I'm the only human here. The only one who can fight for us. I have to try.

"He's lying!" she blurted out as loudly as she could muster. The gasps from the demons in the peanut gallery were like those of children spotting a spider. "They don't want a war! The stones will destroy everything. You just saw what they can do. Joseph wants to do that to the planet—"

Her words were cut off by Chloe's hand clamped over her mouth. Leigh kept shouting, refusing to accept that her rebellion was over and that she would probably be dying now.

The chant had stopped. The Aili clan's eyes returned to floating in silence, awaiting a response from below. Joseph allowed only a brief pause. "You see! You see! This is what we have let the humans become! Brazen. Unafraid. They once believed us gods from the underworld!" He pointed a clawed finger at Leigh. "Lucifer-Aveyl, the Fallen Celestial, has reduced the Archfiend to pitiful, limp creatures!"

The woods filled with an unyielding, burning tension, as the demons roared. Righteous fury soaked the air while Leigh continued to fight for her freedom, but Chloe's grip was unbreakable.

The Medolian leaned down and whispered in her ear, "Those were your last words. Hope they were worth it."

With that, Chloe's hand slipped around Leigh's throat and squeezed. The sensation of boiling water poured down her esophagus, followed by an icy blast of liquid CO_2. The excruciating attack was violent yet contained, directed and pinpointed within her cells. Chloe released her, leaving Leigh's throat feeling charred and ripped asunder, yet somehow free from visible injury.

Whatever warmth remained in her body vanished, leaving her shaking and collapsing under the weight of the pain, clutching her throat desperately. Taking an arduous breath, she released it, producing choked gasps instead of words.

"Every silver tongue is stolen eventually," Chloe said with a callous smirk, leaving Leigh to wallow on her hands and knees in the snow.

Joseph continued his fervent presentation for the demons, who had already moved on from the human's outburst. "Restore the glory of Arros!" he shouted. "Follow our call. The third lord!"

The demons roared in response, breaking from the trees and into the air, swirling, forming a cyclone of smoke and fire overhead.

"*For the Beast! For the Beast! For the Beast!*"

Leigh covered her ears, encompassed all at once by the freezing ground below, the searing pain in her throat, and the howling chaos above. All she wanted was release—to shout, to scream, to curse them back to the pit they'd crawled from. She took one more deep breath, raised her head to the sky, and let loose with a wail, but released only silence.

THIEF AMONG THEM

The sounds and scents of the human police outside the university grew more evident. They'd already set up a perimeter and were beginning to move in. Even from the fourth floor, Mara could hear the order given. *Two teams—one from the south entrance, one from the east. Maybe a minute. Two, tops.*

Looking around the unlikely circle of humans and UnEarth creatures assembled in the partially destroyed lab, she decided that, at least for now, she would hold her tongue. The bizarre situation had escalated when Izaiah, Galinthia, and Fabian arrived almost immediately after Joseph and Chloe's escape.

Mara tensed, recalling the moment she'd entered the lab and seen Chloe shifting away, catching the young Mediolian's eyes for only a second—eyes filled with raw disdain for her former teacher. *Chloe. It makes sense in every way.* Every lesson Mara had ever taught the powerful, Dread-tinted Mediolian was now a weapon to be used against her and the rest of the team. Chloe had been one of Mara's most creative pupils, able to manipulate Mallos in ways Mara had never dreamed possible. Her student's ever-present distress had manifested itself in destructive ways on many occasions over the centuries (*scaring the Eve out of me, usually*), but Mara had always assumed there would be ample time to complete Chloe's training before she could spiral beyond repair. *There should have been time. This shouldn't be happening. Why would she help Joseph? And what are they after?* She glanced at Alex. *Or who?*

Mara's gaze settled on Hannah, standing next to her. Her face, her hair, her hands—everything, even the moth holes in her jacket—was exactly as Mara remembered. The belt buckle she'd "found" during Inferius (*though probably stole, and refused to ever take off*) shone as brightly as the day it was brought home. *I'm impressed. Who knows what filth she's been living in?*

But none of it lessened the shock of seeing her. *How did she even get caught up in this? What would have made General Hypocrite break her code of noninterference? Wait, never mind . . . I know.* Mara shot a hard glance at Izaiah, standing across from her. Next to him, Gale looked ready for war, her fingers dancing along the knife handles lining her chest. Next to her, Fabian's famous neck vein bulged—a thick, bluish-gray bastard that only appeared in times of exceptional stress. Izaiah took a glance around at the fallen shelves of artifacts, broken equipment, and settling dust. Instead of blaming Mara, as she expected, he smiled and clasped his hands.

"Well, am I happy to see you all safe and sound! You wouldn't believe the day I've had. My knees, *ugh*, they feel like hot butter. If I dropped down to beg for forgiveness, I'd just slide right into the wall. *Bam!* But seriously."

"I know what you mean, man," Felix said, raising a fist in solidarity.

"I can still smell her," Galinthia said, with a crimson flash of Wrath in her eyes. "Where is she? I'm gonna tear Chloe's throat out."

"Easy now. Our orders haven't changed," Izaiah said. "We're here to make an arrest. That now includes our own dear Chloe. So, how much did we miss them by?"

"Two minutes, give or take," Hannah answered.

Izaiah muttered nonsense curses as he hobbled over and shook her hand. "General, such an unexpected surprise."

Hannah eyed him with a dubious grin. "Bet it is."

Ugh. Here we go.

Izaiah laughed and sighed as if they were friends meeting for coffee on a crisp autumn afternoon. "How's retirement?"

"Wonderfully boring," Hannah said, then added softly, "Suppose it was a coincidence that Barker and Hunter landed at the Rose the same night Felix and I were there?"

Izaiah looked shocked beyond repair. "*You* were at the Rose that night? Felix too? Oh yes, doesn't he work there? What a wonderful coincidence. I'm glad you found my boys. Speaking of the Rose, how are the Still Rooms these days?"

"Less still than I remember." Hannah gave him a pat on the back.

Ugh. Mara had grown sick of Izaiah and Hannah's friendship and its secret language centuries ago.

Bennett spoke up, looking as disgruntled as ever. "Where you been, man? We've been dealing with some sorry shit."

Izaiah's chin dropped in shame. "I know. I was getting to you next. It seems like I hung you fellas out to dry, but—"

"Seems? *Seems?* You've done it twice now," Alex shouted, his chest releasing a blast of smoke.

"Your word doesn't mean shit from here on out. Ya hear me?" Bennett's nostrils flared.

Izaiah stumbled through a few excuses, starting and stopping so many times that even Mara could tell how sorry he was. "Things didn't go exactly as I'd planned, okay? But I was keeping an eye on you the whole time. I trusted you, and now look at the both of you. Eves as strong as any UnEarth Human's. Maybe even stronger!"

The human authorities were on the second floor, headed for the stairs. Mara sensed their apprehension; some were radiating Fervor, illuminating a deep passion for their work. *Hrm. Honest cops. My least favorite to deal with.* It wouldn't be long until they were kicking the door in. Meanwhile, Izaiah looked as calm as a water lily. *I know he senses them, too.*

"Human authorities on the way. Best get a move on," Mara said.

Izaiah gave a slight nod and returned to his starting position in the circle, both hands on his cane in front of him, looking like an old sage, before coughing twice into his grimy glove. "So . . . anybody heard any good jokes lately?"

As usual, Mara's boss managed to disgust her within moments of his arrival. Though he did manage to get a laugh out of Felix.

"Did you even hear what I said?" she asked.

"Sure did. Just thought the mood could use a little lightening. That's all. But yes, you're right—everything is awful. That's why we're here, isn't it?" Izaiah said dryly.

"We have no idea why you're here," Mara said. "You haven't told us."

"True," he agreed. "Let's do it, then. In the last two days, I traveled from Earth to Arros, then to Hywyn, and finally to Trivium, seeking answers. Sad to say I didn't learn as much as I wanted to, and what I did learn is just dreadful. But . . . how about you all? Anything good? Mara?"

Every pair of eyes fell on her. *Please stop.* She hated being the focus of so many at once.

"I sensed a mess of Wrath and Rapture converging and traveled to the site to investigate," she said. "We're on high alert, after all."

"So, you didn't know I was going to be here?" Hannah asked Mara with a self-assured grin.

You cocky little—

Mara knew the words were meant to get under her skin, and replied bitterly, "No. If I had, I wouldn't have bothered. I know the great Hywyn general neither desires nor requires aid, so . . ."

"Here we go. Fervor Rage," Hannah said.

"There's no such thing!" Mara shouted.

"Whatever you say," Hannah added smugly before turning away. "Izaiah, what was this dreadful news?"

"In a minute," he said, rubbing his dirt-crusted beard. "First, what's this strange signal I'm getting in here? It's . . . bitter. Like black licorice. Something I don't like the taste of."

"Pretty sure it's the stones," Hannah said.

"Or Joseph," Felix added.

Izaiah's gaze turned downward, and he went quiet for a moment before muttering gravely, "The Abyss."

Mara stepped into the circle to interrupt. "We're not entertaining this, are we? The notion of humans soaking rocks in Eve? The demon is smart enough to know better. As are we, yes?"

The sigh Izaiah released seemed to cast a shadow over the circle. "Is it so hard to imagine? Each of us Medolians has an Earthly object imbued with Mallos. Who's to say humanity, a major source of Eve, couldn't do the same? Sadly, we need to entertain the notion of the Gehenna stones, and we must accept that our destinies are about to be determined by the actions of humans from more than four Celestial lifetimes ago. From what I've seen, the Brothers contain more destructive force than the Beast of Arros itself."

Mara laughed at the absurdity of the statement, and yet, Izaiah's wrinkled, Jubilee-laden face looked as somber as ever. "What did you see?" she asked.

"I went to the Seeress," he replied.

"You what?" Galinthia shouted, following with a heated groan.

Now I really don't feel bad for going behind your back. Mara tried to contain her disdain and sound as professional as possible. "You know better than anyone we can't trust her predictions. I warned you of that six months ago, when you first went to her for help in selecting the humans to be imbued. You told me you were only looking for memories."

Izaiah's head hung low, as though the old fool were determined to endure as much shame as possible. "It's true. Only her visions of the past are fact. She sees glimpses of possible outcomes floating in the ether, waiting to be set in stone. But her forecasts have become so strong I can only hope she's wrong this time."

"What sort of glimpses?" asked the smaller human, Alex.

He had healed well, and his Wrath was leagues away from the weak-willed man Mara had seen at the Gathering. *But that's exactly what worries me.* Since learning what lived within Alex Barker, she felt only regret for having saved him and Bennett Hunter from the Wraithians.

"I'm sorry?" Izaiah asked Alex, looking doltish.

"You went to a woman who can see the future? The night we died, you told me that was impossible." The teacher's Wrath leaped up a level.

"It is, kid. Don't listen to this kook," Galinthia assured him.

Alex pressed on. "No, really. What are you saying?"

"I'm with Al. Keep going," Bennett said.

Izaiah put up his hands defensively, surprising Mara with his patience, considering the humans' attitudes. "Easy does it, fellas. The Seeress's visions of the future are like a Plinko machine—those balls can end up anywhere. The reason I'm so scared this time is that every slot at the bottom is filled with some sort of horrific despair."

"What did you see six months ago?" Alex asked again.

Izaiah approached him like a stray dog. "Al, we don't have time to—"

"My name is Alex. Alex James Barker," the human snapped, stopping Izaiah in his tracks. "As far as the world knows, I died on September twentieth, two thousand six, leaving one widow and one fatherless child. I would like to know what you knew. Please."

Mara wondered if Izaiah would reveal to them the full truth. Even with her own bitter personal feelings toward the humans (*and their species as a whole*), she thought they deserved to know why they were chosen and what had truly happened to them. Now was not the time, however.

"Alex, I'm sorry. You deserve the truth, and I know what you're getting at, but I didn't know how that night was going to turn out," Izaiah said.

"Then why were you following me for so long?" Alex pressed.

"It wasn't just you. I only knew two people would die in Prescott sometime soon, on the same night. The timing was too perfect not to utilize. I had no clue who it would be."

Occasionally he lies well.

The humans looked skeptical but said nothing.

"I'm so sorry about what happened to you. And I hope you believe that," Izaiah continued, "but I've seen Joseph and Chloe's plan. If they get all three stones, everything will be over before any of us has a chance to care."

Galinthia scoffed. "What is that dramatic nonsense supposed to mean?"

Mara's senses flared. The human police had reached their floor and were making their way down the hall, whispering among themselves. *Maybe ten seconds to go.* She caught eyes with Izaiah, who nodded in silent agreement.

"I'll answer that, Gale," he said, "but first, I suggest we adjourn this meeting to a different location before we're arrested. Now hold on. As usual, I don't want to lose anybody." Izaiah raised his emerald-topped cane and created a massive Eve gate, which collected the entire group before anyone could protest.

The Shift spat them out onto a wide wooden dock in the dead of night beside a looming cargo ship. The port was rust-colored, engulfed in a mist so thick they could see only a dozen yards in any direction, and all distant sources of light were reduced to puffy orbs. Other than a horn blowing in the fog-filled emptiness at sea, there were no signs of life anywhere. Mara laughed to herself upon arrival, watching the humans react to the Shift—especially Bennett, a man who so clearly cared what others thought, now green in the face.

"Ah, that's better," Izaiah said, glancing around the desolate area. "Now—" He stabbed his cane into the dock and created a Mallos sphere. "Let's get down to it."

The hovering sphere was translucent, another gleaming soap bubble, but with images superimposed across its surface: fuzzy glimpses of what Izaiah had seen in the Seeress's memory potion. He and the images told the tale of Joseph and Chloe, and their quest to halt existence by initiating a chain reaction that would destroy everything, down to the last atom. All of which Mara took with an entire handful of salt. *The universe is too vast. I doubt anything could truly destroy it.* Her boss then explained that Joseph was incapable of harnessing the stones' true power until they were united, but by siphoning off what was essentially residue, he could potentially become more powerful than anyone present. Again, Mara was skeptical.

"If he already has the first two Brothers, and has access to the only person who knows where the third is, then what's the point? Once we feel anything, it'll be too late, right?" Galinthia asked sardonically.

"Hey, yeah. If he'd collected all three, the skies should be turning black and freaking out," Felix added.

"The sky *is* black," Galinthia responded.

"You know what I mean!"

Off to the side, Alex cleared his throat. "Um, about that . . ." All eyes turned to him as he reached into his pants' cargo pocket and revealed the smallest of the Gehenna stones. Like a black oblong baseball, it shimmered, as though freshly polished. With a slight, guilt-ridden shrug, he chuckled. "Joseph doesn't have all three."

Many in the circle on the dock seemed speechless, though Mara couldn't fathom why.

"That was in your pocket this whole time?" Bennett shouted.

"You took it off him? When?" Hannah asked, sounding more troubled than excited.

Alex stared intently at the stone. "Just before Joseph threw me out the window. I think. He was talking. Distracted . . . Guess I forgot about it when I died again. Sorry. There's been a lot going on."

"Good for you! We've got one! Crisis averted!" Felix said, raising a high five to the others around him, which none returned. *Idiot.*

"You're telling me that's it? That's supposed to be a Gehenna stone?" Mara said, gawking at the object. She could barely sense any Eve from it. "Whatever you found, it's a trick. There's no temple, trust me. I've looked. There's no such thing as the Brothers."

"Touch it," Hannah suggested.

Mara found herself taken aback. "What?"

"You want to know if it's the real deal? Go for it," Hannah pushed. "What's there to be afraid of?"

All eyes were on Mara again. *Fine.* Nothing she'd ever experienced had made her believe a rock could hold so much power. Even to her, a being with abilities beyond human comprehension, it seemed impossible—right up until the moment she held out her hand. The stone touched her skin, and a staggering, empty feeling overtook her, turning her insides out and outside in. Her veins filled with ice-cold blood pumping from her palm down her arm, up into her heart, stinging like microscopic needles passing through its chambers. Her breath hitched. She couldn't feel the Eve, the ground beneath her feet, warmth, or sound. She was banished from all sensation save the poison in her veins. Mara shot backward, dropping the stone without ever truly holding it. It hit the ground, immediately stilling the magenta streaks dancing within.

No . . . It can't be. She couldn't believe what she'd just felt, let alone articulate it. A hand then rested on her lower back: Hannah's, helping her find balance. "You okay?" the Celestial asked.

Mara nodded, collecting herself.

Galinthia raised a perplexed eyebrow. "Guess it's real."

"Makes sense, in a messed-up kind of way," Fabian said. "If people could imbue unique rocks with their darkest shades of Eve and really filled those suckers, yeah, I can see it. I mean, you all don't spend much time with humans, but I see their information through my phone's 'web feature,' and let me tell you . . . they are a fucked-up people. For instance, there was this one video recording titled 'hatchet versus genitals,' and—"

"Thank you, Fabian. We believe you," Izaiah interrupted.

Hannah approached the stone, her hand encased in a blue shield, and picked it up. "You should hold on to this." Wincing from its touch, she placed the stone in Izaiah's fingerless-gloved hand.

He reacted as though someone had handed him a hot potato rather than a rock filled with damnation. "Yikes!" He tossed it into his coat pocket and blew on his fingers. "Whoo. That is . . . just hideous. Well done, Mr. Barker. It seems we have one advantage, after all. The question now is what to do with it."

To answer, Mara had to stop her body and lips from trembling.

"The stones are part of the case. Evidence, as well as motive. This one goes right to the Tribunal. We need a new mandate drawn up, one that authorizes drastic action to stop Joseph, preferably without human interference." She didn't bother checking to see if she'd offended Alex or Bennett.

"If it weren't for Al and me, you wouldn't even have that stone, you ungrateful D&D warlock wannabe," Bennett shot back.

Mara narrowly resisted the urge to take his head off with her lance. "Joseph also would never have gotten the second stone, nor snapped your friend's neck, if not for you."

Alex hung his head. She could feel his guilt, mostly Grief, mixed with a little Dread and Rapture. *Good, you deserve it, little bastard.*

"Scuse me, Izaiah," Hannah said, her voice absorbing all the tension in the room, "but what about Hywyn? Can they offer any assistance? Being the majority leader in the Senate, they should be able to do something. Maybe even send Barker and Hunter back home."

"I've already gone to see Gabriel and the Magnus Council," Izaiah answered. "They turned me away and denounced all our findings. Even had the nerve to laugh at me when I hadn't even told them a joke! 'Course—a Celestial wouldn't know a good joke if it took a warm shit on their lawn. No, I think we're on our own. And Mara may be right—the only thing that will convince them is to show them the stone. If Illyana's prediction is correct, we need every soldier both sides can spare to find this guy before it's too late." He then addressed Alex and Bennett. "Sorry, fellas, as of now we still need you. Gotta make sure the Covenant is upheld."

Bennett grunted and shrugged.

Alex waved it away, feigning indifference. "Eh, we're used to being pawns by now."

A look of remorse crossed Izaiah's face. "I showed you what the Seeress showed me. This is an all-hands-on-deck situation."

Mara sighed. "As your second-in-command, I protest. We're already dealing with one outside agent. More boots on the ground could just mean more spies and co-conspirators."

"Noted, but I trust people to do the right thing," Izaiah said, far too cheerful for her liking. *Whatever. I tried.*

"Guess the first thing to do is lock the stone away," Fabian suggested. "Make sure Joseph can never find it. Boom, no mass extinction."

Mara jumped in. "As I said, we are taking it to the Tribunal."

The comment sparked a rousing chorus among the circle. Arguments erupted. Hannah then spoke loudly enough to silence them all. "Hey!" She let the silence settle. "Why is it that the three youngest people here, by thousands of years, are behaving the most like adults?" The circle remained quiet. Heads and eyes were lowered. "They've been through Hell, literally, because of people like us. Maybe it's time we let them have a say in what happens to them and their planet?"

Izaiah took a deep breath and sighed. "As usual, Hannah, you're right. I'm embarrassed to say I don't know your name, young lady."

All eyes turned to the short human with thick-rimmed glasses, who, until now, had been silent. "My name is Casey," she said.

Hannah gave an approving nod and grin. "Casey's the one who got us here. She's been a major help."

"In that case, we owe you a drink and a song," Izaiah said. "And Alex, thank you for being our guiding star, spurring us onward. We've needed it. Bennett, being a military man with experience in strategy, I would like your thoughts on how we proceed."

The humans shared a glance before Bennett took point. "Sure. At the moment we have one stone, and we know Joseph is going after the third, so let's use that. We can send one team to head him off while another follows Mara's suggestion and gets the stone we have to the Tribunal. I've never been there—I don't know what the hell it is, but I doubt Joseph would attack your Senate for the rock unless he's got an army at his disposal or something."

Mara didn't hate the plan. *Provided Joseph still thinks the Barium Guard is on duty guarding the Tribunal. If he calls that bluff . . .*

"But we can't send a team after Joseph and Chloe if we don't know where they went," Fabian interjected.

"I think I know where they went," Casey said, her voice growing louder and more forceful with every word.

Hmm. Mara was finding herself liking her.

"Great! Thank you. Where is it?" Izaiah's face was as bright as a Beaubon's ass. (*A large monkey-creature of a sort. The dominant species on Lanwyn.*)

Casey considered before answering, "I'm not saying, unless you promise I can go with you."

"I don't think that's a good idea, you being a part of this," Alex said— with affection if Mara didn't know better. "We already lost you once."

"Stop being so dramatic. I died for like five seconds." Casey addressed the circle. "The human with Joseph is my boss, Leigh. I think I'm the closest thing she has to a friend, so she's my responsibility. She and I found Gehenna and the stones. I'm sorry it's caused so much trouble, but I saw her face—she's scared. I've never seen her like that. I'm just here to make sure she gets home okay. The end-of-the-world stuff is all yours."

"Come on. There's plenty of humans involved in this thing already," Felix said to Izaiah. "Why not add one more?"

Mara wanted to throw in her two cents but, judging by the look in her commander's eyes, figured it was pointless. *The guy just can't say no to humans.*

Izaiah laughed. "Guess the nine of us are the only thing standing between Joseph and the apparent ruination of everything. We should start calling ourselves the short straws! Like a band name." No one laughed. "Very well, we'll go with Bennett's plan, even though we have no outside support, and it might very well violate dozens of UnEarth statutes."

The head Medolian continued issuing orders. Mara was to lead Galinthia, Fabian, Alex, and Miss Casey in finding the third stone and, hopefully, securing it before Joseph could. Meanwhile, Hannah, Felix, Bennett, and Izaiah were tasked with traveling to Trivium to deliver the stone Alex took from Joseph. At least one human would need to be present for them to make their case.

"Whatever you say, boss, but can they even get to Trivium without—you know . . ." Galinthia made an explosion sound, motioning at Bennett.

Izaiah's jaw hung loose for a moment. "I believe they can. Yes. I'm almost sure of it. They have concentrated Eve within them, and their bodies haven't fallen apart yet. They should be able to squeeze into that part of UnEarth, just no farther." He placed a hand on Bennett's shoulder. "You'll just have to trust me. The good news is you're about to be the first human to travel to yet *another* level of reality!"

Bennett grunted and walked away.

The group began splitting into teams, preparing for what lay ahead and Mara noticed Galinthia and Fabian settling into a conversation with Casey, whom Mara found rather impressive for a human. *She somehow managed to earn even Hannah's trust. There must be a reason why.*

When an opening to speak with Izaiah presented itself, Mara seized it, sidestepping the others. "I need a word."

"Sounds important."

"It is."

"Then, after you." Izaiah excused them for a moment, and they found a secluded spot on the other side of a withered cargo shack.

Mara leaned her staff against the rotted wooden wall and drew back her hood, taking a moment to gaze at the stars. "I have something to tell you. You're not going to like it."

"That you went to Trivium?"

She was only shocked for a moment. "How?"

"Figured that's the only reason you'd mask your energy. I knew the Medolian ban wouldn't work on you. Is this all you wanted to tell me?" Izaiah asked.

"You never thought I was the one working with Joseph? Not even for a second?"

"Just 'cause I know how much you dislike me doesn't mean I think you'd ever turn on us. Nothin's more important to you than the job. I'll always trust you to be you, and to keep me honest," he finished with a dopey grin.

"Would you have let me go if I'd asked?"

"Prob'ly not."

It was as good a start as she could have hoped for. Mara decided against revealing her meeting with Laffler (*he probably knows about that too*), but getting one lie out of the way made delivering her bad news a little easier.

"While there, I decided to go to the Changing Chambers," she said.

"So, that was the smell I couldn't place. What in blazes for?" Izaiah asked. "That place'll kill you—and your Eve."

"Information. We were running around in circles and needed to try something different. To tell you the truth, I wasn't sure what I was looking for until I met a Purged Archfiend scheduled to return to Arros, Niel'Kirean. He was halfway through his transformation, wracked by torment, but could hear and speak well enough. Seems Arros has been approving many remigrations lately. Kirean's Purging was sentenced for abandoning his post during Inferius to possess and murder humans on Earth. No one was better at it, in his own words. The demon's reputation preceded him, and one day, millennia ago, the nameless, not yet called Joseph, came to him for advice. You're right about what he wants. Even back then, he was searching for a grand silencing of life—a way to 'kill misery.' His method was simply different."

Izaiah grumbled, as though not wanting to say it out loud. "The Ire."

"Yes," Mara confirmed. "Joseph traveled to Earth many times and possessed human hosts, trying to ignite a vortex of Wrath, destroying everything around it, feeding the fire until nothing remained. He searched for the angriest, most destructive specimens he could find, but time and again they were consumed by the Wrath. Niel'Kirean thought the nameless demon was insane and sent him away, feeling he was wasting his time. He didn't give it much thought, and certainly wasn't worried, assuming no human could ever contain pure Wrath within them. I did too. Until . . ." She took a quick glance at Alex Barker.

Izaiah shook his head. "I know what you're saying, but he will never go down that road. He's a good man. He wouldn't—no."

"Good people can still get angry and have their judgment clouded," she said. "I know that's the most likely reason you switched Barker and Hunter at the last second before sending them to be imbued. One look at Bennett Hunter and I probably would have done the same thing, but don't forget Wrath can take many forms, and no human is immune to anger. You don't have as much experience with modern high-anxiety humans as I do. Their society is rank with it, and it's getting worse. Joseph may have given up his quest to summon the Ire when he felt Gehenna and the Brothers were close to being found, but that doesn't mean he's forgotten his original strategy."

"What is it you're trying to say, Mara?" Izaiah asked.

"A warning. I'm afraid of the potential Joseph may see in Alex. The imp will do whatever is necessary to win. We should remain vigilant."

"Don't we always?"

After discussing the dangers posed by both Joseph and Alex for a few more minutes, and after Izaiah refuted Mara's multiple requests to execute the teacher, he ended the conversation by thanking her for the warning. He promised to keep it in mind and to closely watch Mr. Barker.

"Just be careful. It's all we can do," Izaiah said. "And please, take care of Alex and Casey. I'm starting to get attached to those guys."

"I'll keep your humans safe. Don't worry." Mara started to walk away.

"Thank you for trusting me with this. Maybe it could be the start of a new friendship?" Izaiah said, bouncing his bushy eyebrows. "What do you think?"

Mara could only respond with, "Maybe."

They rejoined the others. The teams were ready. As Mara passed Hannah, she kept her eyes down, but when she felt a firm yet gentle hand on her shoulder, she couldn't ignore it. Glancing up, she locked eyes with the general's brilliant blue irises, instantly filled with a sense of peace and the belief that everything would be alright in the end—a feeling she hadn't had in a thousand years. Much of her hated it.

I still can't believe you're here. Do we have to do this now?

"It was nice to see you," Hannah said warmly, free of pretense. "You look . . . nice."

"Yeah. Good lucky—*ugh*, no. Good luck . . . I meant to say good luck," Mara stammered, wishing the moment would end. "Take care of the human—we need them both alive." *That was awful.*

Hannah laughed. "Will do. You know, if we're ever on the same planet again, look me up. We could grab a moss or have a fight to the death or something. Sky's the limit."

Mara resisted the urge to smile, laugh, and say all the things she wanted to. Instead, she allowed silence and a nod to be her only reply. Hannah wiped the disappointment from her face to join Izaiah, Felix, and Bennett. Just before they shifted away, Mara caught Hannah's gaze once more. *Should I have said something?* But it was too late. In a flash, they were gone, and Mara was left with Galinthia, Fabian, Alex, and Casey—all staring up at her, ready for war. Despite their presence, she felt utterly alone. Touching the Gehenna stone had drained nearly all her hope, leaving only guilt, shame, and hate to fill the void. *Nothing I can do about it. Bullshit doesn't wait for a bucket.* Shaking off her nerves, she laid out her plan for the newly formed team.

Retrieval jobs were usually easy, and Mara trusted her Medolian partners, but having Alex along made her uneasy. Something about his behavior during the shipyard meeting had seemed off, and she still couldn't figure out how he had held onto the Gehenna stone for so long without realizing he possessed it. When she'd touched it, her reality had been consumed by an all-encompassing experience. His story didn't add up. *Makes me wish I'd tried harder to kill him in front of the school. Just didn't think Hunter had it in him to save him. There might be more to these two than I thought. Could be troublesome.*

"Everyone ready?" she asked. The others gathered around her. Turning to Casey, she said, "You sure you can do this?"

The small human nodded, speaking confidently. "I'll give you as clear a picture as I can."

"Where are we headed?" Alex asked.

Casey still seemed unsure if she should answer, but finally replied, "America."

All hands were placed on Mara's shoulders as she focused on Casey's emotions, pleasantly surprised by their clarity. Though Mara couldn't see Casey's thoughts directly, she could still glean a lot of information from sensing her Eve. Soon, she had enough to pinpoint the northern half of the upper Americas and a dense section of forest. Fortunately—or perhaps unfortunately—a mess of Wrath was directly where they were headed, providing a perfect homing beacon. *Two guesses where we need to go.*

The smart move would have been to abort the Shift right then and there. A mass of energy like that could have been anything, and Mara's intel was thin. The urge to hang back and wait was strong, but the escalating urgency of the situation proved far more compelling.

"Get ready," she said, completing the group Shift, regretting her decision immediately upon landing.

The dark woods around them and the cabin at the center of the clearing were quiet. Too quiet. To a human, it would have seemed like a peaceful winter night, perfect for a midnight stroll. But to Mara and the Medolians, the cold air was thick with palpable hatred and malice. The essence of destruction loomed everywhere, so stifling she almost choked on it. The signal reminded her of what she had sensed upon arriving at the university: multiple presences lurking in the shadows surrounding the campus, which she had dismissed once the excitement with Joseph began. Now, that energy had reappeared.

"We shouldn't be here," Galinthia said, drawing multiple knives from her belt. Fabian followed by suit, taking out his phone.

The humans, oblivious to the approaching threat, began to search the area. "Yeah, this is the place," Casey said. "Maybe it's inside?"

But Mara was too focused on a pile of black ash in the snow near the tree line to pay attention. *No Eve signal whatsoever, and no sign of a fire. What happened here?*

Alex sniffed the air. "I think I'm starting to sense what you guys are talking about. Joseph might have been here."

Casey suddenly shouted, "Leigh!" and rushed to the cabin porch, kneeling next to a curled-up shape against the wooden railing. Mara and the others joined her just in time to hear Casey question her friend, tossing her long-sleeve shirt over Leigh's shoulders and rubbing her shivering body. "What's wrong?" Casey asked. Leigh looked pale, her eyes wide with terror, grabbing at her throat, opening and closing her mouth, but nothing came out. "What's wrong? She can't talk. Why can't she talk?" Casey screamed.

Inside Leigh's throat, concentrated on her ruptured vocal cords, Mara sensed speckles of Eve—both Mallos and Dread. This was a precise attack, the work of a skilled Eve user. *Chloe's been here.*

The other two Medolians were busy eyeing the trees surrounding the cabin. "I've got a really horrible feeling. We need to go," Fabian said, illuminating the tree line with a powerful beam from his phone.

Mara turned to Casey. "Ask your friend where Joseph went."

"Are you kidding? She can't talk!" Casey shouted.

"Figure it out," Mara said, trying to remain calm.

Casey took Leigh's face in both hands and breathed with her, struggling to calm her. "Hey, it's okay. It's okay. I promise. We're going to figure it out. We will. But we need to end it first. Where did they go? Um . . . was the stone here?" Leigh nodded, choking back tears. "Did they get it?" She nodded again.

From the depth of the woods came what sounded like the growling of a monstrous wild animal. The single growl then multiplied throughout the trees, like a fleet of human bulldozers rolling toward them. Shadows crisscrossed in the woods. By now, Mara knew exactly what was coming. *And there are a lot of them.*

Meanwhile, Casey was struggling to communicate with her friend. "Where are they now?" Leigh made a *flying-away* motion.

"That's exactly what we should be doing," Mara said, trying to herd the humans off the porch, regretting her promise to Izaiah that she would get them back safe.

A deep voice came from behind as she urged the humans to move faster. "*Sentries!*" A swarm of blazing red eyes emerged from the trees, surrounding the party.

You guys. Great.

The sea of Archfiend whispered in waves, hissing like rattle-snakes in a barrel. One singular voice within broke through, "*You're too late, Medolians!*"

"Good evening, whoever you are," Mara shouted at the mass. "We are Medolian Sentries of the Tribunal, licensed representatives of the peoples of UnEarth and the majority party, Hywyn. Please state your name, shade, and current affiliation."

The Archfiend hissed in waves in response. A different, gnarled voice shouted back. "*Your efforts are in vain. The nameless knows Mellu has been taken to Trivium. The Brother is being retrieved as we speak!*"

Mara rolled her eyes. "Attention, mysterious Archfiend clan—each and every one of you is on Earth unauthorized, violating the third tenet of Tribunal law. You are all under arrest. Please form a single-file line and prepare for Shift to Trivium. If you resist, you will be brought down. I do have legal authority to do so."

"*No one will be going to Trivium,*" a third voice intoned. "*The nameless will succeed in the quest tonight. Upon the sun's rise, the third war begins!*"

Mara laughed. "How do you think a demon wearing a human shut-in mask is going to get by Izaiah Ezekial? Huh? Thought you guys were smarter."

Multiple voices in the shadows chanted, "*Mallos scum! Mallos scum!*"

Mara whispered to her team, "We're getting dirty here."

Gale readied her knives, Alex sparked his fists to life with potent Wrath, while Fabian asked with a high-pitched whine, "Can't I just take the humans to safety?"

The Archfiend then began pouring out of the trees from all directions, driven into a savage frenzy, blazing eyes wide above elongated jaws filled with teeth, smoke, and boiling acid.

"Not this time," Mara said. "All hands on deck. Like Izaiah said."

Launching herself into the air, Mara neared the first of the demons and began to feel deeply unsure of her team's chances. Normally, she loved it when they didn't come quietly, but they didn't have time for this. A single Archfiend was rarely a problem—usually dispatched or captured without incident—but a few dozen could pose a significant threat, especially with two human civilians to worry about. Then there was Izaiah and his team to consider. *Sorry, boss. Gotta leave you hanging for a minute.* The current situation demanded Mara's full attention. Joseph would have to wait.

Drawing her staff from the sheath across her back, she floated through the air. With a swift spin, illuminated by moonlight, she embedded it in the skull of an Archfiend with burgundy skin. Dark green blood sprayed into the air as the blade came free, and the floating demon dropped to the ground with a wet thud. By the time Mara landed, she'd brought down two more.

PROTECT IT

He hadn't blown up, which was the first good news Bennett had gotten in quite a while. Upon arriving in Trivium, Izaiah looked just as pleasantly surprised by that fact, slapping him on the back—a jolt that felt like he'd jammed a fork into a wall socket. "See! I knew you'd be fine!" the old Medolian exclaimed.

As they trudged through the entrance to the UnEarth city, Bennett felt as stretched as packing tape, buzzing with static electricity. He was basically terrified of touching anything conductive right now. Stranger still, no matter how many steps he took, it felt like his feet weren't actually reaching the ground, which was disconcerting and annoying. Existing on the Eve planet kind of hurt (*just a little, not going to lie*), but he figured he'd tough it out. *After all, who hasn't waltzed down the street in an alternate universe before?*

Stepping away from the tall golden ring they'd Shifted through—one of three—and passing through a gold turnstile, he half-expected to exit into a gift shop, but instead found himself in the heart of an UnEarth urban sprawl. The city stretched for miles, rolling up and down with the landscape, its horizon capped by gray, cone-shaped mountain peaks. The buildings they passed were made of rock or cement, each showcasing a unique, muted color scheme. Some were short, while others soared a few stories tall.

When Bennett asked why they couldn't Shift directly to the Tribunal, Izaiah replied, "The mountains make it nearly impossible to Shift anywhere safely but the city's main entrances. Even for someone like me. Gotta hoof it, I'm afraid."

The group moved briskly, and Bennett had to ignite his Rapture just to keep pace, finding the adverse effects of existing on Trivium lessened the more he did. Continuing like this would be a strain, but the constant flow of Hywyn's energy made remaining on the planet far more bearable. He focused on the lives they could save if their mission succeeded, the destruction they might avert, and tried to imagine what his brother Jerry would have done in each moment. Soon, Bennett wore a brilliant blue radiance, allowing him to move freely and absorb the atmosphere.

There was a mess of smells to discover: some organic, reminding him of the Texas farm his uncle Skip had owned until the bank foreclosed and he was forced into an RV in Arkansas. Other scents were earthy, like copper, recalling an ore mine he'd visited when he was twelve.

As they ventured farther into the city, a murky stink like smokestacks found his nose. Some smells might have been cooking, but others definitely weren't. The businesses they passed had signs out front, just like on Earth, usually featuring a mix of odd symbols and blocky shapes. Many were written in English, Spanish, Mandarin, and a bit of French, but alien languages were definitely king, some of which were just fucking weird. One sign, for example, simply looked like a butthole.

Moving through the seemingly empty civilization, Bennett wished the city would come alive. He wanted to witness how UnEarth society functioned on a typical day. Sure, their current task would have been made harder, but he was curious to see all the crazy shit Izaiah, Hannah, Felix, and the Medolians had spoken about. Of all the creatures described to him so far, he most wanted to see the giant, round beings of Grief—the Lostros. They sounded funny.

Presently, Izaiah and Felix had taken the lead, gabbing back and forth at the front of the expedition, while Bennett and Hannah lagged behind. Throughout the trek, Bennett noticed a twitch in Hannah's right hand, along with a continual licking of her lips—ticks he recognized all too well. *Saw 'em all the time with Lance, and my old man. And me.*

As if sensing his gaze, Hannah clenched and relaxed her fists, sniffing the air. "There's something I don't like here. I've felt it since we arrived. Can you sense it?"

"Not sure. Maybe," Bennett answered.

"Focus. You'll need to multitask. When I was learning to use my power, I thought of every job as being behind a pane of glass in my mind. As long as I kept the glass clean, everything would work out fine. Usually."

Bennett had no idea what she meant. "I think I get it."

"It's a city, a mixture of sensations," Hannah said. "Pick out the ones you want to focus on. Some are nice. Some are not-so-nice. Civilians get to move toward the nice ones. Peacekeepers, the not-so-nice ones."

She spoke to Bennett as though he were at an orientation meeting for a menial nine-to-five. He struggled to find the signal she mentioned, needing to close his eyes to sense Eve, forcing him to alternate between types of vision. Pockets of Grief, Dread, and Madam Daphne's shade, Fervor, surrounded them, but focusing

on everything while maintaining his Rapture shield proved exhausting.

"*Hrm.* Might be nothing," Hannah said. "Too bad we don't have
Mara. She'd know if something were hiding out there."

"Yeah, I heard she hunted down a Beaubon in the Amazon
once," Bennett said, quoting Felix. Kidding, since he had no idea
what it meant.

"Ha! True," Hannah said, sounding proud.

"Forgive me for asking, but what's up with you two?"

Hannah gave him an inquisitive look.

"Bullshit. I saw what happened back there. Fess up."

She scoffed. "You didn't see anything."

Bennett kept a hard stare on her, sick of the baloney.

"Guess it was pretty obvious there's some history," she said.

"Better believe it, sister."

Hannah sighed, sounding less than half-assured for the first
time. "When I met her, we were in the middle of a war. A war she
hated. *Still* hates. One thing you need to understand about Mara
is that she was born just a few centuries before Inferius. She barely
knew what life was like before every friend she ever had killed
themselves in front of her to end something she never understood
the need for."

"Didn't know any of that," Bennett said.

"Nobody talks about it, especially her. Inferius not only took the
closest thing she had to a family; it also introduced her to me,
which is—I'm sure—another reason she hates it so much." Hannah
chuckled to herself before her tone grew serious. "I remember it.
When I first saw her, she was on the battlefield. The most graceful
thing I'd ever seen. For some reason, I remember thinking she was
a blonde. Not that it's important. But after the fight, she was all I
could think of. When it all ended, following the Purge, we actually

lived in TC for a while. A lot of us stayed in the city initially. You were allowed to if you didn't have any contacts or work on Earth. It was a strange time—a transitional period for all of us. Mara and I had a place on the other side of town. Then things went wrong. Really quickly. The fights got too rough, even for me. Not that I regret any of it. We went for it. Least—I know I did—but Celestials and Medolians just can't be together. The diamond and the rainbow, you know? Both want to shine. Especially two high-rankers. It's a conflict of interest, I suppose. Mara would never give up her position. Everything else—and I mean everything else—is second. So when I did what I felt was right—something that would have allowed us to finally be together—she saw it as a betrayal."

"What did you do to piss her off so much?"

"I gave up *my* position."

"As a general?"

"Mm-hm. After the war, I didn't want to live in a society that would perform a mass exodus like that. Plus . . . I was just so tired of being a 'perfect' creature. Being absolute but killing anyway . . . it makes you lose all sense of yourself." Hannah looked away. When her bright blue eyes returned, Bennett realized how much he loathed their absence.

"When I did it—left the Council and became an Eve human—I really thought . . . Mara was going to be happy." Hannah's voice almost cracked. "Shows how little I knew her. Mara Loren, my greatest challenge, and greatest failure. But how about you? Still implosion-free, I see."

Bennett wanted to keep talking with Hannah about her and Mara, which was far more interesting and less distracting than talking about himself, but he could tell she wanted to drop it, so he did. "Being here is about the strangest thing I've ever felt," he said.

"You're not new to it. You've traveled between realities before."

"What do you mean?"

"When they put the Rapture in you, the night you and Alex died, where do you think you went for the procedure?"

"Never thought about it."

"Think about it now."

He did. "Hywyn?"

Hannah nodded. "Congratulations. You're officially—technically—the first human ever to go to Heaven. Though not really."

Bennett wondered if something was wrong with him, seeing as learning this had almost no effect on his psyche. *No time for blue ribbons.* Keeping the Rapture flowing took a lot of his will and all of his focus. "But Izaiah said humans can't go that far into Un-Earth. The only reason I'm in Trivium is that it's located on the first floor or something."

"I'm not sure how they did it—I just know they did," Hannah said. "Maybe someday you'll confront those responsible and ask them not only how but why."

"Pretty sure they did it so I could be useful in situations like this," Bennett said. "But right now, I'm no use at all."

"Discounting yourself and forfeiting are the same in my book," Hannah said. "You throwing in the towel?"

"No, but look at me. I'm a wobbly fuck just trying to balance here. You saw Izaiah's clip show. This is some serious, biblical, heavy-hitter-needed kind of shit, not blue sparklers. I wish I had a big gun in my hands so bad—you have no idea. Bigger the better. Belt-fed would be nice."

"We've been over this. You need to get more creative. Think outside that box," she said. "The Rapture is ready to work for you. Figure out what you want before you begin. Find the clearest thought, grab hold, and ride it all the way to shore. Don't let up. Don't look away."

Bennett finally understood what she meant. Every time he activated his Rapture, it seemed to slip away before he could follow through. He had the same problem with his golf swing.

"When you picked up the smallest Gehenna stone after Mara dropped it, you were focused on making the protective shield, right?" he asked.

"No, on getting the stone to the right place, into the right hands. The goal is key. That's the thing about Rapture—it's not any purer than the other shades of Eve. Hywyn is just as bureaucratic, power-hungry, and full of shit as Arros. It's simply an odd coincidence that Rapture is the shade of Eve ignited by doing what's usually the right thing."

Bennett felt like he was back in preschool, sitting on a soft mat with a big number three and a Tonka truck, being told that hurting other people's feelings is bad and that puppies and turtles are good. "The right thing? That's such cryptic bullshit. How can anyone know—"

Hannah interrupted. "Learn its language. Follow its lead. Odds are your Rapture knows what would benefit the most people in any given situation better than you. Once you think you've got the hang of it, then take back control. Don't try to do too much all at once. Just . . . do whatever good you can. You'll see."

Bennett almost stopped in place, hearing his brother's voice in his head. "*Do what good you can, King Arthur.*"

"What did you say?" Bennett asked.

"Everyone can help. It just depends on how much of themselves they're willing to give," Hannah said. "Everyone has an option in front of them that will lead to joy, wisdom, and tranquility. If you pick the right road, you'll never be steered wrong." She eyed his sudden distance. "You okay?"

Bennett wanted to move on. "Sure, it's just . . . I can't do the things you can. You've known this stuff your whole life—which sounds like a really, really long time."

"It won't all come at once. Just have some faith that it will. You do know what that is, right?" Hannah asked with a suspicious glance.

"Are you asking if I believe in God or something?" Bennett said. "'Cause after all the crap that's happened so far, it's pretty clear he ain't coming. My nanna would be mortified."

She shook her head. "Shut up and listen. I asked if you had faith. Different things. Faith is about believing in something everyone else tells you can never happen, what only you know to be true. Having faith is about watching one result a thousand times and deciding to go once more, believing it will change."

"Some people call that being an idiot," Bennett said.

"And they have a strong case for it, except that change is the only true constant in the universe. So mathematically speaking, the result will eventually change. It just depends on how long you're willing to wait."

"So, you're asking if I think we can succeed?" said Bennett.

"More if you believe in yourself and the moment. Do you believe you belong here? Do you believe you and Alex are part of the whole? Part of this and *every* universe? Or just . . . happenstance?"

"Up until now, I didn't see human beings as anything more than goo in skin suits, walking around, handing out Bibles, eating quarter pounders, being good little barcodes for those in power till they die."

Hannah laughed. "That's one way to look at things. Always amazed me. The holy books of the Earth seem to tell a story of humanity being weak. Sheep. Every great power seems to view the average person as a fragile thing they can control. I never understood it. Not the books, but how people believed it. Why let a book tell you you're powerless? Why let arithmetic or a company do the same? Mortals don't realize they are only worth as much as they believe they are. So, tell me, do you have faith that you—and others—have worth?"

They rounded a corner onto another long gray asphalt lane dotted with streetlamps.

"I guess—I don't know," Bennett answered.

"That's a perfectly reasonable answer. But if you want to unlock this thing inside you . . . might want to start thinking about it."

For some reason, Bennett wanted to continue arguing, then realized he was only arguing against himself. He stayed quiet a few moments until something down the right lane—a bucket—was knocked over, breaking the silence. Looking into the inlet, he saw a dead overhead lamp that left a dark spot, triggering flashbacks of the demon Aili'Eace in the alley in London and the feeling that someone new was watching them from the shadows. A realization set in: he and the others were perfect prey, out in the open with no witnesses or bystanders to disrupt an assault. Bennett's gut dropped. His adrenaline spiked.

"Izaiah?" Hannah asked softly.

The oldest Medolian quickened his pace. "I know. But why?" he said, sounding weary. "Get ready, everybody."

Guess they know something I don't.

Gripping the black and gray marbled knife gifted to him by Hannah, Bennett drew it from its leather sheath. If an attack was coming from anywhere, he figured it would be from the air, so he kept his attention skyward. A moment later, they crossed a second shadowed inlet, which Izaiah and Felix passed in peace, lowering Bennett's defenses one notch too many. As he turned to pass, a sharp whisper came from the darkness on his left.

"*Psst! Hey, buddy!*" Bennett spun toward the open alley just as a flash of smoke and a heap of snot struck his face. What felt like a truck with claws doing eighty miles per hour slammed into his chest, tackling him off his feet.

The goo was some sort of acid, judging by the smell and its clear intent to devour his flesh, but fortunately, the Rapture coursing through him and around him acted as a barrier. Bennett struggled to contain the enormous wild creature on top of him, their razor-sharp talons stretching along the length of their Archfiend body. *Fucker looks like a centipede from down here!*

"*Go to sleep, little human!*" the creature shrieked, trying to bite Bennett's head off.

The soldier howled and gained some ground using the Archfiend's own momentum, able to swing out from under it to top position, and brought the knife down into what he figured was the demon's belly, expecting only to annoy or anger them. Instead, they froze. Their red eyes curled in pain as their whole body drooped, crusting over, becoming like brown rock in the area surrounding the knife wound. As the creature's breath faded, so did Bennett's fear of them. *Well, all right.*

Dozens of human-sized snakes had taken to the sky, growling in unison, forming a rolling thunder over the Trivium block. The Archfiend flowed in streaks of red and brown, swooping through the air like giant ribbons pulled by dancers.

Nearby, Hannah was dealing with a handful of demons. "We have to get the stone to the Tribunal!" she shouted whilst tearing a demon in half.

Bennett dashed toward Izaiah, who was surrounded by a cluster of Archfiend. He dodged snarling jaws swooping from above, but an especially skinny beast grabbed him, screaming with a shrill call that pierced through the chaos. Bennett wrestled it back, quickly realizing that his shield wasn't infallible when the demon clamped its jaws onto his shoulder. To his relief, the Rapture responded, sending a surge of power through his limbs. Using both hands, Bennett was able to get ahold of the Archfiend's protruding teeth from below and yanked down as hard as he could, ripping the creature's jaw open, dropping pools of blood, saliva, and razor-sharp teeth. The demon cried so loudly Bennett thought he might go deaf, and so shut them up by slamming them in the temple, causing the Archfiend's grip on him—and their consciousness—to be released.

As the battle wore on, Bennett dropped three more Archfiend, racking up injuries of his own. Everything felt like it was happening in slow motion, his hands moving as if on their own. Blood sprayed. Fire, ice, and demon acid filled the air. Somewhere on his left, while carving up a demon that had latched onto his leg, an Eve signature approached him. At first, he didn't register it, but then he froze, terror gripping him.

I know that signal.

A blaring crash echoed through the chaos, followed by Felix's cry of pain. Bennett dropped everything and rushed toward the largest mass of turmoil, meeting Hannah along the way. They found their janitor friend on the ground, clutching his side, looking pale and in bad shape.

"They're here!" Felix shouted before a huge ball of Medolian energy with orange highlights coursed over the area, bringing every warrior to their knees.

At the center of the attack stood Chloe, flanked by a figure that resembled Joseph but was larger. The energy radiating from him tore through Bennett like a mountain-sized guitar amp. *Shit! His signature's way more potent and disgusting than last time.* The creature's hood was down, but the white mask remained.

Great. Guess he found the third rock.

The demons backed off following the new arrival, taking to the skies.

"We want what was taken from us," Joseph boomed, his voice like the chaotic force of a thousand tree roots torn asunder.

Izaiah approached the new duo cautiously. "You must be Joseph. We met once before, you might not remember. 'Course, I didn't know at the time you and Chloe were a couple. As the closest thing she's got to a father, I feel it's my duty to approve you. Speaking of which, Chloe, how are you, sweetheart? You look like you haven't been sleeping well."

"I told you he would stall," Chloe muttered to Joseph, who responded without hesitation.

"We won't ask you again!" Joseph's bellows sent a ripple of barks through the Archfiend ranks.

"You can stop with the 'we' nonsense," Izaiah said. "The game is over. I know the boy died months ago. Mason is gone. There's only one of you left in there, and frankly, I find it sick how much joy you're getting outta this."

Joseph's head swiveled back and forth, as though he were considering Izaiah's words. "*Hrm* . . . So, the Seeress was visited after all. Alas, no, we will not be changing. We like it this way. Call it a little bit of fun before the end. Though we were hoping you would make a final plea to speak with the boy—to find the man within the monster. It would have been a wonderful game." Joseph released a low, callous laugh, turning Bennett's gut. Creaking like the bent branches of a dying elm, Joseph's fingers opened, revealing his bare palm. "The Brother."

Izaiah shook his head. "No can do. In fact, I'd like the both of you to surrender peacefully, so this whole thing can end, and everyone can go eat peanuts and ice cream."

"No can do," Joseph responded.

The swarm of Archfiend overhead grew louder, poised for an

attack. Bennett braced himself while keeping an eye on the real action.

"You don't want to do this," Izaiah said to Chloe. "Come on, where's that spunky, swashbuckling Medolian I used to love? The one who was born as lovely as they come, and who annoyed Mara for a thousand years—which I loved—then matured into a powerful, sensitive, intelligent—"

"Shut up!" she wailed, the demons overhead shrieking and hissing in response. "Never again! That's the last time you belittle me. Give us the Brother of Gehenna. Don't make me rip it from you!" Chloe drew her sword, wavering but ready.

Joseph bellowed, "We tire of waiting. Clan Aili, now!"

With a wave of his hand, all Hell broke loose.

The second surge of demons began swooping down. Bennett couldn't keep track of how many there were as claws swiped at his back, then his front, then his back again. Amid the action, he lost all sense of where his teammates ended up. Judging by sound alone, Hannah and Joseph had found one another to tussle, while Chloe and Izaiah were trading gigantic blows packed with frenzied neutral energy.

A particularly ugly demon managed to wrap their entire body around Bennett like a python. "*This one has you!*" the Archfiend hissed into his ear, scorching him with infernal heat pouring from their throat.

Poisonous drool dripped everywhere as they squeezed until Bennett lost his grip on Hannah's knife, which fell, lost to the hysteria. Just before everything went black, a sphere of Mallos—this one with the hue of vibrant green Jubilee—blasted across the block, sending everything in its wake soaring. *That was a Medolian attack!* Bennett and the python Archfiend were sent crashing into a stone column, separated when the creature's coil loosened.

Next thing he knew, Izaiah was helping him up. "Bit of a pickle, huh?" the Medolian said, dusting him off.

Before Bennett could respond, Izaiah slipped the smallest Gehenna stone into his pocket. "It's up to you now. Get to the Tribunal. Just up the road. Can't miss it. Deliver the stone to Senator Laffler, no one else!"

Felix appeared, gripping his side, his dirty T-shirt soaked in red. He seemed in pain, but with a face bright and eager. "How can I help?"

Izaiah kicked them both along. "Get Bennett out of here. To the Tribunal steps. Fastest route possible. Go!"

"What about the demons? And Joseph and Chloe?" Bennett asked, resisting for some stupid reason.

"You let me worry about them!" Izaiah shouted, turning back to face a wave of blistering burgundy skin, thrashing talons, and irate eyes filled with fire. Slamming his cane down, he conjured a fifty-foot cellophane shield. The beasts crashed into it, held at bay while they thrashed, fogging the shield with their hot breath, stacking atop one another like grains of sand in an hourglass.

Felix and Bennett broke into a sprint down the lane. Bennett managed a few glances backward before turning around the next block. Behind the translucent shield, he spotted Hannah and Joseph trading blows, holding the demon at bay. The glow radiating from her was glorious (*never used that word before*), not to mention the ferocity of her hits, which were backing Joseph up. Defensively, he slashed with his claws, which glanced off her Rapture aura with fluorescent sparks. In a swift move, her arm pulled back like a pinball shooter, blurred, and collided with Joseph's mask, cleaving it in two.

The halves drifted to the ground like leaves in the wind—one side clean, the other foul. From a distance, Bennett caught a glimpse of the grotesque mess lying beneath the mask, a chaotic blend of green, brown, and orange smears, with two beady, softly glowing red eyes nestled at its center. Then it vanished, the last thing Bennett saw before he was forced to focus on more pressing issues.

He and Felix banked through turns, and at one point, his Arch-fiend pal took them through a "shortcut" that Bennett prayed was legitimate. *Not that I don't trust Felix—I just . . . don't.*

Soon they were sprinting past an immaculate café with a patio made of cornflower-colored stone and four immense pillars in the corners. Beyond it was a wide-open campus, lined with arching columns along the walkways. A dark shape towered at its center, its shadowed spires rising above the square. Izaiah was right; there was no way Bennett could miss the Tribunal. *Makes the Capitol Building look like a Kleenex box.*

Approaching the three-sectioned ziggurat felt strange (*and wrong*), but they did it anyway. Bennett's heart pounded as he and Felix neared the bottom of the center section's steps, dark and moody as they were, and climbed toward the eighty-foot tear-drop-shaped doors at the top.

"We're home free, so long as nothing else goes wrong," Felix coughed out amid exhausted breaths.

Bennett got a bad feeling about one nanosecond before an Eve gate burst open ahead of them. A Shift, to be sure, but something about this one was savage and raw, reminding him of foul meat burning on a chemical fire. The wave of energy struck him, shoving him backward a couple of steps, and when the flash faded, Joseph was standing there, by himself. *Cripes and fuck, he Shifted!*

Felix gasped. "He can Shift? On Trivium? But that's . . ." His words faded, as though he were too exhausted and shaken to finish.

With the mask gone, Joseph's exposed face was like seeing a wet junkyard from above. A mouth opened amid the bullshit, speaking with a repellent voice made somehow worse by being no longer muffled. "You may stop running."

Felix (*God bless him*) launched an attack so easily dismissed that Joseph never even turned away from Bennett. *He knows I have the stone! Can't beat him to the doors. Can't run. Think! Hannah and Izaiah are coming. Stall!* In that moment, Bennett decided his official mantra was "fuck it," and resolved to live by it. Gathering as much Rapture as he could, he sent every ounce to his right hand, balled it, and hurled it. The fist blazed with violet intensity, streaks of blue flame trailing behind as it soared—directly into Joseph's waiting claw. The soldier's hand was clasped by daggers, squeezing, blinding him with white-hot pain and bringing him to his knees.

"*Arh!* Goddamn it!" he roared, desperately punching the monster in the rib cage with his free hand. The hits thudded against soft flesh and bone. It felt as though his fist would break through to a hollow interior if his assault continued.

Joseph laughed. "All the way to the end! We love it!" His free claw slashed Bennett across the face five times, releasing lines of blood that crawled over the soldier's eyes and dripped onto his chest. The same claw then clasped the Gehenna stone in his pocket and ripped it free, tearing away cloth and a chunk of flesh underneath. Bennett grabbed the wound, attempting to stop the bleeding faucet. Next thing he knew, he was as light as air, tossed away like a banana peel.

He struck the pavement (*or it struck me*) and tumbled down the stairs, stopping only when a pair of helping hands caught him.

"You okay?" Izaiah asked, looming over him on one side while Hannah loomed over the other.

Am I okay? Who the fuck cares?

They helped Bennett up, but there was no time for thank-yous. Their faces were so full of terror that their expressions appeared blank, while behind them, the sky filled with Archfiend on approach. Up the steps, Joseph—the titan shape in soiled rags—lifted his new prize to the sky, the Tribunal and its spires aloft as a curtain behind him. Reaching into his cloak, he revealed the other two Brothers and brought all three together. The reaction was instantaneous and profound.

Bennett's senses were rendered null. His eyes suddenly watered, his fingers began twitching uncontrollably, and he became so tired that he wanted nothing more than to lie down and accept a permanent sleep.

The Gehenna stones were cradled by Joseph as the magenta swirls within them blasted free of their physical bonds, flinging themselves outward in oblong orbits around his body.

"This is it!" he screamed. "The Brothers are set free!"

THE BROTHERS

Towers crumbled. A thunderclap struck overhead. The night sky turned a deep blood red along the horizon, and Izaiah knew, more than ever, he had failed. *So much for my go-with-the-gut approach.* Despite all his efforts and compromises, the Seeress's prophecy of apocalypse was coming true not twenty yards from where he stood. Up the broad stairs, below the imposing doors of the Tribunal, a power transfer was taking place that he had no hope of stopping. Maroon and black mist poured off the stones, blistering and broiling, seeping into Joseph through his eyes, ears, mouth, and wounds, mutating what was once the body of Mason Royans further into a lumbering beast undeserving of the flesh it had stolen.

Manic, shuddering, drunk on the power of the Brothers, Joseph shrieked, "It's endless! Absolutely endless!"

The transfer—how strong is the flow? Are there any breaks? Could I . . . No. Come on, you old fool, something has to work! Izaiah was running on pure instinct, dying to act but unable to, frozen in place by the sheer power radiating off the stones. It was the same story with

Hannah, Bennett, and Felix. Even Chloe—who had joined them on the stairs just before the transfer began—was fighting to stay upright.

"And so . . . with the damnation of the blinding light," Joseph said with an exultant crescendo, "for the countless wasted lives that meant nothing, the nightmare is finally over! We, the nameless, shall create a new order and send this universe into complete, peaceful darkness." He finished and hung his head, like some of the more dramatic priests and poets Izaiah had witnessed over the ages.

There was a scream from within the monster: a wide-eyed release of pain and ecstasy, as Joseph's shoulders jutted upward, as though hoisted by a rope and pulley. Two bone spikes of deep gray rose from his shoulder blades and into the air, where jagged, barbed vines broke away, outstretching and weaving around one another, becoming mangled wings curling into themselves like writhing newborns. Gradually, they drew out, crackling, finding their full breadth. Finalizing his transformation, the trunks opened with sharp, violent sighs, like immense blades over sharpening stones, completing an over forty-foot wingspan.

The smaller Archfiend danced through the sky, chanting, "*For the Beast! For the Beast! For the Beast!*" blissfully unaware of Joseph's true intentions, simply happy their side seemed to be winning. The deed was done. All appeared over, for a moment at least. Then, as Joseph stood proudly—a monolith to sin—the ground began to still. The building behind him ceased collapsing. The stars returned to the sky, twinkling with hope-giving light. Most importantly of all, Joseph— or whatever the nameless had become—stopped growing.

"This can't be—" the monster grunted as the supply of mist from the stones diminished. The smooth black finish on their faces returned. Reality gained its composure. The pressure on Izaiah's body subsided. Like a train slowing, the transfer was gradually coming to a halt. Joseph let out a panicked scream. "No. Noooo. Where is it?"

"Finish the transfer," Chloe called from below, struggling to climb the steps. "Do it. Bring us peace!"

"The Brothers resist!" Joseph cradled the stones, willing them back to life like cold infants in his arms. "They will not open. It . . . it must have been Izaiah. He and his cretins did something to Mellu."

"We didn't do squat to your rock collection," Izaiah shouted back.

Chloe muttered to herself, "Resist you? Why?" She then gasped, shouting above, "Of course. It's Gehenna, my love! The Brothers wish to go home, where the Molochs birthed them and fed them. Where their strength will be amplified. That's where they will open for you."

No kidding? Well—hallelujah! I love second chances. Izaiah's gut then dropped. *Then again, if Joseph can Shift while on Trivium, he might be able to Shift off of Trivium. How the heck did he do that, by the way?*

At first, the monstrosity was placid: a statue, unmoved. His red eyes drifted to the lifeless stones in his arms. "They wish? They wish!?" he bellowed. "We've *given* them everything they've wished! We heard their voices. We did as they asked. They are together, in our arms, and once again, we are a servant! The power is deserved! Ours! Where is it?"

"You have it, my love!" Chloe shouted. "They gave you a taste of their strength so that you may get them home safely. Use it, quickly. Their trust will not be infinite." She spoke with a stern tone, telling her kid not to break their fancy new toy.

Joseph's spine arched forward, shadowing his face and the stones. The wings folded into a gray canopy above. Static shocks of orange lightning coursed around his cloak and claws. The black and red mist filtered out of him, collecting and condensing. Soon, the cloud without shape became a rotating sphere, swirling and expanding. He released a deafening roar, shaking his head. "We brought them together. We obeyed. It should be OURS!"

The sphere turned opaque, swelling with raw power—like a pufferfish the size of a house. Izaiah had never seen such a pure collection of Eve and was willing to bet the thing was unstable. *No one could control something so reckless!* Chloe apparently felt the same way, muttering the word "fool" before jumping into the air, generating a Mallos bubble around herself, and getting the Hell out of there.

Not a bad idea! Izaiah followed her lead, managing to nab Hannah, Felix, Bennett, and a good chunk of the road beneath them in an apple-green Mallos orb of his own. They launched away from the Tribunal as fast as Izaiah could carry them until he couldn't any longer, and the orb collapsed, spewing the team onto asphalt several blocks away in a clean, modest Dolorosian block dominated by yellow and orange housing. "Sorry for the landing, all!" He took cover against the closest wall.

The sound of the Abyss bomb had grown to something akin to thousands of screeching truck brakes overlapping, getting higher and tighter, like a prodigious bottle being filled dangerously close to the top. The old Medolian dared to peer around the corner and spotted the Tribunal stairs through a gap between complexes, just in time to witness the ghostly ball of Abyss start to pitch from side to side like a wobbling top. *Oh no.* Izaiah tackled Bennett and Felix to the same ground they'd just picked themselves up from. "Get down!"

With an ear-splitting explosion, the bomb detonated, sending red and black mist across the sky. The shrill cries of Archfiend burning away filled the air. Foundations and walls crumbled, sending quakes crashing through the surrounding neighborhoods.

Somehow, the structure protecting Izaiah and the others stood, and when the dark Eve faded, the neighborhood descended into a post-shock quiet. Izaiah could no longer feel the energy of the Aili clan. *The ones not caught in the blast must've run off.* He also could not sense Chloe, though something told him she was around.

Creeping out to find a vantage point to survey the damage, Izaiah nearly lost his breath. It looked as though a fire had cleared out five or six blocks of the Trivium landscape, leaving only lifeless ash. Across the barren campus, the Tribunal lay torn open. A laser-precise sphere was cut from all matter in the steps and most of the central hall, where the winged creature that had caused the destruction hovered at its center. *So that's what he plans to do to the universe.*

With a voice powerful enough to reach all of Trivium—or at least anyone still around to hear it—Joseph spoke. "You see, Izaiah! That was only a portion!" He gestured, orating like a twentieth-century Earth dictator, the likes of which Izaiah had never been fond.

What's he waiting for? If he can Shift off-planet, he could do it now and end this. Unless . . .

"Why do you fight us?" Joseph asked. "We fight for you. For everyone! To end pain. Do you enjoy never-ending struggle? The back and forth? Worshipping? Groveling? No creature is above another. Existence bastardizes us all."

Yep, looks like he can't Shift. Either the Abyss is unbalancing him so badly he can't open an Eve gate, or he used up a little too much power with that hissy-fit bomb.

Joseph drifted away from the wreckage of the Tribunal steps and soared over the campus, seemingly searching for something or someone. "You know you can't win this, Izaiah. Come out. End this with dignity."

He can't sense us, either? Well, I'll be. Might be a silver lining trying to shine through here, after all. Izaiah took the chance, getting the attention of Hannah, Bennett, and Felix, who were currently huddled in the shadows of a nearby multidwelling structure. Daring only the softest of whispers, he laid out a plan: Bennett and Felix would go right, Hannah would go left, and he would go up the middle. Hopefully, they could get the drop on Joseph from three sides and maybe (*just maybe*) snag one of the stones before he got bored and headed to the Eb Rings to return to Earth. *Luckily, he's a cocky one.*

Bennett and Felix darted to the right, into the darkness of a greasy alley behind a couple of kitchens, leaving Izaiah to question every move he'd ever made in his entire life—however long that was.

"Got one more joke for the road?" a voice asked, both coarse and soft.

Izaiah turned to Hannah, who gave him a playful punch to the jaw. "Right now, I feel as if I'll never tell another one of those," he said.

"Ah, don't be so dramatic. You will," Hannah said. "'Laughter finds a way in, even when you don't want it to.' Remember?" She gave him a steady pat on the back and a fear-ending smile before starting on her own mission to the left.

"Ah, who told you that drivel?" Izaiah asked, knowing the answer.

"Just some nut." She turned for a wink, then was gone.

Izaiah chuckled to himself, now alone, staring down the middle route, with no idea how any of this was going to turn out and little hope in his heart. If Illyana was at all correct, nothing he could do would affect the coming end. *Doesn't mean I won't try. Just . . . stinks.* He started out as Joseph's voice rolled over the city, echoing down every walkway, filling each passage with his forceful, wretched words.

"You wouldn't believe the things we can do with the Abyss. It's so much more than we ever dreamed! The Brothers are showing us how to unlock it. They know everything, even about you, Izaiah, and your team! Yes, your precious humans, Barker and Hunter. We know why you chose them. We know your plan, pathetic as it was."

Joseph's sick laugh crept into Izaiah's ears as the Medolian hurried without using his cane for support, knowing it would make too much noise. Up a tight cobblestone path, he slipped between brown brick buildings, trying to focus on anything other than his aching knees.

Joseph continued. "Clan Aili! Where have you gone? Did we frighten you away? You have nothing to fear—the Brothers are here to erase all your pain. The war is no longer necessary for peace."

Izaiah spotted a walkway under a stone bridge arch intersecting Joseph's path. Creeping the rest of the way, the monster was revealed through occasional gaps in the awning. Soon Izaiah was tucked below him. Sixty or so feet up, Joseph hovered, luckily still talking, distracting himself. *Keep it going. Tell us how great you are.* Once in position, with his cane pressed firmly into the ground, Izaiah put all his weight on top, planning to launch himself like a circus performer from a cannon. *Piece of cake. Just like the mechanical bull in Fort Worth!*

He had no idea if his teammates were in position or not, but it was now or never. Unable to kiss his own ass goodbye, and with no one else around to do it, Izaiah tapped the green notebook in his chest pocket for good luck and hoped for the best. But he never got the chance to move. In the blink of an eye, a Mallos orb the size of a honeydew crashed into his temple, exploding on impact and sending him sprawling. He spun to defend, but found no one there. *Not now. We were so close!* Another orb appeared behind him. Bam! Then another on his right, like a stone shot from a sling. Bam! "*Agk!*" *Darn it, Chloe! What is this?*

Mallos orbs were popping up all around like fireworks, and the old Medolian couldn't keep up. Izaiah liked dirty fighting as much as the next guy, but this was well beyond underhanded. This was rotten. The fight was over before it began, as blunt orbs jabbed his cranium, neck, and torso until all were tender or cracking. He then felt something small and sharp touch the base of his spine and press forward. Izaiah's breath was stolen when a blade infused with Mallos ripped through his vertebrae and ribs, crunching, pushing its way forward, feeling like billions of tiny, subzero needles had just entered his body. *Boy, she . . . I always knew she was fast, but wow.* Peering down at the rusty cutlass blade sticking more than a foot out of his abdomen, he felt a chill course through the rest of his body. Izaiah's knees buckled, and he tried to drop but was left dangling on the blade, like a hunk of beef on a kabob, bleeding what was essentially saline solution.

This isn't . . . this is bad. Oh no.

He fought to move, partially paralyzed, only able to peer over his left shoulder at Chloe, looming with animus.

"Ah-ah-ah," she whispered. "This time, you don't stop the end."

"I can't believe . . . why?" Izaiah asked, his heart breaking just from the look in her eyes.

Chloe leaned close. "Because my beloved and I are the only ones who understand what's really at stake. Because you think life is a gift, a privilege. Because you're sick. But don't worry, we're going to cure every ailment. What we're doing is a favor for creatures like you most of all."

"By killing everyone? Chloe . . ."

"No. It's not death—it's erasure. Nothing is lost if nothing remembers." Chloe then lifted her head and called to Joseph, "I have him, my love! It's over."

Which is exactly how it felt, watching the winged horror glide into the courtyard and land with a colossal thud.

"Well done," Joseph called, stomping over, sniffing rapidly like a muffled machine gun, then cackling with what could only be described as glee. "Medolian blood. Such a rare, sweet smell! How long we've dreamed of Izaiah's death. Oh! To hear the tale that the deed had been done by a soul of nobility. But now, to know we are the one who will do it? It might give us Jubilee if we'd not diverted so far down the lower shades. That is what those of Earth and Hywyn alike call them, yes? Lower?"

"Sounding like an appropriate title to me," Izaiah said, coughing up his lifeblood. The wound needed to close soon, or he would drain out and fade.

"We don't have time for games. Kill him fast, my love," Chloe snapped. "Then we will take an Eb Gate to Gehenna and complete our task."

"The task is completed. With Izaiah finished, there are none who could stop us." Joseph's mangled face twisted into a smile. "Why can we not enjoy these moments before ending the light of the cosmos?"

"Because creatures out there are in pain. Every moment we wait is another of agony for countless others. Have the Brothers and the Abyss blinded you to that?" Chloe demanded.

Joseph released a cry more akin to a crack of thunder than a voice of flesh and bone. "You know nothing! The Brothers have waited eons for this day. They will wait a few minutes longer." He then set his sights on Izaiah. "The Medolian responsible for so much misery will be tried, judged, and executed."

"Sounds like the jury's in," Izaiah said, growing weaker every second.

A shadow fell over him as Joseph approached, drawing a long claw dripping black and red smoke. Odious Wrath danced up and down the rocklike serrations.

"How does he plead?" Joseph asked.

"I don't," Izaiah responded, using the last of his energy.

Joseph grunted and chuckled. "Wonderful final words." The claw rose above his head, lingered, and came down.

Just before it impaled Izaiah's skull, a blue streak impacted with the winged beast like a demolition ball, sending Joseph—and it— soaring across the street. The black and blue shapes collided with the Un-Earth Bank and Trust on the far corner, a rustic cherry-red building with segments plated in solid gold. *All stolen from Earth.* The lobby imploded, revealing abandoned second-floor offices. A gigantic orb of black glass suspended from the ceiling was knocked loose and exploded among the rubble, blasting out razor-sharp shards.

In the remnants of the bank, a mound of wreckage moved aside, and Hannah rose into view. *My savior!* She coughed on dust and brushed herself off, facing the demon crawling out from under a shattered support beam. "Joe, we gotta have a talk."

"General!" Joseph cried, dropping the support beam, shaking off the last bits of splintered wood and dust like a wet hound. "Well done. Even now, a pathetic, forgotten war hero, you don't disappoint. We've felt your Eve, by the way. We see how much Grief you carry. We know how broken the great Hannah of Cross Station has become. Desperately grasping to her elixir of healing, yet there's never enough of it, is there? Is that why you fight now? To find purpose in a meaningless life? If so, tell us . . ." The demon spread his wings, looming over his minuscule opponent. "With your friend now saved, how will you save yourself?"

Hannah shook her head. "Don't want to. I'm on garbage duty."

"Ha! Not even *you* can stand up to the power of the Brothers!"

With balled fists, unflinching, Hannah calmly replied, "Maybe, but I'm still pretty sure it'll hurt when I shove this up your ass." She raised a fist surrounded by burning Rapture.

"You're out of your league, General, and will never get the chance," Joseph said giddily, swan-diving headfirst into a fight.

His inordinate claws slashed back and forth as he pursued Hannah out of the bank and across the courtyard. With bursts of Rapture from her feet, she nimbly darted between tables and chairs, well out of his grasp, while Joseph charged through like a bulldozer, bellowing his frustrations with each miss. Making him pay for his blinding rage, Hannah landed a roundhouse kick to his face, sending him flying at blistering speed into a bungalow with an orange cocktail-umbrella-style roof, which exploded on impact.

Slow to pick himself back up, Joseph chose instead to remain among the rubble, slamming his fists on the crumpled hut's remains and screaming into the night sky. "Meaningless," he said, finally rising flat bodied, like a vampire from its coffin. "You will have to do much better. If you can. After all, what is a Celestial without her wings?"

"Don't need those anymore," Hannah said. "Found out I never did."

"Then how will you catch us?" With a downward blast, Joseph's skeletal wings flung his massive frame into the air, headed directly toward the South Eb Gate.

No! We need more time! Izaiah fought to move once again, managing to lift his arms only a few inches before they drooped back to dangle at his sides.

"Yes, my love," Chloe said blissfully over his ear.

The wings thrashed forward and back, blasting Joseph into the distance like a plastic bag in a hurricane. From his vantage point, Izaiah guessed he had already spotted the rings and would be there in less than thirty seconds. That was, until flashes of blue and violet light like fireballs struck the monster dead-on and sent him spiraling. A thunderous boom followed a gust of Rapture on the ground, and Hannah's glowing frame was sent blasting into the sky like a rocket. When she missed her target by a few feet, she managed to reach out and snag Joseph's wing, pulling them both to the ground as if that same plastic bag were tied to a small but heavy rock. When they disappeared from Izaiah and Chloe's vision, there was a boom, then a puff of smoke and exploding dirt.

"What does she think she's doing?" Chloe sneered, lifting Izaiah higher, forming a Mallos sphere around them, just cloudy enough to see through. As she launched them toward the impact site, neither Joseph nor Hannah came into sight.

"Where are they?" Chloe called out desperately, landing near the small crater and dissipating the sphere.

You asking me? How am I supposed to know? Izaiah was just glad the ride was over.

They had landed in the middle of a neighborhood known as Ai's Peak. A predominantly Celestial part of town, it was built with precise, simple shapes and not a degree of variance in any corner. *Thank all goodness it's basically deserted. This fight's starting to look rather mayhem-heavy, and nothing makes Celestials clutch their pearls quite like the destruction of private property.*

Before Chloe could ask again, a blast shook the area dead ahead, where the powered-up Celestial general and Abyss behemoth appeared, locked in heated combat. When they crashed through a barrier on the outskirts of a wide courtyard, they split and took a moment to regain their composure before beginning again.

Hannah charged to meet Joseph in the middle of the courtyard as his voice boomed, sounding like concrete blocks smashing into one another. "We'll make you regret this. We swear it!"

Throwing her right arm bowling-style, Hannah released an energy sphere, catching one of Joseph's wings in a brilliant explosion of cobalt blue and violet, sending the beast tumbling head over heels fifty feet, stopped only when he slammed into a blocky lamppost with a clang. Picking himself up quickly this time, he wrapped his claws around the post and tore it from the ground, sending up a shower of sparks. Wielding it like a club, he careened forward, swinging for the fences, knocking away anything in his path. Tables, chairs, benches, and umbrellas were scattered to the wind. After some ducking and dodging, Hannah managed to rip the weapon from his grasp.

Swinging the five-yard pole as easily as a cardboard tube, she punished the monster for losing his weapon. Cracking it against his skull, she knocked Joseph left and right, unable ro conceal her smile while she did. *Always did love a good ass-kicking.* But the punishment of the beast came to an end when Joseph vomited a heap of black sludge. Enveloping the pole, it fed on the UnEarth metal, crawling toward Hannah's grip, making sick gnashing sounds and forcing her to hurl it away before the sludge could reach her.

Joseph laughed with scorn. "If you hold still, it won't hurt so bad. We promise!"

The monster followed Hannah into a courtyard inlet, where three food carts and rolling freezers sat, locked up indefinitely for the Trivium blackout. His wings were on the attack, unrelenting, but had become predictable. As Hannah backed into a corner, she swiftly snatched the left wing out of the air and stomped it under her boot, pinning it to the ground, then seized a nearby freezer in both hands. The metal crumpled in her fists as she heaved the silver cube high and slammed it down like a meteor, blasting thunderous shockwaves and chunks of metal, ice, and frozen food all over the courtyard.

When the proverbial dust had settled, the beast was gone, and Hannah was already on the lookout. *He's fast, that's for sure.* The sound of beating wings was lost among the misty, smoke-covered shadows on the outskirts, ever nearer and also ever farther. Izaiah tried to help Hannah find the menace but could sense no concrete evidence of Joseph, only flashes crisscrossing, as the creature's voice called from the darkness.

"You still don't remember us, do you?"

"Even if I did, I wouldn't tell you, because I don't care," Hannah said, her gaze focused and on the move.

Something then swooped into an alcove behind her with a *whoosh*, but from Izaiah's perspective, nothing was visible.

"We weren't always the nameless," Joseph's scaly voice continued, now echoing from the shadows at the far end of the courtyard. "Once, like all Archfiend, we had a title, a clan. We fought for them. Our enemies were fierce—until the day the nameless killed his commander on the battlefield, looking into your eyes as he did it."

Hannah barely flinched. "You're right. I do remember you. Hard to forget a deserter."

Joseph snickered. "That was the day the nameless chose a new path. He was simply . . . different. Not made for war or to serve like the rest. This one was destined to reach further."

"I assumed you were long dead," Hannah said. "Hard to believe the scrawny little lizard I saw on the field that day has come this far."

"You mock the Brothers' trust in us?" he shouted from all directions.

Hannah remained still, unfazed. "No. Just you."

The silence that followed chilled Izaiah even more than his wound. Only the soft whisper of wind and the rustle of leaves filled the air. Then, without warning, the attack came. He didn't see it until it was too late, unable to comprehend how a creature so massive could move with such agility. It was as if Joseph had been holding back all along, revealing a hidden reservoir of speed and power, making their previous skirmish seem like mere practice.

Hannah reacted, but not soon enough. Amid a flurry of black skeletal wings, Joseph's claws sank deep into her chest, forcing her to call out, gritting her teeth, glaring at him with antipathy. A mist of dark blood appeared on her lips and chin. "You cherry—picking—piece of—shit!"

"Accept it! Accept what we are! End it now! Die!" Joseph's cadaverous jaw flapped wildly, a maniacal gleam in his eyes as he pressed his claws deeper, forcing a scream from Hannah's lips and spraying her blood into the air.

"Do it, my love," Chloe urged, her voice dripping with dark delight over Izaiah's shoulder.

"No!" Izaiah found a flicker of strength to shout, fighting for freedom with everything he had. But Chloe easily quelled his resistance, forcing him to witness an impossible sight. In all his millennia, since the day he'd met her bright, curious Celestial face, he had never seen Hannah lose a fight—neither as a Hywyn general nor as a human. Her tenacity alone made the idea seem impossible. But this monster was unlike anything they had ever fought before: abominable, unstoppable.

And I'm all out of ideas.

The claws within her remained in place as Hannah's breaths grew shallower, more ragged. Rapture ebbed from her until her hands fell limp, and her chin dropped to her chest. The blue glow surrounding her waned.

Joseph cackled with glee. "Yes, go to sleep! Fade!"

No. Come on, you can do this. Find a way out. Do it, Hannah!

Amid Joseph's puerile taunts, a powerful boom resonated, like a heartbeat echoing over Trivium. The demon's laughter faltered as waves of Rapture flooded the area, each pulse building in intensity. A soft glow began to radiate from within Hannah.

"What is this?" Joseph shouted, panic creeping into his voice.

A great swell overcame the area, and with an audible pop, Hannah's eyes open, glowing with an otherworldly brilliance, nearly stark white. Her neck snapped straight, bringing her face-to-face with the beast. She stretched out her arms, palms upward, as a hum grew within her, the Eve inside her expanding, swirling with a potency that rivaled Joseph's, so blinding Izaiah couldn't be sure he was sensing it correctly. All he knew was he liked it.

"How?" the demon called with panic as the wounds in Hannah's chest radiated dazzling white and orchid-blue light. It was now he who was struggling for freedom, straining against her hold. "What is this?" His wings thrashed, trying to gain lift, generating typhoon winds, yet Hannah—and the talons within her—remained fast, firmly embedded.

With a voice from another world that was shimmering, resonant, biting, as though passing through halls of diamond before reaching her lips, she spoke. "This can't go on, Joseph. I won't let it. There are too many souls you've ignored, too many voices beyond your own. You don't know what they wish, and you don't get to make their choices. I'm ending this madness."

"Ours is the only choice *to* make! Only we can accomplish what others call impossible! Only we have the trust of the Brothers!" Joseph roared.

"Are you sure about that?" Hannah replied, her voice calm as ice, yet laced with a power that echoed through Izaiah's bones.

"You are a child! The Brothers are forever," Joseph spat, his voice dripping with contempt.

Hannah laughed once, a sharp, cutting sound. "You're the one trying to get rid of forever."

A sudden chill swept through the courtyard as a mass of blue and indigo Rapture churned around them, coalescing into a raging, donut-shaped whirlwind that obscured their forms. Time and space warped, a high-pitched sound ringing out like an iceberg shattering in the ocean. A flash of blinding light erupted, engulfing Trivium, as if a star were born in the courtyard, luminous enough to rival ten Shifts. Debris spiraled in slow motion, caught in the torrent of Hywyn's power.

Through the veil, Izaiah glimpsed a radiant figure contrasted against the dark silhouette of Joseph. As the storming energy dissipated, the Medolian's breath caught in his throat. Hannah remained clad in her dusty clothes and leather jacket, her dark hair billowing in an ephemeral wind. Yet, the rest of her had transformed into a warrior of radiant blue gemstone, her skin a blend of human and Celestial flesh, tough as steel, yet malleable as rubber. Shimmering like a luminous creature from the deep, her form radiated pure violet sparks—the most potent form of Rapture, akin to the blue core of an Earthly flame.

Poised beneath Joseph, surrounded by chaos, Hannah's stone face wore tranquility. Izaiah, wounded and breathless, was lost in wonder at how she had amassed enough Rapture to become something entirely new—a Human-Celestial hybrid unlike any ever seen. While purged citizens of Hywyn could regain their Celestial forms over months in the Changing Chambers, this was different. Her wings had not returned; she was not a colossus. The glow around her was as intense as if she had fully transformed, yet no such thing had occurred. From Izaiah's perspective, she radiated power surpassing even the oldest, strongest Celestials of the Magnus Council. *How is this possible? Not even Michael had this kind of juice.*

Joseph reeled back, shrieking, his claws singed from the transformation, staring in horror at his missing digits and what Hannah had become. "This is—what have you done? This can't be!"

"It's what you've done," Hannah's crystalline voice thundered. "You will lose, because creatures who think like you—the cowering, the craven—will always defeat themselves."

"*Craven?* You will be the one who dies today. Not us! We promise!" Joseph flexed and screamed, and his claws began to heal, but the demon didn't wait for them to finish. Roaring with determination, he launched himself at her. "The Brothers won't allow it!"

So it began, with a snarl. Hannah unleashed an uppercut that sent Joseph's head sprawling, the impact echoing like a mountain striking an island. Instinctively, his wings jammed into the ground, tearing through concrete to steady himself. With a roar, he charged back, an obsidian bull, launching Hannah into the sky. She plummeted toward Trivium like a ton of bricks, unable to regain control, and landed directly on top of him. The collision sent a shockwave of debris into the air, and Izaiah lost sight of both combatants amid the chaos.

When the dust settled, they reemerged, the fight erupting through a corner bistro, scattering glass, metal, and napkins in a whirlwind of destruction. The winged beast slashed at Hannah's face, the sound cracking like pickaxes striking basalt. Yet, with every hit, she seemed to gleam brighter and push harder. The bout had transformed into a boxing match, each fighter with their heads down, trading blows like titans. Izaiah felt as though he were watching from the nosebleed section, struggling to track their movements as they danced between pillars and structures, their speed nearly matching the sound of their impacts.

One who seemed particularly surprised was Chloe, still hovering close behind Izaiah, breathing down his neck. Always one to be prepared, she'd long had a knack for anticipating bumps in the road, but even she couldn't have predicted what Hannah had just done. Through the blade she'd skewered him with, Izaiah felt tiny quivers in Chloe's hands. Worried sounds were let slip every time the demon was knocked down. Her confidence was clearly fading, her belief in Joseph waning.

As the fight raged on—both combatants dazzling brighter than ever, their strikes landing with the force of a dozen semitrucks—

Hannah delivered a particularly vicious blow that knocked Joseph's head back nearly to the brink of severance, releasing a plume of black and green ichor. His head dangled precariously between his wings, suspended by a grotesque mess of tendons and cartilage. For a moment, it was unclear if he would collapse or recover, until laughter erupted from within his disfigured form—a low, mucus-ridden sound that grew louder, reverberating through his charcoal body.

The flesh remaining on his mutilated corpse quivered as if gripped by a seizure. With grotesque lethargy, Joseph's head seeped back into place with a chattering crunch. The laughter stopped abruptly as he swiveled his head, testing the fit, a twisted grin forming on his mangled lips.

"If the kid wasn't dead yet, he definitely is now!" Joseph erupted into laughter once more, his wings snapping out triumphantly as he exposed his chest. "Do you finally get it? Transform again. Do it a thousand times more—it won't matter. What flows inside us cannot be stopped. We are the hand of destiny."

Hannah stood her ground, seeming ready to continue, as still as a statue. Even with her stoic expression, Izaiah knew the look on her face. She wasn't tired or close to defeated, she was simply running out of ideas. Despite her dominance in the battle thus far, Joseph seemed inexhaustible, a nightmare that would not relent. *What are we going to do?*

When Hannah did not attack for several moments, Joseph scoffed. "Fine." With a powerful thrust, his wings jetted him skyward. "Don't worry, we're not leaving, yet. But when we get back . . . you better not be here."

Breaking away, he ascended, leaving behind a trail of red and black smoke. But Hannah did not give chase. Instead, she planted her feet and waited patiently. As Joseph became a mere dot against the looming Pilomines, he executed a sweeping maneuver, soaring into the upper reaches of Trivium's atmosphere before diving down like an onyx missile.

Izaiah felt Chloe react through the cutlass, a whisper of anguish escaping her lips: "No."

The sight of the creature swooping down to obliterate them was terrifying. But when Izaiah turned to Hannah, hoping to see her charging up a super attack that would make Joseph regret ever starting this, he was met with a gaze that chilled him to the bone. Her brilliant-blue irises had returned, and for some unfathomable reason, she was facing him. In that moment, he knew something was terribly wrong—the serene smile on her face was not one of triumph but of acceptance, as though ready to take a bow, knowing she'd given her all.

No—no, Hannah. Don't you think it!

Before Izaiah could react, she turned to face the oncoming attack, likely aware he would try to stop her.

"We're done holding back!" Joseph's voice boomed from the heavens, his body hurtling at breakneck speed. "This is it!"

"I know," Hannah whispered, so quietly only Izaiah could have heard it.

Clenching her fists, she knelt and sprang into the sky, propelled by a blast of Rapture—a mortar shell locked in a deadly game of chicken with Joseph. In the shadows below, across the courtyard, tucked between two structures, Izaiah caught sight of Felix and Bennett, their distant faces peering out with desperate hope mirroring his own.

KaBOOM! When Joseph and Hannah collided like satellites in orbit, a thunderous shockwave erupted, sent tearing across Trivium. The Celestial and the demon were locked together, fingers entwined, foreheads pressed against one another.

Two orbs of pure Eve erupted into existence, enveloping them in blinding light. One—blue and violet—shielded Hannah, while the other—black and red—encircled Joseph. Rapture and Abyss grappled for supremacy, neither willing to yield an inch. Both combatants roared, pouring every ounce of their power into the struggle. If not for their elevation, the force of their energies would have reduced the city to rubble.

Tables, chairs, and anything not bolted down in the courtyard was sent flying, crashing through windows and doors of nearby buildings. *Don't know how much more of this the city can take.*

Pumping his huge ears with Mallos, Izaiah strained to hear the combatants' words.

Joseph bellowed, "Once you are gone, there will be no one left to stop us. The Brothers will awaken! Everything will end!"

"No," Hannah said, her voice penetrating the chaos. "Life doesn't give up. Life doesn't give in." As she powered up like she never had before, her hands blazed with blue fire, searing Joseph's claws and pulling a primal scream from the brute. "There will always be life."

Joseph matched her intensity, the orbs surrounding them swelling to twice their original size. Deep red and blue lightning split the sky. Of all things to suddenly feel in that moment, Izaiah was not expecting relief to be one of them, when Chloe's cutlass blade was pulled from his gut, granting him the freedom to collapse to his knees.

"No! You can't!" Chloe screamed at the storm of Eve swirling above, suddenly dashing away on foot, her focus solely on the battle. Despite her frantic calls, Joseph was oblivious, locked in a desperate struggle against the newly ascended Hannah, who was taking everything he had—even more than the stones would allow.

"Stop this madness!" Chloe screamed into the blitz, using a Mallos shield to shield herself from the onslaught of power. "You'll destroy yourself—and the Brothers!"

Izaiah leaned heavily on his cane, clutching his gut, trying to staunch the bleeding. He could barely remain conscious enough to watch the action, let alone find a safe distance. Judging by the power building between Hannah and Joseph, he doubted such a thing existed anywhere nearby. With a final, earth-shattering scream, Hannah unleashed a voice so potent it drowned out Joseph entirely, a sound that felt as if it could pierce the very fabric of reality, reaching every corner of UnEarth.

The orbs expanded uncontrollably, soon overtaking everything in their path. For the briefest moment, they reached their zenith before the sphere of Rapture multiplied exponentially, releasing an overwhelming surge of energy.

Izaiah couldn't remember the explosion itself or the moments that followed. All that lingered in his mind was a scream—his friend's voice, giving her all just before everything seemed to invert. White became black, fast became slow, and up somehow down.

A moment later, when Izaiah felt reality calling, the first sensation that came back to him was the wind. A torrential storm swirled around him before subsiding, eventually settling into a gentle breeze. For a fleeting moment, he believed he was lying in the tall grass of one of his favorite lakes up north, near Yellowknife, Canada—a place only he knew. He imagined being asleep under a tall cedar, listening to the frogs and bugs buzzing, enveloped in that peaceful hour just before sunrise when the songbirds began to wake, the only sound a soft draft rustling through the thicket. He could almost hear fish jumping in the pond before everything shattered.

The lake erupted, water boiling, turning a fiery crimson.

Reality came crashing back.

Pain, there was a lot of it. He couldn't see. *Think I'm trapped under something.* Izaiah struggled to lift his cane and press forward, conserving the last of his Mallos for whatever lay ahead. When he finally broke the surface, he found himself surrounded by shadow and dust. The air was thick and putrid, making it hard to breathe, and he began to choke.

No sign of the skyward orbs or their energy remained, which was a monumental relief. Izaiah picked himself up, clutching the wound in his gut. It had already begun healing, but would need much more time to fully close. As he trudged through the devastation, ignoring the debris that clung to him, he passed through clouds of white smoke rising from the scorched earth.

At the center of the chaos, only ash remained, much of it drifting aimlessly through the air. Standing on the barren ground, he felt utterly alone, as if he were on an alien world without a friend in the universe. There was no trace of Bennett or Felix, though their Eves lingered nearby, as did Chloe's. They were out there somewhere. But Joseph was nowhere to be found. Nor was Hannah.

Relief washed over him at the absence of the fiend and his devilry, and the stones of Gehenna seemed to have gone dormant as well. But no matter where he looked, no matter how desperately he searched, he couldn't feel a trace of his friend.

Her light had gone out.

GEHENNA

Controlling the Wrath was getting harder, especially since the attack on the university when Alex had attempted to fend off Joseph. *And failed admirably.* Though the power had proven useful in many situations, the Hellfire within him was anything but welcome. *I'm beginning to understand why Felix had been so reluctant to use it.* Each time Alex allowed Arros in, he could feel his mind shifting, a far scarier transformation than any monster he'd faced in this nightmare. To prevent losing himself further, he decided the Wrath was to be reserved for emergencies only.

Yet as he charged behind Galinthia and Fabian through the dark, surreal city, he was forced to set that apprehension aside, using the power just to keep pace. *Guess everything we do from here on out is an emergency.* Thankfully, the Medolians were kind enough not to abandon him as Mara had; still, they pushed ahead, pulling him along. Despite the added strain, Alex felt a flicker of confidence that he was on top of the Wrath. *Might even be getting the hang of it. Who knows?*

The journey to Trivium City had been chaotic. During the battle with the Archfiend in the Montana forest—*terrifying, FYI*—suddenly, all the UnEarth creatures—demons and Medolians alike—halted mid-fight. In unison, they gazed at the ground, causing Alex to falter in confusion as he wrestled with a large fiend. It was as if an invisible force had compelled them to stop, leaving him baffled. When he followed their gaze, he half-expected something monstrous to erupt from the earth, devouring everyone in its path. Instead, as he would later learn, they were staring at the Earth's core, where Trivium resided, perceived on a higher frequency.

At least, I think that's what he said. Fabian had explained it briefly upon their arrival on the small planet, though Alex didn't absorb much, nodding along anyhow, still grappling with the sheer madness of the overall situation.

Once the fight in the woods ended, many demons fled. Mara then set to work dismantling the few remaining threats. Once the area was clear, she Shifted away without a word, her expression resembling torment. Alex had anticipated a grim comment from Galinthia or a weary remark from Fabian, but surprisingly, neither spoke, which only deepened his unease. Whatever had triggered their UnEarth senses was deadly serious.

Before departing the wintry scene, he caught sight of Casey huddled on the porch of the cabin with Leigh. Leaving them behind felt wrong, yet humans couldn't survive in the higher-frequency realm, or so Izaiah had said. The chances of Alex and Bennett surviving were only slightly better due to the Eve inside them. *That's only a small comfort.*

Much of him longed to stay behind with Casey. *I just feel a little safer around her. Can't explain why.* And after all, what did he *really* have to do with any of this? He didn't belong in a higher plane, fighting a holy war. He didn't even belong in Montana. Yet, without a chance to catch his breath, it was off to the races. Galinthia took Alex by the shoulder and Shifted them away. He and the Medolians landed, alive, if uneasy.

The chase was on.

Presently, they hustled past dead UnEarth shops and restaurants, as fast as Alex could muster. He sensed a resonance lingering in the air, as if a planet-sized bell had been rung, sending waves rolling over the desolation. The smell reminded him of a campfire made from rotten, damp wood, while a thin layer of white ash began to blanket the ground. Galinthia's and Fabian's footprints were stark against the sheets of ash, resembling dry sleet. Alex couldn't help walking in their strides as a sobering sensation approached: unyielding, suffocating, ancient, reminiscent of the feeling of being in the Still Room in La Rose Noire. The air was soaked with it. *I can feel . . . yeah. Rigid and suffocating. Gotta be Rapture.*

Turning a corner, the teacher found himself at the edge of a vast, open expanse—half a mile square of destruction that resembled videos he'd seen online of places ravaged by tsunamis or hurricanes. Few foundations and even fewer buildings remained near the central blast zone, where layers of soot and haze thickened and darkened until they met an elongated shape, a black cloud stretching parallel to the horizon. As they approached, the silhouette revealed itself as a crater, hundreds of yards across and no more than eighty or ninety feet deep.

Galinthia and Fabian hardly acknowledged the hole in the ground, charging off to the right along its rim.

"Barker! Come along!" Galinthia shouted.

Can't we stop for a second? "Coming!" he called.

The desolate scene was eerily quiet, and Alex's paranoia grew as he chased after the Medolians. Raised voices soon broke the silence.

"Where were you?" someone shouted, and Alex zeroed in on a group of gathered figures.

Galinthia and Fabian had joined Izaiah, Mara, and Bennett near a massive block of stone, likely once the cornerstone of a grand UnEarth structure, now reduced to a twelve-foot square. All heads were bowed, faces etched with sorrow. Surprisingly, Felix was off to the side, kneeling near the crater's rim, molten steam rising from his exposed skin. *Look who decided to turn on their Wrath . . . Then again, maybe he didn't.*

The only person Alex couldn't find was Hannah, and judging by the hole in the ground, and the fact that there were no signs of Joseph, he only had one guess as to what may have happened to the both of them. *Guess they took each other out. It's no wonder the others were so spooked—they were feeling the final moment.*

No one acknowledged his arrival, which was fine. Alex wasn't eager to join the heated discussion he'd walked into. Bennett, however, was unmistakably vocal, stunning everyone present when he seized Izaiah by the collar.

"Bring her back!"

"I can't," Izaiah replied, a rag doll in Bennett's hands.

"You can't, or won't?" Bennett demanded.

Izaiah's once vibrant gray eyes drooped, barely open, struggling for awareness. "Look at me. I'm barely here. Lying is pointless."

"What don't you get?" Felix asked from his perch. "Leave it alone. You saw it yourself."

Izaiah's once vibrant gray eyes drooped, barely open, struggling for awareness. "Look at me. I'm barely here. Lying is pointless."

"What don't you get?" Felix interjected from his perch. "Leave it alone. You saw it yourself."

"I didn't see anything! One second, they were there, the next they weren't. Can someone just—" Bennett shook his head, frustration evident. "With all the crazy shit you people can do, there's nothing . . . I brought Al back after he took a fence post to the chest, and I've only had this for a few days. I've seen Celestials do some—"

Felix roared back, "Do you see any Celestials here? Huh? Do you see a body to heal? There's nothing but dust, man. She got what she always wanted,—a big finale."

Alex didn't like seeing Felix like this. *An Archfiend, sure, but he's helped me a lot.* Whether Felix knew it or not, Alex—who had never had so much as a soccer coach before he came along—saw him as a mentor, and it wasn't fun to see a guy he admired losing control. Though there was no denying how much Hannah had meant to him.

As somber as the moment was, Alex couldn't quite pin down his feelings. Hannah had never trusted him—that was obvious—and he had never understood why. *I just assumed it was because I smelled like an Archfiend.* Uneasy in her presence from the start, he felt her high-beam stare lingering on him whenever he turned around. Still, he knew she had saved their lives on several occasions, and the thought of moving forward without her felt daunting, if not impossible, especially with more surprises potentially lurking ahead. Deep down, however, he felt a flicker of relief at the idea of Joseph being gone for good. *That means we're done. I get to go home, right? We did it. We did it!* He wanted to ask someone, just to double check, but it seemed inappropriate at the moment.

"Tell me what happened, then," Bennett said, his voice steadier yet tinged with anguish.

"That's something I would also like to know," Mara said, her arms folded tight, as though trying to bottle her own volatile rage.

"Make it quick. Emergency and disaster teams will already be on their way."

Izaiah spoke simply, "Joseph did it. Collected the Brothers. Then . . . well, Hannah happened. It's over."

"That can't be it. It can't. She wouldn't," Mara retorted, her tone rigid. "It's giving up. If you really knew her, you'd know that—"

"I know," Izaiah interrupted with a groan, struggling to sit on a hunk of concrete. "And yet, you know she would. She had to, and in doing so, became something we'll likely never see again. I couldn't even—" He sighed, staring into the distance. "It was . . . beautiful, if you can imagine."

"I can," Mara snapped. "I imagine you watched the whole thing, and did nothing."

The tension escalated between Izaiah, Mara, and Bennett for another minute, angry but not necessarily at each other, while Alex hung back, relieved the vitriol wasn't directed at him for once. Looking around the circle, he noted the sunk-in, fatigued faces. The others had never looked so unsettled. Outwardly, Fabian seemed the worst off, brought to his knees, tears streaming down his face.

"So many eateries, reduced to nothing!"

Galinthia surveyed the murky scene, giving her partner a comforting back rub. "Screw this idling and wallowing. What's the next move? That's a massive hole, and this mess isn't going to explain itself. Personally, I'm not looking forward to the inquiries. Containment alone . . ."

Mara took charge, her voice firm. "I say we immediately gather the leaders of UnEarth and report this. The Warden Sentry has the authority to call an emergency session. We can send a priority memo, and—"

"A session? To decide what, exactly?" Izaiah asked.

"Repercussions. Finding out who is responsible for this. Deciding the humans' fates," Mara replied, her face taut, lips pressed together. For the first time since Alex had known her, her eyes jittered uneasily.

"I know my fate. I'm going home," the teacher said. "We had a deal."

Izaiah gave a warm smile in return. "Darn right, Al. Glad you could make it, by the way."

Not exactly an answer. But it offered the teacher a little hope. He found Mara shooting him a hard glance, piling on a cold shoulder, though by now he didn't care. *Call me whatever you want! Give me all the mean looks. It doesn't matter anymore! I'm done. I'm out.* His mantra was finally coming true. *Just stay calm, and everything will be fine.*

"This is ridiculous. We know who's responsible," Felix said, rising to join the others. His body shimmered with heat, the smell of singed cotton clinging to him. "Neither of them is around to stand trial."

"You know what I mean," Mara replied. "This will turn into paperwork. Lots of it. Paperwork wants names, and living names are preferred to dead ones. If we're not careful, this could get ugly fast."

It's not ugly now?

Izaiah rubbed his beard, nodding but distracted. "Hmm. Yes, fine. We'll do it your way. But first . . ." He turned to face the crater. "We have to collect the stones."

The group stood still, exchanging confused glances. Bennett was the first to speak. "You're joking, right? They were in Joseph's pocket. No way they survived the blast."

Izaiah grunted with each step. "*Hng* . . . And yet, they did. *Hrn.*

Now please, don't bother offering the grunting old man in pain any help down the slope. No, he's fine. *Hng!*"

The group ignored Izaiah's moans but followed anyway, walking in silence, seemingly out of respect for the dead. It was a rare moment for Alex to catch his breath. For a brief while, there was no Eve, no fire, no UnEarth—just a stroll with ordinary people through a bleak apocalypse.

As they approached the center of the crater, the white and gray ash underfoot turned jet-black.

"That's far enough," Izaiah said, halting three yards from a lumpy, dark mound. The others stayed back as he moved forward. After a swift swipe of his emerald-topped cane, the ash was cast aside, revealing glistening black stones: dormant and quiet, just the way Alex liked them. Twice, Izaiah's hand hovered above them before retracting.

"What are you waiting for?" Galinthia asked.

"Looks like they're back asleep. Should be safe to handle," Fabian added.

"No better place for them than with you, boss," Galinthia said.

Izaiah crossed his arms, studying the stones as if they were modern art. "You know, I'm becoming convinced these are more than just rocks with some juice in them."

Galinthia gave a sarcastic cough. "No shit. What other rocks contain a shade of Eve more volatile than Wrath? Now, let's get the universe nukes out of public view before a crowd gathers, eh?"

"More than all that. It's as though they . . ." Izaiah was staring, entranced, cringing, possibly betrayed by his thoughts. "No. We need to find a way to destroy these without unleashing their Abyss into the cosmos. That may take time."

"If what you said about Hannah's attack is true, and the stones are still unharmed, then what could we possibly do to destroy them?"

Mara pressed, taking a half step forward. "You said we're doing it my way, so the stones will be taken to Speaker Binahq. They're *the* evidence against Joseph."

"I think the particulars can wait, Mara," Izaiah said. "Joseph's dead."

"I know he's dead!" she boomed back.

As the conversation escalated, Alex found his gaze drifting back to the pile of black ash. *A different texture than the rest. And I feel something from it. It's hard to place. Hmm.* Resting in the ash, the smallest stone, the one Joseph called Mellu, caught his attention, holding his gaze with an allure he couldn't understand. *It's the one I stole. The one I touched.* As his vision tightened around the stone, the world around him faded into a fog, and he allowed himself to drift away from the chaos, calling it a moment of rest.

Suddenly, he jolted awake. There was screaming, but he knew it was only in his head. Thoughts swelled as voices clamored for attention. He swore there were at least three or four, radiating from the pile, yet none of the others in the team reacted. *Just me? Great.* The sounds were raspy, furious, their presence overwhelming. He couldn't decipher their words; only their murderous intent was clear, echoing the horrors he'd sensed before the bull insignia appeared on his chest, now even more malignant. Then, as abruptly as they'd started, the voices stopped.

But they're not gone. I can still feel them . . .

The conversation around Alex had stopped as well. Bennett, Mara, and Izaiah stood frozen, all eyes fixed on a shadowy figure emerging from the haze. A crunching, dragging sound broke the stillness as the figure approached, one arm hanging low, dragging a long blade that scraped against the ground, spitting sparks. Chloe limped close enough to make out, appearing soaked from head to toe, her body battered and bruised, gritting her teeth against the pain, her lip swollen and bloodied.

No one moved at first, except Mara, who took a few frustrated steps forward, then seemed to catch herself. "You got some nerve. I ought to fade you right now."

"What's stopping you!?" Chloe barked back.

"I'm in a mood. You better be coming to apologize or turn yourself in," Mara said, gripping her staff.

Chloe halted a few feet out. Her bright gray eyes drifted over the lineup blocking her path. Sneering, she spit at their feet. "Move."

Mara spun her staff and planted it in the ground. "Are you blind? It's over. Joseph and Hannah are gone. I know you feel it."

"Nothing is over. Not yet." Chloe's eyes settled on Alex, sending an old-fashioned chill down his spine.

Izaiah joined Mara by her side. "The Senate will put everything Joseph did on your shoulders, little one. Let us try to make a case in your favor. Help us to help you."

Chloe let out a small laugh, laying out her contempt, brandishing her cutlass. "Let me be clear. I'm taking the Brothers to Gehenna, and I'm ending this nightmare called life. Anyone who gets in my way will be dealt with. I already took down the old man once. I can do it again."

"You can't get past all of us," Mara snapped. "Leave. Flee. We'll catch you later on. Or, come quietly now. Save everyone the trouble. Maybe you'll only spend the rest of your life in a Dread Sling."

"There are none among you I fear. Not even you, dear teacher," Chloe said, her smirk wicked. "I'm much too fast, remember?"

"That wasn't true even before you lost half your Mallos. What happened, get a little too close to the blast?" Mara asked. "Trying to persuade your boyfriend not to blow himself up?"

"Actually, it was Hannah who was the fool. My love simply

chose not to run away. And now look. Look at the pain the general caused. How many in Trivium suffer now because of her? There was only one monster here today." Chloe lifted her blade just under Mara's chin. "Once more, move aside."

"Take your best shot, darling." Mara remained as still as a grave, leaving her staff planted.

Alex fully expected another fight to break out and raised his fists, ready to spark up, until a low tone approached that wasn't so much heard as felt—reminding him of the subwoofer in his neighbor's souped up Pinto across the street. All present took notice as a high-pitched whine joined the vibration, like a kettle of battery acid boiling over. Alex spun back to the pile of ash. *No. No, no. I know that feeling. It's the stones. They're still alive!* The magenta swirls in the Gehenna stones spun like ribbons in a blender, shaking free of the soot. A fourth item was also revealed: a shiny, round object Alex recognized—*Hannah's belt buckle!*

"Look," Fabian said, his voice jittery with terror as he pointed a wilted finger at the circle of ash surrounding the mound.

The jet-black refuse swirled and condensed into a cloud of darkness in the air above them, lifting the stones one at a time. As though controlled by a form of intelligence, the mass swooped over Chloe, who remained still and unwavering. Like a swarm of black wasps, the writhing shape dropped onto the Medolian.

"Chloe!" Mara called. "Stop this!"

"It isn't me!" Chloe screamed, unseen within the mass. The obsidian cloud collected and seeped into her pores as she began to cackle, her arms splaying out. The sounds of pain she initially released transitioned into shouts of pride. "Yes. I see now! I'm here. I'm not afraid!"

The Gehenna stones glowed white-hot, traversing her body, chattering like windup teeth as Chloe lifted into the air, surrounded by a storm of Dread and Abyss. The dark cyclone raged beneath her, jerking and contorting like sparks flying off a Tesla coil, wrenching her body in unison. With a gasp, she opened her eyes wide, then emitted a scream that began as her own but became something much worse along the way. A rattling mixture of voices had taken over. Shadows of heat exuded from her breath, as though a furnace burned deep within her.

"Yes . . . That's it," the voice said.

Egk. Disgusting. The sound coming out of Chloe reminded Alex of the alligators he saw on the side of the road in Florida during fishing trips with his grandpa: all angry hiss and gravel.

"Let it begin," the voice added.

With a shout from Chloe, the ash that had seeped into her broke free of her skin, covering three-quarters of her body in swirling blackness. Long dark blades extended from the rear of her elbows, locking into their final shape with a shrill crack as black gauntlets crystallized around her wrists and hands. The ash armor hardened until it appeared to Alex like steaming volcanic rock, coarse and sharp everywhere except where the Gehenna stones rested. Mellu, faced forward and half-exposed, was centered on her chest, while Raide and Eilam nestled within each shoulder's armor. The final touch of Chloe's transformation was a thin horn that forced its way from her skull, extending from her right temple, drawing back, its base growing to engulf her head.

Chloe (*if that's what this thing still is*) hovered above the others, her gaze turned down as she settled into her new body. Streaks of Eve surged through the cracks in her volcanic armor and skin like white-hot lava. "Ah, Mallos. The purest known." Her hands grazed over her armor. "We find it so . . . balanced."

Izaiah took a few unnerved, cautious steps forward. "Chloe, don't give in! Don't use their power! Don't take what they're offering you! You're better than this, kid."

A midnight-black finger of abrasive stone waved at him. "Whatever do you mean, Izaiah? Use your eyes. Don't you recognize"—her voice crawled further down the scale—"*your darling Chloe?*"

Izaiah shouted, his voice cracking with weakness. "You give her back!"

"Why is it so hard to accept what we are?" Chloe asked. "Is it because the creature before you sends a chill down your spine? Is it because what you feel makes you lose all hope? Did your lack of faith in her betray you, just as she always knew it would? We, however, chose to listen to the child. Chloe has taught us. We see now the strength in what you call balance. The vessel will be shared. We are the Wraith Chloe. We are hope restored."

She played with her sword as though handling it for the first time, and laughed at the Trivium sky. "She is the champion we long desired. That which you cast aside."

"Demon, if this is another one of your games—" Mara bellowed.

"Afraid not. The nameless is not, and never will be again, having gotten exactly what his greed deserved," Chloe said. "The Celestial general's final attack would have faded any UnEarth creature in its wake. The nameless failed to see what was obvious truth and was therefore released. Now, we are forced to finish what he could not. The great silence must come."

"Let me get this straight—am I speaking with Chloe right now or the so-called Brothers of Gehenna?" Izaiah asked. "'Cause if it's the second one, I have a lot more questions. Like a *lot*."

"Names mean nothing to those who are many," Chloe said. "We live, until all do not. When one body of the congregation is destroyed, the movement will continue."

Black ooze crawled over her possessed hand and slid onto

Chloe's cutlass, traveling up the blade. Once fully engulfed, it ignited, a black fire stinging Alex's retinas, as if he were staring at a torrid film negative.

Chloe swung the blade, testing it, and opened a slice in the ground: a clean line of atoms whisked from existence.

"Fascinating," she said, lost in her own little world.

"Chloe, listen up," Izaiah said. "The Brothers are tricking you. Don't let them take over. We need to get whatever this stuff is off you."

"You're joking right?" she said, lifting a rock-encrusted eyebrow.

Mara stepped closer. "Even with this new strength, you can't kill us all, and you know it."

"We don't need to kill you. We just need you out of the way."

Chloe raised her sword and brought it down, generating a dark, brutal Medolian sphere. The energy was laced with Abyss, creating a web of black tendrils powerful enough to toss everyone away and send a surge of pain through Alex's nervous system. He landed in a heap of debris and rolled over crumbled rock before stopping, feeling the effects of the dark sphere and hating being alive to experience it. There was no way he would be on his feet anytime soon. Neither would the others. Even Mara, who was closest to the attack, was down for a few counts.

Meanwhile, with a laugh and a wave aimed directly at Alex, Chloe whispered, "Until next time," before disappearing in a Shift of the same mind-numbing, negative-film quality.

"No!" Mara screamed, the first back on her feet, rousing the party. "Move! Move! We have to head her off! This is go time!"

What followed was a mad scramble. The Medolians each took a passenger. Alex was nabbed by Izaiah and transported via a giant bubble back to the Trivium City entry port, where they'd originally arrived. Stepping up to the huge golden rings, Izaiah took him by the shoulders, stared intensely into his eyes, and said, "Think of Gehenna. Think of the desert. The cave. Think of it now!"

Next thing Alex knew, he stepped through the ring and was back in a place he'd hoped to never see again. A tall canyon face loomed ahead, while an open valley of rolling hills stretched into the distance on the left. To his right was the cave entrance that led to the stairs and the temple where he'd saved Casey. A few yards away, Bennett, Galinthia, and Fabian were running to catch up. Close by, on the other side of the tunnel, Felix and Mara landed. Much of the dig site's equipment remained standing outside the cave, and many tall work lamps were still operating. From over the hill opposite the canyon came the peaceful hum of a generator. *Guess the Wraithians make a few exceptions for modern comforts.*

As rushed as the team's exit from Trivium had been, the area was strangely calm, even with the hundred or so Wraithian birds circling them in the sky, scared into flight upon their arrival.

"No sign of Chloe," Mara said, her head twisting in confusion.

Charging down the tunnel, Felix shouted, "Come on! She must already be inside!"

The others followed, with Mara quickly taking the lead to clear the way. Even from the rear, Alex could see firsthand just how good she was at killing Wraithians. So good, in fact, that none they encountered made a peep before, during, or after their deaths. Jumping over at least three rolling heads along the way, he and the team soon reached the Dead Stairs room, finding it oddly placid and empty. Through the doorway at the top of the eleven steps, there was a rousing call and the raving, chanted replies of hundreds of incensed desert riders. Alex stuck close to the group as Izaiah led them up the stairs. *Okay, stay calm. Just angry enough. Stay calm. Just angry enough . . . I got this.*

The first thing he spotted after stepping out of the entry tunnel was the giant statue of the winged beast with the huge mouth and fat legs on the plateau at the far end. *Still freaks me out.* The hundreds of Wraithians inside were facing away, toward the high pulpit, where yet another sacrificial, pain-inducing ceremony was taking place.

Somehow, no one—not even the Wraithian's pet birds—had noticed the newcomers enter. Izaiah, finding something funny about the situation, chuckled and nudged Bennett with his elbow. He then tucked his fingers in his mouth and whistled so loudly that Alex and about eighty nearby Wraithians flinched, sending most of the birds in the room into the air. A sea of white-tattooed faces turned toward them, many still holding their black stones high in their palms. The woman in white leading the ceremony atop the plateau paused her sermon, looking rightly confused.

Surprisingly, no one said anything for a few seconds.

"So, this is the place?" Izaiah asked eventually. "Thought it might be bigger." He then jammed his cane into the ground and spoke in an absurdly loud voice, echoing around the cave. "Hi-ya. Leave."

One of the Wraithians on the side, a large male with dark, dirt-matted hair, roared and leaped at Izaiah, screaming his head off. Without flinching, Izaiah tapped his cane once, and the Wraithian's head literally popped off when he exploded into a thousand bits and covered all his nearby brethren in him. The Wraithians stared with wide, shocked eyes. Not even they had ever seen something so violent.

"Please," Izaiah said, his normal voice returned.

After sharing some mystified glances, the Wraithians did as requested. Alex and the others stepped aside as the crowd piled through the temple's exit as fast as possible, giving them their fair share of glares on the way out. The majority of the Wraithian hawks and falcons followed suit, also glaring, and within a few minutes the room was cleared.

"I love how disgusting you can be sometimes, boss," Galinthia said.

"Should have killed them all," Mara added.

"Oh, that's your solution to everything," Izaiah said. "Now, obviously we beat Chloe here, which begs the question—if she's not here, where is she? What is she up to? Or do I wanna know . . . Wait, of course I do! I'd love to know—that way it wouldn't be a surprise."

"That thing we saw wasn't Chloe," Fabian said, his brow drooping heavily.

"No, but the bond between her and the Brothers does seem to be healthier than it was with Joseph," Izaiah said. "Either way, they took one of our own, and I won't stand for it."

To help plan a defense, Alex, Bennett, and Felix told the others what they knew of the tunnel system and the structure of the caves. Unanimously, they agreed that any defense should be centered at the entrance to avoid getting lost or risking losing Chloe in the tunnels. "Only one way in and out. We can't Shift directly into the temple, so I'm guessing she can't either," Izaiah said.

The team exited the temple and hiked back to the surface, always tense and ready, not knowing what might arrive at any moment. Stepping out of the entrance, they witnessed the last of the Wraithian horde disappearing into the canyon mouth, headed back toward the camp. Things then grew somewhat peaceful as a light breeze flowed over the valley.

Halting with a sigh, Izaiah cleared his throat. "This is where we'll make our stand."

Galinthia made sure all her knives were in their proper sheaths, ready for throwing. "Can the people who have seen this stuff in action tell us what to expect? I couldn't get a read on how powerful Chloe's become."

"Abyss is hard to pin down or define," Izaiah said. "It seems to be always changing and evolving, but we saw what the sword did. The Brothers are pure emptiness. If they release their full essence, matter will expire. With Chloe's strength added to their own, I can't even imagine how powerful they've become. Sorry, I shouldn't say things like that. I meant—yay, we're going to win."

Mara was busy keeping watch over the desert. "She should be put down as soon as possible. No talking. No distractions. Go high. Not even this new Wraith Chloe, whatever she is, could survive without a head. Could she?"

"Perhaps. Perhaps there are other ways to go about this as well?" Izaiah suggested.

"We can't take that chance or get bogged down worrying about her. Chloe made her choices," Mara said. "This is about everything and everyone, remember?"

"Last time I checked, that includes Chloe," Izaiah said.

Mara closed her eyes and lowered her head. "I don't care, Izaiah. I just . . . want this done. I want to go home."

There was a moment of uneasy quiet, and Alex noticed everyone present was looking in different directions, lost in contemplation. He then found himself staring at the sky, wondering where the stars had gone. Izaiah's lips clicked a couple of times, as though wanting to speak, before he started, "You know, when I was watch-ing Hannah fight—"

"Please don't," Mara interrupted softly.

"I had almost forgotten how to hold on, how to believe," Izaiah continued. "She would have been ashamed of me. Then I saw her take it as far as it needed to go. She didn't wait, didn't hesitate—just did what needed to be done."

"It was a waste," Felix said, breaking the moment. "She didn't stop anything. All she did was trade Joseph for something even worse and left us to deal with it."

"You ungrateful Imp. The Earth would already be gone if not for her," Mara said.

Felix snarled, revealing a long set of fangs. "So what? Nothing we've thrown at this thing works. If Chloe and the Brothers are taking their time getting here, it means they're cooking up something new, which frankly scares the shit out of me, because I don't want to end up like Hannah." He stepped away, out of the light of the lamps. No one moved to stop him.

"I'll never think of her as faded," Izaiah went on, as if nothing had happened. "She can't add to her story, no, but that doesn't mean we can't add to ours in her honor. She was the best I ever knew. We have to learn from her example."

Alex had a few things he wanted to say, and imagined the others did too, but they remained quiet. It wasn't long until Mara looked up into the sky. "Something's coming."

Is this it?

There was a whooshing sound in the distance, which cut off sharply. Footsteps and a silhouette approached. Small red eyes dotted the face. A sword swung by their side, glistening with a fire of shadow and inverted light. Twisting cracks in their armor glowed with molten fire. Wraith Chloe stepped into the light, a vile grin stretched across her face. "Waiting for us?"

"Took you a minute," Mara said. "Stalling?"

"No. Merely ensuring things go our way. The mistakes of the demon will not be repeated."

"For the last time, take your shot or hand over the stones," Mara said firmly. "This ends now."

Wraith Chloe remained in place, grinning, then turned to Alex and Bennett, who were waiting on the side like second-string backups. "The humans. Amazing they've made it this far. We find it shocking the two of you would fight for the likes of Izaiah and the Medolians, considering what they did. What they continue to do. After all, you might still be alive with your loved ones if they hadn't interfered. Or had, perhaps, bothered to save you. Especially you, Alex. Poor, poor Alex."

Alex preemptively hated himself for asking, "What do you mean?"

Bennett grabbed him by the arm. "Don't play along."

"You're not curious to know the truth, Mr. Hunter?" she asked. "You've never wondered what happened that night? Izaiah told you it was random chance, yes? Or has he skirted the subject, hoping you wouldn't ask too many questions?"

"Don't listen, fellas," Izaiah pleaded. "The Brothers are master manipulators."

But Chloe continued. "Mellu found Alex, and Alex found him. It's why he stole the stone. He was eager to take the power the Brother offered. It's why he kept it secret for so long. It felt too good to let go. Meanwhile, Mellu took something in return."

"Is that true?" Bennett asked, looking at Alex, who wasn't sure of the answer. He didn't deny it; he simply stammered, trying to process everything being said. *The rock . . . took something from me?*

"The Brothers are trying to confuse you. Don't listen!" Izaiah insisted.

Wraith Chloe laughed. "Ha! Your choosing wasn't random at all. You were designed to be used as pets. Gophers for the Senate! Izaiah engineered your deaths because they needed you in order to maintain their precious treaty."

"You're lying," Bennett said, now also playing along. "That doesn't make sense. Why us?"

"Ask him," Chloe answered quickly.

Alex looked at Izaiah. Though the old man was shaking his head, his wrinkled face and gray eyes could tell no lie. At least some of what she was saying was true.

"No, it wasn't like that," Izaiah said. "Please. Alex, Bennett, we can't do this now."

No. This can't be the way things are. This can't be why my life is like this. This can't be why I went to Hell. The Wrath was taking hold. Wrestling it down felt like trying to regain control of a spinning car.

Chloe pointed her sword at Izaiah. "We'll explain if he won't. Izaiah used the Seeress to see the boy's past. She showed him the life of the first vessel, Mason. The only problem was, he was not like the others. There were no loved ones to have and to hold. Mason would not have them, nor would they have him. Parents—dead. Younger sister—missing still to this day. In the whole of the boy's short, miserable life, there was no one Izaiah could use to help him. You see, he knew the nameless's bond with the boy was far too permanent. Almost no way to remove the demon. Izaiah had one shot, and he found you two to take it. Two humans, destined to die on the same night. Two who knew the boy."

Alex was already feeling faint. His head was spinning. *Calm down, everything will be fine. Calm down—calm down!*

"This isn't going to work. I never knew that fucking kid," Bennett shouted, his aura of blue flickering.

"You don't remember the recruitment table? In between deployments?" Chloe asked. "You volunteered at the local mall, tasked with finding patriotic teens to manipulate into service for their country. So many faces, so many people to convince of your superiority. We can see it all. Mason's memories are here with us. The boy looked up to you, Mr. Hunter—the proud soldier at the mall, the one man he could see himself being. You spoke with him about weapons, and war, and putting others to death. He loved to hear your tales of Iraq and Afghanistan, of liberation. To hear of the cities and lives you destroyed. He loved to laugh with you, the only one he could laugh with. The only one with a sense of humor as sick as his, as well as a keen love of knights and maidens. Then one day, you—just like all the rest in his life—were gone."

Chloe snickered for a moment, letting Bennett simmer with it. "Ringing a bell? Shy boy? Mad at life? Rather large?"

Alex watched the realization wash across Bennett's face. The soldier knew exactly who Chloe was speaking of, which could only mean—*I knew Mason, too.*

But how?

"Izaiah thought you two would be able to appeal to the human side of Joseph and get Mason to fight back, to free himself," Chloe said. "It's a common practice in exorcisms. The living Eve within the host is usually the best weapon. People close to the afflicted can elicit powerful emotional responses to fight the infection. However, even if you had managed to find the nameless in time, it would not have done you any good. You see, this boy could not be reasoned with. Even the demon was sometimes shocked by the depths to which his thoughts sank. There was no soul there to save."

Alex felt the world closing in on him, tightening. He looked the possessed Medolian in the eye. "How—how did I know the boy?"

"How indeed," Chloe started. "There were many children in your neighborhood, weren't there? Kids would come and go over the years. Grandma and Grandpa always told you to be nice, didn't they? But do you remember a particularly quiet child? A particularly troubled home? Think, Mr. Barker."

Alex remembered the house on the corner of his cul-de-sac,

where the boy a few years younger than him had lived until his family had to move away due to some "problems." *Grandpa never explained exactly what happened, and always changed the subject whenever I brought it up.* Now, Alex's whole life seemed to loop in his mind, a nauseating circle with one frayed end tied directly to the other. Images flickered through his thoughts—games of kickball, tennis, and water balloons. He saw himself and the other kids playing in the street on hot summer days, but his gaze drifted down the block to a little boy sitting on the curb, hands resting between his legs, staring at a bug on the ground.

The bug was dead. They were always dead.

Alex remembered speaking to the boy, who never said much in return, meaning he had to do all the talking himself. He recalled telling the boy secrets—things like the crushes he had on neighborhood girls, assuming the boy was too shy to ever tell anyone about it.

"I remember him," Alex said with a shudder. "The boy. Mason. I can see him."

Chloe smiled, revealing stained black teeth. "Good."

"Are you kidding me?" Galinthia shouted. "Psychological warfare, really? What are you, five dimes old?" She addressed the team loudly enough for Chloe to hear. "Let's just kill her and be done with it. Look at the math. We're in the green."

"Perhaps not so green as you think." Chloe raised her sword high. A flare of negative, inverted light shot into the sky, sending a terrible sensation plummeting into Alex's stomach. The distant sound of several steam engines cut through the air as a cloud of smoke billowed up. Shapes floated within it—long, skinny forms with bursts of steam and glowing orange mouths snapping open and closed.

Again? We just got done dealing with these guys. The approaching creatures looked exactly like Archfiend, but oddly, Alex could find no glowing eyes among them.

The demons swarmed the area, packing behind Chloe in a militaristic formation, baring their teeth and talons, ready to feed. Yet, at the same time, they appeared lifeless and dull, drooling acidic saliva onto the ground. Their once-luminous eyes were now jet-black and desolate, resembling the gaze of a great white shark. These Archfiend were silent, offering no shouts or attempts at leadership. The mass made no sharp movements, swaying gently in loose harmony, breathing together in staccato rhythm.

When Chloe playfully struck one, they remained compliant, continuing to sway. "Beautiful, aren't they? We've forged a new bond with the Aili clan. They now see the beauty of the Brothers and the great peace to come."

"You've made them slaves," Galinthia said.

"We've made them helpful."

Alex was petrified, but Mara wouldn't back down, shrugging dismissively. "Still not enough to get past us."

"Hrm, you are tough to please. Very well." Chloe called over her shoulder, "Bring it up!" With a lick of her lips, she smiled.

There was commotion among the demons, shuffling sounds as something was passed through their ranks. As it drew closer, Alex's heart sank—there was a person, bound, with a hood over their face, making muffled sounds as they were carried forward. The demon at the front took the figure in its claws, and Alex saw auburn hair illuminated like fire in the lamplight. *No.* She screamed again, sounding more and more like her. *Please... please, no.* The Archfiend handed the woman to Chloe.

Alex's cheeks felt like they were melting down his face. His neck tightened, his breath caught in his throat. His brain pounded at his skull, boiling, trying to break free and get some air.

Chloe then pulled the hood off.

There were her dimples, deep into her face, giving her a permanent, warm smile that matched her affectionate soul. There were her green eyes, dark on the outside, pale in the scant light. The smell of her was real, unmistakable. It wasn't a dream. She was here. She was screaming for help. They'd found Melissa.

"You didn't . . ." Alex stammered, his knees weakening. He didn't bother reasoning his next moves; he was reacting. His body lashed out, desperate to take her in his arms, to pull her away from danger. *I have to get to her! I have to!* But someone grabbed him from behind, holding him back. "No. Get off me!" he screamed.

"Hold on one second," Felix said, his breath hot in Alex's ear. Fabian joined him, restraining the teacher.

Alex fought forward with desperation, his fists glowing white-hot. "Melissa!"

He locked eyes with his wife, and the fear and disappointment reflected in her gaze pierced him deeper than any blade. The flicker of joy he hoped to see was overshadowed by terror. He felt the weight of all he had put her through, unsure of the fate of the man he had beaten outside their home, unsure if it was even still his home. Seeing her now hurt more than he could have imagined. She was tormented because of him—because he had once befriended a child who lived on his block.

"Alexander?" she asked through tears.

"Hi, sweetheart. Oh God, are you—are you hurt? Did they hurt you?"

Chloe seized Melissa by the back of the neck, lifting her to present her like a trophy. "We see you two have met!"

"What the Hell is this, Chloe?" Izaiah shouted. "This is too low for you. This has to be the Brothers. Don't let them do this!"

She was probably just at home, watching TV, or . . . Alex strained for freedom. His mind had a singular intent: to reach her. Bennett had since moved in, helping the others keep him restrained. *Get off me!* Alex couldn't move an inch. *She's right there!*

"Let him come to her! This is his one true love, is it not?" Chloe said whimsically. "Mellu knows. He knows everything about Alexander James Barker."

"What is happening?" Melissa shouted.

"Something that has nothing to do with you. Don't worry, we'll figure it out," Alex said. "I can help. You have to trust us. We're getting out of here. I can—help." He wanted to ask her about her day.

"Who is 'us'?" she screamed.

The Wrath was on its way to his surface, and Alex didn't want to fight it. "It's a long story." He longed to take her in his arms, to kiss her warm lips. "Nothing is going to happen to you, you hear me? Nothing. You're going back home tonight." He wanted to ask about their daughter.

"What makes you so sure of that?" Chloe asked, a mocking edge to her voice. "It was you who brought this woman here tonight, Mr. Barker. Mellu learned everything he needed from you when you took him. We must say, a connection as pure as yours and Melissa Klein Barker's is rare. You were lucky, but how many millions of others will never experience the same joy? Is that fair, Mr. Barker?"

Izaiah roared, "Stop this, Chloe, or so help me—"

Chloe interrupted. "What will you do? Will you risk the life of Mr. Barker's one and only? What does the greatest of the Medolians choose?"

"Your fight is with us. If you can't win, you can't win. No need to bring in an innocent," Izaiah said, his voice tense and coarse. As much as Alex didn't trust him at the moment, he had to believe that the old Medolian would get his wife back to him safely.

"Bring in an innocent?" Chloe shouted, jostling Melissa. "As you stand with the humans you yourself brought into this? All because you believed they would appeal to the vessel?"

Chloe forced her hostage to the ground. Melissa searched her surroundings, likely looking for clues that this wasn't real or maybe an exit route. His inability to comfort her was destroying Alex. Screaming in anguish, he looked Bennett in the eye, hoping to break through his callous exterior. "Help me," Alex begged.

"I am, Al," Bennett said.

How can you say that?

"Twenty seconds. If you don't let us by, she will die in front of you," Chloe warned.

Alex's heart plummeted. "No!"

"This is cowardly. Not your style. She has nothing to do with this," Mara said. "Chloe, why are you okay with this?"

"Time is ticking," Wraith Chloe snickered. "What will it be?"

Melissa was crying, shutting her eyes as if trying to wake up from a nightmare. "This isn't real. None of this is happening!"

"She's bargaining with the devil!" Chloe screeched.

"We can beat her. Like Galinthia said," Alex pleaded. "Let's stop this, right now. Come on!" He looked at Mara and Izaiah, the strongest among them, who still wouldn't move. *Why won't you do anything?* He turned to Fabian and Felix. Their faces were cold, impassive. Finally, he found Bennett's gaze. "Bennett. Please don't let my wife die."

Bennett's lips quivered as if he might say something, but he remained silent. His eyes flicked between Chloe and Melissa, then back to Alex. Finally, he nodded and leaned in close. "Okay. When she reaches one."

The thought of waiting so long was torture, but Alex trusted Bennett. At least he trusted the look in his eye.

Turning to his wife, he said, "Don't worry, sweetheart, it will be okay."

Something deep inside told him he'd just lied.

"We can work this out. Let the woman go back to her family," Izaiah pleaded.

Chloe cackled. "Only if you'll let us get in there and blow up the world." Time was counting down, and Alex couldn't bear to lose Melissa again. When her eyes opened—his bright green joys—the same rush he'd gotten since he was a boy sped through him.

"Are you really alive?" she asked.

Alex's jaw trembled. "It's really me. I'm here. That's all that matters."

"Do you know about Patty?"

Patty. That's our daughter's name? Patty? He smiled. It was perfect.

"Fifteen seconds," Chloe said.

Alex nodded at Melissa, striving to keep his composure, if only for her. "Is she strong, like you?"

Melissa almost let out a laugh. "Yes, but also overly cautious, like her dad."

Mara yelled at Chloe as if she were a toddler about to drop a vase, "If you don't stop this right now, you're going to be very sorry."

Chloe's mouth hung open, as though she were considering it, then said, "Ten seconds."

No! God. We move on one? Why one? In a lifetime of feeling powerless, Alex had never felt more so. He looked back at Bennett to confirm their plan was still on. Bennett nodded. Alex readied his Wrath, keeping his gaze locked on Melissa.

"Where have you been? They saw you get shot," she said.

"I know. I know none of this makes any sense," he said.

"Eight seconds," Chloe interrupted.

We go on one. Wait until one.

"Just let the woman go!" Izaiah screamed, taking a step forward.

Chloe raised her sword blade to Melissa's neck, halting him. "Five seconds."

Not knowing what else to do, Alex focused on what was important. He looked his wife in the eye. "Melissa . . . I love you more than anything."

"I know, baby," she said. As if synchronized, Alex and Melissa began speaking over one another, their voices blending while their eyes conveyed what their mouths couldn't.

Exalting above their words, Chloe counted down the final seconds. "Four, three, two . . ."

We go on one! Alex let the Wrath through, opening the floodgates, feeling his hands burn brighter than ever. *Let's do this!*

Once more, Chloe took Melissa by the neck as Bennett's grip on Alex loosened. The teacher was ready to spring.

"Wait!" Izaiah screamed. "Fine. We'll do it."

Everything stopped. A pause fell over the scene. Alex and Bennett stood frozen. Chloe's smile faded like a flower petal caught in a savage wind. "You'll do it?" she asked.

Thank you! Thank God! Alex was dumbfounded and looked at Bennett to make sure he wasn't crazy or imagining things.

"Let her go, and we'll step aside," Izaiah said.

"Absolutely not!" Mara shouted.

"We can't let this happen." Izaiah raised his hands, slowly moving forward. "We can't. Don't worry, Chloe, we'll comply."

Oh, thank you! Thank you, Izaiah!

Wraith Chloe's sick smile returned. "Hmm, tempting, but allow us to end this debate."

Then it happened. With a twist of her hand, she did it. There was a slight snap—a sound as innocent as the clicking of a pen top—and Melissa's head drooped.

The sudden sensation of slipping on ice enveloped Alex, a feeling of waiting to hit the ground. He felt blank, weightless, as if he were a meaningless thing. The lingering emptiness filled with agony and uncertainty. He never expected to land again. Then, through the void, came the same voices he had heard while gazing at the smallest stone, Mellu, brought to life in his mind once more. Finally, his consciousness struck pavement, and everything went black.

HE ASCENDS

Bennett snatched the creatures he'd dubbed Dark Archfiend (*sue me*) out of the air and pummeled them stupid, but no matter how many he put down, more kept coming. Claws swiped at his face. Jaws clamped onto his calves, penetrating his skin. Kicking demons off left and right, he fought forward with a burly shout towards his goal, which required finding the end of the throng.

His knife was missed desperately; Bennett imagined the black and gray marbled blade was out there, missing him in return, likely buried under a mound of debris on Trivium. *We'd grown quite close.* But now his fists had pick up the offensive slack. He unleashed blazing, coordinated strikes at what he hoped were weak spots just below the upper, larger set of legs, each hit expelling blue vapor thick with Rapture, enough to slow the demons in place. It was one of the techniques he'd picked up watching Hannah, but the downside was that it seemed to slow him down as well after each strike. *And she's not around anymore to teach me to refine it. Can't believe this bullshit.*

He pored over the last moments of her war with Joseph, his fists clenching tighter. *Why? Why can't we put this guy down?* The fact that there seemed to be no way to defeat Wraith Chloe—*a fusing of her and the Brothers of Gehenna, who have sentience apparently*— sent pure rage ripping through Bennett, crippling his ability to create Rapture and stunting him in his battle against the mindless Archfiend clan.

Whatever Wraith Chloe and the Brothers of Gehenna had done to gain the clan's obedience had made them fiercer and less remorseful. These demons also fought in silence, which was un- settling as Hell. Turned out, Bennett had already gotten used to talkative Archfiend.

Each step forward felt minuscule. His goal seemed no nearer. For what seemed like hours, he'd been fighting to reach Melissa, a few yards away at most. He was the only Rapture user nearby who could help. *I can save her. I have to!* What frightened him most was not knowing if he could help even if he was able to reach her. He'd only ever healed one wound before, and a fence post through the chest was a far cry from a broken neck.

When Chloe had killed Melissa, and Alex went limp in Bennett's hands, he—for a split second—felt the weight of his partner's an- guish, enough to stagger Bennett in the first crucial moments of the skirmish with the Archfiend. *We were going to save her. I was going to—wasn't I?* He had believed it. But what went wrong? The moment was now a blur. Chloe had been counting down. For some reason, it seemed best to wait and negotiate, despite Alex's pleas. *I thought it would keep her safe.* They had planned to make a move on one. *I was going to get Fabian and Felix off him. It was going to work. It was.*

Alex hadn't moved since it happened. There he sat, dotted among the chaos, his posture stiff, somehow appearing even smaller, his eyes locked low onto Melissa's body. Archfiend swept overhead like wild tendrils of flame, inexplicably ignoring him, possibly because Alex's Wrath had all but dissipated.

This was their plan all along. Chloe was never going to let Melissa live through the night. I'm so sorry, Al. The only question remaining was why the teacher had been chosen to be punished.

As grim as the situation was—battling the horde and the possessed Medolian—it could have been worse. Fabian and Galinthia—the current MVPs in the fight—were holding off most of the clan with a few well-placed maroon and canary-yellow Medolian spheres. But this left two of their heaviest hitters essentially out of commission, leaving Bennett and the others to hold the line against Wraith Chloe and her slave Archfiend.

Felix was allowing himself to be swarmed, which turned out to be helpful, spewing Wrath in ways Bennett had never seen before, his long dragon tongue whipping back and forth from a protruding snout as he assaulted the Archfiend with a ferocity to match their own. His once pale skin had hardened into a shell, cragged and lizard-like, complimented by a small tail poking out from his backside. The acid he spewed tore through the Archfiend as Felix launched himself off the canyon walls, leaving steaming trails behind. Though Bennett didn't like seeing his amiable pal lash out like this, times were desperate, and the guy clearly had some frustrations to get out.

Melissa was now only a few feet away. *I can still save her!* Suddenly, a loud bang rattled him from the left, near where Izaiah and Mara were struggling to contain Chloe. The possessed Medolian's laughter echoed, a taunt that chilled Bennett to the bone. "There! Do you feel it? Her life force has faded! Mrs. Barker truly is no more."

That's what Chloe was waiting for? But Bennett didn't believe her.

A gap then finally opened to Melissa. He rushed in, scooping her up in his arms. She was cold. "This will work!" he shouted, pressing his hand to her chest, forcing out every bit of Rapture he could muster. *Think. Focus!* The aura around them blazed into a brilliant cone of orchid-blue and sapphire. But the Rapture flowed through her and out the other side, unabsorbed.

"No, no, Melissa! Come back! Hear my voice. Follow it." Bennett couldn't accept it, but one glance at Izaiah told him the truth: she'd faded. To a human unable to sense Eve, Melissa would have seemed as alive as ever, her deep green eyes aimed at the night sky, unafraid. But his new senses did not lie, and when Bennett closed his eyes and looked at her, he found no color.

Often, he'd balked whenever Alex would start into a rant about his life before Izaiah. But every word said about Melissa was heard loud and clear. Bennett knew the woman in his arm's favorite food was raspberry tart with rocky road ice cream. He knew she liked to read cheesy romance novels about Spanish lumberjacks and volunteered at the homeless shelter. He knew what she cherished most was rainy days inside with music and coffee, as opposed to sunny ones outdoors. He also understood all the better what he'd sensed from Alex when she passed.

Bennett gently closed her eyes, laid Melissa down, and whispered, "I'm so sorry."

Once she was as safe as could be, he turned his anger outward, finding two willing Archfiend swooping upon him. Lighting his fists in blue fire, he charged just as the fiends tackled him, hoisting him high above the fight. With a furious shout, Bennett drove his hand through the first demon's gut, drawing a howl before it went still, plummeting to the ground. The second fiend flailed, hissing madly, struggling to carry Bennett on their own.

"Damn, Chloe really did a number on you guys, huh?" Bennett

asked as the demon carried him higher, slobbering away. "Up close, you guys get uglier somehow, you know that?"

The beast snarled and snapped at his neck. *No small talk? Fine!* In retaliation, Bennett began tearing off the demon's legs, sending it spiraling and vomiting acid as its screams blended with those below.

Waves of Abyss and Mallos surged through the area as they fell, prompting Bennett to seize the demon midair and thrust them into the energy's path to absorb the brunt of the hit. Sent flying, they both crashed into a nearby canyon wall before crumbling to the ground, rocks tumbling around them. Once again, Bennett used the Archfiend as a shield. The beast didn't even scream as heavy, sharp stone masses crushed it from above, blocking out all light.

Controlling his breathing then became priority, as Bennett knew his claustrophobia would come on strong if he didn't. But after a brief moment, he felt a strange sense of safety within the rubble. The overwhelming fear he expected seemed distant, even as the Abyss continued to surge outside his makeshift cocoon. *That shit stings. I might just stay here for a while—maybe catch a nap.*

But there was no time for complacency. Chloe could slip past their blockade at any moment. Scorching blood oozed from the demon's mushy remains as Bennett fought to extricate himself from the debris, hearing footsteps, lightning-fast, passing by.

That's gotta be her! Someone stop her! Bennett closed his eyes and found the shape of Wraith Chloe, saturated in Abyss, prancing by, unopposed, toward the tunnel entrance and oblivion. Her callous laughter echoed across the cave entrance—a child gleefully opposing their parent's wishes.

"No, goddamn it!" Bennett roared, mustering all his Rapture as he strained to lift the heavy slabs pinning him down. *Don't be a limp dick! What would Sarge say? Come on! Flex that scrote!* Slowly, the debris began to budge, then suddenly gave, rolling off him with a final crash that sent dust billowing into the air.

He was free.

Wiping the hot blood from his face, Bennett sprinted down the tunnel, searching for any sign of Chloe.

A Wrath signature was suddenly beside him on his left. Felix, looking more demonic by the second, kept pace, charging down the tunnel with glazed red eyes fixed on the hunt.

Wind was soon on their backs. A cloak swooped on either side of Bennett and Felix when Mara landed behind them, grabbing them both by the backs of their shirts. "Hang on!" she shouted.

In an instant, a sphere of energy enveloped them, and Bennett felt himself lifted from the ground. They shot down the tunnel at nearly a hundred miles per hour, breaking through tight gaps and carving a clear path with exhilarating speed. Feeling a certain end-of-the-world thrill, he couldn't help but let out an adrenaline-filled shout.

But despite their velocity, Chloe remained frustratingly elusive. Skeptical glances passed between Bennett, Mara, and Felix as they raced deeper into the Earth, finally reaching the last curve that led to the Dead Stairs chamber. As the sphere leapt into the room, a cascade of boulders collapsed behind them, sealing their exit.

Flashes of Abyss lashed out like tendrils of shadow, striking Mara's sphere as they approached. "We're going in! Stop her from opening the Brothers. Whatever it takes!" Mara shouted.

The sphere careened up the steps, smashing through the black doorway and barreling down the entry tunnel, crashing into the temple. Upon entering, the sphere dissipated, dropping the trio to the ground.

Immediately, Bennett was overwhelmed by the weight of the

astronomical energy ricocheting throughout the chamber. The feeling of Abyss was tenfold, a petrifying presence mixed with enough Wrath to make him seriously ill. If the fate of the planet hadn't been at stake, he would have definitely puked then and there.

Ribbons of dust danced through the temple, illuminated by a blinding, anarchic light radiating from the plateau under the great winged statue. Three glowing orbs sat atop the pedestal, their energy pulsating ominously. Looming over them, shrouded in shadow, was Chloe, her hands clamped to the rocks. Loops of magenta energy orbited around her, and as she channeled the power, her cackling echoed throughout the chamber. "You're too late! We are here. It is done!"

Mara didn't hesitate. Launching herself into the air, she released her lance toward the slate-black aura enveloping the pedestal. The blade struck with a jarring impact, eliciting a piercing shriek from the sphere guarding it, as if it were in agonizing pain. But Chloe remained unfazed, her hands still gripping the stones, tendrils of Abyss swirling around her, keeping Mara at bay.

The first wave of tendrils was deflected by her lance, but the second wave detonated against her upon impact. In a blinding flash, Mara was hurled against the temple ceiling, her body going limp as she fell, narrowly avoiding impalement by her own staff. Bennett's heart sank; something told him that last bit of bullshit was likely the final nail in the universe's custom-made coffin.

He and Felix, the last two standing, exchanged frantic glances before charging up the stairs. The steps were agonizingly hot, cooking through Bennett's shoes, searing his toes and heels. Felix's skin began to visibly burn away, yet they pushed on, not even halfway, as the oppressive, demoralizing presence of Eve grew increasingly potent, making each step feel like a battle against a typhoon of hate and despair ready to swallow them whole.

"Felix!" Bennett couldn't help but scream, unable to hear his own voice amid the din.

Fighting a few more steps, his pal was forced to turn back. "It's no use!" Felix shouted, reaching for Bennett. But Bennett pulled away, his legs unwilling to falter. *I'm not dead yet.* Not that he didn't desperately want to go with Felix.

Facing the top stairs, Bennett felt like the poster boy for desperation, but in a strange turn, the Rapture responded tenfold to the emotion. *Whoa. Well, all right.* Using the boon and subsequent clarity, he increased the armor over his body, watching happily as it extended past his arms, over his shoulders, and down the rest of him, encasing him. The final piece slid into place over his head and locked with a clang, and Bennett allowed himself one laugh as he instantly recognized the shape the chunks of Rapture had formed. Inspired by the story that had emboldened him all his life, he'd been garbed in bulky plate armor: a fantastical royal knight of King Arthur's court. For an unrelated reason, he also felt invincible.

With renewed vigor, his pace quickened. The armor pulsed with each black tendril that struck him, releasing a low-pitched scream yet remaining steadfast. *Almost there! Doing it!* But the sheer presence of the stones nearly bowled him over. The Abyss would soon break free from the stones, where it would be amplified by the temple a million times over, and Bennett, for the first time, began to grasp how the Brothers of Gehenna could do something as cosmically large as render all matter nil. Though he was never much for science, he knew space was fucking big, yet somehow the power swelling atop the plateau was proving itself up to the challenge.

As he reached the highest step, tendrils lashed out, striking him square in the chest. Bennett was flung off the stairs, crashing against the far wall of the temple, where he was embedded in the rock.

"Ah, great."

Wriggling free, he dropped fifteen feet amid a rain of rocks onto his ass, startled when a few conked him on the helmet. Gazing up at the plateau, he found Felix across the way, propped against a wall, protecting Mara, who was still unconscious. They caught each other's eyes and nodded—a respectful acknowledgment that they'd given it their best. Bennett wanted one more crack at it, but when he looked at Chloe, he sensed her power was only increasing. There seemed nothing to do but wait. *It's been an . . . okay existence, I guess.* He tried to think if there was anything he wanted to do before ceasing to be, so he scratched his balls and farted, shitting a little.

That's fine.

"Mellu. Raide. Eilam. Show us the beauty of nothingness!" Wraith Chloe screamed, belting out one final laugh for the end of existence as the transfer grew to a fever pitch.

Yeah, good for you.

But the laugh was soon cut off, and Bennett's gaze was pulled to the left, toward the collapsed entry tunnel. *What is that?* Something was approaching—something dark, and powerful. Neither Chloe nor the stones, it was pure Wrath, coming like a freight train just getting rolling. From what Bennett could sense, whatever it was terrified him just as much as the power of the Brothers.

A fierce glow—orange like fire—appeared in the cracks of the boulders blocking the tunnel entrance, swelling until the blockade ruptured into millions of red-hot pieces. Bennett quickly recognized Alex's Eve signature, though he couldn't quite grasp what he was seeing.

Al?

A blazing fireball entered the temple, sending the temperature inside skyrocketing. Rock chunks were torn from the walls and sent spinning through the air. A dark spot in the middle of the fire formed a silhouette, with eyes burning like white spots on the shadowed shape, which took plodding steps toward the center of the room.

"Al! Over here!" Bennett cried, but the teacher continued his march as though he didn't hear, and a whole new bad feeling settled in Bennett's already sensitive gut.

Chloe's voice competed for dominance over the noise of the newcomer. "Yes! Mr. Barker did it! He's found the Ire. The lowest pits of despair! Now it is certain. The collected dark Eve of the universe will be released from this point. Existence ends tonight!"

Bennett tried to wave Alex over, but he didn't seem to hear or see him and would not divert from his path toward the stairs. The ground only remained long enough for him to complete each step before bursting into molten liquid, bubbling in Alex's wake.

"That's far enough!" Chloe called, beginning to sound baffled as Alex planted his foot on the first stair step leading to the plateau. "How are you functioning? The Ire is said to be mindless! Fall!"

This was part of Chloe and Joseph's plan from the beginning? If they couldn't get the job done one way, they would find someone who could do it another? It turned out Alex was the guy, except the results didn't seem to be agreeing with Wraith Chloe. Bennett struggled toward the stairs, unable to find sure footing amid the convulsing cavern. *If I can just talk some sense into him.*

"Al! You can't go up there!"

No response came, and Alex continued higher, seeming more a machine running a program than a man.

"Halt! We order you!" Chloe called.

Again, no response. The steps behind Alex began collapsing, growing into a cascade of lava, forcing Bennett to back off just as he reached the base of the stairs. The walking fire rose into the tight walls enclosing the stairway. *That's not Al.*

The cavern shook. The cave bellowed. Earthquakes mounted. Huge fissures opened in the ground, sending rushing geysers of searing steam. Bennett charged to the relative safety of the far edge of the room as Alex entered the cloud of Abyss and disappeared, and the cavern went dark. It appeared he'd been swallowed, but the aura soon emerged, a sun breaking free from a thunderhead. Alex was whole. His pace was constant. The Abyss whipped at him, catching fire, sometimes striking him, melting away his granite skin, but never slowing him. Reaching the top step, his stride turned toward the pedestal.

As Alex approached, Chloe shrieked in panicked, the charred maliciousness in her voice mixing with remnants of her fragile human form. "The transfer is not complete! You are the Ire! The Ire is destruction! Become it! Finish your fall, damn you! Fall!"

But Alex pressed on. Chloe couldn't pull her hands free as the Brothers continued to use her body as a conduit. More tendrils lashed out, simply burned away in the teacher's presence.

"This is impossible!" Wraith Chloe wailed as Alex took his final, plodding steps toward the pedestal. His arm rose, and he pressed a blistering open palm against her skull. The white-hot, Wrath-imbued hand sliced through her horn and obsidian armor like a scorching knife through soft butter. Chloe's head collapsed into glowing mush over Alex's hand, spilling out and igniting the rest of her body as it traveled downward. A geyser of Abyss erupted from the remains, creating a tower that pierced the cavern's roof, scattering energy into the atmosphere and beyond.

Alex's hands reached through what remained of Wraith Chloe's body, reducing it to liquid fire, which he seemed to toy with like a child playing with hot taffy. Then he turned his attention to the stones. Lifting them, he paused for a moment, head tilted and blazing white eyes fixed, as though simply curious.

A deafening moan arose, drowning out all other sound and sensation. Bennett watched as the stones in Alex's hands glowed from the bottom up and began to droop. A scream resonated from them as the Abyss within soared into the sky through the hole in the temple's ceiling. But Alex remained, his body regenerating faster than it could be burned away by the force. The stones soon dissolved in his palms, dripping through his fingers onto the pedestal in a melting deluge over the collapsing plateau.

An ensuing earthquake jostled Bennett. Across the temple, he spotted Felix and a semi-conscious Mara struggling to rise. A massive slab, shaken loose from the wall, began to topple above them, obscuring his view with dust. "Mara!" Bennett screamed, rushing toward them, uncertain if they had been crushed.

As he moved, the temple began to crumble, starting with the breach above Alex, collapsing in sections. Through the hole, Bennett glimpsed dim gray clouds in the night sky, a reminder that the world was still out there and intact.

Hope it stays that way.

He navigated the crumbling temple and saw Alex atop the plateau, now motionless. The Abyss had vanished, replaced by something equally terrifying. The teacher's head turned upward, and his body lifted limply into the air, rising through the opening overhead and disappearing outside. As he breached, the fiery glow around him illuminated the surface, transforming night into day.

The temple cavern was not going to last long. Bennett briefly forgot about Alex and scrambled, searching for Felix and Mara. Just as he was about to dig through the rubble, a rock slab exploded apart, revealing the pair beneath. Mara's lance was held high.

Medolian spheres began to spring up all around, supporting the fracturing cavern just long enough for the group to escape. Bennett felt little relief as Izaiah, Fabian, and Galinthia entered the cavern to join them.

"Let's get out of here!" the old Medolian shouted.

Encased in Mallos spheres, the party was lifted toward the hole in the roof. Once they were clear, the cavern behind them collapsed completely, dust rising over the desert. Bennett was set down on cold sand and took a deep breath, embracing the chilly desert air in his lungs. He, Izaiah, Mara, Felix, Galinthia, and Fabian had landed on a hill overlooking the valley. A trail of flaming glass led to a blazing light fading over a nearby hill, where the sands sparkled with red and yellow hues.

"You all right?" Izaiah asked, dusting him off.

"Al . . . He's—I don't know what happened. The Brothers and Chloe are gone," Bennett stammered.

"I know. Well done," Izaiah said, waving a hand to keep Bennett's focus. "I don't think they're coming back from that. Which means you're officially off the hook."

"What are we doing about Alex? That's him! What's happening—" Bennett knew he sounded maniacal, he just didn't care.

"Easy, cowboy," Galinthia said.

"You don't need to worry anymore. You did your part," Izaiah reassured him. "This part is ours."

Bennett then noticed the doleful looks on the other Medolians' faces.

"You rest up, partner," Izaiah said, giving Bennett and Felix a respectful nod before moving toward the light on the horizon with the others.

"What are you going to do?" Bennett shouted after them.

"Whatever we can," Mara answered.

Bennett rose to follow, but Izaiah, two steps ahead, snapped his fingers, encasing him in a clear Medolian sphere that immobilized him. "Sorry, pal. You and Felix wouldn't last long out there. Alex is falling into the Ire. The essence of destruction is going to pour out like a river breaking a dam."

"And you expect me to just sit here?" Bennett shouted, unwilling to accept being kept at arm's length.

Before turning away, Izaiah gave him a weak grin, and in that moment, everything Chloe had said about why Bennett and Alex were chosen clicked into place. *Izaiah knew about it the whole time. He knew either of us could fall into this and end the world.* Izaiah had switched them, putting the Rapture in Bennett and Wrath in Alex because he was too afraid of Bennett being the one to succumb to the Ire. As much as Bennett wanted to resent Izaiah, he also understood him more than he ever thought possible. He even grasped why Mara and the others had acted so hostile toward him and Alex: they were flimsy gates holding back the powers of Heaven and Hell.

When the Medolians launched into the distance toward the light, Bennett was released from the sphere. He and Felix followed as closely as they could, but despite their efforts, remained stranded a few hundred yards behind. Soaring over the fire, the Medolians formed a square formation. Bennett was grateful for his enhanced vision, letting him see the Medolians raise their imbued weapons and connect streams of energy, weaving a white sphere that surrounded Alex and the firestorm, blocking it from all senses—a perfect sun dug into the sand, white and opaque, muffling the volcanic squall. He didn't know what it was, but it seemed to be working.

"They're trying to contain it," Felix said, shaking his head. "But it's too much." Bennett didn't want to dignify that negativity with a comment. Felix then dropped to his knees, slumping in the sand.

"It's pointless. Wilbur is gone. That thing's a deity. There's nothing left of him."

As the Medolian bubble grew dense and concentrated, Bennett felt himself being pulled toward it, quickly realizing it was the small bits of metal in his clothing affected by a magnetic field. The white Medolian sphere pulsated, changing size and shape as sharp, riotous clangs erupted from inside, drowning out Izaiah and the others' shouts. They were giving it all they had. The sphere expanded to twice its size before rupturing with a flash visible from space. Neutral energy ripped across the desert, sapping Rapture from Bennett, weakening his armor while momentarily diminishing the effects of Alex and the Ire. The Medolians scattered, and Bennett lost sight of them as he and Felix hit the dirt, buried under clouds of sand.

Lifting himself, Bennett shook like a wet dog, flinging sand from his armor's nooks, only to find the white sphere was gone. The Medolians had vanished, but the fire surrounding Alex remained, ever constant. The blaze dragged on over the next hill and into a mountainous region. *Where you going, Al?* Bennett and Felix helped one another up, their gazes fixed on the blaze drifting away, igniting dry underbrush aflame and spreading smoldering fires across the valley.

Part of Bennett wanted to drop to his knees and give up. "What can we do?"

"Where are the reinforcements?" Felix shrieked. "All of UnEarth should be here to stop this! I guess . . . I honestly have no idea. If the Medolians all together can't contain it . . . I don't know, man. The world really wants to end tonight." Felix laid down in the sand, covering his face with his arm. His Wrath was nearly spent, making him appear once again like the gangly janitor who had risked everything to save Bennett and Alex from Madam Daphne, but all signs of his previous sunny disposition seemed extinguished, possibly for good.

The soldier couldn't help but agree with him. *Does seem like the world wants to put itself out of its own misery.* Every cynical thought he'd ever had suddenly felt justified, and the sand next to Felix looked disgustingly inviting. Yet Bennett found his legs moving him onward. He wanted to stop focusing and let the armor down, even for a second, but it refused, burning brighter around him. Deep within, he felt a warm light coursing up his throat until it erupted as an assertive laugh, startling him. His gaze then drifted to the dark sky. *Must be early morning by now.* On the eastern horizon was the faintest hint—no more than a foggy sliver—of royal blue.

"No," he said. *It doesn't feel like the end. Fuck if I know why, but it doesn't.* "That sun's gonna rise."

Without a second thought, he started down the hill toward the burning dot.

"Are you serious? What are you going to do?" Felix called after him.

"Don't know," Bennett called back. "Whatever I can."

"Alex died with his wife. You're just going to get yourself roasted."

"Along with everyone else, apparently. So, I'll just jump in head-first and let you know how it feels, yeah?" Bennett had no intention of taking this lying down. *Hannah wouldn't. Somewhere in that thing's a fourth-grade teacher who just watched the love of his life die, and he's hurting. I'm not going to let him go through this alone.*

"Good luck!" Felix shouted.

Bennett nodded, knowing he would need it, and trudged on, feeling a deep fatigue settle in. With each step, his body revealed how broken it had become, and the reality dawned on him: he would likely not survive a maneuver as reckless as this, successful or not.

As a wall of flame approached, he turned his mind to thoughts of his brother Jerry, his mother, his team in the Corps, Autumn—the woman he'd assaulted the day he shot himself—Hannah, Alex, and even his truck: all his best ammunition to activate his Rapture.

Once in the fire, Bennett found the bright center of the storm rising, scaling the mountain. Wrath raged around him as he marched on, bolts of red electricity tearing across the landscape.

Only going to get one shot at this.

IRE

Stop the fire! Stop burning! Please, stop!

The Entity knew two things: the burn, and that It was coming. Though the Entity did not know what It was, only that It would be here soon—the thing to stop the fire.

The sky was ablaze, as was ground, and everything in between. There was nothing to feel or experience but the burn. All emotions, thoughts, and feelings were primal, void of reason or conscience. *No more burn. No more fire!* The all-consuming blaze was both the bane and culmination of the Entity's life. There was no way to imagine an end to it, and so the Entity wandered, as it always had, hoping to find one.

Things had been different once, if only for a moment, what seemed like eons ago. There were noises—something, another fire, obsidian. But the Entity's fire, the red fire, burned far hotter than the obsidian. The red fire consumed the black and the bright stones, sending them away. The Entity was proud, despite hating its own red fire.

Step. Step. *Step.* Step. The Entity slammed the (*thing*) below it onto the other (*thing*) beneath it. It did not know the ground or its feet. Words and names were meaningless, but that did not stop the need to move. Moving was all it could do to help ease the burn, even if only in its mind.

The face returned. Her face—the woman—the haunting visage—it always returned. *Why her?—Keep moving!—Do I know her?—Move!—Who is she?*

Step. Step. *Step!* Step.

This time the Entity did not want to let it go and forced its thoughts away from the fire to the plaguing notion of the mystery woman. *Who was she?* A flare was lobbed high, as though triggered by the thought. It pressed on the Entity and found a way to intensify the burn, brighter, as it had every time the Entity tried, punished for seeking the truth. The Entity backed off, as it always had, forcing itself to forget her, to forget the face, to keep moving.

Step. Step. The Entity continued up an incline. *Always higher. Maybe to end the burn. Maybe to some way out.* The pace of the climb was slowed by neither boulder, nor tree, nor rock face. Whole mountainsides dissipated, step by step.

The face. The woman. *No!* She screamed. The Entity could hear it now, as clear as the fire. It was excruciating. *Why was she screaming?* The thoughts bellowed, proclaiming there was a reason for the face. *There has to be!* As the ground below narrowed to a singular path, the Entity stepped higher, observing a fall ahead. Flames rolled over the cliff edge like a fluid river, spreading the fire throughout the valley. The path ended on a precipice. No more ground. No more steps. No more distraction. The journey was over.

This is where It will arrive. It must be. How could it not? Soon, the Entity hoped.

The burn settled deeper, which was fine. Existence could not get worse. The Entity simply wanted It to—*hurry! Now!* If there was anything it could do to speed up the process, the Entity would have.

On the cliff edge, awaiting release, the woman returned to its thoughts. She was reappearing for a reason. She had to be. The Entity wanted to know why before It arrived. As it pondered the woman—who she was and what she meant—something happened to the Entity that it never expected. A voice broke through the torrent. It was faint—a whisper lost on the crashing wildfire shore.

It shouted, "Alex?"

Alex? The name echoed in the Entity's mind. Turning to see a shape through the fire, its head tilted, the Entity wondered if this was truly It. *No, It is within.* The approaching figure was far too small to be of any consequence. Both its hands were held high as it marched forward, blocking its face from the burn—a procession of chilling cold.

Why doesn't it burn?

A man's voice screamed, "Stop this!"

Stop? The Entity didn't know the word.

"I'm here. You're not alone. I'm right here," the man continued, vying to draw closer.

The Entity wondered why. *All other things burned away when they came near.* But the man remained. The red fire clashed with the gleaming, cold blue of the figure, unable to whisk it—or him— away. This neither angered nor pleased the Entity, though it had become curious.

"Don't worry. We can stop this!" the man shouted. "I know we can. Please. Just calm down. You have to calm down!"

The words were putting themselves together, brick by brick. The Entity found the notion of "calm" embedded in the shallow recesses of its psyche. But the momentous weight it brought was neither welcome nor characteristic of its supposed meaning. *Calm? How could there be such a thing?* The existence of such an expectation only made the Entity angrier.

The name Alex carried its own burden. *Why does the man continue to say it? Is he addressing me? Was he the one with the black fire? Was Alex the one like clay, who melted in my hands?*

The man in blue was close—the closest thing the Entity had seen since the obsidian fire, however long ago that was. "Shut it down!" he shouted, fighting for a cause the Entity knew nothing about. Yet the voice was becoming familiar.

Yes, he always called him Al. Al—Al. That's right—never by his name. Alex was angered because of it. Alex . . . Yes, that anger helped fuel my birth. That was the moment the Entity realized Alex and it were connected. What it didn't know was how.

The man's face and words formed pieces—collections of images. The Entity remembered more and grew irate. This fed the fire. The fire expelled itself further, shoving the cobalt-blue stranger backward.

Clutching the ground and pulling himself along, the man roared, "It was my fault you lost Melissa. I should have listened to you. We shouldn't have waited."

Melissa? A wave slammed into the Entity's mind, sobering it. The woman's face was clearer than ever. *Stop! Why does this hurt?* The fire was more than enough pain.

"Don't let this happen. You're stronger than this!" the man bellowed.

Why is this happening? Who is she? What is he talking about? The Entity did not want to be a part of this. The Entity simply wanted It to arrive, but time refused to speed up, or end entirely. The woman's face would not leave it alone. She was smiling. *Stop! It's a lie.* The Entity knew she was dead.

They killed her.

"If you're in there, I'm sorry, Alex. I'm so sorry," the man continued.

Why is he apologizing? Did he kill her? No . . . He wanted to help—didn't he?

Focusing on the image, the woman's face, the Entity saw a house appear through a fog. The home on a desert avenue was beautiful, and a mystery. A dove landed in the dirt yard, which was speckled with green, but without children. *Where are the children?*

The man in cobalt blue crawled within yards of the Entity. "I know you think you can't do it. I know you're scared, but you have to try to get it under control. You can, I promise you can. We've beaten everything they've thrown at us. Come so far. So much further than they thought we could. It was you and me—"

You and me?

"But I failed you," the man continued. "Not just now—I mean through everything! You're better than I treated you, Alex. You deserved better than you got from me. Truth is, you're stronger. You're the best of us."

Much of it was ringing true, but the procession of images and sounds coursing through its mind were only confusing the Entity. *What do they want from me? I don't know what they want!*

"We both know I was supposed to get the Wrath. I was supposed to go to Hell. And not just because I'm a piece of shit! It's because I . . . when I—"

The man stammered, and the Entity did not want to hear any more. The words were beginning to hurt, to choke the Entity, sending it to an incensed rage. *Hell? Yes . . .* It remembered the notion of Hell and lashed out accordingly, releasing a store of heat.

No more! Stop! When the Entity looked back, the man was gone. *Good.*

The wait could resume. The Entity tried again to summon It, but the words and faces would not leave. They would not relent. They wanted its attention. *Why?*

No matter; the fire was growing. *Soon—soon. The burn will end.*

"Alex!?" The man's voice reappeared, approaching in the distance. *How can it be?* The Entity turned to find the man in cobalt blue armor was back, crawling inch by inch.

Why won't he go away from the fire? Why won't he leave me alone?

The man clasped a rock protrusion several yards out and fought to rise. "I told you. I'm not going anywhere. I'm taking you home."

The new words were confusing. *Home?* It sounded free of the burn.

"Joseph is gone! Chloe is gone. The stones are gone. You did that. We're free, Alex. Don't throw away your chance at another life!"

The man was reduced to a knee, barely heard over the fire. "The reason I never told you how I died was that I was ashamed . . . I gave up and threw away every chance I ever had. Every chance you ever wanted. A kid I could have—I just gave up, man. I did. Stole my dad's gun, took the easy way out, and put a bullet in my head."

The man stopped, and the Entity could feel energy flowing through him. It recognized this energy. *Emotions . . . yes.* Some were new, and others were familiar. Guilt was apparent, which the Entity knew well.

The man continued, "The truth is . . . I was always jealous of you. You were a real hero. You saved those people that night in the restaurant. I wouldn't have. I know it. Even though I could've."

Restaurant? More flashes. The Entity saw children sitting on wooden chairs, waiting for food. They were smiling; they were safe. It aided the feeling of calm. *Calm. Yes.* The concept was slowly becoming clearer, however contrary to It, and its promises.

The man fell to his knees and shouted, "Listen to me! I'm trying to tell you I threw my life away. I'm trying to tell you I don't deserve any of this. This fucking Rapture, I don't want it! I want you to be okay."

Something substantial had arrived within. The Entity was inundated with information laced with emotion, all from a singular perspective. *Are these memories? Is this what made Alex? Constructed his mind and soul?*

The Entity knew the name of the man fighting the storm was Bennett. A proud man. A warrior. The Entity knew he was one of many who made Alex angry, but also a man who could be trusted when it mattered.

"My life was gone way before I picked up that gun," Bennett began, his head hung low. "All I did was take from others. All I did was hurt them to prop myself up. You're the only one who ever did the right thing. You—you're the only one who did what a man should. That's why it had to be you, a good person, who endured Hell, because I'm not as strong as you. Don't let yourself fall like I did. Like everyone does. Don't become another shit human. Be better. You are." Bennett thrashed, as though fighting off the endless fire. Whatever strength he possessed could not stop the inevitable. He dropped to his stomach and screamed, suddenly reaching out, as though lost, or as though they might touch. "Gerald?" he called, pleading. "Jer, come home! I know I fucked up! It will be okay."

Gerald? The Entity looked upon the man with increasing curiosity and alarm.

The blue glow around Bennett intensified. "Cody, I—lost him. I—I let him slip through my fingers." He was sobbing, clutching his face in his hands. "You trusted me. You were the only one who trusted me. I promised to take care of him. I promised, but I . . ."

Bennett's blue helm shook. His face lifted to the Entity. "Alex? What—we have to stop this! We have to. . ." His fight faded as he laid his arms at his side, allowing the flames to engulf him.

Once again, he'd called the Entity Alex, and it began to wonder if Bennett wasn't mistaken. He was clearly losing his mind, but also unyielding. *What if he's not wrong?*

Bennett slumped over, speaking softly, his voice nearly consumed by the fire. "Never told you about my brother, did I? Only other good man I know. Killed in action trying to stop a slaughter. But instead of taking my nephew, instead of doing the right thing, I did what I swore to him I never would. I joined up. I ran. Tried to get killed and buried right beside him. They took his son because I failed, but I'm not failing you! Not this time! I'm staying. Not because I'm your friend—I'm not, and we don't have to be. If you want, I could be your brother. We could be each other's family. You're all I have, and if you let go of the anger, I'll catch you. I promise. Just stop this."

Bennett's eyes were closing slowly, seconds from shutting and sending him to nothingness. "Do it. I know you can. Not for me. Not for you . . . for her . . . Don't forget. She's still . . . out there . . . your daughter." His voice trailed off. He lay silent on the ground.

The Entity kept its gaze on Bennett. *Daughter?* There was something special in that word, something important. What was Bennett trying to say? A name appeared in the Entity's mind, as though whispered in its ear: Patty.

Of course. It's perfect.

There was a flare of white as the Entity looked at its hands, seeing the hands of a man. *I am Alex. Alex James Barker.* Another flare launched into the void. *This is the Wrath.* His eyes fell on the fading blue shape below. *Bennett. Rapture. Brother.* A third flare of white rose free from his chest, a column of light and power soaring miles into the sky. His head swung from side to side in a furious arc. A scream rose from his now charred and scaled throat, releasing the pain and anguish of the burn and the fire. The teacher's body was stretched and lifted by his chest as the red typhoon swept into the sky and spread throughout the darkness. With a deafening crack, the fire burst and extinguished itself. Ash waves rolled without exhaust. The sound of searing flesh dominated all others, as dark patches of charred husk appeared over every inch of his body. Alex was aware there was pain but was unable to experience any form of sensation as he slowly came back to Earth.

The only thing in his mind was her face. *Melissa. God, honey. I'm so sorry. This can't be real. Please, I need you to come back—please.*

But he knew it would never be. The first memory to return was the moment he'd lost himself: the moment she'd died. It was also the moment that had brought him back.

The mountain crumbled and shook and did its worst, and soon the ridge lay in silence. The valley below was pitched into stark blackness in the absence of the towering Wrath, almost too dark to be real, allowing Alex to find a wisp of steam playing in his breath. He came upon a crumpled pile on the ground a few feet away, no longer glowing with a cobalt-blue haze, surrounded by shattered stones. Closing his eyes, Alex found his partner's Eve. He was alive, if barely.

Kneeling beside him, Alex placed a hand on his chest, searing the flesh. He quickly pulled away. Sitting with Bennett, gazing at the horizon for all it was worth, witnessing a new day's blue sky fold over the Earth, Alex felt a sense of calm wash over him. He took a deep breath. Others would be arriving soon—help. He sensed as much with his newly acquired sight, something that would take some getting used to.

He wanted to pat his partner on the shoulder, to reassure him, to let him know that he was alive, that he was here for him, and everything would be fine. But he stayed his scorching hand.

Thank you, Bennett. I've got it from here.

THE ALLEY DOOR

Which is funnier, a milkman or a wet nurse? Izaiah leaned over his green notebook, pencil in hand, chewing its end, which was nearly gnawed to a nub, as he struggled to perfect the joke he'd been stewing over for longer than he'd ever admit. *There's a winner in here. I know it.* His mind made up, he scribbled. *Definitely milkman.* A tired sigh escaped his old, chapped lips. Writing jokes was tiring work. He traded the pencil for a silver spoon, immersed in a glass boat next to the notebook, which held six scoops of ice cream, each a different flavor. Taking a bite, he savored the treat. The custom sundae was his third this afternoon. He made a yummy sound, closed his eyes, and enjoyed the cold, sweet indulgence. Even the greatest chefs of UnEarth, with all their wondrous culinary creations, were miniscule contrivances when compared to the glory of human ice cream.

Looking around the blue-walled, yellow-and-white-trimmed soda shop in Prescott, Arizona, he couldn't help tapping his toe to the rock 'n' roll playing on the orange and brown jukebox in the corner. The walls were adorned with all manner of quirky, pseudo decorative crap: decades-old soda pop ads, license plates, fake wanted posters from the Old West, Polaroids of neckless regulars, and inexplicably, numerous bike parts. *There're at least five used bike seats on these walls.* He flipped to a blank page and jotted that down. *Might be a joke in there somewhere.*

After scooping the last bite from the boat, Izaiah let out a burp, a bit louder than intended. *Whoops.* Passing gas was the original joke as far as he was concerned, but Americans could be touchy about such things. The sole administrator of the soda shop, Amanda, a local teenager with glasses the color of ripe avocado, looked up, her conversation with friends in a booth interrupted. *As long as I have her attention.*

Izaiah lifted a pointed finger. "'Scuse me, miss?"

Amanda gave her friends a *one-second* gesture and trotted over. "Can I help you?"

"Yes. I seem to have misplaced my ice cream."

"Looks like it. Should I find you another, what did you call it, rainbow sundae?" She offered an awkward laugh, trying to conceal her braces with bright green rubber bands. Izaiah could tell she was doing her best to be cordial, sometimes forgetting what he looked and smelled like.

"Yes, please. And you don't have to worry about me and money, or anything. I can pay." He pulled out soiled, crumpled bills from his pocket, holding them out like river water cupped in his hands. "See?"

Amanda gave half a smile before hurrying away.

He stuffed the money back in his pockets and checked his watch again: 3:30. *They're late.* Not late enough to panic, but enough to worry him slightly. He busied himself by glancing over the soda shop patrons. Besides the teenagers, there was an older couple sharing a scoop of raspberry sorbet who had been reduced to sparring with their spoons for the last bites. When the scoop was gone, the woman laid her head on the man's shoulder as they licked their spoons clean. Like every other human in Prescott and on the planet, they too were blissfully unaware of what had transpired on the other side of the world just a few nights before. For that, Izaiah was grateful. All of life had nearly ended—twice—but to them, the stars had twinkled, and the sun had risen exactly as it always had, unaware that two of their own were to thank for it.

Izaiah hoped Alex and Bennett would show. He still felt sick thinking of how things had been left between him and his human comrades after Africa. They hated him. He knew it. How could they not? Not an hour had passed that he wasn't haunted by the look on Alex's face the moment Melissa was taken from him. The teacher's eyes hadn't budged, hadn't blinked, not even when tears began to stream down his face.

Then, he fell. *And I was there to see it.*

All sense of Alex Barker had vanished once the Ire arrived. The fireball of godlike fury had nearly vaporized every creature present at the mouth of Gehenna before disappearing into the mountain, leaving the Medolians to deal with the remaining possessed Aili clan. The demons fled into the night, free of their master's bondage (*they were the smart ones*), and the Medolians set to work containing the ever-expanding inferno. However, the Ire lived up to its legend as an unstoppable force. When Izaiah witnessed Bennett march into the fire, he thought he was seeing a suicide. But when the wall of red flame crumbled, and the night became quiet and still, two figures somehow remained. Izaiah and the others arrived to find Alex struggling to come to grips with reality and fiercely protecting Bennett, who was clinging to life. The teacher soon settled, and all trace of the unstoppable Ire was gone. But the area would not stay deserted for long. Everyone in UnEarth had felt what transpired that night. There would be questions. This was going to be what humans referred to as "big news."

After securing Bennett on a makeshift stretcher, Izaiah Shifted the team away, leaving Galinthia and Fabian behind to lead relief efforts. They had a list of instructions to ensure certain tracks were covered while also making sure certain Sentry protocols were technically adhered to. One Medolian was usually enough to supervise an emergency situation on Earth or in Trivium, so he hoped the show of force and solidarity would buy them some time before the Senate's legal authorities, the Counselors, came calling. Luckily, Galinthia was never one to turn down a chance to be devious or to lie at the behest of her boss.

Accompanied by Felix and Mara, Izaiah escorted Alex and Bennett to a Medolian safe house on Earth. It happened to be his favorite, designated the Henhouse for its boxlike design, built with aged cedar planks dyed a rich brown, nestled within the forests of British Columbia near the border of Alberta, a few miles west of the Peace River.

Surprisingly, it was Mara who dressed Bennett's wounds and ground hyuil root for tea. *Never even seen her help an old human across the street, let alone try to heal a young one.* The herb, brought to Earth from the fields of Hyuil in Hywyn, was dense with Rapturous fiber, primarily used to heal citizens and former citizens of the Celestial realm. The only question was whether Bennett was far enough along in his transformation to be healed by the tea rather than poisoned by it. Things were touch and go for a while, but Mr. Hunter's eyes cracked open just in time to witness the dazzling red light of the sun striking the peaks of the Rocky Mountains in the west, lowering on their face as morning rose over Canada.

"Cool," was all he said.

The fellas were fed with the only unspoiled food in the Henhouse:

the same dried biscuits Izaiah had provided them in the desert safe house—dilo cookies. Judging by their reactions, the humans were evidently disgusted by what he'd always found a delightful, crunchy snack. Once convinced they needed to eat to regain their strength, each took half a cookie.

Later, once Bennett was well enough to move, Izaiah escorted them to Prescott, questioning whether he was making the right choice. He forbade the humans from revealing their plans to him, in case they were questioned about their whereabouts sooner than later, and offered his services one last time.

"If you want to go out on your own and try to make it, I won't stop you. I'm not going to take away your chance for normal lives. But if you want to come with me, the door is open—or window . . . no—door. Just know there are sacrifices with either choice. Word will spread fast, and now that everyone's worst fears have been confirmed—the Ire is real—they'll be searching for it. Not just the Senate and its agents, including the Medolians. Every gang and society of UnEarth will be seeking Alex. Rest assured, there are plenty of places to hide. The world of the Eve is mighty immense. Who knows, we might even have a little fun along the way."

Neither Alex nor Bennett committed to the proposal, citing they needed time, which Izaiah had expected. "Totally fine. Just keep your Eves low—low as possible." He then advised them to settle whatever affairs needed settling and, if they wanted to come along, to meet him at the soda shop on Friday at three p.m. Izaiah then Shifted away, uncertain if he would ever see the teacher or soldier again.

The following two days were filled with nothing but UnEarth committee hearings and formal Senate inquiries. With nearly a third of the Tribunal reduced to rubble, one of Trivium's wealthiest citizens, Randal Molm, formerly of the Archfiend clan, had stepped in, allowing proceedings to resume temporarily in the great hall of his compound, Millios, the largest thresh distillery in UnEarth. Randal was a consummate politician and industrialist, and it was long common knowledge that he coveted Arros's Senate seat, whether he admitted it publicly or not. Currently, the position was held by Ariel Van-Mortus, formerly of Clan Vostrus, who did not appear intimidated by the change of setting.

As the highest-ranking Senate official under Arros, second in power only to Lucifer-Aveyl himself, Van-Mortus possessed a hard temper and the slippery tongue of a serpent, both figuratively and literally. In the two thousand years since her appointment, she hadn't lost an election and carried near-boundless reverence within the Senate. This did little to stall Molm or his lofty ambitions, leading to a famous, centuries-old rivalry that neither seemed keen to resign.

Attending only enough formal inquiries to keep up appearances, Izaiah sent letters of profuse apology for his absence from the rest. Political hearings exhausted him; often, he'd doze off in a corner, jolting awake to the sight of some stuffy Nashwyn noble citing that creatures weren't being sensuous enough with one another, or a Scythe lord speaking too softly to be taken earnestly. Yet this was only the tip of the iceberg, and Izaiah had run out of ways to skirt questions about the location of "the humans," a term the citizens of UnEarth had taken to using with the same tenor one would usually reserve for "the economy" during a recession.

He checked his watch again: 3:44. *Hope I'm not wasting my time.*

Amanda returned with sundae number four and a fresh spoon. "Found one."

"M'lady." Izaiah tipped the brim of an imaginary hat. Before diving in, he took a packet of red hots from his pocket, crumpled the candies, and sprinkled the spicy cinnamon dust over the multicolored sundae. *Now we're talking.*

He was halfway through the new treat when the front door opened and a large man wearing a long-sleeve shirt and jeans, with tattoos poking out from every corner, entered. The other customers grew nervous in his presence, their Eves turning the slightest shade of Dread. Izaiah almost didn't recognize Bennett, who'd shaved his scruffy mane and looked much more approachable after a shower. The soldier spotted Izaiah and marched to the table, pausing to let Amanda pass with a tray of sodas for her friends.

Sliding out from the booth, Izaiah welcomed him. "Look at this guy!"

Bennett's polite smile sagged at the sight of the Medolian. Based on his body language, Izaiah let go of any notions of a hug.

"Hello, Izaiah," Bennett said, sliding into the booth. "Sorry I'm late. I walked."

"What happened to the truck?"

"Gave it away." Bennett began flipping through the milkshake menu on his right.

Izaiah sat back down. "I'm shocked. To whom?"

"Still don't know her real name. Goes by Autumn."

Izaiah's head sank at the thought of the young woman. "So, you found her?"

"I drove by her old spot, not expecting much, but she was there. I tried to make amends, but she didn't care. Totally fine. I wouldn't either. She even told me I hit softer than her ninety-six-year-old nanny. *Heh*, pretty good. Anyway, I asked if there was anything I could do. First, she said I could kill myself. When I told her I'd tried that already, she asked for the truck, probably just trying to jerk me around. But I said sure. Got out and left the keys in the ignition. Been walking since. Gotta admit, getting face-to-face with her was a lot harder than losing the truck. But her expression when she realized it was worth it."

"I think you did the right thing."

"Yeah, well, a truck's not much use to someone with warrants out for their arrest in multiple parallel universes."

That got Izaiah stirring in his seat. "Does this mean you've chosen to accept my offer? Ooo! You won't regret it. I promise to—no—no more promises! But I swear."

Bennett made a pump-the-brakes motion. "I haven't agreed to anything yet. I just . . . if what you said is true, and people will be coming after Al, I need to be there with him. If he doesn't show today, I may need your help finding him. God knows what might happen if someone else gets to him before we do."

Amanda shuffled up to the table and took out her notebook, making minimal eye contact with Bennett. "Hi, um, can I get you anything?"

"I'm very hungry, yes. What do you have in the way of meal-ish food?"

"Well, we've got like mostly candy and ice cream. That's kind of, like, the theme. But I don't know if you have, like, a sweet tooth, or, um, we also have, like, hot dogs and waffles and stuff. We don't have, like, a grill, but I could microwave some stuff. If you want." Her cheeks were flushing red.

"Perfect. May I have eight hot dogs and eight waffles, please? Lots of butter and extra syrup. If you added sprinkles, I would not be ungrateful. Thank you," Bennett said.

Amanda scribbled into her notebook and pocketed it. "Uh, sure thing. Give me a minute?" She ran off with urgency, no doubt for what was surely a monumental task.

"I'm surprised you and Alex didn't arrive together," Izaiah said.

Bennett nodded as he took a glance around the shop. "Said he had some things to do. I think he just wanted to be alone for a bit. I don't like it, but I get it. Just hope he's okay."

"I'm sure he's doing as well as he can."

"Couldn't tell what was going on with him the last day, to tell you the truth. What the fuck kind of help can I be, right? I mean, to someone who went through something like that?" There was a silence. Bennett cracked his knuckles and folded his hands on the table. "Sorry."

"It's fine. Any anger coming my way is well deserved. If there's anyone to blame for all this, it's me."

"Don't be ridiculous. There's always someone to blame—the trigerman. Unfortunately, when things like this happen, those people tend not to live to see repercussions. They're the cowards. It's the survivors who have to live with the horrible shit others do. You're not to blame—Joseph is. And I'd be a poor excuse for a Rapture user if I didn't admit I've done my fair share of lying for the 'greater good.' I've done a lot of shitty things in the name of good, actually. Just part of being human, I guess, or whatever you are."

"I may be Medolian, but I live on the same planet as you. Just 'cause I'm not born like other people doesn't mean I don't walk these streets—don't enjoy the culture."

"How the Hell *are* you born, Izzy?"

A flash went off in Izaiah's mind. *Izzy? Was that a nickname?* No one had ever called him that before. All his life, he'd hoped for a nickname, and now that he had one, he didn't know what to do with it. The Medolian's heart fluttered, making it hard to keep his cool. *Don't be uncool, now. People with nicknames stay cool. Don't spoil it!*

Izaiah (*Izzy*) leaned back, nice and cool. "If you must know, we're basically born from a flash of light once an energy quota's been filled, which I admit is pretty much the most agamic way of reproducing possible. But still"—he laughed, then took a somber turn he himself wasn't expecting—"when I look in the mirror, I don't see a Beaubon, or a Celestial, or a Lostros. I see an old, ugly man, with wrinkles carved into his face, and a mess-a hair in the crack of his ass—as human as anybody else in this town."

Bennett grinned. "Good enough for me."

"In so many ways, and I hate to say it, I see Chloe's point of view," Izaiah continued. "We Medolians—let's just say it's a rough gig. I mean, human uprisings, religious cults, rogue government factions. The Senate even put our branch in charge of human corporation oversight. Really? What do I know about computers, stocks, or email banking? Whatever the Hell that is. Four Medolians even stopped a nuclear warhead from exploding in a populated area once—just barely. A fantastic tale, sure, but also terrifying. Nineteen forty-nine, I think. You'll have to ask Di Xiao about it sometime—she's great. The point is, when a Medolian is born, they have a choice: serve the Tribunal and keep the balance, or accept banishment from UnEarth forever. You might be surprised how many choose the latter."

"Not a great deal." . . .

"No, but most of us grow to accept it. I don't have much choice because there aren't any other elders left—none as active Sentries, anyhow. I'm the last to have seen Unos. Only Mara and I came home from the Battle of Die Muneris. Luckily, we both live for the job, but the others . . . they didn't ask for this life. I don't condone what Chloe did—Lord knows I'll carry her actions with me to the end of my days. But she was never meant to keep others in line. She wanted to be free. We tried to cage her, and she said no."

Izaiah realized he was gazing out the window like a doe-eyed teen at the brown and red mountains in the distance. He snapped back to the moment. "I'm sorry, where was I?"

"Nowhere," Bennett said. "Just know everything is okay."

"Splendid!"

Amanda arrived, balancing a waffle and hot dog on separate

plates, along with a syrup caddy featuring four different flavors—something Izaiah always found odd since no one ever used the other three, just maple. "Um, sorry, I didn't want these to get cold. Should I, like—"

"Yes. Perfect. Keep 'em coming. You're an angel." Bennett made room for the spread, tucking a napkin into his shirt. Amanda set down the plates and reached into her apron pocket for a bottle of sprinkles, earning a hearty laugh from Bennett, who even clapped. "Thank you."

She laughed along, completely unaware that this was the same man who'd likely terrified her dozens of times when she'd taken out the garbage, with his mangled beard and liquored-up grunts and gurgles. The man across from Izaiah brought none of that weight through the soda shop door. This man's Eve was as light as air and as strong as granite.

"Do you want, uh, some extra syrup?" Amanda asked.

"Yes, thank you," Bennett said.

"I could also get you, like, more butter. Or ketchup. Or mustard. We might have, like, some relish in the back."

Bennett waved away the offers with a grin and a hearty laugh. "No, I couldn't be better. What's your name?"

"Amanda Hodgins," she said with newfound gusto, no longer afraid to show off her braces.

"Thank you, Amanda Hodgins. As long as you keep a train of hot dogs and waffles headed my way, I'll be the happiest camper ever. And, on second thought, may I please have a root beer float? Got a sudden sweet tooth."

"You got it!" Amanda hurried behind the counter.

Bennett turned his attention to the plates, and the hot dog was gone in two bites.

"We've talked about Alex. Now how about Bennett?" Izaiah asked.

Bennett answered while chewing, spitting bits of bun onto his plate. "Whh bt Bnnt?"

"What's he been doing with his time back?"

Bennett swallowed. "Does it matter?"

Izaiah watched him douse his waffles in syrup, happily avoiding any serious inquiry. "You know, that was a very brave thing you did for Alex. In Africa."

"Someone had to do something."

"Someone did. You."

"Where you going with this?" Bennett asked, applying sprinkles generously.

Izaiah sighed, deciding to move on. "I went by the gas station. It wasn't there anymore."

Bennett folded the waffle like a taco and ate the front half. Syrup and sprinkles drizzled out the back. "That's 'cause I burned it to the ground."

"So that's where all the black ash and cinder came from."

"*Heh*, yeah. She went up quick, too. Dad and his cheap-ass materials. Also box after box of bogus receipts. If you ever need shitty money laundering advice, look up my old man."

"Oh? And where is he?"

"Six feet in the ground. Died five years ago."

Izaiah could sense a calmness and clarity in Bennett, a genuine confidence, far removed from the false bravado he had grown accustomed to. "How'd it feel? The burning of the station, I mean."

"Revelatory." Bennett closed shop on the waffle, licked his fingers, and finished with a monstrous burp. *Atta boy.*

"I'm not normally one to promote arson, but seeing as it was your property, and seems to have done you some good—"

"Not my property anymore." Bennett pulled a stack of papers from his back pocket and slapped them on the table.

Izaiah read them over. "You transferred the title to your nephew?"

"Cody gets the plot next year when he turns eighteen, as long as he keeps his scholarships and maintains a few academic honors. There's no name on the form; he won't know where it came from. He can sell it, develop it—whatever. The kid's smart as shit. Not a loser. Hopefully, it'll give him a head start. 'Bout time someone from this family does."

"I take it this means you saw him?" Izaiah asked.

"I always knew where he ended up, up off 89, north of Flagstaff. Nice couple took him in, name of Jones. Always knew, never had the guts to go see him, which is exactly why it's better he never knew me. As we recently learned, I don't have a great track record influencing the youth. He was adopted pretty quickly after my old man gave him to the state, put him in the system. Just two years old when it happened, so they're the only family Cody's ever known."

"Did you go?"

"I drove out there, sat outside for a bit, checked things out. Wonderfully boring place. But no, didn't go up to the door."

"If you think that's best. Though if I may say, Bennett—you're not a detriment. People make mistakes. Lives fall off the track. I've seen it time and again. The difference is whether someone wants to get better, if they want to push past their mistakes. If you have ghosts that haunt you, it means you're still alive, and things can change."

"Can't change what I did to Jerry, or his boyfriend Ryan, or Cody."

"No, but I doubt your brother would like to hear you say those things."

"You didn't know Jer."

"That's both true and not."

Bennett stopped chewing. "What are you talking about?"

"When I went to the Seeress to ask for her help finding the humans for the Joseph Mandate, I didn't just look into Mason's past. I also saw yours. Once a soul on Earth has been released, Illyana can see its Eve as it passes into UnEarth, revealing the lives of the dead. She found your brother's Eve. I saw your life through his eyes. I know what Tony, your father, did—to both of you. He was a cold, cruel man. I saw how fiercely Jerry wanted to protect you, but always felt he couldn't, like he wasn't good enough, wasn't strong enough."

"Jer thought that?"

Izaiah nodded. "When Jerry left home, it wasn't because of you. He never hated you. He did what he did to find a way out—for both of you. When he passed, I'm sure you thought going to war in his place was the only answer. It was the only way to escape your father. Remember, he brought hate into your home. He was too ashamed of his son to help raise his grandson. His Eve was nothing but Grief and Dread. Jerry would never have blamed you for what happened to Cody, and he never stopped loving you. Trust me."

"I appreciate what you're saying. Thank you, but—" Bennett's eyes were glued to the table. Izaiah could feel his Rapture flaring, solid and fully integrated into his being. "I'm done making excuses for the bad things I've done. Cody is my biggest regret, in a life full of them, and I'm going to have to learn to live with that. Sooner the better."

Izaiah held back a smile. *He's found it. Always knew he would.*

Bennett grew quiet as Amanda arrived with a new plate—two waffles, two hot dogs, and an overflowing root beer float.

"Thank the Eve, this looks wonderful," Bennett said, earning a giggle from Amanda.

"If it's not too much trouble, Miss, may I . . ." Izaiah held out his empty sundae dish.

"Going for five?" she asked.

"Please," he answered with a scrunch of his nose.

Amanda disappeared into the kitchen just as the front door opened. The teenagers in the corner fell silent as a short, dark figure entered the soda shop. A hood was pulled over their face. Despite the nearly one hundred-degree heat outside, Alex Barker looked ready to shiver, drowning in a sweatshirt three sizes too big. He shuffled through the shop, and as Izaiah rose to greet him, he spotted scabbed-over skin on burnt cheeks beneath the hood, and a pair of downcast eyes glowing faintly orange. Ignoring Izaiah, Alex nodded at Bennett, who rose to let him into the booth.

"Alex, I'm so glad you could come. You look well," Izaiah said.

Alex stayed quiet as he slid against the wall, slumping into himself, hands buried in the pockets of his coat, hood low. Bennett offered him a sip of his float, but Alex waved it off, clutching his stomach as if the thought of it made him sick.

Amanda exited the kitchen and hurried over to drop off Izaiah's new sundae. "Oh hi, we have a new friend! Is there anything I can—" She paused, having just caught a glimpse under Alex's hood. "Um, get you? Sorry, I don't mean to stare, Mister."

When Alex coughed, it sounded like a cloud of dust being expelled. His whisper was hoarse, sharp as a rusty razor, gritty as sand. "*Water. Please.*"

Amanda smiled brightly, like she would to any other customer. "Sure thing!" She hurried off.

"Probably thinks you're a burn victim," Bennett said.

Alex coughed out a laugh, wincing and holding his side before returning to his sullen demeanor. "*Can we make this quick?*"

Izaiah nodded. "I will, but before we get to why we're here, I wanted to ask about Melissa's funeral. Did it go well? I'm sorry I wasn't able to make it. They would have surely followed me."

Bennett nodded, answering for Alex. "It was nice. What little we could see, anyway. Unfortunately, we had to keep our distance.

Weather was good. Beautiful spot. She's buried at the top of the hill, under a large oak, right beside Al's tombstone."

"Seems only proper," Izaiah said, keeping an eye on Alex, whose Eve was surprisingly placid.

Amanda returned with waters for the table, and Bennett asked her to bring back a couple of pitchers. Alex reached for a glass, revealing a red hand speckled with dark scabs.

Bennett continued. "Of course, Patty is too young to remember any of this, which is for the best. She's living with Melissa's sister, Rachel, for now. They're good people. She'll be taken care of, have a nice life. And deep down, her parents will always be with her." Bennett finished his current helping of waffles as Amanda dropped off the rest of his order, proceeding to make it disappear while Alex pulled glass after glass of water under his hood, returning them empty.

Izaiah grew nervous asking his next question, unsure if he might set either of them off. "And the man? From the night the scars appeared?"

Alex's dejected eyes drifted to Bennett, who again answered. "Yeah. Daniel Cuthmoore. First thing we did when we got back to town was check on him. Found him at Yavapai Regional. I pretended to be the air-conditioning repair guy and snuck in. He'd been brought in already dead but was resuscitated. The guy's likely going to have brain damage, but he'll live. Luckily, his jaw was healed enough that he could talk a bit. Barely. A few more surgeries, and he gets to go home. Turned out he was an old friend of Melissa's who'd recently moved back to town and tried to help when Al went missing. He might have had a crush on her, but no, he's more of a puppy than Al. Even felt bad he couldn't shake my hand. Nothing was going on. Melissa never gave up hope he was coming home."

Alex and Bennett held each other's gaze, as though communicating telepathically. The teacher's guilt was palpable.

"What happened to you both was a tragedy," Izaiah began. "Our worlds were never meant to collide. But sometimes choices other than our own determine the way things go. I owe you both apologies—for a lot. What I'm most sorry for is not warning you about your deaths. If I could go back and change it, I would. Hell, I'd take both your places if I had the power. I'd never been in a position like that before and couldn't wrap my head around what I was supposed to do with the job and the information I was given. Humans have written enough books about time travel and tampering with it to scare me into second-guessing every step I took. Seriously. I never knew if I was altering the future or ensuring it. The Seeress's visions are powerful—sometimes helpful—but she can only see so far up the road. Once you get there, things always seem different. Looking back is easy. We know where we've been, but up ahead . . .

"I wasn't positive your deaths would come to pass, so I tried to warn you instead, and did a half-assed job of it. Bennett, do you remember our talk in the alley behind this shop? We talked about choices, and I told you to lay off the booze, just a little. And Alex, I know this won't help, but I spoke to him—the boy in the red hat. The one who shot you. His name was Lionel Trent, at least until he hung himself a month ago when Illyana discovered his Eve crossing over. Just like Mason Royans, Lionel was disturbed and angry, with no outlet and nothing but time. Part of my job as a Medolian Sentry is to prevent humans from reaching such extremes, but somehow, I've missed whatever this is, and it's rising. Scares me to think how many Masons or Lionels may be out there. I stopped paying attention to the details and spent too much time fighting to keep things afloat. Got a wake-up call I never knew I needed. Sad thing is it might have been too late. Looking into Mason's mind taught me more about the human condition than any of my years on Earth, and if I'm honest, what I saw chilled me to the bone.

There was nothing resembling home, kindness, or joy in his heart. Nothing I would call a friend, or a desire for one—except you two. Alex and Bennett. You fellas were my only hope of reaching that kid . . . but it turned out, even before we started, we were too late. Mason was gone. There was only Joseph."

Izaiah took a break to sip some water. This confession was turning into a marathon, and as usual, he was getting off topic.

"I kept trying . . . trying to keep you both out of harm's way entirely. I forced things, trying to fix them, then I realized sometimes things just need to play out. Nobody— and I mean nobody—has control, which I'm sure must be disappointing to hear. Almost as disappointing as dying and meeting me instead of God. It turns out it's not just one death, or one level higher. In fact, it might take a very long while before anyone truly understands what created all this. Even Michael the Great, known for his boundless wisdom, was filled with childlike curiosity, left guessing what started life, just like the rest of us. Nobody knows it all, fellas, and anyone who claims otherwise shouldn't be listened to."

"Don't worry," Bennett said. "I stopped looking for God a long time ago. I figure if He wants to talk, He knows where to find me." The soldier and Alex shared a glance, and Alex shrugged. "As far as the rest of it, forget it. We both just want to move on."

"Really? Do you mean it? You don't hate me?" Izaiah asked, feeling his cheeks flush. *First a nickname, now this?*

"At the end of it all, reality is still here," Bennett said. "Who knows what might have happened if things had gone any different?" Alex finished the second pitcher of water and gave Bennett a hard stare. "Oh, right. Thank you," Bennett added. "Al wants to know about Casey. Is she okay? And her friend, the professor. Have you seen or heard from them?"

"Yes, I meant to tell you," Izaiah started. "Fabian went back to the cabin the day after Gehenna but couldn't find Casey or Professor Evans. Snowmobile tracks led into a southern valley, but the snow had melted, and he lost the trail. He believes they made it safely to civilization. Said they exchanged numbers—or some such. You'd have to ask him, but I'm sure wherever they are, they're well."

Bennett looked at Alex, who gave an approving nod, satisfied.

"Well . . . I think that about sums things up." Izaiah wiped his hands with a paper napkin and adjusted his gray knitted cap, about to rise when he suddenly remembered. "Oh! Almost forgot. I have something for each of you." Reaching into his coat, he produced Hannah's belt buckle, freshly polished to a crisp silver sheen.

"Hannah's buckle. You found it?" Bennett exclaimed.

"Tough ol' thing. You know she won it in a game of poker a few hundred years before Inferius? At least that's what she told me. Wore it all through the war, even during the Battle of Cross Station, where she helped halt the Beast and Lucifer's army. Made him awful mad, let me tell ya. No one ever got under ol' Lucy's skin quite like Hannah. Yeah, this buckle's seen it all. When I found it, I knew I had to make sure it found a good home. So, I gave it a wash and offered it to Mara. Strangely enough, she didn't want it. We both talked and decided who it should go to." He slid it across the table to Bennett, who held still, eyeing the buckle, then Izaiah.

"I don't understand. Why me?" Bennett asked.

"It belongs with a Rapture user."

"I can't accept this. She hardly knew me. I—"

"No. Hannah cared about you more than you know. She would be glad to know you had it. And this is a rare gesture from Mara, which shouldn't be taken lightly. That buckle was meant for you. Who knows, it could even end up being your lucky charm."

Bennett took the buckle. "I'm honored." His fingers grazed over the front. "This symbol, the eye—I saw it in the Wraithian temple.

The same symbol was smeared in blood on the walls in the town where we met Yuri, and I saw a woman with it tattooed on her neck in La Rose Noire. What does it mean?"

"The eye is the symbol of the Eve," Izaiah explained, just as his mentor had done for him. "Many millennia ago, when the worlds of UnEarth first became aware of one another, there was no common written language or tongue. When traveling to other worlds, banners, tattoos, and body markings showed one's allegiance. The eye—the one common element of all risen Earthly creatures—was the key. If the top lid was thicker or accented with a Higher Shaded color, it signified they swore allegiance to the upper shades of Eve. If the lower lid was accented, they saw only the lower shades. But not all wanted war. Those who accented both lids indicated they witnessed all sides as equal and valid, necessary for life to thrive. It was only when the old realms discovered Earth, and with it the Medolians, that a common language was born, and the first war for humanity began—forty-five thousand years ago, lasting nearly six thousand."

"Hell of a war," Bennett said, mopping up the last of his meal.

"Yes. My mentor, Batia Tulis'uace Ungun Meleria, creator of the first order of Sentries, led the fight for balance, eventually joining Michael, the Celestials, Lucifer-Aveyl, and the forces of Hywyn to expel the armies of Arros from Trivium."

Izaiah motioned at the buckle in Bennett's hand. "Hannah expelled herself from Hywyn because she saw with both lids wide. She believed in balance. Now, it's up to a new generation to carry on that mission."

Bennett pocketed the buckle with a nod. "Thank you."

Izaiah then turned to Alex. "But enough about old wars. Alex, my friend, you'll never guess what I found." Reaching into his coat, he revealed a familiar blue baseball cap and set it on the table. It was scuffed but had survived mostly intact. "Ta-da!"

The hat sat untouched. Alex didn't budge. "*No thanks.*"

Izaiah's grin drooped. "You don't want it?"

"*No.*"

"I don't understand." Izaiah reached for the hat, then left it alone. "I thought you'd be happy to see it."

"*I said no,*" Alex said sharply.

Yikes. Izaiah snatched the hat away and stuffed it back into his pocket. "Tell you what, I'll hold on to it for you—just until you want it back. No pressure."

"So, what happens now?" Bennett asked before a silence could linger.

"I have a place lined up for you to stay in Trivium while you transition into your new lives. Gonna have to lay low for a while, you understand. If you come along, it'll be rough for a bit. Fair warning."

"A place to stay? Like an apartment?" Bennett asked. "Or another safe house?"

"Somewhere in between I think."

"Feeling welcome in UnEarth already," Bennett said dryly.

"You should!" Izaiah said. "There are so many wonderful creatures to meet, so many new experiences to have! New foods, new sights, new places, and did I mention new foods? We will, of course, need to make up backstories for you fellas. No one can ever know you were the humans of the Joseph Mandate. The good news is 'Alex and Bennett' are already becoming household names. The bad news is they must never be heard from again. So . . . you win some, you lose some. Shall we adjourn?"

Bennett leaned back in his seat with a grunt—a man satisfied with his meal—folded his arms, and lifted an eyebrow at Izaiah. "What do you say, Al? Should we give this old kook one last chance?"

Alex peered up from under the hood with a faint grin.

Izaiah clapped, overjoyed. "Great!" With that, he slid out from behind the table. "Let's head somewhere less conspicuous. How about the alley?"

"What is it with you and alleys?" Bennett asked, rising.

"I'm not sure what you mean." Izaiah stretched a little before they headed out, his joints sounding like bendable straws opening and closing.

Once Amanda was paid for the meal (*with a little extra for being so kind to an old fool*), Izaiah, Bennett, and Alex started toward the rear exit. "I was working on some new material while I waited for you fellas," Izaiah said. "Think I've got some good stuff. You want to hear?" He took out his green notebook and flipped through the pages, hearing whispered groans and sensing eyes rolling behind their lids but not caring. *World's not ending anymore. You got no excuse now.*

"Too bad. You're listening." He found the page. "Here we go. So, a milkman, a priest, and a barber walk into a bar. The bartender says, 'Must be our lucky night. A baby boy was just born in our bathroom, and then you three walked in!' The trio says, 'Congrats on the kid, but what's that got to do with us?' The bartender says, 'Well, now we can get him fed, blessed, and brissed!'"

Izaiah waited. *Come on, nothing?* He'd worked too hard on that one to get nothing. "'Cause the barber is there . . . and a priest wouldn't—"

"No, yeah," Bennett said. "I get it."

As they reached the back door, a smile crept up Bennett's cheeks, and by the time they entered the alley, he was full blown chuckling. "Pretty good," he said.

Darn right. Izaiah even swore he heard a raspy snicker from Alex.

"I'm marking that one down as a success." He tucked the pencil into his notebook, contented, and slid it into his coat's breast pocket, stepping toward an alcove out of view of the street. It felt odd being back where it all began—where he'd first told Alex and Bennett they were all but dead and would be forced to join him on a harrowing quest across two planets to catch a renegade demon. *And somehow, it worked out. For now, anyway.*

Feeling on a roll, he thought he would try one more. "Tell me what you think of this one. What's worse than biting into an apple and finding a worm inside?"

"I've heard this one," Bennett said.

"Really? About finding a rotten orange?" Izaiah asked.

Bennett raised an eyebrow. "No. About finding half a worm."

Izaiah considered him as he hoisted his emerald-topped cane and focused on their destination. "You're right. That's much better."

Ivory light overtook them as Izaiah filled with Jubilee at the thought of his new nickname and what the unknown future might hold for him, Alex and Bennett. Hardly able to contain his excitement, the old Medolian Shifted them away, smiling ear to ear, feeling for the first time in however many tens-of-thousands of years that he'd finally made human friends.

THE END

EPILOGUE

(A BOOK II PRELUDE)

With a final, exhausting swing, the seven-pound pickax wedged itself deep into the gap between boulders, sending a jolt through Leigh's weary arms, down her spine, and straight to her toes. She twisted her torso and legs, straining to pry the slabs apart with every ounce of strength left in her. A microscopic shift in the rock drove her on. Mud cracked like tearing fabric as the upper slab budged, rising like a massive arm lifting a bridge. Finally, it rolled free, tumbling down the slope with a dense thud and a puff of dust—the fruit of half a day's labor, bringing her five feet closer to breaking through the vent in the hill to the Temple of the Beast.

Gazing across the vast African desert stretching to an empty horizon, Leigh felt an unsettling mix of familiarity and isolation.

This time, she was utterly alone. No Casey, no Wraithians, no Joseph—just her and endless hills of sand. She had arrived five days earlier, prepared to battle murderous tribespeople, only to find Gehenna deserted. The three-axle truck she rented, loaded with tools for digging and blasting—including dynamite—was also equipped for defense: toxic gas grenades, four cases of ammo, and two brand-new Daewoo Precision Industries K3 machine guns. She was relieved not to need them, but felt safer keeping the weapons close, just in case the Wraithians returned, though that seemed unlikely after more than fourteen months.

The camp that had once belonged to her and her crew lay desolate upon her arrival, nearly swallowed by the Chadian desert. The canyon leading to the Gehenna cave entrance was mysteriously blocked by a colossal cylindrical rock, its surface splattered with dried blood like traincar graffiti. As she worked her way into the canyon, she discovered the temple cave entrance had collapsed, reduced to a slanted pile of rubble. It felt as if the universe were pointing at her with infinite middle fingers, laughing with galaxy-sized buckteeth.

After a futile day trying to clear the blockage, it became painfully clear she wouldn't get into the temple; the system had likely caved in all the way to the Dead Stairs. Disheartened, she began her return trip, wishing for a tail to tuck between her legs. But just as she was leaving, something caught her eye—a glimmer of what appeared to be a freshwater river flowing into the distant hills. *I couldn't be hallucinating already.*

Upon closer inspection, the river revealed itself to be long stretches of unnatural glass winding westward. The murky substance resisted her tools. Following the glass road, she discovered its origin: a hill riddled with deep fissures and a ten-yard hole punctured through the Earth's crust. Rifts snaked out from the breach, hundreds of yards in every direction. The location of the collapsed vent seemed too perfectly aligned with the tunnel system that led to the temple. Leigh knew it well, having walked it more than a hundred times. It couldn't be a coincidence—the statue of the beast was directly beneath her feet. She would bet the farm on it, though it was impossible to know how far down it lay as she hadn't packed any radar sensors. *Didn't even have space for wet wipes.*

On the second day, following the glass trail, Leigh hiked into a rocky area saturated with reds and browns. Towering cliffs rose around her as she approached the summit. The path carved by the glass was eerily devoid of life, as if a radical force of nature had swept everything away. As the terrain opened to the blue sky above, she reached a broken cliff's edge: half a mountainside lay in ruins. *This was where it happened—whatever it was. But we're still here. Joseph failed. For now, at least.* More convinced than ever of her mission, Leigh hurried back to the cracked hill. If the creatures invading her world wielded such power, what else could they do? Time was of the essence. She parked the truck, set up camp, and resumed clearing the collapsed vent—her shortcut to the temple.

Hardly aware of whether she was shivering, boiling, or sweating, she pressed on, pushing past human need and weakness. Each passing second made the obstructed hole feel more likely to give way beneath her in a deadly cascade, yet she felt no need for a helmet, rope, or harness. *So far, it's been fine. Nothing to worry about.* She tapped the slab beneath her boot for reassurance. *See?*

The closer she got to breaking through the obstruction, the more she believed the prize was near—waiting to be uncovered. The Wraithian dagger was rumored to be much more than just a weapon for sacrifice, but she wouldn't know its true potential without a chance to test it. Her return mission to Gehenna was one of retrieval, based only on a hypothesis backed by conjecture, but if she was right (*pretty sure I am*), Leigh stood to gain incredible power of her own.

Presently, hoisting the pickax with every intention of continuing, she stumbled and had to catch herself from falling. There was no fighting it: after spending three hours this morning with an electric jackhammer then two more with the pickax, she needed a breather. Removing her dusty wide-brimmed hat, she wiped her forehead with her shirt sleeve—once white, now stained a mixture of cream, brown, and whatever yellowish color sweat was.

Leaning against the truck, she took a drink and opened a nutrient bar (*strawberry cream*), setting her watch alarm for ten minutes. The water was ice-cold and refreshing—the only thing she ensured to bring in excess, stored in an eighty-gallon tank with a solar-powered refrigeration unit. Every drop had been meticulously accounted for, a habit instilled in her by Casey's fastidious bookkeeping.

Casey. Thinking of her slowed Leigh's heart, and also made it heavy with burden. Leaving her behind had been one of the hardest decisions Leigh had ever made, but no one could know about her return to Gehenna. *Especially not Casey.* If she found out, she would surely follow, and this mission was far too dangerous for Leigh's former assistant. Even if everything went smoothly, the journey would only become more perilous. Casey had been put through enough. She belonged somewhere with pillows, friends, and hot cocoa. Leigh was the one that belonged in nature, covered in dirt.

She thought of the night she'd lost her voice—the night she'd seen (*goddamned*) demons with her own eyes, floating through the trees around her parents' cabin. It was the night she truly lost all sense of what was possible and what wasn't. She and Casey had stayed as long as they could, but with no food, water, gas, or power, one night was enough. The only comfort the cabin offered—once they'd broken inside—was three scratchy, moldy blankets and a slanted, rotting couch. Hours spent shivering, hoping someone might rescue them had led to ultimate disappointment when the sun rose, and no one came. All night, Casey had repeated the same tired lines: "Don't worry. They're coming. They're good people." *Bleh bleh bleh.* But they hadn't, and they weren't.

The snowmobile Leigh's father had left in the shed started up, but the fuel gauge read only half full—not enough to reach Red Lodge. It was their only shot, though. After a brief discussion, they decided to take the risk. Two solid hours of fighting through the woods led to the snowmobile sputtering and dying, forcing them to hike the remaining five or six miles. They trudged through banks of snow that reached their knees, icy wind stinging their cheeks like tiny needles. Eventually, after losing the trail twice and nearly succumbing to frostbite, they reached the outskirts of town. The first building they encountered was the sheriff's station, which felt like a miraculous blessing at the time.

That brief spark of hope quickly dimmed once it became clear the deputies inside were anything but helpful. One—a lanky twentysomething named Elvis in a uniform two sizes too small—was paired with an elderly man named Bill, whose forehead shimmered like morning sun on the Atlantic. The duo were as inept and disorganized as their lopsided badges and coffee-stained coats suggested. Leigh thought she and Casey would be in and out in no time, perhaps even with a ride into town. But then Casey told them the truth: they'd been teleported to Montana by spirit-warrior people and almost witnessed the end of the world at the hands of a demon in a hockey mask. If only Leigh had had her voice in that moment—there were plenty of things she would have liked to say. Instead, she watched as Bill and Elvis struggled to contain their laughter.

Of course, they didn't believe the tall tale, which initially seemed like a lucky break. However, Leigh's optimism quickly proved misplaced when Casey mentioned Jeff, the Scotsman. On a whim, Bill—the diligent one, apparently—decided to input Jeff's full name into an international missing persons database. To their surprise, they got a hit: Jeff's family had reported him missing the week prior. Suddenly, the deputies were all ears, detaining and questioning Leigh and Casey separately for hours about Jeff Clatcher's whereabouts and the mysterious group claiming to be from another world.

For the first time, Leigh's muteness worked in her favor. Unable to incriminate herself, she spent her time shaking her head and eventually directed them to the wrinkled business card she'd received from the anonymous donor who'd funded the African dig. She was amazed to find it still in her pocket, alongside her I.D. and two credit cards. Though they would likely find nothing, she secretly hoped the Red Lodge Sheriff's Department could help identify the woman that sent her to Chad in the first place: the one she knew only as Aluqa. *Just a nice, friendly chat. Promise.*

After twenty-seven hours, and six increasingly threatening phone calls from Leigh's lawyer, they were allowed to leave the cramped, fluorescent-lit office. They emerged with dual citations—free of criminal charges but under limited surveillance until Jeff's disappearance was resolved. They could fly home but would be placed on travel watch lists until further notice.

"I'm sorry you had to go through that," Casey said, exasperated, as they slumped out of the station, zipping up the thin, ugly plastic jacket Elvis had kindly given her. "I mean, with Jeff. It must have been awful to relive all that, and then to have to lie . . . I just can't imagine . . ."

At first, Leigh didn't understand. Then she remembered the nights spent with Jeff in the tent and felt . . . nothing. There was no heartbreak or sorrow for a lost love, no despondency at the thought of never seeing his face again. Shocked by her own lack of remorse, it dawned on Leigh how much she had changed—never to be the same again. Jeff was a memory, and survival dictated moving on. Without blinking or an ounce of regret, Leigh nodded and wrote a note to Casey: *Call us a taxi to the airport.*

Casey's eyes went wide. "No! We have to get to a hospital. There might be a chance we can save your voice."

Leigh wanted to laugh but instead shook her head vigorously. What Chloe had done was obvious; her days of speaking were over. No hospital on Earth could change that, but Casey refused to accept it. As they continued to argue, Leigh made her way to the nearest bus station and bought two tickets to Billings. Reluctantly, Casey took the second ticket and followed. Any hope of silence during the trip was squashed as Casey buzzed with excitement about returning to Michigan to stay with her parents, which sounded perfect—for her.

"They'll be so surprised to see me, but also thrilled! They have a spare room, and I can see my brothers and sisters again!" she gushed while Leigh absently flipped through a travel magazine someone had left in the seatback pocket. *Can't wait to see the latest trend in fingernail fashion.* "Seriously," Casey half-shrieked, "we shouldn't be alone right now—especially you. You're more than welcome to stay at my mom and dad's. I know you're technically my boss, but we need to be careful, take it easy, you know? We're just getting started on our road to healing."

Sometimes, Casey's relentless positivity was hard to stomach.

Being around others was the last thing Leigh desired. All she wanted was a hot bath, a bottle of something single-malt, heavy metal in her ears, and time to think. When they arrived at Billings Logan International Airport, Leigh took her time studying the departures board, hoping for a destination that called to her. With nothing standing out, going back to London seemed as good an idea as any. She purchased Casey's ticket back to Michigan as a final gift, then her own.

When Casey realized they were splitting up, her reaction was slightly less than distraught. After a long, one-sided discussion, Leigh convinced her it was for the best with a final written note that read: *PLEASE. Go home. Need time alone.*

Casey wiped away a tear and nodded. "Okay, yeah, sure," she said, wrapping up their woeful goodbye, pretending not to care when she realized there would be no reciprocation. "Thank you for the ticket, Professor Evans," she said with a final sniff. "Now, if you'll excuse me, I'll be going, and I'll be taking some time off before seeking new avenues of employment. I appreciate all the time you dedicated toward me, and . . . *ugh*, never mind." With a heavy roll of her tired eyes, Casey walked away, never looking back.

It took three hours for the airport to approve Leigh's travel without a passport, which was a pleasant surprise. *I wasn't sure they could do that.* The few identification documents she had helped, but it was a call to the sheriff's office and Elvis's testimony (*or was it Bill's? Don't forget Bill*) that provided the legal legitimacy needed to get her approved. When she finally boarded the plane, she buckled in and fell asleep before the flight attendants could even begin their safety lecture, sleeping through the entire flight home.

Leigh was surprised when a letter from the law courts upholding the charge came through upon her return. She honestly hadn't expected the systems to be so connected. But official or not, she'd seen how the deputies had reacted when Casey mentioned Joseph, Mara, Izaiah, and the others. There was no way she'd play that hand against professionals. The summons and all subsequent letters went straight into the trash.

Back in her flat in London, nothing was as Leigh remembered. Each day felt dimmer than the last. Without her voice, the world seemed dead, constrictive, and merciless. Communicating with regular citizens was excruciating, and the smug, deaf assholes she occasionally encountered signed too quickly for her to follow. Not that she didn't understand—having read a few volumes on ASL and studied dozens of sign language charts, she had memorized most of the language, including many American dialects. However, signing still felt cumbersome, and she was too distracted to engage in any casual conversation, even if her voice hadn't been burned away.

No matter how hard she tried, Leigh couldn't stop reliving her time with Joseph—the demons' eyes floating in the trees, the instant transmission of her body over thousands of miles, the night she'd endured the void.

Most of the first six weeks back were spent indoors, watching TV and ordering delivery. Cabin fever set in quickly as Leigh grew restless, aided by the unhelpful responses from the university, which continued to send bland replies every time she requested an assignment. They even restricted her from returning to the department building to retrieve her personal belongings. *But . . . my cactus is in there.* No firm in town would return her emails, and she had no idea why. It might have been the news of Jeff's disappearance spreading, though that seemed unlikely since he had been a contract worker from Scotland. *More likely, the world thinks I need to be protected. Babied.*

Reborn as she was, Professor Evans recognized her vulnerability at her core, which had been nearly shattered but never broken. To survive in this world without her greatest weapon was perilous, and without words, she felt utterly defenseless. Chloe might as well have taken her life.

Each day, as the world moved on without her, new thoughts and notions emerged—things she would have once deemed shady, counterproductive, or outright sinister began to gain appeal. For the world wasn't what you wanted it to be; it was simply what it was. That was one of the lessons she'd learned from Joseph, however unfortunate. The demon was efficient and effective. He knew his strengths, utilized them, focused on his goal, and came irritatingly close to victory. But he didn't know his weaknesses because he didn't want to. That ignorance had surely led to his downfall. Leigh, on the other hand, knew hers all too well.

As she ventured further into the world, walking the streets and interacting with others, she realized how often speech served as a crutch, mindlessly spewed out without purpose. As she adapted to her silence, she discovered the unexpected strengths that came with never having to speak. Her cynicism and malaise transformed into something deeper. She saw how much she had given away in the past by dominating conversations. Words could capture attention, but true knowledge was gained through listening. For more than a century, government agents had been trained to let silence elicit the truth. With a mute like Leigh, that left ample space to be filled.

Casey continued to call and text daily from the States. Occasionally, Leigh listened to the voice messages; it was comforting to hear her voice and know how she was doing. Yet, she couldn't bring herself to reciprocate or share in Casey's enthusiasm. A new idea had taken root in Leigh's mind, and it was growing without

restraint. A universe had been revealed to her, one where fire dragons spit acid and warriors from another realm with powers beyond
comprehension walked among humans since time immemorial.
She was determined to find proof, to uncover what really happened to souls after death, and—if fortune felt like smiling—to
ignite a rebellion against their "afterlife" oppressors.

The clues were hidden in plain sight, scattered throughout history. One simply needed to know where to begin.

With no credible sources on UnEarth, and after weeks of sift-
ing through libraries and online databases in London, Leigh had
gathered little more than hearsay. To uncover the truth, she realized
she would need to leave the country. Over the years, she had built
a network of connections across various universities and libraries
globally—the keepers of the world's oldest secrets. Surely, one of
them could shed light on Joseph's origins and the threats posed by
such places. The challenge lay in escaping London without arous-
ing suspicion. Jeff's case remained open, and if authorities caught
wind of her travel plans, it could have led to serious consequences.

Acquiring a fake passport and identity marked the first in a series of illicit steps she took over the past year. When she walked
as casually as possible away from a dingy warehouse in Stoke-on-
Trent with a manila envelope full of falsified documents, a rush of
exhilaration had coursed through her. *Not going to lie—I liked it.*
Leigh had never dealt with underworld figures before, especially
those who carried shotguns and Rottweilers, staring into her eyes
as if they could read her soul. Yet, when she did, she found herself unnervingly calm. Even when it came time to buy explosives
and firearms on the North African black market months later, her
hands remained steady. After her experiences with Joseph, nothing
seemed capable of frightening her ever again.

Having traversed thousands of miles across five countries—

Wales, Italy, France, Sweden—and nearly depleting her savings, Leigh's search had drawn close to an end, with next to nothing to show for it. Then, in Nuremberg, Germany, her first breakthrough came.

For three days she'd walked the same path to the city library, and for three days she'd missed it. Then, on the fourth morning, the day she was set to leave the country, a bronze statue in a grassy lot beside a bike path caught her attention. Recognizing the eye from the Temple of the Beast, she approached the sculpture and read the plaque beneath: it was titled *"Mallos."* The statue had been donated by an anonymous benefactor. *The demons called Chloe "Mallos scum."*

A bit of metaphorical digging led Leigh to a single entry in the city's public art index, which revealed the artist's name: Lenae Monsato. Tracking down Monsato in Madrid, Leigh discovered that while the artist knew nothing of UnEarth, she did recall the commissioner mentioning the term. Initially instructed to maintain secrecy about the piece, Monsato seemed comfortable breaking her silence after twenty-six years. "What's the worst that can happen?" she shrugged.

When Leigh asked if such a demand had seemed suspicious at the time, Monsato replied nonchalantly, "It felt like a basic, non-partisan symbol. I didn't think much of it. Just took the money and did the job. Gotta take what I can get."

Monsato then pointed Leigh to a website run by the commissioner: Velondir Manor Incorporated. The site was mostly filled with overpriced modern art, but a few pieces piqued Leigh's interest, including a haunting painting of glowing red eyes in the dark. *Someone's seen an Archfiend or two.* The names of the pieces caught her attention as well: *Mallos, Eve, Lanwyn, Long Live Michael, Long Live Molm'Ursuth, Barium Guard, Wyst,* among others. Diving deeper, Leigh discovered a subculture of UnEarth believers online, where survivors of encounters with mysterious creatures shared stories without fear of ridicule. There were accounts of man-sized cocoons hunting people in the woods of Georgia and terrifying jellyfish-like beings abducting sailors for centuries. Surprisingly, many entries about the latter were told in a positive light, with some eager to relive the experience, fervidly, willing to pay good money for it.

The pieces of the UnEarth puzzle were starting to connect, but the picture remained incomplete. A miraculous second breakthrough occurred during a visit to her friend and former classmate, Sal Twincy, in Spain. By sheer luck, Leigh stumbled upon handwritten pages in the senate reading room in Madrid, tucked inside volume three of the *Spiritual Mason's Guidebook*—a text documenting the experiences of the more open-minded ancient Freemasons from the fifteenth century. No one must have opened the book since the pages were stashed there, likely in the mid-twentieth century.

Written by Professor Francisco Emul, a botanist from Murcia specializing in biophysics, the pages told of the day that sparked his passion for science at eight years old. He recounted meeting a mysterious woman with bright gray hair and blue eyes, adorned with an amulet containing a vibrant blue gemstone. "She appeared at least seventy, but even then, her presence filled me with awe," he wrote. "Her joyous laughter evoked a reaction from me that left me feeling small, like an insect, blinded, lost in awe."

Emul and his friend, Tommy, had found the woman asleep in the weeds alongside the road. Fearing she was dead, they tried to wake her, relieved when she rolled over and smiled. Neither of the boys was frightened of the woman, and after a brief conversation she revealed she was once an angel who had fallen to Earth many centuries ago. While Tommy laughed and moved on, Emul was captivated and spent the afternoon with her, discussing everything from the stars' alignment to the color of grass.

"Would you like to see something special?" she asked with an affectionate grin. When the boy nodded, she revealed a stunning, crystalline plant from her pack, shimmering with vibrant blues and sparkling violets. Mesmerized, Emul accepted a fruit from the plant.

"Just don't take food from anyone else you don't know. Only me. Only this once," she warned.

He agreed. The fruit was cold and dense, the size of a cherry yet light as air. When he popped it into his mouth, a wave of flavor overwhelmed his taste buds—spicy, sweet, sour, salty—all boundless and vivid. Years later, as he penned his memories, Emul would recall how that cold fruit made him feel stronger, steadier, and unshakable. He claimed to have grown an inch that day, convinced the mysterious plant was responsible for his towering stature as an adult. At six foot five and two hundred thirty-five pounds, Emul remained lean and fit, akin to an Olympian, despite never having worked out. Even as the powers of the fruit faded with age, he remained healthier than most of his peers.

The woman had vanished with her plant that day, leaving an indelible mark on young Francisco's mind. His yearning for another taste of that wondrous fruit would drive nearly every action in his life from then on, leading him across the globe, spending every last penny in search of it. But despite decades of searching, Professor Emul never encountered anything resembling that childhood wonder. His career crumbled, and he found himself alone. Near penniless and invalid, he spent his days feeding pigeons in the park, even after suffering back-to-back strokes in his mid-eighties. Life had finally caught up with him.

One day, while watching the birds and unable to toss breadcrumbs any longer, a woman passed by, igniting memories and joy within his heart. Even half-blind, he recognized her: the woman who had offered him the divine fruit. At ninety-three, he had become a shadow of his former self, but she seemed ageless, now the younger looking of the two, appearing twenty years younger than him. The moment their eyes met, she approached his wheelchair, introducing herself as Ilsa. Astonishingly, she still remembered him and offered to heal his ailments. Emul "nearly laughed," not surprised by her gesture but politely refusing. "I've lived my life, luckier than most could ever hope to be. I'll gladly accept my fate. I'm just happy to see you one more time."

Feeling he did not possess a threat to her or her kind, Ilsa began visiting the old man weekly, sharing stories from her world. A friendship blossomed, and she blessed him to publish their conversations in his journal. Against all odds, defying every word from his doctors, Emul lived for another four years, mostly bedridden, during which he meticulously documented his talks with Ilsa. By the time he passed, he had been rejected for publication sixteen times; no one believed the tale.

The entries in his journal ceased in April 1897, where Leigh discovered a clipping—Emul's obituary—dated May nineteenth. He died in his sleep, found a week later by his building's superintendent: a sad end to a fascinating life, but one that would not be in vain. Armed with Emul's pages and the insights they provided, Leigh had more than enough to begin her mission. These creatures of UnEarth were not higher beings; they were aliens invading Earth, and someone had to act. One crucial detail tucked in the margins changed everything: a weapon existed—one wielded by humanity—that could turn the tide of the coming war. The sign had arrived. Leigh knew what she had to do. She was going to return to Gehenna.

Her watch's alarm went off. *Break's over.* With the pickax in hand, she got up and returned to work, hoping to breach the obstruction by nightfall.

A buzzing soon came from her pack: another message from Casey. But Leigh couldn't risk revealing the truth. Silence was safer. She had to keep Casey waiting a little longer. With a resigned sigh, she tucked her sat-phone away and focused on her task. By the time the sun dipped below the sandy hills in the distance, a gap began to form in the obstructed vent. Several times, she had to leap to safety as rocks shifted and reorganized. Low-frequency rumbles echoed through the vent from whatever lay below, reinforcing her belief that she was getting close. As the sun made its final descent, she retrieved four solar-powered, yard-high LED towers with tripod legs from the truck, setting up stations at each corner of the rubble pile. Fully charged from a day in the sun, they would provide around seven hours of light—*limited, but worth the effort.* With the area illuminated, she rigged up the electric drill.

Two hours into the night dig, after switching back to her pickax, a massive boulder gave way, crashing in front of her. Desperately, she reached for a rock ledge, clamping down as hard as she could, holding on for dear life as the ground fell away beneath her. The debris plunged into the abyss, thundering with a series of booming crashes that reverberated through the pickax she clung to. Coughing and covering her face, she peered into the hole. The beam from her headlamp barely grazed the tops of the boulders below, at the end of the narrow fifty-foot vent. With a swing of her right leg, she caught the ledge and pulled herself back up. Rolling onto her side, a smile spread across her face. The vent was open.

It took more than an hour to secure a safe anchor bolt into the rock for her descent. After tying a double figure-eight knot above her harness, she double-checked her pack and headlamp, swung the pickax over her shoulder, and prepared to go.

Dropping several flares into the void confirmed the temple floor was about eighty feet down. *Eighty-ish. Doable.* She began lowering herself into the darkness, feeling as though she were descending into a vast natural well, its walls scalded to a stark black. Moments later, the vent opened into a sprawling space as she entered the temple. The area nearest the entrance was littered with rubble and fallen chunks from the walls.

Her light swept over the cavern, revealing the same destruction as the vent. *What kind of fire could do this?* As she approached the plateau, her headlamp illuminated the wings of a great creature buried beneath the collapsed ceiling. Most of the beast lay hidden under rubble, which was somewhat reassuring, though what was visible appeared suspiciously intact. *Can only guess what that thing is made of.*

Leigh's toes touched down on a broad, flat-faced rock. After testing its stability a dozen times, she released the belay rope. Moonlight poured through the vent above, casting a foggy column at the room's center. For a long while, she sat in the darkness, soaking in the silence. Once intimidating, this place no longer held any power over her. Any feelings of anxiety had dissipated. The temple felt expired, and she sensed that what she sought was nearby. Climbing the mass covering the plateau—which seemed the logical starting point—she allowed the rocks beneath her feet to shift and settle, making her ascent agonizingly slow.

Once midway, she swung the pickax from over her shoulder and began digging, hitting, and tossing debris for hours on end.

When a larger rock was disturbed, it tumbled down the slope, taking many of its companions with it. The resulting rockslide pushed her to the safety of the exposed flat top, but she didn't mind; half the work was done for her. Once the rubble settled and the last pebble stopped rolling, she found the beast statue nearly revealed, its wide, mangled jaw jutting out filled with rock, as though eating it for breakfast.

Clearing the plateau, Leigh looked up the vent and noticed a deep blue creeping into the night sky. Daylight would arrive soon, which suited her just fine. She was content to remain in the coolness below, ready for her search to continue indefinitely. The prize would be found. It was here, somewhere within reach.

As she examined the flat ground of the plateau, the pedestal came into view. Crouching low, she shone her headlamp into the nooks and crannies, finding nothing but black dust. Just as she was about to move on, something caught her eye: a small shape, out of place. Leaning closer, she realized it resembled a handle. *There!* She reached out, but it was just beyond her grasp. After an hour of clearing rocks away, she finally inched close enough to slip her hand through the crevice. *Just a little farther!* Sharp edges scraped her arm and stung her chest. Skin might have been breaking, but she pressed on, her fingers finally wrapping around the object.

From the tight, stinging crevice, Leigh pulled out a Wraithian dagger, its surface covered in a fine black powder. Blowing it clean, she marveled at what she had come so far to find. The blade, forged from a single piece of charcoal-colored metal, was inscribed with symbols she was only beginning to comprehend. It was clear: the true prize was never the Gehenna stones themselves, but the weapon that had created them. Joseph had done his research, but he had missed the most crucial detail. The power within them was immense, but what use was strength without control? *Joe never sought control because he never wanted it.*

But Leigh did.

As she touched the dagger's blade, it drew blood from her finger.

Somehow, the edge remained as sharp as ever. The sunlight beginning to stream through the vent gleamed off the dagger's coarse metal, and she couldn't help but bask in its reverence. None of them truly understood its significance. Even the Wraithians were unaware of the power they possessed in the blade: one of the most powerful weapons in all of UnEarth, entirely neutral in its charge, capable of amplifying and drawing out the Eve of any creature and bestowing it upon the one wielding it.

Watching the blood drip down her finger, a smile crept across Leigh's face.

A marvel.

Acknowledgments

This book would not have been possible without the boundless support, advice, and necessary critical abuse of Michelle Kowalski, Alison Tafel, David Hill, Bret Eagleston, Zach Bruning, Adina Cohen, Jeff Delaroy, and Tammy Salyer.

Thank you, all.

APPENDIX

UnEarth Senate:

<u>Majority Party:</u> Hywyn
<u>Home World Ruler:</u> High Lord Gabriel
<u>Ruling Body:</u> The Magnus Council
<u>Current Senator:</u> Honorable Speaker Binahq

The oldest of the six worlds of UnEarth, Hywyn formed four point one billion years ago out of Rapture, the shade of Eve manifested by the acts and will of creation. For tens of millions of years, the Celestials lived peacefully, creating anything and everything possible, until the other worlds of UnEarth were discovered and conflict first came to the world of purity. Though it took many millennia for Celestials to learn basic combat, Hywyn eventually led the worlds of UnEarth to victory in both major UnEarth wars, Unos and Inferius, and helped found the Tribunal and Senate, placing themselves as the majority party, never to give up the slot.

<u>Second Majority Party:</u> Arros
<u>Home World Ruler:</u> King Lucifer-Aveyl
<u>Ruling Body:</u> Alus Conclave
<u>Current Senator:</u> Ariel Van-Mortus

The second world of UnEarth to form, Arros is made of Wrath, the shade of Eve manifested by the acts and will of destruction. Since the dominant species on the world, the Archfiend, operate similarly to a hive mind, a governing body was not needed for many millions of years, until the first skirmishes with the high shaded worlds of the Eve began. The strongest of these chosen leaders, Molm'Ursuth, led Arros into the first UnEarth war, Unos, and was defeated by the newly discovered Medolians of Earth, Michael the Great, the united peoples of UnEarth, and Lucifer-Aveyl of Hywyn, who would later be banished to rule as king of Arros, continuing his rule in seclusion to this day.

Minority Party: Nashwyn
Home World Ruler: Queen Regent Bau-ni Reyo (*ruling in stead of her mentee, King Bauq-un Reyo, currently in pupal stage.*)
Ruling Body: The Queen's Council
Current Senator: Minority Leader Mau-auvt Bo

Nashwyn and the Wysts are created from Fervor, the shade of Eve manifested by life's passions. The Wysts were the first higher-shaded creatures to discover the temporary gateways that open between like shaded worlds as their orbits convene. This is how they discovered the Celestials over one million years ago. Though the two species shared few traits, diplomatic relations were pursued, and the worlds began to form the first common UnEarth language. When the armies of the lower shades began to show themselves, Nashwyn and Hywyn joined forces, creating the first UnEarth union.

Of the higher shades, Wysts are the most zealous and likely to enter into a conflict.

<u>Second Minority Party:</u> Fovos
<u>Home World Ruler:</u> Mistress Tennille
<u>Ruling Body:</u> N/A
<u>Current Senator:</u> Head of the Cavern States Claude Malcolm Rowse

Fovos formed a few millennia after Arros from Dread, the shade of Eve manifested by fear and doubt. Existing alongside Nashwyn in the second pocket of the UnEarth universe (*Universe Delta, à la Professor Francisco Emul's notes*), Fovos is perpetually dim, never truly in night, and never truly in day. Most of its life originated beneath the crust, near the planet's core where it's warm, though many of the planet's creatures make the cold, dark surface their home, living among the dead forests and bogs covering its landscape. The Scythe's current leader, Mistress Tennille, has lived far longer than any of her predecessors by siphoning Eve from her constituents, which they have given up gladly for thousands of years.

<u>Third Minority Party:</u> Lanwyn
<u>Home World Ruler:</u> Premiere Meese Linski
<u>Ruling Body:</u> The Leew Union
<u>Current Senator:</u> Afton Laffler

Lanwyn, the world of green, and its tree-dwelling citizens, the Beaubons, were formed from Jubilee, the shade of Eve manifested by joy, excitement, and contentment. Lanwyn and its sister-world, Doloros, both exist in the same subpocket universe as Trivium, which is always visible, especially at night, where it glows like a warm, soft sun.

The Beaubons of Lanwyn, though relatively small, and with a cheeriness sometimes hard to tolerate, have proven themselves mighty warriors and trustworthy companions to the higher shades of UnEarth.

Fourth Minority Party: Doloros
Home World Ruler: Governor Monty Mulmin
Ruling Body: The Klepper Lostros Club
Current Senator: Prime Minister Yaddo

Created from Grief, the shade of Eve manifested by despondency and sadness, Doloros is a world of golden mountains and sand. Though slow to move, as well as to leap into action, the Lostros are strong, powerful creatures, able to lift many times their own, already notable, weight. Though the Lostros fought exclusively for the lower shades in Unos, their loyalty to Arros and Fovos was put into question when Doloros switched sides in the final years of Inferius, helping to turn the tide against Lucifer-Aveyl and the Archfiend's attack on Hywyn, helping to bring about the longest reign of unequivocal peace in modern UnEarth history.

Universe Alpha

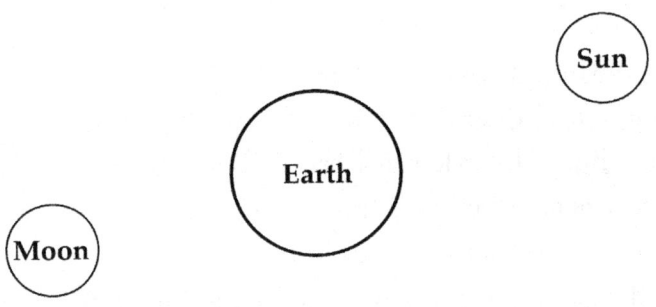

Note: Images not to scale

Universe Delta (UnEarth)

The sun emits Eve, making it visible in Universe Delta.

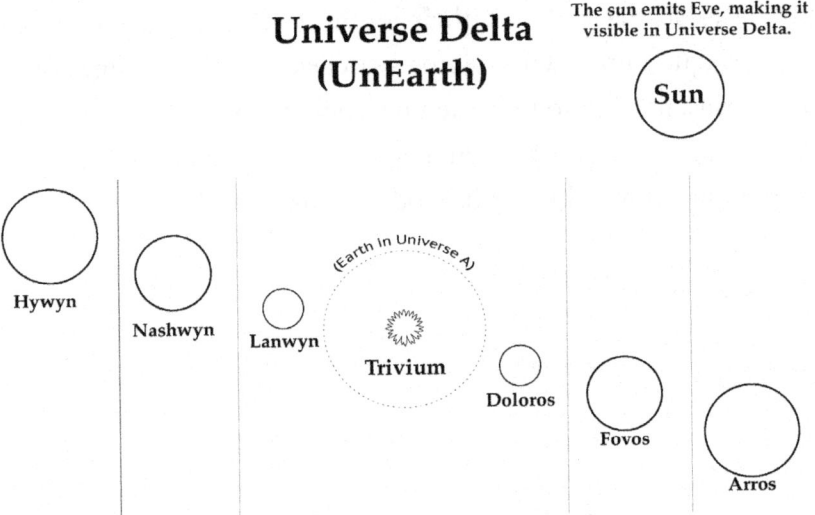

Universe Delta
(UnEarth)

UnEarth World		Eve Shade	
Hywyn	⬭	Rapture	
Nashwyn	⬭	Fervor	
Lanwyn	⬭	Jubilee	
Trivium	✺	Mallos	
Doloros	⬭	Grief	
Fovos	⬭	Dread	
Arros	⬭	Wrath	

Note: Images not to scale

UnEarth Timeline

13.8 Billion YA -	- Life begins with the Great Expansion.
5 Billion YA -	- Natural evolution of Universe Alpha solidifies Universe Delta.
4.5 Billion YA -	- Trivium is fully formed in Universe Delta.
500 Million YA -	- First Eve creatures appear on Hywyn.
2 Million YA -	- Temporary portals between UnEarth worlds are discovered.
50,000 YA -	- Michael, of OA and Lucifer, of Aveyl are born the same year.
42,000 BC - **37,000** BC -	- UNOS, the first great UnEarth war, takes place.
28,000 BC -	- "Lucifer's Coup" - Following its failure, he is cast out of Hywyn.
3109 BC -	- INFERIUS begins.
3101 BC -	- Michael is killed in the Battle of Lannion Peninsula by Lucifer.
3026 BC -	- Gabriel assumes mantle of Overseer.
86 BC -	- Uhl'k, under Lucifer's control, makes landfall in Hywyn.
YEAR ZERO -	- Begins with Die Muneris. INFERIUS ends.
YEAR 1 -	- The Covenant is sealed. The Purge begins.
March, **2000** AD -	- First official sighting of the nameless demon by Nigel Roe.
February, **2006** AD -	- The UnEarth Senate votes to approve the Joseph Mandate.

Made in the USA
Middletown, DE
16 June 2025